BRAMBLEWELL

AND THE ASPECTS OF

VENUS

1 Northbay Inn
Isle of Barra
HS9 5XY

Published by Victoria Somerled Books

Paperback ISBN-13: 978-1-7398120-0-3
eBook ISBN-13: 978-1-7398120-1-0

Cover design and layout by www.spiffingcovers.com

BRAMBLEWELL

AND THE ASPECTS OF

VENUS

VICTORIA SOMERLED

PRINCIPAL CHARACTERS

THE HOUSE OF BRAMBLEWELL

Lord Bramblewell of Bramblewell Manor,
benefactor of Bramblewell School

Susie Sutton, his fiancée

Lady Artemis Aethelfreda Bramblewell-Eurlinn, his sister

Julian Bramblewell-Eurlinn, Lady Artemis' son

Horatio Bramblewell-Eurlinn, Julian's elder brother

Gwenny, Horatio's wife

Mrs. Oliver, Lord Bramblewell's housekeeper

THE SOMERLAND FAMILY

Gylen Somerland, a surgeon

Rosalind Somerland, his daughter

John Somerland, his son

Liz Laurier, his former wife and
the mother of Rosalind and John

THE HOUSE OF SAUZON

Count Henri, the head of the family

Countess Marie-Christine, his wife

Jacqueline de Sauzon, his daughter

Héloïse de Sauzon, Jacqueline's younger sister

Marie-Colette de Sauzon, Jacqueline's youngest sister

Jérôme de Sauzon, Jacqueline's brother

Jacqui Galant, Jacqueline's husband

THE TRAVERSI FAMILY

Ida Traversi, a boarder at Bramblewell School

Caterina Traversi, Ida's eldest sister

Beatrice Traversi, Ida's elder sister

Signora Elisabetta, the Travesri girls' aunt

Adelina, Caterina's friend and housekeeper

BRAMBLEWELL SCHOOL

Miss Hilary Trimm, the former head-mistress of the school

Lynn James, the current head-mistress

Teddy Laurence, Lynn's deputy

Margaret Devere, headmitress of the Prep. School

Thetis Ravenswood, teacher of Latin and Greek

Barbara Merrivale, teacher of Elocution and Drama

Savannah Rock, teacher of Chemistry

Anna Layne, teacher of Mathematics

Lydia Dacre-Hill, teacher of English

Stella Lomas, head girl

Talitha Appleby, a pupil

Portia Price, a pupil

Rosalind Somerland, a pupil

Ida Traversi, a pupil

Irene Miller, a new girl

Isolde Delamar, Miss James' personal assistant
and former fiancée of Lord Bramblewell

Eva Derbyshire, a former head girl

BORDEAUX

Madame Gabrielle de Talence, mother of the Countess de Sauzon

Agnès Seurelle, her hairdresser

Pierre Laurier, a film director and Liz Laurier's second husband

ELLESMERE PORT

Dorothy Trimm, Hilary Trimm's mother

Kath Yarrington, Dorothy's confidante

LIVERPOOL

Louis Lindsey, Portia Price's boyfriend

PARIS

Antoine du Crâne, Madame Gabrielle's nephew

THE WIRRAL

Kit Mallory, a musician

CONTENTS

PROLOGUE

"I must confess, Liz, that I expected you to be living at the other end of Ellesmere Port," said Dorothy Trimm, addressing the younger woman, who was sitting opposite her in an artfully decorated sitting room. "Obviously, I'm referring to the part of Ellesmere Port that used to be quite separate and was called Whitby Village. Do you know what I'm talking about? In those days, the Port hadn't yet spread up to Whitby. In fact, I used to think of Whitby, at that time, as being practically within the boundary of Chester."

"Chester? I think that would have been a bit of a stretch, Dorothy," protested Liz Laurier, in a light-hearted way. "I take it you, yourself, live in Whitby, though. Do you?"

"Well, yes! Of course I do!" exclaimed Dorothy, taking off her wrist-length gloves and placing them beside her on the white sofa on which she had made herself comfortable. "Honestly, Liz! I don't know why you want to live in this part of town. I mean, it's more like Merseyside than West Cheshire down here. Wouldn't you say so?"

"Oh, Dorothy! Come on!" exclaimed Liz, trying to suppress the laughter that was rising up inside her. "You remind me of people I used to know: New Yorkers who would say disparaging things about New Jersey, without stepping back to assess, objectively, what New Jersey was really like."

"Are you criticising me?" asked Dorothy, lifting her eyebrows.

"I simply want to point out that you are not seeing Merseyside, and Liverpool, specifically, I guess, from the point of view of a visitor to the area: someone who might acknowledge its attractions more readily. You know, I, myself, love Liverpool! I'm definitely not the sort of person who would create a fuss about being allotted an L for Liverpool post-code, instead of a CH for Chester one!

Given Liverpool's gloriously adventurous past and its promotion of high culture now, why should I not want to be associated with it? Dorothy, are you, yourself, not in danger of falling for a myth, dreamed up by those less knowledgeable than you? A myth that would persuade one that Merseyside and Liverpool are replete with shortcomings? I see the area from the reasonably detached perspective of an outsider. And what I see, I like. It's alive, Dorothy! It's alive! Why would you undermine the place where you live by implying it is an undesirable location for habitation?"

Dorothy, momentarily, looked too shocked to speak, but then, she regained her composure. Adopting a patient expression, as if she were about to explain a difficult concept to a child, she said:

"I don't want to sound rude, Liz, but - how can I put this? - you seem to be deliberately overlooking the fact that we do not live in Liverpool, you and I. Ellesmere Port is on the edge of the Wirral, it is true, but I refuse to accept that the Wirral is in any way connected with Liverpool. It simply isn't. Anyway, Ellesmere Port is now officially in West Cheshire. And don't pretend you don't know how close it is to the city of Chester, itself. You've been to Chester and back often enough! Honestly, Liz! What is wrong with you? You are being jolly annoying on purpose, aren't you?"

"I shall not labour the point I am making any further," said Liz, smiling pleasantly, "except to say that, in my view, Liverpool is one of the most fascinating cities in the world."

Dorothy sighed, as if in exasperation, but stopped herself from asking sharply, "Oh, really? You are qualified to make a judgement like that, are you?" for she did not know, in fact, how far Liz had travelled during her life. Dorothy knew she had lived in France and in America, but Liz was not one to babble about her past and details had never been forthcoming. Why! She had even concealed her real identity from her own daughter, until it, her identity, had been dramatically revealed the previous summer. What a to-do there had been about that! Yet, there she was, sitting calmly on her sofa, as if she had led a prim and faultless life and was quite prepared to pass judgement on others! Talk about complacent!

Liz, catching the glint in Dorothy's eyes, frowned. She pushed her hand through her dark, shoulder-length hair and said:

"This part of Ellesmere Port is on the way up, anyway."

"Oh?"

"Yes. I foresee a great future for it," she added, as a teasing smile lit up her oval face.

"Hm! Touchée!" muttered Dorothy, lifting an eyebrow with an air of hauteur, as she realised Liz had been playfully referring to an astrologer's supposed ability to predict what lay ahead. But, affronted by Liz's attitude and suspecting that she, Liz, considered her to be provincial, Dorothy then said:

"May I ask you a rather direct question?"

"Please do."

"Since you, yourself, have brought up the subject of astrology, Liz, albeit obliquely, maybe you will explain to me why you consider it to be acceptable for you to set yourself up as an astrological consultant, specialising in relationships - relationships, mind you! - when you, yourself, have two failed marriages behind you? Can you understand why I think your choice of career is odd, given your own inability to be happy in a relationship? You don't even know how to communicate with your son, John, do you? "

Dorothy's hands were clasped upon her knees and she was now looking at Liz in what appeared to be a genuinely perplexed manner.

As if tired of hearing questions that had been asked by others, Liz breathed out audibly but softly, her eyes lowered. She had been told, by teachers at Bramblewell School, near Chester, while she had spent a year there, controversially tutoring teenage girls in astrology, that Dorothy, the mother of Hilary Trimm, who had been headmistress at that time, was the type of person who was inclined to home in on lapses in other people's behaviour, while appearing to be unaware of her own offensive bluntness.

"I dread Dorothy's visits," Thetis Ravenswood, the teacher of

Latin and Greek, had said one day, in the staffroom. "I cringe whenever she interrupts a conversation, because I know she is about to embarrass someone."

"Who is Dorothy?" Liz had asked.

"Who is Dorothy? What is she?" Lydia Dacre-Hill, the teacher of English, had murmured, adding more loudly, "The mother of the headmistress, I'm afraid. Hilary's Mama."

"But not the power behind the throne," Anna Layne, the Maths teacher, had stated firmly. "You must admit that Hilary does stop Dorothy in her tracks when she becomes pushy."

Pushy! That word, Liz now thought, summed up Dorothy's behaviour well. The fact that Miss Hilary Trimm, headmistress of Bramblewell School until seven months previously, had grown up to be a gracious woman, at ease in social situations, suggested that her nanny, rather than her mother, had taught her how to conduct herself, as a child.

Liz stood up and sauntered towards the bay window which was allowing the muted light of an early evening in Spring to enter the white-painted sitting room, a room which had something of an air of a small, modern art gallery about it, given the number of paintings hanging on the walls. Outside, the sun had started to go down over the rooftops of Ellesmere Port. Dorothy watched Liz. The younger woman's silence was making her reflect on what she, herself, had just said. Her motivation in asking the pointed questions had had its source in genuine curiosity, she had convinced herself, rather than in the desire to be awkward. Had Liz thought she had been over-intrusive? Surely not! Her questions had been reasonable ones to pose, given the nature of Liz's work, had they not?

"I think my own experiences in life have given me an insight into the problems my clients encounter," said Liz, then, suspecting, at the same time, that Dorothy would not consider two failed marriages and two abandoned children a qualification for anything other than a life darkened by guilt. Would Dorothy be sympathetic were Liz to tell her that the pain, caused by the separation from her children, had never gone away? Probably not.

Dorothy shifted her position on the sofa. Liz still had her back to her and she was beginning to feel uncomfortable.

"Shall we leave it at that?" asked Liz, turning around, then. "I'm expecting a client shortly."

"Well, I'd still..." Dorothy began. But she stopped and blandly stated, instead, "You'd like me to leave fairly soon."

Liz gave a shrug that implied both regret and apology. It was obvious she was not at her best and so Dorothy picked up the box-shaped handbag she had left at her feet, when she had arrived, and started to put on her short, white, cotton gloves.

"You have every right to enquire," said Liz, then, making an effort to sound warm. She walked to the centre of the room, her long, slim dress, coloured flame, making a whooshing sound, where it flared out slightly, near her ankles."Your question was perfectly valid," she added. "It just took me by surprise. And, by the way, you still haven't told me why you wanted to come to see me this evening. I doubt that you were planning to make an appointment for an astrological consultation, given your opposition to my presence in Bramblewell School, last year!"

Liz picked up one end of the length of violet silk she had tied around her waist in place of a belt and clutched it tightly, suggesting, through that gesture, that she was on edge.

"No, Liz, I didn't come here to make an appointment for anything," said Dorothy, reaching for the beige, linen jacket that she had draped over the back of the sofa where she had been sitting.

"So, what exactly can I do for you?" asked Liz, sounding a little impatient, having glanced at the wrist watch that she had left on a small, lacquered table nearby. Her client would be making an appearance before long. Given Dorothy's gossipy nature, she did not want the two, Dorothy and her client, to meet on the stairs, outside her apartment, because they knew each other.

"I want to invite you to a 'do,'" said Dorothy. "A terribly inadequate word that I don't much like using, but you know what I mean. And you've probably already guessed that I'm arranging it for Hilary. She left Bramblewell School very abruptly, last summer, but then, when one's heart is broken, one makes rash decisions, unfortunately. But, anyway, as a result, nobody really had the opportunity to say 'Good-bye' properly to her. In fact, only Lynn James and a couple of others saw her driving away. Oh! Lynn James, herself, had been planning to arrange something for Hilary, but I said, 'No, Lynn! You have enough to do, being acting head of the school. Lord Bramblewell, in fact, asked me to organise the event for you, when I broached the subject the last time I was talking to him.' Lynn was agreeable to my suggestions – she's a born diplomat, that girl!! - and so I made a few notes."

"Lovely!" said Liz quickly, conscious of the passing minutes.

"I was thinking of a sit-down dinner sort of affair. Or a buffet, although, personally, I find buffets a bit uncomfortable, don't you? I could book tables in a restaurant in Birkenhead, or in Chester or the Fleuve Chéri, in Liverpool. What do you say? Will you come along?"

"Actually...I mean, yes. I shall, Dorothy. Thank you."

"It would give you a chance to meet again the friends you made among the Bramblewell teachers, wouldn't it?"

"Yes. That would be very nice."

"Jolly good! Anyway, I can tell that you are becoming a bit anxious, Liz, and so, I should go."

Liz helped Dorothy to put on her smart jacket, while, at the same time, feeling rather guilty about the fact that she was pleased Dorothy was leaving. She knew that Dorothy was not, essentially, a malicious person, despite her apparent inability to stop herself from being outspoken and inquisitive. She meant well, she wanted to help others and, fundamentally, she was a good sort. Dorothy made for the door of the apartment, saying, "I do hope, dear, your client isn't down in the hall and on the point of coming up to see you. I'd like you to have time to have, at least, a cup of tea before you start your evening's work."

Liz smiled, somewhat benignly, and opened the door. Dorothy stepped on to the landing, stretching out her hand to grasp the banister rail.

"I'll go ahead of you," said Liz. "The stairs are steep."

"Oh! Good! I can't see anyone standing down there," said Dorothy, loudly, as if to suppress any further suggestions, on Liz's part, that she needed help to descend. "And by the way, Liz," she added, "have you noticed how many people no longer say, 'standing there'?"

"What?"

"Oh, my dear! Countless people say 'stood there' now! Have you not noticed? 'Stood there'! I ask you! Oh! And 'sat there' instead of 'sitting there'. It goes on and on. Even educated people do it. I'd love to know what The Beatles would have thought of it all."

"The Beatles?"

"Well! They saw her standing there, didn't they, dear? She wasn't stood there, was she?"

"I see what you mean."

"And don't let me start talking about the way people misuse 'disrespect', apparently believing it to be a transitive verb."

"I shouldn't dream of persuading you to. Are you managing, Dorothy? These steps really are very steep."

"Yes, thank you. I'm fine. Nearly there, anyway. Who lives on the ground floor?"

"Oh! A very quiet couple. I hardly see them."

Having reached the last step, then, Dorothy looked around her.

"You know, this is a nifty arrangement," she said. "It would never have crossed my mind, before, that dividing a semi into two flats would work, but it seems to. Do you like living on the upper floor?"

"Yes. I have a good view of the sky! And the stars!"

"Oh! Very amusing, Liz! Anyway, I'll say 'Good-bye' or

perhaps I should say, 'A demain,' as I expect I'll see you tomorrow morning."

Dorothy's eyes had lit up in a way that suggested she was looking forward to attending the high society wedding - that being Lord Bramblewell's marriage to Miss Susie Sutton - which was going to be celebrated in Chester Cathedral, the following day.

"Yes. You probably will!" answered Liz.

"And little Rosalind will look adorable in her bridesmaid's dress!"

"Little Rosalind is not so little! She's fifteen, Dorothy, and growing up fast."

"Yes. Of course. And it must irk you, now, to reflect on the fact that you missed being with her and your son, throughout their childhood. I know, dear, you must regret, at times, having walked away from the two of them, when they were so young."

"I'm trying to make up for it, Dorothy."

"And how are you doing that, dear?"

"As a start, I'm writing a book for Rosalind,"

"About the story of your life?"

"No. It's a sort of astrological guide to help her make her way wisely through her teenage years. I plan to call it 'The Aspects of Venus', Venus, being, in astrology, a planet very much associated with relationships. All kinds of relationships."

"Well, that's very nice, dear. I'm sure Rosalind will find your advice very helpful. And will you publish the book?"

"I'll see. I've been writing the book mainly for Rosalind and a few of her friends," replied Liz, remembering, then, that she had been told, at Bramblewell School, that Dorothy owned a small publishing company, in the Wirral. Liz was tempted to ask, opportunistically, "Would you consider publishing my book, Dorothy?" but since Dorothy, herself, did not offer to look at the manuscript, Liz was quiet.

"And now, I'd better be on my way!" Dorothy was saying, instead, her expression inscrutable. "Cheerio! Thank you for coming with me down the stairs. They are, indeed, jolly steep."

Liz watched as Dorothy made her way across the quiet side road to the spot where she had left her car, parked in the shade of the red brick houses opposite. Then, she, Liz, sped back upstairs, holding on to the skirt of her dress, to avoid tripping over it. Once inside her apartment, she looked at her watch. Maybe she would have time to eat something, quickly, before her client arrived. Toast and white Cheshire cheese with a cup of tea, à l'anglaise. She would dine properly, after the consultation was over.

It was Susie Sutton, the following day's Chester bride, who had requested an appointment with Liz, that evening. Liz knew that, had Dorothy seen Susie arriving, she would have wasted no time in spreading gossip about what she would have surmised to have been Susie's reasons for rushing to see an astrologer. "What do you think?" she would have asked, after locating the mobile numbers of her closest friends, while relishing every moment of suspense. "Last minute doubts? Panic?" Her friends would never have heard the end of it, as poor Susie's motivations would have been discussed ad infinitum. Liz, though, was not thinking so much of Susie, in wanting to avoid such an occurrence, as her own reputation. The success of her astrological practice depended on her being discreet and discretion, she felt, covered making appointments in such a way that clients were unlikely to cross paths. Liz ate toast in an absent-minded way, while she mulled over what she was going to say that evening. Susie was not always easy to handle. She was rarely relaxed and seemed to be desperate to cover up the fact that she could not compete with Liz, in serious conversation, her formal schooling having been affected by the unfortunate conditions at home that had prevented her from concentrating on school work, when she had been a child. She tended to dress rather splendidly whenever she knew she would be meeting Liz, though, so that she would be seen to be out-doing the glamorous astrologer in, at least, one area, that being fashion. Liz tried to make all clients feel at ease, but she always put on good, rather than casual, clothes for consultations and she felt that she should not alter that habit, simply to make Susie Sutton feel superior. She, therefore, went into her bedroom and changed into a long dress of pale blue velvet, which had bell-shaped sleeves. From her make-up tray, she chose a deep pink lipstick, of American provenance.

While Liz was carrying out her preparations for the session ahead, Susie Sutton was already making her way, in her low, convertible car, towards the gates of Bramblewell Manor, on the outskirts of Chester, along a gravel drive that took her through the manor's parkland and past the grounds of Bramblewell School, which were enclosed in Bramblewell territory. Susie was not sure if it was wise for her to make such a sortie, on the eve of her wedding to Lord Bramblewell, her beloved Rupert. Perhaps it would have been better for her to have stayed in her suite of rooms at the manor, to rest and prepare for the events that would unfold the following day. Having reached the gates, where the drive met the public road, she paused, therefore, for a moment or two, to reflect on what she was about to do. But then, abruptly, she turned the car to the left and headed for Ellesmere Port.

Her journey, taking her, for the most part, past lush, still light-infused meadows, bordered by the tall, densely-aligned, stately trees of west Cheshire, was, she noticed, beginning to calm her. She opened the window beside her to allow cool air to flow over her brow, hot with the fever that had been induced by the ragged state of her nerves. She felt better, but could not stop herself from brooding on the fact that Lord Bramblewell's former fiancée, Isolde Delamar, destabilised by jealousy, would be wishing her ill, that very night.

After she had been driving for fifteen minutes, Susie slowed the car down, as she approached a roundabout. Road signs directed her on to the route that would take her to Ellesmere Port and soon, she was within its official boundary. Before long, she found herself in Whitby Village. The territory was familiar: familiar because it was there that her own semi-detached house was located. She had no intention of selling that house of hers, despite the fact that Bramblewell Manor had already become her principal residence. Her house in Whitby Village, she now regarded as being a bolt hole, a private sanctuary to which she could withdraw, from time to time, or even return, permanently, were her marriage to go awry.

The house was situated near the end of Silvermere Road. There were trees where the road ended and, beyond them, a green field, where there was a pond in which water-lilies grew and sticklebacks swam in clear, shallow water. Susie's father, who had been missing for long periods during her childhood, a childhood which had been spent in Camden Town, in London, in a flat above a shop, and later, in rented accommodation in Chester, had re-appeared, briefly, in her life, when she had been twenty. Having, unexpectedly, come into money, he had spent it all, in one go, on the acquisition of the house in Whitby Village and he had given it, as a present, to her, his neglected daughter, before disappearing again. She had been grateful, of course. The fact that she had been given a house of her own had compensated, in part, for the insecurity of her early years. Some of her first evenings in the house had, touchingly, been spent going from room to room, running her hand along the walls and, then, the stairs, as if to ascertain that they, the rooms, walls and stairs, were real.

As she approached Silvermere Road, Susie felt tempted to switch on the car's indicator, to signal that she was going to turn left into it. To spend just a few minutes within her own house would do her good, she reckoned. She could forget, there, the new responsibilities that were being loaded on to her fragile shoulders. She could forget those who were hoping she would fail. She could forget Isolde Delamar. She glanced at the time on the dashboard clock. Dicey! Even a quick visit to her house would be unwise. Were she to go there, she would risk being late for her appointment with Liz Laurier and the future Lady Bramblewell had to learn to be on time, along with so much else that she had been required to change about her ways.

Susie had prepared diligently for her new rôle, though. Following advice given to her by Gwenny, who lived in Ywen Manor in Wales, with her husband, Horatio, one of Lord Bramblewell's two nephews - the other being Julian - Susie had read several books on how to run a large house and estate correctly, how to host dinner parties on a big scale and how to manage a social calendar, with specific reference to county life in Cheshire. Gwenny had given her many tips on how to behave when merely conversing informally, also. She had warned Susie that, in general conversation, it would be considered inappropriate to bring up the topics of politics, money or religion, for example, for fear of giving offence and, furthermore, that it would be best to try not to cry in public. Were she to cry, she risked making other people feel distressed and at a loss as to how to respond. Bramblewell ladies were expected to exercise self-control.

Conscious of her lack of adequate education, Susie had studied, in a broad way, literature, music and art and she reckoned she now knew enough to help her to bluff her way through superficial conversations, at formal dinners. She had, additionally, visited theatres, to see performances of serious plays in the Wirral peninsula, as well as in Chester. She had attended ballets in New Brighton. She had visited all the art galleries in the region, not only to be enlightened, but also to be seen to be patronising them. Had she done enough? Would she succeed in her rôle as Lady Bramblewell? She had to! Throughout her insecure childhood, when money had been tied to a tight budget, mainly because her father had often been missing, she had thought of nothing other than her dream of, one day, being comfortably off, having nice clothes and, above all, being warm in winter. The dream was about to become a reality. But firstly, she had to make a success of her wedding day.

The plans for the celebration had been in place for months. Susie's five bridesmaids, four of them being fifteen-year-old girls from Bramblewell School and the fifth, June Jones, a close friend who had worked with Susie in the past, had been put through their paces, had been supplied with dresses which suited them and which they liked and had been allotted bedrooms in the Manor for the night before the wedding. The banquet had been arranged. The music and flowers had been chosen. What could go wrong? Susie laughed softly, but in a subdued manner, as if the joy she should have been feeling had bubbled away, leaving behind only a sense of foreboding.

Isolde Delamar, who had been Lord Bramblewell's fiancée, ten years previously, had now been working in Chester, and, specifically, in Bramblewell School, for seven months, her aim having blatantly been the recapturing of Lord Bramblewell's heart. She had not achieved her goal. However, Susie was now wondering if Isolde would make one last desperate attempt to regain Lord Bramblewell's love. Failing that, would she wreck the marriage by bringing the ceremony to a halt in a dramatic fashion? Would she produce a trump card that would shock everyone present, while the wedding was in progress? Susie breathed in sharply, but tried, then, to put Isolde out of her mind, as she drove, at a lesser speed, past the shopping centre in Ellesmere Port and then, more slowly, towards Westminster Bridge, the road bridge over the railway. Beyond it, in the older part of town, she turned into a side street on the right.

Dorothy Trimm, sitting in her car, which was parked opposite the house in which Liz Laurier's apartment was situated, had been speaking to her daughter, Hilary, on her mobile phone, for several minutes and was still engaged in that conversation when Susie Sutton's car drew up.

"Oh! Wait, Hils!" Dorothy said, lowering her voice, as soon as she had spied Susie. "You are NOT going to believe who Liz's client is! What? NO! Not Teddy Laurence! Be sensible! It's SUSIE SUTTON! Yes! I KNOW! Hm? What? No. I don't think she has seen me. She has got out of her car and she has pressed the buzzer on the panel at the side of the door. Hang on! The door has opened and she has gone in, now. What? Well! I don't know, do I? Maybe she wants to know if she is doing the right thing. I can't help feeling sorry for her. She should be looking forward to a happy day and she would be, if you hadn't meddled. What? What was that? Oh! Stop, Hils! Yes! I DO blame you! How could I not? You know quite well that Susie has been in agony since Isolde Delamar turned up. What? No! Don't say you had nothing to do with Isolde's appearance on the Bramblewell scene! You jolly well know that you did! We're not going to go over that old ground, are we? What? Fine! Fine! I'll call you when I reach home. No! Of course I'm not going to wait here to see when Susie comes out of the house! What sort of busybody do you think I am?"

Dorothy drove away, annoyed at Hilary's continuing failure to face up to the fact that she had been largely responsible for Isolde Delamar's appointment to an administrative position in Bramblewell School. "Shame on you, Hils!" Dorothy muttered, as, vexed and ill at ease, she headed for Whitby Village. "Shame on you! Shame on you!" she repeated, her hands tightening on the steering wheel. Was it a sudden desire to make reparation for her daughter's misdeed that overwhelmed her, at that point? Or did she simply feel compassion for the future Lady Bramblewell, an outsider because of her background, who had been described, disparagingly, by some of her, Dorothy's, acquaintances, as "the fake-blonde fortune-hunter with the red shoes"? Whatever the reason, Dorothy decided that, instead of stopping in Whitby, she would drive on along the main road, her intention being to go as far as Chester, and there, to visit the Cathedral, to check that preparations for the wedding were in full swing and that nothing had been forgotten. She liked organising, anyway, and she had such an air of authority about her that people usually deferred to her without posing questions. Yes. She would go to the cathedral to check that all was as it should be. It was the least she could do for poor Susie.

Meanwhile, opening the door of her upper- floor apartment, Liz Laurier was raising her eyebrows, upon seeing what Susie Sutton was wearing that evening. The future Lady Bramblewell was dressed in a soft-pink skirt suit. Her tiny handbag, constructed of quilted, pink leather, was attached to a thin, gold chain. Her shoes, which had very high heels, were pink, also, the colour, though, being the creamier shade of a strawberry ice. "Rather de trop," Liz thought to herself, wondering, simultaneously, if Susie had been deliberately trying to control the way people responded to her, by dressing in that delicate way. Pale pink on a slim, blonde woman! It created such a picture of fragility that most individuals would be unlikely to treat Susie in any way other than kindly, Liz suspected.

Liz's suspicions regarding psychological manipulation on Susie's part, though, were pushed to the back of her mind, when she noticed the young blonde's demeanour. Susie had visited Liz's apartment before and was well acquainted with it. For that reason, Liz was taken aback to see how nervous Susie seemed to be. She shivered, visibly, as she sat down on one of the two white sofas. So pale was her face that it seemed to have drained colour out of the layer of make-up that had been skilfully applied. Susie's lipstick was of a vibrant red shade, but it was signalling only a false confidence.

"Would you like some tea or a cup of coffee?" asked Liz, as she sat down opposite Susie. "A glass of water?"

"No. Thank you. I'm in a bit of a hurry. Did you receive the birth data I sent you?"

"Your own and Lord Bramblewell's? Yes," answered Liz.

Susie had been clutching her pink handbag, but now, she placed it on the floor, under the long, glass-topped coffee table in front of her.

"What did you think?" she asked.

"I should like to begin with a brief analysis of your own chart," said Liz, taking out of a folder, lying on the glass table, two hand-drawn astrological charts. She could have resorted to using charts that had been created by her computer, or rather, by one of its programs, but she, personally, found it easier to analyse charts that had been drawn by her own hand.

"Listen! I just want to know if my marriage will last. That's all," said Susie, leaning forward. "I just want to know if it will actually take place and if it will last. You don't have to analyse my chart, Liz. I know what people think I am and I can't say I blame them. After all, I latched on to Teddy Laurence because I thought he was a teacher on the up, but then, Gylen Somerland - sorry! - came along and I ditched Teddy for Gylen, because, obviously, Gylen, being a surgeon, was earning more money than Teddy was. Then, when I got to know Lord Bramblewell, through Gylen of course, I made the most of my opportunities. I do absolutely know what I am, Liz. A social climber. And that would be putting it mildly. But, do I love Lord Bramblewell? Yes! I do! I really do, Liz. And I don't want to lose him. I'm determined to be a good wife and a perfect Lady Bramblewell. I want Lord Bramblewell to be proud of me."

Liz, who had flinched upon hearing Gylen Somerland's name being mentioned - he had, after all, been her own first husband and the father of her children, Rosalind and John - adjusted her position on the sofa and leaned back. She had now slipped into the rôle of astrologer and her expression was serious. She was conscious of the responsibilities she bore and how much trust was being placed in her by the client sitting before her. She had to be careful about the expressions that flitted across her face and the words she chose to use. She was aware, too, of her duty to abide by a code of ethics, both personal and professional. An astrologer could not, for example, be a gossip.

"Will my marriage last, Liz?" asked Susie again.

"Oh, Susie!" murmured Liz, softly, "All marriages require a certain amount of nurturing. Compromises have to be made and one has to be patient. I have said, repeatedly, perhaps not to you, but to others, that astrology cannot be used to predict the future in specific detail. One can pinpoint times when opportunities for development could gainfully be seized and, conversely, times when…"

"Liz!" interrupted Susie, apparently exasperated. "Forgive me, but I still have a lot to do tonight and I shall have to return to the manor soon! Could you simply tell me if Rupert - Lord Bramblewell - and I are compatible and if the marriage will last?"

"Very well," said Liz. "I'll condense what I was going to say."

"Please tell me quickly!"

"When judging the sort of person to whom a man is likely to be attracted, consciously or unconsciously, an astrologer will look at the sign on the cusp of the Seventh House in his astrological chart. When I talk about 'the cusp', incidentally, I am referring to the sign at the beginning of each House, a House being one of the twelve slices into which a chart is divided, like a cake, and which are numbered in an anti-clockwise direction, from the Ascendant, which will be marked on the chart, often, by the letters, ASC."

Susie nodded, but was looking impatient.

"One, also, looks at the Moon's sign and the connections, or aspects, it, the Moon, makes to the Sun and planets and, of course, one looks at Venus and its connections, or aspects, to the Sun and planets also."

"Oh, Liz!" Susie exclaimed. "Forget Venus! Just get to the point, will you? Can't you see I'm at the end of my tether? I suppose I came here hoping you would say to me, 'Everything will be all right, Susie. You'll have a lovely day tomorrow and then, you will live happily ever after.' But nothing is ever that simple, is it?"

"Listen, Susie!" said Liz, gently. "Are you sure you wouldn't like a cup of tea?"

Susie shook her head. And then, she leaned forward, her expression serious.

"When I came to see you,, some months ago," she began, "asking you to analyse Isolde Delamar's astrological chart for me, why didn't you do it? I've been puzzling over that for ages. Why was it acceptable for you to know something I was not allowed to know?"

"Ah!" said Liz, leaning back into the white cushions on her sofa. How was she going to answer such a pointed question? She could argue that years of study under the guidance of erudite tutors, whose knowledge had been passed on, carefully distilled, had taught her the dangers of revealing, too readily, information that could be misinterpreted and misconstrued. But instead, she said:

"You were very upset that night, Susie. I didn't think you would have taken in all that I'd have had to say."

Susie sat very still for a moment or two. Then, as if overcome by panic, she stood up and started to wander around the room, in a distracted fashion.

"What if she does something awful tomorrow, Liz?" she asked, leaning against a wall, with both hands behind her back.

"Who?"

"Isolde Delamar, of course!"

"What could she possibly do at this stage, Susie?"

"Oh! Don't be silly, Liz!"

"Listen! Throughout the marriage ceremony, you'll be surrounded and protected by people who love you and wish you well. Remember that!"

"I shan't be able to sleep, tonight. Isolde knows I shan't, of course. She will want me to look exhausted and miserable and on edge, tomorrow morning."

"Everything will be fine! Come on, now! This won't do!"

"You know," said Susie, walking, then, towards the window, to look up at the darkening sky, "I'll never understand why Hilary Trimm disliked me so much that she would offer a job to Isolde Delamar, just to upset me. Just to be spiteful. Other people say she's a fair-minded woman, but, I can't agree. She could have deleted Isolde's application from the screen of her computer, knowing how much trouble she would cause were she to return to Bramblewell. Hilary could have told her she wasn't suitable. But, Hilary didn't, did she? You know, I knew, on the day that Hilary mailed Isolde's application form to Lord Bramblewell, that something had changed in his attitude to me. It was the way he said Isolde Delamar's name, when he told me about Miss Trimm's message. He spoke softly, Liz, when he said her name. A man thinks he can hide things from a woman, but he can't, can he? He can't change the way he says the name of the woman he really loves. Not unless he's a cad who is used to deceiving."

"The woman he USED to love, Susie," said Liz kindly. "You know very well that Lord Bramblewell doesn't love Isolde Delamar now."

"Yes…I do think you're right," agreed Susie, while forcing herself to breathe in a measured way. "Teddy Laurence told me that Rupert had spoken really angrily to Isolde, in a corridor in the school. But, that telling-off would have just made her hate me more. She's bound to have something up her sleeve. She won't let the wedding go ahead, tomorrow, without causing a commotion."

"You are allowing this woman to deplete your strength. Why are you giving her so much power over you? Put her out of your mind by distracting yourself. Think of something else. Your beautiful dress! The honeymoon! Are you listening to me?"

Susie was gazing into the evening skies, through the window, as if she were, now, paying no heed to Liz's words. "You do know," she said then, "that Hilary Trimm's message was mailed to Lord Bramblewell when we were at the Château du Crâne last summer, don't you? Hilary knew that we would be having a lovely time there, in France, but it appears she wanted to spoil our happiness. 'Isolde Delamar has applied for the job of P.A. to the headmistress of Bramblewell School,' Hilary told Rupert. How could he not have been taken aback to hear that piece of information? And can't you imagine how smug Hilary would have been, knowing that I'd have been upset? That's when my troubles began, of course. And, oh! Life in France, down by Bordeaux, had been so lovely before then, Liz! Did Rosalind tell you about that holiday? She must have done! She was having a wonderful time with her three best friends from school. And Teddy Laurence was there as well, of course. And Julian! And that French girl, Héloïse de Sauzon, that Julian liked. Everyone was so nice! It was like living in a fairy tale. But then, Hilary Trimm put her two cents in, to use one of your own expressions, Liz. I'm not sure if I am using the expression correctly, but it sounds right to me. Hilary put her two cents in, like a jealous snake in Paradise..."

CHAPTER 1

Ida

Having sat up in the high, four-poster bed that was now familiar to her, since she had already been staying in the Château du Crâne, near Bordeaux, for three weeks, Rosalind Somerland switched on her bedside lamp while hoping that its light would not waken her school-friend, Ida Traversi, who was sleeping in an identical bed, close to her own. Ida wore pyjamas of pure silk and as Rosalind leaned back into her French pillows and bolster, she supposed, in a dreamily impressed kind of way, that Ida slept in silk because her family was enormously rich and practically aristocratic. And it occurred to Rosalind, then, that she would never have thought it possible that she, herself, would ever have met anyone like Ida, when, little more than a year before, she had been living in Bristol, being raised by her grandmother.

A move to Ellesmere Port, in West Cheshire, with her young brother, John, in order to stay with their father, followed by her subsequent enrolment in Bramblewell School, on the edge of Chester, had changed Rosalind's life in a way that only a novelist could have imagined - or so she believed. In the space of a year, she had discovered that one of her teachers, at Bramblewell School, had been her long-lost mother, she, herself, had written a play, "The Quest of Angélique," which was in the process of being turned into a film and she had come into contact with three families which she would previously have described, in demotic fashion, as being so "posh" that, in her girlish opinion, they would probably have been completely beyond her reach.

Ida, the youngest daughter of the founder of one of the most important publishing houses in Europe, had been the first to give her a glimpse into a more adorned world. Next, she had come into contact with the family of Lord Bramblewell, owner of Bramblewell Manor and patron of Bramblewell School, through her father's former girlfriend, Susie Sutton, who was now engaged to him: to Lord Bramblewell. And finally, she had become acquainted with Héloïse de Sauzon, one of the three daughters of the aristocratic, Breton family that inhabited the Château de Sauzon, in Belle-Isle, off the coast of Brittany. Héloïse, with her fine cheek bones, amber-brown eyes and long, pale blonde hair, which rippled down her back in gentle waves, was, in Rosalind's opinion, simply beautiful. She was one of the leading actresses in the film being shot at the Château du Crâne and Rosalind longed to look like her. Rosalind, in fact, had borrowed a book of facial exercises from Ida and when Ida was asleep, in the morning or at night, she would study the book and would try to do the exercises described in it, in the hope of losing some of the chubbiness lying along her jaw line, her intention being to become more Héloïse-like, in appearance. Rosalind had toyed with the idea of colouring her brown hair blonde, but she knew her father would be livid, if she were to return to Ellesmere Port, after her sojourn in France, looking less like a school girl. He would point out that she was only fifteen and that there would be time enough for "nonsense" when she would be older.

Appearance apart, what Rosalind admired about Héloïse was the arch and sophisticated way she was dealing with her crush on Teddy Laurence, the science teacher from Bramblewell School, who, on the insistence of Susie Sutton, had been given the leading male rôle in the film, or rather, had had it foisted upon him. Rosalind had had a crush on Mr. Laurence, herself, the previous year, but her mother - who, at the time, Rosalind knew only as the mysterious Miss Laurier, one of her teachers - had helped her to direct her feelings into properly structured pieces of writing. Rosalind had, subsequently, set about writing an historical play about the quest of a servant girl, Angélique: a play which had been based on a centuries-old letter that she and Ida, along with their two best friends, Portia Price and Talitha Appleby, had found during a school trip. The outcome had been the play Rosalind had written, with some fervour, since her crush on Mr. Laurence had provided her with the energy to try to impress him by making a success of it. It had been performed at Christmas, by Bramblewell School's dramatic society, The Eliza Club, of which Ida, Portia, Talitha and Rosalind were the most prominent members. The play had interested Pierre Laurier, a French film director and, formerly, Miss Laurier's second husband. Thanks to funding provided by Lord Bramblewell, then, Pierre had arranged for the play to be turned into a film which, he, himself, had spent the summer directing at the Château du Crâne. Rosalind, Portia, Talitha and Ida, having been so deeply involved in the writing or the staging of the play, had been invited, under the supervision of their elocution and drama teacher, Mrs. Merrivale, to watch the filming at the château.

Rosalind reached for the book of facial exercises that was lying on her bedside table and began to study it. She stretched her mouth and smiled widely. She could feel the muscles of her jaw tightening. She felt sure the facial exercises would be effective, eventually, even though she had not yet noticed any visible changes in her appearance. "It is important to persevere, when faced with a challenge," her father, Gylen Somerland, had said in connection with something else: her Maths homework, probably. Rosalind now pondered on her father's words. The ability to persevere was probably one of the secrets of worldly success. But if a girl had a crush on a boy, was it not better to pretend to him that she was not interested in persevering? Debbie, Rosalind's best friend during her former schooldays in Bristol, had once said that she had been told by an older cousin that "the pretence of insouciance" was the best strategy to adopt. The pretence of insouciance! When Rosalind had first heard those words, she had not known what they had meant. But, having consulted a dictionary, she was now convinced that the pretence of insouciance was the strategy Héloïse was adopting in her effort to capture the heart of Mr. Teddy Laurence!

The light of early morning was seeping through the gaps in the old wooden shutters that were closed every night. Rosalind slid down from her bed. In her cream, cotton pyjamas, she made her way, barefoot, to the window, which she opened slightly, pushing back the dark shutters, also. She felt the gentle air of the Gironde upon her face. The morning was lovely, as all the mornings had been at the Château du Crâne, that summer. Rosalind reached out for the long, pale shawl that was lying on a faux Louis XIV chair, nearby. She flung it, theatrically, around her shoulders, giving expression to the actress within. Susie Sutton, the fiancée of Lord Bramblewell, had given the shawl to her, as a present, for no specific reason. But, Susie was like that: spontaneous and generous.

Susie had come to the Château du Crâne, with Lord Bramblewell, for a brief stay that summer and it had been noticeable how life had started to sparkle, as soon as she had appeared. Her blonde hair, cascading in waves to her shoulders, had been glamorously styled and she had worn at least three chic outfits every day, in order to brighten the lives of those who were observing her. Upon watching her, happy in her new rôle as the future Lady Bramblewell, Rosalind had understood why Lord Bramblewell had been attracted to her: why any educated man - despite the fact that Susie, herself, had had only rudimentary schooling - would have been attracted to her, really. Any educated man, including, in the past, Rosalind's own father, Gylen, and, to Rosalind's dismay, Mr. Teddy Lawrence, also. In a period of eighteen months, in fact, Susie had progressed from being the girlfriend of a teacher, to that of a surgeon and, ultimately, to that of a lord of the manor, simply by relying on her blonde hair and a cultivated air of helplessness, which she knew would arouse in men, the instinct to protect and to be chivalrous. A social climber she might determinedly have been, but warm-hearted Susie had, nevertheless, lit up the lives of the men she had known and, for that reason, she had remained unforgettable.

During her stay at the Château du Crâne, Susie had often sat, at lunch time, with Rosalind and her three friends, Ida, Portia and Talitha. Susie had made the four of them laugh, with her self-deprecating stories about her introduction to life at Bramblewell Manor and the faux-pas she had committed - or rather, those actions of hers which the forbidding housekeeper, Mrs. Oliver, had considered to have been her faux-pas. Rosalind had noticed that Susie had seemed to have wanted to make everyone she liked feel special. Had that been the reason she had insisted that Mr. Teddy Laurence be given the leading male rôle in the film, even though he had, initially, been furious at having been emotionally forced into accepting it? It was as if - Rosalind thought - Susie had cast herself in the rôle of a lady overflowing with generosity, benevolence and charity, having become engaged to Lord Bramblewell. It had struck Rosalind that Susie would have always wanted to have been as kind to friends, but that previously, she had had neither the money nor the influence to indulge her wishes.

All had been well for days. The sun had poured its rays down on the green, Girondin meadows, around the moat-encircled château and the air had been scented by wild flowers, stirred by the heat. But then, out of the blue, there had been a set-back. What had happened, exactly, had not been clear and Susie had given no explanation. Lord Bramblewell had simply announced that it was necessary for him to return to England. Susie, mysteriously looking perplexed one minute and dejected the next, had accompanied him. Portia Price had sent a text message to her boyfriend, Louis, in Liverpool, to ask him if, by chance, he had heard of anything unusual happening in the vicinity of Bramblewell Manor. "Not my territory, love," had been the reply: a reply encompassing more than one meaning. Then, Portia had tried asking her younger brother, Lance, at home in Chester, the same question. Lance had sent a reply, by text, to tell Portia that he had heard nothing out of the ordinary happening at the Manor, but obligingly, had added that he would try to find out if anything was amiss. Lance had become more compliant and helpful than he had been in the past, Portia had been surprised to discover. Perhaps he had acquired a girlfriend.

Rosalind, standing at her bedroom window at the Château du Crâne, now stretched out her arms and breathed deeply. She could hear, beyond the walls of the château and its moat, the sounds of the film crew, engaged in preparations for the day's shoot. The crew would already have had breakfast in the dining room, two floors below the two bedrooms which had been allocated to the four Bramblewell girls, a breakfast that would have consisted of baguettes, fresh from a bordelais bakery, flaky croissants, charentais butter, hot milk and good coffee. Rosalind started to feel hungry and was about to move away from the window, when Teddy Laurence came into view, walking across the courtyard of the château. Rosalind hesitated.

In readiness for the day's filming, Teddy was already in costume. His loosely-fitting, white shirt, resembling that of a poet, in a portrait from a bygone age - a portrait of Byron, perhaps, or Shelley or Keats - bestowed on him the aura of a carefree hero of the Romantic type. The heels of his tall, polished boots clicked on the flag stones beneath his feet as he made his way, briskly, towards the arched passage that led to the drawbridge over the moat and the pastures and woods beyond. Teddy's slim, blue breeches, Rosalind knew, had been styled, by a costume designer, to be, anachronistically, like those of one of Napoléon's aides-de-camp, although the action of the film was, supposedly, taking place during the Reign of Terror, some years before the Napoleonic era. However, it had been decided that the focus of the film would be on romance, rather than exactitude and so, the director, Pierre Laurier, had shrugged when the mistake had been pointed out by a consultant historian, visiting the film set. "They fit," Pierre had said, referring to the breeches. "They are appropriate."

In Rosalind's opinion, the breeches did, indeed, look appropriate, as Pierre had stated. Their pale blue colour enhanced, rather than detracted from, Teddy's handsomeness. And as he was crossing the courtyard, he rolled back the cuffs of the sleeves of his white shirt, to reveal his tanned wrists, as if he were about to take part in a sword fight: a morning duel. Yet, he seemed not to be concentrating fully on what he was doing. It was as if his mind was preoccupied with other matters. Rosalind wondered if he was thinking of Bramblewell School and the duties that would be awaiting him there, when the next term began. Was he pondering, also, on how he could have allowed himself to have been persuaded by Susie Sutton to take part in the film: a film which, though broadly historically-based in content, he had clearly found too lacking in academic weight to have been of interest to him. Although he had played his part well, in order to satisfy the demands of the contract he had signed, he had always seemed to have been emotionally detached, upon leaving the film set and even somewhat impatient, as if his time had been wasted, or as if he could not wait to go back home to Liverpool and, specifically, to his apartment, overlooking the cool River Mersey. Perhaps he was longing to return to Rebecca Hampton, the American student who was spending the summer in his apartment, during his absence. The rumours that had been circulating among Bramblewell girls in the know, before the previous summer term had come to an end, had suggested that she had gone there.

"You still like him, don't you?"

Rosalind gave a start, upon hearing Ida Traversi's words. She had not heard Ida slipping out of bed and crossing the room to join her at the window.

"No! Not really!" Rosalind protested.

"Are you sure?"

"Absolutely."

Rosalind was feeling uncomfortable and so, decided to channel the conversation into another direction.

"Did you sleep well?" she asked. "I woke up once and imagined you were awake, too, but I didn't say anything."

"I can never sleep the night before I travel anywhere," replied Ida, kindly pretending not to notice Rosalind's confusion. "Even if I am going home."

Ida stretched out her arms, then, in an elegant gesture that Rosalind judged to be natural to her, rather than practised. Ida always exuded a graceful confidence, a confidence that had its source in the fact that she had been brought up in a family in which she had probably been supported by the loving attention of her parents: an Italian, business-oriented father and a cultured, English mother. There were female siblings as well. No doubt they were all close, Ida and her sisters.

"It's a pity you have to leave today," said Rosalind. "Talitha, as well. Portia and I will be lost without the two of you."

"I know that Talitha would like to stay, but her parents want her to spend time with them in New York, before the new term starts at Bramblewell. And my own parents want me to meet them at the Traversi apartment in Forte dei Marmi. My family always goes there at this time of year. It would have been difficult for me to have said, 'No!' My father, being Italian, I suppose, is keen on traditions and keeping the family together. My mother, being English, doesn't mind as much, you know. But, I feel I have to go, rather than stay."

"Of course you must go!" insisted Rosalind. "Family comes first."

Ida looked embarrassed, as if she were wondering if she had been insensitive in bringing up the topic of family traditions, given the fact that Rosalind's own experience of family life had been so broken.

"I love to hear you talking about your family," said Rosalind, then, sensing her friend's consternation. "Honestly I do! I can imagine you all in that big apartment, with its marble pillars and balconies, overlooking the sea, having a lovely time. It's nice to think about a family living like that."

"Listen, Rosie," said Ida, her expression grave. "Conventional family life, even ours, can be as difficult as your life has been. I mean that. I have two sisters, for example, who are older than I am, by ten years and seven years, and life with them has never been..."

Ida stopped as if wondering how to continue.

"Go on," urged Rosalind.

Ida turned to look out of the window, without seeming to focus on anything in particular.

"One of them, Caterina, is very beautiful," she said.

"What does she look like?" asked Rosalind, curiosity evident in her voice.

"She has dark hair. It reaches her shoulders, but she scoops it up on one side and holds it in place with a fancy clasp or a jewelled slider, if she is wearing an evening dress. She often looks rather haughty or proud, but really, that look is just a façade and behind that façade, there is a sensitive person. Should I go on?"

"Definitely," replied Rosalind, now fascinated.

"My sister, Beatrice, who is younger than Caterina, is Mamma's pet. She always has been. I could see that Beatrice was the favoured one, even when I was very young. I, also, realised then, partly by observation and partly by intuition, that Beatrice was cunning. She would behave badly, but Mamma would always take her side and make excuses for her. Caterina, unlike Beatrice, was not allowed to be naughty. She was not allowed to be a child. She would protest, 'You are not being fair! You have never been fair, Mamma!' However, Mamma would take no notice of Caterina, or else, would scold her for speaking in that way. It was always so. I saw Beatrice deliberately forcing a wedge between Caterina and Mamma and I grew up knowing that Beatrice was treacherous, that Caterina was vulnerable and that not all mothers are scrupulously just in the way they bring up their children."

"Oh!" murmured Rosalind, not knowing what to say.

"My sisters are twenty-two and twenty-five, now," continued Ida. "But they are as suspicious of each other as they were in childhood. I know that Caterina will never trust Beatrice and that her relationship with Mamma will always be frosty. I also know that Caterina does not value herself, now."

"What do you mean?"

"Well! When Caterina was in her late teens - a bit older than we are - she became quite rebellious. She would flirt with rich, mature, but spoilt men and, occasionally, with cultured, erudite men who were a lot older than she was. Both types were difficult to attract, but, by persuading them to show an interest in her, if only for a while, Caterina would temporarily manage to convince herself that she was worth knowing. Then, she would say to herself, 'If he likes me that much, he must actually have a poor sense of judgement, because not even my mother has ever found anything about me that was worth liking.'"

"Did Caterina tell you that?"

"Yes. She did."

"That's awful!"

"Yes. And she carried on destroying her chances of happiness as she became older. When she was in her twenties, she tended to be attracted to a certain type of young Roman, who was rich, but only because his parents were rich: the type of young man who was obsessed with 'cars, clothes and currency,' as Papa would say. Caterina would pursue this type of man doggedly, but also with panache. I think that's the right word. She would buy presents for him, in order to impress him with her good taste and generosity. Papa had, at that point, acquired an apartment for her, in Rome, because she had said she had wanted to study Fine Art seriously. He had also engaged a cook, Adelina, to take care of her and make sure she ate well. When Caterina would invite a gentleman for dinner, she would ask Adelina to prepare something special. A rare type of risotto with figs cooked in Tuscan wine, for example, or soufflés, floating over dark cherries, in prosciutto. Caterina would dress in gowns made of luxurious fabrics and would wear her finest jewellery. Then, when the privileged young man had become captivated and had started to show a genuine interest in her, 'the game would be up' as she, herself, would say. She would cease communicating with him, no longer having an inclination to do so. "

"But, that's so sad!"

Ida sighed. She leaned out of the window, resting her arms on the sill, while gazing down at the courtyard."

"Have you seen Julian this morning?" she asked.

"Julian? No. Why?"

"Just wondered."

"Why?"

Ida did not answer, but instead, turned around so that she was facing into the bedroom.

"Mamma never showed any interest in Caterina while she was at school," she said, as if suddenly remembering another aspect of the tense, mother-daughter relationship. "Whenever Caterina achieved anything, Mamma would just shrug and look away or would say, at the most, 'Your teachers must have been pleased.' She would never admit that she, herself, was pleased. Caterina ended up believing that everything she did was worthless and, by extension, that she, herself, had no value."

"But, didn't her father like her?"

"Yes. But she said Mamma's opinion mattered more."

"Why?"

"You know, I'm sure your own mother, being a qualified astrologer, would be able to give you the answer. I can't. I did look up the planetary positions for the day of Mamma's birth and of Caterina's birth, though."

"And?"

"I did notice that Mamma's Pluto was in conjunction with Caterina's Venus."

"But, you don't know what Pluto clashing with Venus will do

to people."

"No. Do you?"

"I have no idea. I think Miss Laurier - Mum, I mean - didn't reach Pluto with Venus when she was teaching me. I'll ask her about it."

Despondent now, like Ida, Rosalind looked down into the courtyard. Talking loudly, members of the film crew were crossing it, followed by Héloïse de Sauzon, in a long dress of apple green chiffon, lined with silk. Suddenly seeing the anachronistically designed but lovely dress, Rosalind knew how she could make Ida feel cheerier.

"I have something to tell you" she said, before firmly adding, "but you'll have to keep it to yourself for a while. Promise?"

"Yes. All right. What is it?"

"Two or three days before she left, Susie Sutton told me something which she said I could tell you and Portia and Talitha eventually, but no one else."

"What did she say?"

"She wants the four of us to be her bridesmaids when she marries, next Spring."

"The four of us?"

"Yes. The four of us. And a friend of hers called June Jones, as well. I think June Jones will be the chief bridesmaid, as she is older than we are."

"That's incredible. I mean, I hardly know Susie Sutton. Will she be getting married in Chester Cathedral?"

"Yes."

"That's so romantic! I can't believe she wants three girls she hardly knows to be her bridesmaids, though. I mean, she really doesn't know Portia or Talitha any better than she knows me."

"I think Susie wants you and Talitha and Portia to be there to please me. She really appreciated the way the three of you helped me to settle down at Bramblewell School last year. Susie was almost engaged to Dad at the time and she thought of herself as being a sort of step-mother to John and me for a short while. She felt guilty when her relationship with Dad collapsed, because that made life difficult for us at home. She knows how big a part you three played in keeping me going. She said she thought of the three of you as my sisters."

"Sisters!" exclaimed Ida, suddenly laughing. "I think I'd prefer to imagine us as friends, Rosie! We don't want to end up like Caterina and Beatrice, do we?"

"I'm sorry that you have to worry about them."

"I imagine they have already arrived in Forte dei Marmi and tomorrow, I'll be there as well and I shall, inevitably, be drawn into the maelstrom. One cannot avoid being affected by the atmosphere created by Beatrice and Caterina and Mamma, too, unfortunately. There is always a confrontation of some sort: a prova di forza. It's un-nerving. Maybe you, Rosie, find family life easier and cosier than I do, after all.

At that moment, both girls were startled as the door of their bedroom flew open and Portia and Talitha, still in pyjamas, rushed in.

"You're not going to believe this!" exclaimed Portia, sitting down on Ida's bed while holding up her mobile phone as if it were a trophy.

"What?" asked Ida."What?"

"A text message from Lance has just arrived," said Portia, obviously eager to divulge the news her brother had passed on, but wanting to keep her friends in suspense at the same time.

"And? What did he say?" asked Rosalind. "Tell us!"

"Lance overheard some Bramblewell girls talking in a riverside café, in Chester and..."

"We'll have a new headmistress next term!" exclaimed Talitha, unable to control her excitement. "Miss Trimm is leaving Bramblewell!"

CHAPTER 2

The Red Dress

"That red dress, again!" Miss Hilary Trimm said to herself, as, from her office window, she watched Susie Sutton approaching Bramblewell School, through the trees. Susie, Miss Trimm noted with displeasure, was walking hand in hand with her fiancé, Lord Bramblewell. Tall and solid in stature, his silvery- blond hair giving him a Saxon appearance, Rupert, as Miss Trimm called him in private, was twenty years older than his future bride. Susie, by his side, looked as fresh and delicate as a porcelain doll. But, she was wearing what Miss Trimm had, once before, described as "an unwisely chosen cocktail dress." Now, in the grounds of Bramblewell School, the dress looked even less appropriate, in Miss Trimm's estimation. It was a hot, Cheshire afternoon, but the startlingly scarlet dress was not one that could have been described as a tea dress. In other words, it was not the sort of garment that Miss Trimm would have considered to be "comme il faut" for an afternoon visit to a prestigious school for nice girls, situated on the outskirts of elegant Chester, of all places, and, of course, it was unquestionably not what one would wear when visiting the headmistress, herself. And how had Miss Sutton managed to walk with such aplomb along a woody path, rendered uneven and bumpy by the roots of oaks and sycamores, wearing those backless, high heeled, red shoes of hers?

Miss Trimm had seen the shoes before, of course. Miss Sutton had been wearing them on the night she had caused such a stir at a reception held at Bramblewell Manor, the previous year. Arriving without Gylen Somerland, the surgeon to whom she had apparently been unofficially engaged at the time, Miss Sutton had feigned anguish and weakness, fainting implausibly at Lord Bramblewell's feet. Naturally, the fainting fit had been nothing more than a performance, staged to arouse Lord Bramblewell's protective instinct. The damsel in distress and all that! Miss Trimm had seen through the act straight away, as had probably every other woman present in the room. What had been baffling, though, had been the sight of a highly intelligent man like Lord Bramblewell apparently allowing himself to be taken in by a show of such obvious trickery! He had been seduced by Miss Sutton's beauty, of course. The shoulder-length, blonde hair, gleaming and swinging softly, when she had moved her head, the dark-blue eyes, carefully made up and the red lipstick had all created an illusion of a woman who, to him, would have seemed alluringly beautiful, in an old fashioned, film-starry sort of way: not one who was brazenly bold, as Miss Trimm would have it.

Red, as Miss Sutton clearly knew, was a colour that stirred the blood of a man, just as a red cloth aroused the passions of a bull. And the brighter the red, the wilder the response, Miss Trimm had deduced. The night of the reception at Bramblewell Manor, when Susie had staged her fainting act, Miss Trimm, herself, had been wearing black. A nondescript, black cocktail dress, with unobtrusive jewellery. She had looked lady-like, naturally, as was always the case, but she might as well have condemned herself to an evening lurking in the shadows. And now, that cunning minx, Miss Susie Sutton, was engaged to Lord Bramblewell! And one would soon have to start thinking of her, not as Miss Sutton, but as Lady Bramblewell and furthermore, one would have to address her in that way! The very thought of being forced into the humiliating position of having to treat Miss Sutton as if she were a social superior, by a long shot, made Miss Trimm feel so inwardly angry that the polished veneer of sophistication she had cultivated over many years felt as if it were about to crack.

When Miss Trimm had first arrived in Bramblewell School, five years previously, to take up her post as head-mistress, she, herself, had secretly set her cap at Lord Bramblewell, hoping that, one day, he would ask her to be his bride. Seeing him, on her first day in Bramblewell territory, a well-built, strong-looking figure striding across the grass, his blond hair blown by a soft breeze and with a dark cloak clasped to his shoulders, she had fallen for him rather helplessly, in the style of the heroines of the sorts of romantic novels she had always claimed she did not read, but in fact did skim through, in camera. However, she had been too intelligent, too well-educated and too honest a woman to have descended to using the kinds of tactics Susie had employed to capture Lord Bramblewell's heart. What had appalled her, after the night of the reception at the manor, had been the fact that Lord Bramblewell, whom she had known to be an intellectual of some repute, had fallen so quickly and so completely for Miss Sutton's chicaneries. Before she had realised what had been happening, Lord Bramblewell had started to talk about Miss Sutton as if she had been a stray kitten, limping helplessly through the world, in desperate need of his care! Miss Trimm had known that Lord Bramblewell had never been a shallow man and had not shown himself to be unsophisticated, either. Why had he been unable to see Susie for what she was? Why had he not perceived, behind the dazzle, an ill-educated, mistress of deception, who would embarrass him socially and bore him, eventually, simply because her conversation would be restricted by her lack of learning?

Miss Trimm had met Miss Sutton before that fateful night at the manor. On that first occasion, Susie had been on a lower rung of the social ladder. She had, in fact, been accompanying Gylen Somerland, on a visit to Bramblewell School. Like Lord Bramblewell, Mr. Somerland had clearly been considerably older than the young woman by his side. Nevertheless, it had been his intention to marry her, apparently, thus making her, not only his wife, but also step-mother to his two children, Rosalind and John: the two children he had summoned to the Wirral, from Bristol, to stay with him. Mr. Somerland had requested an appointment with

Miss Trimm to talk about the possibility of his daughter becoming a pupil at the school. And as Miss Trimm had sized up both her visitors, it had occurred to her that Susie had seemed unsure of herself. She had sat stiffly in her chair, hardly moving, and had refused the offer of coffee because Mr. Somerland had refused. It had occurred to Miss Trimm, that she, Susie, had been reluctant to make even the least significant of decisions on her own, through lack of confidence. She had been a nice enough girl, Miss Trimm had reckoned, but one who had been entirely unsuitable to be a future consort to a well-established surgeon in the Wirral: a man with considerable social know-how, poise and urbane tastes.

Much later, Miss Trimm had picked up, through the medium of staffroom gossip relayed to her by Lee Chan, her loyal personal assistant, the information that Susie Sutton had once - incredibly, in Lee's opinion - been the girlfriend of Mr. Teddy Laurence, the decent, young Physics teacher, who had not been in the school for long. Miss Sutton had broken his heart and he had been shocked by the reason she had given for leaving him. However, at least, he had conceded, she had been honest in telling him she had wanted a higher earner as a boyfriend. And having gone up in the world, subsequently, thanks to Gylen Somerland, and having met Lord Bramblewell, as a consequence, Miss Sutton had, then, apparently, realised she could better her lot to an even greater extent. When she had, finally, managed to enchant Lord Bramblewell and he had proposed marriage to her, offering her the cabochon ring that had belonged to one of his ancestors, the founder of Bramblewell School, Susie had known that her conquest of the social heights had reached its zenith, that she would be comfortable for the rest of her life and that, crucially, she would never be cold in winter again.

What had galled Miss Trimm most, at that point, had been the fact that she, herself, had spent all her years, at Bramblewell School, preparing for the day when Lord Bramblewell would finally notice that she would be able to play the part of Lady Bramblewell splendidly. In a blatant attempt to please him, she had curbed her natural inclination towards independence. She had stopped herself from stamping her own personality on Bramblewell School, so as to accommodate his vision of what it should be like. Some of his innovative ideas had caused dissension among the staff, the introduction of astrology, as an optional subject, having been one of them. Even taking into consideration the fact that Lord Bramblewell had always been the chief benefactor of Bramblewell School, providing scholarships for fifty per cent of the pupils and funding much else besides, and, therefore, had to be placated to some extent, Miss Trimm had still been too lenient with him, in the estimation of her staff. She had surrendered too much control. When challenged by the more experienced teachers in the school, Miss Trimm had energetically argued that the connection with the Bramblewell family had to be maintained, because of the school's history, but in the evenings, alone in her large house in Chester, she had often admitted to herself that, on occasions, she should, in fact, have put her foot down, when dealing with Lord Bramblewell and, furthermore, should not have used the school's policies as part of her strategy to win him over, for her own gain.

With the arrival of Miss Susie Sutton in Lord Bramblewell's life, Miss Trimm had, in a professional manner, continued to behave as if nothing had disturbed her. But, she had begun to regret, bitterly, all that she had done to please Lord Bramblewell over five years, at a high cost to her own reputation as a teacher. Her heart had started to ice up. How could she, now, remain in Bramblewell School, knowing that, only yards away, Miss Sutton would be enjoying the life-style she, herself, had coveted for so long?

Susie Sutton, in her red dress, and Lord Bramblewell had left the small but ancient wood that was situated between the school and the manor house. Lord Bramblewell had tenderly helped Susie down the slope from the rise on which the tall oaks, sycamores and horse chestnut trees had been planted, long in the past. On lower ground, they had followed the path skirting the side of the tennis courts. And now, they were climbing up the steps that would lead them in the direction of the back door of the main building of the school, a neo-Gothic construction which had once been the home of one of Lord Bramblewell's ancestors. Miss Trimm stepped closer to the window of her office. Was it possible to see the expression on Miss Sutton's face? Could Lord Bramblewell have already told her that his former fiancée, Isolde Delamar, had been appointed to a post within the school?

It was not in Miss Trimm's nature to be revengeful. Really, it was not. However, when Lee Chan, her personal assistant, had resigned in order to move to an administrative position in Hong Kong, Miss Trimm had found temptation thrown in her path. She had been astonished to find that one of the applicants for Miss Chan's post had been Isolde Delamar, of all people! How had Miss Delamar had the nerve to apply? Had she read that Lord Bramblewell had become engaged to Miss Susie Sutton and, riled by that piece of news, had she thought she should remind him that she, herself, had been his first fiancée? Was she hoping that he would remember how much he had loved her and that his attachment to Miss Sutton would look insignificant in comparison? It was well known in Chester and elsewhere, that, ten years previously, Lord Bramblewell had been engaged to Miss Delamar. Their engagement photo had been printed in all of Cheshire's society magazines and a date had been set for a grand wedding in Chester Cathedral. But then, shockingly, Miss Delamar, had abruptly broken off the engagement, in order to follow to London a young man who had turned out to have been a scoundrel and a complete cad. Possibly feeling foolish at having made such an ill-considered blunder, Miss Delamar had remained in London for years. But obviously, she had no scruples about returning to Cheshire, after all. And by applying for a post in Bramblewell School, which she would know Lord Bramblewell visited several times each week, her intentions had been clear enough. Clear to another woman, anyway. The temptation to appoint her to the post had been considerable. If Miss Trimm could not have Lord Bramblewell, why should she allow Miss Sutton to walk away with him, as if she had scooped a prize, without effort? If the appointment of Isolde Delamar would upset Lord Bramblewell, it would undoubtedly un-nerve Miss Sutton as well. Did she not deserve to be un-nerved, at least for the cold way she had dismissed Teddy Laurence from her life?

Miss Trimm had been torn between the way she knew she should behave and the way she had been tempted to behave. In the end, she had allowed Lord Bramblewell to choose Miss Chan's successor. She had sent him, by e-mail, while he had been on holiday in France, the names and career records of three candidates for the post. Isolde Delamar's name had been one of the three. Lord Bramblewell had chosen Isolde.

Miss Trimm watched as Lord Bramblewell and Susie Sutton started up the short flight of steps that led to the back door of the school. From her window, she, now, had a clear view of them. She stepped back, so that she, herself, would not be noticed, by her visitors, but not before she had taken in the fact that Susie was looking dejected and possibly nervous.

"She knows," Miss Trimm thought to herself. "She knows."

CHAPTER 3

The Aspects of Venus

"The Age of Aquarius," murmured Liz Laurier, as she watched a piece of paper spilling out of the printer positioned beside the computer in her study. She was not reflecting on the Aquarian Age in a general way, but rather, on one of its manifestations which had rapidly become commonplace: electronic mail. And although she found it riveting to observe how scientifically-oriented Aquarius was seeping into the psyche of humanity - in the increasing use of robots, for example - she had certain misgivings about the direction in which it, Aquarius, would ultimately lead the world's peoples. Liz could not, in fact, imagine what lay in store for humanity without, also, feeling a nostalgic yearning for the age that had preceded the Aquarian Age: that of Pisces. The Piscean Age, after all – stretching over two thousand years - had been a time when the world had been left in the hands of warm-fleshed humans rather more than in the care of programmed machines, as was increasingly the case.

The message that had arrived by e-mail had been sent by Liz's daughter, Rosalind Somerland. Liz studied it, leaning against the table on which the computer had been wired up. She had, in fact, been looking forward to reading news of Rosalind's holiday in France and so, was disappointed to find that the message, although long, consisted, principally, of a request which concerned the sister of Ida Traversi, one of Rosalind's closest school friends. Ida's sister, Caterina, had had a difficult relationship with her mother, Signora Traversi, throughout her life. According to Ida, who, like Rosalind, had studied astrology for a short time at Bramblewell School, Venus, in Caterina's astrological birth chart, was in conjunction with Pluto, in her mother's chart. In other words, Caterina's Venus occupied the same degree and sign of the Zodiac as Signora Traversi's Pluto did, or else, the two planets were very close, an orb of four degrees, either side of exactitude, being allowed. Rosalind wanted to know if Liz would confirm Ida's belief that this conjunction was at the root of Caterina's problem. Rosalind promised she would be careful in the way she passed on information to Ida and she knew that Ida would be equally cautious were she to have the opportunity to talk to Caterina about the conjunction. Ida was not sure, in fact, if Caterina, being a few years older than she was, herself, would be receptive to receiving advice from a kid sister and so, she would have to be subtle. But, that aside, Rosalind wanted to know how the conjunction would affect the lives of both Caterina and Signora Traversi in order to satisfy her own curiosity and to extend her own knowledge. She had been intrigued by Ida's description of Caterina.

Liz wished Rosalind had been able to send the two astrological charts in their entirety, but since they were not available, she would have to confine herself to writing general comments. Yes. Pluto in one birth chart in conjunction with Venus, in another chart, could be experienced as being over-controlling and even oppressive, especially in a parent-child relationship. But conversely, Pluto, when operating in a helpful manner, could support and guide a Venus who was, say, inclined to be naïve and incapable of good judgement. In the Traversis' situation, Plutonic heaviness had, seemingly, been experienced by Caterina, in a way that had consistently not been conducive to her happiness. Liz reckoned that the tension that existed between Signora Traversi and Caterina would ease as Caterina became older and lived independently, to the extent that she could. But any invisible wounds, inflicted in childhood, would possibly not heal quickly.

Liz put down Rosalind's message and began to pace the small room that she used as an office, as she often did when an idea which would, perhaps, lead to a course of action had begun to form in her head. She walked towards a window that provided her with a view of the roof-tops of Ellesmere Port and the sky. The evening was quiet; the air was still. Then, Liz heard voices, down in the street. A young couple, who lived in the flat below hers, had started to get into their car. The man was saying something to his young wife. Liz could not hear what was being said, exactly, but the cadences of the man's Cheshire accent were soothing and made her feel peaceful. And then, just as Liz was allowing her mind to free itself of tension, a fresh idea came into her head. She would write a book for Rosalind! She would write a useful book that would have, as its focus, the planets and their connections with each other - or aspects, as they were called - occurring across charts. And she would write it in a straightforward and simple way, as if she were preparing the scripts for lessons of the type she would once have delivered to her young pupils at Bramblewell School. It would be a book which, she hoped, would be of interest to all teenagers who were struggling to understand the forces at work in their relationships with parents, siblings, teachers and friends. But, principally, it would be a book for Rosalind. It would centre on her world and the people in it. And the book would be dedicated to her.

Liz conjured up an image, in her head, of the page on which the dedication would be written. It would bear the legend, "To Rosalind," or simply, "To my daughter." Liz wondered which one Rosalind would prefer. And then, there was her son, John, to consider. Should she dedicate the book to him, as well? Maybe he would balk at the thought of being mentioned in a book written by her, though.

Liz went into her sitting room, curled up on a white sofa and started to jot down on the back of the page on which the message had been printed, a list of the relationships which were preoccupying Rosalind, at that moment, as they would be the focus of the book's chapters. The girl's relationship with her school-friends, Ida, Portia and Talitha were obvious starting points. Then, there was Héloïse de Sauzon. Why Rosalind had, suddenly, become fascinated by the Sauzon girl, whom she had met at the Château du Crâne, would remain a mystery until Liz had had a chance to examine the French girl's astrological birth chart, but, in the meantime, the fact that Rosalind seemed to have been walking in Héloïse's shadow all summer irritated her. Rosalind had relayed news of Héloïse's cool, Parisian style of dressing, her logical way of approaching problems and her sophisticated control of her emotions, with gushing enthusiasm. But what had dazzled Rosalind most of all had, apparently, been the fact that Héloïse had confessed to having a crush on Teddy Laurence. "Just like me last year, Mum," Rosalind had written in the breathless style of a girl who believed that that connection alone had conferred on her a little of Héloïse's glamour. "And she's mad about Julian Bramblewell-Eurlinn , as well!" Liz had raised her eyebrows in dismay at the thought of the cold strategist, that Héloïse seemed to be, befriending Julian, with his decent,

English-style niceness, his perfect manners and his polite modesty: a modesty that concealed inner grandeur.

Liz had already realised that she was reacting strongly and negatively to the possibility of a liaison developing between Héloïse and Julian because she had begun to hope – in the manner of an unattractively pushy mother - that when Rosalind was old enough to marry, Julian might still be - well! - looking for a bride.

Accepting that she had begun to think in the same way as a character in a novel by Jane Austen - Mrs. Bennet, for example - Liz smiled ruefully and then, sighed. She had to concentrate on reality: on her own book. She needed a title to help her to focus. What would be appropriate? All planets played a part in establishing the nature of human interactions, but, traditionally, Venus was the planet that was associated most with relationships. What if the book were to be called "The Aspects of Venus"? A title such as that would suggest to the person who had little knowledge of astrology that different characteristics of Venus and

Venus' sphere of influence would be described. But the astrologer, proper, would know that "aspects" was the word used to describe significant connections created by angular distances between planets. All of that having been taken into account, Liz decided that "The Aspects of Venus" would serve her well as a title and, consequently, the evening drew to a close with her feeling pleased.

Two hours later, as she made her way to the kitchen, prior to retiring for the night, Liz removed copies of "Pride and Prejudice" and "Emma" from a bookshelf, as she passed by. She tucked the books under her arm, as, some minutes later, a cup of hot cocoa in her hand, she headed for her bedroom. If anyone understood the nature of relationship and its value, it was the pragmatic, but still romantic, Jane Austen. The Age of Pisces, in which Miss Austen had lived, could not be dismissed as being redundant, after all.

CHAPTER 4

A Bride and June

"What exactly does a man mean when he says 'I love you'?" asked Susie Sutton, flicking a lock of glossy, blonde hair out of her eyes.

Susie's companion, June Jones, a woman younger by two or three years, did not reply but, instead, shook her head. She put both her hands around the tall glass of caffè-latte in front of her and waited, as if assuming the question had been a rhetorical one.

"I'll tell you what he means," Susie continued, as expected. "He means, 'I'll be devoted to you, until I notice someone who is more attractive than you and more interesting.' That's what he means."

"Oh! Hush, Susie!" urged June, leaning across the table, while keeping her voice low. "That's not true. And don't talk so loudly. Remember who you are, now."

June looked to her left and right in surreptitious fashion, but the other customers in the café, on the upper floor of the large book-store in Liverpool One, were either engaged in conversations of their own, or were reading novels they had just bought. No one seemed to be paying attention to the blonde in the chic, beige dress sitting opposite June, despite the fact that she, Susie, was now clearly agitated. She bent down to pick up from the floor the turquoise handbag she had left at her feet, pushing out of her way the large cardboard box with the name of a shop, SHE-LI, written on its side.

"Lord Bramblewell hasn't actually done anything wrong," June said gently, watching, with furrowed brow, what Susie was doing.

Susie had pulled out of her turquoise handbag a tiny, round mirror. She carefully looked at the reflection of her mouth in it. Then, being satisfied that her bright lipstick was in place, she put down the mirror on the table at which she and June were sitting. Catching June's eye and realising her greatest friend was tempted to chide her for attending to her make-up at the table, she smiled. "Of course you are right. Rupert hasn't done anything wrong," she said. "But I know he is THINKING about her. Oh! June! How can I put up with it? Every day, she will be working just yards away from Bramblewell Manor! I don't know how I'll be able to stand it!"

"Susie! Calm down! You are raising your voice again!" said June, now looking strained. "You haven't explained why you are so worried, anyway. I mean, she's just a girl from Lord Bramblewell's past. So what? Don't forget that you have an 'ex' actually teaching in Bramblewell School, after all, Has Lord Bramblewell ever complained about your past relationship with Teddy Laurence? I bet he hasn't! This girl can be ignored, Susie. Don't forget that you are the one wearing the engagement ring. Come on, now! It isn't like you to be so…"

"So…what?"

"I don't know. It's just that, usually, you don't seem to look upon any obstacle as a problem, really. You just deal with obstacles. You jump over them. I haven't ever seen you looking as unhappy as you are now."

Susie looked down at the cabochon engagement ring on her pale hand, and she breathed in audibly. To June, the sound seemed to be half way between a sob and a sigh. Susie was, then, silent. She sat back in her chair and looked around her, without focusing on anything in particular. She seemed to be wondering what she should divulge next. Eventually, she said:

"June, as soon as I saw her, I knew I had been outclassed."

"What do you mean?"

"I mean that the girl looked fabulous. She was tall and she had dark-blonde hair. It wasn't brown-ish, but it wasn't bright blonde either. She didn't seem to have coloured it, but it still looked attractive. No…Not attractive. It looked amazing. It really suited her. She had plaited it. It was in two plaits, just slightly longer than shoulder-length."

"Two plaits?" exclaimed June, obviously taken aback. "Didn't she look ridiculous? I mean, if she was tall..."

"No. She didn't look ridiculous. She was stunning. She looked as if she would stand out in a crowd - any crowd - just because she was so unusually beautiful. There was something a bit continental about her. I thought she could have been half Swiss and half French. Oh! I don't know...She had that sort of pale tan that some French women have all year round."

"But, she is English."

"Oh! Yes! She is definitely English. She comes from Cheshire. I'd say, though, that going by the way she was dressed, she must be one of those Cheshire women who are used to living in high style."

"What was she wearing?"

Susie smiled kindly, before replying. June was fascinated by clothes, possibly because she could not afford to buy many of her own.

"She was wearing a trouser suit. A corduroy trouser suit in a dark, maroon shade. And the trousers were very well cut."

"Expensive, then?"

"Definitely."

"And you said her name was..."

"Isolde Delamar. Apparently, she's a cousin of Eva Derbyshire, last year's head girl at Bramblewell."

"Oh!" exclaimed June, as if she had suddenly resolved a puzzle. "That explains everything! Eva would have told her about the vacancy at the school. Maybe this... Isolde?...was tired of travelling on the London tube every morning and just wanted to return to Cheshire. The explanation for her coming here could be as simple as that. Would Eva Derbyshire have been able to put in a good word for her?"

"No. Not Eva Derbyshire," said Susie softly, placing her elbows on the table, although she knew, now, she should not. She rested her head in her hands. Her shiny hair, having been washed and brushed by a stylist from Chester, who had visited Bramblewell Manor earlier that morning, fell forward like a glossily rippling curtain.

"Is there something you haven't told me?" asked June.

"Rupert was deeply in love with her for years," answered Susie, looking up. "Years. Even after she left him, he could not forget her."

June stared at her friend in silence.

"How do you know?" she asked, then. "Did he tell you, himself?"

"Mrs. Oliver, the housekeeper, told me that he kept her photo by his bedside for absolutely ages."

"Hang on! You once told me that Mrs. Oliver didn't like you. She might have lied just to hurt you. Some people are cunning enough to do something like that, Susie."

"I know...but..."

"I'll fetch some more coffee," June then said, standing up abruptly, as if to indicate she needed time to herself, perhaps to work out what Susie's strategy should be.

Susie watched as June made her way to the counter to place her order. She noticed that the bones in June's shoulders could be perceived through the thin material of her cheap dress. A wave of kindness, mixed with resolve, swept over her, then. She knew what it was like to struggle financially. She did not want to return to being in that difficult position, herself. And at that moment, she knew that she was going to fight to hang on to Lord Bramblewell and the style of life he would be able to provide for her. She would outsmart Isolde Delamar, Mrs. Oliver and everyone else who wished her ill. She would marry Lord Bramblewell, in Chester Cathedral, no matter what she would have to do to achieve her goal. And on that wedding day, when June would be her chief bridesmaid, she would make sure that June's dress would be a work of art, a picture of opulence.

It now seemed so long since the two of them had worked together as administrative assistants at the Tectum letting agency, in Chester. June was still employed there, but when Susie had become engaged to Lord Bramblewell, he had asked her to leave. June had been sorry to lose Susie's companionship, but, at the same time, she had been thrilled to discover that Susie's dreams of a fairy-tale romance had actually been realised. However, she had, at times, plainly expressed her reservations about the way Susie had achieved her goals. In June's opinion, Susie's cold rejection of Teddy Laurence had been shocking. Susie had tried to make amends, but had ended up making Teddy even more annoyed with her.

June returned from the counter carrying glasses of coffee on a tray.

"I've been thinking…" she said, as she sat down, but she did not finish the sentence.

"What have you been thinking?"

"Lord Bramblewell is not a stupid person, Susie. He must know that this girl is unreliable. She's not made of the right stuff."

With a spoon, Susie slowly scooped the foam from the top of the glass that June had handed to her.

"I might as well tell you," she said then, "that I, myself, realised that Rupert still loved her when we were in France."

"You mean…a couple of weeks ago?"

"Yes. When Miss Trimm sent a message to ask him to choose someone to replace Lee Chan as personal assistant in the school, he chose her. Miss Trimm apparently sent him the names of three candidates and he chose her."

"HE chose her? This Isolde girl? HE chose her?"

"Yes."

"And how did he explain what he had done? What did he say to you?"

"Oh! He said he believed Isolde Delamar was possibly down on her luck or worn out. London was a tough place in which to work.

He wanted to give her the opportunity to make a fresh start, back home. He did ask me if I thought he had made the right decision."

"Really? What did you say?"

"I told him he had probably made the right decision."

"WHAT? Why on earth did you say such a thing? You should have told him to choose one of the other two!"

"How could I?"

"Easily!"

Susie sighed, then, and leaned back in her chair.

"Listen!" she said. "If I had told him to choose someone else, I might as well have said to him that I didn't trust him. I'd have looked mean-spirited. The thought of poor Isolde, desperate to return home, would have been preying on his mind forever. Can't you see that?"

"But, Susie! He won't just be thinking of her now, will he? He'll be seeing her every time he goes into the school! You should have said 'No!' You were taking a big risk."

"I was going to lose either way. It was like one of those jams chess players dread, or so I have read. A knight fork, or something like that. My only option lay in giving Rupert the impression that I trusted him."

"And how did he behave when he saw Isolde again? Do you know?"

"Yes. I do. When we returned from France, Rupert said he was going to walk over to the school, from the manor, through the wood. Did I want to go with him? I said that I did."

"I'm assuming Isolde had already started working in the school?"

"Yes. She had. Although it was August and the schoolgirls were on holiday still, there was a lot of administrative work that needed attention. Anyway, we went through the wood and as soon as we had arrived in the school, Rupert took me into the main office and there she was, in her trouser suit and plaits."

"Go on!" urged June, leaning forward.

"I had put on my scarlet dress."

"Oh! No! You weren't wearing your backless sandals as well, were you?"

"I was! "

Susie smiled at June, knowing that June had always found the sandals rather louche.

"Why didn't you wear something nice?" June asked, trying not to frown.

"I wore red because I wanted to give this Isolde Delamar the message that I was not going to be pushed into the shadows."

"And what happened?"

"You know, I could practically sense a crackling of electricity in the air. Honestly! One could have imagined an electrical current flowing between them. I might as well have been invisible. My scarlet dress seemed to make no impression at all on Isolde Delamar. She ignored me. She glanced quickly in my direction and then seemed to dismiss me, as being someone who wasn't important. She must have concluded, straight away, that she wasn't going to find it difficult to frighten me away."

"How dare she?"

"Yes. Exactly. How dare she? My marriage to Rupert, all being well, will take place in seven months' time. Isolde Delamar has seven months to try to persuade Rupert to marry her, instead. But if she thinks I am going to be pushed out of the way easily, she can think again. I shall not attack her, but I shall defend myself, June."

"Good girl!"

"But, I'll need your support, June," said Susie, earnestly. "I've leaned on you in the past, but I'll need you more than ever in the months to come."

Suddenly, Susie bent down and lifted up the large cardboard box that had been lying by her feet.

"This is for you," she said.

"'SHE-LI'?" gasped June, staring at the name of the boutique, written on the side of the box. "Susie! You can't…That's so extravagant! What is it?"

"A dress. I want you to have it."

Susie had bought the elegant, slim dress earlier, intending to wear it herself that evening. It was well cut, had a good lining and generously covered seams. It had occurred to her, though, that June needed the dress more. June, in fact, would really appreciate the way it had been constructed and sewn and she would treasure it. Its colour was pale lemon, into the bargain. Susie knew, from experience, that lemon would lend warmth and brightness to pale skin. It would light up June's face and caramel-coloured hair, becomingly.

"But Susie!" protested June, peeking inside the box.

"Please! Just take it," said Susie. "To make me happy! It's an advance present for my best bridesmaid."

June acquiesced graciously then, her eyes shining with excitement.

Half an hour later, they, Susie and June, parted company. Susie wandered through Liverpool One, alone. It was Saturday afternoon and the streets were crowded. A fresh breeze blew up from the Mersey, but it was a warm day and Susie found the breeze as refreshing as cool cologne, infused with lime zest, sprayed upon her face. She turned her head to look in the direction of the river and realised that Teddy Laurence's flat was possibly down there, by the water's edge, in a parallel position to where she was standing. She wondered if the rumour was true: the rumour that would have it that he had allowed Rebecca Hampton, the American student he knew, to stay in his flat throughout the summer. Teddy, himself, was in France, of course, and was probably still angry over the fact that she, Susie, had compelled him to appear in the film being shot there. So great had been his annoyance that Susie now wished she had not forced him to accept the rôle.

She had meant well, though. She had wanted to make Teddy a star, in order to enable him to earn a large amount of money: enough to make it possible for him to buy nice things, to travel extensively and to meet interesting people. She had wanted to give him what she had considered to have been the gift of happiness, to make up for the insensitive way she had treated him previously. But, Teddy had berated her for thinking her approach had been acceptable. He had made it clear that he had found her attempt to control his behaviour exceptionally crass.

Reflecting on Teddy's reaction later, Susie had had to admit to herself that Teddy's anger had been justified. She had told him that she, herself, had persuaded Lord Bramblewell to provide funding for the film, implying that the money would be withdrawn, were she to request its withdrawal. She had made it clear she would demand that the film not be made if Teddy were to refuse to appear in it. If the film were not shot, the four Bramblewell girls who had been responsible for the staging of the school play that had been the basis of the film script, would not be paid for their idea. If the Bramblewell girls were not thus rewarded, one of them, Talitha Appleby, would not be able to pay for her school fees and, as a consequence, would be required to leave Bramblewell School, her parents having fallen into financial difficulties. She, Talitha, was not clever enough, seemingly, to win a Bramblewell scholarship.

"A great deal hangs on your decision, Teddy," Susie had stated.

Teddy had, momentarily, wondered if Susie had been bluffing. He had reckoned that the shooting of the film would proceed whether he had a rôle in it or not. But, could he be sure? Susie had appeared to be so ruthlessly determined, that day, dressed in her fine, new clothes, that he had not risked crossing her. Susie shivered as she remembered the way Teddy had looked at her, in the restaurant in Chester, where she had arranged to meet him to unveil her proposal. She had realised later, the extent to which she must have hurt his male pride. She had insulted him, that day, in a way he would not forget.

Susie wondered, now, if Teddy would react, in some unexpected fashion, to the way he had been forced to spend his summer holiday. He was capable of springing surprises, after all.

Pondering on this fact, a dismaying thought suddenly struck her. A chill, simultaneously, went down her back and her head seemed to grow cold, also. She thought she might faint and so, she put out her hand to touch a wall, in order to steady herself.

"Are you all right, love?" asked a man who was passing by.

Susie nodded and forced herself to smile. She saw a café, then, a block away and she made her way to it. She went to the counter, ordered tea and walked with it to the nearest small table. She drank half of the tea in the cup, before pausing to consider the question that had de-stabilised her: what if Teddy were to resign from his post at Bramblewell School?

Life without Teddy, somewhere in the background, was unthinkable, she now realised. Even after she had abandoned him in order to become, first of all, Gylan Somerland's girlfriend, she had still turned to him in times of distress and he had always responded with kindness. She had taken it for granted that he would always be within reach. How could she possibly deal with Isolde Delamar on her own, without his help? June Jones would offer sympathy, of course, but June would not be able to think of strategic solutions to problems in the way Teddy would.

"Oh! Teddy!" thought Susie, as she felt an inner panic gripping her. "Don't leave me!"

CHAPTER 5

Madame Gabrielle

"I'd like to look younger. Is it possible to make me look younger?" asked Madame Gabrielle de Talence, addressing Agnès, the young woman with the smooth pony tail, who had arrived a few minutes earlier, at her residence in the Cours de la Victoire, in one of the elegant quarters of Bordeaux.

Agnès Seurelle, aged only eighteen, but already a mistress of diplomacy and discretion, stepped back to look at the reflection of her client in the long mirror, which had been placed on the dressing table at which Madame Gabrielle had sat down, straight-backed.

"Ah! Oui, madame," she replied, her voice low and soft and her expression appropriately serious. "But would Madame allow me to cut her hair, instead of simply styling it as usual?"

Agnès would not have been surprised had her uncharacteristically bold request been refused with a sharp "Non!" However, Madame Gabrielle, after a moment of thought, gave her consent with a nod, saying then:

"A little. Just a little."

Agnès had been feeling tired when she had arrived at the Cours de la Victoire. She had had to deal with many clients that day, at the hairdressing salon at which she was employed, in the centre of Bordeaux, since two of the senior stylists had been absent, having been summoned to work on the set of a film being made at the Château du Crâne, not far from the city. Nevertheless, the thought of creating a new look for Madame Gabrielle, one of the private clients whom she visited weekly, gave Agnès a lift that evening. She felt as if she had drunk a cupful of creative energy.

Agnès began to remove pins and small combs from Madame Gabrielle's essentially grey hair: hair which she, Agnès, tinted once a week with a silver-white wash. On Fridays, when she normally carried out this task, she would, first of all, leave the salon, her hours of work there having been completed, and then, she would make her way, on foot, along the rue Sainte-Catherine, before walking through the Place de la Comédie and past the impressive Esplanade des Quinconces. Upon reaching the Cours de Verdun, she would turn right and head in the direction of Madame Gabrielle's house. There were times when, exhausted on a Friday evening, she would momentarily consider going straight home to the small flat she shared with her mother, down a side street, close to the River Gironde. But, on those occasions, she would remind herself of the fact that Madame Gabrielle always paid at once, in cash, tipped well and lived in the kind of stylish surroundings that she, Agnès, longed to inhabit. Agnès' imagination was fed, in fact, by her Friday visits to the Cours de la Victoire.

Five steps led up to the polished door of Madame Gabrielle's residence. Behind it, a few more steps, these glossy, took Agnès to an entrance hall rendered imposing by marble pillars that advertised the wealth of the owner of the house, Agnès felt. Madame Gabrielle had been a widow for ten years, but her husband, an unostentatiously rich man, had invested his money in ways that had ensured Madame Gabrielle would live in comfort and without worries of a financial kind, for the rest of her life. Agnès had gleaned this information from the gossip of clients at the salon and her observation of Madame's habits had confirmed what she had heard. Agnès' weekly visits drew her into a world, therefore, with which she was largely unfamiliar, her own life having been lived in a less wealth-infused part of the city. However, having had a glimpse of Madame Gabrielle's highly bourgeois existence, Agnès longed to better her own lot.

Habitually, Madame Gabrielle's hair was brushed away from her face and, in part, piled high at the crown of her head, the rest, being pinned in a neat roll at the back. Viewed from the front, the style was reminiscent of that which had been favoured by ladies living in France at the end of the eighteenth century. There was a touch of the Ancien Régime about it. The style was excessively old-fashioned, in Agnès' judgement, but she conceded that it did suit Madame Gabrielle, visually. Madame had a high forehead that was almost unlined, despite the fact that she was, after all, a grandmother. She had, indeed, a forehead which gave her, immediately, the appearance of an exalted aristocrat, belonging to that bygone century which had given birth, eventually, to the turbulent Revolution. In Agnès' opinion, Madame looked like those ladies on the covers of eau-de-rose, romantic novels that she, Agnès, liked to read, but which, of course, she would not admit to buying when in the company of former school-friends who were, now, more intellectually focused, being students at the Faculté des Lettres: friends she met in cafés, near the Cours Pasteur, from time to time.

Agnès often wondered what Madame Gabrielle's life had been like when she had been young. Had she had sentimental and interesting encounters with handsome men who had, perhaps, broken her heart? She appeared sad, on occasions, as if she were reflecting on a past that could have been lived in other ways, but although Agnès had been attending to Madame's hair for more than a year, she knew little, really, about her private life and Madame Gabrielle knew equally little about her own, aside from the fact that the apartment she, Agnès, shared with her mother provided a view of the river. Madame Gabrielle and Agnès conversed rarely, in fact, being separated by almost five decades, when it came to age. However, as time had passed, Agnès had accumulated information about Madame's lifestyle and tastes, through observation mainly, but also, at rare moments, through having been present, fortuitously, when Madame had dropped her guard. There had been, for example, "the Jacqueline revelation" as Agnès had called it. That revelation had been triggered by the fact that Agnès' eyes had been drawn to one of the silver-framed photographs standing on the mantelpiece, in the room in which Madame had been in the habit of paying her, at the end of each Friday visit, and Madame had noticed. With unusual candour, Madame had casually mentioned, then, that the three teenage girls and younger boy, posing in the photo with their parents, were her daughter's children. "This one," Madame Gabrielle had stated, pointing to one of the girls, "is called Jacqueline. I chose her name, my daughter having allowed me to. I chose it because I admired Mrs. Jacqueline Kennedy so much, at the time. I still do. Being so young, yourself, you possibly are not aware of the fact that Mrs. Kennedy was the wife of the 35th President of the United States. She loved France, you know. She loved our style of living and thinking. She dressed very elegantly. I collected photos of her, cut out of newspapers and magazines, and I kept them in scrapbooks." Amazed, Agnès had been able to respond with only an "Ah bon, madame?"

Agnès always carried out her hair-styling duties in a spacious dressing-room which was an ante-chamber to Madame's bedroom. There were two trunks and three large wardrobes in the chamber: pieces of furniture in which, presumably, Madame's clothes were kept. The wardrobes, constructed of dark, carved wood, were endowed with ornate, brass key-holes through which drifted the scent of lavender. In the room, there was, also, the dressing-table at which Madame sat, to have her hair done. She, Madame, had once said that it was a replica of one which could be seen at Malmaison, a residence near Paris, in which, in times past, Napoleon's wife, the Empress Joséphine, had lived. This piece of information had appealed to the romantic side of Agnès and while, thereafter, attending to Madame's hair, usually in silence, she would imagine herself living in a different era. She wondered if Madame, too, pictured herself in an historical setting, but having reflected on this notion, she thought not. Madame appeared too cold and too self-disciplined to yield easily to the fanciful.

Three steps led from the scented ante-chamber up to Madame's bedroom, proper, a room into which light entered in abundance, through a large window which overlooked the Cours de la Victoire. The light, though, was filtered through the five finely-meshed, muslin panels of a screen which stood on the floor, in front of the window. Agnès had added to the points of etiquette or, more correctly, "savoir-vivre", that she had absorbed through having had contact with Madame Gabrielle, the rule that people outside in the street should not be allowed to catch a glimpse of the contents of a private room within a home, and, above all, not a bedroom.

The pins having been removed from Madame Gabrielle's hair and having been laid in a porcelain dish on the dressing-table, along with little combs, Agnès stood and, again, studied Madame's reflection in the looking-glass.

"I could cut your hair so that it would skin your shoulders, Madame," she said. "Then, I could add a fringe. Finally, I could dye the centre parting, covering two centimetres on either side, using two shades of dark brown, when doing that. The dark tints would give an observer the impression that the white-blonde colour was fake. The apparently dark roots would suggest youthfulness. I think, Madame, that you had dark hair when you were younger, had you not? I could dye a few locks, here and there, in dark brown shades, as well."

Madame Gabrielle sat still, in silence, for a moment or two. Then, she nodded.

"Oui," she said, with a casual shrug, her mouth forming a partial pout.

What Agnès had proposed had not been what Madame Gabrielle had had in mind. She had imagined that Agnès would have wanted to tint her hair, more conventionally, in, say, the pale blonde shade that was naturally the colour of the long, glossy tresses of two of her grand-daughters: Héloïse and Jacqueline de Sauzon. A long, white-blonde bob, with startlingly dark roots, which was effectively what Agnès had envisaged, would require a touch of audacity on Madame's part, when appearing in public with her new style. "But, why not?" she thought, as if disengaging herself from self-imposed restrictions.

Agnès removed long scissors from a transparent, zipped bag she had taken from the attaché case she carried with her when visiting private clients. Madame Gabrielle uttered a sigh, apparently of resignation and started to let her thoughts drift. She was normally disinclined to speak at all when Agnès was engaged in her tasks. On the few occasions when she had felt the urge to chat, she had strayed no further than general topics: the effect the weather would have on that year's Cabernet Sauvignon and Merlot grapes, growing in the vineyards around Bordeaux, for example. It occurred to her that Agnès' interpretation of her reticence might be that she, Madame, had no wish to talk to a young girl with whom she would normally have no contact, socially. Truly, there was a time when she would have felt it unwise to converse other than in a formal manner with Agnès, but in recent months, she had realised she was becoming more tempted to cross social boundaries and to revisit a side of herself that, for decades, she had suppressed. Maybe, that evening, as Agnès set about her task, she, Madame, would tell her exactly why she wanted to look more youthful. Maybe she would tell Agnès about the musician ...But, no! What utter folly that would be! Desipience! Agnès looked discreet and quiet, but in another environment, she might turn into an untrustworthy gossip. No. She could not confide in anyone. She would keep to herself the information that, soon, she would see him again: the man who had illuminated a moment of her life with what she now, effusively, considered to be his dazzling presence. She knew she was thinking in the way an unattractively ingénue adolescent would, but as long as her daughter and grandchildren did not find out about her thoughts and plans, what did it matter, for once, if she were to allow herself the indulgence of a flight of fancy? She was becoming older and, with increasing age, she had realised, suddenly, that she had been, perhaps, too harsh with herself and with others, during her life.

Madame Gabrielle closed her eyes. Her memory of the day, in the previous year, when she had heard the musician's voice again, after an interval of decades, was hazy, because on that day, she had been feeling unwell and her perception of events had been affected by her physical pain. She had been at the Château de Sauzon, the home of her son-in-law, Henri, the Comte de Sauzon and of her daughter, Marie-Christine, the Comtesse de Sauzon, in Belle-Isle, off the coast of Brittany. A garden party had been planned to celebrate the engagement of Jacqueline, the couple's first-born daughter, to Teddy Laurence, a teacher she had met during a gap year between school and university: a year which she had spent in England, and specifically, in Liverpool. It had been a hot day. Madame Gabrielle could picture in her mind how the sun had blazed down on the green lawns of the château and, beyond those stretches of glistening grass, the glittering, Breton sea, which had been languorously washing the eastern shores of the beautiful island. Madame Gabrielle remembered asking Jèrôme, her grand-son, to carry a heavy chair for her, to a shady grove, some distance away from the large lawns where most of the guests were gathering. Marie-Colette, her youngest grand-daughter, had helped Jérôme, she remembered, because the people who had been employed to work at the château, that day, had been exceptionally busy and old Albert, the gardener, had not been up to carrying much. Marie-Colette's hair, long and dark and so unlike that of her two blonde sisters, had reminded Madame Gabrielle of her own hair when she had been young and still at school, so unaware, then, of what was to happen in the years ahead of her.

Madame Gabrielle had sat in the grove, in the shade of its tall, dark trees, reflecting on how kind and decent Count Henri's and Countess Marie-Christine's children had turned out to be: all four of them. She had felt uncomfortable, then, when she had thought of how mean-spirited she, herself, had been in her attitude to

Teddy Laurence, Jacqueline's fiancé. What had it mattered, after all, if Teddy had not been French, had been devoid of blue blood and had been unable to provide much information about his antecedents, in the centuries that had gone before? He had clearly been intelligent, thoughtful and kind. She should have been more accommodating in the way she had treated him. She should not have accused him of being an arriviste and a fortune hunter. After all, he had shown himself to have been more honourable than Jacqueline, in the end. As those thoughts had bothered her, Madame Gabrielle had leaned forward, as if weakened. The sun had started to make her forehead feel hot. She had seen Jacqueline walking towards her. At the same time, somewhere in the grounds of the château, a band of musicians had started to play in the open air. Madame Gabrielle had recognised, at once, the voice of the principal singer, or rather, the song he had been singing. Like bubbles escaping from champagne, memories had swirled to the surface of her mind. She had remembered that she had seen that singer when she, herself, had been young and a foreign student in Liverpool. Whence had he re-appeared, out of the blue, after so many decades? Why had he come to her son-in-law's château, of all places? Madame Gabrielle had lost consciousness, then, she supposed.

She had awoken in the bedroom which she had habitually occupied during her visits to the Château de Sauzon. She had been in the habit of visiting four times a year, much to Count Henri's apparent displeasure. However, on the day that she had collapsed, she had been struck, upon wakening, by the strained and anxious look on Count Henri's face, as he had stood by her bedside with Marie-Christine.

"We have sent for a doctor," he had said. "You will soon be well. It is nothing."

"I hope I did not spoil the afternoon for Jacqueline," Madame Gabrielle remembered having said, her voice weak.

"Oh, no!" Countess Marie-Christine had retorted, with

uncharacteristic iciness. "Jacqueline managed to spoil the afternoon, all by herself."

Later, Madame Gabrielle had found out that Jacqueline's former boyfriend, Jacqui, had arrived, although uninvited, dressed in his naval officer's uniform. Having seen him, and no doubt having remembered the way she had felt about him in former times, Jacqueline had run into his arms, leaving Teddy Laurence abandoned and bereft.

"How disgraceful!" Madame Gabrielle had thought, while lying in her bed, her temperature having risen, in response to her anger and horror at the way the entire Sauzon family had been dishonoured by this one thoughtless action. "What impropriety! What shame!"

Her bedroom window had been open and later, through it, she had heard Teddy Laurence's voice. He had been talking, down in the courtyard, to the musicians who had played, earlier, in the open air. They had offered him a lift to England.

"Where are you heading?" he had asked.

"To Liverpool! Where else?" had been the reply.

Liverpool! Liverpool: the city in which she, Madame Gabrielle, had once been young and carefree and happier than she had allowed herself to be, in the years since then. Weak still, and unable to rise, she had turned on her side and tears from her eyes had flowed into her pillow.

Some days later, when stronger and composed, Madame Gabrielle had discussed with Countess Marie-Christine how Jacqueline's reputation could be salvaged. She would have to marry Jacqui Galant, of course. There was nothing else that could be done, in the circumstances. Who else would want to consort with such a reckless girl, after all? A marriage would have to be arranged.

To divert her attention from these unhappy thoughts, Madame Gabrielle had allowed herself to wonder, with increasing curiosity, how the musicians she had heard, al fresco, had happened to be at the Château de Sauzon, that dramatic day. Had she imagined they had been there? She had asked Jérôme if he had known if Teddy Laurence had invited them, but Jérôme, twelve years of age and having no interest in such music as theirs, had been unable to provide any information whatsoever.

Madame had recovered the musicians' name from her memory, eventually: The Mermen. They had played in cellar clubs in Liverpool in 1967, the year she had been a student there. It was odd, really, that, decades later, Jacqueline, without any knowledge of her grand-mother's stay in the city- Countess Marie-Christine had not even known about it - had chosen Liverpool as her own gap year destination. Sometimes, Madame Gabrielle had wondered if there had been forces at work in the universe of which Jacqueline had been unaware, but then, she had shrugged and had placed Jacqueline's choice in the category of mere coincidence.

Performing on the stages of Liverpool's clubs, The Mermen had been much admired in the 1960s. The principal singer, dark eyed and haughty in bearing, had dressed in the style of Lord Byron and other poets of the Romantic era. One evening, making his way through the throng of spectators, he had, briefly, brushed past Madame Gabrielle, who had been standing in the crowd. The scent of lemon-infused cologne had trailed behind him, intoxicating Madame, with its freshness, in the hot air of the small club and she had subsequently associated him, the singer, in her imagination, with cool lemon groves, by the blue Mediterranean, as if he had been the hero of some novel written in those sunny climes. Sometimes, when he had been on stage, he had looked deeply into her eyes, or so she had imagined. But then, he had invariably disappeared, after the show, like a chimera. Had he really been at the Château de Sauzon a few days previously? She had not dared ask Marie-Christine about him, for fear of unveiling too much interest, on her own part.

Eventually, Madame had been able to return to Bordeaux and her residence, in the Cours de la Victoire. She had a computer there, which she had previously felt obliged to buy. She had not liked it, but she had accepted the fact that she had to keep up with the times. And it did have its uses, after all. She had typed "Mermen - Liverpool" into the Search bar. Information about the band had duly presented itself, to her amazement. The Mermen still performed, from time to time, it seemed, but all members of the band belonged additionally to other professions, now. Kit Mallory, the dark-eyed principal singer, was, apparently, a well-established architect, working mainly in the Wirral and Merseyside. An architect! How impressive! Having looked at the web site, daily, from then on, Madame Gabrielle had noted, a week previously, with interest and increasing tension, that he, Kit Mallory, would be performing, with The Mermen, in nostalgic fashion, as well as delivering a series of lectures, about his architectural work, aboard a cruise ship, departing from Liverpool, that September. Within a few weeks' time, in other words!

Madame Gabrielle had booked a state room, with an adjoining sitting room and bathroom, aboard the ship. The logical part of her brain was informing her, coldly, that she was behaving ridiculously and with even less propriety than that displayed by Jacqueline on the day of her engagement party, at the Château de Sauzon, when she had run, with unguarded impulsiveness, into the arms of Jacqui Galant. However, Madame Gabrielle's heart, for once, was over-riding her cool brain. It was persuading her, with overwhelming force, to go away on the voyage into unknown territory. The cruise was to last fifteen days. She would have fifteen days in which to change her destiny, the direction of her life, everything…if only the dark-eyed musician were to remember the girl he had enchanted with the lingering glances he had given her, while on stage, so many years before. If only…

Agnès had cut Madame Gabrielle's hair in such a way that it skimmed her shoulders with joyful jauntiness. A fringe with a flick was now beginning to appear as well. Madame stared at her own reflection, a little shocked by the transformation in her appearance. Even though the dark tinting of her parting had not begun, she was looking more youthful, already. She appeared to be less haughty and forbidding, in fact. Softer. She almost smiled with pleasure.

"Your life will be different, now, Madame," said Agnès, daringly. "One change leads to another."

CHAPTER 6

A Writer's Anguish

Sitting on the floor of her apartment, her back to a sofa and a piece of paper, on a large book, resting against her hunched-up knees, Liz Laurier expressed, with a sharp sigh, her exasperation over her inability to overcome the tricky, psychological block that was preventing her from putting pen to paper. She had thought that the production of a book for Rosalind, her teenage daughter, would have been a task that would have been quickly, and even joyfully, accomplished. However, after an hour spent on false beginnings, she was still finding it difficult to home in on the "mots justes," the correct words to use, in the opening phrases. "If the first sentence sounds right, the rest will flow," she had been told by an American writer, to whom she had chatted once, at a book-signing session in New York City. His words had remained lodged in her memory. And she worried about them, that important first sentence in her own book having yet to be written. The evidence of her rejected efforts lay around her, in the form of scrunched up pieces of paper.

Liz was baffled as to why she could not make a start. After all, she was anxious to write "The Aspects of Venus," the astrological guide to relationships which she hoped would help her daughter, Rosalind, to steer a steady course through her teenage years. Had she, Liz, drawn a blank because she had already toyed with the idea of attempting to have the book published, not just privately for a handful of girls at Bramblewell School, but through a bigger imprint, with a larger readership in mind? Was it the unconscious fear of wider exposure and concomitant criticism that had unexpectedly induced in her a writer's block? Surely not! She could handle rejection. And furthermore, if she could write an astrological report of sixty or seventy pages for a client, she could manage to write a book which, essentially, would be little more than a series of astrological reports joined together. Besides, she loved to write! At least, she usually did.

She reckoned there had to be some way to break the inhibiting spell. Some trick she could employ. What if she were to start to write the middle of the book first, instead of the opening pages? She knew that she was going to devote each chapter of the work to the astrological aspects dominating one of Rosalind's friendships. What if she were to pick one of those friendships in arbitrary fashion,, in order to begin to write about it freely, as if it were not to be contained within the structure of a book? But, even when giving herself this licence to write as she wished, Liz could not make a start.

Restlessly, she threw down her pen and hauled herself to her feet. She made her way from the sitting room to the kitchen, where she switched on the electric kettle. It was early. 5.45 a.m. She opened a window slightly, to allow the cool air of morning to enter the apartment. The Port was beginning to wake up. She could hear the noise of vehicles in the distance. She guessed they were heading for the oil refineries. She imagined how blue the Manchester Ship Canal would look, that morning. Its name, Manchester Ship Canal, possibly conjured up, in the minds of those who were not au fait with its appearance, images of docks, clanging locks and greyness. But, in reality, the blue waters, flowing peacefully along by the River Mersey, were bordered by beautiful countryside. Liz, prior to moving from New York to the Wirral, had not been aware of the prettiness of the terrain. In fact, when she had discovered, through secretly having had a long-established contact with Gylen Somerland's mother - her first former mother-in-law, in other words - that her children, Rosalind and John, were going to leave Bristol in order to live with their father in Ellesmere Port, Liz had, initially, been alarmed, wondering if they would be growing up in a less cerebrally enriching environment than the one that had, until then, been provided by Bristol. However, the Port, with Chester nearby, had turned out to be more culturally stimulating than she had expected and the Wirral, she had found as green and pleasant, in summer, as Somerset.

Liz realised she was allowing her mind to wander. She was procrastinating, of course: delaying the moment when she would sit down again, in front of the blank page. "Oh! Just get on with it!" Liz then said to herself, aloud and sharply. She made French coffee in the hope that it would spark the pre-frontal cortex of her brain into activity so that she could focus.

Back in the sitting room, she curled up in the corner of a sofa. It occurred to Liz,then, that the more emotionally engaged she was with what she was writing, the more easily words might stream on to the paper. Which of Rosalind's relationships, then, was most likely to arouse an emotional response within her? Rosalind's crush on Teddy Lawrence, the previous year, came to mind first, as it had made Liz anxious and upset and fearful that her daughter might behave stupidly. That crush had been contained - damped down, rather - but a residue of attachment still remained, Liz suspected, and Rosalind would possibly benefit from being reminded of the consequences of folly. How ardently Liz wished that her daughter would turn her attention to the younger and more desirable Julian Bramblewell-Eurlinn, if only to admire him, romantically, from afar.

Suddenly, Liz stood and made her way to her study. From a locked drawer, she removed the small, white, leather-covered book, in which she kept hand-written records of the birth data of people in whom she had a personal interest: not clients. She wrote no dates in the book: only the planetary positions on the day of birth. And there were no names: just single initials. She found the page devoted to Julian, easily. She had studied it with some care not long before, when wondering, in a day-dreaming sort of way, what sort of significant aspects, or connections, if any, bound Julian's chart to Rosalind's.

The seductive thought that Rosalind, one day, might marry the heir to the Château du Crâne was one that had fixed itself in Liz's head. Was it not natural, she persuaded herself, that a caring mother might dream of her daughter marrying the sort of handsome prince who brought so many fairy tales to a satisfactory end? A quick glance at the positions of the planets on the day Julian had been born had been enough to inform Liz that Julian's Venus was in aspect to Rosalind's Ascendant, Midheaven, Saturn, Uranus and Pluto. Quite a collection! How easy it was to convince herself that the number of Venusian aspects, alone, boded well! And that the potentially serious and duty-filled character of the relationship, described by, say, Saturn, pointed to nothing more than the responsibilities and obligations that would be placed on Rosalind's shoulders, were a marriage to take place, eventually.

Were she an ambitious mother, in a novel written in the nineteenth century, Liz knew she would be making plans, at that moment, to bring Rosalind and Julian together - at a ball, perhaps - in the hope that a romantic attachment would be the result. In the twenty-first century, mothers arranged cosy dinner parties, with the same sorts of aims in mind, she assumed. Being an astrologer and party to the astrological data of Rosalind and Julian, Liz could not indulge in manipulative practices of that sort, though. Such behaviour would be judged, quite rightly, to be unethical. But one thing was certain: her wish to write about Rosalind and Julian had suddenly set alight in her the desire to start to work, with eagerness, on the comparison of the two charts, at that very moment. Her writer's block had vanished.

CHAPTER 7

Jacqueline

It was a hot evening in Paris. Having bought a fresh baguette, wrapped in tissue paper, to eat with dinner, a meal she would have alone as was her custom now, Jacqueline de Sauzon, or Jacqueline Galant - the name she used when she was obliged to acknowledge her marriage to Jacqui Galant - walked along the Boulevard Saint-Michel, heading in the direction of the second-floor flat on a corner, which, since her marriage to Jacqui, had been her home. It was the flat to which Jacqui, her husband - and how difficult it was for her to accustom herself to the use of the word 'husband' - would speedily travel to find her, from the naval college of Lanvéoc-Poulmic near Brest, whenever he could. He had to study in Brittany; she had to study in Paris. There had been nothing for it but to accept and endure the separation. They, the two of them, had decided from the start - that is to say, from the time of their marriage four months previously - that Paris would be their base. It was the logical choice. Even if Jacqueline had been free to live in Brest, there would have been occasions when she would not have seen Jacqui for long periods. He would, for example, have been away at sea for training.

The thudding realisation that such partings would take place, that marriage to Jacqui would force her to accept separation and solitude throughout the years to come, was making Jacqueline panic. She had not had the courage to tell Jacqui how she had felt about living in that way, though. She had not told him she would not be able to cope with long, endless nights alone, without his reassuring presence in the flat. But, surely he knew her well enough - they had been friends throughout their schooldays - to realise that she had always drawn strength from companionship. She had grown up with her two sisters, Héloïse and Marie-Colette, and her brother, Jérôme, after all. Did Jacqui not have the wit to understand the effect loneliness would have on her? Maybe he did not. Maybe he was too engrossed in his own career to notice. Maybe she would have to explain to him how a sort of depression would fall on her, as she left the crowds in the streets of Paris behind and opened the door to the flat, where no one would be awaiting her, to converse with her, or listen to her, or boost her enthusiasm for living with inspiring ideas or gentle humour.

Were she to explain all that to Jacqui, though, she felt sure she would see a look of dismay in his eyes. It would be best, she had often thought, to tell him about her feelings over a good meal of, perhaps, small fish and fried cubes of bread, sprinkled with lemon juice, followed by a good chicken with onions, cooked in wine. Men were more inclined to listen, after eating, were they not? She could picture, on such an occasion, Jacqui's lightly-tanned skin and his brown hair, cut short, illuminated by candle-light. The French Navy, through the imposition of discipline and physical exercise, had changed his appearance, but the new look suited him. He seemed taller and stronger. But was he robust enough, psychologically, to deal with her fears? She suspected that, were she to reveal to him her misgivings, he would become afraid that she would leave him and she would end up having to reassure him, quickly, that naturally she would be able to manage after all, and that everything would be fine.

In reality, though, she was finding it difficult to cope, not only with solitude, night after night, but also with the restriction marriage had imposed on her day-to-day behaviour. She had not anticipated, prior to her marriage, that her freedom would be curtailed by her change in status. Before her marriage had taken place, for example, she had thought she would be able to go to cafés in the evening, where groups of her friends would meet to discuss literature, cultural events and politics, until very late.

But having married, she felt she no longer had the freedom to pursue that lifestyle. She felt constrained. Jacqui would telephone her, after dinner, to ask "What are you doing? Are you in the apartment? When will you sleep?" It was hard to tolerate the constant questioning. She hoped it would end once the novelty of being married had worn off.

If only her family lived nearby! Belle-Isle and the Château de Sauzon seemed so distant, now. Jacqueline had an aunt and an uncle in Paris, of course, living in the Boulevard Saint-Germain, but both of them were experts on ancient history and often went away, on long, cultural excursions, to places far and wide. In any case, Jacqueline did not want to intrude on her relatives' private life excessively, now that she was twenty and married. During her first excursions to Paris, she had stayed with them, but the time had come for her, now, she felt, to stand on her own two feet, without their support. She believed that, being married, she should be able to endure, in a mature way, life's follies and obstacles, without running to her aunt and uncle, several times a week, expecting to be cosseted, as if she were a child.

Sometimes, though, she did feel as if she were still a child, or rather, she longed to be treated as if she were still one. In other words, she wanted the responsibilities of adulthood - and specifically, of married life - to be lifted from her shoulders. She wanted to be the most important person in her own world again, instead of having to take into consideration the habits and expectations of another. She missed living at her family's château in Belle-Isle, intensely. She now recognised how carefree her childhood and adolescence, there, had been. Her parents had carried the financial, practical and psychological burdens life had imposed on them, while she, like her siblings, had been given the liberty to live without being conscious of them. What had seemed to have been overwhelming teenage problems, when she had been growing up, now seemed unsubstantial. She had recognised, at last, all that had been done for her by her parents, and the thought of having to face similar problems to theirs, in the years that were to come, made her flesh turn cold with fright.

It was a pity that her sister, Héloïse, once her most trusted and closest confidante, and only two years younger than she, had decided to avail herself of the opportunity to spend a gap year, between school and university, to do as she pleased. It was what Jacqueline, herself, had done, of course, and she did not really begrudge her sister a year of freedom from intense study at the University of Paris. Nevertheless, had Héloïse not decided to delay her studying for a year, she could have been beginning her student life in Paris, that very autumn and Jacqueline would have been able to enjoy and depend upon her companionship.

Héloïse was, in fact, at that very moment, still near Bordeaux. The casual job she had sought, as a film extra, during the summer months, had led to her being offered a more substantial rôle, as one of the leading characters, in the film being shot at the Château du Crâne. When she had heard that Teddy Laurence, her sister's former fiancé, had been chosen to be one of the other principal players, she had accepted the offer. Teddy Laurence! The young man whose heart Jacqueline had broken! In fact, Jacqueline had humiliated him, in public, and he was, naturally, now determined to try to forget his association with the entire Sauzon family, but Héloïse knew that Jacqueline, herself, could not forget Teddy. Jacqueline had told Héloïse, in fact, how often she had stayed awake at night thinking of the pain she had inflicted on him and reflecting, also, on how dejected he must have felt on his way back to England, after her shocking rejection of him. Jacqueline clearly wished that the harm she had done could be undone and that she could, at least, be Teddy's friend again. Héloïse had not told her that she, herself, had become besotted with Teddy, although, having a cool mind, she had, now and again, wondered if the reason for her attachment had had its source, principally, in Teddy's unavailability. She suspected that she was the type of girl who could not resist a challenge: the challenge of winning Teddy's heart, in any case. How Jacqueline would react, were she, Héloïse, to attract his attention was a problem that would be considered only if it were to arise.

However, Jacqueline was familiar enough with the signs of infatuation to have recognised them, already, in her sister's behaviour. Héloïse, for example, would seize upon every opportunity that presented itself to her, to mention Teddy's name. But Jacqueline did not have the time to dwell on this complication, as there was another matter to consider more urgently and it was this: Jacqueline's mother, the Countess de Sauzon, had sent a message, by e-mail, in which she had expressed her concern about her own mother, Madame Gabrielle de Talence. It seemed that Madame Gabrielle was planning to go away on holiday, on a cruise ship. "A cruise ship!" the Countess had written, as if the idea had been completely outrageous, adding, "Imagine! Alone!"And, to add fat to the fire, it was not even to be a French cruise ship! It was to be one that would depart from Liverpool! "Liverpool! At her age!" the Countess had continued, as if at the end of her tether. What had dismayed the Countess, above all, had been the fact that she, herself, had suggested she accompany her mother, but the offer had been declined. Madame Gabrielle had specified that she wanted no member of her family to accompany her. "Why?" the Countess has asked, as if she had expected Jacqueline to provide an answer. "What was Madame Gabrielle planning to do? What if she were to become ill? What if she were to collapse, as she had done before, with no one from her close family with her to help her? What would people think of a daughter who had allowed her mother to go away on a long journey without support? What if the ship were to capsize, or if some other calamity were to befall it? How would Madame Gabrielle cope? Did she know enough English to convey her through a difficult episode?"

"Grand'maman can speak English well," Jacqueline had replied. "Have you forgotten that she spent a year in England, when she was young?"

The Countess had not been reassured. She had wondered if Jacqueline had met anyone, during her own stay in Liverpool, who might be free and willing to go on holiday on the cruise ship as well, to keep an eye, discreetly, on Madame Gabrielle. The Countess, of course, would pay for the voyage. An individual from Liverpool would be the ideal choice for this clandestine task, since such a person would blend with the other passengers without stimulating suspicious thoughts in Madame Gabrielle's head. Could Jacqueline think of anyone who might be suitable?

At first, Jacqueline had expressed her horror at the suggestion her mother had made.

"A spy, Maman? You want to hire someone to spy on Grand'maman?"

The Countess de Sauzon had protested that she had no desire to engage someone to spy on her mother, exactly. She simply wanted a companionable individual to keep watch over her from a distance, and to step into the picture only if Madame Gabrielle were to find herself in a difficult situation.

In the end, Jacqueline had agreed that her mother's plan had some merit and was probably sensible, given Madame Gabrielle's worrying stubbornness. She had conceded it was probably a step that the Countess was being forced to take, and that it was unquestionably one she was finding disagreeable, but necessary. "Allow me to have a night or two to think about this, Maman," she had said to the Countess. "When does the ship leave Liverpool?"

"At the beginning of September. Very shortly, in other words," the Countess had replied.

Later that night, sitting up in bed, Jacqueline had, slowly, brushed her long, pale, silky hair, while reflecting on her mother's plan. She could imagine the scene that would have taken place, at the Château de Sauzon, when her mother had brought up the topic of Madame Gabrielle's proposed voyage, possibly the previous night and, probably, over dinner. The candles would have been lit on the long table and Marie-Colette and Jérôme would have been dressed, semi-formally, as was the custom at the Château, in the evenings. Count Henri, her father, would have raised his eyebrows and, with a shrug, would have said:

"If she wants to go, let her go!"

"Henri!" the Countess would have protested, putting down her soup spoon, while looking aghast. "You don't mean that, surely! Do take this problem seriously!"

Marie-Colette would have looked down at her soup plate, nervously and Jérôme, now fourteen and starting to become vocally rebellious, might have sighed audibly and impolitely, with exaggerated exasperation, at what he might have judged to have been a silly, parental argument.

Jacqueline had put down the silver-backed hairbrush on her bedside table and then, had leaned back so that she had been supported by her bolster and pillow. She had closed her eyes, as she had wondered what sort of person would be likely to take up her mother's offer of a voyage on a cruise ship, in return for a light duty. A teacher from Bramblewell School would be the ideal sort of person to approach, but the ship would be due to leave port as the new term at Bramblewell School would be beginning. Jacqueline had been certain of that. Maybe one of the teachers, though, had a relative who would be happy to have a holiday on board ship. But, how could she, Jacqueline, make her approach to those teachers to find out if that was the case? Having rejected Teddy Laurence, whom they, the teachers at Bramblewell School, held in esteem, Jacqueline had felt she could not do so, without appearing to be brazen. Teddy, himself, in fact, would, ironically, be the best person to contact, as he would be more forgiving, she had reckoned. But, in the end, she had realised she would not have the nerve to send him a message, directly. There was another way of communicating with Teddy, though. Rebecca Hampton, the American student with whom she, Jacqueline, had shared a flat in Liverpool, during her gap year there, had returned to England, that summer, for a holiday and Teddy had allowed her to stay in his apartment, during his absence. Perhaps Rebecca would be willing to act as a go-between.

Jacqueline had decided to contact her, there and then. She had had no idea as to how close Rebecca had become to Teddy, but she had felt no resentment as she had written the message. She had always liked and respected the raven-haired, cool, optimistic and ambitious Rebecca and she had known, too, that Teddy had been intrigued by her. But, as she had pressed "Send", Jacqueline had felt a heaviness within.

"Maybe you will end up having what I could have had, Rebecca," she had thought, but not without wistfulness.

She had, later, read one of Françoise Sagan's novels, before going to sleep. "If one is obliged to be unhappy in love, one might as well be stylish about it," she had told herself, pretending she had stepped into the world, described in the paperback's pages, at least for a while.

CHAPTER 8

Dorothy in Distress

Unsmilingly, Dorothy Trimm entered the office of the head-mistress of Bramblewell School and closed the heavy, Pugin-esque door behind her, with care.

"No. Don't get up, Hilary!" she said to the smartly dressed woman, sitting at the wide, polished desk, occupying the centre of the room.

Noticing that the window was open, Dorothy made her way to it and breathed in the fresh, but noticeably flower-scented air, deeply. For a moment or two, she gazed down at the school's playing field, a field which was situated on lower ground, but was not far, really, from the school's principal, neo-Gothic building. The field was largely unoccupied, because the month was August and the school's pupils, apart from a few boarders, were still on holiday. Dorothy, who heartily appreciated the beauty of the countryside, took in the way the grass in the field and the leaves on the centuries-old trees, along the perimeter, seemed to be infused with the dazzling light of a Chester summer.

Dorothy, then, turned and sat down on a leather sofa, close to the window. She placed her varnished, straw, box-shaped handbag at her feet, smoothed a few creases out of her beige, tailored dress and took off her white, cotton gloves.

"I saw Eva Derbyshire, a few minutes ago," she said then, referring to the pupil who had been head-girl of the school during the previous, scholastic session. "She was wearing her striped blazer and tennis whites. I was surprised. I thought she had left school."

"Really, Mother?" said Hilary Trimm, looking up from her

paper work. She removed her rimless spectacles and pushed a lock of her stylishly-cut, short hair away from her eyes, before adding, "She must have dropped in to use the tennis courts or maybe she wanted to talk to one of my teachers about her exam results. I think Thetis and Ann are on the premises. Lynn James, as well."

"Young people are so sure of themselves, these days," said Dorothy, as if she had not been listening to her daughter's words. "How many are modest and shy and deferential, in the way pupils used to be in my day?"

Not seeming to be expecting an answer to her question, Dorothy sighed and turned her head to look in the direction of the window. Impatiently, she tapped her left wrist with the fingers of her right hand, as if wondering what to say next.

"Her hair's a shade or two darker, wouldn't you say, Hilary?" she then asked, out of the blue, with a sharp edge to her voice.

"Whose? Eva's?"

"Don't be absurd!" retorted Dorothy, unexpectedly snappily. "Oh! Don't pretend, Hilary! You know perfectly well to whom I am referring! Do you think I am someone with whom you can play verbally, as if I were a recalcitrant pupil?"

Hilary Trimm leaned back in her chair and raised her eyebrows slightly.

"What's on your mind, Mother?" she wearily asked. "It's clear something is annoying you."

"Annoying me? Honestly, Hilary! You know that..."

Dorothy stopped as if to prevent herself from giving expression to uncontrolled anger. Then, she said:

"That girl out there! How could you? How COULD you?"

"You are talking about Miss Delamar, my new secretary?"

"Of course I am talking about Miss Delamar, your new secretary!"

"May I explain how and why that appointment was made?"

"Oh, please! Don't insult me! Don't you think it is obvious to me that you waited until Lord Bramblewell and Miss Sutton had gone to France and then…"

"May I explain?" Hilary interrupted, leaning forward.

"Very well! Explain!" exclaimed Dorothy, raising her hand in a theatrical gesture.

"At the beginning of last term, began Hilary calmly, " Lee Chan told me that she was going to resign from her post as the school's secretary, because she had been offered an interesting, administrative post in Hong Kong. She felt she could not turn the offer down, given the fact that it would give her the opportunity to further her career."

"Yes. I did know about Lee's resignation, but you didn't have to…"

"May I continue?"

"Please do," said Dorothy coldly.

"I asked Lee if she knew anyone she would recommend as a replacement for herself. Lee said that one person came to mind: a Chinese girl who was living in Liverpool. However, when contacted, this girl, Hoi-Lo, informed us she was still a student and would not be able to take up any post, full time, for quite a while. Lee, then, suggested we advertise the position widely and this, we did."

"Go on."

"Lee, herself, helped me to sift through the applications we received. We chose the three best. Isolde Delamar was one of the three."

"And you selected her, knowing quite well that…"

"Please let me finish, Mother!"

Dorothy looked directly at her daughter and shook her head, as if in disbelief or disapproval.

"Continue!" she then said, with a sigh of resignation.

"Isolde Delamar had worked in London for a number of years and, in fact, had been promoted to quite a responsible position in a company."

"Oh, stop, Hilary! Stop! I can't listen to you!"

"Mother, please! Everything is going to be fine!"

"Fine? How could anything possibly be fine? Don't be so silly! Isolde Delamar broke Lord Bramblewell's heart! It may have happened ten or eleven years ago, but don't imagine poor Rupert has forgotten the pain or has, in fact, recovered from it! How old is Miss Delamar now? Thirty-two, perhaps? She would have been twenty-one at the time of her engagement. Rupert was ten years older than she was. As were you, yourself, Hilary. Of course, you weren't interested in Rupert, at that time, were you? But, you must have seen the engagement photographs taken of him and Isolde Delamar. They appeared in every society magazine in the county. Isolde Delamar, with her pearls and that waist-length, blonde hair of hers. Obviously, she must have been bleaching it, then, if her natural colour is the one I've just seen. There was a terrible to-do, you know, when she broke off her engagement to Rupert and went away to London. There was a rumour that she had gone there in pursuit of some other man. The silly girl! The man who had lured her away from an English lord must have thought she was stupid and 'easy,' if I may express myself that crudely. No wonder the man in question seemed to have had little respect for her, in the end. He discarded her, of course. But anyway, questions now have to be posed. Why, for instance, has she decided to return to Chester, at this point, and, more pertinently, why has she chosen to take up a post in Bramblewell School, knowing that what could have been her home- Bramblewell Manor- will be only a short walk away from her place of work? Hm, Hilary? The answer is rather obvious, wouldn't you say? And, incidentally, I must mention, en passant, that she doesn't seem to be up to the rigours of the job, here, from what I observed in the ante-room, a few minutes ago. She was typing- if one could call what she was doing by that name- very slowly, while looking at the computer's keyboard, rather than at the computer's screen."

"Mother!"

"I am disappointed in you, Hilary. I cannot believe a daughter of mine could sink as low as to play games with the heart and emotions of a good man who has never wished anyone any harm. Frankly, I am appalled. This behaviour is beneath you, Hils. Lord Bramblewell is engaged to Susie Sutton now, and you should have left them to enjoy their engagement in peace. Instead, you had to meddle. Dismiss this Isolde before Lord Bramblewell becomes enthralled with her again and - believe me! - he will. You do have grounds for dismissing her. My guess is that she lied about her qualifications. Isolde Delamar is nothing but a schemer. I can tell. And no matter how unworthy of marriage to Lord Bramblewell you think Susie Sutton is and no matter how jealous you are of her..."

"I can't get rid of Isolde Delamar," Hilary interrupted, blushing slightly at the suggestion that she was jealous of Miss Sutton.

"I can scarcely recognise you as my own daughter, then," said Dorothy, clearly disappointed. "Do you know that? I can scarcely recognise you as my own daughter. I am utterly shocked. You wanted to marry Lord Bramblewell, yourself, but when he fell for Miss Sutton, your heart broke into bits. You resented the fact that he had chosen, as his future bride, a younger woman and a poorly-educated one, at that. Compared with you, she seemed to be of inferior stock. That was what you thought, didn't you? And you are hoping, now, that Lord Bramblewell will break off his engagement to Miss Sutton, when his love for Isolde Delamar is rekindled. That's your plan. It is, isn't it, Hils? Isn't it? And will you sit back and watch the drama unfolding and - even worse – you will enjoy watching it? Hm? Talk about Schadenfreude! That's the word the Germans use to describe the enjoyment of other people's distress. I never thought the day would come when I'd attach that word to your behaviour, Hils. I am utterly ashamed of you and very distressed."

Dorothy Trimm picked up her handbag and began to search inside it, as if looking for a handkerchief. She took out of the bag, instead, a tiny bottle of Eau de Cologne and began to sprinkle a little of the liquid on her wrists and hands, as if she felt she had been infected by her daughter's presence and needed to make some gesture to show she was cleansing herself.

Hilary stood up and walked over to the sofa. She sat down beside her mother.

"You haven't given me a chance to explain properly," she said gently.

"When Lee Chan and I had chosen the three best candidates, we mailed the details of their employment records to Lord Bramblewell, who, as you correctly pointed out, was in France, at the time. It was he who decided Isolde Delamar would be the new secretary of Bramblewell School. He reckoned she had fallen on hard times and needed to be given a chance to get on her feet, again. He acted out of kindness."

"Oh! I see!" exclaimed Dorothy scathingly, giving her daughter an imperious look. "You want me to say that I have misjudged you! Do you? Do you, Hils? Well! I am not going to say that! What I am going to say is that you should never, ever have sent Isolde Delamar's application form to Lord Bramblewell. You should have deleted it from your computer's screen and forgotten it. You know perfectly well that that is what you should have done. Don't try to convince yourself that your behaviour can be excused because Lord Bramblewell did the choosing. You are being pathetic. I feel nothing for you but contempt. And, you know, your behaviour is not rational, either. Even if you were to destroy the relationship existing between Susie Sutton and Lord Bramblewell, you would still have to endure the pain of seeing him with someone other than you: Isolde Delamar! Please explain to me where the advantage to you lies in this strategy you have adopted! How will you be able to tolerate the presence of Isolde Delamar in the room next to yours, at school, if Lord Bramblewell..."

"I shall not have to tolerate the presence of Isolde Delamar," interrupted Hilary.

"What? What do you mean?"

"Unknown to you, some weeks ago, I applied for the post of Principal of the Christina Quayle College of Languages, in Liverpool. I was interviewed and the job was offered to me."

"Q-COLL? You are going to be the Principal of Q-COLL?"

"Yes."

"Oh! Hilary! You are not going to leave Bramblewel, are you? I mean, leaving Bramblewell…Well! You've loved being here! You are so deeply attached to the school! Are you sure you have made the right decision? When will you be obliged to take up your new post, if you do accept the offer? I'm assuming you'll stay at Bramblewell for another term or so."

"I'll be starting work at Q-COLL at the end of September."

"So…you will stay at Bramblewell for only five more weeks? Six more weeks?"

"I've arranged to leave Bramblewell in a day or two."

"But…you can't! Who will replace you?"

"Really, Mother! Lynn James, of course! She's the Deputy Headmistress, isn't she? She'll step in, until interviews for the permanent post will take place. I hope she will apply for the permanent post, incidentally, but I know Thetis might, also, be keen to have it."

"I'm flabbergasted. I really don't know what to say, Hils."

Dorothy had put her hand up to her forehead, as if confused.

"Teddy Laurence won't, of course, apply for my post, given his youth and inexperience," continued Hilary, "but I hope he'll apply for the job of acting deputy, once Lynn steps up. Lord Bramblewell does like Teddy and Lord Bramblewell's word carries a lot of weight, obviously. Teddy should take advantage of that fact, but I bet he won't. He's as scrupulous as you are, Mother. Maybe Lynn will be able to persuade him, though."

"What are you babbling about, now? I assume Lynn has been told about your plans."

"Yes. I told her, yesterday. She was shocked, of course. But, you know, underneath that calm exterior of hers, she has strong nerves. She'll be fine. She'll find out, though, that there's a difference between functioning as a deputy headmistress and being a headmistress, proper."

"Hilary!"

"Yes, Mother."

"When you telephoned me this morning, I was under the impression that you were asking me to come here to see you because there was something else that you had on your mind. You mentioned an offer of some sort. Did I misunderstand you? I wasn't expecting to hear anything like the piece of news you have just given me, I must say."

"Oh, yes! I had almost forgotten," said Hilary, rising from the sofa and returning to her desk. "Would you like to go on a cruise with me, Mother? Since I shall have a little free time between my leaving here and taking up my new post, I thought we could go on a cruise together, during that period. A suitable cruise ship leaves Liverpool in a couple of weeks' time."

"A cruise?"

"I imagined we could both benefit from having a good holiday."

Dorothy scrutinised her daughter's face and wondered if the mentioning of a holiday was little more that a ruse to distract attention away from the plot to wreck Susie's social advancement.

"Consider my proposition and let me know, soon, what you have decided," Hilary went on.

"What put the idea of a cruise, specifically, into your head?" asked Dorothy, her voice tinged with suspicion.

"Well!" said Hilary, leaning forward, her forearms crossed on the desk. "I received a telephone call from Teddy Laurence, two days ago, during the course of which he told me he had been contacted by his American friend, Rebecca Hampton, about an interesting request which she had been asked to pass on to him. To cut a long story short, the American girl had said that a distinguished French lady, of a certain age - your age, Mother - was planning to go on a cruise, alone. The lady's family, concerned about her safety, was offering to pay for someone to watch over her, from a discreet distance. The cruise ship would be leaving from Liverpool and would head for the Canaries and the western Mediterranean. Teddy wanted to know if I knew anyone who would be willing to keep a watchful eye on this lady. He thought that, given the sorts of circles in which I moved, I might know someone who would be free to go. I told him I'd possibly be able to help, but that the friends I knew would not want payment. I asked for Rebecca Hampton's e-mail address and said I'd contact her. Teddy, then, told me the French lady's name and as soon as I had heard it, I realised she was the grand-mother of the French girl to whom he, Teddy, had been engaged. Do you remember, Mother? I was invited to the engagement party, at the château in Brittany. Poor Teddy! Anyway! It occurred to me that I might go on the cruise, myself, and that you might like to accompany me."

"You mean…You want us to behave like a couple of sleuths?"

"Well! Not exactly."

"I think the idea is outrageous. Were I to go on a cruise, I'd be appalled if you were to send someone along to watch me, on the quiet."

"Mother, this French lady is not well. She collapsed at Teddy's engagement party."

"But, if she was at the engagement party, she'll recognise you, won't she?"

"No. She didn't see me. She fell ill before she could meet anyone. I'm not surprised her family is worried. I can't help wondering, myself, why she would want to go off on her own to a strange place."

"To escape from her interfering relatives, obviously."

"Don't you think there could be some other reason?"

"Some other reason? What are you talking about?"

"What if she has fallen prey to the charms of a fortune hunter?"

"Oh! Hils! Please!"

"Mother, that sort of thing happens in Europe."

"Rarely, Hils. Be sensible! I can think of numerous reasons as to why she might want to go on a cruise at her age."

"That's why I think you should come with me. You will, additionally, be provided with the opportunity to begin writing that book you have been saying, for years, that you will write, one day. I mean, it's time your Nightshade Press branched out into fiction, isn't it? Why don't you write a fictional work of your own, to set the ball rolling? Thrillers always sell. Write a thriller about a lady who goes on a cruise, alone!"

"A thriller?" said Dorothy, an expression on her face that was half way between bemusement and disgust. It was as if Hilary had suggested she read a tabloid newspaper. The small publishing house she owned in the Wirral specialised in books on the etiquette to be observed at county events taking place in Cheshire. There were also books on good manners in the modern world, gardening in allotments and numerous ways to hold garden parties, in small spaces, such as back gardens. She was thinking of publishing a range of books on the promotion of good health, for people of advanced years, too. But, thrillers? Fiction? The thought threw her, but, simultaneously, it occurred to her ever-lively mind that a cruise holiday, by widening her horizons, might awaken in her the desire to become more adventurous in the world of publishing. It was her belief that one should always keep the door to fresh ideas ajar, after all, if only slightly.

"Mother! Are you coming or not?" asked Hilary, sharply interrupting Dorothy's musings.

"Let me think about it, Hils," said Dorothy, deliberately adopting a languid air.

But, the sparkle that had appeared, suddenly, in Dorothy's eyes informed Hilary of the fact that her mother's answer would probably be "Yes."

CHAPTER 9

Julian

The information delivered briefly by Lynn James, in a morning telephone call, had shocked Teddy Laurence. Miss Trimm, headmistress of Bramblewell School, had gone! But, where? And why? Lynn had been unable to answer those questions. Teddy, therefore, had been left perplexed, not least because Miss Trimm had not mentioned giving up her post a few days earlier, when he, himself, had been in touch with her, in connection with a request that Rebecca Hampton, his American girlfriend, had made in another morning call. To be exact, the request had not been made by Rebecca, herself: she had simply been an intermediary. Indirectly, it had come from Jacqueline de Sauzon, Teddy's former fiancée. Seemingly, Jacqueline, given the way she had previously let Teddy down, had felt she could not contact him directly and so had asked Rebecca, formerly her flat-mate, when they had both been students in Liverpool, to explain what had been on her mind. Curiously, Jacqueline had wanted Teddy to arrange for someone to go away on holiday on a cruise ship, at her family's expense, but with the obligation of keeping a watchful eye on Madame Gabrielle de Talence, Jacqueline's grand-mother, who would also be on the ship. Teddy had been astonished that Jacqueline could have been bold enough to have considered it admissible to approach him for any reason, let alone one so outré. However, for Rebecca's sake, but with reluctance, he had passed on the request to Miss Trimm, who, after all, had already met Jacqueline, having been one of the guests at the engagement party, held in the grounds of the Château de Sauzon, Jacqueline's family home, the previous year. Teddy knew Miss Trimm to be acquainted with leisured ladies in Chester and in the Wirral: ladies who had the time to meet for lunch in elegant restaurants and to spend afternoons playing bridge or planning charity work. Perhaps one of these friends or acquaintances might, also, be inclined to go away on holiday on a cruise ship, departing conveniently from Liverpool. And maybe this person might be intrigued enough, as well, to agree to the unusual terms.

Teddy, sitting pensively on the edge of the four-poster bed in his room in the Château du Crâne, put down his mobile phone on the blue, silken quilt. He stood and walked across to the window facing east and pushed it wide open. He looked out and breathed in the softly scented air of France. The sun shining down on the walls of the château and the acres of land beyond, he found hot, even though it was only ten o' clock in the morning. It would be nine o' clock in Chester, where Lynn was. She must have driven to Bramblewell School at the time she would normally have left home to go there, had the new term begun. But, two weeks of the holiday remained before Bramblewell School would, in fact, re-open for the autumn term: the long prelude to Christmas. To Teddy, who had already spent four weeks of the summer holiday in France, the world of Bramblewell School seemed to be a distant one to which he had become partly detached. However, it would be necessary, in a few days' time, to plan his return there and to focus his mind, once again, on his regular routines, scholastic targets and all the rest of it.

Teddy gazed out, with appreciation, at the green meadows shot through with light beyond the château, the dark trees thickly bordering them and, above them, the tender, blue sky over the Gironde. Teddy wanted to retain an image of the scene in his mind, just as it was at that moment. A photo, of course, would remind him of it, even bringing to his attention, perhaps later, details previously un-noticed. But a photo could not reproduce the feeling of warmth on his skin as the sun hit it, or the scent of wild herbs growing by the château's walls.

That morning, Teddy was dressed in his usual eighteenth century costume: a white shirt, breeches and boots. Filming had started at six, four hours earlier. Teddy now felt hungry. When he had risen, at five, he had eaten only a few biscottes and had drunk one cup of coffee. An interval for proper breakfast was now taking place and soon, Teddy would go downstairs from his room, where he had been resting briefly, to make his way to one of the great halls of the château, where he would be served café au lait, out of large, stainless steel jugs containing hot milk, frothy at the top, and equally hot, dark coffee. There would be fresh baguettes to eat: long loaves, transported from a bakery in Bordeaux, earlier. Croissants, in abundance, would be flaky and soft and butter would taste of salt and cream, as if it had come straight out of a churn on a farm.

Teddy was about to turn away from the window when he noticed a tall, young man, in jeans and a white cotton shirt, walking across the courtyard of the château. Teddy leaned out to call to him, but then, drew back; he would catch up with him down in the breakfast hall, the place to which the young aristo, Julian Bramblewell-Eurlinn, probable heir to the Château du Crâne and the surrounding lands, was presumably going.

The second son of Lady Artemis Aethelfreda Bramblewell-Eurlinn, Lord Bramblewell's sister, Julian strode across the courtyard with an air of confidence born of an upbringing in an educated family that had provided him with emotional security, material comfort and the knowledge that he belonged to a line of Bramblewells of impressive lineage. Yet, he was not an arrogant young man, Teddy had observed. Indeed, what Teddy had liked about Julian, upon becoming acquainted with him, had been his direct manner - he played with a straight bat- and his lack of self-obsession. And conversations with Julian had always been fascinating, as he had seemed to possess a paradoxical nature. Although he would appear to be detached in his judgements, in the way a scientist would be, he could also surprise, by displaying a passion that powered an inner drive. He would, frequently, be serious and reflective, but, on other occasions, he might put on show all the enthusiasm and dash of his youthful years. He was barely twenty, Teddy knew, but nevertheless, he was already able to compel one to accept him as a responsible and natural leader: one whom Teddy could respect. Additionally, Teddy had noticed that, like his uncle, Lord Bramblewell, Julian was chivalrous, in an attractively old-style way. Teddy supposed that Julian would be of the type of intuitive young man who would be inclined to treat girlfriends with faultless politeness and a kind of tender respect. He thought it was a failing on Héloïse de Sauzon's part that she had not yet realised what she had been missing, in paying insufficient attention to Julian, but then, was Héloïse really interested in anyone other than herself?

Julian had spoken to Teddy about his attraction to Héloïse, one evening after dinner. He had explained that, since the shooting of the film had begun and Héloïse had appeared, day after day, in long dresses made of rose or apple green chiffon, lined with silk, her pale, blonde hair rippling down her back, like a river of champagne, her skin lightly tanned to look like honey and her brown eyes shining with intelligence, he had been able to think of little else. But, he had noticed, of course, the extent to which Héloïse had seemed to have been drawn to Teddy: how she had, invariably, followed him with her eyes. Was Teddy interested in establishing a relationship with her?

"Certainly not!" Teddy had replied and with such force that Julian had been taken aback, when he had posed the question.

Having seen the surprised look in Julian's eyes, Teddy had explained that, two years previously, he had become close to Jacqueline, Héloïse's sister. However the relationship had ended badly, with Jacqueline hurting and humiliating him. He, now, wanted to forget the entire Sauzon family. A relationship with Héloïse, even if he were attracted to her - and he was not - would have been impossible for him even to imagine.

"But, you agreed to take part in the film," Julian had pointed out, puzzled. "Did you not know Héloïse would be in it?"

"I was coerced into appearing in the film."

"Coerced by whom? By my uncle?"

"No. Not your uncle. Of course not."

Julian, having the instinct of a natural diplomat, had asked no more questions. But Teddy had suspected that Julian had realised that Susie Sutton, his uncle's fiancée, had played a part in forcing him to accept the rôle.

"Anyway, it worked out all right," Teddy had added. "I managed to persuade Pierre Laurier to change the ending of the film, so that I was never actually alone with Héloïse in a scene. But, listen! Don't think for a moment that Héloïse is anything like Jacqueline in character. She is not. Jacqueline is an impulsive and sometimes thoughtless romantic. Héloïse is more cool and logical in her approach to life."

"But, the way she looks at you would suggest…"

"She does not like to lose. That is what is annoying her. She is trying to work out what to do next. You might bring out another side of her, though. I don't doubt, in fact, that you will uncover what is best in her nature."

"You are sure you have no interest in her."

"Absolutely none. I have a girlfriend waiting for me, in Liverpool, anyway. Rebecca."

Teddy frowned as he remembered that conversation. He turned away from the open window and walked back into the shade of the room. He sat on the edge of the bed again and, in an absent-minded way, pulled at the cord attached to one of the blue curtains of the four poster bed. He, then, leaned forward, resting his elbows on his thighs. Relationships were complicated. What right had he to offer anyone advice, given his own failure to establish a relationship of his own successfully? He was not sure, even, if his friendship with Rebecca would last. She would soon have to return to her college, on the east coast of America.

Would the two of them be able to sustain their attachment to each other with such a distance between them? And when Rebecca had graduated, would she be prepared to pursue a career in Chester, in the Wirral or in Liverpool? Would she expect him to move to America, instead? If only the future could be predicted!

With a wry smile, Teddy thought of Liz Laurier and her astrological practice. How often he had made disparaging remarks about her fortune telling, as he had erroneously described it, when she had been employed in Bramblewell School! For a second, Teddy wondered how Liz would react were he to ask her if she would help him to work out how to proceed in his relationship with Rebecca. Of course, at once, he dismissed the idea from his mind as being ridiculous. He was a scientist, after all! Besides, if Rebecca were to find out that he had even considered discussing his feelings for her with a third party, and an astrologer into the bargain, she would be hurt and offended. She would believe such an action to be an unforgiveable intrusion into her private life.

The mobile phone lying on the bed beside Teddy rang. He picked it up. Lynn James was calling again.

"Hello, Teddy," she said. "Have you been thinking about what I told you earlier?"

"I find it hard to believe, Lynn. I mean, why would Miss Trimm leave so suddenly? I was talking to her just a few days ago. There wasn't a hint in her conversation that anything unusual was about to happen."

"Well! She has gone, Teddy. I'm in her office just now and there is nothing here that belongs to her. Have you worked out the implications?"

"What do you mean, exactly?"

"I am now acting head of the school. Obviously, my previous position of deputy head will have to be filled by a new acting deputy head."

"Thetis might step in to hold the fort. Or Savannah. Or Barbara Merrivale, even. She's good at administration, and..."

"Teddy!" Lynn interrupted. "I want you to apply for the post."

"Don't be absurd, Lynn. I'm twenty-four. I haven't spent enough years teaching in a classroom. I haven't held a position of minor responsibility, even."

"I want you to apply for the post, Teddy. I don't see your lack of experience as being an obstacle. I was considered to be very young when I became deputy head. One learns while doing the job."

Teddy was becoming aware of an uncharacteristically urgent edge to Lynn's voice. Since she was normally calm, no matter how demanding the task before her, he was disturbed by this. He sensed she was obliquely asking him for help. What was she concealing?

"When I return to Bramblewell, we'll talk about this," Teddy said, trying to sound reassuring. "I'll be there soon, Lynn. I promise."

CHAPTER 10

Pressure and Persuasion

Summer was drawing to a close and Rosalind Somerland would soon be leaving France in order to resume her life in West Cheshire and Chester. Liz Laurier was looking forward to seeing her daughter again, even though she knew that her meetings with Rosalind would be confined, for the most part, to weekends, once the new term at Bramblewell School had begun. But she, Liz, knew too that she would be fortunate to have the opportunity to be accorded even those few hours of Rosalind's time, weekly. Although Gylen Somerland, her first husband, had, actually, never stipulated how much time she could spend with Rosalind, she felt morally compelled to respect the fact that he had been granted custody of the children - the children she had abandoned when they had been very young - and so, she had never asked for favours but had accepted that her rôle in the children's lives would be much less important than his. Additionally, she was grateful to Gylen for never having spoken ill of her to the children. And she had appreciated the fact that only once had he said to her, in private, "Can you imagine, Liz, what it was like to have had to deal with Rosalind and John, the day you went away? They couldn't stop crying. Rosalind asked again and again, 'Where's Mummy? Where's Mummy?' Her distress nearly crushed me." But, he had not spoken in anger, the way he once would have done. The days when his voice would have been full of force and his face red were now in the past, it seemed. In fact, he had asked his question calmly and had never repeated it. Maybe he had realised that Liz would already have been suffering: especially at night, in the dark, when the distractions of the day would have no longer been able to divert her attention away from what had long lain hidden in her heart. Gylen's few words, though, had added to Liz's concealed misery, having conjured up in her head a picture of her abandoned children: one which she had not been able to erase. And time and time again, she would now wake up at night knowing that she had been dreaming of those infants calling out to her, "Mummy! Mummy!" Then, her heart would feel heavy as if a weight had been leaning on it and she would wonder if she would ever be free of the guilt which had been clinging to her, like wet strands of sea-weed, amongst which she had become entangled.

Driven by a mixture of guilt and the desire to help Rosalind along the path to a happy adulthood, Liz had devoted night after night to writing notes for "The Aspects of Venus", the book which she hoped would help her daughter to understand the forces at work in her relationships with other people. But now, the work was becoming tiring. The preparations for writing the book were making more demands on her than she had anticipated. A multitude of questions were spinning around in her head. How frank should she be when describing what was really happening in Rosalind's friendship group, for example? Should she describe all the planetary connections across the charts, or focus on just one or two for the sake of clarity? Of course, she would have to create new names for the people described in the book, if she were thinking of having it published and, probably, she would have to disguise their life-styles, also. Would they still be recognisable? The complications were stacking up.

It occurred to her one night, when she put her notes away, before making a bed time drink, that not only school children could be rendered uncomfortable by their classmates' planets. Teachers, too, might find the scatter of planets in their own charts to be challenged by those of their pupils, like pieces in a game of chess. Maybe she should write a book to warn her former colleagues of the possibility of that unhappy occurrence. And maybe they would be persuaded, thus, to look with more favour on astrology.

But, oh! She could imagine Teddy Laurence's appalled expression if she were to present him with a copy! And he was not the only teacher at Bramblewell School who had looked upon astrology with distaste, while she, Liz, had been in post there. In the staff-room, she had often felt as if she had been in a hostile zone. But who could blame those teachers, really? They associated astrology with newspaper horoscopes and fairground entertainers and not with the works of those serious astrologers who had studied in respectable centres of learning.

Liz shook her head as she poured hot milk into a cup. She knew she was feeling downhearted because her writing-session had gone badly that evening. Maybe she would show what she had written to Rosalind once the girl had settled down after her holiday. Perhaps she, Rosalind, would be able to offer advice on how to make the book attractive to teenagers, in fact. She was gifted in that way.

CHAPTER 11

Coffee and Cakes

Dorothy Trimm had a long-standing arrangement with her friend, Kathleen - "Kath" - Yarrington, whereby they would meet, once a fortnight on a Thursday, either at Dorothy's house or at Kath's, for morning coffee or for afternoon tea, unless there were pressing matters to which one of them had to attend. Like Dorothy, Kath lived in the Whitby Village suburb of Ellesmere Port, but whereas Dorothy's house was in the part closest to Ellesmere Port proper, Kath's was located further out, in the direction of the Strawberry Roundabout and the extreme boundary of the Port, as Ellesmere Port was known, locally.

Kath was married to a cardiologist and her house was slightly larger than Dorothy's, but Dorothy was gracious in her acceptance of her friend's good fortune. Besides, Kath was refined and educated and did not affect those unattractive airs and graces that one occasionally found being adopted by other women who had married "well". Kath was too intelligent to be uppity.

On the Thursday following her encounter with her daughter, Hilary, in Hilary's office in Bramblewell School, Dorothy made her way to Kath's house, all agog with the desire to relate the latest piece of gossip. She walked down the paved path, through Kath's cottage garden at the front and then, went directly along the side of the house to the back, where she guessed Kath would be planning to have coffee on the patio, since the morning was clear and warm.

"Coo-ee!" she called, as she rounded the corner of the extension, with an eager step.

"In here!" Kath replied, raising her voice so that it would be heard, through the kitchen door, which was only slightly ajar. "I've made cakes!"

That morning, Kath was dressed in a nutmeg brown, silk blouse, white slacks and two-tone, white and brown shoes. She did not look as if she hadspent an hour or two fussily baking in the kitchen, but the cakes that had been removed from the oven, a few moments before, were warm and a recipe book could be seen propped up on a small, wooden book-stand, open at the page which had been consulted. Dorothy, therefore, while inspecting the scene, had to concede that the cakes had, indeed, been made by Kath herself, despite the absence of messy patches of flour on the kitchen's work tops.

"I hope you'll like these," said Kath. "I used a Swiss recipe."

"We're having coffee outside, are we?" asked Dorothy, avoiding commenting on what Kath had just said. Rarely straying from traditional British recipes, she, herself, had a repertoire that leaned towards less elaborate butterfly cakes and custard flans, rather than the foreign delicacies that Kath attempted to bake, in remembrance of her numerous holidays.

A table had already been positioned in the shade of a tree, Dorothy had noticed. Kath had placed on it a large tray, covered in a white cloth, upon which cups and saucers, side-plates, linen napkins and silver knives and forks had been arrayed neatly, in rows.

"Take this out, will you?" said Kath, handing her friend a three-tiered cake stand, on which small sandwiches, cut into rectangles, along with scones and the freshly baked cakes had been arranged. "I'll fetch the coffee."

A few minutes later, Dorothy and Kath were sitting at the table outside, tucking into the small feast before them and talking about the fine weather, as a polite prelude to more gripping topics. Dorothy commented on Kath's outfit, mentioning how chic it looked. Kath, by this time, had put on a wide-brimmed, straw hat, with a fuchsia-coloured hatband, possibly to add zing to the brown outfit, but also, because the heat of the sun was increasing and she did not want the colour of her tinted hair to fade.

"Very smart," Dorothy added.

"As is your dress, dear," said Kath, leaning back in her chair to study the yellow and white, fitted dress that Dorothy was wearing. "I do congratulate you on wearing that very pale nail lacquer with it. I'm so appalled by the current fad for wearing scarlet nail varnish, aren't you? I suppose one could get away with it if one were wearing a bright red dress, but not a dress of any other colour, surely. I mean, when we were young, dear, red nail varnish was regarded as being vulgar, wasn't it? I know all sorts of rules are being relaxed, these days, but even so…Those red talons!"

"Mm," said Dorothy. "You should write a book, dear, on the art of being lady-like."

"Oh!" said Kath, pretending that she had found the suggestion ridiculous, while she smiled with pleasure, all the same. She wrapped a linen cloth around the handle of the cafetière and started to pour the coffee into the cups. "Anyway, now that we have compliments out of the way," she said, "let's get down to business, shall we? What, exactly, were you talking about on the 'phone, when you said you were going away on a cruise with Hilary? Did you really say you were going to spy on a French lady or did I imagine that you said something like that? What did you mean? Come on! I'm all ears!"

"Oh, my dear! I shouldn't have said 'spy'! We've simply been asked to keep an eye on a French lady, in case she falls ill. I've made the trip sound more exciting than it actually will be, I'm sure!"

"But who is this French lady? Where did you meet her?"

"Well! Do you remember my mentioning an engagement party to which Hilary had been invited some months ago? Last year, in fact. It took place in France."

"Oh! Yes! I actually do! What an awful time the young teacher must have had! Imagine! Wasn't his name Teddy Laurence?"

"Yes. Teddy Laurence. The experience must have been just

ghastly for him! Anyway, the lady we shall be observing, if I can put it like that, is the grandmother of the girl who - if I can resort to the demotic - ditched Teddy at that engagement party."

"No! Really? How on earth did you make contact with whoever it was who wanted you to look after this grandmother?"

"Well! That's the strangest part of the story. It seems the French girl who rejected Teddy Laurence - Jacqueline something or other - got in touch with him through a mutual friend, to ask him if he could think of anyone who would look after her grandmother, while she, the grandmother, was on a cruise."

"What? And he responded to her request?"

"Well! He got in touch with Hilary and she told him she would sort out the problem for him."

"But, you would think - wouldn't you?- that he would simply have told this Jacqueline whatever- her - name - is that he had absolutely no wish to have anything to do with her. Why did he even pass the request on to Hilary? Had I been in Hilary's position, I'd have said to him, 'Listen! Since that girl treated you with complete contempt, you really should have nothing at all to do with her. She has a nerve to approach you!'That's what I'd have said."

"I am inclined to agree with you that he should have ignored the request, but Hilary didn't offer him advice. She simply said she'd attend to the matter. It makes one suspect, though, that Mr. Teddy Laurence is still emotionally attached to the French girl. And she, also, must be longing to have some sort of contact with him."

"Yes. She probably regrets giving him up, now. Didn't another boyfriend of hers turn up at the party? Something like that?"

"Yes. Jacqui somebody - or - other appeared out of the blue. He hadn't been invited. Anyway, she married him."

"She married him? And she's still trying to keep in touch with Mr. Laurence! Well! My guess is that she has realised she has made a catastrophic mistake. Maybe her marriage has disappointed her.

Maybe she's the romantic type: the type that thinks love should be all dash and excitement, the way it is in novels. Oh dear! She must have thought marriage would be easy."

"I really don't care what she thinks, Kath, but I do care about poor Teddy Laurence. He's had such bad luck when it comes to relationships. He used to date Susie Sutton, you know. She hurt him as well. Really badly."

Kath started coughing, having swallowed a mouthful of coffee too quickly, so great had been her surprise at what Dorothy had said.

"What?" she exclaimed. "The future Lady Bramblewell?"

"Exactly. The future Lady Bramblewell."

"Oh! My word! I'm surprised the unfortunate Teddy hasn't left Bramblewell School."

"I don't rule out the possibility that he might. But anyway, to return to the topic of this cruise and the French lady..."

"Did you say, earlier, you were asked to keep watch over her in case she became ill?"

"Yes. The task shouldn't be too arduous."

"I bet there's more to this than meets the eye."

"What do you mean?"

"Oh, come on, Dorothy! Has it not crossed your mind that her family might be afraid she'll meet a fortune hunter on the cruise?"

"Oh! Not you too! Hilary said the same thing! But, be sensible! The woman is in OUR age group and she's, presumably, an educated person! She wouldn't be taken in by a fortune hunter!"

Really, Dorothy? REALLY?"

"Kath, be serious!"

"Excuse me," said Kath, indignation obvious in her voice. "I can assure you that education provides no barrier to self-deception when it comes to affairs of the heart, to use a popular phrase. And age and experience, it seems, provide no barrier either. Furthermore, families who want to keep an eye on a fortune that they might potentially inherit are legion, in every culture. They certainly exist in France. We're talking about the pragmatic land of Molière, after all. I can think of lots of examples of well-to-do women, in Europe, who have kept the grimier newspapers going because, unfortunately, they have wasted their money, in their later years, on scoundrels."

"Of course," said Dorothy, staring out at the long lawn beyond the patio, as if deep in thought. "Unscrupulous men can be very persuasive, I'm sure. You know, it hadn't crossed my mind that there might have been a hidden motive attached to the request made by Teddy's French girlfriend, I must admit. The French grandmother might even have arranged to meet someone on board the ship. A gentleman, I mean. You have certainly given me food for thought, Kath."

"Food for thought!" echoed Kath, while removing the plate of Swiss pastries from the cake stand. She handed it to Dorothy, saying cheerily, "Eat up!"

CHAPTER 12

Lynn

Lynn James was awoken by the noise of a young business man, who lived in the apartment below hers, starting his car. The soft whirr of the engine, heard invariably as she was waking up, always comforted her, just as, during her childhood, the gentle sound of a milk float arriving in the road in which her home had been located, had, in a similar way, let her know that all was normal and that the distortions of reality, seen in dreams, had been chimeras.

Lynn lay still for a few moments, feeling cosy after a long sleep, but then, she sat up abruptly, remembering in a rush what she would be required to accomplish during the day ahead. Miss Trimm had left Bramblewell School - left! - and she, Lynn, was now in charge. There was so much to do before the new term would begin, in fifteen days' time, and the prospect of being wholly responsible for the completion of all necessary tasks was, frankly, daunting. Miss Trimm had always been well-prepared at times such as this. Always quick off the blocks. It would be necessary to be as polished as the impeccable Miss Trimm had been, if not more so, in order to impress the Bramblewell teachers and, crucially, to justify receiving the elevated salary that would now be hers.

Lynn pushed the white sheet and matching, padded, down quilt, covering her, to one side, rose from her bed and grabbed the pale blue, silken robe lying on a white arm-chair, nearby. She slipped the robe over her nightdress: one she particularly liked, because it had been styled to look like the sort of elegant, floor-length, evening gown that a lady in the 1930s might have worn. Lynn felt sophisticated when wearing it and, having become aware of the effect it, and other clothes she possessed, had on her mood, she had realised that the rôle played by fashion in a woman's life was not one that should be underestimated. She would have to bear that in mind as she chose an outfit to wear that day: effectively her first, duty-filled day as head of Bramblewell. She looked under the arm-chair for the satin mules, with kitten heels, that she wore in the morning and then, made her way through the apartment, following her usual routine, while simultaneously trying to focus on what was in her wardrobe, as well as what her priorities would be, upon her arrival in the school.

Lynn would not have been on edge, to the same extent, had it not been for the fact that she was sure there would be a number of experienced teachers in the school, even though, theoretically, they were on holiday, still. These ultra-conscientious ones would be anxious to make a start on preparations for the new scholastic year which was about to begin. Lynn wondered if she should make an announcement in the staff room, to those present there, that Miss Trimm had left unexpectedly and would not be returning. Or would it be more correct to wait until the first day of term, when all teachers would be present in the school, before saying anything, formally, about the departure? She, herself, did not think it mattered what she did, one way or another, but she knew some teachers at Bramblewell were tetchy about precedence and would object to colleagues, whom they considered to be undeserving, being granted what they, themselves, would judge to be favours. Perhaps she should send an e-mail message, that morning, to everyone on the staff. Or, maybe she should not. Would the arrival of an e-mail message about school be perceived to be an unwelcome intrusion during holiday time? Miss Trimm had made the position of headmistress seem easy, but easy it was not. If only there was a deputy- head already in situ: one with whom she could discuss matters that required diplomatic solutions! If only Teddy Laurence had already been appointed! Thetis Ravenswood, the Latin teacher, might apply for the post, but Lynn did not know her well. Thetis had been in the school for decades and was unquestionably discreet, but she had an aloof character and Lynn could not imagine herself confiding in her. In fact, Lynn suspected Thetis' answer to all problems disclosed would be, "Chin up! Pull yourself together, girl! Show them who is boss!" And, in any case, would Thetis, given her age and experience, want to be seen playing second fiddle to a younger woman? No. Thetis would not apply for the deputy's position. As usual, she would remain on the side-lines, as it were, insinuating, through her attitudes and behaviour, that she was an unbranded maverick, who was not at all tempted to climb the ladder to promotion, given the sort of compromises that would have to be accommodated. How Lynn wished, though, that when she would arrive in the school that morning, she would not be obliged to face the day, with no one, really, to whom she could turn. Not even Lee Chan, the school secretary - who had been more than a secretary, in fact, given her ability to be cool and rational while all about her were in a tizz - would be at her desk. Isolde Delamar, Lee's replacement, was not in the same league as Lee, in Lynn's estimation. Nowhere near it.

The little kitten heels on Lynn's mules clattered on the red, tiled floor of the kitchen. Lynn reached for a tin of ground Arabica coffee beans, which she kept, in readiness, on the granite work-top next to the cooker and then, she pulled forward the coffee-making machine, also standing there. The morning was already warm. Lynn put thoughts of comfort food - porridge, for example - to one side and opted for a breakfast of muesli with nuts, plain yoghurt and a handful of grapes. Then, it occurred to her that she should give her brain a boost with protein and so, she toasted a slice of bread with Cheshire cheese on top of it. She had still not made up her mind as to what she would wear. A skirt suit? A formal looking jacket with a slim, fitted dress? Or would a slightly more casual outfit be appropriate, given the fact that it was still holiday-time? Besides, looking out of the window, she could see clear skies over Hoylake. The day ahead was likely to be hot, probably all over the Wirral. Maybe she should wear her white, sleeveless dress, with red and tangerine poppies printed on it, along with peep-toe, high-heeled shoes. She had bought the dress, while on holiday in Dallas, Texas, two years previously, and despite the fact that it was a summer dress, it had a certain air of sophistication about it. She would carry a light jacket, just in case the afternoon would turn cool in Chester.

Half an hour later, Lynn made her way to her car, parked in the courtyard in front of the house divided into two apartments, where she had lived for three years. Having started the car's engine, she drove slowly in the direction of Birkenhead Road. She opened the window beside her and, a minute or two later, although it was out of sight, she could sense the presence of the sea - the blue water of the Bay of Liverpool - on her left.

Lynn invariably enjoyed her morning drive through the Wirral, from north to south and then, onwards to Chester. She varied the routes she took. Sometimes, she would choose the westerly road. On other days, she would veer to the east. Driving through the quiet areas of the lush, green peninsula, she had time to think and plan. There were no tall mountains to throw bleak shadows on to the landscape and into her thoughts. The sun was allowed to shine down freely, making the fields, the villages and the small towns sparkle.

Bramblewell School was situated on the outskirts of Chester, proper, and within the grounds of Bramblewell Manor. Lynn, having finished her journey that morning, turned her car into the school's drive, through the wrought iron gates at the entrance and between the tall, rhododendron bushes, on either side. Shortly afterwards, she parked the car in front of the school's main building: the neo-Gothic construction which, initially, had been intended to have been a large house, but which its owner, a Lady Bramblewell from times past, one of Lord Bramblewell's ancestors, had turned into a school for the education of girls. Originally, the girls had been taught, by the teachers employed, to be refined and well-mannered to the exclusion of all else, but then, the pioneering owner had intervened and had insisted that "her girls" be encouraged to read widely, to think independently and to embrace innovation. Lord Bramblewell had always impressed on Miss Trimm the importance of bearing in mind the educational direction in which his revered ancestor had wanted to push the school. "Innovation, Miss Trimm!" he had been inclined to repeat. "Innovation and independent thinking!"

Lynn saw no one in the entrance hall of Bramblewell School, when she entered the building. No sound could be heard, either. Lynn paused, for a moment. The ridiculous thought occurred to her that the school seemed to be looking different, now that she was in charge. She gazed at the imposing staircase and the large paintings, Pre-Raphaelite in style, which were hanging, darkly, on the walls, as if she were observing them for the first time. Lord Bramblewell, of course, had insisted that the paintings be displayed in the school, since they had been the work of his adored ancestor, Lady Maureen, and, in fact, they had been in position for years, but Lynn had not really studied them before, dismissing them as the work of an amateur. Now, she realised that they had merit. Perhaps the school's founder had been a woman of genuine talent, after all, rather than a dilettante, dabbling in this and that.

Lynn, then, realised that she had been allowing her mind to meander because she could not decide what she should do first. Should she go to the staff room to see who was there? Or should she go directly to Miss Trimm's office, to evaluate what had to be done that morning and to become properly acquainted with Miss Isolde Delamar, in the ante-room? Lynn had, previously, come across Isolde only fleetingly, but had noted, with interest, that, although she, Isolde, had willingly deferred to Miss Trimm, she had barely acknowledged Lynn's presence. In fact, she had avoided looking straight into Lynn's eyes. Of course, she was only two or three years younger than Lynn and, therefore, perhaps resentful of the superior position held by her, Lynn, within the school.

But, now that Lynn was headmistress, Isolde would surely try to improve her attitude, so as to avoid repercussions.

Deciding to tackle Isolde first, Lynn opened the door of the ante-room, which was situated on the ground floor, to the right of the school's main entrance. It served as Isolde's work area and Lynn had to cross it to reach Miss Trimm's office, or rather, to reach the room which would now be her own office. Isolde was sitting at her desk, poised and apparently at ease. She looked up, at once, when Lynn entered and surprisingly, smiled widely, thus placing on view her perfect teeth. That morning, she had put on a white, collarless blouse, with three quarter - length sleeves, that looked new. She had chosen to wear with it, a pale grey, pencil skirt and beige, court shoes with very high, stiletto heels. Her hair had been brushed into a shiny, pony tail style. She looked glossy, as if she had prepared herself for a fashion-shoot, rather than a day in a busy office and Lynn wondered if she was going to use her clothes as one of the ways in which she would try to upstage her new boss, or, at least, would attempt to do so. Isolde's smile looked friendly, but Lynn had already noticed that there was a glitter in the young woman's eyes: a glitter that suggested to Lynn that, behind the smile, there was coldness and enmity. Lynn, at once, suspected that Isolde Delamar would not be supportive. In fact, she knew in the way women instinctively do, that Isolde would actively try to undermine her. How could she, Lynn, work with a secretary like that? But of course, Isolde would be hard to unseat, given her previous association with Lord Bramblewell. It would be Lynn who would, probably, have to tread carefully. If she wanted to secure, for herself, the position of headmistress permanently, she would have to appease Lord Bramblewell, the school's benefactor, at least during her first months as acting head. Isolde would know that. The situation was tricky. Isolde might not be immensely clever, but people with a nature like hers often, disagreeably, compensated for their deficiencies through the use of cunning.

It occurred to Lynn that, during that day, Isolde would be testing the water, as it were, to see what sort of relationship with Lynn could be established. A point had to be made. Lynn was not keen on the idea of ostensibly pulling rank. She was far too subtle a person to enjoy the parading of her status. But boundaries had to be put in place, to avoid her relationship with Isolde, from then on, being excessively stressful.

"Good morning, Isolde," she said, calmly, making her way across the ante-room. When she had reached the door of her new office, she turned to add, "Would you bring coffee to my room, please? And could you find a cup and saucer somewhere? I don't like drinking from mugs. Oh! And after that, would you phone Miss Laurier for me? Her number will be on file. Tell her that Miss James, headmistress of Bramblewell School, would like to speak to her."

Isolde had been staring at Lynn, her eyes wide. But then, as if suddenly shaken out of a state of shock, she said, "Yes, Miss James," in a tone that was cool.

Lynn gave her a brief nod, before opening the door of the office and stepping inside Miss Trimm had left the room, as Lynn had noticed a couple of days before, in faultless order. The wide, polished desk was devoid of everything, except a computer, a telephone and a reading lamp. The bookshelves contained only boxed materials, connected with the management of schools and the implementation of those national policies, which were compulsory. Miss Trimm's personal books had been removed. There was no visible trace remaining of the woman who had served Bramblewell School diligently for a number of years.

"I really am on my own," thought Lynn, as she placed her handbag on the desk and, impulsively, took out of it her mobile phone. She was an independent, ambitious and talented woman, but she was also prudent and she knew when it was wise to seek support, if only support of the emotional kind. Isolde, and certain teachers on the staff, even, would resent the fact that, although only thirty five, she was now acting as head of the prestigious school, locally known simply as Bramblewell. She needed what was colloquially known as "back-up." A buffer between her and those who would not wish her well. She would call Teddy Laurence, if only just to hear his voice and to be told again that he would soon be returning.

CHAPTER 13

A Prince of Legend

Evening had fallen over the Gironde. The day's filming had been satisfactory and so, the film crew had repaired, in good spirits, to the dining room of the Château du Crâne, where the household staff had served clear soup, chicken with rice, salad and. later, slices of glazed, apricot tarts.

Héloïse de Sauzon had reluctantly denied herself the carbohydrate-rich, apricot tart that she had been offered at the end of the meal, her mind having been on the tightly-laced costume she would be required to wear the following morning. Now, it was eleven o'clock and, presumably because she had spent two hours after dinner learning lines in her room, thus using up energy cerebrally, she felt hungry again. She knew that food, that was easily accessible, was usually left in the kitchen for anyone who needed a late-night snack and she was considering leaving her room to go downstairs, when her mother, the Countess de Sauzon, dialled her mobile phone number. Had she, Héloïse, received any news of Grand'maman, the countess wanted to know. Had Grand'maman been in touch, since the cruise on which she had embarked, had begun, in fact? The Countess, herself, had heard nothing - and neither had Jacqueline.

"But Grand'maman has been away for only a day," Héloïse responded calmly. "Even when she is at home, she calls you only once a week, at the most. Give her time to settle! There are people on the ship who are watching over her, after all. If she becomes ill, someone will let you know."

After a few minutes, calmed by Héloïse's cool logic, the Countess conceded that she had been worrying un-necessarily and so, Héloïse ended the conversation, trusting that her mother would stop torturing herself by imagining mishaps that would never occur. Grand'maman, after all, was possibly having a delightful time in a place where she was not known, improbable though that might seem. Annoyingly, though, it had not been the first time that Héloïse had found herself cast in the rôle of counsellor to her own mother and it felt odd to her to have to play the part of the parent, as it were. Sometimes, she felt as if she had never been allowed to have been a child and, occasionally, she would feel an urge to do something wholly unconventional, in order to surprise her mother or even to shock her. She knew, for example, that it had been the rebellious side of her that had come to the fore when she had decided to accept the offer of a part in the film that was being shot at the Château du Crâne, thus risking subsequent exclusion from those social circles, in which acting was still regarded as being unacceptable as a profession.

The air was cool, at night, in the corridors and on the dark stairs of the Château du Crâne. Being aware of this, Héloïse slipped a navy jumper, with a V-neck, over her white tee-shirt: a tee-shirt which had been shortened to reach only her waist. She changed her shoes, then, replacing her comfortable, canvas espadrilles with coral-coloured sandals, which had platform soles that increased her height by seven centimetres. She had a major rôle to play in the film and, consequently, she felt she had to look glamorous every time she stepped out of her room, in case a casual employee, working in the château, took a photo of her, inconspicuously, on a mobile phone. One had to be careful. In that respect, being a leading actress in the film was starting to become a chore. There were days, in fact, when she longed to be home, at the Château de Sauzon, in Belle-Isle. There, she could wander along beaches, incognita, wearing sea-bleached jeans and espadrilles, if she wanted to. Who would care? She wondered, then, if she had been wise to invite her younger sister, the shy, home-loving Marie-Colette, to the film set. A few days before, the director of the film, Pierre Laurier, had seen a photo of Marie-Colette: one that Héloïse had stored on her electronic tablet. He had said, at once, that Marie-Colette might look "unforgettable" were she to play a part in the film, given her striking appearance. "An actress has dropped out," he had said, giving the sort of shrug that implied Marie-Colette could replace her. Héloïse had thought about his suggestion, carefully. On the one hand, it was possible that Marie-Colette might blossom, in the sort of rôle Pierre might create for her. Shy people often did benefit from attending speech and drama lessons, after all. On the other hand, there was a danger that, given her sensitivity, Marie-Colette might be crushed by the experience, especially if exposed to Pierre's outbursts of temper and impatience. But of course, the Countess de Sauzon would never allow Marie-Colette to appear in a film and so, there was no point in considering Pierre's idea. The Countess might not even allow Marie-Colette to visit the film-set although it would do the young girl good to attempt to travel to Bordeaux, alone. Were she to manage to do so, her confidence would be boosted. The journey to Vannes, across the water from Belle-Isle, to attend school had, previously, been all that she had been expected to do on her own.

The stone stairs in the Château du Crâne reminded Héloïse of those that had been familiar to her, all through her life, in the Château de Sauzon. As she made her way down, she thought wistfully of her family at home. In the evenings, she often did think of her family: Papa and Maman, her sisters and even, with the sort of affection that accompanies distance, the sometimes insufferable Jérôme, who, amusingly, had left behind the mischievous child he had once been and had, in early adolescence, turned himself, instead, into a rather uppity know-it-all. Héloïse suspected he had been encouraged to be snobbish by Grand'maman, who often talked to him on the telephone. Indeed, Jérôme seemed to spend more time in conversation with Madame Gabrielle than with the other members of the family, all put together.

Lost in rêverie, Hèloïse was taken aback when she saw Julian

Bramblewell-Eurlinn making his way upstairs. His blond hair looked glossy in the glow of the electric lights, placed in small globes, at regular intervals, in high sconces along the wall. Although she was aware of the fact that she was allowing herself to be as romantic as her sister, Jacqueline, Hêloïse wondered what Julian would have looked like in centuries past, when flaming torches would have been attached to the same walls and he would have been dressed differently. It occurred to her that Jacqueline would have written poems about him, describing him as a prince of legend, cultured, studious and adventurous. Unknown to Julian, Héloïse, herself, had often watched him, during meal times, at the Château du Crâne, and had rather regretted the fact that her heart had been taken over by an irrational attraction to Teddy Laurence. Irrational, because she knew her feelings for him would never be reciprocated. It was as clear as water that she was effectively wasting her time pining for Teddy, but she, also, knew she could not hurry the process of emotionally detaching herself from him. She would have to wait for indifference to liberate her. Often, despairing of the hold Teddy had on her, she had wondered what had been at the root of her attraction to him and when, precisely, it - her attraction to him - had begun. On Christmas Eve, on the first occasion he had visited the Château de Sauzon? Madame Gabrielle, on that night, had tried to persuade the naïve Marie-Colette, to give Teddy a copy of "Le Rouge et le Noir" as a Christmas present, thus implying that Teddy, like the leading character in the book, had been an arriviste, a parvenu or a manipulator. Héloïse had been horrified and, unknown to Madame Gabrielle, had exchanged the book for another. Hêloïse had considered Madame Gabrielle's behaviour, that Christmas, to have been unforgivable. Sitting beside Teddy, during the Réveillon meal, late on Christmas Eve, she, Héloïse, had surreptitiously glanced, from time to time, at his fine profile, while also taking note of his behaviour. His good manners, his sense of fair play and, she had to admit, his faultless choice of clothes for the occasion, had left an impression on her that time had not eradicated.

"Hi!" said Julian, upon reaching Héloïse. "Are you going for a walk?"

When he had first met Héloïse, Julian had addressed her in better than passable French, but having realised that she was able to speak English with ease and liked to do so, he had, thenceforth, reverted to his own language whenever he had run into her.

"No. I'm not going for a walk," answered Héloïse, unable to stop herself from smiling. "I am going to the kitchen."

"Hungry?"

"A little."

"I'll come with you, if you like. I'll show you where some really nice food is stored."

"Ah! Quel rêve!" exclaimed Hêloïse softly, bowing slightly to show assent, while becoming aware of a desire to behave a little flirtatiously.

As they went down the stairs together, Hêloïse found herself reflecting on Julian's politeness, his even temper, his straightforwardness. his savoir- vivre, his polish, his story-book, prince-like appearance…A romantically-inclined girl, who read eau-de-rose novels, would find him dreamily irresistible, she had no doubt. She, herself, could pretend to be entranced by him, while waiting for lassitude to replace her obsession with Teddy Laurence, but she recoiled at the thought of having recourse to the tricks that another woman might employ. She was disinclined to dissemble, and anyway, Julian was too perceptive to be taken in by feminine trickery and simply too nice to be treated in that way.

Once in the kitchen, Julian invited Hêloïse to sit at a long, wooden table, while he went in search of food, in faraway refrigerators. He returned with a tray of Grosvenor pies, English cheeses, French butter, still fresh bread, milk and Darjeeling tea along with a basket of figs and apples, shiny and good.

"Tuck in!" said Julian, adding, thoughtfully, "It's a bit rustic, isn't it? Would you prefer an omelette or something? I could, perhaps, make one."

"Mais, non!" exclaimed Hêloïse, laughing. "How very English you are!"

Julian looked at her quizzically, but then, rather than question her as to what she had meant exactly, he urged her to taste the Grosvenor pie. He placed a large slice on a plate and put it in front of her, with a knife and fork.

Hêloïse looked up at him, smiling, but she felt like sighing, because she wanted to talk to him frankly, but knew she had better not try to do so. Not at that moment, anyway. English men did not like to talk about emotions, she believed. Was she being unfair or presumptuous, though? She wondered how Julian would react, in fact, if she were to explain to him that Teddy Laurence had a grip on her which she could not explain, really. Perhaps when she knew Julian better she would talk about such things - the stupidity underlying her obsession, the illogical nature of it - but at that moment, she felt she had to endure a deep pain in her heart, while appearing to focus on something other than her emotionally-driven confusion.

Julian had started to make tea for her, in a competent, English way.

"How are your historical investigations progressing?" asked Hêloïse, trying to keep her voice level and hoping a discussion about the history of the château would steady her mind.

Julian seemed to have been shaken out of a day-dream by her question. He pushed back a lock of blond hair that had fallen across his face.

"Well, as you know," he said, sitting down opposite her, at the table, "the starting-point of my research has been the story of Angêlique, the young woman played by you, in the film. You are aware of the fact that this Angêlique was sent to France, from the Isle of South Uist, in Scotland, by her mother, to find the descendants of a man who had wronged her grand-mother. Angêlique's grandmother, I should specify. The grand- mother, when she, herself, had been young, had been abandoned by that frankly irresponsible man, even though she had been expecting his child. He had, in fact, left her to face social opprobrium, on her own, while he had followed Bonnie Prince Charlie into France, after the Battle of Culloden, in 1746."

"Angêlique must have known the man's name, even though she did not reveal it in the diary that was found in this château."

"You know about the diary?

"I know that four Bramblewell schoolgirls found it during a school trip, That is why they were invited to come back here, to watch the film being shot, I believe. Was it the diary that provided you with most of your information or had you found other rich sources?"

"I did find out about Angêlique's existence from another source, but the diary, apparently written in Angélique's own words, filled in gaps in the information that I had uncovered already."

"The story in the diary sounds so improbable to me. The descendants of the mystery man - shall we call him Monsieur X? - must have been almost impossible to find, not least because of the disarray into which France had been plunged in the late 18th century, when Angélique had, apparently, been sent on her journey. And how was it possible, anyway, for a young woman to travel alone, from Scotland to France, at that time? It seems inconceivable that the story could be true."

"She may have been disguised as a young boy. As a theological student, attached to the Scots College, in Paris, for example. Students travelled from Scotland to Paris and back quite often, I have discovered, and this practice continued until the college was seized, at some point, by revolutionaries. Angélique may even have been accompanied by one of the students."

"That had not crossed my mind. The disguise of a theological student would have been an odd one for her, though, given the fact that she was dabbling in superstition."

"You're referring to the curse?"

"Yes. The grandmother cursed the man who had wronged her, did she not? She cursed him as he was fleeing, saying that he and his descendants would find no happiness until one of them had married one of her descendants."

"And, presumably, Angélique was sent to France in order to find and to marry one of the man's descendants."

"It's astonishing that she obeyed! Did she really believe that lives would be improved, if the curse were to be broken? Did she convince herself that that was possible? Can this story actually be true?"

"One has to remember the culture of that age and Angélique's limited access to books. I doubt that she would have read the works of Voltaire! The grand-mother, incidentally, believed that she would go to hell, upon her death, unless the curse had been broken. That aspect of the story was mentioned in the play, written by the Bramblewell girls: the play that was staged at Bramblewell School. I saw it. When the grand-mother was old and death was approaching, she became fearful, thinking that she would not find rest after death, if the curse had not been broken. I think Angélique had been persuaded that it was her duty to save her grand-mother's soul from a terrible fate. It was considered to be a grave sin to curse someone."

"Have you found out anything else? What became of the baby: the one who would have been the child of Monsieur X?"

"The baby was still-born. Some years later, the mother of that baby - Angélique's grandmother - married and had another child, a girl, who grew up to be Angélique's mother."

"I understand. It's quite complicated, though. And I still think it's odd that a young woman like Angélique, who had obviously had some education - she could write with fluidity, after all - could be so superstitious, but, as you have pointed out, she probably did come from a culture where superstition reigned. I know that the inhabitants of Brittany, also, would have leaned towards superstitious practices, at that time. One still hears about the

Ankou, actually, or images appearing in water."

"You are prepared to dismiss what is believed to be superstition as something that has no rational basis?"

"What are you implying? That curses hit their mark? That is nonsense. If a curse appears to work, it is because the victim believes, fervently, that the curse that has been hurled at him - or her - will be effective. By allowing himself, or herself, to be taken in, by believing in the power of the curse, the victim colludes with the agents of his or her own downfall."

"Do you believe in prayer?"

"What do you mean?"

"Do you believe that people can help others by praying for them?"

"Héloïse gazed at Julian, wondering what he thought her answer would be. His expression was serious.

"Why do you ask that question?" she said then, with curiosity evident in her voice.

"Consider this: if you believe in prayer, is it not logical that you should also believe in curses? Is it not possible that the people whom you described as being superstitious were simply being logical?"

"You mean curses are the opposite of prayer, just as darkness is the opposite of light, or rather, just as the forces of darkness are opposite the forces of light, in the spiritual sense?"

"Are you talking about dualism?"

Thrown by the question, Héloïse looked at Julian with new interest.

"We are in deep waters, now," she said evasively.

"Well!" said Julian, gently. "Let's leave all that for another day! Where were we? Oh, yes! Angélique found her way to France, one way or another, and she ended up in Bordeaux, working here, in the Château du Crâne."

"Yes," said Héloïse, recovering her composure, "I know that she worked, as a maid, for the Countess du Crâne, who was living in the château at the time. Angélique must have slept in a small room, at the top of one of the turrets, because that was where the diary was found."

"It is clear that she, then, went to Paris," said Julian, thoughtfully. "It would have been a dangerous, bloodthirsty place, as the French Revolution would have been in full swing, by then. But, she seemed, according to her own account, to have managed to become acquainted with an aristocrat."

"She claimed she had had his child."

"Yes. She appeared to have had his child. A little boy. Regrettably, she, then, died, perhaps as a consequence of childbirth. The child was taken to the Château du Crâne, by someone who had known her and the child was left in the care of the Countess du Crâne. The countess brought up the child as if he were a future little count, her husband and her own son having been killed by revolutionaries."

"And the baby boy, when he grew up, was actually given the title of the Count du Crâne. It's like a fairy tale. Too much so."

"But, all the Counts du Crïne, since then, have apparently, been descendants of the child. In other words, they have all been descended from Angélique. But the question, now, is this: was the father of Angélique's child really an aristocrat or did Angélique actually find the man whom she had been seeking? In other words, was the curse broken or not? It's possible that Angélique, while dying, had described the baby's father as having been 'an aristocrat', because she had hoped that a noble lineage would increase the baby's chances of being brought up by the Countess du Crâne, herself. Who knows? It's possible we shall never know."

"The film ends with a question, too," said Héloïse, frowning. "It was originally going to have been a straightforward, romantic film, which would have had a happy ending. Now, it ends with a question. I find that an un-satisfactory way to end it. One is left in suspense, rather than with a warm feeling of completion."

"I know what you mean," agreed Julian, leaning back and pushing a lock of blond hair out of his eyes, as if he had, thankfully, completed a piece of concentrated work. "I'd love to know what really became of Monsieur X. Following the Battle of Culloden, lots of Scots and others fled into exile, taking refuge in France. Quite a lot of them settled in the Loire Valley. In Sancerre. There must be some evidence of what became of the young man, somewhere. It's possible that he joined the army, fighting for the French king."

"Why does the story mean so much to you?" asked Héloïse, becoming aware of the urgency suddenly evident in Julian's voice. "You seem to be really anxious to discover the truth. I know that you are likely to inherit the Château du Crâne. Are you interested in its history only for that reason or is there another reason?"

"Ah!" said Julian, as if some hidden motive had been perceived. "I have to confess that my interest was increased by my memory of something my father used to claim. He would say that, on his side of the family, the Eurlinn side, there was an ancestor who had fought at the Battle of Culloden, a chap who had fled to France. I rather fancifully imagined that that person could havebeen the one who had known Angélique's grandmother."

"That's a long shot. A very long shot."

"I know, but I do wonder, at times, if it's a complete coincidence that I have ended up in the Château du Crâne. Are there forces guiding our lives of which we are unaware?"

Héloïse thought for a moment.

"If you are descended from Monsieur X," she said, then, with a pout, "you should, perhaps, marry a descendant of Angélique's child. Then, the spell will be broken for sure. But, obviously, the Château du Crâne is no longer owned by the Counts du Crâne. Do you know what became of them and their families?"

"I have traced the ones who sold the Château du Crâne to my grand-mother. There were three brothers and a sister, I believe. The sister's name was Gabrielle du Crâne. My grand-mother never met her. She met the brothers, only."

Gabrielle du Crâne, did you say?"

"Yes."

Héloïse leaned forward, looking puzzled. Gabrielle was a common enough name. It was her own grand-mother's name, in fact. Her grand-mother was called Gabrielle de Talence. At least, that became her name after her marriage. It occurred to Héloïse, then, that she did not know her grand-mother's maiden name. And, suddenly, into her mind came the memory of the evening, two years previously, when she had found her grand-mother's journal in the Château de Sauzon. That evening, there had been a wild storm and a gale had blown open a window in the room in which Madame Gabrielle habitually slept, during visits to her daughter and grand-children. After attempting to close the window, Héloïse had found the journal on the floor, and not realising what it was, had taken it to her own room, running along the cold corridor in her silken robe, her hair streaming down her back, like a river of pale gold. She remembered that evening well. She remembered jumping into her cosy, four-poster bed, covering herself with the copious bed covers and then, opening the book. She had discovered that Gabrielle de Talence had written it in order to reveal, to her descendants, facts about her past: a past to which she had, previously, made no allusion. Héloïse, being one of Madame Gabrielle's descendants, had judged it acceptable for her to continue reading. And now, one of the sentences she had read, that night, unexpectedly jumped into her mind. It had been:

"I went to meet him at the Gare Saint-Jean in Bordeaux, with my brother, Julien, who drove us back to the château."

The château? Which château? WHICH château? How odd that it had not crossed Héloïse's mind to ask the question, before. But then, the rest of the story had been so disturbing and distracting that questions about the château had not arisen. Besides, no one in the Sauzon family would ever have dared to try to find out, anyway, Madame Gabrielle being so prickly about being interrogated about her past. Even Héloïse's mother had been kept in the dark about her mother's upbringing, all through her life. For a while, then, as a result of reading the journal, only Héloïse had been party to the knowledge of Madame Gabrielle's behaviour in 1968, when she had marched in student demonstrations in Paris. Her father, an ardent Gaullist, had, shockingly, banished her from the family home, as a consequence.

"Julian, would it be possible for you to find out if one of the Counts du Crâne had your name? Was he, also, called Julian?" asked Héloïse, thoughtfully.

"I could look at the bills of sale. I am sure my mother has kept copies, here. Why?"

"I have a feeling - and yes! I know it's unusual for me to say something like this - but I have a feeling I may be descended from the Counts du Crâne."

"Really?"

"Facts are piling into my brain at a speed which one would normally associate with intuition. The point I am about to make is that..."

"If you are descended from the Counts du Crâne and I am really descended from Monsieur X, we..."

"Could break the curse," interrupted Héloïse, in a tone that betrayed no emotion. "But first," she continued, "we must find out who we really are, mustn't we?"

Julian looked at Héloïse in a quizzical manner. She appeared to be neither shocked nor surprised. Sitting up straight in her chair, she nonchalantly picked up a fork from the table and using it, she cut a small corner from the pie on her plate. Then, she looked up at Julian and smiled at him, in a bemused and fetching way.

"Maybe it's not a coincidence that I am here, either," she said.

CHAPTER 14

Illusion

"The sooner a distance exists between Rosalind and that girl, the better," Liz Laurier muttered to herself, as she read the message that had just arrived from her daughter, Rosalind. As had increasingly been the case during Rosalind's time in France, it contained little news of day to day life at the Château du Crâne, really, but plenty of information about the obviously extensive wardrobe of Héloïse de Sauzon! Héloïse wore this yesterday! Héloïse wore that the day before! Héloïse had "tons" of skinny jeans! Héloïse had shoes with heels that were seven and a half centimetres high! "Imagine, Mum!" Well, yes! Liz could imagine the situation quite accurately: that of a young girl deluded by her association with a more glamorous older one into thinking that, simply by being in her company, she, Rosalind, could absorb a little of the other's style, sophistication and cool way of looking at the world, as if by osmosis. "Am I being over-critical?" Liz wondered, as she re-read the message. Was it not normal for a young girl with her Ascendant in Pisces, as was the case with Rosalind, to be dazzled and delighted by a vision of what she believed to be beauty? What Liz feared, though, was the possibility that Rosalind's other friends would resent being neglected by her, after all that they had done to help her to settle down at Bramblewell School and, indeed, to enable her to shine. "Loyalty is important, Rosie!" Liz muttered to herself. "This Héloïse won't be with you at Bramblewell next term, but the other girls will!"

There was a post script to the message that pleased Liz, though. Rosalind had, somehow, managed to acquire Héloïse's birth data: something that Liz, in exasperation, had requested that she do.

"It wasn't easy, Mum," Rosalind had written. "Héloïse doesn't APPROVE of astrology." "No! Of course she doesn't," Liz said sourly and aloud. "But isn't it a bit impolite of her to make you doubt your mother's intelligence? Hm?" However, although she was feeling rattled, Liz, assuming that the birth date and time provided were accurate, left to one side the cup of early morning tea she had made and pressed by curiosity, looked for paper so that she could calculate Héloïse de Sauzon's astrological chart, without delay. Then, she fetched the white book – the one in which she kept birth data - from a drawer which she kept locked. She flicked through the book's pages until she had found a blank space. Then she stopped and looked up. "What are you doing?" she asked herself. "WHAT are you doing?" she repeated. "You're turning into a manipulative monster! Stop this now! Let it be!"

She went into the kitchen, poured herself a glass of water and opened a window. "Sorry, Rosie," she whispered to the air. "I almost crossed a line."

CHAPTER 15

Ida's Italian Sojourn

Ida Traversi's paternal great-aunt, Signora Elisabetta, was the only member of the Traversi family in whom Ida was inclined to confide. Ida felt comfortable and secure in Signora Elisabetta's company, possibly because she, the Signora, had a knack of offering advice diplomatically and in such a subtle way that it never, overtly, appeared to be criticism. Despite her age - she was seventy-five, Ida believed - Signora Elisabetta had an eager interest in all that was new, especially in the domain of fashion. She subscribed to glossy fashion magazines from New York, London, Paris, South America and the Far East. However, after perusing them, she would habitually express her conviction that Italian designers were still the finest promoters of style in the world. She, herself, championed those quiet, Italian couturiers who did not make a song-and-dance out of the promotion of their fashion houses, but who, nevertheless, attracted a discreet and wealthy clientèle.

Signora Elisabetta had not regularly attended family gatherings at the Traversi apartment, in Forte dei Marmi, and so, when Ida arrived there, after her journey from the Château du Crâne, she, Ida, was pleased to find her great-aunt already in residence. Ida, though, was startled to see that Signora Elisabetta was wandering, uncharacteristically restlessly, around the spacious apartment's five reception rooms, as if working off anger which she was too polite to express. Dressed in mandarin-coloured palazzo trousers and a white, silken blouse, she left, in her wake, the scent of a new perfume which, Ida discovered later, she had had created for her in Florence. Ida's mother and father and her sister, Beatrice, had already arrived at the apartment also, along with her paternal grand-parents. But there was no sign of Caterina.

"Dov'è Caterina?" Ida asked, but Beatrice shrugged and her mother said that Caterina had gone off, in one of her moods, and would not be joining them. Ida sensed the two of them had a secret to which they did not want her to be party and this annoyed her. After all, she was fifteen, but she was being treated as if she were still a child. Signora Elisabetta, though, drew her to one side and said, "Follow me!" before setting off along the corridor that led to her bedroom.

"There was a serious quarrel," explained Signora Elisabetta, once Ida had reached her room and had sat down on the chaise longue, in front of the tall window which led to a balcony overlooking the sea. The window was ajar and Ida could hear, not far away, the sounds of people on the beach and, distantly, the purr of cars.

"A quarrel?" said Ida. She had been expecting to hear a story about yet another potential beau having been rejected by Caterina, much to her mother's annoyance. That pattern of behaviour was a familiar one. The sophisticated Caterina, though, rarely quarrelled. She would pout and she would flounce away to her bed room, but she was always reluctant to engage in situations which demanded confrontation and, least of all, confrontations which were potentially of a combustible nature. What could possibly have driven her to have become involved in a serious quarrel? Had she entered into an entirely unsuitable liaison of some sort?

Signora Elisabetta was pouring sparkling water into two glass goblets that were standing on a silver tray, on top of a small, round table. She handed one to Ida and then, turned to look out of the window, in the direction of the baby-blue and glittering Tyrennhian Sea. She sipped water from her glass, slowly.

"So," said Ida, after a moment or two. "What was the quarrel about?"

Signora Elisabetta sighed softly.

"Caterina quarrelled with Beatrice," she replied. "Caterina said things which, I suspect, she had been longing to say for most of her life, but which it would have been better she had left unsaid, in my view. However, I think inner pressure had reached a point at which resentment simply had to be given expression. It was as if the lid had been blown off the top of a pressure cooker. Do you know what that is? It doesn't matter. You can imagine it."

"What did Caterina say?"

"Oh! She had heard about something disparaging Beatrice had said about her to someone outside of the family and she was understandably livid. She was white with anger, in fact. She raised her voice in a way I had never heard her raise her voice before. Her mother was horrified, of course, because the household staff could hear her. Everyone in the apartment heard her, including poor Adelina, whom Caterina had brought with her, from Rome. Adelina had been in the kitchen, preparing soup. Her hands started shaking so much, when she heard Caterina castigating Beatrice for her lack of sisterly loyalty, that she could not finish her work."

"Then, what happened?"

"Beatrice retaliated. She pointed out that Caterina had a nerve to talk about loyalty when, on several occasions, she had disgraced her family's name by behaving without discretion. Her lack of dignity, in the way she had dated men, one after another, indiscriminately, was the talk of Mamma's social circle and Mamma had had to live with the consequences. Did she, Caterina, ever think of anyone other than herself? When, for example, was she going to help the family by actually doing some work? She, herself, Beatrice, had been appointed to a responsible post in the family's company, thus making a useful contribution to the family's wealth while, simultaneously, learning the ropes, while Caterina, at the age of twenty-five, still thought it acceptable to depend on her father for the provision of an income and a luxurious life-style. Had she no shame?"

"Oh, no!" said Ida softly. "Caterina would hate to hear someone saying something like that to her."

"She was very angry. 'Fine! Fine!' she screamed. 'I'll find a job!' She turned to look at the rest of us and I could see she was on the point of a break-down or perhaps, a break-through. Anyway, it was obvious to me that something was going to change. She could not return to being the Caterina she had been before. I really believed that. I took a step towards her, but she turned on her heels and went to her room. I had never known anyone, in the Traversi family, to express anger in that undisciplined way before. Caterina had really lost control of herself, but Beatrice had been as bad. Anyway, two hours later,

Caterina emerged from her room, her bags packed. She went to the kitchen, to talk to Adelina.

"She had packed her bags, by herself? Do you think she was planning to go back to Rome and to take Adelina with her?"

"We all assumed she would go back to Rome and your Papa said, 'Let her be! She'll cool down.' She left with Adelina and two days later, he, your Papa, received a call from her on his mobile phone. She had gone to England."

"To England?"

"Yes. She told him she would be looking for a job."

"A job? You mean she meant it when she said she would find one?"

"Yes. She seems to have meant it. Of course, she hasn't a clue as to what people in normal employment have to endure. Her eyes will be opened."

"But what if she makes a mess of things?"

Signora Elisabetta shrugged.

"She knows that her Papa will be somewhere in the background and that he will pick her up if she falls. That knowledge is what endows her with confidence. That knowledge is what endows all you girls with confidence. You know you have a safety net."

Ida nodded. As a child, she, herself, had regarded her father as being omnipotent: the solver of all problems, no matter how trivial they were. "My Maths homework, Papa! I cannot do it!" That had been a common complaint of hers, as a child. Papa would finish her homework, while simultaneously talking on the telephone to a business associate. As a teenager, though, she had started to think of her Papa in a more realistic way. He was too strict, she believed. Too demanding. He expected too much of her. One day, he had said to her:

"Of the three of you, I can rely on only you. Beatrice overestimates her own ability. Caterina is unable to set realistic goals for herself and she lacks self-discipline. But you, Ida, are the intelligent one. You are like me."

Since then, instead of being happy, Ida had felt that an added burden had been placed on her shoulders. Only when she was at Bramblewell School, among her friends, could she forget it. At Bramblewell School, instead of feeling burdened, she felt free and creative.

Signora Elisabetta turned away from the window and sat down on the chaise longue, beside Ida. Bracelets of Venetian glass beads slipped up her arm as she finished drinking her goblet of water.

"It's fortunate that Caterina speaks English as well as you do," she said, then. "It's to one's advantage to speak a few languages well. It was your mother who decided to send all of you to Bramblewell School. Your Papa was not sure: he'd have preferred a boarding school in Switzerland, I think. But, I believe Bramblewell has served you all well."

"Maybe Caterina has gone to Chester, as she knows her way around it so well. She knows it better than she knows London," said Ida. "I think she would go to a familiar place, first."

"Yes. Perhaps she plans to see you, there, when you return to school."

"You don't think she would actually apply for a job at my school, do you?" asked Ida, then, wondering if the post of school secretary had actually been filled, as rumoured. But, quickly, she dismissed the idea as being silly. She simply could not imagine

Caterina in an administrative rôle.

"She'll find something to do," said Signora Elisabetta. "She's not a kid. And I think she has realised she cannot be a dilettante all her life, without losing self-respect and the respect of others. I have faith in her, you know. I'm hoping she will return, triumphant, having surprised us all."

CHAPTER 16

Direction: Chester

After the departure of Ida Traversi and Talitha Appleby from the Château du Crâne, as the summer holiday drew to a close, Portia Price expected that she would spend most of her time in the company of Rosalind Somerland, but, to her surprise, she found that Rosalind still appeared to prefer that of Héloïse de Sauzon. In fact, whenever Héloïse was not filming, Rosalind seemed to be with her, accompanying her, often, during walks around the grounds of the château. Rosalind, in long, flower-printed, cotton dresses, looked like a French person's idea of a nicely - educated and bourgeoise, English girl, Portia suspected, whereas Héloïse, in denim shorts and sleeveless blouses, looked Parisian, even though she was not.

Portia, somewhat miffed at having been excluded from these walks, assumed, at first, that what had drawn the two girls together had been their shared admiration of Mr. Teddy Laurence. Was it not understandable, after all, that Rosalind would seek the company of a girl who would talk about Mr. Laurence as adoringly as she, herself, had once done, rather than be with a Bramblewell girl who would remind her of how childishly silly she had been? Portia had not encouraged Rosalind to talk over much about Teddy Laurence, while at the château, fearing that Rosalind's ardour might be re-ignited, in the languorous atmosphere of the Girondin summer. Instead, she had emphasised the fact that Rosalind's imagined romance could have led to folly and much embarrassment, had she previously acted foolishly and impulsively.

After observing the direction in which Rosalind and Héloïse would walk, while taking the air, though, it occurred to Portia, then, that she had perhaps jumped to the wrong conclusion. The two of them, Héloïse clearly leading, invariably walked past the windows of the rooms occupied by Julian Bramblewell-Eurlinn. Why would Héloïse want to walk past the windows of the young heir to the château, when she had declared herself to be attracted to Teddy Laurence? And was Rosalind completely unaware of the fact that she was being used as an accomplice in Héloïse's game, whatever that game was? One had to wonder if Héloïse was trying to make Teddy Laurence jealous. Or was she beginning to have a genuine interest in Julian? Whatever her motive and strategy, it was wrong of her to use Rosalind, unwittingly, as a pawn in her game, her jeu d'amour. Perhaps it was fortuitous that the summer holiday was drawing to a close and that Rosalind would soon be back at Bramblewell, in the cool atmosphere of an early Cheshire autumn, where she would resume her rightful place as a member of the friendship group of four.

When the holiday did end, Portia and Rosalind travelled homewards in the company of their teacher, Mrs. Barbara Merrivale. With mixed feelings, they left the Gare Saint- Jean, in the Cours de la Marne in Bordeaux, one morning, taking the fast train to Paris. The holiday at the Château du Crâne had been culturally enriching, as well as good for their health, but they were anxious, now, to see their families again. Rosalind wondered how her young brother, John, would have managed without her at home. Would he have grown up a bit?

In Paris, they spent the night in the small hotel in which they had stayed during a previous school trip. The black and white tiled floor in the entrance hall; the Art Nouveau-styled lift that looked as if it had been constructed in the 1900s; the rooms with shuttered windows and tiny balconies that overlooked Montparnasse: all were familiar. Even the scent of faded lavender petals in the wardrobes evoked memories of the previous visit. The teacher and girls felt at ease and slept well.

The following morning, after a breakfast of bread, butter,

apricot jam, croissants and coffee, served in a small dining room, where the tables were round and the waiter was a careful youth who wore a white apron that reached his ankles, they set off for their journey, by rail and sea, to London. From there, they would travel to Chester, via Crewe.

During the first part, the long stretch on the train between Bordeaux and Paris, Rosalind and Portia had spoken little, when in the presence of their teacher. All the same, Mrs. Merrivale had paid little attention to them, having preferred to read a novel, by Wilkie Collins, in which she seemed to have lost herself. After Paris had been left behind, though, the girls' conversation became light and mirthful, as mishaps that had occurred during the holiday were recalled and plans for the future were discussed with abandon. At times, Portia and Rosalind came close to forgetting that Mrs. Merrivale was their teacher, but, as if to remind them that a barrier existed between them, one which they were not to cross, Mrs. Merrivale would, occasionally, put down her book and would look frostily around the carriage, as if counting imaginary pupils. The two girls would rein in their conversation then and would become more guarded. Mrs. Merrivale's unspoken message was clear enough. The names of other teachers were not to be mentioned in her presence: not even that of Mr. Teddy Laurence, although he had been with them all summer, at the Château du Crâne.

Rosalind and Portia liked Mrs. Merrivale, though. Despite the fact that she was in her early forties, she looked girlish, especially since she had had her hair cut, in a gamine style, in a salon in the centre of Bordeaux: one that had been recommended by Héloïse de Sauzon. Furthermore, she, Mrs. Merrivale, was in the habit of dressing flamboyantly, displaying a certain penchant for wearing jangling bracelets and large necklaces of polished stones. Being a teacher of what Miss Trimm had always called Elocution and Drama, Mrs. Merrivale had helped Rosalind, Portia, Ida and Talitha considerably, when, as members of The Eliza Club, the dramatic society which Portia, herself, had founded at school, they had written and staged the play upon which Pierre Laurier's film script had been based. That was why Mrs. Merrivale had been chosen to accompany the girls to France, after all.

When the three of them, teacher and girls, had reached London, had changed stations and were safely seated on a train bound for Crewe, Mrs. Merrivale, surprisingly, became more chatty, though. It was as if a weight had been removed from her shoulders, since they were on the last stage of the journey.

"Are you happy to hand over the running of The Eliza Club to someone else?" she asked Portia, suggesting, through her tone, what she expected the answer to be.

Portia's reply was unequivocal.

"Of course not, Mrs. Merrivale," she said bluntly, adding, "and that is because, quite honestly, I cannot think of anyone further down the school who is really capable of running it. I don't want to sound arrogant, but..."

Portia did not finish the sentence, as Rosalind had given her a look of shocked surprise. It was unlike Portia to be dismissive of other girls' talents or boastful of her own. Perhaps she had spoken in the way she had because she thought of The Eliza Club as her own possession and did not understand why she would be obliged to hand it over to someone who would not work as hard as she had, herself, to promote it.

"The pupil who would take it over would have to be able to write and direct plays, hold auditions and keep pupils, taking part in productions, enthused throughout rehearsals, for weeks, as you always did in the past," acknowledged Mrs.Merrivale, adding, "and, of course, you are right. I, myself, cannot think, at the moment, of anyone, who would be capable of stepping into your shoes. However, years in teaching have taught me that one should not underestimate pupils who, at first glance, seem to be lacking in talent, ability or the will to work. I do know that once pupils are given the opportunity to demonstrate what they can do, some do reveal facets of their character which would have remained hidden, had they not been given the chance to shine. Let's hope for the best, then! I must say though, Portia, that during the term ahead, you will be missed from the club. You too, Rosalind."

"Is there even a slight chance that we could stay in the club?" asked Rosalind.

"You know what Miss Trimm's rule is, don't you?" said Mrs. Merrivale sympathetically. "Pupils who will be sitting important exams at the end of a scholastic year are not allowed to take part in activities that will use up important studying time, or else will distract them from their studies. I think it is fairly evident, given the amount of time you normally spend on The Eliza Club's projects, that you would be likely to be discouraged from running the club."

"But, Mrs. Merrivale," protested Portia, "sports are not included in that rule. Sporty pupils can spend as much time as they like in the gym or on the sports field. I don't think that's fair."

"And anyway," Rosalind began to say, "Miss Trimm won't…"

She stopped herself from continuing the sentence, as she did not know if Mrs. Merrivale was au fait with the news to which she and Portia were party, thanks to the message sent by Portia's brother, Lancelot.

"Miss Trimm won't…what?" asked Mrs. Merrivale, frowning.

Portia closed her eyes as if pained, but then, stated calmly:

"My brother overheard some Bramblewell girls talking in a café in Chester. They were saying that Miss Trimm was going to leave the school."

Mrs. Merrivale sighed and looked out of the window of the train, now gathering speed.

"Actually, Miss Trimm has already left," she said, after a pause. "If Bramblewell girls are already in possession of the news, there is no point in concealing the fact that she has accepted the offer of a post elsewhere. At the Christina Quayle College of Languages, to be exact."

"Q-COLL?" exclaimed Rosalind.

"Yes."

"So, is there a chance that the rule about not participating in activities ...?" Portia began to say, opportunistically.

"Might be waived? I'll let you know, Portia," said Mrs. Merrivale. "Miss James, being deputy head, will automatically take over Miss Trimm's position as headmistress, for a while anyway, and she may reconsider the rule. I, myself, don't have any objections, at all, to your continuing to run The Eliza Club...but, we'll see."

Mrs. Merrivale leaned back in her seat and closed her eyes as if signalling that she did not want to talk any longer. Perhaps she suspected she had already said too much, having been caught in the trap into which teachers on school trips can easily fall.

The rest of the journey passed uneventfully. Rosalind and Portia felt tired and tried to sleep. At Crewe, though, they had to change trains and, as the small train to Chester set off, Portia's heart leapt, when familiar landmarks, in the flat, Cheshire countryside, came into view. She began to think about Louis, her secret boyfriend, who lived in Liverpool. She had not dared to mention to her mother the fact that such a person existed. Her mother, who aspired to seeing her married, one day, to a man of property, living grandly in Cheshire, probably in a large house in Alderley Edge or thereabouts, would balk at the thought of her consorting, at a tender age, with a boy such as Louis: a nice enough boy, but one who was not supported by a moneyed background. It was true that he lived with his father, who was unwell and that their house was in an unremarkable area. But, Portia knew that Louis was ambitious and she felt sure that all would be well, in the end.

The train slowed down and stopped in Chester's station. Rosalind was going to be met by Mrs. Stanley, her father's housekeeper. Portia, on the other hand, had been told that her mother would pick her up, and so, she steeled herself to receive the onslaught of criticism that her mother would probably deliver upon seeing her. Why was she looking so thin? Why was she not wearing her jacket? Why was her face so tanned? Had she not worn a hat when out in the sun? Those were the questions that Portia expected to be directed at her with coldness. However, when she caught sight of her mother, standing at the end of the platform, Portia noticed the strained expression on her face, as her eyes darted from one person to another, looking for her daughter.

"Maybe she actually missed me," Portia thought, momentarily, but then, decided that her absence could not possibly have been the reason for her mother's apparent anxiety. All the same, just for a second, Portia felt an urge to run into her mother's arms and to say, "I'm home!" Just for a second, too, she felt the urge to cry, but instead, she walked casually along the platform and said, without emotion, "Hello, Mother."

Mrs. Price immediately stiffened her shoulders.

"I'm parked at the front," was all she said, as she fussily checked the case on wheels that Portia had been pulling behind her.

"Where is the rest of your luggage?" she asked. "Haven't you any other bags?"

At that moment, Portia saw, beyond her mother, a tall, blond boy with intelligent eyes, gazing at her.

"Louis!" she thought, but uttered not a word.

Louis lifted his hand, in solemn greeting, and then, turned and walked away.

CHAPTER 17

Maternal Possessiveness

Liz Laurier was in a state of alert as she waited for the door-bell of her apartment to buzz. It was the Saturday following Rosalind's return from France and, since the girl had been away from her home country for more than four weeks, Liz was anxious to question her about life at the Château du Crâne during that period. Gylen Somerland had kindly agreed to Liz's suggestion that Rosalind be allowed to spend the entire weekend with her. And Rosalind, herself, had expressed her enthusiasm upon being told of the proposed plan, when she had been in contact with her mother by telephone.

"It'll be great, Mum!" she had exclaimed. "I have so much to tell you!"

Rosalind's words had been bubbling with excitement, but Liz had not been able to share her daughter's joie de vivre, when it had become clear that Rosalind had already visited Susie Sutton. In fact, Rosalind had visited Susie the morning after her arrival in the Wirral. In other words, her visit to Susie had been granted priority over her visit to her own mother!

"How nice for Susie!" Liz had commented blandly.

"But, just wait till I tell you what she said to me while I was in France!" Rosalind had continued, her enthusiasm undiminished by her mother's restrained tone. "She wants me to be one of her bridesmaids next Easter! Can you believe it? In Chester Cathedral! Can't you just imagine what her wedding there will be like? It will be so romantic! And Susie doesn't want me to be on my own, either! She wants Ida, Portia and Talitha to be with me as well, so that I shan't feel lonely! Isn't that nice of her? She's going to order the dresses soon! I think they're going to be lovely! It'll be amazing! Won't it be amazing, Mum?"

"Yes! Lovely!" Liz had said, feigning delight. "I can't wait to see your dress!"

Liz had made an effort not to make any derogatory comments about Rosalind's obviously warm and easy friendship with Susie. There had been no sour remarks about Susie's lack of education or her unsuitable choice of clothes, on occasions. Liz had known that such poisonous words would have had their source in jealousy after all, and jealousy was always unattractive. Instead, she had pushed aside her emotional response in order to examine Rosalind's loyal attachment to Susie from a reasonable point of view. Why should she, Liz, expect her daughter to elevate her above the other people in her life - people like Susie - when she had been so neglectful of the girl for years, after all? It could be argued, in fact, that, from Rosalind's and John's perspective, Susie had been more of a mother to them than she, Liz, had ever been, since it had been Susie who had looked after them at a difficult period in their lives, when they had first arrived in Ellesmere Port, in order to live in their father's house. At that time, Susie had been unofficially engaged to Gylen and it had been she who had prepared a meal for the children every evening, had checked that their homework had been done properly, had looked after them when they had been feeling unwell and had kept them calm and reassured, on the night that their father had lost his temper and had abruptly left the house, banging the door. It had even been Susie who had bought their school uniforms and had washed and ironed them. It had also been Susie who had managed to befriend Rosalind, in such a warm-hearted and guile-less way that the girl now regarded her, Susie, as being a sort of big sister in whom she could confide.

Liz, of course, had realised that, given her own past behaviour, she would have to tread carefully, if she were ever fully to win Rosalind's respect and trust. The girl had been friendly and chatty, once she had recovered from the shock of learning that Liz had not only been her teacher for a year, but also her mother. However, naturally, she had been wary too. Her mother had deserted her once. Would she do so again?

Liz had checked the spare bedroom several times that morning but, nevertheless, did so again. Rosalind had never previously spent a night in the down - town apartment and Liz wanted her to feel comfortable during this, her first weekend - long visit. Would she like the look of the room in which she would be spending the night? The décor was mostly white-ish. Only a large, black and white, framed photograph of a morning scene in 5th Avenue stood out. It was on the floor, leaning at an angle to the wall opposite the bed. Would Rosalind regard it as being a sort of objet d'art or would she think it had been left there casually and was still to be hung up? Was the look of the room, in fact, too New York-ish to appeal to her? If Rosalind was going to make a habit of spending weekends at the apartment - and she might - Liz felt she should suggest that Rosalind decorate the room in any way that she pleased. On the other hand, could she, Liz, endure living with Rosalind's preferences in furnishings and art-work? Liz had not yet visited Gylen's house and consequently, had no idea as to what the girl's home environment was like. Liz's own ideas when it came to interior decoration and design veered towards the stark and the chic. How would she cope with a teenager whose tastes were less evolved or more baroque?

Liz, though, was wary of imposing her own tastes too forcefully on Rosalind. She knew, after all, that if one were to compare her own astrological chart with Rosalind's, one of the aspects that would stand out would be the square formed by her own Saturn at seventeen degrees of Libra and Rosalind's Venus at fourteen degrees of Cancer. Such a Saturn-Venus aspect occurring across charts could be a source of great discomfort. Saturn, although perhaps initially dazzled by Venus, would nevertheless eventually feel driven to criticise Venus' tastes in all matters artistic, including self-presentation. Venus' confidence would be weakened, if Saturn did not take steps to rein in the impulse to undermine.

Liz had been aware of the fact that the closer she had become to Rosalind, the more Saturn had been making its presence felt in her relationship with the girl. She had been angered by Rosalind's admiration of Héloïse de Sauzon's style of dressing and would-be sophisticated way of behaving, for example, without ever having had contact with Héloïse, herself. And the status- conscious side of Saturn had been making her anxious to encourage the establishment of a friendship between Rosalind and Julian Bramblewell-Eurlinn, without her having any idea as to how Rosalind would feel about such a development. As for Julian, he would, no doubt, have been appalled had he learnt about the plans and intentions that had been spinning around in her, Liz's, head. She, herself, was appalled now, too. It would all have to stop. Saturn would have to be acknowledged, in some way - through providing a structure or practical direction for Rosalind's artistic and literary ventures, perhaps - but its excesses would have to be contained.

Liz walked into her sitting room and swept her hand along a bookshelf. She pulled out, from the row of books, a slim volume of Keats' poems. Rosalind should like Keats. She would put the book on the table beside Rosalind's bed and would leave her interference with the girl's tastes at that.

In another part of town, Rosalind had decided to walk from her father's house to her mother's apartment down - town, even though she had reckoned it would take her almost an hour to reach her destination. While on her way, she had decided to lengthen her journey by a quarter of an hour or so by cutting down Deeside, a side road which had led her in the direction of Whitby Park. There was a path in the park that she liked, as it was lined on both sides by tall, old, densely leafed trees which, for some reason, made her feel secure. And as she was walking along that path, now, she began to think about an e-mail message that Portia had sent to her the previous evening.

For once, Portia had seemed to be all at sea. Louis had just sent a long message to her via his computer. He wanted to see her, of course, but since she had arrived back from France only a few days previously, she could think of no reasonable excuse that she could use to persuade her mother to allow her to go to Liverpool for an afternoon.

"Why do you want to go all that way?" her mother would be sure to ask, with suspicion evident in her voice. "You can buy all you need for school here in Chester."

Portia had previously told Rosalind that she had caught a glimpse of Louis at Chester Station. Perhaps he had hoped, after her return, to have a rendezvous with Portia there, but then, she remembered being told that Portia's mother had friends in every corner of Chester and that at least one of them would be bound to catch a glimpse of Portia with her beau were they to meet on her home ground - even in the station - and, furthermore, would be equally certain to telephone to her mother immediately, to relate what had been seen. Mrs. Price would be enraged. "Who is he? Do we know his family? What do you know about him?" Portia would never hear the end of it.

Rosalind stopped for a while and leaned against a tree. Portia had seemed miserable and she, Rosalind, wished, now, that she could help her friend in a practical way. She recalled, then, that before going away to France she had asked her mother if she would miss teaching astrology at Bramblewell School and her mother had said, "Yes. I think I shall." Then, in a flippant fashion, she had added, "Maybe I'll write a book for you all, to replace the lessons I'd have given, had I stayed." What if she were, now, to be persuaded to embark on a project of that type? Rosalind was sure that there were many questions that she, herself, as well as her three friends would be anxious to pose. Portia, for example, would want to know if she should continue her friendship with Louis or if there would too many obstacles placed in her way to make the effort worthwhile. No doubt Talitha would want to discover what sort of career she should choose when it would be time for her to leave school. She was not really academically inclined, but she loved ballet. And Ida would be wondering what would become of her sister, Caterina. What would make Caterina happy? Rosalind envisaged the book as being structured rather like the problem pages in magazines. There could be a simple question on each of the book's pages, followed by a lengthy answer. She would talk to her mother about it. Enthused by her idea, she set off in the direction of Ellesmere Port, proper.

CHAPTER 18

All Aboard!

Madame Gabrielle de Talence moved her long fringe out of her eyes with a flick of her hand and a slight shake of her head. Her new hairstyle, she had to admit, was making her feel youthful, mentally fresh and more adventurous, really, as if she were looking forward to what life still had to offer, instead of back, with regret, to a past she wished she could forget. At the same time, the part of her brain that, throughout most of her life, had reined in her emotions, allowing cold logic to dominate and dictate to her how to behave was now asking her, "What exactly do you think you are going to do, madame? What would your grand-children think of you if they could watch you during this voyage? You are not going to be foolish, are you?" Nevertheless, for once, Madame Gabrielle was trying to ignore this stern, inner rule-maker and was allowing her softer side - suppressed too often, in the past - to rise to the surface, in order to persuade her to conduct herself in a less disciplined manner.

That morning, she, Madame Gabrielle, was dressed in stylish, white slacks, wide at the ankles. She had never seen photos of her life-long fashion idol, the young Jacqueline Bouvier Kennedy, wearing ones as wide as her own, but she felt that they, her white trousers, nevertheless had such a hint of the Cape Cod-sporty look about them that she could not resist conjuring up, in her mind, pictures of the grounds of stately, American houses, where slim, fit people played games like tennis, attractively, on the green lawns or else, made preparations to go sailing on the sparkling, East coast sea, nearby. A navy blouse with short, slightly puffed sleeves completed Madame Gabrielle's maritime look, along with two-tone shoes in navy and white. Madame Gabrielle occasionally wore the stylish outfit when walking by the beach in Deauville, the chic resort in Normandy, much frequented by Parisians, when seeking respite from the city. She knew it went down well in Deauville, but that morning, she was fretting a little, wondering if the navy and white theme would be considered de trop by the other passengers aboard the cruise ship, the *Sabine Estelle.* She had fastened a navy and white scarf around her waist, instead of a belt. Had she taken a step too far? Would a leather belt have been more fitting? What about the colours of her shoes? Madame Gabrielle allowed herself to sigh, audibly - there was no one near- but decided not to worry any longer, that day, about her appearance. Perhaps no one aboard the *Sabine Estelle* would question her taste, anyway. She was not in the company of her competitive friends in Bordeaux, after all.

Sitting on the fifth deck of the ship, in one of the observation lounges, as they were officially called - those areas set aside for resting, day-dreaming and drinking tea - Madame Gabrielle decided to allow herself a few minutes of repose, in the comfortable armchair she was occupying. She closed her eyes and started to direct her attention to pleasant memories of events that had taken place not long before: her arrival in Liverpool, for example, and her re-acquaintance with streets and buildings she had known during the year she had spent in the city, when young. Her intention, earlier, had been simply to read. In fact, on her lap lay a book she had brought with her: "This Side of Paradise" by F. Scott Fitzgerald. She had intended to spend much of her time, while at sea, improving her knowledge of American idioms, specifically, but already, she had begun to be distracted by passengers walking to and fro and by strangers trying to engage her in conversation. She felt tired, too, even though she had slept well the previous night: her first night on board. Could the sea air have been making her drowsy? Or was she simply exhausted, as a result of having had to deal with new experiences?

The evening before, there had not been much time to pause.

Shortly after Madame Gabrielle had boarded the ship and had located her cabin, her luggage having already been delivered there, she had started to unpack, but then, she had been startled to discover that it was necessary for her to take part in a lifeboat drill. Surprisingly, the drill had been immediately followed by dinner. Madame Gabrielle had been directed to a table, in a dining hall on the fourth deck, where five individuals of approximately her own age, she had guessed, had, also, been seated. They had seemed pleasant enough, even though one of them, Dorothy, had been over-inclined to express her opinions, in intransigent manner. Despite the fact that Madame Gabrielle could read English with ease, she had not spoken it, at length, for many years and, consequently, she had found the effort of making conversation in the language stressful.

Before the pudding course, she had gone out on deck, for a minute or two, to breathe cool air, to be alone and to think in French, again. Her excuse for leaving the table had been, she had claimed, her wish to see the lights of Liverpool, as the ship had slipped out of port, making its way towards the mouth of the Mersey and the sea beyond. She had heard the engines starting up, minutes before. Tears had, in fact, come unexpectedly and embarrassingly into her eyes, as she had watched the lights of Liverpool fading away on the starboard side. She had silently said, "Au revoir!" to the great, exotic city of dreams that she had once loved. The sadness that had come over her, like a mist, had perplexed her though, given the fact that it had no logical basis. After all, the person who had made Liverpool particularly dear to her, in the past, had embarked on the same voyage, on the same ship, the *Sabine Estelle*. But, where was he to be found? She had fifteen days to find out, before the ship would return to Liverpool, after its journey to sunny climes.

"Oh! There you are!" Madame Gabrielle had heard a woman's voice exclaiming, then, and she realised Dorothy had followed her out on to the deck.

"Your pudding has been served, dear," Dorothy had continued, as if, curiously, she had assigned to herself the task of looking after Madame Gabrielle. "You won't catch a chill, will you?"

"No, madame," had answered the surprised Madame Gabrielle, turning to look at Dorothy, who had joined her at the rail on which she, Madame Gabrielle, had been leaning.

"You won't lean too far out on that rail, will you?" Dorothy had said, then, but Madame Gabrielle had not responded as, at that moment, she had noticed a man emerging from a door at the other end of the deck. He had stood, in a relaxed manner, by the rail, but had gazed in the direction of Liverpool, as if saying "Good-bye," also. Madame Gabrielle had given no indication to Dorothy of having recognised him, but her heart had given a lurch and, for a second, she had felt light-headed, although, outwardly, she had remained composed. Madame Gabrielle had recognised the man as having been Kit Mallory of The Mermen, since she had previously found photos of him on-line. Of course, he had not resembled the young musician he had once been, the one who had played in the cellar clubs of Liverpool with The Mermen, while she, a young, French student, had watched and listened, so many years before. But he had still had a certain aura, Madame Gabrielle had thought. Even under the subdued deck lights, she had been able to see that he could still command attention. She had wondered, momentarily, if she should approach him, but the presence of Dorothy had immediately driven that thought out of her mind. She had sensed that he would not have enjoyed verbal engagement with the imperious Dorothy, who would undoubtedly have taken over the conversation. Besides, given her own age and social status, such behaviour on her part - such impropriety in attempting to speak to the man, without having been properly introduced, as if she were a mere "fan" - would have been unseemly. How shockingly uncharacteristic of her even to have considered such action!

Dorothy, then, had said that it would be better to go back into the dining saloon and Madame Gabrielle had felt compelled to acquiesce. What else could she have done? Before turning away, though, she had thrown one last glance in the direction of Kit Mallory, but he had paid no attention either to her or the chattering Dorothy. As a consequence, by the time she had reached the dining table, Madame Gabrielle had been feeling dejected. She had looked at the dish of meringues, strawberries and cream awaiting her without pleasure, her mind having been elsewhere. She had wondered how she could make Kit Mallory notice her, were their paths to cross again. But, she had, simultaneously, been angry with herself for allowing such a thought to enter her head. She, after all, was the daughter of the Count du Crâne and an aristocrat of France. France! That mattered.

"Well! There you are, dear! Having a little sleep, are you? This is a nice observation lounge, isn't it? Mind if I join you?"

Madame Gabrielle, startled, opened her eyes. Had she fallen asleep, really? She adjusted her position in her arm chair, sighing quietly, as she recognised the voice now familiar to her. She watched the woman who had spoken, smartly attired in a yellow and white patterned dress, settling herself in a chair next to her own.

"I didn't introduce myself to you properly last night," added Dorothy, for it was she who had interrupted Madame Gabrielle's rêverie. "I'm Dorothy Trimm."

"And I am Gabrielle de Talence. How do you do?"

"I'm travelling with my daughter, Hilary," Dorothy explained in a sort of conspiratorial way. "Well! Actually, not with her, exactly! We have separate cabins. And we have decided to part company during most of the day and to dine at separate tables in the evening. In that way, we meet a variety of interesting people. It's the best way to travel, don't you think?"

"Ah! Yes!"

Dorothy interpreted Madame Gabrielle's "Yes" as permission for her to describe, at length, individuals she had met at breakfast time, but, as she was in the throes of doing so, Madame Gabrielle became conscious of the figure of a man who had entered the observation lounge and was standing at a distance of just a few paces behind Dorothy and slightly to her right. Madame Gabrielle felt her skin turning cold. The man was Kit Mallory. She was sure of it, even though she was seeing him only out of the corner of her eye. Once again, she did not display, outwardly, any sign of recognition or emotional disturbance, but she wondered, whimsically, if he would always appear, as if by magic, whenever Dorothy unexpectedly did. She continued to allow not a flicker of delight to flit across her face, but pretended, instead, to be fascinated by what Dorothy was saying. And without looking directly at the subject of her excited thoughts, Madame Gabrielle sensed rather than saw that he seemed to be wondering whether to stay in the observation lounge or to leave.

"Stay! Please, stay!" Madame Gabrielle silently commanded him.

She wondered, then, if she should, at least, cast a glance in his direction. Was it possible that he might remember her amber-brown eyes? He had gazed into them, so often, when he had been a young musician on the stages of clubs in Liverpool, and she had been in the audience, as near to him as it had been possible for her to be. She decided there would be no harm in throwing a glance in his direction, as if wondering why he was standing there. She turned her head in a deliberate fashion, and looked straight at him, then. For a second, her eyes met his, but he looked away, almost at once and, a few seconds later, turned and left the room. He had shown no sign at all of having remembered Madame Gabrielle. But, of course, she was no longer the girl she had once been. She had long lost her allure.

Displaying no disappointment, nor giving any indication of the fact that she had humiliated herself, Madame Gabrielle continued to feign interest in Dorothy's conversation, occasionally interjecting, "Really?" or "How wonderful!" Her heart felt heavy though, now that all hope had been taken away. But, when she considered what had happened in a detached manner, she had to conclude that she should have guessed what the outcome of her gauche behaviour would have been. What had she realistically expected Kit Mallory to have done? Had she really imagined he would recognise her and would sweep her off her feet, as if she had been a fairy-tale princess? "Oh! Gabrielle! Gabrielle!" she admonished herself, silently and sadly. "Look in the mirror!"

She realised, then, that Dorothy Trimm's voice was softening.

"I think I'm tiring you, dear," she was saying. "I do go on a bit, don't I?"

"Oh, no!" Madame Gabrielle protested, out of politeness. But Dorothy only smiled kindly and, then, looked at her watch.

"Oh! My!" she exclaimed. "I arranged to meet my daughter, Hilary, in my own room at eleven, for coffee. Would you like to join us? No? Some other time, perhaps?"

"Yes. Some other time. I'd like that."

Slipping her white, leather handbag, with chunky handles, over her arm, Dorothy went off to locate her own room, or rather, rooms. Hilary had opted for single occupancy of a double cabin, but Dorothy had chosen for herself a suite with a comfortable sitting room and large bathroom, in addition to a bedroom. She had thought it wise to have a sitting room with sofa at her disposal, in case Madame Gabrielle were to become ill or were to dread being left alone, while in that condition. A bed could be made up for her on the sofa, in that event.

Hilary had been given a spare key card which allowed her to gain entry to her mother's quarters. She was already there, looking elegant in a sleeveless, silver grey dress. She was arranging sandwiches on a plate when her mother arrived, in a state of excitement.

"I say, Hils!" Dorothy exclaimed, as she was closing the door of her suite, behind her. "I think I have solved the mystery, but it has only led to another problem."

"What are you talking about, Mother?" asked Hilary, sitting down on the sofa and, being in holiday mood, casually crossing her legs at the knees. "What mystery? And do sit down, won't you? The coffee has arrived."

"I do believe I know why Madame Gabrielle has chosen to be on this cruise ship!" said Dorothy, as she headed for an armchair.

"Go on!" urged Hilary, now intrigued.

"Well! Last night, Madame Gabrielle went out on deck before the pudding course had been served. 'How strange!' I thought to myself. But, anyway, I followed her out, fearing that, feeling hot and dizzy, she might have collapsed and fallen overboard."

"We had only just left Liverpool, at that point, Mother!"

"I know! I know! But anyway, at first I thought she had gone out only to have a look at Liverpool's lights, but then, a man appeared on deck and it seemed to me that Madame Gabrielle definitely recognised him, even though her expression did not really change. Her eyes gave her away, you see. I think the man must have seen her, even though he did not acknowledge her. I honestly suspect he went out on deck on purpose because she was there, but did not say anything to her, because I was with her."

"Mother! You are imagining things!"

"I could have been imagining things, but my suspicions were confirmed just a few minutes ago, when Madame Gabrielle and I were sitting in the observation lounge. Would you believe it? The man appeared again!"

"Yes, but the ship isn't very big, Mother! I am sure you will run into this man of mystery on other occasions! It's almost inevitable that you will!"

"But, leaving that obvious fact aside, Hilary, I should tell you that Madame Gabrielle definitely- but - definitely seemed to be troubled by his presence. She glanced in his direction furtively. Oh! I pretended not to notice what was going on, of course! But I saw what I saw!"

"What do you think is going on, then?"

"Well! Madame Gabrielle didn't want any members of her family to be with her, on this cruise, did she? What does that imply? That she wanted to meet this man in secret?"

"But, why did she have to go on holiday on a cruise ship to do that, when she could have met him, in secret, anywhere in France?"

"That is the crux of the mystery, isn't it?"

"Just out of interest, what does the man look like?"

"He's tall and he has dark hair with silver streaks in it and he is good-looking in a conventionally handsome way, but I'd say he's around Madame Gabrielle's age. And mine, of course. He seems to be very confident. He carries around with him that 'air of entitlement' I've heard Americans mentioning, in connection with the famous."

"An air of entitlement? To what does he think he is entitled? Attention? His face wasn't familiar, was it?"

"Well, no?"

"I wonder who he is."

Dorothy Trimm frowned. She stood and, deep in thought, walked towards the ceiling- to-floor window that led on to a small balcony that provided a view of the glittering ocean.

"I don't know who he is, Hils," she stated, absent-mindedly beating her fingers against the frame of the window, "but I think it is our duty to find out, before Madame Gabrielle does something silly."

CHAPTER 19

Introducing Mr. Mallory

"You are reading Racine, Mother?" said Hilary Trimm, while raising her eyebrows, upon catching sight of the collected works of the famous French playwright, as she entered her mother's suite on the *Sabine Estelle*, the following morning. The book was lying on a sofa. Dorothy, elegantly dressed in fuchsia pink, was sitting beside it, her reading glasses pushed into her hair.

"You seem to be surprised, Hilary, but you have surely not forgotten that I adore Racine's tragedies," said Dorothy, theatrically making an arc- like gesture in the air, as if she were on stage. "Those Alexandrine lines!" she added, before Hilary could stop her. "Those rhyming couplets! And in addition to the fine writing, I have to say that Racine intrigues me because his plays are pertinent to our present situation."

"What are you talking about, Mother? Racine wrote tragedies, didn't he? How can his plays possibly be relevant to our situation? Are you referring to the consequences of unbridled passion? I suppose you are!"

"Well, of course I am. You know, when I was a teenager and in the sixth form at school, the plays of Racine along with those of that other French playwright, Corneille, were used as a means of teaching girls how to behave and how not to behave. Corneille's heroines placed duty to their family and family honour above their personal passions and they were rewarded, in one way or another. Racine's heroines did not possess self-control, the result of their folly being, invariably, self-destruction and, often, the destruction of others as well. The lessons couldn't have been clearer."

"Your knowledge of French culture never fails to impress me,

Mother," said Hilary, as if wearily. "Anyway, I take it all this is leading up to the subject of Madame Gabrielle. Are you suggesting that she needs to be reminded of these lessons in decorum that Racine and Corneille considered to be appropriate in…the seventeenth century? Were I in Madame Gabrielle's shoes, I think I'd be stunned if you tried to tell me how to behave. You have been asked to watch this woman from a discreet distance. You have not been requested to intervene in her private life. Honestly, Mother! I think you should examine your own behaviour."

"Mock me not, Hilary! I wonder what you will have to say for yourself when I tell you that the man who is shadowing Madame Gabrielle used to be…just wait till you hear this…a rock star."

"A rock star? Oh! Well! Of course! What else? Who has concocted this unlikely tale, may I ask? Some gossip, with a vivid imagination, no doubt. A gossip whom you have encountered during your meandering around the ship?"

"I don't know how I put up with you, Hilary, or why I agreed to accompany you on this trip. The rock star is an architect of sorts as well as being a musician, as it happens…but it is the rock star side of him that, obviously, should worry us. I mean, Madame Gabrielle and a rock star! Such a liaison is unimaginable! What does she think she is doing? No wonder she didn't want anyone from her family to come with her on this cruise! She would know her daughter would collapse with shock, were she to discover that her mother was consorting with…"

"With…what?"

"Well! A rock star! A rock star from the 1960s! Imagine! It's so…improbable!"

"Who was your source of information, may I ask?"

"Oh! My stewardess told me. Nice girl. Very chatty. The chap's name is Kit Mallory. He has a suite on the same floor as mine. During the cruise, he will deliver three lectures on architecture. But, his band mates, The Mermen - they played together in the 1960s - are with him as well. They are all scheduled to play, on stage, on at least three occasions, also."

"Well! You are well informed...or rather, your stewardess is. I don't understand why you are so het up at the thought of Madame Gabrielle embarking on a relationship with this man, though. And why would Madame Gabrielle's daughter object to her associating with him?"

"Oh, Hilary! Please! Are you really unaware of the fact that ladies, in France, of Madame Gabrielle's social class, don't invite people, who perform on stage, into their private social circles? It's not 'the done thing'."

"Times have changed, Mother."

"Not that much, Hilary. And certainly not for women in Madame Gabrielle's age group. Madame is in danger of making a fool of herself if her aim is, stupidly, to pursue this man. My fear is that he will break her heart."

"Oh! Mother! She is a sophisticated woman: not a teenager."

"One can be sophisticated and yet, when it comes to matters of the heart, be taken unawares. I am genuinely worried. You know, it's not out of the question that the two of them arranged to come on this cruise so that they could be together, without her family knowing."

"That theory simply doesn't hold water. This Kit Mallory, or whatever his name is, could have visited Madame Gabrielle, in a discreet way, at her home, in Bordeaux, if she, or indeed he, had wanted to keep the relationship hidden. And why would they arrange a rendezvous on this outlandish cruise, where the two of them would risk being observed by numerous people? Is it not possible that you are imagining that something is afoot, because you are so diligent when it comes to carrying out a duty - any duty - that you have become over-vigilant? My guess is that the two of them don't even know each other and that you are imagining impropriety, or even danger, where none exists!"

Dorothy stood up and walked towards the window of her sitting room, in order to allow the light of day to lift her spirits and help her to think clearly. The *Sabine Estelle* was passing the mouth of the Severn, she reckoned, or had passed it, shortly before. The sea looked a little rough. Cut through by the bow of the ship, the mesmerising waves, green and blue, separated cleanly, before flowing bouncily by.

"What you are arguing is perfectly feasible," Dorothy said after a pause. "But I cannot help feeling…sensing, if you like… that something upsetting is about to happen and I am disturbed by that feeling."

"It's not like you to be so fanciful, Mother," said Hilary, frowning.

"I know. It isn't like me, at all."

"Listen!" said Hilary, clasping her hands on her knees and leaning forward a little, in the armchair which was facing the window. "To ease your mind, why don't we bring matters to a head, quickly?"

"What do you mean? How?" asked Dorothy, turning round to look at her.

"We could observe Madame Gabrielle and her rock star in a managed environment."

"A managed environment? Speak in English, Hilary! You've been teaching too long, obviously! All those made-up words and phrases you've been obliged to read, in silly, ill-considered documents, have lodged themselves in your brain and now, you can't get rid of them. You should read Dickens every evening, in order to re-stock your head with what is considered to be normal English vocabulary."

"Last night," said Hilary, ignoring her mother's comment, "I could not sleep and so I made a cup of cocoa and started to look at the brochures that were stacked in a rack in my cabin."

"Have you not brought any books with you? That surprises me. I'll let you borrow my copy of "'Great Expectations'. Or a book of letters people have written to their mothers. That might be more appropriate. I don't want you to think I'm likening you to Miss

Havisham. I bought the book in Blackler's decades ago. Do you remember Blackler's, in Liverpool? No. Of course not. You're too young."

"Mother! May I continue?"

"Yes. Go on."

"In one brochure, I read that private parties may be held in one's suite and that food will be provided, if a request is made. Since you have a suite, Mother, couldn't you have a little cocktail party, one evening, around six, say? You could invite the people who sit, habitually, at your table, for dinner, Madame Gabrielle being one of them. You could also invite Kit Mallory."

"Kit Mallory? Don't be absurd, Hilary! How could I possibly extend an invitation to Kit Mallory: a man I do not know? Is your brain functioning properly?"

"I am sure that 'celebrities' like Kit Mallory - who, as you have informed me, is a rock star, from times past - are used to being invited to parties by people they do not know," responded Hilary calmly, ignoring the insult. "Especially on cruises. Do invite The Mermen, also. It will look as if you simply want to sprinkle your party guests with star dust! Write out a nice invitation and ask someone at the Reception desk to deliver it to Mr. Mallory."

"You have not explained what the purpose of this party would be. Presumably, you want Kit Mallory and Madame Gabrielle to meet in a semi-formal setting, so that you and I can observe them and see if my suspicions about them are correct. It's a manipulative and mean-spirited thing to do, as you know quite well."

"Is it any more mean-spirited than gossiping about Madame Gabrielle and this rock star, who may or may not know her? Unless you have a party of that sort, in your own quarters, how will you be able to discover, quickly, what is going on? How will you be able to become acquainted with Kit Mallory? And how can you possibly find out if he is an honourable man or a cad, if you don't furnish yourself with an opportunity to talk to him, to listen to what he says and to watch how he behaves?"

Dorothy gave a sigh.

"It's a vaguely unpleasant thing to do, given the hidden agenda, but I fear you are right and we have no option but to proceed," she said. "However, if I'd known, before coming on this cruise, that complications such as this were likely to arise, I'd have stayed at home. I don't know what Kath will think of all this cloak and dagger stuff, when I tell her about it, once I'm back in Cheshire."

"I'm sure Kath will lap it up, Mother. Don't try to persuade me that the two of you do not spend your coffee mornings and afternoon tea sessions, gossiping. I shan't believe you!"

The following day, Dorothy made enquiries at the Reception desk about private parties and, being satisfied with the information given, she handed to one of the receptionists an invitation addressed to Mr. Kit Mallory and The Mermen, to attend a small, pre-dinner party in her suite, the following Monday. To Dorothy's surprise, a hand-written letter, accepting her invitation with grace, was delivered before the end of the day. Having received this prompt reply, Dorothy was able to mention the party, that very evening, to her dining companions. Casually, she told them that Mr. Kit Mallory, the rock star from the 1960s, who was in a suite not far from her own, would be present, also. A woman, of a certain age, who was sitting opposite Dorothy at the table, became flustered, in a noticeable way.

"Ooh!" she exclaimed. "I knew he was on the ship, but I didn't think I'd be meeting him! I used to be in his fan club!"

A buzz of excitement went around the table. Dorothy noticed that Madame Gabrielle was looking pleased, as she sipped sparkling water from a wine glass.

Monday evening arrived, after a weekend of planning that seemed to zip by. Hilary, elegant in a slim, ivory dress and stylish costume jewellery - stud ear-rings and a bracelet- arrived early, to help with the laying out of canapés, along with polished cutlery, linen napkins, plates and glasses. Dorothy, wearing a bronze-coloured dress, with three-quarter-length sleeves, seemed all in a tizz.

"I hope this won't end in disaster, Hils," she said.

"What can go wrong? It will be fine. Don't worry!"

Dorothy had expected that the excited dining companion, the woman who had once been in Kit Mallory's fan club, would be the first to arrive. But, most unexpectedly, it was Kit Mallory, himself, who knocked on the door first. He was accompanied by The Mermen. "Come in, won't you?" said Dorothy. "Allow me to introduce myself. I am Dorothy Trimm and this is my daughter, Hilary."

Kit Mallory was polite, but reserved. His voice was low and he spoke with dignity: not jollity. He did not appear to be a man whom one would describe as being "the life and soul of a party." Hilary decided, straight away, that he was, rather, the sort of person who was sometimes described as being "very private." Yet, she was conscious of the fact, also, that he was not a man whom one could ignore. Just by being in the room, he commanded it, she had to admit, but she reckoned that he did so partly through being tall and partly by being dressed, not casually, but immaculately correctly, in a well-tailored, dark suit, a white shirt and a sober, grey tie. He sat down at one end of the sofa: there was room for only one other person to sit beside him.

The other guests, these being Nigel, Abigail, Jeremy and the excited Eileen, began to arrive, Madame Gabrielle knocking on the door last of all. Hilary noticed that Madame had chosen to dress, in a restrained and bourgeois way, in wine-coloured silk. Her jewellery announced her wealth only to those capable of recognising its value. She walked into the room, head held high, appearing confident and at ease and she looked, at once, in the direction of Kit Mallory, as if she had known, before entering the room, where he would be sitting. She allowed her gaze to linger on him for a second and then, she lowered her eyes, as if remembering who she was. Something about her- the poised way in which she was standing, perhaps - seemed to trigger a memory in Kit Mallory's brain. He looked puzzled. Dorothy had handed him a glass, previously, but he had barely touched the drink within it. He put it down on the coffee table and stood up, as if expecting an introduction to be made. He looked at Dorothy as if waiting for her to say something.

"Do you already know Madame Gabrielle?" Dorothy felt compelled to ask.

"No. I don't think so," answered Kit, although his eyes seemed to suggest he was not sure.

"This is Kit Mallory, formerly of The Mermen," explained Dorothy, turning to Madame Gabrielle. "He's an architect, now."

Kit held out his hand and Madame Gabrielle hesitated. Hilary remembered that, in France, a woman invites a man to shake hands, by holding out her own hand first, but Madame Gabrielle's apparent dismay over this breach of French savoir-vivre lasted only a moment. She, then, smiled and shook Kit Mallory's hand and he indicated to her that there was an empty spot on the sofa, next to where he had been sitting. Madame Gabrielle demurely sat down there, but turned her head away, as if to suggest she was not eager to converse with him. As if bowing to her wishes, Kit did not attempt to engage her in conversation, but glanced at her, from time to time, as if wondering who she was.

The atmosphere in the room, at first one of contrived high spiritedness, developed into a more relaxed one after a while and conversation started to flow easily. Madame Gabrielle, alone, remained a person apart, communicating little. Dorothy reckoned she was used to more formality in her social encounters and was not sure how to conduct herself, in a situation strange to her.

Then, there was an unexpected knock on the door and Hilary went to see who was there. A pleasant, calm voice, that of a woman with a cultured, English accent- the type of accent one practised in élite language schools, Hilary thought - was heard to say:

"I am Caterina Traversi, personal assistant to Mr. Mallory."

"Oh! Do come in," said Hilary, a note of surprise evident in her own voice.

The newcomer, Hilary guessed, was in her early twenties. Her dark hair, parted at the side, was styled so that it swung to a level just below her shoulders, in soft waves, like that of a film star in the 1940s. Her eyes, Hilary had to admit, were beautiful, being dark and yet, sparkling. She was wearing a lemon-coloured, sleeveless cocktail dress. Her shoes, which had very high heels, matched the colour of the dress. Her demeanour was that of a young woman who was used to having her wishes granted, rather than of one who was obliged to jump to the orders of someone else. Her gaze fell monetarily upon Kit Mallory and Madame Gabrielle sitting beside him, but, behaving like someone too well brought up to stare, she turned her head away quickly, raising her fine eyebrows only slightly. But, this slight indication of surprise, or even disapproval, had been noticed by Madame Gabrielle. She put down the glass that Dorothy had handed to her minutes before, on the coffee table in front of her and she picked up, from the floor, her small, quilted evening bag, as if she were preparing herself to leave the room.

Dorothy looked at Hilary. Her eyes seemed to be saying, "What now?"

CHAPTER 20

After the Party

Madame Gabrielle leaned over the rail of Deck 4 as the *Sabine Estelle* cut through the ocean smoothly. She was not able to observe much out in the sea, its being too dark at that post-cocktail hour, but she realised that waves would be bobbing along by the side of the ship and would be leaving a froth of foam, trailing behind the stern. Madame Gabrielle tried to think of nothing but those waves. She was as unsuccessful, though, as she was whenever she tried to meditate. And anyway, how could she empty her mind of thought when the fresh memory of her stupidity was repeatedly taunting her? Had she had a trusted companion with her, one in whom she would have been able to confide, she might have managed to laugh away her hasty retreat from Dorothy Trimm's party and dismissed, with a shrug, her fear that her unexplained disappearance would give rise to gossip. But she was alone and her problems were magnified by her solitude. She remembered now that, shamefully, she had not even turned to say "Good-bye" to the other guests present at the cocktail party! And, even worse, she had not exchanged a single word with her hostess before heading for the door. This breach of savoir-vivre was plaguing her as much as everything else that had gone awry.

Madame Gabrielle turned and leaned her back against the rail. She stared downwards at her shoes, then, in the way a child who had behaved naughtily might. "How could I have conducted myself in that way?" she asked herself, as she felt a flush of embarrassment beginning to warm her face. "And, at my age, how could I have been so gauche?"

With a sad heart, Madame Gabrielle took a pace towards the

wooden door that gave access to the interior of the ship and she hauled it open. She stepped into a corridor and the warmth that immediately surrounded her made her feel better. It occurred to her that she should not have gone out on to an exterior deck, at night, without having put on a coat, first, but of course, she had not been thinking sensibly. She made her way, quickly, in the direction of her own quarters, hoping that she would not meet anyone who had been at the party, while on her way there. She did not. And once she had gained entry to her own rooms, she bolted the door. A stewardess had left chocolates on her pillow. She ate them, because she had no intention of having dinner in the dining room, that night. She really did not possess the sang-froid, at that moment, to face anyone, let alone her habitual dinner table companions. She was aware of the fact, though, that deprived of her presence, they would, undoubtedly, be spending time indulging in chit-chat about her and expressing their theories on why she had disappeared so quickly, as soon as Mr, Kit Mallory's attractive and young assistant had arrived. It was unbearable to think that she, who was normally so inscrutable, would become the subject of such intrusive debate.

Madame Gabrielle sat on her bed and grasped hold of a pillow which she held tightly in front of her, as if she were attempting to relieve some interior, physical pain. It occurred to her, then, that she would have to provide her dining companions with an excuse for her hasty exit, the next time she saw them. What could she say? That she had felt the approach of a migraine headache and had been compelled to rush away to swallow tablets, which would halt its development? That excuse seemed plausible enough and it was not entirely devoid of truth. Her head was hurting now and she was feeling exhausted. In fact, her forehead was pounding. She lay down on her bed, thus crushing her elegant dress, but her crushed dress was the least of her worries, she felt. She had tried not to think of Kit Mallory, but she started to wonder, now, what he must have thought of her behaviour. And what would his assistant, his young and attractive assistant, have concluded? That she was ill-educated, awkward and unable to behave in a sophisticated manner? How awful! How shameful! What a spectacle she had made of herself!

Madame Gabrielle sat up and tried to smooth away the wrinkles that had appeared in her dress. But then, she stopped. Why was she bothering? What had been the point of spending hours packing dresses that had had a certain allure and elegance, when Mr. Mallory was not going to give them, or their wearer, a second glance? And why would he pay attention to her, no matter how well-dressed she was, when the glamorous Caterina Traversi was on board?

She, Madame Gabrielle, had wasted time, obviously, having her hair cut and styled in a jaunty way, when it was evident that her face was not memorable! Why had it not occurred to her, before, that her dreams would possibly end in the way they had? Why had she bothered to book a berth on the cruise ship, at all, when her sole motivation for doing so had been the obviously misguided and ridiculous notion that Kit Mallory, leader of The Mermen, upon seeing her, would romantically sweep her off her feet, remembering her as she had once been? What self - delusion! Had she really convinced herself that her first meeting with him, after decades apart, would have resulted in the coup de foudre for him? "Oh! Gabrielle! Gabrielle!" she thought, piteously. "How could you have fallen into such an abyss of self-deception?"

At base level, she reminded herself, Kit Mallory was a man like any other troubadour. No matter how sophisticated and knowing he appeared to be, he was as capable of being entranced by youthful beauty as any other rock star, when he was dealing with still-adoring fans, vying for his attention. A younger woman would always be preferred to an older one, were a choice to be made available. And who could blame the man for paying attention to a girl with fresh skin and sparkling eyes, who looked up to him, or appeared to be doing so, even if he were aware of the fact that the girl was behaving cynically? A man of maturity and wit would wryly enjoy being seen with a pretty, young girl, no matter what he assumed her motives to be. Caterina Traversi had beautiful eyes, young, unlined skin and glossy hair. It was inconceivable that Kit Mallory, given his age, would not be pleased to be the object of her unfaltering attention. He had obviously appointed her to the position of personal assistant, in order to endow her with a certain status. But it was unlikely that she actually worked. Any woman examining Miss Traversi's appearance would suspect that she spent her days exercising in the gym and enjoying beauty treatments, rather than attending to administrative duties.

Madame Gabrielle shivered even though the bedroom was warm, as she realised the extent to which she had let herself down, that evening. So much for French savoir-vivre, the code of behaviour she had taught to her daughter and grand children! What would they think of her, if they could see her, in disarray, having lost control of her feelings? Why, they would wonder, had she not managed her emotions more intelligently? Why had she not stayed at the party, to contribute to the frivolity of the event, by indulging in light conversation with the other guests?

It occurred to Madame Gavrielle, then, so advanced was her distress, that, to avoid being made to feel odd and humiliated, she should not dine in the ship's dining room again, but instead, should ask the stewardess to deliver her meals to her cabin. But such a solution to her dilemma struck her, then, as being extreme and over-dramatic. Had she forgotten who she was? Surely a woman of her class should be able to step over the blunder she had committed, with aplomb. She would find a way to make amends, and, on reflection, the correct way to proceed was obvious. First of all, she would send a hand-written letter to Dorothy Trimm, to apologise for her rapid departure and her failure to add to the jollity of the evening. Then, in the dining room, she would talk about her "migraine" and its sudden onset with feeling, while expressing her deep regret at having missed the party. Had the evening, in fact, been marvellous and amusing? Maybe there would be others, for them all to enjoy. She would talk and talk with enthusiasm and, in that way, she would convince her listeners that her excuse for absconding, with haste, had been a genuine one and that they had been mistaken, if they had thought otherwise.

And if, later, she were to come across Mr. Kit Mallory and Miss Caterina Traversi in some corridor or on some deck, she would be polite but distant, as if they were of little interest to her. Would she be able to manage to do all of that? In a day or two, perhaps.

CHAPTER 21

Caterina Traversi

In her cabin bedroom, Caterina Traversi switched on the TV set, selecting the cruise ship's own channel, and sat down in a swivel chair to watch The Mermen performing in one of the ship's theatres. The cocktail party in Dorothy Trimm's quarters, which she had felt obliged to attend earlier, had left her feeling listless, partly because she had been bored by it, but also, conversely, because she had been on edge while there, in case, given the cosy conviviality of the occasion, she might have been asked intrusive questions which she would have been disinclined to answer. She had not stayed at the party for long, in fact, realising that she preferred distance in social intercourse, rather than excessive friendliness. She had chosen not even to mix with other passengers on board the ship, when dining. Adelina, who was voyaging with her, had been charged with the duty of bringing meals to her rooms. Caterina could not bear to deal with the questions she imagined that people would ask, at table, while on holiday - "Who are you?" "Where do you come from?" "Are you travelling alone?" – in expectation of answers overflowing with detail.

Some weeks before, after leaving Forte Dei Marmi in a huff, following her exchange of heated words with her sister, Beatrice, Caterina had intended, initially, to go to Chester and to spend some time there. Having once been a pupil, one of the boarders, at Bramblewell School, like her sister Ida, who was studying there, she knew the area well. She had hoped, in fact, to find employment in some kind of business. She had been looking for a job, of an administrative nature, that would equip her with knowledge of how a company - even a small one - was run, how working practices differed from those in Italy and how employees were treated. After a year, or so, she would return to Italy to say to Beatrice, "There! I have experience of working in another country. Have you? Furthermore, what I have achieved, I have achieved alone, without any help from Papa. Can you say that? No?"

Upon arriving in Chester, Caterina had checked into a hotel in the city centre, late in the afternoon, and after making her room comfortable, had gone for an early evening walk, just as the shops were closing. Chester had looked pretty at that hour, as the streets were emptying. Caterina had been surrounded by Italy's beautiful cities all her life and had been well acquainted with the Mediaeval and the antique in urban design, but Chester, with its mixture of Roman, Norman, Tudor and even fake Tudor buildings, had enchanted her as a schoolgirl and had delighted her even more, that evening, as she had re-acquainted herself with her surroundings. "It's like a film set!" she had thought, as she had wandered around the city's centre.

In a side street, she had entered, on a whim, a small, fast food restaurant, incongruously situated on the ground floor of an historic building. She had ordered fish and chips at the counter and then, had sat down at a table that had been vacant. On the chair beside hers, a previous customer had left a city newspaper, folded in such a way as to display a column of small advertisements. One such advertisement had caught Caterina's eye. It had announced that a temporary administrative assistant was being sought, for a period of two to three weeks. The job would involve travelling abroad. It had occurred to Caterina, at once, that temporary work of that nature might prove to be a good starting point for her. Even if the duties were to prove to be onerous, she could surely tolerate them for a short while.

The next morning, Caterina had telephoned to the number given in the advertisement and had said to the girl - presumably a secretary - who had answered her call that she would be happy to be interviewed for the post that had been advertised and that she would telephone later in the day to suggest a time and location where the interview could take place.

"No. You don't understand," the secretary had said, speaking slowly. "We shall tell you when the interview will take place and where it will take place. Anyway, you will have to fill in forms, first."

Mr. Kit Mallory, for whom the secretary worked, had obviously been present in her, the secretary's, office when the call had been received, because at that point, intrigued, he had asked the secretary to put the call through to his office. After conversing with Caterina for a while, he had arranged to meet her the following morning, in the foyer of the hotel where she was staying, for morning coffee and, perhaps later, for lunch. As a result of that encounter, Caterina had been offered the temporary job and she had accepted the offer.

Caterina's task, she had been told, would require her to accompany Mr. Mallory, architect and occasional musician, playing with The Mermen, on a cruise ship, leaving from Liverpool. Mr. Mallory's permanently employed personal assistant would be on a holiday elsewhere at that time, and Caterina would be obliged to take over her duties. Caterina had not mentioned to Mr. Mallory, at that point, for fear of stepping over a line into over-familiarity, that his name had not been unknown to her. She had recalled seeing it, as a child, on the covers of The Mermen's English L.P.s that had been collected by her maternal grand-mother, as a teenager, along with continental records that had borne the names of Rocky Roberts and Richard Anthony. She had remembered, in particular, the photos of Kit Mallory that had appeared on The Mermen's L.P.s since they, The Mermen, had struck her as being Byronic. Mr. Mallory's dark hair had fallen on to his forehead, in a poetic way. He had been handsome then and he was still good-looking, Caterina had to admit, despite her avowed preference for Italian men.

Back in her hotel room, Caterina had surveyed the clothes she had brought with her from Forte dei Marmi. Adelina had packed her luggage in haste and had put into her case only three cocktail dresses, two evening gowns and jeans. These were not going to serve her well on a working trip. With Adelina, therefore, she had taken a taxi ride to Ellesmere Port and, specifically, to Cheshire Oaks, a retail centre, where she had stocked up, buying navy crew-necked jumpers in cashmere and plain, white blouses in cotton poplin, white trousers in a cool fabric for the heat and a selection of white and pink sun dresses. For deck sports, she had chosen white shorts, navy shirts and white gym shoes. Back in Chester, she had bought jewellery in Eastgate and The Rows. Satisfied, then, she had returned to the hotel, knowing that a few days would pass before Mr. Mallory would contact her to give her further instructions. She had been intrigued to observe that she had unexpectedly felt excited at the thought of working - and earning her own money-without Papa watching over what she did.

Caterina, realising she had been allowing her mind to wander, sat up straight in her swivel chair. On the ship's TV, The Mermen had finished their set. Caterina hoped she would not be summoned now, by Mr. Mallory, to undertake some duty and that she could spend the rest of the evening attending to her own needs. In Rome, she would pass two or three afternoons each week, in beauty salons. Italian women would consider such behaviour to be normal. But, as a consequence of having accepted her job, she had had to restrict herself to one or two hours, at the end of each day, for beautifying tasks and she was beginning to find the restrictions placed on her private time, stressful. How could she possibly be expected to look glamorous, or even presentable, when she had so little time to attend to the care of her hair, the polishing of her nails and the moisturising of her skin? Kit Mallory, she was beginning to discover, could be over-demanding. "Do this...! Do that...!" he would order her, as if she were an unexceptional employee. Of course, that is exactly what she was, but she had not expected to have had so much to do. She had, in fact, supposed that her job would have been little more than a sinecure. The fact that

Mr. Mallory had actually expected her to work hard had shocked her. She had, after some reflection, explained to him who she was, in the expectation of indulgence, when she had been interviewed by him for the post, but he had merely shrugged, as if her surname had meant nothing to him.

Caterina had guessed that one of the reasons as to why she had to work long hours, well into the evening rather often, was the fact that Mr. Mallory, long-divorced, tended to attract single women, as quickly as a magnet might attract iron filings. Part of Caterina's job was to accompany him to social events in the evening, in order to make women hesitate before considering approaching him. "Is Caterina Traversi a girlfriend?" they might cautiously ask themselves, upon becoming aware of her presence. "A permanent attachment?"

Caterina had been asked by Mr. Mallory to attend a cocktail party in Mrs. Dorothy Trimm's suite, earlier that evening, for that very purpose, she had assumed. Upon entering the suite, she had seen Mr. Mallory sitting on a sofa with an elegant lady, dressed in burgundy, by his side. What had she, Caterina, been supposed to do? Had she been expected to confect an excuse to draw him away from the lady? She had glanced at one and then, the other. Perhaps she had looked marginally longer than required at the lady in burgundy. Affronted perhaps, the lady had picked up her handbag and had left the room. Had she, Caterina, been responsible for that hasty exit? She had noticed the way Mr. Mallory had watched the departure. There had seemed to have been a look of regret in his eyes.

Caterina's mobile phone rang, disturbing her perplexing thoughts. She had left the phone on the coffee table, in front of the beige sofa and after a moment's hesitation, she picked it up. The call was from Ida. Caterina sighed. Although she had previously ignored calls from Beatrice and her mother, deigning to speak only to her father, she knew she would feel mean were she not to chat to young Ida, who was a good sort, after all. "Ciao!" she said, feeling remorse, then, upon hearing the relief in Ida's voice as she responded with, "Caterina! Ciao, cara!"

Ida went on to explain that she knew Caterina was in England, but where exactly was she? Was she anywhere near Bramblewell School? Everyone at home was worried about her and sorry about the circumstances that had led to her departure. Was she in good health? Caterina explained she was working on a cruise ship, but that upon her return, she would meet Ida, certainly, when the new term had begun at Bramblewell School and they would, then, go to dinner in nice restaurants and on trips in pleasure boats on the river, and additionally, they would set off on excursions to interesting locations in North Wales. They would have such fun! Ida was not to worry. All was well.

In reality, Caterina knew all was not well. She was beginning to change and not for the better, she feared. As a result of having to take orders from Mr. Mallory and to having had to respond positively to them, without making a fuss, she had begun to feel diminished. Smaller. She was starting to wonder what it had to be like to take orders, day in, day out, for an entire working lifetime. People who worked in Papa's organisation had to endure that indignity. In fact, most people in the world had to work under those conditions. It had never struck her before what it had to be like to spend one's life obeying orders, instead of being privileged enough to be able to give them. How long could she stand being treated without favour by Mr.Mallory when she had been so used to being Papa's indulged daughter? Just by standing beside Mr. Mallory, she could feel her confidence being drawn out of her, like lemonade through a straw. Mr. Mallory obviously believed himself to be superior to her. He conveyed this belief, of course, in the arch way he spoke to her in the presence of others. Caterina was learning that her boss's approach was not conducive to encouraging her to be positive in her attitude to her work and she began to reflect on ways she could make people happier within Papa's organisation. Was she being naïve in thinking she could accomplish what others had failed to do? Was it possible to enable people to feel self-reliant within a strict system of management? She would have to give some thought to the problem.

Caterina walked into the bathroom, adjacent to her sitting room. She gazed at her reflection in the mirror above the sink. She who had once looked at men haughtily now seemed to be only jaded and tired. But why was she allowing herself to be crushed by the demanding Mr. Mallory? How dare he treat her as if she were no one of any significance, in fact! Did he not realise that she could resign from her job that very evening and could move to a much grander suite, for the remainder of the cruise, using her own money? Obviously not! Were she to resign, unexpectedly, in that way, what fun it would be to see the startled look on his face, though! How would he manage without a personal assistant? Why! He would have to do his own administrative work!

What should she do? The seductive thought of spending the rest of the trip lounging on the pool deck danced into her brain and filled her with glee. But then, the honourable side of her nature declared war on this childish response to her dilemma. She had agreed to take the job. In doing so, she had deprived someone else of the opportunity of earning money. Having signed a contract, she should see the job through. Mr. Malory had actually done nothing wrong. She was feeling the way she was feeling because she, herself, had not anticipated what would lie ahead of her. The cruise would last for a little more than two weeks. Surely she could continue in post for sixteen days! She was a Traversi, after all. She would step over difficulties and would rise above them. And, afterwards, when she had returned to Italy, she would laugh at the experiences she had had working for Mr. Mallory and would really begin to appreciate the privileged life she led in Italy - or perhaps, instead, she would ask Papa for a job in the family's firm, starting at the bottom of the ladder, of course, so as to understand the psychology of those who would, one day, work for her, when she would be in charge.

CHAPTER 22

Dorothy Investigates

"She has simply disappeared from view, Hilary!" exclaimed Dorothy Trimm, entering her daughter's cabin."Two days, now! Two days without a sighting of her!"

"Who?" asked Hilary, although not quite focusing on what was being said, having slept late.

"Oh! Wake up, Hils!" urged Dorothy, putting her straw and leather handbag down on the floor with a thump, before switching on the electric kettle, which was standing on a brass tray, on a darkly veneered desk.

"You are referring to Madame Gabrielle?" asked Hilary calmly.

"Of course I am referring to Madame Gabrielle! I spoke to a stewardess who was working in her corridor and she assured me that Madame was fine but that she wanted her meals to be served in her room, for two or three days, until her headache had gone away. But, I'd guess that all that is wrong with Madame is nothing more than the fact that she wants to avoid situations in which she would be obliged to speak to other passengers and explain her behaviour at our party. We've really made a mess of things, Hilary, haven't we?"

"No! We haven't, Mother!" responded Hilary in a determined way, while dabbing her forehead with a cloth soaked in Eau de Cologne. "We've simply..."

"What is wrong with you?" interrupted Dorothy. "What is wrong with your head?"

"There's nothing wrong with me. I've just overslept. That's all!"

"Too much sleep deprivation!" snapped Dorothy. "That has been your problem for years! That's why you have always been so tetchy! And now, your body is trying to make up for all that lost sleep."

"Mother! As I was saying…"

"What were you saying?"

"I was saying, or rather, going to say, that it isn't our fault that Madame Gabrielle has been behaving in the way she has. If her current behaviour has any connection with the soirée that we held in your suite, that does not mean that we can be blamed for the way she reacted to a certain situation. Madame Gabrielle decided to leave the soirée of her own volition, as soon as Miss Traversi appeared. We could not have predicted that she would have objected to Miss Traversi's presence. We did not even invite Miss Traversi. Who is she, anyway?"

"I don't know…but I'll find out. I wonder if she has had any dealings with Madame Gabrielle in the past…Or did Madame simply reckon she was a rival?"

"Mother! I don't think you should meddle."

"I shan't make my intention obvious, Hilary."

"Really? Don't you realise how blunt you sometimes come across as being and the extent to which I often cringe when I am with you, in company?"

"You worry too much, Hilary! Incidentally, I've told you before that that red blouse you are wearing doesn't suit you. The red blouse and white trousers combination may look fine on fashion models but not on you, dear. Red becomes far too strident a colour when placed beside your complexion, Hilary."

"Thank you, Mother. How could I possibly get through life without your invaluable guidance? Now! Are you going to make offee, or are you going to stand there all day with the kettle in your hand? Hm!"

Later that day, Dorothy observed, on the news-sheet announcing the evening's activities, that The Mermen would be performing in one of the lounges, as they were called, on Deck 3. Normally, Dorothy would have opted for a more sedate way to end the day, but given the fact that Miss Traversi would possibly be present, Dorothy made her way to the lounge after dinner, having first assured Hilary that her presence would not be required.

Dorothy located an empty table near the door, her intention being to leave, unobtrusively and without fuss, from that secluded position, should Miss Traversi not appear. Dorothy settled herself in a chair which had upholstered arms. She ordered a long drink, with fruit in it, from a passing waiter. Then, she glanced at her watch, which she had decided to wear even though she knew it was considered incorrect to wear a watch with an evening dress. She simply felt uneasy without it. Eight forty-five. How long would she have to wait?

Five minutes later, Dorothy was pleased to see Miss Traversi entering the lounge with the confident glide of a lady who expected to be noticed by those present. Proud in bearing, slim in build and dazzling in dress, Miss Traversi paused and looked around the room, as if assessing which would be the most appropriate part in which to sit. Dorothy wondered what was on her mind. Was she looking for a spot in which she would best be seen and admired by many? Or, was she deciding where she would have the clearest view of the stage?

Dorothy, with an air of carefree spontaneity, called out:

"Miss Traversi! Coo-ee! Miss Traversi! Over here! Would you like to join me?"

Arching her fine eyebrows, in apparent surprise, Caterina Traversi turned her head to look in Dorothy's direction. She seemed to hesitate, momentarily, as if perplexed, but then, she dropped her haughty pose and smiled widely and engagingly, in Italian style. Hoisting up, with one hand, a piece of the material of her slim, almost tight, scarlet evening dress, shimmering with tiny sequins, she made her way, in small steps, to Dorothy's table.

"I'm so pleased to see you!" she exclaimed, in a warm, soft voice, placing her tiny evening bag on the table before transferring it to her lap, when she had sat down opposite Dorothy. Her glossy, dark hair, brushed to one side of her head, in a mass of confected waves, held in place with a silver clasp, her jewellery - a diamond bracelet and one, matching drop ear-ring - and her carefully applied, pretty make-up endowed her with that aura of glamour that Dorothy usually associated with the unreachable stars of Hollywood, in earlier times. Despite the slight flashiness of her appearance, Miss Traversi, though, was retaining, through her natural poise, the air of a well-bred European, brought up to be discreet. Dorothy could not help imagining her at the opera in Milan, her graceful arms covered in long, pale gloves, or at the casino in Deauville, dramatically wearing red lipstick, while dressed in black velvet, or at the Carnival in Venice, masked and glittering in an elaborate costume. Those were surely the milieux in which Miss Traversi belonged.

"I've been hoping to run into you, to thank you for the lovely party I attended in your rooms," she said, her English accent sounding almost perfect. Dorothy had detected only one word, "lovely," that had given the game away, but had she not been paying rapt attention, it would have escaped her notice.

"Oh! My dear!" exclaimed Dorothy, then. "We received your very nice note and the chocolates, ostensibly sent on behalf of Mr. Mallory, but which, I suspect, came from you."

"Mr. Mallory asked me to thank you. It was part of my job, but I'd have sent a note, anyway, as it was so nice of you to arrange an evening like that for him. For all of us."

"Forgive me for asking this, but how long have you been working for Mr. Mallory, dear? I'll be frank. Your job doesn't seem to me to be the sort that I should normally imagine you taking seriously."

Caterina Traversi laughed. She leaned back in her chair and looked up at the ceiling for a moment.

"I have agreed to do this job for only the duration of the cruise," she said, before adding, "and to gain experience, rather than to earn money."

Caterina observed Dorothy's surprised look and smiled indulgently at the older woman's obvious curiosity. Hesitating only for an instant, she then revealed:

"I wanted to understand what it was like to do a regular job, to take orders and carry them out and to be dependent on money earned and nothing else. I must say, though, that I'd hate to take orders all through my working life. There must be a better way of managing the work place."

"Some people prefer to obey orders rather than be responsible for a project, dear. You are imagining that everyone thinks in the way that you do, but that is not necessarily the case. However, your mistake is a common one. But, you know, you, now, strike me as being younger than I had thought you were. I had reckoned that you might have been in your mid twenties, and yet, you seem not to have had much experience of the world of work. Is that the case? Have you never had a proper job before?"

"I have never had to work, before," replied Caterina, chastened by Dorothy's remarks. "I have never had to, because Papa has always given me an allowance. My father owns a large publishing company in Italy and I thought that having experience of the way people worked, in all sorts of other jobs, would be of use to me, before I asked him if I could be trained in the family's business. At the moment, Papa thinks I am not a serious person. But, I actually want to be involved in the company and to be given the chance to work in it, at a high level. I want to convince Papa that I am not an extravagant doll, fit only for marriage."

"Now, now, dear!" Dorothy interrupted. "Don't undervalue marriage! Running a household is pretty much like running a business. One has to establish daily, weekly and monthly routines, manage a budget, pay attention to stock control and review systems annually. It is not easy and…"

"I don't undervalue marriage!" said Caterina, in a heated way, stopping Dorothy in mid-sentence. "Really, I don't! I want to marry. But, I do want to know how the family business operates, as well. What is wrong with that?"

"Nothing, dear! Nothing! I've combined work with marriage, myself, during my life. But, anyway, leaving that aside, you said your father was in publishing, did you? Imagine! Publishing! Now, isn't that a coincidence?"

"Coincidence?"

"Let me explain..." began Dorothy, her face suddenly aglow with interest. "I, myself, own a small publishing business, a small press, in the Wirral. Do you know where that is?"

"Yes. I went to Bramblewell School when I was a teenager. I know Chester, the Wirral...Liverpool even. I know all the places around there."

"Well!"

"Please continue. You were saying you own a small press?"

"Yes. The Nightshade Press. I am very attached to it and I don't want to give it up, but I am not as energetic as I used to be and I want to find somebody who will help me to run it. Someone who can put up with my irascible character, admittedly. My daughter, Hilary, has her own career and we couldn't work well together, anyway. And so, I wonder, dear, if you would be interested in working for me for a while?"

"What sorts of books do you publish?" asked Caterina, without hesitation.

"I publish books about etiquette and how to behave at various social events in Cheshire, specifically. Gymkhanas, garden parties...That sort of thing. I, also, publish books about interior decorating and garden design. Life-style, in a word. Or rather, two words."

"Style and behaviour are very important. Nice style and good manners make life pleasant for everyone. I am Italian and so, obviously, I really believe what I have just said!"

"Of course. So..."

"If I may, I'll have a look at your business when the voyage is over. Could I work with you for a week, initially?"

"Oh, yes! Do!"

"I have a sister, Ida, who is a boarder at Bramblewell School. I think she'll be happy to have me near. Even if I think I shall not be able to work for you, long-term, I'll ask Papa, once I am back in Italy, if he can suggest how you can be helped. Maybe one of my cousins would come over, for work experience, if nothing else."

"That would be very kind of you," said Dorothy, suddenly dumbfounded, as she took in what was being said. Caterina belonged to a family that owned a large publishing house in Italy? And Caterina was going to ask her father to help her, Dorothy, to run a small press in the Wirral? Dorothy did not know what to think. Should she be excited? Or wary?

"You are the one doing me a favour, Mrs. Trimm," said Caterina calmly, noting Dorothy's confusion. "Papa will be convinced that I am taking the family's line of work seriously, when I tell him about you. Meeting you has been a stroke of luck for me. Do you believe in fate?"

"I've never given it much thought. I've been too busy creating my own destiny, through hard work."

Miss Traversi nodded, but said nothing. Her mind was filling up with images of her family's reaction upon learning about her work experiences in England. Papa would discover that his Caterina was no longer a dilettante. In fact, she had grown up. And Beatrice? Well! She would have to make more of a splash, if she wanted to avoid being eclipsed.

CHAPTER 23

A Night in Topaz and Black Velvet

Madame Gabrielle awoke, unsure of where she was, being still anaesthetised by the world of dreams. And then, as had been the case, three mornings in a row, she started to remember the night of Mrs. Dorothy Trimm's cocktail party. The memory of each moment began to flow into her brain. She thought of Mr. Kit Mallory's initial solicitude, the arrival of Caterina Traversi and then, her own undignified exit and, as she did so, she cringed under the white sheets and duvet quilt covering her.

It was not yet seven o' clock. Normally, Madame Gabrielle would have remained in bed at that hour and would have attempted to sleep a little longer, but she felt, on that morning, that a certain discipline was required. Three days had passed since the party, but she had not yet summoned the courage to leave her room to join her usual dining companions for dinner in the evening. Her meals, including breakfast, had been brought to her suite by a stewardess. But she knew she could not continue to be reclusive, taking the air only on her balcony. She simply had to conquer her embarrassment. Possibly no one else had even noticed the rapidity of her unexpected departure, on the night of the cocktail party, after all. Why would anyone bother to comment on it?

Madame Gabrielle rose and bathed and then dressed, choosing navy slacks, a navy jumper, a red belt and a red handbag, red being a colour she believed to be a conveyer of courage. Having left her cabin then, she made her way to the breakfast room, her head high. She was conscious of the fact, though, that her heart was thumping and that her stress level was elevated, her anxiety being generated, no doubt, by a fear that she would encounter Kit Mallory, or even worse, Caterina Traversi. Were she to see Caterina Traversi again, in fact, she knew she would be obliged to return to her rooms at once, in order to quench the jealous feelings that would be aroused by the young woman's presence. However, there were not many passengers in the breakfast room and Madame Gabrielle recognised no one. She felt calmer. Her appetite had faded away all the same, and although there was a vast buffet of hot and cold dishes on offer, she chose to take from it only slices of water melon and pineapple and a large cup of café au lait.

A middle-aged woman, whom Madame Gabrielle had not seen before, joined her at the table where she, Madame Gabrielle, had decided to sit, because it gave her a view of the entrance to the room.

"Do you mind if I sit here?" the woman asked.

Madame Gabrielle shrugged and smiled. She would have preferred to have been alone, but perhaps it was time she attempted to be sociable.

The newcomer was chatty and extractive. Where did Madame Gabrielle come from, she wanted to know. Was she voyaging with friends? And which evening shows had she attended? Not any? Oh! She would simply have to go to the lounge on Deck 4 where The Mermen were engaged to play some nights. When they were not playing music, they were often there, anyway, talking to passengers. They were so accommodating. They did not seem to be annoyed when asked to sign autographs, endlessly.

"You know, you should go there: to Deck 4!" the chatty woman urged. "You can sit with us, if you like."

She had not specified to whom she had been referring when mentioning "us," but Madame Gabrielle assumed she meant a group of friends or her family, even.

As soon as she had finished her coffee, Madame Gabrielle excused herself, saying she had to attend to a few obligations. She had not enjoyed the chatty encounter, but at least, it had provided her with information about Mr. Mallory's group, The Mermen.

They spent their evenings on Deck 4? She had not dared to ask if Mr. Mallory was always with them.

During the rest of that morning, Madame Gabrielle tried to push out of her mind thoughts of The Mermen, or rather, of Kit Mallory, but she found she could not concentrate on anything else. Her heart was beating with some force again and it occurred to her that it was not advisable to subject it to so much pressure. She knew that she was allowing herself to behave like a silly teenager, chasing a hopeless dream, and yet, she could not stop herself from looking through her wardrobe, in order to choose what would be suitable to wear that evening, should she decide to visit the lounge on Deck 4. She would never behave in such an inappropriate way in France, of course. It would be unthinkable of her to do so.

Madame Gabrielle remembered reading, in one of the leaflets left by her bed, that the "smart-casual" look was acceptable on the ship, on most occasions. The description, "smart-casual," struck her as being an oxymoron, but she had a vague idea as to what it meant. If she were to decide to go to Deck 4 that evening, would white cord trousers, a lime-coloured blouse and peridot ear-rings be considered to be both smart and casual? Or would it be more appropriate for her, given her age and the time of day, to wear black velvet trousers, with a topaz coloured blouse and amber ear-rings? After some thought, she decided to opt for her black velvet and topaz outfit, bearing in mind, of course, the fact that she would probably not need it since, by evening, she would probably have decided to behave sensibly, by remaining in her cabin, reading a novel. She wanted to make a start on one by Victoria Holt, after all. It would take her to a different place and a different time and she would forget where she was and what she was missing.

Madame Gabrielle was calmed by these thoughts and she spent the rest of the morning sitting by her balcony, taking the air. However, at lunch time, she started to feel agitated again, when the stewardess asked her if she wanted to have lunch in her rooms or if she was well enough to go to the dining room. Madame Gabrielle said she wanted to stay in her rooms, but realised, then, that the incident at Dorothy Trimm's cocktail party had affected her so deeply that her mind must have been flooded with unhelpful thoughts that had made her panic and were continuing to make her panic. What was the information about fight-flight-freeze that she had once read? And more pertinently, what could she do to help herself? Could rational thinking overcome the stupidity of the way she was continuing to react to an imagined threat? She believed herself to be Cartesian when it came to creating order in her life. Had she forgotten that? Had she, in fact, forgotten that she was proudly French?

The afternoon passed slowly. Madame lay down on her bed and read a little. But around four, she decided to wash her hair, since it had absorbed salt from the sea air, when she had been out on the balcony. At least she managed to convince herself that that was the reason she was effectively beautifying it. At six, she ordered soup to be brought to her room, saying she was too unwell to consume anything more substantial. In reality, her appetite had been suppressed by the nervousness which had started to bother her again.

Around nine o' clock, dressed elegantly now in black velvet and topaz, Madame Gabrielle surrounded herself with the soft mist of a perfume that exuded the scent of roses and, trying not to ponder too deeply on what she was doing, left her rooms and made her way to the appointed place. She was hoping that Kit Mallory would not have a large number of people around him, but she had made up her mind that, even if Caterina Traversi were present, she would stay in the lounge for a while and would behave as if she were at ease. Were she to find Kit Mallory on his own, however, using well-chosen words, she would speak to him about that era, in the 1960s, when she, herself, had been a foreign student in Liverpool and he had been a young rock star in the making, rendering teenage girls weak at the knees with his haughty expression and tender voice, both of which appeared to have been de rigueur, at the time. It was the juxtaposition of apparent arrogance and unexpected gentleness that had intrigued, of course: the melding of the dark and the light. "Do you remember me?" she planned to ask, looking straight into his eyes. "I was the French girl with the long dark hair who stood by the stage when you were playing. Sometimes you would look at me and I used to think you recognised me and wanted to talk to me, but you never did."

Madame Gabriele reflected on her plan for a moment. It would not, perhaps, be wise to say so much, at first. She would drop hints, instead, and would leave him to work out who she was. Yes. That would be the better strategy.

Madame Gabrielle knew it would be perfectly acceptable for her to walk into the lounge alone and to sit at a table on her own, but nevertheless, she felt uncomfortable, when she arrived there. The room was occupied by only a few people, however, and there was no sign of Kit Mallory. Madame sat down at a small table, in the centre of the room- she was not going to hide in the shadows- and busied herself tying the black silk scarf she had brought with her to the handle of her black, velvet evening bag, before placing it on the chair beside her own. A waiter in a short, white jacket and black trousers approached. She ordered, whimsically, lemonade with a scoop of lime ice cream in it. Could such a drink be concocted? The waiter said he would make one, but he would have to fetch the ice cream from elsewhere. Could Madame wait? She could. Ten minutes later, he arrived with the drink and a long spoon.

The room began to fill up, but neither Kit Mallory, nor anyone associated with him, had yet appeared. The chatty woman who, that morning, had recommended that Madame Gabrielle go to the lounge in the evening had not arrived either. Every five minutes or so, Madame looked at her watch. Then, at ten o' clock, when the room had started to look crowded, two people asked her if they could join her at her table. Madame decided to leave. In the rock and roll world inhabited by Kit Mallory, maybe evenings began late: as late as eleven o' clock. However, she, Madame Gabrielle, did not intend to find out if that was the case. Dejected, but still proud in bearing, she made her way to the door.

Back in her own quarters, Madame Gabrielle walked the floor of her sitting room for a while, to work off her anger with herself, her frustration and her disappointment. Why had she fallen for the inane chatter of the woman she had encountered at breakfast time? Why had she persuaded herself that Kit Mallory, the master of hauteur, would appear and would make her childish dreams come true? Had she really been foolish enough to believe that life was a fairy tale? Madame walked into the bathroom and stared at her own reflection in the mirror before her. What did she suppose she had been doing? She, Madame Gabrielle de Talence, once the cherished daughter of the Count du Crâne, had spent an evening sitting in a bar, effectively looking, at best, abandoned and silly and, at worst, predatory. How demeaned she felt!

Her heart seemed to be turning to ice. Her skin felt cold. She would endure the rest of the voyage as best she could, hoping she would not run into Kit Mallory again, or even hear his name being mentioned. She would continue to eat in her rooms, at least for a while, and would walk on the outside decks only in the evenings, when most passengers were occupied in other ways. Her life would be restricted but such restriction would be preferable to further humiliation. She thought, then, of a line from Racine's "Phèdre":

"Le ciel mit dans mon sein une flame funeste."

A deadly flame had been lit within her, but she would extinguish it with the icy water of reason and good sense. Had emotion ever served her well after all? Indubitably not.

CHAPTER 24

Home Truths

"I've been calling Kath, Hils," said Dorothy Trimm, as she was entering her rooms aboard the cruise ship, where Hilary was already preparing the coffee that they had decided to have together, around eleven o' clock every morning. "I managed to pick up a telephone signal on one of the top decks."

"How is she?" asked Hilary, who had met Kathleen on a few occasions when she, Kathleen, had been visiting Dorothy.

"Well! She told me she had been to an evening reception at Margaret Devere's house. I didn't know she knew Margaret Devere. Did you, Hils?"

"Who? Kathleen? No. I don't know anything about her. Only what you have told me. She lives on the west side of the Wirral, doesn't she?

"Kath?

"No. Sorry. I meant Margaret Devere."

"Yes. It seems so. In a lovely house overlooking the River Dee. She served canapés outside, on a large patio that overlooked a terraced garden. And she was wearing one of those wide-skirted dresses of hers. You know: the kind of dresses that nearly reach the ankles. The type that Grace Kelly used to wear in films. Did you know her well when you were head of Bramblewell?"

"Margaret? Well, I saw her now and again. She attended some of my staff meetings. She was head of the prep school, of course, and ran it in her own way. Whenever I spoke to her, I found her ideas on education to be very sensible. She thought changes should be introduced slowly and cautiously and I agreed with her, obviously."

"Obviously? I think not, Hilary! Would you say that your introduction of astrology as an optional subject at Bramblewell School had been done slowly and cautiously? You would not, because you could not! What did Margare Devere think of astrology being introduced as a subject? I imagine she found it a step too far in the direction of absurdity. It was certainly introduced without much regard for the opinions of the teachers on your own staff. I mean, more than half of them were opposed to the idea, weren't they? But you brushed their objections to one side and appointed an astrology tutor, just because Lord Bramblewell had wanted you to do so. The fact that your teachers treated Liz Laurier with such civility, when she arrived in the school, says a lot for their character and upbringing, I must say. Oh! Love makes us all behave stupidly at one time or another, Hils, but to respond to the whim of Lord Bramblewell against your better judgement was to be exceedingly silly. You should have stood up to him and said, 'No, Rupert. That's too controversial an innovation. The school isn't ready for it.' Anyway, I hope you have learnt something from the experience."

"Can we change the subject? I have left Bramblewell School. I don't want to talk about it or Lord Bramblewell any longer."

"You will surely go back to the school, at some point in the months ahead, though, Hilary! I mean, the teachers at Bramblewell, in spite of what they thought about some of your decisions, will want to say 'Good-bye' to you, properly. You scooted off without saying as much as a 'Thank you' to them. You simply MUST go back! You must show that you did not leave in a hurry because you were emotionally upset. You must pull yourself together and behave with the dignity that becomes you. And I am sure that, when you meet your teachers again, you will deliver a speech with grace and dignity, in the way you always used to, even if Lord Bramblewell and Susie Sutton are present. I know it will be difficult for you to see those two there, together, but you mustn't show that you are in the least bit disturbed. I'll talk to Lord Bramblewell and

Lynn about arranging some sort of dinner in a nice restaurant for you and the teachers you are leaving behind. Now! Don't argue! It's 'the done thing' and you must do it. What's wrong? Hm? Hilary... I'll leave you alone for a minute."

Dorothy had seen tears appearing in Hilary's eyes and had thought the better of continuing to deliver unsolicited advice. She had not seen Hilary crying since she had been a little girl and the sight of her now, breaking down, alarmed her. She went out on deck and leaned on the rail, allowing the breeze from the sea to cool her face and ruffle her hair. She had always thought that her daughter was so strong that she could cope with criticism. It had not occurred to her, before, that Hilary, in fact, could be hurt by her words. Maybe more attention should have been paid to Hilary's behaviour, during the weeks that had just passed, also. When a post in Bramblewell School had been offered to Isolde Delamar, for example, Dorothy should have realised that her daughter's faculty of judgement had become faulty.

Dorothy looked over the edge of the railing and gazed as if mesmerised at the green waves topped with white foam. They dipped down and then bounced along as if dancing. The ship was heading for the Canary Islands: the warm south. It occurred to Dorothy, then, that Hilary would benefit from walking in the sun. A bit of heat would warm her skin and deliver a shot of Vitamin D. Maybe that was what she needed. Dorothy did not often feel maternal - Hilary had been brought up by nannies, mainly - but she did not like to see her daughter suffering, either. She would do her best to help Hilary through the difficult period she was silently enduring, even though her prickly pride would make any intervention difficult. And then, there was Madame Gabrielle! She was suffering also. It was a mistake to think that love could be experienced only by the young, although the young might find that fact hard to swallow.

CHAPTER 25

Teddy Comes Home

Teddy Laurence descended the flight of steps outside Lime Street Station, in Liverpool, wondering if he should walk down in the direction of the river, dragging his trolley case behind him, or if it would be preferable to hail a taxi. He was tempted to make his way to his riverside apartment on foot, taking in, slowly, the sights of Liverpool, once again, and sensing the excitement that was ever present in the air. He longed to hear, in the streets, the familiar accents of the city's denizens and to become aware of the scent of the sea, borne by sharp breezes, from the Bay of Liverpool, to his beloved city.

Teddy had been away from home for only a month, but he felt as if he had been absent for a year. Rebecca Hampton, the dark-haired and intelligent, American student who had been staying in his apartment, by the River Mersey, during his absence, had sent him messages frequently, to keep him au fait with what had been happening in the city, but now, arriving there, he felt as if he had been somewhat cast adrift: a stranger in his own town. He wondered, then, with the excitement which accompanies hope, what would be ahead of him, when he would turn the key in the lock of his apartment. Rebecca had told him that she would be leaving Liverpool before his arrival. There was studying that would have to be done in America, prior to her return to her east coast college for the Fall, as she called it. She was going back for her last year and she had to be prepared. But Teddy was hoping she had decided to delay her departure. He hoped, in fact, that she would be waiting for him in his apartment, when he arrived, and that she would be full of questions and anxious to converse with him in that calm, grown-up - sounding accent of hers, which encouraged him to believe that life was manageable, no matter what was actually happening in it. He had realised, in France, perhaps because he had felt lonely, that he could scarcely wait to see her again and, in the end, he had longed for every day of filming to pass quickly, so that he could return to her. He hailed a taxi. Silence, however, hung in the air outside Teddy's front door, on the first landing of the building in which his apartment was situated. When he put the key in the lock and pushed the door open, he sensed only emptiness.

"Rebecca!" he called, just in case his intuition had misinformed him. But, there was no reply.

He left his trolley case in the hall and wandered from room to room. Rebecca had left the flat in a state of perfect cleanliness. Everything was in order. No belongings had been left behind. Not even one last discarded paper-tissue lay in a bin. On the kitchen table, there was only a folded note, saying, "Welcome home!" And under it, there was an envelope containing money which Teddy had neither requested nor wanted. There was also a little present in a white box tied with gold ribbon. The box contained gold cuff links, tastefully plain.

Teddy walked through the rooms of the apartment again, looking for signs of Rebecca's presence. A book? A pen, even? There was nothing tangible to be seen. But, here and there, he thought he could detect the slightest traces of her favourite scent, hanging in the air. It was American. Sophisticated. He remembered it well.

The door bell rang.

"Rebecca?" said Teddy, quietly. Simultaneously, his heart gave a lurch. He turned to walk briskly towards the door. However, on the threshold, stood not Rebecca, but Susie Sutton. Teddy stared at her, as if not comprehending why she should be there. Her expression was troubled. Had something happened to Rebecca? But surely, if something had happened to Rebecca, Susie would not be the one delivering the news! Teddy's mind was in a spin, but he managed to remain looking calm.

"May I come in?" asked Susie, falteringly.

"Yes. Of course," replied Teddy, his manner business-like. "I'm sorry…I've just got back."

"I know. I telephoned Lady Aethelfreda to find out the time you had left the Château du Crâne. I worked out which flight you would have taken to London. Or rather, I asked Tamsin to work it all out for me. The 'plane and your train and everything."

"Tamsin? Oh! Tamsin who works in Bramblewell Manor."

"Yes."

"So…do you want to talk to me about something specific? Come into the sitting-room! Would you like some coffee?"

"No, thank you. Not at this moment, Teddy," said Susie walking towards a sofa and allowing herself, then, to sink into it, as if she were drained of energy. "But, have some, yourself. Do! I'll just rest here."

Susie turned her head, to gaze up at the sky through the floor to ceiling window, which took the place of almost an entire wall. Teddy looked at her. She was wearing a pink coat, which covered a creased, red dress. The jarring combination of pink and red surprised him. Susie, he knew, had started to pay more attention to her outfits, as she believed she conveyed her new status - she was Lord Bramblewell's fiancée, after all - through her clothes, as much as in the way she behaved. On this occasion, though, her newly acquired good taste seemed to have been replaced by the less taxing standards of the old Susie.

"Are you quite sure I can't bring you something to drink?" asked Teddy. "How about tea?"

"No. Really. Look after yourself, Teddy! You say you've just arrived?

"Yes. Five minutes ago."

In the kitchen, Teddy discovered that Rebecca had left the fridge, freezer and cupboards fully stocked. He found a tin of ground coffee, made from rare beans. Rebecca must have bought it in a shop she knew he liked. He opened the tin. The scent always made him feel comfortable. He looked for the percolator and five minutes later, he was pouring good, hot coffee into a mug, one of a white set that Rebecca must have bought also. Musing on Rebecca's behaviour, he next went into the sitting room, mug in hand. He walked over to the window and gazed down at the River Mersey, gently and wisely flowing by.

"Well!" he said, turning round, after a few seconds, to look at Susie. One of his eyebrows was raised, in a questioning way.

Susie smiled at him. She remembered that she had found his habit of raising one eyebrow, when puzzled, rather endearing, when she had been his girlfriend. He was handsome, but not so impassively perfect that his face lacked interest. Many expressions flitted across his face and Susie knew them all. She also knew - or rather, sensed - that he was still fond of her, in spite of the cold way she had terminated her relationship with him, before climbing up the social ladder. She felt that there would always be a bond existing between them and that if she were ever in trouble, Teddy would help her. He had done so, after all, on the day Gylen Somerland's son, John, had run away from his home, in Ellesmere Port. She had been frantic, as John had been left in her care, but Teddy, after she had called him in tears, had summoned the help of boys from the youth club he ran in Liverpool, and one of them, Louis Lindsey, had found the boy sleeping on a bench, at Pierhead, in the shadow of the tall and stately Royal Liver Building. Teddy had been her knight in shining armour, that day. Now, she needed him again.

"Susie?" said Teddy, since she had said not a word. "What is wrong? Are you going to tell me?"

Susie sat up straight. She picked up a cushion and clutched it, as if it were a comforting hot water bottle.

"I want you to do me a favour," she then explained.

"Go on," urged Teddy, adding as an afterthought, "I'm really tired, you know."

"The new secretary at Bramblewell School, Isolde Delamar, used to be engaged to Lord Bramblewell," said Susie sadly.

"I had heard that piece of news."

"Who told you?"

"I've been in touch with Lynn James."

"Lynn? Of course. Lynn…Actually, Lynn does not think Isolde Delamar is a very nice person. I can assure you of that!"

"Am I to assume that you want me to keep an eye on this Isolde Delamar? Is that what you want me to do?"

"More than that, Teddy. I want you to distract her, totally. I want you to ask her to go out on dates."

"Don't be absurd! I've never met this woman!"

"Teddy, please! Just date her until I am married?"

"No, Susie!"

"Please. I'll be married in seven months' time!"

"Seven months!"

"Please,Teddy."

"No, Susie. This time you are asking me to do something that I cannot do. Anyway, this Isolde Delamar is older than I am. About ten years older. Why would she want to hang around with someone who is as young as I am? But that aside, why are you so frightened of this woman? Lord Bramblewell is a man of honour. He asked you to marry him and he will marry you. This other woman deceived him and broke his heart. How can he possibly trust her again?"

Susie flinched, with embarrassment. Teddy's words had reminded her of the fact that she, herself, had deceived the young man now admonishing her and had broken his heart. Did he hold her in low esteem because of that? She looked directly into Teddy's eyes and found sadness in them.

"Lord Bramblewell will never trust Isolde Delamer again," reiterated Teddy. "He'd be foolish if he were to do so."

Susie stood up, walked towards Teddy and unexpectedly stretched out her arms in supplication.

"I am pleading with you," she said, softly.

Teddy sighed with exasperation. Susie looked up at him, her blue eyes open wide, a small frown creasing her forehead. The rays of the setting sun were streaming through the window from the west and were settling on her blonde hair.

"Stop this, Susie," said Teddy gently. "You are too upset to be able to think clearly. I wouldn't date that woman even if I wanted to. Romantic relationships at work are ill-advised. A big mistake."

"Then," said Susie, "you must apply for the post of deputy-head of that school so that you can watch Isolde and monitor everything that she does. Rupert wants you to accept the position anyway. He told me so."

"I'm thinking about it, Susie."

"Do more than think about it!"

"I'll think about it very carefully."

Susie returned to the sofa and sat down. She leaned forward and looked up at Teddy, giving him a coaxing smile.

"Will you come back to the manor with me now?" she asked. You could have dinner with Rupert and me. You must be hungry after travelling."

"It's kind of you to invite me, but I'm very tired, Susie. I'll stay here, tonight, if you don't mind. Rebecca has left a fridge full of food. I'll be fine."

"Rebecca?"

"She stayed here during the holiday."

"Did she? Rebecca Hampton?"

"Yes."

Susie looked away. So, the rumours had been true! Teddy and Rebecca were close!

"Well! You're tired and I must go. I'll leave you in peace," said Susie, then, affecting a brightness that she hoped would conceal her dismay. She pulled up the pink coat which had slipped off her shoulders. Teddy accompanied her to the door. He noticed that her pink handbag was tiny. He found himself smiling at what he had always judged to be her attractive femininity.

On the landing, outside the apartment, Susie said, "I'll take the stairs, rather than the lift" and she made her way towards the door that led to them, calling over her shoulder, "'Bye! I'll be in touch tomorrow!"

As Susie was about to put her hand on the door, it was pulled open from the other side by a young man, who looked as if he had been running and was out of breath.

"Sorry, love," he said and stood back, as Susie passed by.

"Louis?" exclaimed Teddy, who was still standing in his doorway, having recognised the young man as being Louis Lindsey, now the most senior member of his youth club.

"I wanted to see you, sir," said Louis, as he approached, with quick steps. "I know you can't be long back, but…"

"Come in!" said Teddy. "What's the problem?"

"I can't apply to Cambridge. I can't go there," said Louis without preamble, as soon as he was inside the apartment.

"Hang on!" Teddy began to say, but was interrupted.

"No, sir! I can't," insisted Louis. "I'm very grateful for the tuition you have given me, but, I know I can't go any further."

Teddy looked at Louis thoughtfully. The young man's eyes were devoid of their usual sparkle.

"Can you tell me why you have made this decision?" asked Teddy.

"It's my Dad. He's ill again and he needs me. I don't want to leave him in the care of strangers. He wouldn't want strangers coming into his home and neither would I, quite frankly. I think it's the thought of being left with strangers that has made him ill again and so, I feel I have no option other than to stay."

Teddy did not doubt that Louis was telling the truth, but wondered why he had been so desperate to come to tell him about his dilemma on the very evening that he, Teddy, had returned from France. It was as if Louis had been dreading telling Teddy about the problem that had developed at home and had not wanted to wait any longer, to see what his, Teddy's, reaction would be.

Teddy hid his own disappointment. He had been tutoring Louis in Maths and Physics for some months, mainly at weekends, and had hoped that Louis would eventually fulfil a dream that he had poignantly nurtured since boyhood: a dream of being accepted at Cambridge and making his Dad proud of him. The excuse Louis had given for not being able to go to fulfil the cherished dream was entirely plausible, but something about it, or perhaps the way in which it had been communicated, persuaded Teddy that there was more to the story than had been revealed. And then, he remembered young Portia Price's attachment to Louis. Would her dreams be scuppered, also, by this twist of fate?

"That's all I wanted to tell you, sir," said Louis, "I'd better go home, now, to my Dad."

"Yes. But we'll talk about this some other time."

Louis left with what Teddy judged to be an easier step and, no doubt, a lighter heart. Teddy followed him to the head of the stairs and watched him descending rapidly. Teddy, then, heard the door on the ground floor opening and he felt on his face the jet of cool, river air that had entered at that moment and had risen.

"What a night this has turned out to be!" Teddy thought to himself, as he made his way back to his apartment. Once inside, he went to the sitting-room and picked up the white mug which he had left on the floor by the window. What with Susie having behaved as if she had been auditioning, in amateurish fashion, for a rôle as a would-be Greek tragedienne and Louis having declared long-held hopes to have been dashed, the return to Liverpool had been more dramatic than he had anticipated. Teddy took the mug to the kitchen and noted again the money that Rebecca had left in the envelope on the table. Rebecca was generous in the way many Americans were, but it struck him that, by leaving it, she could additionally have been conveying to him the message that she wanted to owe him nothing. He had to be careful, of course, not to project on to her his own interpretation of her behaviour, but he could not help wondering if the money she had left was a symbol of severance: an acknowledgement of the fact that the two of them might meet again only sporadically, if at all. Teddy sighed. He would reflect on Rebecca's intentions at another time. Emotionally, as well as physically, drained now, all he wanted to do, at that moment, was to go to bed and to drift into a long sleep.

CHAPTER 26

Miss James Visits

"Down town Ellesmere Port is really different from the part where your Dad lives up in Whitby," said Portia Price in a pensive way, upon reaching the summit of Westminster Bridge, the hump-backed bridge which carried traffic over the railway line that served the pretty, rural-like station nearby. "Whitby seems to be..."

"Getting bigger?" suggested Rosalind Somerland, who was sauntering by her friend's side. "Busier?"

"Something like that," said Portia, and then was silent, as if her mind had suddenly started to wander.

It was a Saturday afternoon and the sun was shining. Having walked for three quarters of an hour from Gylen Somerland's house, amidst the tree and rose filled gardens at the other end of the Port, the two friends were slackening the pace they had set for each other in the beginning.

"Yes. Whitby is expanding," Portia went on, then, as if re-focusing on what Rosalind had said. "But beyond the bridge, the Port looks a bit desolate, really. Don't you think so?"

She stopped, to take in the appearance of the main road ahead with its buildings in mercantile, Cheshire-red brick, standing tall on either side of it. Once a busy thoroughfare, the road was now quiet, a by-pass having filtered heavy traffic away. Rosalind, who had continued walking, now looked back and waited for Portia to catch up, but Portia was leaning against the wall at the side of the bridge.

"You know, it's rather like a painting by Edward Hopper," she said. "Do you know the paintings I mean? People have written about the still atmosphere in them. It's the sort of stillness you feel before there's a thunderstorm orsomething like that. You can almost feel the heat in others and, in some of the paintings, you'd almost think that aliens from space were about to land in a rural landscape. I totally love those paintings."

"I've never heard of Edward Hopper," said Rosalind. "Anyway, are you going to walk with me or not?"

"You must have seen them," insisted Portia, standing up straight again. "You probably have seen them but you don't realise you've seen them."

Rosalind shrugged and tried to pout in the way Héloïse de Sauzon might have done, had she been present. Portia's occasional references to writers and artists with whom she, Rosalind, was not familiar annoyed her, since she disliked being ill-informed. She had recently resorted to "becoming Héloïse", in a manner of speaking, in those moments when she felt inferior to her more cultured friend, by adopting the mannerisms of the sophisticated French girl whom she had known at the Château du Crâne. Her new mode of behaviour, though, irritated Portia, in turn.

The walk over Westminster Bridge and, then, the road beyond it continued as the sun, now becoming hotter, streamed down on to the girls' heads and the buildings on either side of the road: buildings which once had been fully occupied but now, were not.

"Mum said this part of town is on the verge of becoming livelier," said Rosalind in an apologetic kind of way. "She thinks it's on the way up, in fact."

"Really? Is that why she lives down here?"

"Well! Sort of. But she said she wanted to live at this end of the Port, also, because it's secluded and clients can visit her discreetly. You know what people are like. They consult astrologers, but don't want anyone to know they've been to see one. Mum says it's normal for people to behave in that way. She doesn't bear them grudges. But I think it's awful that astrologers like her are placed in the same category as…I don't know…."

"Fairground fortune tellers?"

"Mum would be horrified if she heard you saying that!"

"I can't get used to hearing you calling Miss Laurier 'Mum'!" said Portia, quickly, while blushing a bit, as if annoyed. "I don't know how you've coped. One minute she's your teacher and the next, you find out that she's your long-lost mother and that she kept the secret from you even though she was teaching you for a year! What sort of mother could do that to her daughter? How can you be so forgiving?"

"I have no choice, Portia! What do you expect me to do? If I become angry and tell her that I never want to see her again, I'll have lost her forever. I'd rather get to know her. Anyway, she used to live in New York and in France...and she's an astrologer! She's cool!"

"Well! If you say so...but I don't know how I'll get through this lunch with her without saying something about the way she deceived you. I'll be tempted to, Rosie. She's not my teacher any longer after all."

"No! Don't! She'll think I've been talking about her! Please, Portia! Don't say anything!"

"All right, I shan't."

"Promise?"

"I promise...but I still think her behaviour was awful. I haven't forgotten, even if you have, that you said, last year, that you'd never trust her again. You know...when you told her you had a crush on Mr. Laurence and she told him what you'd said to her. She shouldn't have done that, Rosie."

"But, she was my teacher then and you know what teachers are like. They always tell each other things - don't they? - because they're never sure of what to do. Anyway, it was for the best, in the end."

"How can you say that? Mr. Laurence totally ignored you from then on and you felt dreadful!"

"No. It really was for the best, Portia. I was hanging around the science corridor and he put an end to that. He got fed-up."

"He got scared, you mean, because he was ambitious and he didn't want anything or anyone to get in the way of his promotion. Anyway, is your Mum's place much further? Where exactly are we going?"

"We turn right here."

In the residential side road in which Liz Laurier lived, there were semi-detached houses built in glossy, dark red brick in two rows facing each other. It was a quiet place. No one could be seen walking on the pavements, but cars were parked here and there.

"That's the house! Mum lives in the upper apartment," said Rosalind, pointing out a building near the entrance to the road.

"The one with Miss James' car in front of it?"

"What?"

"That's Miss James' car, Rosie."

"She must be visiting. What shall we do? Shall we just go in? Mum will tell her she's expecting up for lunch. Maybe she'll stay."

"I don't think so! She won't want to have a meal with two of her pupils, will she? She's probably just checking that your Mum is O.K. We'll just have to wait until she goes away."

"We could go to Ted's."

"Ted's?"

"It's a café around the corner, in the main road. Mum said it has been there for decades. She read about it on a web site. Shipping agents from Stuart's Wharf used to go there a lot, a long time ago."

"So, it doesn't belong to Teddy Laurence?"

"No! Of course not! Honestly, Portia! You do go on! I hope it's open."

Ted's was open.

When the two girls entered, Portia stood still for a moment or two, taking in the appearance of the long counter, the two women in summer frocks, who were drinking sodas through straws at one table and the solitary man, in a sports jacket, hovering over a cup of tea at another.

"What's wrong?" asked Rosalind.

"It reminds me of something...I know! 'Night hawks'!"

"What are you talking about?"

"'Night hawks'! A painting by Edward Hopper. I told you about him a minute ago. Sit by the window and keep watch, Rosie. I'll fetch something for us from the counter."

"What am I supposed to be watching out for?"

"Miss James' car, of course, so that we'll know when to leave! You can see the entrance to your Mum's road from here, can't you? Wake up!"

At that moment, Lynn James was making her way up the stairs to Liz Laurier's apartment. Liz greeted her at the door and led her into the sitting room, where she, Lynn, then made herself comfortable on one of the white sofas, well endowed with pale cushions. She slanted her slim legs to one side and crossed them, neatly, at the ankles. Her two tone caramel and white shoes looked both sophisticated and new and her pale bouclé skirt suit with a cardigan-style, short jacket looked simply elegant. She tossed back her long dark hair which she had left loose but which had obviously been trimmed and shaped in a professional way. "It was kind of you to see me at such short notice," she began.

"Before you say anything else, may I offer you my congratulations?" interrupted Liz. "I should have sent you a note. I'm really pleased. I wish you all the luck in the world, Lynn!"

"Thank you! I know it's not going to be an easy job. I'm only now realising why Hilary was as strict as she was. She had to be like that. People try to take advantage of perceived gentleness, assuming it's weakness. You'd be surprised at..."

"No! I wouldn't be surprised, Lynn!" Liz interrupted again.

"No. Of course not. Anyway, I shall not take up too much of your time."

"Oh! Don't hurry! Please! There's no need to. I'm expecting only my daughter and one of her school friends for lunch. Won't you join us?"

"It's kind of you to invite me, but I really do have another appointment. Thank you, though. But actually, I did want to mention your daughter. Will she be staying with her father or with you, next year? Should I amend the school register and her profile?"

"Rosalind will remain with her father. He has custody of both my children. He has kindly told me, though, that he will allow the children to visit me when they want to and whenever I'd like them to. He has behaved generously in that respect, I must say."

"Good… Good."

"Was there anything else?"

It occurred to Lynn that Liz was on edge. Had she been expecting to be admonished for her hasty departure from Bramblewell School, or more seriously, her deception in hiding her true identity from her daughter and former colleagues? Lynn decided to keep the conversation light.

"The other matter concerns Hilary Trimm" she said. "I'll have to arrange some sort of event – by the end of the session - at which the staff at Bramblewell School will be able to say 'Good-bye' to their former headmistress properly. Like you, she left in a hurry and I was wondering if you would like a separate event for yourself or if you'd like a presentation to be made to you during Hilary's event."

"Oh, Lynn!" exclaimed Liz. "How sweet of you to suggest such a thing, but an arranged event for me would be inconceivable. You know how my appointment as astrological tutor was viewed by over half the teachers in Bramblewell School! With complete horror! Teddy Laurence was appalled at first and he was not the only one!"

"So…" said Lynn, now looking slightly uncomfortable. "Not even a dinner party for a few teachers to whom you were close?"

Liz smiled.

"No, Lynn, Thank you, but I think not. I was never completely at ease in Bramblewell School. Not in the staff-room, anyway."

"The pupils will miss you."

"And I shall miss teaching them. I felt as if I had a lot to offer them. Astrology arouses one's curiosity...and not least, the desire to study so many other subjects. History! Psychology! Astronomy! By the way, I was thinking about writing a book..."

"Oh! Good! Good! I look forward to reading that," said Lynn, politely. "And now, I should go, I think. I really have taken up too much of your time."

"You were always a good friend to me Lynn. I appreciated the fact that you did not judge me harshly. Won't you wait to have one cup of coffee? I don't know why those girls are so late! They should have 'phoned!"

"Maybe they saw my car and are hanging around in the street waiting for me to go! I'll have that cup of coffee some other time Liz. It was lovely to see you again! Keep in touch! Oh, and even though you don't want your own year at Bramblewell to be recognised in any way, you will come to Hilary's party, won't you? Please! I think you'd be surprised to find how many people will be delighted to see you. Teddy will. I know he will. And so will Thetis and Anna. Give it some thought, anyway."

In Ted's café, Rosalind was sighing with impatience.

"Would you like to sit here?" she asked Portia, finally. "I'm tired of keeping watch."

"All right. But, switch quickly so that we won't miss her."

The two girls exchanged places, Portia taking up the position beside the window.

"I wish I'd brought my sun-glasses," she commented. "The light is shining into my eyes."

She leaned back in the wooden chair and stretched out her legs. She looked for a moment or two at her apple-green ballerina shoes, wondering if she should have worn them with blue jeans. Did the colours clash too much? In an absent-minded way, she sipped sarsaparilla cordial through a straw.

Rosalind's frothy coffee, in a transparent cup with a wide rim, was now cold, but she finished it off, nevertheless.

"It's very quiet," she said, then, looking around the café. "You could…"

"I could what?"

"You could meet Louis Lindsey here. You could have secret rendezvous in this café. Easily. Ellesmere Port's station is just a couple of minutes' walk away and Louis could travel there by Mersey-rail. You, yourself, could take a bus from Chester to the bus centre, near Ellesmere Port's library. Then, you could walk down to Westminster Bridge, and carry on here to Ted's. Your mother's gossipy friends would never come near this place. If they were to come to Ellesmere Port at all, they wouldn't wander any further than Cheshire Oaks, would they?"

"There's no point, Rosie."

"What do you mean?"

"I don't know…It's all going wrong."

"Why?"

"It's because of my background. I make Louis aware of all he doesn't know. It seems to bother him a lot. He thinks the Wirral is posh and that Chester is posher and that he isn't good enough for me!"

"But, that's your own fault, Portia! When you first met him - at Mr. Laurence's youth club's Christmas party - remember? - he became really annoyed with you for staring at him, while he was giving a speech, and you said to him that you were a Cheshire girl and that he was obviously not used to talking to girls like you! You might as well have said that you were superior."

"Yes. I remember all of that. But, he WAS rude, Rosie! It doesn't matter now, anyway. Maybe I should just forget him."

"Oh! Come on! You're crazy about him! And he must be crazy about you! Why else would he leave a flower on the wall beside the school gates, just because you would be walking past it?"

Portia sighed.

"I know all that, but if I make him feel awkward and unhappy…"

"Don't give up, Portia!"

"I haven't quite..."

Portia stared out of the window for a moment or two, leaning her arm on the back of her chair. Then, she sat up straight.

"There's Miss James' car," she said. "Listen, Rosie! Don't say a word to your mother about Louis! Please don't! I'd be so embarrassed. And so would he be, if he thought I had been discussing him with an astrologer."

"I shan't tell her but I bet she'd have been able to help you."

"I know, but I can't ask her. I just can't. I don't know her well enough. You are so lucky, being so close to her. She can help you with all your relationships."

"She said she'd never interfere unless she saw I'd become attached to someone whose Pluto was square, opposite or in conjunction with my Venus or Mars. Then, she'd advise me to be cautious."

"Pluto square, opposite or conjunct Venus or Mars," repeated Portia, simultaneously remembering that Louis Lindsey's Pluto at seven degrees of Sagittarius was in conjunction with her own Mars. She felt unsettled. She would think of nothing other than the Pluto - Mars connection on the way home on the bus! She was sure of that. What was to be done?

CHAPTER 27

On the Beach

It was late August and although the sun shone over Belle-Isle, as it had done all summer, there was, in the air, a tingle of freshness that made the island's young aware of the fact that the start of the autumn term at school – la rentrée - was imminent. Soon, the long days of freedom would be used up and time on the beaches and in cafés would be limited and largely replaced by hours of concentrated studying.

Marie-Colette de Sauzon, who was approaching the age of sixteen, was walking on the shore near her family's château, the Château de Sauzon, trying not to think of the scholastic term that would begin soon and the daunting, highly pressured year that would follow. To distract herself, she watched the waves rippling on to the sand and then, sliding away again, while she thought, wistfully, of the way her sister, Jacqueline, after throwing off her canvas espadrilles, would have danced along the edge of the water lightly, when she had been happy and younger. Jacqueline's best friend, Jacqui, would have invariably been with her, laughing as he watched her. They had been inseparable, the two of them. Now they were twenty and married and living in Paris. Or rather, Jacqueline was living in Paris, while Jacqui was still in Brittany. Their lives had altered and Marie-Colette could scarcely believe the extent to which the two of them had changed in character, also. Jacqueline was so serious now, so grown up and stylishly Parisian in her tastes. She read novels written by fashionable modern authors, listened to the music of Jacques Loussier and talked about Left Bank café society, repeatedly. Jacqui, for his part, had become rather distant.

Although Marie-Colette had always been closer to Héloïse than to Jacqueline -only two years separated her from Héloïse in age, whereas Jacqueline was four years older - she longed for the return of the sensitive Jacqueline, the old Jacqueline, who had been romantic in her literary tastes, loving the lengthy novels written in the nineteenth century and the poetry of Verlaine. When Jacqueline had initially left home, to spend a gap year between school and university in Liverpool, Marie- Colette had missed her presence from home so deeply that she had found the year hard to endure. She would go into Jacqueline's empty room in the château in order to remove the tops of the bottles of sun-protection lotion, the jars of face cream and the tiny pots of lip balm which Jacqueline had habitually used, in order to release into the air their mingled scents. In that way, she could pretend that Jacqueline was still using them and was, therefore, not far away. She would, even now, seek refuge in Jacqueline's old room on evenings when Maman had scolded her at dinner for saying something illogical or stupid. But, despite the way Maman sometimes spoke to her, Marie-Colette did not want to leave home, as her sisters had. She did not like change: she wanted childhood, or rather the teen years, to last indefinitely. She wanted to be protected by the strong walls of the Château de Sauzon and had no desire to venture out into the daunting world beyond, in order to experience what it, the world, had to offer. Naturally, she had not wanted any of her siblings to leave home either and sometimes she felt a sense of desperation overwhelming her when she was forced to accept that two had already gone and possibly would return only for brief stays.

Héloïse, although loyal, had not always understood how stressful Marie-Colette's shyness and apparent passivity were. The expression of her, Héloïse's compassion, when offered, had always been less emotionally charged than that of Jacqueline. She would say, in a cool and detached way, "You mustn't worry about Maman's criticisms. She means well but doesn't realise how hurtful her words can be. Accept that deficiency in her understanding and do your best to please her." Jacqueline, however, had always tended to respond with obvious sympathy, a consoling "Chérie! Ne t'en fais pas!" and, the offer of, perhaps, a gentle book to read. The two sisters, Jacqueline and Héloïse, were different in nature and cerebral direction and yet, both, with their sparkling, amber-brown eyes and long, blonde hair, streaming like pale golden water down their backs, possessed the confidence their obvious beauty endowed. Marie-Colette's long dark hair and eyes as deep blue as the ocean intensified her feeling of being different and of being socially clumsy. When she looked in a mirror, she was unable to acknowledge her own attractiveness, seeing, inaccurately, only awkwardness and flaws. She wanted to be confident and clever and articulate, but her undermining shyness made her heart pound and her voice weak, whenever she tried to behave in the easy way her sisters did, when among strangers. Héloïse, no doubt desiring to help her to overcome her handicap, had suggested she visit the Château du Crâne, during the last days of filming. "Why not come for a day or two before your return to school," she had said. "The break will do you good." Héloïse had not mentioned the fact that it had been Pierre Laurier's idea that Marie- Colette visit, after seeing her photo. Pierre had thought that Marie-Colette would be ideal for the rôle of Angélique's grandmother, since, despite her dark hair, she resembled Héloïse enough in looks to play the part of the grandmother in the film, convincingly. Héloïse had not informed Marie-Colette, in advance, of what the real purpose of the visit would be, since she knew the girl would be disconcerted if she thought she would be closely scrutinised.

"Listen, Pierre," Héloïse had said. "Marie Colette is very sensitive. She is the sort of girl who thinks she hears the whispers of the dead outside, in the dark, on Christmas Eve. You are Breton, yourself. You know what I am talking about. Maman always tells her not to be so silly, but Papa then interrupts to say, 'Let her be. She has a Breton soul. You do not understand.' But, you would understand her, wouldn't you Pierre? She is not the sort of girl you would allow to attend a 'noz-veil', for example, on the night someone died. You will speak to her gently, won't you? I hope you won't shout!"

"Shout?"

"Yes. Shout! And furthermore, should you offer her a rôle in the film, kindly remember that you will not be able to film her during term time. Scholastically, the year ahead will be a crucial one for her."

"I had intended to film her scenes at Easter, anyway."

"In Brittany?"

"No.No. In the Hebrides."

"The Hebrides?"

"Yes. Is there anything else that you want to say?"

"It's just that Maman will have to be told…"

"Mademoiselle, that, I regret, will be your problem. I have done enough."

Realising that Pierre had become irritated and not wanting to arouse his temper, Héloïse had said no more, but the thought of how she would approach Maman with the news that another of her daughters was to be an actress now began to trouble her. How would Maman react, should Marie-Colette be enthusiastic about appearing in the film? Héloïse had decided not to think about that problem until it arose. After all, how likely was it that Marie-Colette would agree to the proposition?

Marie-Colette ran along the sand. The waves were now reaching her slim, sun-tanned ankles, under her rolled-up jeans. She began to think about a message she had received from Héloïse a few days previously. It had contained the suggestion that she, Marie-Colette, join Héloïse for the last few days that would be spent filming at the Château du Crâne. Marie-Colette wanted to go, but the thought of travelling to Bordeaux on her own made her feel ill at ease. On the other hand, how difficult could such a journey be? After all, Bordeaux was simply one train journey away, after she had reached Paris, where Jacqueline would be waiting.

Héloïse would meet her at the Gare Saint-Jean de Bprdeaux. It would be easy.

The sun was obscured by a cloud. Marie-Colette stopped to turn to look in the direction of Sauzon. Maybe she would, now, go to the café, where Jacqueline would once have gone, with Jacqui, to drink tea with lemon. She, Jacqueline, would say, later, that she had pretended to be a Russian ballerina, from a century past, visiting Sarah Bernhardt, at her holiday retreat in Belle-Isle. She had quite an imagination! Smiling at that recollection, Marie-Colette braced herself. She hated going into a café on her own and drawing to herself the looks of other teenagers whom she did not know well. But, maybe she could do what Jacqueline habitually had done, when growing up. Maybe she could pretend to be someone else: someone poised and graceful. In any case, she could try. She was nearly sixteen. It was time she tried to conquer her debilitating shyness. She had to become more rational. Perhaps she would never be as Cartesian as Héloïse was, but she could make an attempt to apply enough logic to make life more manageable.

Marie-Colette set off in the direction of Sauzon, saying to herself, "I am a Russian ballerina. I am poised. And I am going to drink tea!" To her surprise, she began to feel calmer. Had she, out of the blue, hit upon a psychological technique that could help her? If she had, maybe the year ahead would be bearable.

CHAPTER 28

Julian's Inheritance

"Another fine morning," thought Julian Bramblewell - Eurlinn, looking out of the window of his study in the Château du Crâne, while simultaneously smiling as it occurred to him that, mentally, he was still in England. There, in his own country, he could not count on one lovely day following another with the degree of certainty that he could in the south-west of France. In Bordeaux, morning brightness would develop into heat, predictably, day after day, it seemed to him. Only occasionally, out of the blue, would there be a cloudburst, followed by a fall of what Julian considered to be the most surprisingly warm rain: rain which enlivened his senses and heightened his appreciation of the natural world. Julian had discovered that even the sharp scent of nettle leaves could be rendered sweeter by rainfall of the Bordelais type.

While Julian was looking up at the sky, down in the courtyard of the château, her pale golden hair shining in the early rays of sunshine, Héloïse de Sauzon was walking, or rather, sauntering, as if heading in the direction of the arched passage that led to the drawbridge across the moat. She caught Julian's eye, of course, but he could not help himself from suspecting that it was her intention to attract his attention. After all, there was no reason for her to be up at such an early hour. Although filming was still continuing at the château, the scenes in which Héloïse appeared had already been completed and there was no need for her to arise at dawn. And clothed in a long gown, comprised of floating white chiffon, she was not dressed for morning exercise. Knowing that Julian would possibly see her through his window, was it not likely that she was parading her beauty for his benefit? Teddy Laurence had gone away. Was that why she was trying to stir up the emotions of another beau? How unsubtle she was, though! And how disappointing!

Julian turned away. He was drawn to Héloïse's beauty- who would not be? - but the fineness of character that he had previously attributed to her was beginning to appear to have been misplaced. Initially, he had reckoned that she had the potential, at least, to be an interesting companion in conversation, but he had begun to realise that, logical though her mind was, it lacked some of the depth that only wide reading could provide. No doubt he was being over-critical, though. How likely was it that she would have read the books with which he, himself, was familiar, when, naturally, she would have been drawn to the works of French writers who were mostly unknown to him.

Julian sat down at the desk where he would sit most mornings. On it, he had already placed maps and books - including a very old copy of Cocks and Féret- which he intended to peruse. He was anxious to study the history of the vineyards of Bordeaux and those across the river, in the Saint - Emilion and Libournais areas. He already knew that, on the traditionally aristocratic left bank of the river, the Cabernet Sauvignon and Sauvignon Franc grapes were favoured. On the right bank, Merlot predominated. But those were just the ones that were used to make red wine. There were, also, Sauvignon Blanc and Sémillon grapes that required study: those that were pressed into the production of white wine. The soil and the climate affected them all, of course. In a word: the terroir.

Julian had walked on the land around the Château du Crâne on many occasions, but now he realised he had never read any documents or books about the composition of its soil. Was it predominantly of sand or limestone or gravel? He wanted to know. He had imagined that he could detect traces of straight lines in the ground, suggesting that the château had once had a vineyard of its own. He had wondered when it had been in use, if, indeed, it had existed. In the pre-revolutionary era? Surely, if a vineyard had existed as far back as the 18th century, though, traces of it would not be seen still in the ground. The soil, over time, would have levelled itself. No. Had a vineyard existed, it would have had to have been cultivated in times more recent than that. Yet, when his grandmother had bought the château from the Counts du Crâne, who had owned it in indivision, there had been no suggestion of an old vineyard or the traces of an old vineyard having been a part of the sale. Julian had questioned his mother about the existence of vines, but she had been unable to provide any answers.

"Are you considering resurrecting a vineyard?" she had asked him, instead. "It would take years to do it and would be labour-intensive. When I hand over the château to you, formally, you will have to find another way to make money - and jolly quickly too. I'm relying on you to think of something." Julian sighed as he reflected on his mother's words. Perhaps he was being over-romantic in thinking he could have a vineyard of his own, but that morning, he thought there would be no harm in finding out what the process of wine-making would involve. There was so much to understand about the practice of viticulture, though, and so many French terms, like coulure, floraison and pourriture grise, which had to be fully investigated.

Feeling restless, Julian stood up and made his way towards the window again. Héloïse had not walked towards the drawbridge, after all. She was, instead, sitting on the ground, opposite Julian's window, and leaning against the wall of the château. Her head was held up to the sun, as if she were sun-bathing. Surely, she who was so focused on the way she looked knew that soft, feminine, facial skin could not stand up to extreme exposure to the direct rays of the sun. No doubt she had applied a protecting lotion, but even so, she was being rather reckless. Why was she behaving in that way, anyway? Was she waiting for him to lean out of his window to call, "Hi!"? Julian balked at such an obvious attempt on her part to attract his attention. Had the girl no shame? Or was this just the opening move in another elaborate jeu de l'amour?

It occurred to Julian that marked differences were evident in the way he would expect an educated British girl to behave and the way Héloïse was behaving. No doubt the differences had their origins in culture. But, frankly, he preferred the straightforwardness of the British girls he knew. And yet, he could not help being intrigued by the increasingly alluring Héloïse. She looked like a mediaeval princess in her contrived and recherché apparel. He began to wonder what sorts of music she liked. Who were her favourite composers? The romantics of the 19th century? Or ones who were more cerebrally challenging?

Julian pushed away a lock of golden hair that had fallen into his eyes as he watched the beautiful girl who was sitting still in the sunshine. Could he marry her? One advantage that she possessed, he reminded himself, was the fact that she had been brought up in a château. She would not, therefore, find the running of the Château du Crâne daunting: it would be just like home. But was this enough to ensure compatibility in a long-lasting relationship - or would the lack of emotional rapport lead ultimately to the rapid collapse of the union, were, in fact, Héloïse to consent to marry him, one day? Would the differences in their expectations lead to indifference and a slow drifting into separation? Maybe the two of them would end up living in different wings of the château.

Julian suddenly turned and hit the table at which he had been previously sitting, as if an important idea had unexpectedly revealed itself to him. Separation! Of course! Would it not be possible to divide the Château du Crâne into separate apartments, so as to provide accommodation for tourists? Or longer-term residents? Would such a venture be financially viable? Crudely put, would he make money out of it? Consumed with a new excitement, Julian sat down and took sheets of paper out of a drawer in his desk. He would have to talk to his mother's French lawyers of course and perhaps, an acquaintance at the Kedge Business School, but his idea was surely a sound one. Julian began to draw rough plans and make calculations. Héloïse, sitting outside in the courtyard, was forgotten.

CHAPTER 29

Héloïse Regrets

Héloïse de Sauzon knew that her behaviour, over a period of more than a year, had been out of character, in the sense that it had been at odds with that of the emotionally-controlled, academically inclined girl she had once been and, in essence, still was. In her - admittedly few - conversations with Teddy Laurence and in her increasingly intriguing encounters with Julian Bramblewell-Eurlinn, she believed she had been propelled into play-acting. It was as if she had decided, on an unconscious level, to adopt the mannerisms and speech of some imagined young woman: one whom she had, ultimately, not respected and in whose company she had felt uncomfortable. But it occurred to her, now, that she had been behaving in that way because she had not known, instinctively, what to say or what to do or how to react to prompts and, therefore, she had felt obliged to make an ill-conceived attempt at flirting. Flirting! What a fool! Reflecting on her behaviour, Héloïse felt demeaned, but also puzzled. What was she to do now? Without appearing to be excessively forward, how should she encourage Julian to deepen their friendship, if indeed, their friendship still existed? She was French, though! She should know how to behave by instinct, or at least, she should have learnt how to, by now, through mere observation of other women! But the rules of the game had been, and still were. unknown to her. Of course, the fact that she was thinking of the establishment of a relationship as "a game" pointed to a certain shallowness in her approach. Maybe Julian would respect her more if she were to be simply honest in the expression of her feelings. What had she to lose, after all? Initially, he had shown an interest in her. But, although he was still faultlessly polite when speaking to her, he had suddenly become detached and cool. As a consequence, she had become alarmed. What if she had lost him forever? When that thought had struck her, she had felt a panic arising within.

It was late in the afternoon. Héloïse knew that, by parading around, earlier in the day, in the courtyard of the Château du Crâne, she must havelooked like a feather-brained coquette. She had been hoping that Julian might have caught a glimpse of her through a window, if he had been working in his rooms. But what had she expected him to do? Had she hoped he would race downstairs to run towards her and sweep her off her feet? Julian, if he had seen her, would probably have glanced away, giving a shrug that indicated indifference. Or contempt.

Héloïse shivered visibly. She would have to pull herself together - not least because Marie-Colette would be arriving in Bordeaux soon and then, she, Héloïse, would have to resume her rôle as the wise, emotionally-stable sister. And, before Marie-Colette's arrival, she would have to try to persuade Julian to revise his opinion of her, because she could not behave normally when dealing with Marie-Colette, if her mind was weighed down with her guilt over the way she had mis-managed her relationship with the golden-haired, English heir to the Château du Crâne.

Héloïse's brain was never at its sharpest during the afternoon and so she decided to wait until evening before approaching Julian. She thought it likely that she would see him at dinner and, therefore, she dressed with care beforehand, after deciding to wear a short, white dress with white shoes. She left her hair casually loose, but brushed it until it looked like blonde silk. And then, although her heart was fluttering, she set off for the stairs which led down to the dining hall, holding her head up, in order to look as if she had not lost any of her confidence.

Julian was already in the hall, sitting at a long table, engaged in conversation with Pierre Laurier and members of the film crew. Héloïse wondered if she should saunter towards their table in order to join them. But immediately, she thought the better of doing so. It struck her that Julian might find such a move unseemly, somehow. Too casual. Or too "needy": a word which she had once heard an English girl using. She had realised, instinctively, what it had meant. She would sit elsewhere and wait to be noticed. She sat at an empty table, where Julian's view of her would not be obscured by others and where she could pretend to be preoccupied with studying the baguettes, tubs of yoghurt and fresh fruit on a long table near to her.

Pasta soup and omelette aux fines herbes were on the menu that evening. Héloïse drank the soup and ate the omelette without paying much attention to them. Her heart had now started to thump. Why was Julian having this effect on her? She felt so much younger than she actually was. And gauche. And silly. Then, Julian stood up. Oh no! He was preparing to leave and he had not thrown as much as a glance in her direction! How could she draw his attention to her? She stood, also, and made her way to the table on which the bread was displayed. She pretended to be looking for a baguette that had already been cut into pieces. She picked up a pot of yoghurt instead. She was hoping she would hear Julian saying, "Hello!" and she was preparing to spin round as if startled and then, to respond with a smile. But, by giving a quick sideways look, she saw that he was leaving the room with Pierre Laurier. Had he not noticed her? Or worse, had he noticed her and had decided not to say "Hello"?

Héloïse remained in the dining hall for a while, slowly eating yoghurt with a small spoon. What should she do? Return to her room or knock on Julian's door and hope he would be in the mood to chat to her? She left the dining hall and hesitated. Then, purposefully, she made her way in the direction of Julian's rooms. She stood outside the heavy wooden door behind which she knew he would be working at his desk and she tried to compose herself and to decide what she was going to say. Then, the door flew open.

"Héloïse!"

"I was just going to knock on the door."

"Come in."

"Were you going somewhere?"

"Only to talk to Pierre about something, but it doesn't matter. Come in."

Héloïse entered the room, noticing at once the pile of maps and books on the desk, in front of the window. Had Julian been sitting there, that morning, he would have seen her."

"Julian…about this morning…" she started to say.

"Please, sit down."

"No. I don't want to waste your time. You are busy. I just wanted to explain that, this morning…You must have seen me and…"

"Having had an early start and, then, being in need of a rest, you thought you would sit in the sun rather than be cooped up in your bedroom. Isn't that right?"

"Yes…Yes. That's right."

"Englishmen could be so diplomatic! She should have known Julian would be gallant. He must have suspected, from observing her dejected expression, what she had been about to say. Understanding that she was in a state of anxiety, he had helped her, by providing an excuse for her behaviour.

"I…" she began, in a chastened way, but then, realising that Julian had indicated, in fact, that he had wanted to keep the tone of the conversation light, she said, impulsively:

"If you are ever in Paris, please do stay with my sister, Jacqueline, in her apartment on the Left Bank. She is alone so much and I'm sure she would love to have your company. You would be doing her a favour. I'll mention to her the fact that I've invited you and I'm sure she'll be pleased. I'd be pleased, too, of course."

Had she gone too far in hinting that she wanted to stay in touch with Julian? He seemed not to have interpreted her words in that way.

"It's very kind of you to make that suggestion," he said gravely.

"Well! You're busy…and so, I'll leave you, for the present."

"Don't let the sight of the books on my desk chase you away."

"I'd better…I'll leave you. Yes…Until tomorrow. A demain!"

Julian nodded and Héloïse made for the door. She thought he would stop her, but he did not. Still, the encounter had not been as painful as she had imagined it would be. And although he had not said he would stay with Jacqueline, he had not said, either, that he would not. Maybe, he would, in fact, give her, Héloïse, a chance to reclaim his respect and interest, in time. She would have to think about her next move with care, though."

CHAPTER 30

Consternation

When Talitha Appleby awoke, she looked up at the ceiling, in a disoriented sort of way for a moment or two, before she remembered that she was in Portia Price's parents' house in Chester and not in her own parents' rented apartment in New York. She had been invited to stay at Portia's for a week or so, prior to the start of the new term at Bramblewell School, and although she had already been there for two days, she had not yet become accustomed to her new surroundings and the house rules. Therefore, once fully alert, she rose quickly, not wanting to appear to be an inconsiderate guest. Besides, on that morning, a Saturday morning, she knew that she would be accompanying Portia to Bramblewell Manor to have a look at the early sketches for the dresses she and Portia, as well as Rosalind Somerland and Ida Traversi, would be wearing as bridesmaids at Susie Sutton's wedding in the spring. Rosalind had also been asked to go to the manor that morning, but Ida, who was still in Italy, would have to meet the seamstress on another occasion.

The session at Bramblewell Manor, which began promptly at ten o' clock, went well, in fact. Made of a heavy material, the dresses were to be long, straight, fitted and white, although not quite as white as Susie's sparkling gown, which would be studded with little crystals. Rosalind wondered if Susie had disingenuously chosen to dress up girlishly, imagining herself as a doll-like princess, or if she had calculated that her dress would enhance the dramatic impact a bride always had when she appeared in a semi-dark church. A little of both, perhaps. It was obvious, on that Saturday morning, that Susie, in any case, was impressively paying attention to every aspect of the mise en scène, as it were.

Once the girls had finished examining the sketches, Susie looked at the three of them in a thoughtful kind of way, for a moment or two, as if wondering if she had forgotten some aspect of their appearance. Then, as if unexpectedly exhilarated, she exclaimed, "Shoes! Your shoes! I thought you might like white satin ones with kitten heels! What do you say?"

"Oh! Lovely!" said Portia, approvingly. She was already envisaging herself following Susie down the aisle of the cathedral, her own Cleopatra-dark hair dressed with green leaves and white flowers, her hands and arms in long, white gloves, her bearing, imperious. She would feel like a debutante at her first society ball and she was now finding it difficult to conceal how thrilled she was. She was determined to appear to be calm, though. She feared that if she were to look too emotionally stirred, she would seem to be unsophisticated and somewhat naïve and naivety was not a trait of character with which Portia wanted to be associated. Appearances had to be kept up!

Noticing that Portia had brought a bag of books with her and that Talitha had been carrying a sketch pad, Susie, during the light buffet lunch she had arranged for the girls in one of the manor's dining rooms, after the seamstress's departure, asked them where they were planning to go, during the afternoon. Their intention, Rosalind explained, had been to go down to the River Dee, to sit and to watch the swans floating by, probably.

"You could stay here, though!" exclaimed Susie, as if reluctant to let them leave. "Why don't you look for a shady spot by the little lake in the grounds? You know where it is, don't you? You could come back into the manor for afternoon tea with me at four o' clock. Would that suit you? Please! I'd like you to!"

It was difficult to refuse any request made by warm-hearted, generous Susie, especially since - as Portia was to point out later - a hint of loneliness could be detected in her voice. The girls, therefore, made their way towards the extensive stretches of lawns and gardens surrounding the manor, carrying with them the grey and white, woollen blanket which Susie had insisted they take with them. They placed the blanket on the ground in the shade of a large oak tree and then, they all sat down on it. Talitha, her back against the tree's trunk and her sketch book resting against her hunched up knees, started to draw, her source of inspiration not being the verdant scene before her, one rendered vital by the light of the sun, but rather, one of her favourite characters from a previous era: Chatterton, the doomed, young poet. From time to time, Rosalind glanced at what she was drawing with admiration, but also, with some dismay.

"It's a very good picture, but it's so sad," she commented finally.

"It's based on the Wallis painting in Tate Britain," Talitha explained. "There's nothing original about my sketch really. I'm just copying from memory."

She, then, pulled another page from the back of her sketch pad.

"I like what I've drawn here better," she said.

Seeing Rosalind's questioning expression, she added:

"It's Steerforth from 'David Copperfield'. Steerforth, on the beach."

"Another tragic character?" Rosalind was about to say aloud, but then did not, in case the comment would sound disapproving. On the other hand, she did disapprove. She was concerned about the fact that Talitha had become attracted to the concept of sadness in youth. A healthy, half-American golden girl, who had not long before been full of a joyful enthusiasm for living, Talitha had now become worryingly introspective. Rosalind thought, though, that it had been touching to see the way she, Talitha, had pretended to be happy while in the presence of Susie earlier in the day, not wanting to spoil the atmosphere in the room. It had been obvious to Rosalind, too, that Talitha had simply been playing the part of the high-spirited school-girl, in order to please and to fit in.

Rosalind knew that Talitha had been deeply shocked during the previous year by the news that had been given to her about her parents' financial difficulties: news which had come out of the blue like a bolt of lightning. However, thanks to the money that had been transferred to her by Pierre Laurier, in acknowledgement of her contribution to the plot of "The Quest of Angélique", her school fees would be covered until it was time for her to leave Bramblewell. She would no longer have to fear that she would be required to quit her school and her friends in order to move to America and an educational system with which she was not familiar. Perhaps what had happened to her parents, though, had left a residue of darkness within, along with the de-stabilising realisation that nothing in life was certain.

"Would you like to go to art college?" asked Rosalind suddenly, in an attempt to encourage her friend to focus on a positive goal.

"I'm not good enough," was the answer, but it was uttered as a plain statement rather than an expression of regret. "I wanted to be a ballerina, once," Talitha went on, "but I don't think I'm good enough to be a dancer, either. Not even in the corps de ballet. I think I'm more likely to end up like Meg in 'Good Wives.' You know...staying at home and making jelly and baking cookies and stuff. I'd need a husband, of course. You wouldn't think I'd wasted my education if I just married, would you?"

Rosalind, taken aback, frowned as if considering her response, but before she could reply, Portia, who was looking in the direction of the small lake a short distance away, cheerfully said:

"There's Julian! You could marry someone like him, Talitha. You know...like an American lady in one of Edith Wharton's books."

Following Portia's gaze, Rosalind saw Julian Bramblewell-Eurlinn, deep in conversation with Lord Bramblewell, at the water's edge.

"What do you think they are talking about?" asked Talitha.

"I don't know," answered Rosalind, in a vague sort of way. "The château in France?"

"Or Héloïse?" suggested Portia.

Rosalind wondered if there was something Portia knew that she, herself, did not know. Had Portia's comment been a shot in the dark, only?

Portia said nothing more, though. She shrugged. Julian was looking in the direction of the oak tree and so, she lifted her arm and waved. Julian turned away, as if to say "Good-bye" to Lord Bramblewell and then, started to head across the grass towards the girls. With his blond hair shining in the sunlight, his jeans very blue, his shirt very white, he looked rather magnificent, Rosalind thought. She sighed and looking down at the book she had been reading: *Dusty Answer.* She wondered how the writer, Rosamond Lehmann, would have described Julian. With unforgettable sensitivity, she reckoned.

"He's very nice," said Talitha, somewhat wistfully.

Rosalind nodded.

"He's more your type and Portia's, Rosalind," Talitha continued. "I'm not bright enough."

"He's Héloïse's type," stated Rosalind firmly. "At least, I think so."

"Hi, Julian!" she called then, as if signalling to Talitha that the conversation was at an end.

The young scion of the House of Bramblewell-Eurlinn came closer.

"Room for me?" he asked, as he reached the girls, but in such a way as to suggest that he would not mind were the answer to be "No."

"Of course!" Rosalind answered quickly, moving books out of the way. "You mustn't sit on the grass, Julian. No matter how fine the weather, the ground will always be cold and very bad for you. That's what Susie said."

Julian smiled in acquiescence, as he sat down on the edge of Susie's blanket, without comment. But, his expression became immediately quizzical as he noticed the books Rosalind and Portia were reading.

"Rosamond Lehmann's *Dusty Answer* is presumably a romantic novel for a thoughtful girl," he said, "but Portia, I'd not have thought that 'Game of Spies' by Paddy Ashdown would have been the sort of book you'd normally read."

"Actually, I can't put it down," said Portia. "It's about Bordeaux in World War II. Rosalind's mother gave it to Rosalind and Rosalind has lent it to me. I'm a bit shocked by it. Civilians during that war must have been under an enormous strain in Bordeaux. They couldn't trust anyone. Honestly! You wouldn't believe…"

"Oh! I think I could," interrupted Julian. "War places everyone under unbearable pressure. Some never recover."

"Before I read the book myself," said Rosalind, "I didn't know that people were so changed by war. Really changed."

"War is best avoided, Rosie," said Julian looking grim, but uttered not another word on that subject. Instead, he leaned towards Talitha to look at her drawing. "Chatterton? Gosh! His was a very sad tale," he said.

"My mother once told me," said Rosalind, "that if she could save one young person from falling into despair - just one - she would think that all the years she had spent studying astrology - and all the abusive or scathing comments that had been directed at her because of her interest in astrology - would have been worthwhile."

"Abusive comments," said Julian, thoughtfully, "are another way of waging war. Words can inflict serious wounds."

"That never mend," added Talitha.

Portia and Rosalind, both unsettled by Talitha's comment, exchanged a look, as if wondering what sorts of memories hovered in the mental hinterland of the friend they thought they knew. Then, Portia, adopting an uppity tone, said:

"That's why high brow culture is so important. Do you remember, Rosie, that your mother, when she was teaching at Bramblewell, used to say that Libra, the sign of culture, elegance and beauty was opposite Aries, the sign of conquest, in all its forms and that one was a balance for the other? An antidote for the excesses of the other? We spent this morning talking about dresses and shoes and it might have seemed to you to have been a superficial way to spend the time, Julian, but actually. I don't think it was. The creation of beauty is terribly important. I think so, anyway. Your mother would say so, too, wouldn't she, Rosie? That's why Lorenzo the Magnificent, at the time of the Italian Renaissance, became a patron of artists, sculptors, poets and musicians and..."

Portia did not finish the sentence, realising she must have sounded as if she had been showing off.

Rosalind noticed that Julian was smiling in a gentle but bemused way.

It crossed Rosalind's mind, then, that Julian probably considered all three of them, Portia, Talitha and herself, to be terribly young. A bit like ingénues, or kid sisters, who still had a long way to travel on the road to sophistication. What did he think of Héloïse, though? Had Paddy Ashdown's book brought memories of Bordeaux and, by association, Héloïse, to mind? At that moment, Rosalind rather wished Portia had left the book at home.

Julian was now leaning on his elbow, very close to Rosalind. She suddenly felt tempted to touch his arm, as if to suggest that she was not a child, but a young woman with feelings. But then, she remembered that she had read, in *Dusty Answer* that the perceived forwardness of the heroine had been judged to have been unbecoming, by a young man in that book, and so, she kept very still instead. She did not want Julian to think she was "easy". She knew, also, that she owed a certain loyalty to Héloïse, since they were friends, and Héloïse was obviously enamoured of Julian. On that warm Cheshire day, though, with Julian beside her, Rosalind felt trapped by those ties of loyalty that were binding her to her French friend. Putting down her romantic novel, she sighed in a way that was both angry and dispirited. Julian looked at her in surprise. Rosalind wondered what he was really thinking. Would she ever know?

CHAPTER 31

Destination: Bordeaux

It occurred to Jacqueline de Sauzon, having been summoned to the door of her apartment by a hesitant ringing of the bell, that her youngest sister, Marie-Colette, who was standing on the threshold, had turned into a young girl of intriguing attractiveness, within the period of a few months. Marie-Colette had always been pretty, but her prettiness was on the point of evolving into a more mature and mysterious beauty, Jacqueline thought. Outwardly, at that moment, there was no evidence of that shyness that habitually made life difficult for the girl and placed pressure on her nerves. Jacqueline hoped that her other sister, Héloïse, had been right in assuming that simply by playing a part in the film which was in the process of being directed by Pierre Laurier at the Château du Crâne, Marie-Colette would blossom, shedding her fears and feelings of insignificance, as she turned her head to face the cameras. And with her silky, dark brown hair, tumbling down her back in waves and the irises of her eyes looking navy blue, one minute, and violet the next, she was surely capable of dazzling a spectator by appearance alone, in the way a beautiful, dark rose, leaning over water might.

Relief could be seen appearing in the navy blue eyes as Marie-Colette stepped into Jacqueline's apartment: the relief of a girl entering a place of sanctuary. Jacqueline led the way to the kitchen.

"Café au lait?" she asked.

"Please," answered Marie-Colette, sitting down at the kitchen table, while casting a glance around the room. "It's pretty," she added.

Jacqueline smiled, but sadly. Had the kitchen looked anything other than pretty, Marie-Colette would have said something complimentary, nonetheless. "It's so cosy" or "It's homely." She had adopted the habit of doling out compliments, her policy apparently being one of appeasement, in order to deflect real or imagined hostility.

After enquiring if the trip from Brittany to the French capital had been smooth and having received polite assurances that the journey had been pleasant, Jacqueline sat down opposite her sister: a sister who was now trembling. Perhaps she was simply winding down after being on edge during her solitary journey, or maybe she was beginning to dread what lay ahead: a journey to a place unknown alone. Had Héloïse been thinking sensibly when she had invited Marie-Colette to visit the film set and meet Pierre Laurier? Might Marie-Colette, in fact, be ill-equipped to play the part Héloïse hoped she would play in the film? Was she, frankly, too Breton, too psychically inclined, to accept a rôle that would evoke, forcefully, memories of books read and stories heard about ghosts and spirits? Could the mingling of two cultures, Breton and Gaelic, produce disturbances that Marie-Colette, being fragile, would not be able to handle? Jacqueline knew that Héloïse would scoff at such an idea, but being more sensitive and less Cartesian than Héloïse, she, herself, felt ill at ease.

Jacqueline pondered, then, on the part Marie-Colette would be asked to play. What if it was a mistake to think she would be overwhelmed by the challenge of playing the part of Angélique's grandmother as a young woman? Perhaps her extreme sensitivity, after all, would help her to convey the inner anguish of a young woman bearing an unborn child who was being abandoned by the equally youthful, Jacobite father of the child. Would she be able to put enough vehemence into her voice as she called out the words of the curse, though? Would those words be tinged with the modicum of regret that would show that the young woman had once loved the young man who was leaving her to a fate that would be characterised by poverty and social opprobrium? Would

Marie-Colette's words, indeed, be able to convey the woman's anguish as well as her thirst for revenge? Suddenly, Jacqueline, herself, shivered as the thought crossed her mind that Marie-Colette's body might be invaded by the ghost of the abandoned woman, but she banished the thought from her mind at once. It was ridiculous.

Jacqueline, helped by Jeanne, a girl who worked as a cook in a café in the Saint-Germain area, and whose services Jacqueline had hired for one morning, had already partly prepared a meal for Marie-Colette. Jacqueline now served the first part - a clear soup - while she finished off cooking a roasted chicken, green beans, shallots, and potatoes au gratin. "There is a salad and fresh fruit,also," she said. "Eat what you want."

Later, Marie-Colette was shown the room that would be hers. It was comfortable rather than classically elegant. A bolster and numerous, white pillows were piled up on the bed. A tall, glass vase of mixed blossoms stood on the dressing table and a couple of soft toys - a teddy bear and a rag doll, both being souvenirs of Jacqueline's sojourn in England - were sitting on a chair.

"Did you do all this, yourself?" asked Marie-Colette, as if not believing Jacqueline was capable of housecraft.

"I had a little help," said Jacqueline disingenuously. Jeanne, the girl from the café, had helped with the laundry as well as the cooking, but Jacqueline did not want to admit to Marie-Colette that she was finding housework draining because Jacqui was not present to provide a reason for doing it impressively well. "University classes have not started, obviously," Jacqueline went on. "I have plenty of time to devote to the decoration of the apartment."

Of course she had plenty of time. Jacqui had not been in Paris for a month. His telephone calls had been irregular; his text messages, rare. Jacqueline knew he would be finding studying at the college in Lanvéoc-Poulmic difficult. But, she was his wife! He should not have been neglecting her to the extent he had been.

At that moment, Jacqueline wished she could confide in Marie-Colette in the way she would once have confided in Héloïse, but Marie-Colette was not the sort of sister with whom Jacqueline could exchange confidences. She was, as yet, incapable of mature judgement and would feel unstable and unhappy were Jacqueline to talk about her own fears. Were Héloïse present, in the place of Marie-Colette, it would be possible to reveal that all was not well. She, Jacqueline, would be able, too, to talk about caring, intelligent Teddy Laurence as Héloïse would understand how she felt. Héloïse, after all, had started to hint that she, herself, had been beginning to appreciate Teddy's qualities.

Coldly, the realisation hit Jacqueline then, like hail-stones out of season, that Héloïse might have been trying to tell her that she, Héloïse, had fallen for Teddy Laurence and that her feelings had been reciprocated. Surely not, though! Surely Teddy would not have wanted to become involved with the Sauzon family again! Not after the way she, Jacqueline, had treated him! Or would he? How could she find out what Héloïse had been on the point of divulging? How could she uncover, in fact, what had been happening at the Château du Crâne that summer? But, one moment! The solution had surely presented itself when Marie-Colette had arrived that evening! Of course! She, Jacqueline, would accompany Marie-Colette to Bordeaux! She would spend a day or so in the south-west! Why not? Did she not deserve a break? And, anyway, if Jacqui were to arrive in Paris during her absence – well! – he would have only himself to blame if he were to find the apartment empty, would he not?

The next morning, Marie-Colette seemed to be in such a state of unease when she entered the kitchen, that Jacqueline decided to tell her immediately that she would not be alone during her journey to Bordeaux. The look of relief on Marie-Colette's face assured Jacqueline that the correct decision had been made. She hoped, furthermore, that Héloïse, upon becoming aware of Marie-Colette's nervousness, would not suspect that Jacqueline had travelled to Bordeaux for any reason other than to support the girl.

The Countess de Sauzon telephoned after breakfast. Would Jacqueline take Marie-Colette, at least, to the Gare Paris - Montparnasse to catch the train to Bordeaux?

"Ecoutez, Maman! J'ai décidé de l'accomapagner à Bordeaux. Oui, oui. Tout va bien," said Jacqueline, in a calming way.

The Countess expressed her relief, revealing that she had been on edge, not only because of Marie-Colette's journey but also because Jérôme had been behaving nonsensically at dinner, the previous evening, claiming that his opinions were never taken seriously and that he was, therefore, going to run away to join the Knights of Malta! His father had laconically shrugged and had said that the gesture would be a noble one but that Jérôme would be wasting his time. One could not join the Knights of Malta without having been invited to do so. Had Jérôme received an invitation? No? The Count had shrugged again and had continued to eat the steak on his plate. Jérôme, in a huff, had risen from the table and had gone to his room without asking permission to do so. The Countess had been so shocked at witnessing such a flagrant display of bad manners that she had had to lie down, in a dark room, with a bandage soaked in cologne on her forehead. She had, later, had to drink several tisanes before being able to sleep.

The Countess still seemed to be in a considerable tizz and in order to pacify her, Jacqueline asked if she wanted to speak to Marie-Colette, to assure herself that the girl was well.

"It will not be necessary," said the Countess. "You will be with her. I am satisfied with that."

The answer did not surprise Jacqueline. The Countess found Marie-Colette annoying even at the best of times, the girl's shyness and passivity being the trigger for outbursts of otherwise unwarranted anger. It was clear-thinking Héloïse who had once pointed out that the Countess was not actually angry with the fragile Marie-Colette, but with the young girl she, herself, had once been and of whom she was constantly reminded by her youngest daughter. Héloïse knew that it had been the dreamily conceived wish of the Countess, when she had been young, to have created beauty products out of flora growing beside the clear waters around Brittany and to have headed a business selling them, but her mother, Madame Gabrielle de Talence, had crushed her ideas, telling her that young ladies of worth would never consider working in that way. Young ladies, in fact, did not meddle with the world of business in any manner whatsoever, unless they had married an aristocrat who had inherited a vineyard along with a château! The Countess had submitted herself to her mother's will without a murmur of complaint. But Héloïse suspected that her mother, the Countess, was still living a life blighted by repressed ambition and ensuing resentment.

The morning seemed to pass quickly and after a simple lunch – salade de tomates, poisson-frites, fruits- Jacqueline and Marie-Colette made their way to the Gare Montparnasse. The train left at 3p.m. Having settled in her seat, Marie - Colette took out of her leather bag a book, "Le Grand Meaulnes," which she had found on one of Jacqueline's bookshelves and which she had asked if she could read, during the journey. Jacqueline looked sadly out of the window, the book having evoked memories that induced feelings of guilt. She remembered that she had given a copy of the book to Jacqui, on the day that she had been leaving Belle-Isle to spend a gap year in Liverpool. She had realised too late that the novel's principal plot, centred on a lost love, had probably been inappropriate, as Jacqui had been likely to have interpreted her choice as having been insensitive, rather than dreamily romantic. He had not, after all, wanted her to leave France. She had realised, later, that she had hurt him. Was he punishing her now with his show of apparent indifference? Of course, when she had become engaged to Teddy Laurence, during her year away in England, he, Jacqui, had been filled not just with hurt but with despair. However, the existence of a rival had compelled him to join the

French Navy and to make something of his life, in an attempt to win Jacqueline back.

A shiver went down Jacqueline's spine as she thought of the day of her engagement party in the grounds of the Château de Sauzon, when Jacqui had arrived, unexpectedly in his smart uniform and she, like a foolish, guileless ingénue, had run into his arms, thus humiliating Teddy, her fiancé, in front of the guests there assembled. She shivered again.

"Tu as froid?" asked Marie-Colette.

Jacqueline shook her head and smiled. No. She was not cold. She was simply horrified at how childish she had been. She felt so much older now and so sorry about the fact that she had acted with such a lack of decorum. Inevitably, she wondered how she would be able to face Teddy Lawrence, in the event of his still being at the Château du Crâne. She had not seen him since the day that she had rejected and crushed him so cruelly. Of course, the consequence had been her marriage to Jacqui and her subsequent constrained life of boredom. Yes. Boredom. She might as well admit it.

Jacqueline closed her eyes and tried to sleep, lulled by the movement of the train. Marie-Colette was silent for most of the journey, engrossed in her book, and did not disturb her. The hours passed and then, Jacqueline came to as the train slipped into the Gare Saint-Jean, in Bordeaux, where Héloïse was waiting. Alerted earlier that day that Jacqueline would be with Marie-Colette, she had arranged for rooms to be prepared at the Château du Crâne, She assured Jacqueline that there was plenty of space as most of the actors and actresses had already departed along with most of the film crew. Only Pierre Laurier and a few assistants remained, really. Teddy Lawrence had been one of the first to leave.

Jacqueline had imagined that Héloïse had been watching her face with interest when she had mentioned Teddy's name, but Jacqueline had learnt the art of fixing her expression in such a way as to conceal her true feelings and so was able to hide them. Was Héloïse interested in Teddy or not? Once, Héloïse had been her closest confidante. Was she now to be a rival? Over what though? A prize that would never be attained by either of them?

Pierre Laurier had been warned by Héloïse not to alarm Marie-Colette.Héloïse, in fact, was helping Marie-Colette to settle in her room when he knocked quietly on the door. Dressed in a short, leather jacket, a tie-less shirt and jeans, he looked artistically bohemian, but he greeted Marie-Colette in an exquisitely correct and formal way and thus, made her feel at ease.

"Perfect!" he said to Héloïse, later. "The oval face, the symmetry of her features...Her voice is weak. All the same, we can work on that."

"Don't forget that the filming must take place during her Easter holidays," said Héloïse. "That is crucial."

"Yes! Yes!" snapped Pierre. "Are you her agent? Yes or no?"

He shrugged and walked away as if angry, but Héloïse knew that, at least visually, Mare-Colette had lived up to his expectations.

"But, how do I tell her?" Héloïse now silently asked herself. "And how do I tell Maman?" The Countess had to be told about the chance Marie-Colette would be given to appear in the film, but how likely was it that she, the Countess, would allow a second daughter to act professionally? She still had not recovered from the shock of having to cope with Héloïse's decision to accept a leading rôle in the film. She would not be able to bear the thought of Marie-Colette doing the same, given the sort of reputation professional actresses had had in France, at least in times past. There would be a frightful fuss. The Countess would suffer from a succession of headaches and she would call upon the Count to insist that his daughter pay attention to the family's honour. The tears and the prolonged silences, when all else had failed, would be never-ending.

Héloïse sighed and made her way to Marie-Colette's room. She would tell Marie-Colette, first, what was being offered. After all, if Marie-Colette balked at the thought of appearing on film, there would be no need to alarm the Countess, would there?

Out in the grounds of the Château du Crâne, Jacqueline was taking a walk. She was imagining Teddy Laurence there, strolling through the meadows, in eighteenth century costume. It had been disappointing to hear that he had gone away and Jacqueline wondered where he was at that moment. In Chester? In Liverpool? Dreamily, she began to ponder on where the two of them would be living, if she had married him. It was pointless and painful to allow her thoughts to drift in that direction, though. After all, Rebecca Hampton had apparently slipped back into Teddy's life. The cool and intelligent Rebecca Hampton! Who would have believed, at one time, that such a development would have been likely? Jacqueline felt a little betrayed. But, of course, she deserved no better than to suffer in that way. She knew that. It occurred to her, then, that if Teddy had, indeed, fallen for Rebecca, he could, at least, thank her, Jacqueline, for having introduced him to the American girl in the first place. Would he consider that happy introduction to be adequate compensation for the way she had hurt him? Would he ever tell her so?

CHAPTER 32

Susie's Broken Heart

"How long can one love a man who is constantly thinking of another woman?" wondered Susie Sutton, as, through one of the large windows of a first floor corridor in Bramblewell Manor, she watched her fiancé, Lord Bramblewell, setting off for a morning stroll. With his dark cloak thrown over his broad shoulders - to shield him from the nip in the air - and his blond hair gleaming in the light of the weak, early morning sun, he looked, to Susie, like a figure on the cover of a romantic novel. But a romantic hero, Susie knew, being an avid reader of the literary genre, would not leave his beloved, in order to place himself within the proximity of another woman, less worthy of attention. And yet, there was Lord Bramblewell, her supposedly loyal Rupert, heading in the direction of the small wood, through which there was a path that led to a door in the grey, stone wall: a door which would take him into the grounds of Bramblewell School. If questioned, upon his return to the Manor, he would explain that he had gone to the school to offer his support to Lynn James, as she was in the throes of taking over Miss Trimm's rôle as headmistress. His excuse would sound plausible. Lynn, after all, had had the responsibility thrust upon her unexpectedly. But, how could Susie not suspect that he had been drawn to the school, in reality, in order to catch a glimpse of Isolde Delamar?

A white mist rose from the lush lawns that stretched out in front of the manor, as the sun heated the dew on the grass. Susie sighed. There was a time when she would have settled for all of that - the extensive grounds, the manor, itself, the soon to be acquired title of Lady Bramblewell - and would have been content.

But, she had become so deeply attached to Lord Bramblewell that the thought of him being distracted by another woman made her heart ache.

"Ah! There you are, madam! Will you be going downstairs for breakfast, this morning, or shall I bring you something on a tray?"

Susie turned round quickly, having heard behind her, the cold voice of Mrs. Oliver, the housekeeper. Tall and severe, her dark hair pulled back into a sleek chignon, Mrs. Oliver was always correct in the way she used words, when addressing Susie, but her tone was never warm. Susie knew Mrs. Oliver regarded her as being unworthy of respect. She had once, in fact, overhead Mrs. Oliver describing her as "an upstart from the lower orders," when, one day, she, Susie, had got lost in the manor and had found herself in a passageway that led to the kitchens. Susie had not related to Lord Bramblewell what had been said, but she had mentally noted that Mrs. Oliver was one not to be trusted. Now, as she looked at Mrs. Oliver's gleaming eyes and observed the hint of a smirk on her lips, Susie pulled herself together. She realised that Mrs. Oliver would have guessed that she, Susie, had been watching Lord Bramblewell, as he had made his way towards Bramblewell School, but she was not going to allow the malicious housekeeper to perceive how upset she was.

"I'll be down, presently," said Susie, her voice steady.

"Very well, madam," said Mrs. Oliver, still smirking as she walked away, the thick heels of her laced-up, black shoes now clattering on the polished floor of the corridor, whereas upon her approach, they had made no sound.

"Schadenfreude," thought Susie, remembering a German word she had heard Dorothy Trimm once using. Dorothy had told her that it meant "an enjoyment of another's distress" and that it filled her with horror. "Me, too, Dorothy," thought Susie, as she made her way slowly along the corridor, musing on Mrs. Oliver's attitude. It had its roots in envy, of course. There had been no mistress of Bramblewell since Rupert had inherited the manor and he, Rupert, had allowed Mrs. Oliver to run the establishment without much interference on his part. No doubt Mrs. Oliver was fearful of the day when Susie would become Lady Bramblewell and would be in a position to dictate changes, if she thought they were required. Susie could understand Mrs. Oliver's anxiety, but nevertheless, could not overlook her malevolence.

The corridor was lined with portraits on one side. Susie stopped in front on one of Lady Maureen Athena Bramblewell, one of Lord Bramblewell's ancestors and the founder, in fact, of Bramblewell School. In the portrair, Lady Maureen Athena was wearing the very cabochon ring which Lord Bramblewell had given to Susie as an engagement ring. When Susie had gazed at the portrait and others like it, in the past, she had been filled with a resolve to live up to expectations and to work hard to become, like the revered ancestor, worthy of the greatest respect. However, that morning, deflated by Lord Bramblewell's early departure for Bramblewell School and by Mrs. Oliver's gloating, she felt she could not summon the strength to do anything other than to survive the day.

In the breakfast room, watched by Tamsin, the house maid, who stood respectfully to one side, in her black dress and white apron, Susie helped herself to scrambled eggs, sausages and fried bread, from the dishes laid out on the sideboard, before sitting down at the long table, in the middle of the room. It then occurred to her that she felt so downhearted that it would be the best of plans to discuss her problems with a confidant or confidante - as Rosalind Somerland had been inclined to describe close friends, during her sojourn in France - rather than to continue to allow those problems to spoil the entire day. But, to whom could she talk about her personal misgivings? Effectively, her weaknesses? To very few. And she had already approached Teddy Laurence and had made a fool of herself, by pleading with him, in exaggerated style, on the night he had arrived back home from France, to do something silly. She could not contact him again. Not for a while, in any case. She trusted Julian, but he was Lord Bramblewell's nephew and she could hardly talk to him about his uncle's behaviour: it would not be fair to do so. Besides, Julian would be preparing for his return to Bristol for another year of studying and would be preoccupied. It then occurred to Susie that she could ask Liz Laurier for an appointment for an astrological consultation. As a professional astrologer, Liz would be bound by oath not to divulge what was said during a consultation, would she not? Of course she would! Giving herself no time to ponder on what she was doing, Susie decisively telephoned to Liz, after breakfast and arranged to visit her in Ellesmere Port, in the afternoon.

During lunch, upon Lord Bramblewell's return, Susie did not mention his morning visit, but later, drove off to see Liz, without telling him where she was going. She arrived at Liz's apartment in a haze of soft scent, but she was more casually dressed than usual, her choice of outfit consisting of blue jeans, a white jumper with a V-neck and white ballerina shoes.

"How may I help you?" asked Liz, sounding formal, as she invited Susie to sit on one of the white sofas in her sitting room.

"I expect you know there is a new secretary at Bramblewell School," began Susie. "Rosalind has probably mentioned her."

Liz sat down opposite Susie and nodded.

"Well!" said Susie, her voice beginning to tremble. "I managed to get hold of her date of birth. I simply asked Lord Bramblewell for it, you see, on the day he received Miss Trimm's message in France, telling him there were three suitable candidates for the post of secretary. He thought I just wanted to know Isolde Delamar's age. I did want to know that, of course, but I also knew her birth data might be useful, one day, and so I hung on to it. And now, I'm wondering if you would compare Lord Bramblewell's astrological chart with hers."

Liz hesitated. So, that was it! That was the reason Susie had sounded so agitated when making the appointment by telephone that morning and seemed to be so ill at ease now. Essentially, she wanted Liz to tell her that there was no evidence that a relationship between Lord Bramblewell and Isolde Delamar would ever be established. She wanted Liz to wave a magic wand and make Miss Delamar disappear, effectively. Many of Liz's clients wanted her to solve their problems as if by magic and so, Susie's attitude was not particularly unusual, even though it was naïve. Liz hated disillusioning clients, but if she was to help them, they had to realise that their rôle would not be a passive one. And she could not help Susie at all, of course, however much she would like to.

"Susie, listen!" she said, gently, her voice signalling regret. "I cannot compare those two charts without having the permission of at least one of the two people concerned to do so."

Susie looked at Liz, as if not understanding what she had said.

"Couldn't you just have a quick look at Isolde's, then?" she asked, standing up and handing Liz the piece of white paper on which the dates of birth were written.

Liz took the paper from Susie's hand and glanced at it. She wanted to help Susie, as she would want to help anyone who was troubled, but her personal code of behaviour was stopping her from proceeding with the consultation. She did not want to swim in the muddy waters into which the young blonde was drawing her. Simultaneously, she was wondering if she was being too scrupulous. Susie, after all, was seeking nothing more than peace of mind. What, though, if the charts were to reveal the potential for deep compatibility? How would she explain that to Susie without causing her more pain? She could not take the risk of hurting the young woman more than she already had been hurt. Liz handed back the paper.

Susie stood, walked over to the window and looked down into the street.

"You won't do it," she said.

Liz could tell she was struggling to control tears.

"Susie," she said. "There are web sites that will compare charts for you. Some are better than others but I can recommend a few that are..."

"If there are web sites that will do this for me, why won't you?" Susie interrupted, turning round and sounding more plaintive than angry. "Oh! It doesn't matter," she added, immediately, giving a shrug. "Don't answer."

She crossed the room and picked up the tiny white handbag she had left on the floor by the sofa.

"Thank you for seeing me," she said, then, remembering to be polite.

After accompanying Susie downstairs to the front door, Liz went back up to her apartment feeling guilty, rather than satisfied that she had followed the correct procedure. She could not help remembering how distressed she, herself, had been when her marriage to her second husband, Pierre Laurier, had been going awry, in France. A young American girl, a tourist in Paris, had helped her then, by setting up her astrological chart and that of Pierre's, casually, in a café. At a time of great distress, Liz had been given hope. What was the use of astrology, if it did not give one hope? Was that not its greatest gift?

Liz had only glanced at the piece of paper that Susie had handed to her, but she remembered what Isolde Delamar's birthday had been. And out of the blue, it struck her that the Sun in Isolde's chart would be making a connection with Teddy Laurence's Pluto. She knew Teddy Laurence's chart well and she remembered where his Pluto was situated on the astrological wheel. Pluto –Sun connected could point to a battle of wills.

Liz's mobile phone was lying on the glass topped coffee table in front of the sofa where she had been sitting. She waited until she reckoned Susie had arrived home and then, she called her number.

"Susie," she said. "I don't think you will need to worry much about Isolde Delamar. She'll probably be too busy dealing with Teddy Laurence to be able to focus on much else. That's all I can tell you."

"Thank you," said Susie, at first relieved, but then alarmed. Isolde and Teddy? Was that worse?

CHAPTER 33

Rose Petals Fall

"Dad! Where's John?" asked Rosalind Somerland, walking into the garden of her father's house. "He isn't in his room."

"Hm? Oh! Mrs. Stanley took him to visit a dentist, out in the Rivacre direction, I think."

"Rivacre? Why?"

"I wasn't paying attention," answered Gylen Somerland, putting down the sheaf of papers he had been studying. "I did ask Mrs. Stanley to bring back an itemised receipt, so that I could check, at some point, what had been done."

"Oh!" said Rosalind, taken aback by what she considered to be her father's lackadaisical attitude to the welfare of his son.

Seeing a frown appearing on her forehead, Gylen added wearily, "I do care for your brother, you know!"

Sitting at the edge of a sun lounger, on a light-infused lawn, beside a rose bush patch, with papers stacked in three piles beside him, Gylen, Rosalind had to acknowledge, was looking tired, even though, in principle, he was enjoying a day away from work.

"Would you like to sit down?" he asked, moving the papers so as to make a space for her.

"No. No, Dad. I just wanted to ask you where John was," said Rosalind, not wanting to disturb a man who was clearly preoccupied.

Gylen moved the papers, anyway.

"Sit, Rosie. I want to talk to you," he said.

"About what, Dad?"

Rosalind lowered herself on to the grass, leaning one elbow on the lounger.

"No! Don't sit on the grass! Here put this beneath you!" ordered Gylen, handing Rosalind a copy of "The Cheshire Chronicle."

"You're not going to give me a lecture, are you Dad?" asked Rosalind, spreading out the newspaper. "I know all the stuff about not letting moisture from the ground seep into the body. Susie told me all about it."

"I want to talk to you about John," said Gylen, ignoring her words.

"What about him?"

"Do you know if he's happy at school?"

"Happy at school?"

"Yes. Is he?"

"Well! I think so. I know he misses Bristol a lot. He's been away from his friends, there, for more than a year, but I know he misses them still. By the way, could I...?

Rosalind stopped. She had been about to ask if she, herself, could go to Bristol to stay with Debbie, her former school friend, there, for a day or two, before the start of the new term at Bramblewell School, not least because she hoped to catch a glimpse of the student on whom she had once, secretly, had a crush. She had called the student Peregrine-Hugo. Later, she had discovered his true name to have been Owen Banks. She knew he would be sharing a flat with Julian Bramblewell-Eurlinn and with another friend called Pomeroy, in the Clifton area, where Debbie lived. She wanted to see him again, out of nostalgic curiosity - romantic thoughts about him had often sustained her, during her school-days, in Bristol - but, observing her father's suddenly darkening expression, she decided to leave her request for another time.

"Is there something wrong?" she asked instead.

"It's interesting that you should mention John's attachment to Bristol," said Gylen. "I was actually thinking of sending him back there. In fact, I was looking at this..."

Gylen stopped in mid-sentence and took a brochure from the bottom of one of the piles of papers and handed it to Rosalind. It was an advertisement for a boarding school in Somerset. There was a coloured photo of the school on the front of the leaflet. The building was attractive in appearance, to be sure, formerly having been a large Georgian house, surrounded by parkland and lovely trees. Rosalind, though, was aghast at what her father was considering doing.

"A boarding school?" she exclaimed."Oh! No, Dad! You're not really thinking of sending John away, are you?"

Gylen sighed.

"When Susie Sutton was here, looking after the two of you," he began after a short pause, "she advised me that the best place for John would be a boarding school where he would be looked after and given proper support. I was angry with poor Susie at the time, but now, I am wondering if she was right after all. I don't have the time to give John the guidance he needs."

"But Dad, John isn't the kind of boy who would settle down in a boarding school. He'd be unhappy all of the time. Really, he would. I remember the night that Susie said to you that John should be sent to a boarding school. You didn't know this, but John and I were sitting on the stairs, as you talked to Susie downstairs, and we could hear every word that was said. John was shivering with fright, Dad. I put my arm around him and I could feel his little body shaking. That night, I promised him that I wouldn't let you send him away. But then, a few weeks later, I went to France, on a school trip - remember? - and while I was on that trip, John began to imagine that Susie would send him to boarding school, while I wasn't at home to protect him. And so, he ran away from home, didn't he? I still haven't been told all the details of what happened that day. John won't talk about it. But, I do know he gave Susie and you a fright and I know the boys in Mr. Laurence's youth club were looking for him all over Liverpool. Do you want him to run away again? If you sent him to boarding school, he'd never forgive you, Dad. It's the worst thing you could do to him."

Gylen, who had been listening to Rosalind's outburst, with his head bowed, sat up straight, then.

"John is older now, Rosie," he said, as if he thought her words had been irrelevant. "He will have changed. We all change."

"No, Dad! Honestly! He hasn't. Please, believe me!" urged Rosalind, sounding as if she were desperate to persuade.

"Well!" said Gylen, gazing into the distance, beyond the garden. "Something will have to be done. He doesn't want to have anything to do with Liz, of course. Your mother, I mean."

"Are you surprised, Dad? Don't forget, he was even younger than I was when she walked out of our lives. I remember hearing him crying at night, because she wasn't at home. And then, last year, out of the blue, she turned up! She had been my teacher for a year and she hadn't told me she was my mother. I can see the funny side of it, now, I suppose."

"The funny side? Can you?"

"Well, yes. I quite like her. She's interesting. She's not like other mothers, is she? But John got such a shock when he discovered who she was that he nearly passed out. I think he had grown up believing she had died, you see. I don't think he has recovered from the shock, yet. Haven't you noticed how pale he is? You're the doctor, Dad! You're supposed to pay attention to these things!"

"I could have handled the situation better. I do realise John reacted badly when he met your mother. I should have broken the news to him with more care. I can see him now, sitting down on a log, in the grounds of your school, looking stunned. I should have taken him straight home."

"But, you were shocked too, Dad. I could tell."

"I was an adult. You, two, were not."

"Dad, why don't you talk to Mum about John and work out what to do about him, together?"

"Don't start, Rosie!"

"But Dad, you should talk to her!"

"Don't!"

"So, what exactly are you going to do, then?"

Gylen leaned forward and picked up the brochure that Rosalind had placed on the grass beside her. He gazed at the photograph of the elegant-looking school on the cover.

"I don't know," he said, placing the brochure under the sheaf of papers, lying next to him. "I'll let you know when I have made a decision."

Rosalind looked up at the cornflower-blue sky. Although summer had entered its last phase, the days were still warm in West Cheshire. The pale pink petals on the roses, in the garden, were beginning to lose their soft, velvet bloom, but their scent was lingering. Rosalind remembered that Héloïse de Sauzon, earlier that summer, had talked about the perfumes of flowers, while she had been at the Château du Crâne. To put herself in an eighteenth century mood, she had explained, she had been reading a book, written by Elisabeth de Feydeau, about Jean-Louis Fargeon, the perfumer of Queen Marie-Antoinette and, as a consequence of reading that book, she had started to spray her room, at the château, nightly, with the scents of French lavender, lemon and thyme. Those scents were lovely, Rosalind had agreed, but she had thought, secretly, that the scent of English roses, after summer rainfall, was even nicer. Rosalind stood and walked over to the patch of rose bushes, close to where her father was sitting. She touched one pale pink rose and its soft petals fell slowly to the ground. Rosalind watched the petals drifting down with a look of profound sadness in her eyes. The destruction of beauty disturbed her, but she was more alarmed by the fact that change seemed inevitable. It was part of "the human condition," as Héloïse had frequently and rather grandly stated.

"You're too beautiful to die!" thought Rosalind, as she picked up a handful of rose petals from the ground. Everything was in a state of flux. She knew she had absorbed this idea from Héloïse, who had been inclined to quote lines from the work of Montaigne, her favourite French philosopher - or so she had claimed. Flux! Upheaval! Were they really unavoidable? What Rosalind and her fragile brother craved, at that moment in their lives, was stability.

"Gylen, looking up from his papers, noticed the strained expression on Rosalind's face as she gazed upon the fallen rose petals. He did not want her to be unhappy. He did not want either of his children to be unhappy. He frowned. What if Rosie was right? What if John needed to stay at home for a while longer to settle his nerves?

"Do you really think John should stay here?" he asked, finally.

"Dad, I know that he'd miss us if…"

"All right!" said Gylen, interrupting her with an exaggerated sigh. "All right! I'll find another way to help John. You win!"

He returned to his papers.

Rosalind felt as if her legs had been weakened with relief, but her mind, relieved of a burden, seemed fresh and new. Suddenly the world appeared to be full of possibilities, rather than ominous changes.

CHAPTER 34

Stella

Stella Lomas' small, rectangular phone, placed by her side on the rug on which she was lying, started to play a jingly-jazzy tune. Stella, who had been drifting into a day dream, while enjoying the warmth of the afternoon sun which had been shining down, without aggression, on to the large garden behind her parents' house in Chester - a garden that descended, in terraced, flowery steps, to the river and a small landing stage - propped herself up on the pillows she had placed beneath her head.

"Not exactly in the Jacques Loussier class, is it?" called her brother, Ralph, from the garden room, his voice sounding languid, in the way it did when he was affecting disdain.

Ignoring his remark, Stella picked up the noisy phone and stared at its small screen. The number displayed was unfamiliar. Still, she answered the call.

"Hello?" she said, puzzled.

"Stella? Stella Lomas?"

"Yes."

"This is Eva Derbyshire. You gave me your number last term. Remember? I thought we could meet, before your return to school. I did say I'd give you some tips on how to be a head girl."

"Oh! Gosh! That would be useful. Thank you."

"It was Miss Trimm's suggestion. Not mine. Where would you like to meet?

"Anywhere that suits you, I suppose. I don't mind. Where are you, exactly?"

"I live in Eastham."

"And I'm in Chester."

"I do know that. I could come to Chester."

"Really?"

"I could be there in an hour's time."

"What? You mean…this afternoon?"

"Is the timing inconvenient?"

"No! I mean…No! It's all right."

"Would you rather not meet?

"Oh! I do want to meet you. Yes. Listen! I'll wait for you in the Rows, in the part nearest Eastgate. I'll be there in an hour's time, if that suits you."

"Yes. It does. 'Bye!"

Stella pushed her brown fringe out of her eyes and stood up, brushing blades of cut grass from her white jeans. She put her phone in her pocket and walked into the house, through the glass doors of the garden room, where Ralph was stretched out on a comfortably upholstered, pale sofa. His head on an apple-green, silk cushion, he was engrossed in working out the solutions to the clues in that morning's "Telegraph."

"Going out," said Stella, as she was passing him.

"Hm?"

"Meeting Eva Derbyshire," she added.

"Who's Eva Derbyshire?"

"Last year's head girl."

"Oh!" exclaimed Ralph. "The one who looks like Jane Morris in the Pre-Raphaelite paintings!"

"No! SHE thinks she looks like Jane Morris in the Pre-Raphaelite paintings."

"Am I getting the impression you two don't get along?"

"Well! She has a nerve! I mean, she more or less ordered me to meet her in an hour's time!"

"Why didn't you say, 'No'?"

"She gave me the impression she wouldn't give me another chance! Well! She didn't say that exactly…but her tone wasn't friendly."

"Good luck, then!"

"Well! You're a lot of help!"

"What do you mean? You haven't asked for my help! What could I do anyway?"

"Oh! Go back to your crossword!"

"Fine!"

"Fine!"

Stella went up the stairs to her bedroom, fuming. Ralph had a way of making her feel childish, even when she was trying to communicate with him in a mature manner. She hoped persuading the girls of Bramblewell School that she deserved their respect would be easier, for she had been chosen to be head girl of the school for the duration of the scholastic year ahead of her. Of course, the thought of living up to expectations was daunting, but she had set about preparing herself for the task in a practical way, instead of allowing herself to wallow in self-destructive thoughts. In front of a mirror, she had daily practised speaking with dignity and standing in such a way that she exuded an air of authority. She reminded herself constantly that the younger girls in the school would look up to her, expecting her to be their rôle model. In anticipation of such an occurrence, Stella had jotted down a few ideas on how she could help these younger girls to grow up to be confident and responsible young women.

Stella smiled to herself, ruefully, as she changed her tee-shirt for the rendezvous with Eva Derbyshire. Would she be able to hold her own when dealing with the arrogance of the previous year's head girl? Stella had been taken aback at how abrupt Eva had sounded. No Bramblewell girl, even a former one, should have behaved in that impolite way, as if she had not had the benefit of a good education. Of course, Stella had often wondered how Eva had managed to retain her position as head girl of the school, during the previous scholastic year. Admittedly, Eva had worked hard during most of her school life, had organised charitable events and had played with appropriate enthusiasm on the netball and tennis courts. However, in her final year, her performance, academically, had been lacklustre and her leadership skills had shown themselves to have been deficient. Even Portia Price, as the president of The Eliza Club, the school's dramatic society, although much younger than Eva, had been considered to have been more inspiring.

Given her low opinion of Eva Derbyshire, Stella should not have been surprised that the former head girl should have arrived late at the Rows, the mediaeval shopping terrace in the centre of Chester. Yet, given the precise nature of the arrangement Eva had made, Stella was surprised, nevertheless. She had been wandering up and down the Rows, window-shopping, for forty-five minutes before Eva appeared, sauntering towards her, while affecting an air of nonchalance.

"Got held up," said Eva, pushing her long, thick, dark hair away from her face. "Sorry. It was my mother's fault. She offered to give me a lift and then, she made a telephone call that went on and on. You know what it's like."

"You could have phoned to tell me," Stella was on the point of retorting, but decided, then, not to react to the provocation. She chose, instead, to behave in a restrained manner, as was befitting a future head girl.

Eva was wearing a long, grey-blue dress, in a chiffon-like material. It reminded Stella of a dress worn by a lady in a painting in the Lady Lever Gallery, on the east side of the Wirral. She noticed Eva taking in the way that she, herself, was neatly attired in her nicely-tailored, white jeans, a white tee shirt and a cricket cardigan.

"Preppy!" was all that Eva said, though.

"Where would you like to go?" asked Stella, hoping she sounded arch.

"Let's walk around for a bit...on the wall."

Stella acquiesced with a nod and so, they made their way to the reddish, Roman wall nearby. They went up steps to the well

– trodden path on which Roman soldiers would have marched in a bygone age and then, they both turned right, as if by mutual agreement, in order to walk in the direction of the river. Eva was silent as she made her way between the wall's ramparts, until the glistening waters of the Dee were in sight.

"Let's go down to a café," she said.

They found one where tables had been placed outside in the sun and they sat there, watching swans gliding by and pleasure boats passing, as if they were taking part in a scene in a painting by Renoir or Manet. They both ordered iced tea with mint.

"Was there anything in particular you wanted to say to me?" asked Stella.

"Just that…with Miss Chan gone, you must be prepared to help the new school secretary to settle down."

"Help the new secretary? Me? Why? I mean, I'm sure Miss Chan left systems in place and clear instructions on how to proceed from Day 1. You know how meticulous she was. She would not have gone away without making sure her successor would have no difficulty in understanding what to do."

Eva was quiet for a moment, appearing to be nonplussed.

"Was that all?" asked Stella.

"No. I wanted to tell you, as well, that there will be a new girl in Portia Price's class. She'll actually be a boarder, but she might go home at weekends. Her parents live in London."

"Oh?"

"She likes ballet. She wants to go to London at weekends, so that she can continue having lessons there."

"But she could go to ballet classes at Bramblewell!"

"Don't be so provincial! The ballet teacher in London is Russian. The new girl probably thinks Mrs. Merrivale is not in the same league!"

"How do you know all this?" asked Stella sharply, angered at having been accused of being provincial. "Miss Trimm would never have discussed the private lives of pupils with another pupil:

not even with a head girl."

Eva's face turned slightly pink.

"There was another thing I was going to tell you, but actually, I don't think I should, now," she said, primly. "Actually, I think I should go, now," she added.

Before Stella could speak, Eva stood and looked straight into her eyes.

"Good luck," she said and for once, there seemed to be a hint of kindness in her voice.

Stella watched, baffled, as Eva walked away quickly along the river's edge. What had been the point of the meeting? It had seemed to have been an attempt, on Eva's part, to persuade Stella to help the new school secretary. But why? Was the new school secretary completely incompetent? Or did Eva know her socially? Was she a friend?

Stella finished her iced tea. As she did so, it occurred to her that with the meeting with Eva having been cut short, she had time on her hands, before she would need to return home. Her mother and father had gone to a three-day conference and, as was the custom when her parents were away, she took it in turns with her brother to prepare meals. That evening, it would be Ralph's turn to cook. There was no requirement on her part, therefore, to hurry back home. And then, it occurred to her that rather than wandering around shops, she could go along to Bramblewell School, where, no doubt, the mysteriously incompetent, new school secretary would already be in situ. With these thoughts in her head, Stella left the café and made her way to the bus station.

Bramblewell School was situated on the outskirts of the city but the city was not large and so, within a short time, Stella was entering the main, Neo-Gothic building of the school and hearing raised voices coming from the secretary's room, on the ground floor.

"You don't understand!" a teenage girl was shouting in apparent exasperation. "I am Irene Miller. "

"Yes. I know. You keep telling me what your name is," a woman replied with icy anger evident in her voice. "But I don't care who you are! You will still have to share a room with another girl."

"Don't speak to me in that way! Who are you, anyway? My father will insist that I have a room of my own."

"Listen!" the woman's voice was heard to retort with more force than before. "You will be sharing a room and, as far as I am concerned, you can take it or leave it. I don't care, quite frankly. And don't YOU speak to ME in the tone you have been using!"

"Do you REALLY not know who I am?" the girl shouted, sounding shocked. "How DARE you talk to me so rudely? How dare you?"

Stella, now standing outside the open door of the secretary's room, was amazed. No Bramblewell girl would normally ever dream of speaking to members of the school staff in such a peremptory manner. Stella approached the doorway and looked into the room. A tall, striking-looking young woman was standing behind the wide, polished desk. Her fine eyes were flashing with temper. Standing before her was a young girl. Although her back was turned towards Stella, it was obvious, from her stance, that she was equally annoyed.

"I share with no one," the girl was continuing to insist. "And what is more, you must hire a special ballet teacher for me. See to it!"

"Mrs. Merrivale teaches ballet here, as well as speech and drama," the tall young woman - obviously the new secretary - was saying, in a drawling sort of way.

"No! I don't want a teacher who teaches other things!" the young girl shouted, unreasonably.

Stella gasped on hearing those words and the new secretary threw her a curious look. At that moment, a door opened and Lynn James appeared, from her adjoining headmistress's room.

"Hello, Irene," she said calmly. "I could not help overhearing what you were saying. I shouldn't have, because Bramblewell girls are expected not to raise their voices, even when they find themselves in situations which they find irritating. Now, Miss Trimm, the previous headmistress of this school, left notes which state, clearly, that your father agreed with the school's policy on sharing, for the first five years. I understand your misgivings. I really do. But this school is quite small and there are restrictions on space. We try to accommodate girls comfortably, but what we can't do, we can't do. If you would prefer to go to another school, perhaps I could talk to your father on the telephone about that. Would you like me to telephone him in London, this evening?"

"Oh! No! Please don't talk to my father! I want to stay here."

"Good! Well! I see Stella, our new head girl standing there in the doorway. Perhaps, Stella, you would like to show Irene around the school. I think this is just a casual visit, on Irene's part. You are visiting just for an afternoon, aren't you?"

Yes…uh…"

"Miss James."

"Yes, Miss James."

Irene turned to give Stella a warm smile. It lit up her face and made her grey eyes sparkle.Once outside the secretary's room, though, Stella thought she had better sternly make clear to Irene what the school's expectations would be, but Irene interrupted her, before she could start.

"Listen! I know I was rude," she said, "but that woman…"

"Who? The new secretary?"

"Yes. She looked at me as if she were doing me a favour by talking to me."

"I expect she'll settle down."

"Oh! You are SO diplomatic! By the way, I didn't mean to insult the school's ballet teacher."

"Mrs. Merrivale."

"Yes. Mrs. Merrivale. I'm sure she is very good. I just got carried away. I usually go to ballet classes in London, you know. Oh! And you should see my ballet teacher's son! He is just GORGEOUS!

He's Russian, of course. Rudi."

"Really?," said Stella with a smile. "Gorgeous?"

"Absolutely! If Dad will let me go to London at weekends, I'll see him at ballet class."

"He dances too?"

"Oh yes! He loves everything to do with the arts. You know… galleries, museums, literature…He loves going to theatres to see plays."

"Oh! Maybe you should join the school's dramatic society, then. It might impress him!" said Stella, trying to sound helpful.

"You have a dramatic society? Are plays actually staged?"

"Oh gosh! Yes! We have a little theatre called The Woodlanders."

"Will you take me to see it? Now?"

"Yes. Of course!"

"Amazing! What If I became the star of a play at Bramblewell School and I asked Rudi to come to watch it?"

"Oh! I'm sure Rudi would be really impressed," said Stella warmly, while silently wondering, with some misgivings, how the stardom of a newcomer would go down with Portia Price and her friends.

CHAPTER 35

Dinner in Hoylake

"I'm glad you could make it," said Lynn James, her tone suggesting she was relieved that her future deputy-head - or rather, the young man who would be her future deputy-head, were her hopes for his rapid promotion to be realised - had accepted her invitation to dine in her apartment in Hoylake. She had extended the invitation to him five days earlier, just hours after his return from France. Now, on the eve of the start of the new term at Bramblewell School, or rather, on the eve of the two days set aside for a preparatory session for teachers, prior to the term beginning properly, he, Teddy Laurence, was standing at her door.

Teddy had not visited Lynn at home before, and, while driving through the Mersey Tunnel on the way to Hoylake, he had wondered what sort of private environment she had created for herself. He had imagined her surrounded by pictures on white walls, in rooms that resembled spaces in a museum of modern art and so, it was with interest that he walked through her door, finally, somewhat curious to discover what he would find. He noticed, as he was led along a corridor, on the way to a sitting room, a large, framed painting hanging on a pale wall. He would not have described the picture as an example of representational art, but in his opinion, it was not completely abstract either. The colours were muted – soft greys and misty blues, mainly - and they depicted, he imagined, an interestingly Gothic landscape.

"This is an original piece, obviously," said Teddy. "Your own work?"

It occurred to him that he had no idea how Lynn passed her spare time, but it was not inconceivable, he felt, that she painted pictures, in order to escape from the world of education, for a while. However, Lynn said she had bought the painting from a small gallery in the Wirral, adding:

"I don't have only originals on my walls, though. There are some prints I cannot live without.

There was, in fact, a single, large print, framed in heavy gilt, in the sitting room, the original painting having been a Rembrandt. Teddy was surprised. Had he been asked to guess Lynn's tastes in artists, he would have opted for those working in Paris in the early twentieth century. It was a mistake, of course, to presume to know the direction in which a discerning lady's tastes would lie. He had guessed correctly, all the same, that Lynn, being sensitive to beauty, would like fine art. And, he remembered, then, that Jacqueline de Sauzon, two years previously, had explained to him the extent to which she, herself, had depended on the chic, effervescent paintings of Raoul Dufy to cheer her, whenever she had been low in spirits and as that memory of Jacqueline intruded on his thoughts, he felt as if his heart had been jabbed.

"I sometimes think I'd like to see an exhibition of twentieth century American art," he said, for no reason other than to take his own mind off Jacqueline.

"Oh?" said Lynn, as if in expectation of development.

Teddy realised, then, that Lynn would be wondering what had brought American art to mind. She might have associated his statement with his rumoured attachment to Rebecca Hampton, but, weary of wondering if he would ever see Rebecca again, he was disinclined to start to explain to Lynn how he felt about the American girl. He did not want to mention her, at all. However, he found he could not banish, from his mind, imagined scenes of college quads and Rebecca strolling through them, with books under her arm, her stride confident and her expression eager. Why had he thought she would be waiting for him in Liverpool when she had said she would not be there? It had been foolish of him to have pictured her emerging from the kitchen, as he had entered his apartment upon his return from France, saying "Surprise!" She did not tease and was too smart to be indecisive.

"I do like some American art," Lynn was saying and adding, "Listen, Teddy. Make yourself at home. I have to keep an eye on what is cooking in the kitchen. Do pour yourself a drink, if you would like one. The remote for the TV is on that shelf." She made for the door. Teddy noticed that the colour of the slim, sleeveless dress she was wearing matched the soft lavender colour of one of the cushions in the otherwise white room and he wondered if she had worn the dress deliberately to create an artistic effect. Teddy smiled. Lynn's attention to detail always enchanted him, as did her natural sophistication, her unpretentious charm and her appreciation of finesse.

Teddy walked around the room. One wall was lined with glass shelves on which there were books, which were foreign as well as English. Teddy glanced at the authors. Stendhal…Proust…De Gaulle…The memoirs of De Gaulle? Teddy thought of Gabrielle de Talence and the fate that had befallen her when she had taken part in student demonstrations in 1968. Her father, interpreting her behaviour as being anti-Gaullist, had punished her in a way that had affected her entire life. Teddy leaned over to take the book from the shelf, but then, stopped. He believed that one should not touch people's belongings, in an intrusive way, in their own homes.

Teddy sat down on a white sofa, then, and gazed, without concentrating, at the small, flat-screened TV, standing unobtrusively on a shelf in an alcove. Its size reflected, perhaps, the lack of importance Lynn attached to it. He imagined she watched the News and art programmes and foreign films, but little else. The TV had, in fact, been tuned to a News channel, but the sound had been turned down to zero. Teddy tried to make sense of what was appearing on the screen, but then, the call to dinner came.

The dining room was cosy, a polished, oval table taking up two thirds of the space. Lynn had laid out silver cutlery and beautiful glassware and Teddy felt honoured to have been treated to such a display of sophistication. He suspected the food would be very good. He also surmised that it would be inspired by foreign dishes, since Lynn had travelled widely at holiday times. He had heard her mentioning, in the past, that she liked to cook lobster bisque with cream and a stew flavoured with tamarind and he was prepared to be surprised. However, that evening, Lynn had made bone broth and had cooked good beef, served with vegetables, in a traditional way. For pudding, there was trifle, the recipe having been adapted from an eighteenth century receipt. Teddy, who occasionally cooked for himself, but who, more often than not, now, bought a ready-made meal from a store, on his way home after a hard day's work at school, much appreciated home cooking, when he had the opportunity to tuck in.

"That was really good, Lynn," he said with sincerity, the meal over. "I honestly didn't realise you were so accomplished, when it came to cooking." He hoped that his words had sounded like a compliment, rather than a patronising remark. He was not sure, but Lynn seemed to read his mind and laughed.

Back in the sitting room, she served coffee and Teddy sank back into the abundance of white cushions piled behind him, on the sofa. However, the coffee quickened his mind and he leaned forward, as if he had suddenly come to his senses.

"So!" he said. "Tomorrow!"

"Yes. Tomorrow," echoed Lynn, sitting down opposite Teddy.

She settled her gaze on the window behind him. The long, heavy, white curtains were open and she could see that the sky was starting to darken over Hoylake and beyond it, the Bay of Liverpool. To Teddy, she appeared to be trying to recall something that needed to be remembered, Her agenda for the following day, he supposed. She would be required to address the teachers of Bramblewell School, as head mistress, for the first time and so, would have to be well prepared.

"I imagine the first day's session will last until four o' clock?"

said Teddy, then, looking at Lynn in a questioning way.

"I know Miss Trimm would have gone on and on," responded Lynn, "but I'm thinking of using only the morning for staff meetings. I plan to allow teachers to spend the afternoon doing what they, themselves, think is necessary in their classrooms."

"That's generous of you," said Teddy. "And it's a good idea."

"Let's face it Teddy. I'm not going to find tomorrow easy," Lynn reflected. "Some teachers, who might have been prepared to tolerate my position as deputy-headmistress, will balk at the thought of seeing me in complete charge of the school, and of them, to some extent. Naturally, they will be resentful of the fact that I have stepped into Miss Trimm's shoes."

"They, themselves, will have the opportunity to apply for the permanent headship post, if they want to do so…and fairly soon, I should imagine. They know that. In the meantime, you, obviously, have to step into the breach. I don't think criticism will be thrown in your direction. Anyone who aspires to the post will take care not to put a foot wrong. Besides, teachers place more value on your work than you think. If any do grumble, take no notice. In a week or two, they will have got used to the idea that you are in charge. In fact, they will be coming to you to ask for favours. Act as if that day has already arrived. Act as if you have been in the post for years."

"Easier said than done."

"I know, but I also know you will carry it off, even though you are so young."

"I'm thirty-five but I'm glad that you brought up the question of age, Teddy. I know you, yourself are very young."

"Twenty-four."

"As I was saying, I know you are very young, but you will apply for the deputy-head's post, won't you?"

"I did tell you I'd consider applying for the post."

"And?"

Teddy looked at the floor as if he were studying it closely. After a second or two, he said, "I was thinking of moving to another school, at the north end of the Wirral. But actually, from the point of view of my career, it would make more sense to stay at Bramblewell School, if that deputy's post were, in fact, on offer."

"I know Lord Bramblewell would be keen to see you in the post," said Lynn, her expression brightening with relief. "Obviously, his opinion carries a lot of weight."

"We'll see. There will be other candidates. I haven't even been a head of department. It would be extraordinary if I were to be chosen."

"You have shown leadership in other areas and there are courses you could do, while in the acting deputy's post."

Teddy leaned back into the cushions.

"Anyway," he said. "I want to talk to you about another matter: the new school secretary."

Lynn stood up and poured coffee into the small cups on the low table in front of her from a tall, silver coffee pot.

"Isolde Delamar," she said, sitting down again, while pushing her long, waist-length, brown hair, which had swung forward, back over her shoulders.

"Yes," said Teddy. "Isolde Delamar."

His tone, it seemed to Lynn, sounded cold. Had he already met her? Lynn raised an eyebrow questioningly and Teddy noticed.

"I was visited by Susie Sutton, the evening I arrived back from France," he offered by way of explanation.

"Miss Sutton is very obviously ill at ease in Miss Delamar's presence," said Lynn. "To put it bluntly, Isolde seems to be a thorn in Susie's flesh. Let's speak plainly, Teddy. If Susie visited you, she was asking for help, wasn't she? Presumably, she wants you to unseat her rival."

"She left me in no doubt of what she wanted me to do, but I could not go along with her ill-conceived and frankly embarrassing plan."

"What sort of plan?" asked Lynn, curious to know what Susie

had had in mind.

"She wanted me to date Isolde."

"That's funny!"

"Yes. I suppose it is."

"But, you know, dating you might take Isolde's mind off mischief making! Don't forget that I find that young woman really troublesome, also. It's her attitude that annoys. She's like one of those teenagers in a classroom who knows how to annoy a teacher without doing or actually saying anything that the teacher could identify as an act of wrong-doing. You know what I'm talking about, Teddy. The sneer on the face…the mocking smile…the silent sniggering behind the hand… Isolde Delamar is a grown-up version of the type of girl who would behave in that way."

"She sounds horrible."

"I'm sorry to have to say this, but that actually is the word that comes to mind."

"Hm!" said Teddy, his expression thoughtful.

Lynn looked at him in surprise. Then, she frowned. She had once read that there were men who found women, whom other women disliked, to be rather intriguing! But, surely Teddy was not a man of that unattractive type, was he? Surely she could trust him, couldn't she?

CHAPTER 36

Grumbles in the Staff-Room

Had the air been sharper, the teachers' return to Bramblewell School, for the prelude to the new term proper, might have been easier. But the morning was warm and the rays of the sun, streaming through the windows of the staff- room, were more conducive to memories of holidays than thoughts of timetables, future work programmes and the results of examinations. At 8.30 a.m., the atmosphere in the principal staff-room was a dispirited one.

"You know," said Thetis Ravenswood, teacher of Latin and Ancient Greek, "people, in general, feel sorry for pupils who are waiting for exam results, throughout the summer holidays, and quite rightly. But, there is little sympathy for teachers who go through that waiting process year after year! I mean, these days, the subject you teach can stand or fall, in status, when the results obtained by the pupils you happened to have in a class are published! Your pupils might have been downright lazy, rather than desirably hard-working, but that fact isn't considered when results are released! And we teachers can't even write the truth in report books! Witty or pithy remarks are no longer permitted! Everything written about a child has to be bland, bland, bland! Oh! I despair!"

Anna Layne, teacher of mathematics, smiled at Thetis' outburst, but decided to lighten the atmosphere by turning to speak to Barbara Merrivale, who was sitting near her in a white, leather arm chair, one of a number of comfortable, white chairs, scattered in groups around the spacious room, each group separated from the others by large, palm-like plants in heavy pots.

"So, Barbara, are you going to tell us all about it?" she asked, cheerily.

"The holiday in France?"

"Yes."

Anna placed the mug of tea she had been holding on to its saucer on the low table in front of her. She looked at Barbara with expectation.

"You've had your hair cut!" Lydia Dacre-Hill, the teacher of English in the upper school, exclaimed then, before Barbara could begin. "It suits you!"

"Yes. It's shorter," said Barbara, ruffling her hair with her fingers. "I had it done in Bordeaux. The girl who cut it - I think her name was Agnès - made a sketch of what the style would look like, before she picked up her scissors. She gave me time to think about what she had suggested."

"That was helpful," said Lydia. "Communication in foreign beauty salons can sometimes be difficult. One ends up speaking slowly and loudly and, of course, looking ridiculous."

"What about the important part of the holiday?" interrupted Thetis, who was now placing books she had brought with her on an empty shelf, in the nearest glass-fronted book case. "Did everything proceed as expected? One can never be sure of what will happen when taking teenage girls abroad and believe me, I speak from experience! I think the sun affects girls' brains! The troubles I have had when taking parties of even the most serious Latin scholars to see Roman ruins! You have no idea!"

"Oh! Thetis! It was fine!" said Barbara reassuringly. "The weather was lovely, of course, and the food was really nice. Lord Bramblewell and Susie Sutton stayed for a bit, but they left rather unexpectedly, I have to say. Oh! By the way, on the way back on the train, I had only Portia Price and Rosalind Somerland with me and it quickly became clear to me that they were aware of Miss Trimm's departure."

"Oh! I think everyone knows about Miss Trimm, now," said

Savannah Rock, the chemistry teacher. "During the holiday, Susie Sutton would have found out what Miss Trimm had decided to do and she would probably have broken the news to Rosalind Somerland and Rosalind would have told her friends and before long, the whole school would have known, thanks to mobile phones."

The conversation was halted, at that point, by a tall, young woman, dressed in a smartly tailored, maroon trouser suit, who strolled, nonchalantly, into the staff-room. Her dark blonde hair, falling smoothly to her shoulders, added to the air of sophistication that she conveyed through the erectness of her carriage as well as the elegance of her gait - an elegance which Barbara, for one, associated with early lessons in ballet or later training, perhaps, at a school for fashion models. The newcomer was carrying a bundle of plastic folders in her arms. Without preamble and using an accent she might have acquired in Chelsea, but which was overlain with an affected American drawl, she said:

"I am Isolde Delamar, the new P.A. to the headmistress. I have a folder for each of you. Please read what is in it, before proceeding to the staff meeting which will be held in the Assembly Hall at 9 a.m. precisely. Who is Mrs. Hill?"

"Miss Dacre-Hill," Lydia corrected the self-introduced Isolde, stretching out her arm to receive the folder.

Isolde did not respond as expected. Not deigning to move forward to hand the folder to Lydia, she placed it, instead, on the table.

"Who is Mrs. Ravenswood?" she asked, then, in peremptory fashion.

"Over here!" stated Thetis, using her grandest accent, one she normally toned down, when conversing with friends.

Again, the young woman in the maroon suit made no attempt to approach the teacher whose name she had called, but placed the folder on the table.

"And who is Mrs. Rock?" she then asked, apparently now

weary of her task.

"I am," said Savannah, calmly, putting up her hand.

"Is that your real name or one you've made up?" asked Isolde, a sneer in her voice. "Do you teach geology?"

There was a rustle of silk as a teacher rose from her seat, amidst a cluster of armchairs, nearby. Mrs. Margaret Devere, head of the prep. school, approached the teachers Isolde was addressing. Looking splendid in a sea-blue, full skirted dress, which almost reached her ankles and skimmed her high-heeled, court shoes, she stood slightly apart, as if monitoring what was happening. Then, she calmly said:

"Why don't you leave the folders here and return to your office? You are wasting everyone's time."

"I'll leave them, then!" said Isolde crossly, placing the bundle of folders on the table with a thump.

"I think you had better," said Barbara Merrivale, coldly.

"Well! You can sort them out by yourselves," said Isolde, as she made for the door of the staffroom, still hoity-toity in her manner of speaking and arrogant in her bearing.

Just as she reached the door, it was pushed open, from the other side, by Teddy Laurence, dressed soberly, that morning, in a charcoal grey suit , a white shirt and a grey tie.

"Sorry, Isolde," he said, dispassionately, as he stood aside to allow the young woman to pass. He did not look at her, but he frowned as he became aware of the scent of patchouli that trailed behind her. He, then, walked into the staffroom and recognised, at once, that tension was hanging in the air.

"I can't believe what I have just witnessed," said Margaret Devere, as she sat down in a vacant seat, beside Anna Layne.

"What's up?" asked Teddy, sitting beside Savannah.

"That girl has to go!" said Bunty West, the Biology teacher, who had been silent until then. "She simply does not know how to conduct herself. I mean, she's clueless!"

"Lynn has already found working with her a strain," said

Teddy, with a sigh of exasperation.

"A strain?" gasped Barbara Merrivale. "Surely you mean that Lynn has found working with her tantamount to being a nightmare! How can you possibly allow her to remain in the school office, answering telephone calls and talking to parents? She can't possibly be allowed to represent the school!"

"How could she possibly have been appointed in the first place?" asked Lydia Dacre-Hill, her voice laden with disbelief. "I know about Lord Bramblewell's past involvement with her, but he's an intelligent man and…"

Lydia stopped as Anna Layne turned to look at her, with one eyebrow raised cynically.

"Yes. All right, Anna! Arguably, his judgement in choosing Susie Sutton as a future bride could call into question his judgement of suitability when it comes to women, in general," conceded Lydia. "But given the way this Isolde Delamar treated him in the past, one would have thought he'd not have wanted to see her again. I don't understand him. I really don't! And why has she come back now, after all these years? Has she suddenly become desperate because he is going to marry someone else? Did she think he would stay un-married forever because she had left him? More fool her!"

"Never underestimate the effect that a rival can have on a woman's behaviour," said Thetis, peering over the pin-hole glasses she used for reading.

"Can you find a way to release this Isolde Delamar from her contract, Teddy?" Savannah asked, then, turning towards him. "I assume you'll be acting deputy head. Incidentally, when will your appointment be made official?"

"Hold your horses! Other people will be applying for the post," said Teddy, taken aback at the way Savannah was speaking, as if his appointment had been a fait accompli. "I'm sure you want to apply, Thetis," he added. "You have so much experience and Lynn could do with…"

However, Thetis put up her hand to interrupt him.

"No, thank you, my dear!" she said. "The job is yours as far as I am concerned. Besides, if you will be required to work with the young woman who has now ensconced herself in the school office, I don't envy you,"

"Agreed!" said Savannah, with some force, aggrieved over the fact that she could still feel, within her, the soreness and frustration that accompany public humiliation, no matter how slight. She had been astonished when the ill-mannered Isolde had made fun of her name. She, herself, would never have dreamt of making fun of a person's name, and especially not that of a pupil, no matter how outrageous the child's parents' choice of name had been. She had always believed her own surname, Rock, to have been a derivation of Petroc and she was proud of it, given the fact that she had Cornish antecedents.

Various conversations started up among the teachers in the group, on the subject of Isolde, then. Teddy leaned towards Savannah.

"What happened, exactly?" he asked softly.

Moved by Teddy's gentle approach, Savannah suddenly found she could no longer hold back the tears that were coming into her eyes.

"What happened?" Teddy repeated, more insistently. He had never seen the sensible, mature and strong Savannah losing control of her emotions before.

"Oh! That girl took me by surprise. That's all. Throw beginning-of-term-blues into the mix and everything seems worse, anyway. Don't worry Teds! It's all right!"

Teddy looked at Savannah for a moment or two, saying nothing. Then, he rose and left the room, his expression angry.

CHAPTER 37

A Different Point of View

Susie Sutton had told Lord Bramblewell that she had decided to spend a few days at Ywen Manor, in the south of Wales, an invitation having been extended to her by Gwenny, the wife of his nephew, Horatio Bramblewell-Eurlinn.

"It will do you good," Lord Bramblewell had said, congenially, having taken in the strained look on Susie's face, "but, perhaps you would prefer to have another holiday in France. I could take you to the south of France. Would you like to go there?"

Susie, remembering how careful she had once had to be when using money - saving up for this and depriving herself of that - had been taken aback at the idea of having two holidays within a short period of time, and in France no less, but she had realised, too, why Lord Bramblewell had made the suggestion. Looking at her reflection in a mirror, she had had to admit that she had lost weight very rapidly and with it, her former joie de vivre. Of course, the loss of weight had given her face what beauticians would have called "contours," but Susie had known that she had looked more attractive when her face had had more volume. She had been tempted to accept the offer, naturally. Momentarily, she had imagined herself enjoying warm evenings on the Côte d'Azur, sitting on the terraces of restaurants, sipping continental, iced drinks, while gazing, with a child-like fascination, at the lights of casinos and smart hotels along the coast and at glamorously lit yachts, on the dark waters of the Mediterranean. However, she had very much wanted to talk to Gwenny, whose judgement she had learnt to trust, and so she had declined Lord Bramblewell's kind invitation.

"I'd really like to talk to Gwenny about the wedding," she had explained. "Women sometimes need to talk to other women about things like that."

Lord Bramblewell had said he had understood and consequently, one clear morning,, Susie drove out of the gates of Bramblewell Manor and headed for Wales. She was feeling better than she had felt for a while and as she was driving, the thought crossed her mind that the change of air and location would, indeed, do her good. When she was outside of Chester, she followed the road signs for Wrexham, over the border, and before long, she was in the midst of countryside that was different from Cheshire's but lovely in another way. As she drove, she caught glimpses of Welsh hills and meadows through gaps in the trees, and, here and there, of farm houses surrounded by fields of livestock. She wondered what the décor inside those houses would be like. At Bramblewell Manor, she had begun to reflect on the way the ambiance created by a building had an effect on the way one felt. The high ceilings of the manor made her thoughts soar usually, but she had also discovered that when one was tortured by a pressing problem - the existence of Isolde Delamar, for example, - all of one's thoughts and, in fact, one's perception of the world were darkened by it, no matter how beautiful one's surroundings.

The journey lasted several hours, because Susie did not drive fast and, furthermore, because she stopped now and again, to eat or to have a cup of tea in a café. She considered making detours to visit Betwys-y-Coed, in order to visit souvenir shops, which she loved, or, alternatively, the bookshops of Llangollen, but she decided ultimately that she had better press on. As she made her way south, she imagined she could feel the pull of the Severn, but knew she was probably being fanciful.

Towards evening, she turned into the long drive that led up to Ywen Manor, the magnificent, stone building that stood amidst Bramblewell-Eurlinn lands. Gwenny, her long dark hair ruffled by a breeze, ran down the steps to greet her, when her car came to a halt, before the great door.

"Oh! You made it!" Gwenny exclaimed. "How lovely to see you! Julian is here and so is his university friend, Pomeroy and Pomeroy's girlfriend, Tansy. You remember Tansy, don't you?"

"Oh, yes! I remember Tansy!" said Susie, swivelling in the front seat to swing her legs out of the car in lady-like fashion and noticing, as she did so, that Julian was running down the steps to greet her, also.

"Oh! Thank Goodness!" she thought. She had never previously realised the extent to which Julian made her feel peaceful and secure, but she was becoming aware of it now. She had become used to his reassuring presence while at the Château du Crâne and had missed him when she had left. She wondered, momentarily, if she could confess to him what her fears regarding Isolde Delamar were, but then, she decided it would be unfair to burden him with them when he was about to return to university to start another term of study. She had heard that he was about to inherit the Château du Crâne, officially, as well. He had quite enough, in fact, to occupy his thoughts, without her adding to his problems.

"Where's your luggage?" Julian asked. "I'll take care of it! It's good to see you!"

Dressed in blue jeans, a white shirt and a navy blue jacket, with braided button-holes, that looked as if it had been cut and sewn in the eighteenth century, Julian cut a dash, Susie thought, especially since he was wearing high, polished boots as well. Gwenny, in a baby-blue skirt that reached her ankles and a loose, beige jumper, looked as attractive as ever. Susie remembered, ruefully, how she, herself, had been dressed, the first time she had visited the manor. In her high-heeled shoes and city suit, she had hardly been prepared for walks in the country.

"I've put you in the same room as before," said Gwenny. "You liked the view, didn't you? Come on!"

Inside the manor, Susie followed Gwenny up the remarkable, wide staircase, feeling increasingly at ease, because she sensed she was among friends who would be on her side, were there ever to be friction between her and Isolde. The room was familiar and, once Gwenny had left, Susie sat on her bed and focused her thoughts on nothing more daunting than what she would wear for dinner.

That evening, in fact, she went downstairs wearing beige trousers, pink ballerina shoes and a plain, pink blouse. The outfit was informal but gave one the impression, as well, that she had made an effort to look pretty.

"Hi!" called Tansy, once Susie had walked through the door of the huge kitchen. "How lovely to see you again!"

Tansy, as accommodating of Susie's hesitancy as she had been before, walked forward to greet her and to accompany her, across the vast space between door and table. Although the atmosphere was deliberately casual, Horatio, Julian and Pomeroy who had already been sitting around the long table, chatting, stood, as Susie approached and she was visibly moved by their old-school charm. Susie held out her hand to Horatio, who was nearest to her when she reached the table. "Hello!" she said, cheerfully, while privately thinking, "I'm getting good at this."

Like his brother, Julian, Horatio was dressed in a white shirt and blue jeans, but his jacket was a red, Romantic-era one. The brothers' penchant for the extraordinary in jackets, Susie found quite in keeping with their surroundings.

Wanting to be useful, she offered to help Gwenny and Tansy transport dishes from huge oven to long, oak table, but Gwenny would not allow her to do so.

"Not tonight! You are our guest!" Gwenny insisted, as she paraded dishes of lamb stew, potatoes au gratin, French beans cooked with onions, carrots and peas, various salads and champagne ice cream before all assembled.

After eating, Susie felt sleepy, but later in the evening, she was still up and drinking cocoa in the corner of the manor's library with Tansy, Gwenny and Julian, while Horatio took Pomeroy to have a look at the fish in the garden ponds.

"I knew that something wasn't quite right when I spoke to you on the telephone, Susie," said Gwenny gently. "Do you want to talk about whatever is bothering you, now?"

"Should I be here?" asked Julian quickly. "Should I go?"

"Gosh! No!" said Susie. "Please stay…if you want to!"

"Is something in particular preying on your mind?" pressed Gwenny. "Does it concern Rupert?"

Since Gwenny was not beating about the bush, Susie saw no point in doing so, either. After all, she trusted all three people present.

"Rupert has appointed to a plum, administrative post in Bramblewell School, a woman to whom he was once engaged: Isolde Delamar. I don't know how he could have done this without realising how insecure his action would make me feel. Rupert can protest as much as he likes that Isolde means nothing to him, now. If she means nothing to him, why has he felt so compelled to give her a job? That's what I'd like to know. If Isolde means nothing to him, he should not behave as if she does, should he? Do you follow what I am saying? Anyway, what is really annoying is the fact that Isolde looks like a fashion model and obviously doesn't think I could ever compete with her, even if I tried to do so. She ignores me, in fact. She looks through me as if I don't exist. I suspect she is completely convinced she will win Rupert back and that she will be the one walking down the aisle with him in Chester Cathedral, in seven months' time. What should I do?"

Susie looked imploringly at Julian, but he was sitting with his hands clasped between his knees and his head bowed. Of course, he greatly admired his Uncle Rupert. It occurred to Susie she should not have criticised Lord Bramblewell so harshly in front of him.

"Gosh!" said Tansy, softly, then, to break the spell of silence.

Gwenny leaned back so that her head was resting against a book-laden shelf.

"Listen, Susie," she said. "I know what all three of us are

thinking and I hope you will not mind my pointing out what is obvious to us. It is this: is it not true that a former boyfriend of your own is employed at Bramblewell School?"

"You mean…Teddy Laurence?" said Susie, sounding incredulous.

"Yes. Obviously."

"But, Teddy means nothing to me. I mean, he's just a friend."

"Oh, Susie! Listen to yourself!" protested Gwenny, kindly. "You have just said, 'He means nothing to me' and 'He's just a friend.' I don't doubt that you are telling the truth, but is it not true that Rupert will have said similar things about Isolde Delamar? And doesn't it occur to you that Teddy Laurence's presence in the school might dismay Rupert as much as Isolde Delamar's presence dismays you?"

"But Rupert likes Teddy!" insisted Susie. "I know Rupert actually respects Teddy."

"That may well be the case," said Gwenny patiently. "But the fact remains, that Teddy is a former boyfriend of yours and he is ever-present."

"The difference being," interrupted Tansy, that this Teddy Laurence is probably an honourable chap, whereas Isolde whatever-her-name-is sounds as if she could be plotting Susie's downfall."

"I just wanted to point out that both a former girlfriend and a former boyfriend were in the school," said Gwenny. "And I'm not sure, Susie, if the thought that Rupert might have been concerned about Teddy's presence ever even crossed your mind."

"It didn't" admitted Susie. "Maybe I should have been more sensitive."

"I don't want to go on and on," said Gwenny, "but I feel I should also mention the fact that you did arrange for Teddy Laurence to be the star of the film that was shot at the Château du Crâne and that you persuaded Rupert to pay the lion's share of the funding for the film. How do you think your action might have been judged by the detached observer? What if Isolde Delamar had become aware of the arrangement and had concluded you were making a fool of Rupert? What if she had decided to save him from making a terrible mistake in marrying you? What if she had thought he deserved better than a woman who was bent on using his money to turn a previous boyfriend into a film star?"

"No! I wasn't doing that!" gasped Susie, turning pink from anger as well as embarrassment. "I had to twist Teddy's arm to make him appear in the film! He was really annoyed with me! I actually wanted to have the film made for Rosalind Somerland's sake!"

"Ah! Yes!" said Gwenny, mercilessly. "The daughter of another ex-boyfriend!"

"That's enough, Gwenny!" interrupted Julian. "The story's more complicated than that."

"Listen, Susie," said Gwenny more gently. "I'm just trying to explain to you what people will think. You will have to manage people's perception of your behaviour more carefully, when you will be Lady Bramblewell."

"What did you say to Teddy to make him accept the rôle in the film?" asked Tansy then, in an attempt to help Susie save face.

"I told him that if he didn't accept the part, the film would simply not be made and if it wasn't made, the girls whose play was the basis of the film script wouldn't be paid anything and then, one of them, Talitha Appleby, wouldn't be able to stay at Bramblewell School, since she needed the money to pay for her school fees. Her parents had run into financial difficulties and she wasn't clever enough to win a Lord Bramblewell scholarship."

"Oh! I see," said Tansy, re-framing the picture she had had in her mind of Susie. She glanced at Julian but she could not interpret his thoughtful expression.

"You think I'm an awful person," said Susie, looking from Tansy to Gwenny and then, to Julian, who was now gazing at the ground. "Well! I'm not! I wanted Teddy to appear in the film so that he'd have a lot of money. There! I've said it! I wanted him to be happy! I wanted him to be able to travel and see places he had read about, to make up for the way I had treated him in the past."

Suddenly, Gwenny sat upright and said briskly:

"Listen, Susiie! I think you should return to Bramblewell Manor and spend the time between now and the wedding concentrating on turning yourself into a truly irreplaceable Lady Bramblewell. Find out what a lady of the manor would, traditionally, have been expected to do and using that knowledge as a guide, start to prepare for what lies ahead. You might consider, for example, supporting local charities, in practical ways, by asking Rupert if he would consider throwing open parts of the grounds for garden parties, once or twice a year, to raise funds. You once told me that you still had nightmares about having no home. Why not offer to help a charity for the homeless? You could also ask Lord Bramblewell if he would consider establishing a scholarship in your name. It could be given to a girl or even to one of the few boys who enter the school at sixth form level. It could be awarded to a pupil who could demonstrate he or she had a talent for - shall we say? - enterprise."

Tansy gave Gwenny a glance, wondering if she was being ironic, but Gwenny's expression was inscrutable.

"Wow! Gwenny!" said Susie, with enthusiasm. "I think that's an amazing idea."

"Yes," said Gwenny. "I think that is how you should proceed. And if Isolde continues to ignore you - well! - you can reciprocate by ignoring her. Once the new term begins properly at Bramblewell School, she will be too busy to focus on anything, anyway, other than the work piling up on her desk."

"I think, also," interjected Tansy, "that you should stop mentioning her name to Lord Bramblewell."

"Yes," agreed Gwenny. "Keep your conversations with Rupert light. Look cheerful and have a list of other things to discuss each evening. Don't allow him to think you are mean-spirited. I think

Rupert would prefer you to be generous and to trust him."

"I know you are right," said Susie. "What you suggest is the only civilised way in which I can deal with the Isolde problem."

After a pause, she added with a sigh, "And if I lose, I lose."

Julian stood and walked over to a window, to watch the setting sun.

"Well! That was an eye-opener," he said softly, as Tansy joined him.

CHAPTER 38

The Gardens of Ywen Manor

Susie did not sleep well during the first night of her visit to Ywen Manor, although her bed was large and firm, the sheets of fine linen and the pillows lightly scented with lavender. After slipping into sleep, she would wake up minutes later, her thoughts returning repeatedly to the conversation she had had with Gwenny, Tansy and Julian, after dinner. The revelation that she had forced her former boyfriend, Teddy Laurence, that summer, to appear in a film for which she had asked Lord Bramblewell to provide funding, had seemed to shock Tansy. Naturally, Tansy, who was the epitome of well brought up niceness, had made no comment about her apparent misgivings and had continued to speak to Susie with friendly warmth. But, Susie had noticed the way Tansy had averted her eyes more than before, when talking to her and she had been aware, also, on an intuitive level, of a slight withdrawal of favour on Tansy's part: a withdrawal stemming, no doubt, from her disappointment over what she would have perceived to have been Susie's gaucheness and lack of sensitivity in dealing with ever-patient Lord Bramblewell.

After that restless night, Susie rose early the next morning. After bathing, she dressed herself in blue jeans , a white, knitted jumper and little, white ankle boots, before leaving her room quietly and making her way down the wide, grand staircase to the ground floor. She found a door that was easy to open near the spacious kitchen and she walked out into the gardens, conscious of the fact that the air, though fresh, was already scented with the perfumes of flowers. The grass was dewy and so she kept to the paths and soon, she found herself going up steps to an arch in a thick hedge that led her in the direction of an old sundial. Julian Bramblewell-Eurlinn, his throat-length, pale golden hair glinting in the light of the rising sun, was standing looking at the sundial, occasionally glancing in one direction and then another, as if making mental calculations, involving time and distance. Dressed in jeans and a jacket of deep blue velvet,he looked like a handsome, princely youth in a painting by Edward Burne-Jones, Susie thought, her acquaintance with the Pre-Raphaelites, though recent, now approaching adequacy. She stopped and watched Julian, reluctant to interrupt his thoughts by walking nearer to him, but then, he caught sight of her.

"Hi!" he called as he came towards her. "You're up early!"

Noticing Susie's drawn expression, he frowned and pushed back a lock of golden hair that had fallen forward, over his eyes.

"Let's take a turn around the gardens, as they say in Miss Austen's books," he suggested. "Let's take a turn around the gardens, Miss Sutton!"

He offered Susie his arm and she gratefully accepted the offer of physical support. It was comforting for her to be near Julian, since he exuded peace combined with strength and he was decent, amusing and kind. On her previous visit to Ywen Manor, she had expected to have been confronted with some hostility on the part of the Bramblewell-Eurlinn family, given her lack of obvious qualifications for the rôle of Lady Bramblewell. She was not formally well-educated, after all and was lacking, considerably, in social graces. However, both Horatio Bramblewell-Eurlinn and Julian had treated her with courtesy and respect, making not one allusion to her deficiencies. Gwenny had been almost maternal in her delivering of reassurance and guidance.

Susie allowed herself to be led by Julian past pools of water in which little fish swam and then, into a Tudor garden. On Julian's invitation, she sat with him on an oak bench, looking at the views of trees and meadows that stretched, verdantly, beyond the manor for miles. Susie wanted to ask Julian what he had thought, honestly, about all that she had - no doubt, unwisely- said the previous evening, when talking about Teddy Laurence and Lord Bramblewell. However, words and courage could not be summoned. She, then, started to ask him about Héloïse de Sauzon, but realising that a direct enquiry might be judged to be blunderingly clumsy, she went no further than, "Are you in touch with…?" before lapsing into a silence. Julian smiled, though.

"You were going to ask me about Héloïse, I think," he said. "I expect you realised I was drawn to her while we were at the Chấreau du Crâne. Was it very obvious?"

"Well…No. Not really. I just wondered…"

"We send each other messages now and again, but not often. I'm investigating the history of the family that lived at the Château du Crâne, as you possibly know and Héloïse sometimes sends me snippets of information that have come her way. It's important for me to know the history of the château as I am thinking of ways to make it pay for its own repairs. My mother had been hoping to make some money by renting it to the film crew this summer, but after totting up her sums, she found she had made only enough money to renovate one quarter of it, if that much. It's a problem."

"Neither of you would sell it, though, would you?"

"No. She is going to hand it over to me soon, but she is hoping that I shall look at it with fresh eyes and will come up with a way to make it viable as a business project."

"Lord Bramblewell would help," Susie began to say impulsively, but then, stopped, remembering Tansy's reaction to the revelation of the night before. Susie had realised that Tansy had considered it inappropriate for her to determine the ways in which Lord Bramblwell's money could be lavishly spent.

"Oh! I know Uncle Rupert would very obligingly help," said Julian, choosing not to notice Susie's private consternation. "But, I want to deal with this project on my own to the extent that I can. I do have some ideas but, at the moment, they will have to remain at the planning stage. I'll really have to get my degree from Bristol first. Working for my degree takes priority at the moment. 'Vim promovet insitam,' as they say. I have just one more year to go and then, I'll start to consider what to do with the château. I thought of bringing the vineyard back to life."

"Could Héloïse help you in any way?"

"Ah!" said Julian, leaning back on the bench and looking up at the brightening sky. "Héloïse suspects she may be descended from the Counts du Crâne who owned the château, before…but I don't know if she has a natural ability when it comes to growing vines!"

"Oh."

"You do realise," said Julian then, "that I suspect Héloïse was more attracted to Teddy Laurence than to me."

"Teddy Laurence?"

"Yes."

"Her sister's former fiancé?"

"Well, yes."

"Héloïse must know that Teddy Laurence wouldn't want to have any contact with her family, after the way her sister treated him. I'd bet that she is just playing games. She wants to see if she can crush his pride completely. She's…dangerous."

"No. You have misunderstood her."

"I don't think so. Be careful, Julian!"

"She has arranged for me to stay with her sister, Jacqueline, when I go to Paris, before the university term begins. I want to do some investigations into the lineage of the Counts du Crâne, you see. I think one of them lives in Paris."

"So…you are going to stay with Jacqueline? You do know that Teddy can barely tolerate hearing her name being mentioned, don't you?"

"I was aware of some friction."

"Julian…"

"Oh! Don't look so worried, Miss Sutton!" exclaimed Julian with a laugh, interrupting her before she could say more. "I can look after myself! Come on! Let's go inside and have breakfast!"

Julian stood and held out his hand to Susie, to help her to her feet.

"My lady!" he said.

He was smiling down at Susie and she noticed that the look in his eyes was warm, but that there was something else, in his look, that she could not decipher. She wondered if he thought that she truly deserved the title of "lady" or if, given her performance the previous evening, he believed she was undeserving of it. She would not blame him if he thought badly of her, for that morning, she, herself, felt shallow. What right had she to criticise Héloïse, or indeed, anyone else, given the thoughtless selfishness of her own behaviour?

CHAPTER 39

First Term

The first morning of the first term of the new scholastic year, for Bramblewell girls, was invariably one marked by chatter, amiability or, in some quarters, despondency. Having met in the grounds of Bramblewell School early, Rosalind Somerland, Ida Traversi, Talitha Appleby and Portia Price were spending their last minutes, prior to the ringing of the bell for morning assembly, reminiscing about their summer in France and then, in giving each other accounts of how they had spent their time afterwards. While talking, they had wandered up to the high piece of ground, the rise that overlooked the school's two tennis courts, which were situated on lower ground, and beyond them, the lush, green sports field, edged thickly with trees and bushes. Talitha and Ida were now sitting on a felled log, their legs stretched out in front of them, Ida stylishly wearing the new knee-length, navy socks which had been introduced as an optional part of the school uniform, thanks to Miss James.

Portia was standing close to the edge of the rise, her hands in the pockets of her striped, summer blazer: one which Bramblewell pupils were allowed to wear until October, when the navy blue blazer became obligatory. She was watching a group of girls, on the lower ground, making their way to the glassy building near them. It housed four of the school's classrooms, in addition to the library, the science corridor, the ballet practice room and the little theatre known as The Woodlanders. The theatre was Portia's favourite space in the entire school and she was already silently making plans to spend her spare time there.

Rosalind was leaning against an old, solid oak tree, appreciating the comforting closeness, also, of sycamores, beech trees and horse chestnuts. The leaves of the trees were rustling in a breeze which was cooling her brow, left fevered by her state of uncertainty. What lay ahead? Would she pass her exams at the end of the year? Her mind was not at ease. But, curiously, that morning, she felt a kind of excitement, also: one triggered by an expectation of the new experiences the year ahead would bring.

Rosalind noticed that Portia was looking pensively in the direction of the theatre and, eager to bring up the topic of The Eliza Club, she asked:

"Shouldn't we start talking about the Christmas play? I know it's a bit early, but the play will have to be written and... You know...

"What?" asked Portia, turning round to face her friend. "Oh... Yes! You're right. We'd better get down to deciding what we are going to do, this year. What do you all think? Any ideas?"

As she was addressing her three friends, Portia noticed, behind them, two Bramblewell girls who were approaching, through the trees. One was Stella Lomas, the new head girl. The other, a tall girl with long hair and an attractive face, Portia had never seen before.

"Hi," said Stella, as she reached the little group. "I'm assuming this is a meeting of The Eliza Club. Is it?"

"Not officially," answered Portia, "although, funnily enough, we were about to talk about the Christmas play."

"Right - oh," said Stella. "I'm glad to see you're quick off the mark."

"We'd better get down to it," said Portia, sounding all grown-up, because she wanted to impress Stella, who had now acquired some kudos, being the bearer of a Head Girl's badge. "This will obviously be a heavy year for us, academically," she continued, importantly, "but Mrs. Merrivale has managed to persuade Miss James to let us carry on running the club more or less as before. We shan't have any time to waste dithering, though."

"Of course not," said Stella, apparently impressed by Portia's business-like manner. "Anyway," she added, turning to encourage her companion to step forward, "this is Irene Miller."

Irene, who had been silently watchful, now smiled.

"Hello!" she said, brightly.

"Come over here! Sit beside us," invited Ida, in a friendly way, while moving closer to Talitha, on the log. "Are you a boarder or a day girl?"

"A boarder, but I shall go home to London at weekends." replied Irene. "I am sharing a room, here, with Araminta Smythe. Do you know her?"

"Ah!" said Portia, wondering if she should point out that, the previous year, Araminta had acquired a reputation for being a childish sort of bully. She quickly concluded she had better not mention that fact to a new girl, though. After all, Araminta might have grown up during the holiday and might have acquired more sophistication, in the process. Besides, she did not want Stella to think she was a gossip and so, she said, diplomatically: "Araminta didn't really mix with us."

"No," said Rosalind, who had been subjected to the derision of Araminta and her little côterie of friends, when she, Rosalind, had first arrived in the school. "She had her own favourites."

"Who arranged for you to share with Araminta?" asked Talitha.

"Oh! Miss Delamar, the new secretary did," explained Stella, answering for Irene.

There was a hint of displeasure in Stella's voice and Portia, sensitive, always, to changes in tone, expression and mood, surmised that the new secretary had made an unfavourable impression on the head girl.

"You can always move to another room, Irene, if you have nothing in common with Araminta," Talitha suggested helpfully. "Ida and I are boarders, too, and we'll help you move if you find you are not getting along with Araminta."

"Well!" said Stella, looking pleased. "You can talk about that later, Irene. I'll leave you now as I have to return to the new building. Miss James wants to see me before assembly."

"I can't believe Miss Trimm has actually gone," said Rosalind, as Stella walked away. "I wonder what Miss James will be like as head of the school."

"I don't think it will be Miss James who will rock the boat," said Portia, frowning. "Eva Derbyshire was hopeless, but at least she left us alone! I imagine Stella could be a lot stricter."

"Were you talking about plays?" interrupted Irene, as if impatient. "I love the theatre! I'm not scared of performing! And I can dance!"

"Can you actually act?" asked Portia, looking interested.

"Of course!" exclaimed Irene, as if the question had been un-necessary. "Did you say you were going to stage a play at Christmas? Which one?"

"We haven't decided," said Ida. "We could make up a play based on some historical event, as we did last year. Or rather, as Rosalind did, last year. Or we could adapt the plot of a book."

"I love 'The Age of Innocence' by Edith Wharton," said Talitha, who had developed a taste for American literature. "I think it would be easy to adapt."

"Oh no! Please do 'Anna Karenina'!" said Irene, interrupting without hesitation. "It's the favourite book of my Russian ballet teacher's son! His name is Rudi, by the way. It's such a sad story. It's full of Russian sadness."

"Do you think people would want to watch a play full of Russian sadness at Christmas?" asked Rosalind, but Irene ignored her question and, instead, turned to Portia, her grey-green eyes wide.

"Oh! Please!" she pleaded.

"Well…!" began Portia, taking her hands out of her blazer pockets and leaning against the trunk of a sycamore tree. "Actually, we could use some of the costumes we used last year for the ballroom scenes. We would have to make very few changes to the costumes if we did stage 'Anna Karenina'."

"I can help to paint the back cloth," said Irene eagerly. "And design the sets. I can do anything, really."

"Well! You're quite a find, aren't you?" said Portia, frowning now, as if deep in thought.

"What is the story of the book, again?" asked Rosalind, pushing a lock of her shoulder-length brown hair behind her ear. "Who wrote it, anyway? Pasternak?"

"Oh! No!" gasped Irene as if aghast. "Don't be stupid! It was Tolstoy! The heroïne of the book is Anna, of course. She misbehaves and ends up being shunned by her social circle. She is a mother, but does not behave responsibly. She's …just awful, really."

Rosalind felt her face turning pink with discomfort as well as anger as if it had been her own mother who had been insulted.

"I'm not sure if it will be suitable, actually," said Talitha quickly, noticing Rosalind's unease. "At Christmas, people expect to be happy."

"Wait! If handled carefully, it would be no more alarming than a Greek drama," said Portia, thoughtfully. "In fact, it might be good for girls to be reminded of the fact that they shouldn't let their hearts rule their heads completely."

"How likely is it that teenage girls of our age will pay attention to that message?" asked Talitha, with American-like candour.

"I don't know," said Ida, joining the conversation, "but what I do know is that we're going to have to make a decision fairly soon about the play we're going to do at Christmas, and this one is unusual enough to cause a bit of a stir."

"Some of the scenes could be pretty upsetting, though," said Talitha, "It doesn't strike me as being a Christmas play at all."

"We could leave out the upsetting scenes," said Ida. "Couldn't we? It wasn't unknown in European drama, centuries ago, to have upsetting events happening off stage. Someone could run on stage, saying "I have bad news about Anna!"

"Yes," agreed Portia. "But I have doubts about meddling with the text."

"Oh! Come on!" exclaimed Irene. "Are we going to do 'Anna Karenina' or not?"

"What do you all think?" asked Portia. "You first, Ida?"

"I think it might be all right but I'd be happier if we asked Mrs. Merrivale for her views also."

"Talitha?"

"We'd obviously save time if we were going to re-use costumes, but I think that we should wait a couple of days before deciding what to do."

"Rosalind?"

"I don't mind," said Rosalind. She did mind, though. She had been hoping she would have been given the opportunity to write a play of her own invention. Furthermore, she did not like the way Irene was beginning to dominate the group.

"I think the character of Kostya Levin should be emphasised in the production and I, also, think that Anna's tragic end should played down," said Ida, then. "In fact, I'd like our play to focus on the ideals and sensitivity of Kostya. His high mindedness could be contrasted with the shabbiness of the man who destroys Anna's reputation. I hate men like that!"

Irene pouted, but everyone else was paying attention to Ida. Rosalind was noting the way she had seemed to have grown up a bit in the short space of time between the holiday at the Château du Crâne and the return to school. Had something extraordinary happened in Forte dei Marmi? Had Ida, perhaps, witnessed some familial event that had forced her to view the world less as a child and more as an adult? Rosalind was longing to know, but she knew she would have to wait for Ida to confide in her, when she was ready to.

"I know there will be about ten boys in the sixth year this year," said Portia, then, not sure how to reply to Ida's suggestion, as she had not read the book in full. "I hope that they will pull their weight and take part in the play."

"And may I have a part in the play, too?" interrupted Irene, showing impatience. "I'd like to be Anna, of course."

"You may become a member of The Eliza Club if you are willing to work," said Portia, calmly.

"Yes! Of course!" exclaimed Irene. "I'll work! And if you must make Kostya Levin into the principal character, I'll play the part of Princess Kitty!"

Portia breathed in deeply and raised her eyebrows, as if hoping she had not made a mistake in allowing Irene to join the club before she had had time to assess what she was like. "Don't make friends too quickly," her mother had always warned her. "Don't trust too soon!"

"There will be auditions for the major parts," she said.

"Yes," said Rosalind. "Everyone must attend the auditions. No one can expect to be given a part without reading lines in front of Portia. She's in charge!"

Suddenly, Irene jumped up and faced Rosalind, who was still leaning against the tree.

"You don't like me, do you?" she asked in a peremptory fashion. "I saw the way you looked at me, when I turned up with the head girl!"

"I don't know what you are talking about!" exclaimed Rosalind, taken aback. "I didn't know who you were! Who are you, anyway?"

"There! How is that for acting?" asked Irene, turning towards Portia and bursting into laughter.

But Portia responded with a blank look.

At that moment, exactly, the school's electric bell trilled throughout the school's buildings.

"Andiamo!" said Ida softly and with relief.

Portia straightened her blazer and gave her glossy, Cleopatra hairstyle a pat.

"I wonder what Miss James will be wearing," said Talitha, to lift the mood. "I hope she hasn't put up her hair. It looks so lovely when it is loose. She has always looked like a fashion model, hasn't she? A fashion model who has wandered into the school by mistake. I hope she doesn't change."

"She will," said Portia, assuming the air of a girl in possession of worldly wisdom. "You'll see!"

Rosalind lagged behind as Ida, Talitha and Portia made their way, with Irene, towards the school's main building. Irene had placed herself between Talitha and Portia. And as they were descending the rise, Irene put her arms around the waists of the two girls to steady herself. She threw her head back and laughed loudly.

"She's awful!" Rosalind thought and then remembered a proverb that her grandmother, in Bristol, had been fond of repeating, the proverb being, "All that glistens is not gold." Irene had been busily trying to promote herself, with verve, as a golden girl, but was there real ability behind the dazzle?

CHAPTER 40

Mother and Daughter

Liz Laurier had made an arrangement with Gylen Somerland that, on the first day of Rosalind's new term at Bramblewell School, she, Liz, would prepare dinner for Rosalind and her brother, John, after school, in her apartment. Gylen had told his children about the plan, but John had declined the invitation. Therefore, after classes had finished for the day, Rosalind, with her leather school-bag slung over one shoulder, set off alone to where her mother lived, after taking a bus from Chester to the centre of Ellesmere Port, first.

Upon seeing her, Liz Laurier realised, at once, that the day had not gone well. But she waited until Rosalind was seated at the table and the first course of the meal had been served before she gently started to ask questions. Was Rosalind missing the stability of Miss Trimm's régime? Had changes, which were not suiting her, taken place? Surely Teddy Laurence had not left abruptly, had he?

"No. No, Mum. Nothing like that," Rosalind assured her. "It's just that…Well! There's a new girl in our class and I don't like her. I really, really don't like her."

"Oh? Why?"

"She's splitting us up!"

"Splitting you up? Who? You and Ida? Or Portia and Talitha?"

"She's playing games with all four of us. I know she is. She's a player."

"A player? What do you mean exactly?"

"She knows what she is doing, but she's pretending to be oh-so-innocent. You must know what I'm talking about."

"But the four of you are so close! How did this new girl manage to push her way into the group?"

"Oh! This morning, Stella Lomas brought her along to meet us, because she was going to be in our class. She didn't actually need Stella to help her to settle. She may have been a new girl but she certainly wasn't shy! One minute she didn't know us and the next, she was deciding for us which play we'd be doing at Christmas! Her name is Irene Miller. Portia knew I wanted to write the play for Christmas and yet, she listened to what this girl was saying and now, I think we're going to base the Christmas play on the book that was her choice."

"Whose choice? This Irene Miller's?"

"Yes! It's so unfair, Mum! It's really, really annoying. I thought Portia was my friend!"

"Portia may have a lot on her mind. Didn't you tell me that she was worried about Louis Lindsey?"

"That's not an excuse, Mum. She's supposed to be loyal to me. I wouldn't have done to her what she has done to me."

"Listen! Most disagreements like this sort themselves out over the course of a few days. Don't show that you are reacting in any way just now. Wait until the term is in full swing and then, talk quietly to Portia about the way you were hurt by her behaviour. She'll probably be shocked. She probably didn't realise, today, how her behaviour had affected you. She wasn't deliberately hurting you, was she?"

"No. Not deliberately. She was just being thoughtless, I suppose. But this Irene, is going to be..."

"Troublesome?"

"Probably."

"Well! We'll deal with the problems that arise as they come along. Can you put Irene out of your mind for an evening?"

"Yes. I think so."

"Good. Finish your soup. I'll fetch the cottage pie."

In the kitchen, Liz reflected on Rosalind's anguished appearance when she had entered the apartment. Teenage life did not become easier as the years progressed, obviously, and the field of relationships, in particular, was potentially a source of setbacks and disappointments. During the previous scholastic year, Rosalind had endured severe emotional pain as a result of her crush on Teddy Laurence. Now, another challenge was presenting itself in the form of a new girl who was pushing her way into Rosalind's group of friends. Dealing with challenges such as that required skills that could be learnt. She, Liz, would have to speed up her writing of the book she was preparing for Rosalind, though. Never previously had it been so obvious that it was needed. Knowledge did not eradicate emotional pain, but understanding surely made it more tolerable.

Liz brought the dish containing the cottage pie out of the oven and arranged a green salad on a large, flat dish. Rosalind would feel better once she had eaten nourishing food. Liz had become a great believer in the healing quality of comforting meals. How unfortunate, though, that it was only now that she was beginning to cultivate the mothering side of her nature! She could not blot out the past, but she could try to help at least one of her children to deal with the teenage years and eventually step over the threshold into a successful and happy adulthood, couldn't she? Couldn't she? Liz gripped the side of the kitchen table as a wave of emotion, arising from guilt and regret, unexpectedly swept over her.

"Mum? Are you all right?" asked Rosalind, entering the kitchen at that moment, anxiety evident in her voice as she looked in amazement at the mother, who was normally so cool and in control of her emotions, pushing back tears.

"Yes, Of course," said Liz, regaining her composure. "I've a head ache. That's all. Don't worry, pet. Let's carry these plates to the table."

Liz was tempted to confide in her daughter and reveal what her own fears were, but she believed it was unfair for a mother to act as if she were one of her daughter's friends, thus burdening her, rather than making life easier for her. She was Rosalind's mother and that meant that she had to be the wise one and the strong one, until her children were safely out of the rapids. It was time for her to shoulder her responsibilities and finally and effectively, to grow up, instead of playing "houses" like a little girl, herself.

CHAPTER 41

Autumn in Paris

Julian Bramblewell-Eurlinn had been to Paris before, on several occasions, but he had never, previously, stayed on the Left Bank, and specifically, in the Latin Quarter, despite the fact that the area was the one in which students were found in great numbers, frequenting bookshops, pensively making their way to classes or endowing neighbourhood cafés with an air of seriousness.

Héloïse de Sauzon had insisted Julian stay in this part of the French capital with her sister, Jacqueline, during his visit, although Julian, himself, would have preferred to have opted for an hotel near the Rue St. Honoré, on the Right Bank, this being his usual practice. And had he been able to stay longer in Paris, prior to returning to Bristol, for the start of the new term, he would have considered taking out a short lease on a studio or flat. However, given the fact that his attitude to Héloïse had started to soften after their last conversation, he had surrendered to her wishes, on this occasion.

Jacqueline's apartment was situated near the Rue St. Jacques, a street Julian knew to be associated with historically interesting buildings and long-serving places of learning. He observed his surroundings with appreciation, as the taxi he had taken from the Gare du Nord made its way to where Jacqueline lived. Contrary to what he had been told about Parisian taxi drivers, Julian found the man driving the car amenable enough. He even pointed out places that might be of interest to a tourist. What more could anyone want?

Greeting him warmly, even though they had not met previously, Jacqueline told Julian he should feel as much at ease in her apartment as if he were in his own home. She was glad to have his company, she assured him. Startled at how similar she was to Héloïse, in appearance - both sisters had flaxen hair and what Julian decided were caramel-brown eyes – he noted quickly that Jacqueline was less direct in her gaze than Héloîse was and that she occasionally tended to go off-piste, as it were, while conversing. It was as if she had been distracted by passing thoughts. Héloîse, in contrast, was nclined to progress to the point she was making without deviation.

With an apologetic air, Jacqueline told Julian that she had no idea as to what he liked to eat, but she had bought a gigot and had made an apple tart, flavoured with Calvados. Having lived in England, she knew English men liked apple pie, or any pudding with apples in it, really.

"But, I wasn't able to buy English custard," she said, looking disappointed. "The powder that is sold in tins, in England, I mean."

"But, you didn't have to cook for me!" exclaimed Julian, surprised by the effort Jacqueline had made. "I intended to invite you out to a restaurant."

"Vous m'invitez?" asked Jacqueline, her eyes suddenly sparkling. Then, she hesitated. "Some other night, perhaps," she said.

"Yes. Good!" responded Julian, not sure if he had unsuspectingly upset her or not, by making such a suggestion. She seemed to have become downcast, suddenly, as if he had triggered a delicate memory that was causing her pain. Her vague air of mystery was beginning to intrigue him.

The only spare room in Jacqueline's flat was the one that had previously been used by Marie-Colette and vestiges of the young girl's presence remained. Popular, French, romantic novels had been left on a shelf, but Jacqueline had added to them books written in English, these being well-known ones by Dickens, Trollope and Henry James. Julian read late into the night, but finally, tired by his journey and the experience of becoming accustomed to his new surroundings, he fell, eventually, into a deep slumber, lulled by the sound of Jacqueline walking around her flat, while talking softly into her phone.

Waking up early, the next morning, Julian knew, at once, he was in France. The very air he was breathing seemed different from the air he breathed in England, as was the noise of the traffic outside and the scent of French coffee drifting under the door.

When he had made his way to the kitchen, Jacqueline asked him if he would like croissants and tartines au beurre. "Or something more English?" she suggested, with a trace of anxiety in her voice, being conscious of the fact that English men liked to eat a copious breakfast in the morning.

"Coffee will be fine," Julian said, politely. "Please don't go to any trouble."

But, Jacqueline had already started to cut into a baguette and to cover each slice with good butter for him. Momentarily, he thought of Tansy, whizzing a jar of marmalade across the table in the direction of Pomeroy, in the flat he, Julian, shared with Pomeroy and Owen Banks in Bristol, while she, Tansy, muttered that Pomeroy should be perfectly capable of fixing his own food. Julian smiled ruefully and was about to say that Jacqueline's attempts at dutifully buttering bread for him were not necessary, when he remembered how she had reacted the night before to something he had unwittingly said. He decided, therefore, to eat without protest. He did not want to open any fresh wounds, originally inflicted by Jacqui, he assumed. Or had Jacqueline's pain been connected with her failed relationship with Teddy Laurence?

Jacqueline looked quizzically at Julian, as if wondering why he had stopped speaking.

"What are your plans for today?" she asked.

"I have arranged to meet the grand-son of one of those Counts du Crâne, who sold the Château du Crâne to my grand-mother."

"Ah! Hëloîse mentioned something about your research," said Jacqueline. "You want to uncover the history of the château, because, of course, you will own it."

"Yes. I imagine so," said Julian, wondering how much Héloïse had told Jacqueline. Had she mentioned her own suspicion that her grandmother, Madame Gabrielle de Talence, might be a sister of the Counts du Crâne? However, Jacqueline made no mention of Héloïse's speculation and therefore, Julian did not mention it either.

The appointment with Antoine du Crâne, as the grandson was called, had been arranged for eleven o' clock that morning. Julian, initially, went to the Odéon métro station, but reckoning that, given his own lack of familiarity with the system and the time that would be spent, upon his arrival in the 16th arrondissement, walking from the métro to Antoine's apartment, it would be preferable for him to take a taxi.

Antoine du Crâne lived in a desirable, second-floor flat in what could have been a Haussmann building. Brown haired, brown-eyed and handsome, in a fine-boned, French kind of way, he greeted Julian in the library of his apartment where he, Julian, had been left by a housekeeper of a certain age in a smart dress.

"Won't you sit down?" said Antoine, in good English, indicating a comfortable-looking, leather chair. "I was intrigued by your request. You say your mother owns the Château du Crâne at present, but that she is about to pass it on to you."

"Yes. And I want to make a go of it," said Julian, simultaneously wondering if Antoine understood colloquial English. He seemed to, for he said:

"And presumably, you want to encourage tourists to visit the château and, furthermore, you want to provide them with information that will fascinate them."

"Yes. Precisely."

"Let me see..." said Antoine, walking towards one of the sets of bookshelves that lined the walls. "By the way, would you like a drink? Coffee? Are you hungry? Continental breakfasts don't add up to much, do they?"

"No. Nothing, thank you. Not just now."

"Perhaps we can have lunch later?"

"Yes. Of course," answered Julian, realising the invitation meant Antoine was taking his request seriously and that, with luck, a fair amount of information would be forthcoming.

Antoine ran his hand along the books on the shelf he had chosen to peruse: a shelf that was level with his head. Then, he lifted down two leather-bound volumes. He laid them carefully on a polished table in the centre of the room.

"The Counts du Crâne were descended from…" he began.

"I know the story about Angélique," Julian broke in. "I'm sorry. I should not have interrupted. But, you see, a film was shot at the Château du Crâne, during the summer, this year: a film which was based on Angélique's diary."

"Ah, yes!" said Antoine, thoughtfully. "I read about the film."

"Do you know what drove Angélique to come to France, initially? Do you know about her grand-mother's curse and all that?"

"Oh, yes! The story is actually recounted in one of these books," said Antoine, opening the first of the heavy tomes, at a page marked by a red silk ribbon.

Julian stood and approached the table.

"Is there any information there about the young man whose descendants Angélique had been sent to find?" he asked eagerly. He knew he was sounding impatient, but his curiosity over-rode his usual strict adherence to the rules of decorum.

"You are assuming he existed," said Antoine, bemused.

"Did he exist? I mean, I assume he must have existed unless Angélique's diary was a work of fiction."

Antoine gave Julian a quiet smile and then, returned to the bookshelves in order to remove a slimmer volume into which notes on paper had been inserted. Returning to the table with the book, Antoine said:

"From the information my father gleaned over a number of

years, we have come to the conclusion that, after his escape to France, in 1746, following the Battle of Culloden, the young man, like so many of his countrymen, settled in Sancerre, in the Loire Valley. He possibly joined one of the regiments of the French army. The famous Ogilvy's regiment, perhaps. He probably married and had children, also. We suspect one of the children, a boy, may have also joined the army, fighting for France. The boy would have used a Scottish name that was easy for the French to pronounce. One as easy to pronounce as Macdonald, the one used by the famous Maréchal Macdonald, whose father was Scottish."

"So, what was the real name of the young man we are talking about?"

"We don't know. What we do know is that, at the time of the Reign of Terror, the boy changed his name to Aubaine, because Scots with recognisable Scottish names, at the time, were being questioned by revolutionaries. Scots, you see, were assumed to be royalists, given the fact that their countrymen had fought for their Bonnie Prince at Culloden. That prince, as you probably know, was a relative of the French king."

"Aubaine?" said Julian, puzzled.

"We thought he had chosen that name because it sounded like Oban," explained Antoine, with a shrug. "It actually means, 'Godsend'."

"And so, do you know what happened to this Aubaine? What was his first name, anyway?"

"John, we think."

"Do you know what happened to him?"

Antoine, who had been leaning over the books, straightened his back and said, with humour in his voice:

"Permit me to overstep the boundary of propriety for a moment. I hope you will forgive me if I say this, but it seems to me that your interest in this story extends beyond a desire to provide tourists with fascinating tales about the Château du Crâne. Am I correct?"

Julian sighed.

"I think I may be descended from the young man Angélique was seeking. But my belief is based only on a hunch. My father used to say an ancestor of his had fought at Culloden and had, later, gone to France."

"The evidence you present is very flimsy, I must say! It hardly exists! Many men fought at Culloden and went into exile in France, afterwards. There was quite a colony of them, in Sancerre alone!"

"I accept my hope is based on very little," agreed Julian.

Antoine clasped his hands behind his back, walked over to the bookshelf and turned, to lean against it.

"Forgive me for the indiscretion of this question," he said, "but in pursuing this research of yours, is your intention to impress a young lady? I ask only because, in France, there is almost always a beautiful lady inspiring every adventure. Every quest."

Julian, taken aback, hesitated before replying.

"There is a girl called Héloïse de Sauzon…" he began, then.

"Ah!" interrupted Antoine, raising his hand in an elegant, ""I knew it!" sort of gesture. "My cousin!"

"Really?" asked Julian, trying to conceal his excitement. If Héloïse was Antoine's cousin, Gabrielle de Talence was almost definitely the sister of the Counts du Crâne.

"Oh! Yes!" said Antoine, giving a shrug. "She probably doesn't know she is my cousin. The relationship, I suspect, will be her grandmother's secret."

"I know that she suspects she might be," said Julian, "but I don't think she has spoken to anyone else in her family about her suspicions."

"No? Well! Maybe Gabrielle du Crâne, if she is still alive, would not want to talk about her banishment from the family home, either. She joined the students who were demonstrating in the street of Paris in 1968, you see," said Antoine.

"Is that all?"

"You ask if that is all? The demonstrations were anti-Gaullist.

Have you any conception of how a man of my grand-father's lineage and political direction would have felt about her behaviour? He believed she had dishonoured her family and disgraced him, above all. He never forgave her. Never."

Julian looked serious but said nothing.

"To return to your supposition," continued Antoine. "I am imagining that you are guessing that you are descended from the fellow Angélique was seeking because fate has brought you into contact with Héloïse and you think there must be a reason as to why this has happened. You cannot have been brought together by mere chance. In the throes of blossoming love, young people always feel that way, I have observed. They think fate is at work and that they are part of a mysterious plan. Is that really how the world is ordered? I have a Cartesian mind and I think not. It is likely the man who took the surname Aubaine was badly injured at the Battle of La Trebbia, in Italy, during the Napoleonic years. He would not have survived."

"Are you sure?"

"You can peruse the evidence in this book, if you like," said Antoine. "I think you will come to the same conclusion as I."

"Well!" said Julian, trying to hide his disappointment. "That's that."

CHAPTER 42

Santa Cruz

After days at sea, the *Sabine Estelle* arrived in the Canary Islands and, specifically, at Santa Cruz de la Palma. The ship was to stay tied up at the quayside for one day, from early morning until evening.

Energised by the warmth of the sun and tired of her self-imposed isolation, Madame Gabrielle de Talence decided to go ashore, after breakfast, to stretch her legs and to have a look at the town. Shops were always a draw and it was invariably interesting to see what women were wearing in foreign places. Madame Gabrielle, herself, put on a cream dress and a straw hat which had a wide brim and a brown ribbon around the crown. A bag, though! Would she take the straw one with the leather handles or the small, cream shoulder bag? She opted for the straw bag.

Once off the gang-way, Madame Gabrielle found herself enjoying being on firm ground. She became aware of the fact that her senses were freshly coming alive, as if she were on the point of embarking on an adventure. She strolled towards the shops, noticing the sub-tropical nature of the vegetation, at the sides of the roads, with interest and pleasure.

In a busy street, Madame Gabrielle bought scent at a perfumery and then, sat on the terrace of a café and ordered a lemon soda. She enjoyed being in foreign places, incognita, even though her well established adherence to the rules of etiquette and a certain stiffness of demeanour prevented her from letting down her guard. Her soda drunk, she decided to wander a little further and she made her way along what appeared to be a principal street. Music was being played at the entrances to shops and although such modern music would not normally have been to her taste, it gave her a lift, that day. It was with a light heart, therefore, that she continued her exploratory walk, while the sun warmed her skin gently. Then, she saw a church and she thought of Saint-Martial, back home in Bordeaux.

The door of the Santa Cruz church was open and Madame Gabriele went in. When rocked by emotional upsets, she, herself, had, on occasions, gone to the church of Saint-Martial, near her home, in the hope of tapping into some source of goodness that would offer succour. Sometimes, she had found peace from doing so. She had not cared, really, what sort of psychological mechanism had been in operation, at times like that; she had merely been grateful for the change in outlook that had been effected. She shrugged, then, and reflected on the fact that when asked for her own views on religion, her replies would generally verge towards secular cynicism, but she would also have had to admit, at least to herself, that ever since her daughter, Marie – Christine, had married the Comte de Sauzon, she, Madame Gabrielle, had become privately intrigued by stories about spirits and ghostly apparitions that had been embedded in the folklore of Brittany. Whenever she had visited the Château de Sauzon, in fact, she had invariably chosen, for her bed-time reading, a book about strange tales and superstitions attached to certain Breton practices, from the large collection in the library of her son-in-law, le Comte Henri. She had, as a result, in recent months, been interested to hear that the script of the film in which her grand-daughter, Héloïse, had been taking part, had been based on the story of a curse that had emanated from another Celtic land. And she could not help musing on the circumstances that had led Héloïse to agreeing to appear in that film, unaware of the fact that it was to be shot in the very Château where her grand-mother had been born and had grown up. It had been assumed that she, Madame Gabrielle, would be appalled at the idea of Héloïse becoming an actress – and, of course, that had been the case - but she had been even more disturbed by the fact that Héloïse had gained entrée to the Château du Crâne. Had this direction in which Héloïse had been pointed been a part of a mysterious plan? And how many other people in the world were being pulled by invisible threads that took them in directions, for reasons of which they were unaware, through not knowing their family's wounded history?

Madame Gabrielle immersed in thought, lost track of time. When she did look at her watch, she realised that she had been sitting in the church for more than an hour and so, she picked up her bag, and made haste to leave.

There were stewards on duty on the *Sabine Estelle* putting passengers' purchases through a machine that checked contents. Madame Gabrielle took her wrapped up perfume out of her straw bag, in readiness for inspection, Then, as she was about to step on to the gang-way, she felt a compulsion to look up. On a higher deck, she saw, looking down at her, Kit Mallory and the beautiful Caterina Traversi, standing beside him. Wearing a white sun dress, a deep pink lipstick and large sun-glasses, pushed back on her head, Miss Traversi seemed to be as glamorous as any continental film star. Madame Gabrielle was thankful that she, herself, managed to look nonchalant as, with an unfaltering step, she made her way on to the ship. At least, she supposed that she had convincingly appeared to be uncaring, but how could she know for sure? Madame Gabrielle knew her heart had lurched at the moment she had caught sight of Kit Mallory standing so close to Miss Traversi. Could Miss Traversi have divined how she had reacted, emotionally, despite outward appearances? Some women were highly perceptive in such matters. They enjoyed witnessing the inner disarray of others, not so much because they were given to Schadenfreude, exactly, as the fact that they derived a certain satisfaction from being in a more composed state, themselves. They homed in on tell-tale signs, like the shadow that might momentarily pass over a woman's face or a lack of adroitness in the way she might move her hands or the way her voice might weaken.

Madame Gabrielle placed her straw bag and wrapped- up scent on to the small conveyer belt that would take them through the checking machine. A second or two later, she collected them and made her way quickly to her cabin. As she closed its door, she realised she was feeling numb. She removed her hat and her shoes and lay down on her bed, pulling the white quilt over her. She knew that lying down always helped when she was feeling upset. It was better to lie down than to try to perk oneself up with coffee, she felt. She tried, then, to clear her mind of any thoughts, but as always, she found a discipline of that nature impossible. Questions began to spin around in her head. Why had Kit Mallory and Caterina Traversi been looking down at her as if they had had a reason for doing so? Had they found her behaviour so odd at Dorothy Trimm's party that they had been talking about her clumsy departure afterwards? Had they come to the conclusion that she was eccentric or socially inept? How humiliating it was to have one's conduct discussed! Madame Gabrielle hoped, at least, that she was not being pitied.

Sighing, although she was not sure if she was sighing from pique or sadness, Madame Gabrielle allowed herself to become drowsy for a while, but then, sat up with a start as she heard someone knocking on her door. She looked at the alarm clock on her bed-side table. Only half an hour had passed since her arrival back on the ship. Madame Gabrielle judged the soft knock to have been that of a woman. Maybe the stewardess wanted to ask a question or give her information. She rose, slipped her feet into her sandals and walked to the door, pushing her hand through her hair to smooth it.

To her consternation, Madame Gabrielle found, standing outside, the beautifully groomed Caterina Traversi, looking even more ostentatiously glamorous at close quarters than she had looked on the outer deck.

"I wonder if I may talk to you for a moment, signora," she said gently.

"But why?" asked Madame Gabrielle, betraying her annoyance with the sharpness of her tone. She was not in the mood for entertaining the Italian girl or even for being nice. Besides, as far as Madame Gabrielle was concerned, her rooms on board ship were her home for the duration of the voyage and, in France, one did not invite strangers into one's home: one arranged to meet them in a restaurant. At least, people who shared her outlook still did.

"Oh! Forgive me, signora!" exclaimed Caterina, as if guessing what was on Madame Gabrielle's mind. "I am not asking you to invite me into your rooms. I thought that we might have tea, later, on Deck 4."

Madame Gabrielle hesitated for a second, but then, being curious to know what Miss Traversi wanted to say, acquiesced and an arrangement was made for four o' clock.

"Thank you, signora," said Miss Traversi, smiling in a sweet way.

Madame Gabrielle shut the door, wondering if the Italian girl wanted to talk to her for some reason of her own or if she had been persuaded by Kit Mallory to extract information about her. Was Kit Mallory, himself, perhaps planning to make an appearance, on Deck 4, on the pretext of needing to talk to Miss Traversi? Madame Gabrielle's heart began to thump as that thought crossed her mind. She showered and changed into a slim, lemon-coloured dress. She sprayed her wrist and neck lightly with the scent she had bought in the Calle O' Daly and looked at her reflection carefully in the mirror in the bathroom. Her neck, thankfully, was not looking as old as it sometimes did, but she covered it in a layer of cream nevertheless.

Four o' clock. Miss Traversi was already seated in the open-plan café when Madame Gabrielle arrived there. She, Miss Traversi, had changed into a sleeveless dress, one on which large, exotic orchids were printed on a white background. She stood up as Madame

Gabrielle approached and held out her hand to be shaken.

"Shall I order tea and sandwiches or would you prefer coffee or a cold drink?" she asked.

"Just a lemonade soda," said Madame Gabrielle, sitting down.

She watched Miss Traversi winding her elegant way through largely empty tables to find a waiter and returning with one who placed a long glass of sparkling liquid in front of her along with a cup of lemon tea for Miss Traversi.

"I wanted to introduce myself, really," said Miss Traversi, then, in a chatty way, placing her white shoulder bag on the floor, before sitting down.

"We didn't really have a chance to speak at that soirée to which we were invited," she continued, picking up the cup of lemon tea in an elegant way.

"I am flattered that you would want to get to know me, after such a fleeting acquaintance," said Madame Gabrielle, suddenly feeling anger rising within, perhaps because the girl was not being respectfully distant enough. Was she, Madame Gabrielle, expected to be grateful that a young woman like Miss Traversi would want to make friends with her?

"In what direction do you want the conversation to proceed?" she added sharply, wondering what sort of information Miss Traversi was going to try to extract.

Miss Traversi hesitated as if not expecting that response. And then, she blenched as Madame Gabrielle leaned forward, her eyes cold, now.

"What do you really want to know, Miss Traversi?" she asked bluntly.

Normally, it would be inconceivable that Madame Gabrielle would speak so directly in a situation where light remarks and tact were required, but an inner intuition had suddenly convinced her that Kit Mallory had asked the young woman to make enquiries about her. In other words, he had humiliated her, by not making contact with her himself, directly. Why had he not arrived in person at her door, to invite her to tea, after all? Why had he not invited her to a soirée of his own, by hand-written letter?

Madame Gabrielle rose. She was not going to be treated any longer as if she were a person unworthy of being approached, with dignity, by Kit Malory, himself. She was finding the situation demeaning. Who did he think he was? What did he think she was? A dispensable admirer who was mildly entertaining?

"You must excuse me," she said. "I have a head-ache. The heat… is overwhelming, in the afternoon."

She walked away, knowing that her excuse had been ridiculous. The ship possessed an air conditioning system which cooled the air on board. She knew she had broken rules that she had learnt, even as a child, about the art of savoir-vivre. However, with her emotions having been churned by disappoint and anger and, additionally, by envy of Miss Traversi's youth, beauty and confident manner, for once, she did not care.

CHAPTER 43

Remorse

Feeling like a schoolgirl standing outside the head's room, Caterina Traversi paused before knocking gently on Kit Mallory's cabin door. When the door was opened, Caterina stood, with eyes lowered, saying nothing.

"Look at me," said Kit Mallory, brusquely. "What have you done?"

Caterina raised her eyes. Kit was gazing at her, with one eyebrow raised in the quizzical way that had become familiar to her.

"I invited Madame Gabrielle to tea," said Caterina.

"And?"

"I don't know...Something I said triggered a reaction in her. She became angry and left."

Kit Mallory sighed as if disappointed, but also, as if resigned to dealing with the consequences, whatever they might be.

"Come in," he said, standing aside to allow Caterina to pass. He indicated that she sit in the comfortable arm chair nearest the door to the balcony. That door was open and as Caterina sat down, she felt the warmth of the sun upon her back. She, then, noticed a pile of documents on the sofa and she realised that Kit must have been working on them and that she had interrupted him, but there was now no annoyance evident in his voice when he spoke.

"What exactly did you say to Madame Gabrielle?" he asked, as he sat down in a chair opposite the balcony.

"Something along the lines of our not having had a chance to speak previously," replied Caterina. "Then, she snapped at me, asking me what I really wanted."

“That reaction must have seemed a bit odd to you, I imagine,” mused Kit, “but obviously, Madame Gabrielle thought you had had an ulterior motive in approaching her. Did you?”

“Did I what? Did I have an ulterior motive?”

“Well? Did you? Why did you knock on her door?”

“To invite her to tea! To make friends with her! No more than that!”

Caterina sighed and leaned back into the armchair, placing both arms behind her head.

“All right!” she said then. “I saw the look on your face when you saw her coming on board earlier and I thought…”

“You thought you would be able to persuade her to agree to attend some sort of social gathering that would bring us together? Oh! Caterina! Caterina! You should have known better than to have tried to blunder your way into the life of a woman like Madame Gabrielle. She would have seen through the ruse and, of course, she would have resented your interference. Women of Madame Gabrielle’s age group - my age group - have been deceived too often to be trusting. We have been disappointed too often to be spontaneous. I know you meant well, but I am asking you not to invite Madame Gabrielle to any kind of social event from now on, without having a word with me first. Got that?”

Caterina nodded and looked down at the floor. She felt tears gathering in her eyes. She knew she could summon tears at will, to impress or persuade, but that afternoon, her tears were real and were not under her control. Her growing respect for Kit Mallory, arising, in part, from her bafflement over his refusal to defer to her, in spite of her family’s money and status in Italy, intrigued her and, additionally, encouraged her to want to work for him in a way that would make him think she was an asset. She turned her head away. She felt sure that if he were to see the tears glistening in her eyes, he would regard them as being an unseemly and embarrassing display of weakness.

“I’d better go,” said Caterina, standing up. “I’m sorry if I…”

She bent down to pick up her hand bag from the floor, where she had placed it. When she straightened up, Kit Mallory was standing in front of her.

"Hey!" he said, softly. "Come here!"

He was holding his arms open and, scarcely believing he was inviting her fall into them, Caterina hesitated, but then, allowed herself to be enclosed in an embrace and as she did so, she began to cry. She became aware of the fact that the front of Kit Mallory's shirt was being soaked by her freely flowing tears and stained by her mascara, but he did not seem to mind. He was holding her gently, allowing her to empty herself of emotion. Eventually, she looked up at him. He was gazing over her shoulder at some point beyond the door of the balcony. He looked down at her, then, his brown eyes softer than she had seen them before.

"Feeling better?" he asked.

She nodded, wondering if she should now go or stay. But he pushed her away from him gently but firmly.

"You'd better wash your face. You can do that here, but I expect you'd rather go back to your cabin, wouldn't you?" he said.

Caterina could tell, by the tone of Kit's voice, that he wanted her to leave.

"Yes. I'll go back to my room," she said quietly.

She picked up her hand bag and made for the door.

"Take the evening off," said Kit, without turning round. " I'll see you in the morning."

CHAPTER 44

Teddy Solves a Problem

Although it was only the first day of the new term proper at Bramblewell School, Lynn James was feeling as if she had been at her desk for weeks, so numerous had been the queries that she had had to answer in the course of the morning. She found that she was gathering strength from dealing with challenges, though, rather than being laid low by them. Of course, despite the fact that she was only in her mid-thirties, she had plenty of experience on which to draw. Prior to having been appointed to the post of deputy-head in Bramblewell School, she had worked in two other schools. She was well acquainted, therefore, with the array of difficult people that could cross the path of a class-room teacher. Lynn had witnessed the entire cavalcade of poor behaviour and had been shocked by it. But now, armed with her knowledge, she was determined to make good judgements, while occupying the post of headmistress in the prestigious school that was now in her care. She had to admit, all the same, that the phenomenon of the personal assistant, bent on trying to up-stage her, in underhand ways, was new territory, which would require the application of novel strategies.

Thankfully, Lynn knew she was not alone in finding much to criticise in the behaviour of Isolde Delamar. The personal assistant had managed to enrage the rest of the teaching staff also, as a result of her attack on Savannah Rock in the staffroom, two days previously, before the start of an in-service session.

"You must DO something about her, Lynn," Barbara Merrivale had insisted later.

"Do what, exactly?" Lynn might justifiably had enquired,

being well aware of Isolde Delamar's one-time relationship with Lord Bramblewell and the probable need to tread carefully as a consequence.

It was Teddy Laurence, who decisively homed in on the solution, though, on the first morning proper of the new term. Lynn had asked him to do the work of acting deputy-head, even though his appointment had not been formalised, and it was in this capacity, conferred on him by Lynn, that he took control of the situation. Miss Lee Chan, the previous school secretary, had had a part-time assistant, who had never been replaced. Could another girl not be appointed to do some of the office work in the school, therefore? Could this new girl not occupy the ante- room next to Lynn's office, so that Isolde Delamar could be moved to the small room at the end of the science corridor, where he, Teddy, could keep an eye on her and supply her with tasks related to his own rôle as deputy-head? After all, he would be in charge of the bulk of day-to-day administrative work. There would be much to do. It was only sensible that he should be given the secretary with the most experience.

"I'll keep her busy," Teddy promised the teachers assembled in the staff-room on the first morning of term. "And out of everyone else's way."

"I'm not sure about that, Teddy," Savannah Rock had interjected. "If she is going to be ensconced at the end of the science corridor, I'll be running into her daily!"

The humour evident in Savannah's voice raised laughter. Those who had heard Isolde Delamar's remarks about Savannah's surname had been smouldering with anger for two days, but Teddy's solution cheered them mightily.

The science corridor was situated in the relatively new, glassy block of classrooms constructed on ground that was lower than that on which the main, neo-Gothic building had been built. When Isolde Delamar would be located there, she would have a less visible rôle to play in the school. She would be furious, of course, but Teddy was ready to deal with her tantrums and he was prepared, also, to endure long-term sulking on Isolde's part in order to spare Lynn any further distress.

A telephone call made to Lord Bramblewell by Teddy, out of courtesy, to explain his reason for moving the personal assistant to the science corridor, or rather, to provide a diplomatic excuse for relocating her, was well received. Lord Bramblewell, having much respect for Teddy, accepted his decision to move Miss Delamar and added, during the course of the telephone call, that he looked forward to formalising Teddy's appointment to the post of deputy-head within a short period.

"I've rung an agency and I've been told that a girl called Karen Tasker can start work as your secretary almost immediately," Teddy then told Lynn. "She's apparently quiet but efficient and likely to learn the ropes quickly." Susie Sutton, who had been told by Lord Bramblewell of Isolde's move to the science quarter, was naturally pleased that Lord Bramblewell would no longer be traversing Isolde's work space when going to see Lynn, but she was now worried about the fact that Isolde would be working exclusively for Teddy. She hoped he would not be drawn into the web of the woman she had judged to be darkly predatory.

Lynn felt much relieved when she realised she was on the point of being delivered of the undermining presence of Isolde. Telephone calls from Isolde to the main office would now be fielded by Karen. The occasions on which Lynn would be required to talk directly to Isolde, in fact, would be rare. Teddy, Lynn knew, could have chosen to use any room in the main building as his office and he did, in fact, intend to use one on the first floor when he stayed in school in the evening, but he nevertheless now assured Lynn that he would do the bulk of his work in the science corridor and Lynn realised he had made the decision to do this, in order to make life easier for her. She wondered how Isolde would react when Teddy told her of his decision to move her. She hoped Teddy would do so that morning.

Lynn flicked through the notes she had written for the speech she intended to deliver at Assembly. She had found it difficult, when wondering what she would say, to strike a balance between seriousness and approachability. It was natural to want to be liked, but sensible teachers quickly learned that they were not employed to be popular but rather to instruct their pupils in an effective manner. The rôle of the headmistress was somewhat different, of course, but when dealing with teachers as well as pupils, a proper balance had to be struck. Miss Trimm had carried out her duties with aplomb. She had been an expert in her craft and Lynn knew it would be in her own interests to reflect on how Miss Trimm had behaved, even though, in her previous rôle as deputy-head, Lynn had often criticised her former head-mistress.

There was a knock on the door and Teddy Laurence entered.

"Ready?" he asked. "Everyone is in the Assembly Hall."

"How do I look?" asked Lynn, with a touch of uncertainty in her voice.

"Perfect," said Teddy, glancing admiringly at her new, soft lavender suit and her long hair, flowing glossily past her shoulders. Then, he added, quickly, "Let's go!"

Teddy stood aside as Lynn walked out of her office. She noticed at once that Isolde was not in the ante-room. "I sent her on an errand," explained Teddy. "I didn't want anyone to upset you before you faced the crowd."

Lynn looked at Teddy with curiosity in her eyes, but she made no comment.

CHAPTER 45

The Darkness Within

When Teddy Laurence told Isolde Delamar that she was about to be moved from her office - prestigiously located next to that of Lynn James - to a smaller room, at the end of the science corridor, it became clear to him, at once, that his instruction was being interpreted by the proud, young woman as a lowering of her status. The range of emotions, suggested by her facial expressions, as Teddy spoke, progressed from surprise to shock, from shock to anger and from anger to dark fury: a fury that startled Teddy, given the obvious ferocity driving it.

While observing the way Isolde was reacting, Teddy, himself, remained expressionless, not wanting to give her, Isolde, the satisfaction of knowing that she had had an effect on him. At the same time, he was realising that he would have to reconsider his opinion of her. He had, of course, believed Lynn James when she had told him that Isolde Delamar had constantly been trying to undermine her, but in such an underhand fashion that there had never been clear grounds for dismissing her. Lynn had obviously been irked by Isolde's ways of behaving, but, although Teddy had trusted Lynn's judgement, he, himself, had mentally placed Isolde in the category of the spoilt, vain and self-absorbed type: the sort of woman who was capable of behaving spitefully towards those she considered to be rivals, but who - being vapid and incapable of calculated strategy- was essentially more harmless than dangerous. Now, however, as he saw the malevolence smouldering in Isolde's eyes, he realised he had previously - to some extent, at least - been duped by her.

He should, of course, have fully trusted Lynn's judgement and, for that matter, that of Savannah Rock and Thetis Ravenswood. Women were intuitively capable of perceiving what other women were in essence and he should have reminded himself of that fact. He remembered, then, that he had once read in some scientific journal, that a man's faculty of discrimination stopped functioning efficiently when he was in the presence of feminine prettiness. To what extent had he, himself, fallen prey to that cerebral phenomenon? Certainly, he would have to admit that when he had initially fallen for Susie Sutton, he had not been thinking clearly. She had had a rather unsophisticated way of dressing and a passion for unsuitable, backless shoes, but he had seen only an angel, with blonde hair and an air of child-like vulnerability. He had quickly become aware of the fact that her favourite topics of conversation had been confined to fashion, dining out and desired holidays on sunny beaches, but in the beginning, he had not cared, his ability to judge the outcome of the relationship having been impaired, obviously. Now, he looked at Isolde Delamar - her dark, blonde hair falling in loose waves around her shoulders that morning, her eyes carefully emphasised with grey shadow, her lipstick bright - and he realised that, although he had previously been tetchy and impatient in the way he had spoken to her, he had, in fact, been over-lenient too. Were he to be honest with himself, he would admit that he had always been attracted to her and had been suppressing his feelings, because so many of the teachers in Bramblewell School had told him she, Isolde, had been behaving dreadfully and he had not wanted to look as if he had been an immature fool, by protesting that Isolde had not been as bad as all that. Of course, Isolde, herself, would have sensed that he could be as weak as other men in her presence and thus, she would have been aware of the power that she could potentially wield. No doubt her attitude of near-insolence, when she had been dealing with Lynn, had been supported by her belief that Teddy had been secretly attracted to her charm and had been impressed by her hoity-toity ways.

Teddy felt his back turning cold. Reflecting on Lynn's integrity, dignity and mysterious remoteness- qualities reminiscent of those of a beauty in a Renaissance painting - his face became pale. He wondered if she had sensed how mixed his thoughts had been, when she had spoken to him about Isolde previously. Had she seen through him? Had she found his attitude disappointing? Teddy felt as if he had let her down and the guilt stemming from his belief that he had done so made him angry. He now returned Isolde's hateful stare with an icy and unflinching gaze of his own and then, he shrugged as if indifferent to her reaction.

"I'll arrange to have cardboard boxes brought to your room," he said.calmly. "You may start packing your belongings into them this morning. You will be able to find your way around the science block by yourself, won't you? As I explained, your new room will be at the end of the corridor."

"You do realise that Lord Bramblewell will hear about this," said Isolde coldly.

"He already knows," Teddy replied.

"I don't believe, you."

"Please yourself, love," said Teddy unexpectedly, insinuating, through the casualness of those words, that what she did was of no interest to him.

For the remainder of the day, Isolde seethed with the sort of resentment that led to thoughts of revenge. She would pay Teddy Laurence back for the way he had treated her! She would destroy him and Susie Sutton, too. She detested them both with a dark passion. But, how would she go about ruining their lives? Perhaps she needed an accomplice.

Isolde's anger, combined with the stress of moving quarters, drained her of energy and therefore, when it was time for her to go home in the late afternoon, she felt exhausted. She decided to visit the Grosvenor Shopping Centre before returning to her parents' house. She would have a nice cup of coffee somewhere there to cheer herself up. She turned the key in her car, to start the engine, but then, turned it off. She sat for a moment as an idea formed itself in her head. She got out of the car then and, having looked to the left and to the right to check that no one was watching her, she made her way towards the wood, up on the rise above the tennis courts.

The cestrian air was cool and so, she buttoned up her jacket as she slipped through the trees. The quaint, wooden door in the grey, stone wall was quite easy to open. The heavy latch and bolt must have been greased. Isolde held her breath as she went into Lord Barmblewell's territory, proper. She knew the way through the grounds: she remembered it from ten years before, when she had been engaged to Lord Bramblewell, herself. Walking swiftly, she was soon within sight of the manor. "All this could have been mine," she could not help saying, remembering a novel she had read as a schoolgirl, but then, she laughed coldly at herself, knowing the extent to which she did not resemble Jane Austen's heroine, Eliza Bennet and never would. She cautiously skirted the east side of the manor, keeping close to the wall, and soon found herself before the kitchen door. She opened it and walked in.

"Mrs. Oliver!" she exclaimed, upon catching sight of the housekeeper, stern and prim as ever. "Remember me?"

CHAPTER 46

An Unexpected Rebuke

Isolde Delamar positioned her desk in her new office, at the end of the science corridor in Bramblewell School, so that it, the desk, was opposite the office door which she intended to leave open, while she was occupying the room. The open door, though, would not be an invitation to any passing teacher, pupil or stranger to drop in. Isolde's cool expression and hoity-toity manner would soon remove the notion of an acceptance of familiarity from the mind of anyone who might mistakenly judge her to be approachable. The door would be left open, in fact, so that Isolde would be able to view the white painted corridor in front of her and, specifically, the entrances to the science classrooms, the library and, at the far end of the corridor, the rehearsal rooms for ballet and theatrical work. The move to the science corridor would, perhaps, turn out to be more interesting than anticipated, Isolde was beginning to think. She had initially felt as if she were being sent into exile, away from the centre of activity in the school and the seat of power, as it were. However, the new location was now not looking quite as bleak as it had previously. After all, she would be able to keep an eye on people who went in and out of Teddy Lawrence's classroom. And oh! How she would relish watching every move Teddy, himself, made: he who had been so high and mighty when he had told her, brusquely, to pack her belongings and to move out of the ante-room, beside Lynn James' room! She would have her revenge, though! She would watch him with cold eyes until the day he made a mistake and then, she would scoff and sneer.

Isolde looked around her new office. It was smaller than the one she had vacated in the main building, but it was, nevertheless, sizeable. She would not admit, of course, to anyone in Bramblewell School, what she, herself, had had to acknowledge: the fact that it was considerably larger than the one in which she had previously worked in London and which she had had to share with a younger woman with whom she had not been on the best of terms. She had not had much of a window in her London office, either, but here, in her new abode, there was a large one, on her right hand side, which provided her with a view of trees in the grounds of Bramblewell School, and, if she craned her neck, she could see, also, the grey, stone wall which separated the school's grounds from those of Bramblewell Manor. Maybe she would be able to catch a glimpse of Lord Bramblewell coming through the old wooden door in the wall, on those days when he would choose to walk through the woods, in order to reach the school.

On the desk in front of Isolde, there was a flat screen computer, a land-line telephone and a shiny, black stand for pens. The desk, itself, had six drawers, three on each side. Isolde had already placed a tray of make-up in one and having done that, she started to feel comfortable in her surroundings. However, she was beginning to feel concerned about the fact that pupils in the school might perceive her position to be a diminished one, because she had been asked to move from the main building. It irked her to think that mere pupils might look down on her because they had calculated that she had been given a less important rôle than the one she had had initially. Furthermore, her chances of being able to talk to Lord Bramblewell, on a regular basis, had been greatly reduced. She would possibly not see him when he would drop into the school, weekly, to talk to Lynn James. Would he ever visit Teddy's classroom? She thought he probably would not, but would meet Teddy in Lynn's room, instead.

However, one afternoon, towards the end of the second week of term, Lord Bramblewell did, in fact, make his way to Teddy's science classroom. The bell marking the end of a lesson had rung and Teddy's pupils were on the way out of class when Lord

Bramblewell appeared. Tall, blond and well-built, with his dark cloak hanging off his shoulders, he almost blocked the doorway of Teddy's room.

"May I?" Isolde heard him saying, his voice pleasant but commanding, as he asked permission from Teddy to enter.

Isolde stood, walked to the front of her desk and leaned against it, while watching the corridor in the way a predator might. She had to be ready to attract Lord Bramblewell's attention as soon as he had left Teddy. She picked up the burgundy coloured handbag on her desk and took out of it a small magnifying mirror. Carefully, she inspected her pale tan make-up and her lipstick. She reckoned her artwork looked perfect. She began, then, to become impatient as minutes passed, but finally, Lord Bramblewell appeared. Without throwing a glance in the direction of his former fiancée's office, he set off along the corridor.

"Rupert! Rupert!" called Isolde, beginning to run after him, although hampered by her inability to move quickly in high-heeled shoes. Hearing her voice, Lord Bramblewell turned round. The expression on his face surprised Isolde, though, and brought her to a halt. He was not looking at her with coldness, exactly, but rather with indifference.

"Rupert, could I have a word with you?" she asked, nevertheless.

"What is it, Isolde?" asked Lord Brameblewell, curtly. "I'm in a hurry."

"I'll talk quickly," said Isolde, softening her voice, having realised that charm rather than an expression of annoyance was required. "I've been moved out of the office in the main building and I feel a bit left out of things," she continued plaintively.

"Do you?"

"I was wondering if you had sanctioned the decision to move me or if Mr. Laurence had made the decision by himself."

"Isolde," said Lord Bramblewell icily. "Mr. Laurence is, or soon will be, the deputy head of this school. The decisions he makes and, indeed, the decisions Miss James makes, are no concern of mine. Miss James and Mr. Laurence run the school. I do not."

"But you could persuade Mr. Laurence, surely, to..."

"To what?"

"To give me my old office back."

"Isolde, if Mr. Laurence wants you to be situated in the science corridor, there you must stay. Who am I to question his decision?"

"But, Rupert..."

"Listen, Isolde! I shall repeat that the day-to-day running of the school is not my concern."

"But, Mr. Laurence hates me! He really does! He has moved me out of the main building because one of his precious science teachers - that Savannah person, I mean - complained about me. I'm sure she did. The move was completely unjustified and I don't know why you are taking his side against mine, anyway. What is wrong with you? And what you have just said is not true! When Miss Trimm was head-mistress, you interfered in the running of the school all the time. Miss Trimm complied with every crazy idea you had. Everyone says so! And so, don't try to tell me that you couldn't re-instate me in the main building: you could if you wanted to. You won't because that silly girl you are going to marry doesn't like me either. I don't know what it is about her that you find attractive. In fact, nobody else I know can understand what you find attractive about her. When you come to your senses, you are going to feel such an idiot!"

The angry words had poured out of Isolde's mouth in a stream and although tears of frustration were now gathering in her eyes, she looked up unflinchingly and proudly at Lord Bramblewell. Her verbal attack on him, she knew, had had little connection with his indifference to her being moved from one office to another. What had fuelled her anger had been her own failure to entice him away from Susie Sutton. She realised that her outburst would mean that there was no chance, now, of her ever being Lady Bramblewell but, strangely, she did not feel regretful for having revealed her true feelings. She felt relieved. She was scheming, but she preferred not to be hypocritical, really.

Lord Brambelwell was looking at her in astonishment.

"You are clearly upset" he said, after hesitating for a moment to reflect. Then, raising his voice he added:

"But your being upset does not excuse you for your lack of good manners. The insults you have directed at Mr. Laurence and his colleague and, additionally, at me, specifically, and most shockingly of all, at my future wife, will not easily be forgotten. It is true that I have appeared to have had some influence over the previous head-mistress of this school, Miss Trimm, but I can assure you that had Miss Trimm's objectives differed from mine in matters related to the school, I should have deferred to her wishes. You, yourself, have benefited from the fact that Miss Trimm consulted me on many issues, in any case. It was she who put your name forward for consideration for the position which you currently hold: not I. Admittedly, I suggested that you be given a position here, but only because, frankly, I wanted to give you a chance or break, if you like, in the event of your being down on your luck. But Miss Trimm had no need to comply with my suggestion. And I did not care one way or the other whether you were appointed to the post or not. Let me repeat what I have just said. I did not care. Is that clear? Since your arrival in the school, Isolde, you have distinguished yourself by being rude to several teachers, including Mr. Laurence and you did not over-exert yourself, when working for Miss James. That is why you now find yourself in this corridor. Miss James told me she would rather have an inexperienced but enthusiastic office girl working for her than a sullen thirty-five year old with previous experience of office duties. Be thankful, Isolde, that you are still employed in this school, as, to date, you have not lived up to expectations. It is very obvious to me that you are not aware of the strong work ethic that underpinned the life of your predecessor, Miss Chan. My advice to you would be to pull up your socks or you might find yourself looking for a new job by Christmas. And by the way, don't let me ever hear you uttering another derogatory word about my fiancée. Susie is my guiding star: something you never were and could never hope to be."

Lord Brambewell turned and briskly walked along the corridor, cloak and blond hair flying. Isolde, chastened, returned to her room and closed the door.

Teddy Laurence had heard every word exchanged during the verbal intercourse that had taken place in the corridor, since Lord Bramblewell, when exiting his classroom, had left the door open. Teddy had been standing, mesmerised, but now he sat down on the edge of his table. He looked out of the window, in the direction of the playing field, but without paying attention to the way the early autumnal sun was shining brightly on the grass or the way a breeze was playing gently with the leaves on the trees marking the perimeter. It occurred to Teddy that Isolde was not the type to sink into the background, although she must have realised that she had had the rug pulled from under her feet. He had heard her closing the door of her office quietly, but for how long would she be licking her wounds? He had detected something of a wild quality in her anger. She would plot her revenge: there was no doubt about that. And there would be consequences for those towards whom she bore a grudge. He would have to be vigilant for his own sake but also for Susie's.

CHAPTER 47

A Detour

It was Friday and Teddy Laurence was furious with Isolde Delamar. Throughout the entire school week, which was ending, she had been clearly seeking opportunities to annoy him, in his view, entering his classroom to ask foolish questions and deliberately making mistakes with the intention of provoking an angry response from him. She had crowned her efforts, after the lunch hour that day, by feeding incorrect information into the school's digital system for recording absences and attendances and so he, Teddy, was going to have to stay in school, after every other teacher had departed, to untangle the technological web Isolde had woven.

Teddy had restrained himself from losing his temper during most of the week, but that afternoon, he had finally gone over the edge, so to speak.

"I'll tell you what I'll do, Isolde," he had said in exasperation. "I'll buy a set of those old blue, cardboard covered registers that teachers used to be given in schools, decades ago, and I'll distribute them to form teachers to use for registration each morning and afternoon. We'll see how you will enjoy extrapolating information from the blue registers and adding up the numbers of absences and attendances in the old way, at the end of each week, shall we? If you can't cope with technology, it's the only solution left to us."

Obviously enjoying the sight of Teddy finally revealing how annoyed he was, Isolde had smirked before saying, with an expression of fake innocence on her face, and with her shoulders hunched in an exaggerated shrug:

"Well! If you will insist on forcing me to work in this tiny office, you must also expect me to make mistakes! I am used to having more space in an office. In fact, I am used to having a room where I can breathe properly."

Isolde had histrionically stretched out her arms sideways, as she had uttered "breathe," in the way a teacher of relaxation might have done: slowly and with emphasis.

Rather than allow Isolde to provoke him further, Teddy had decided to say no more. He had realised that she had been goading him on purpose, in the hope that he would express his anger, so that she could quote what he had said later, verbatim. He had realised, too, that, out of context, his words might sound inappropriate. He was well aware of the dangers of falling into the sort of trap she had set. Smug pupils played the game as well and, therefore, teachers had to be on their guard, when dealing with it. Teddy, wisely, had walked away from Isolde without saying another word.

Now, at 6p.m., he had finally completed the unravelling of Isolde's muddle and he knew he could go home. Usually, he loved the drive to his riverside apartment in Liverpool, after school on a Friday, since an entire weekend of freedom would be stretching before him. He left the science corridor after locking cupboards and made his way up to the space outside the main building, where his car was parked. He drove slowly towards the gates of Bramblewell School, noticing how sombre the leaves of the rhododendron bushes looked, on each side of the drive. He slowed the car to a standstill, as he approached the main road. Should he turn right to head to Chester's city centre, where he could buy supplies for his evening meal or should he turn left and shop in late - night stores in Liverpool? He looked at his watch. Some of his favourite shops in Chester would have closed, he realised. He turned left.

Outside of the boundary of Chester, the fertile, lush fields of Cheshire and the Wirral stretched out on each side of the road. Teddy felt his mood changing. The memory of the week-long battle of wills in which he had been engaged with Isolde was thankfully beginning to fade and yet, he knew it would be sensible to spend at least part of the weekend pondering on how to deal with the young woman effectively. It crossed his mind that he could move her to a room on the top floor of the main building, but she would be unsupervised there and who knew what sorts of mischievous plans she might execute? No. The safest location for her was the office at the end of the science corridor, but he, himself, would have to tread carefully until there were clear grounds for dismissing her. What he had always found annoying about people who were objectionable was the fact that they forced one into a position of dropping one's own standards in order to put up a suitable defence or even, in some cases, in order to survive in a job.

Teddy realised the car was approaching a roundabout and he slowed it down. Giving way to as sudden impulse, then, he set off in the direction of Ellesmere Port, rather than heading for the north of the Wirral and the Mersey Tunnel. Why Liz Laurier's name had flashed into his mind, he was not sure, but he suspected it was because she was good at listening and reliably discreet.

In a side road by Whitby Park, some distance from down-town Ellesmere Port, Teddy stopped the car and located Liz's number on his mobile phone.

"Liz?"

"Hi, Teddy!"

"Are you busy? Do you have a client with you? I was wondering if I could drop in."

"I have no one with me and I'd love to see you."

"I'm on my way."

Liz must have been keeping watch to see Teddy's car arriving because she had run downstairs to open the main door of the house in which her apartment was located, before he rang the bell.

"It's great to see you, Teddy!" she said, holding her head at a slight tilt, so that he could kiss her on the cheek. "Come on up!"

Teddy sank into one of Liz's squashy, white sofas in her sitting room and he became aware, then, of how weary he felt. He noticed a tall pile of cardboard folders and papers on the glass coffee table in front of him. Was it fair to load his troubles on to Liz's shoulders when she was so preoccupied with her own lists of clients? Probably not.

"Maybe I shouldn't have come here," he said. "You have enough on your plate, Liz. I should go."

"No! No!" exclaimed Liz, as Teddy stood up. "Of course you shouldn't go! Come on, Teddy! There's something wrong. How can I help you?"

There had been not a word from Liz about the way Teddy had been inclined to make disparaging remarks about her work as an astrologer, when she had been employed in Brambelwell School. She had been too kind or too diplomatic to point out his previous lack of graciousness when speaking to her on that subject, even though she was possibly wondering if he had come to her for astrological advice that evening. But no! Surely not! Yet, he was troubled.

"Let me fetch you something to drink and eat," said Liz, solicitously. "You must be starving, after a day's work."

"No! No, Liz! I'm not staying long! Really. I just want your opinion on what I should do about Isolde Delamar."

"I take it you don't want any advice based on pseudo-science, as you once called it!"

"Astrology, you mean?"

"Yes."

"Listen, Liz. I know I've been unforgivably mean to you in the past, but, at the moment, I don't mind what sort of source you use as a basis for your opinions. I'd just like to hear what a woman has to say about Isolde."

"Ah! Teddy! I can tell you that your Pluto is in conjunction with her Sun and square her Mars. There! Are you going to ask me what those two configurations mean or would you rather I didn't?"

Teddy leaned forward, his hands clasped in front of him, while he looked at the floor.

"Is it bad news for me?" he asked then.

"Actually, it's bad news for Isolde, as you will be the one in control, really, but goaded by your Pluto, she could be quite irksome."

"There's just one other question I want to ask, but I'm not sure if I should, as I know you have a strict code of ethics that you follow."

"Ask anyway."

"Is Susie in danger from Isolde?"

Liz hesitated, but said:

"I know that you are discreet and that you have integrity, Teddy, but all that I can tell you is that you should keep a careful watch over Susie until she is safely married to Lord Bramblewell."

"So, she is in danger."

"It depends on how strong Isolde's moral centre is."

Teddy stared at Liz, as if not understanding what she was saying.

"So, she really is in some kind of danger," he said, finally.

"Not necessarily. Isolde isn't stupid, is she? She'll be careful. But keep a watch on Susie all the same."

"I should go," said Teddy abruptly, as if he could endure no more.

"Teddy," said Liz softly, then. "My feeling is that, on the way home, you will be annoyed with yourself for allowing me to have had the opportunity to prattle on about astrology."

"No! I shan't! And you didn't! But…thank you for listening."

"My pleasure, Teddy. Wait! I'll come downstairs with you."

When Teddy reached the main door on the ground floor, he turned to say, before leaving, "Be sure to drop into the school when you feel like doing so, Liz. We'd all love to see you there again."

"Thank you."

"And be assured I'll watch over Susie."

"Yes," murmured Liz, as she closed the door behind him. "I know you will…because you still love her."

CHAPTER 48

Louis Disappoints

On a moderately warm Saturday afternoon in Chester, while Lancelot Price was engrossed in reading text messages on his mobile phone, his sister, Portia, slipped past his open bedroom door without being noticed and for that, she was thankful. Lancelot, mean-spirited as a child, was becoming more personable as the years progressed, but that afternoon, Portia wanted to avoid him as she had no desire to answer questions prompted by his curiosity.

Portia descended the stairs, her heart throbbing in a way which made her alarmingly conscious of its beat. It was not in her nature to deceive and so, she was hoping to be able to leave the house quietly, while her mother was chatting to friends in the sitting room, feeding them sandwiches and cakes and pouring tea into what she was inclined to call "proper porcelain tea-cups: not those awful mugs." Were her mother to catch sight of her, Portia knew she would probably be placed in a position in which she would be forced to pull the wool over her mother's eyes, if only by omitting information. Deception being alien to her nature, she knew she would feel uncomfortable. Subsequently, a cloud would be cast over the rest of the afternoon. But how could she tell her mother that she intended to meet Louis Lindsey?

It was Genevieve, one of Portia's mother's friends, who caught sight of her as she passed the sitting room door, in fact.

"Coo-ee! Portia!" Genevieve called. "I haven't seen you for ages! Come here, dear! Are you going to a Girl Guides' meeting or something like that?"

Portia paused and then, entered the room, but she remained

standing near the door, as if to make it clear that she was in a hurry and anxious to be on her way.

A low table covered in a white, linen cloth, that hung over the table's edges and almost reached the floor, was laden with plates, ashets and a three tiered cake stand. There were napkins of white linen and heavy silver forks, knives and tea spoons. It was a sight that Portia knew her old head mistress, Hilary Trimm, would have described as being "de trop" given the situation, but Portia's mother seemed to have wanted to put on a show.

Portia recognised the second guest in the room as being Pamela, a neighbour newly arrived in the road. Portia's mother had already mentioned that Pamela was the type who liked to "do the teas" at the cricket club, to which her husband belonged. No doubt, she, Portia's mother, would have wanted to make it plain to Pamela who the Queen Bee was, when it came to making sandwiches and little cakes.

"We were just talking about you," said Genevieve addressing Portia. "Your mother was telling us how much she was looking forward to your wedding day. It's such an important moment in the life of the mother of the bride, isn't it?"

"What?" asked Portia, as if startled.

"Don't look so shocked, Portia!" exclaimed Mrs. Price. "Of course we KNOW you won't be getting married for years, yet, but all the same, it's important to plan events like weddings well in advance. We were considering the advantages of having a marquee a minute ago. What do you think about that?"

Although utterly flummoxed, Portia, nevertheless, managed to keep her voice steady. She ignored the question and said, instead:

"Mum, I'm going to Ellesmere Port for a couple of hours."

"Oh? Are you? To see Rosalind? Well! You'll be back in time for dinner, I hope."

"Yes. I shan't be late."

Fifteen minutes later, Portia was on the bus to Ellesmere Port, her mind in turmoil. For her mother to discuss her wedding day when she was only fifteen and still at school was an act of such presumptuous silliness that Portia almost gawped, just thinking about it. Of course, she realised that, given her mother's desire for social recognition, it was not surprising that the planning of a big wedding - marquee and all - would be one of her dreams. A favourite mental pastime, it was sure to become. And if Portia were to choose a husband who did not pass muster, her mother's disappointment would be overwhelming, as indeed, would be her perceived fall in status in her social circle.

Portia had never had an easy relationship with her mother. Even as a small child, she had never been able to please Mrs. Price. No achievement had ever been good enough. And it occurred to Portia, therefore, that if she were to do as she herself desired, when it came to choosing her destiny in adulthood, surely no one who knew the strictures imposed upon her during her childhood would blame her for ignoring her mother's preferences.

At the same time, the thought of disappointing Mrs. Price worried Portia. She did not really want to hurt the woman who had raised her and who probably, in her own way, had wanted what was best for her. But, what was to be done? Had Louis followed his original plan to try to be accepted as a student at Cambridge University, Mrs. Price might have approved of an association with him. But Portia's hopes had been crushed as Louis had changed his plans along with the direction of his life. Portia was as strongly attracted to Louis as she had been before, but suddenly, the future which had previously seemed so sparkling, now looked dull and exhausting. A struggle, really.

Ted's café, in down-town Ellesmere Port, was only half full when Portia entered and so, she was able to spot Louis immediately, sitting at a discreet table, by a faraway wall, where he, nevertheless, had a good view of the door. He stood up as Portia approached and pushed her chair gently towards the table as she sat down. A Saturday waitress - a sixth former probably - approached and Louis ordered a cappuccino for Portia and a cup of tea for himself.

"You should have heard the way my mother was talking before I left the house," said Portia exuberantly, her boyfriend's presence having given her spirits a lift. She leaned forward before adding, "Can you BELIEVE that she was actually planning my wedding? There she was, in the middle of the sitting room with her friends, practically on the point of ordering a marquee! Oh! I'm sorry. I'm forgetting what is really important. Is your father any better?"

"It's difficult to say," replied Louis with a shrug that suggested helplessness in the face of fate. "Listen, Portia," he then added, straightening his back. "I think we should call it a day."

"What do you mean?"

Portia felt momentarily immobilised with shock. She could sense that blood was draining from her face. It was beginning to feel numb. Her hands felt limp. Louis took hold of one and began to stroke it as if trying to bring life back into it. His touch was gentle, but Portia wanted to pull her hand away from his. She felt as if he were mocking her by being sympathetic.

"The way I am placed at the moment," said Louis, "means that I can't promise you anything. You need someone who will buy a nice house for you, one day, and will take you on long holidays to interesting places. I can't see myself as being able to provide anything like that. Not for a long, long time, anyway. I think it would be better if we were to part company now. I don't want you to waste your time waiting for me, Portia. I don't want you to hang on and on expecting me to make something of my life, only to end up disappointed."

"But, we'd manage," said Portia.

She knew her voice had weakened, but she tried not to sound desperate or pathetic. And she did not dare add, "If I get into Bristol and get a good degree, I could earn enough money for the two of us." She knew that, given his background, Louis would not be able to tolerate a dependent rôle in a relationship. Intellectually, he might accept the situation, but emotionally, he would feel diminished.

There was a pause. Louis looked away as if distracted by people who had just come into Ted's and were choosing a table. It was as if he did not want to engage in conversation. It occurred to Portia that she should not have mentioned her mother's plans for a wedding. Louis must have been consumed by panic upon hearing about them. Perhaps the words he had uttered had been no more than a normal masculine reaction to the feeling of having his life ordered by others. Maybe he was balking at the thought of having a mother-in-law like Mrs. Price.

"We could at least wait until it's time for me to go away to university, couldn't we?" suggested Portia. "And that won't happen for another two and a half years, will it?"

Louis looked directly at Portia, not saying anything.

"Will it?" she persisted.

"Fine," said Louis, but without enthusiasm. "We'll hang on for a bit."

The moment of panic was over, but as it faded away, Portia was aware of the fact that the relationship had changed its nature. Some of the fizz, as it were, had evaporated. The fairy-tale prince had shown himself to be a mortal, after all.

Portia leaned back in her chair. She did not want to entertain the negative thoughts that were beginning to enter her mind, but she could not stop them from seeping in, either. She looked at Louis with his grave, grey eyes, his short blond hair and the remnants of a sun-tan, acquired, probably, while sitting on the steps of Pierhead, looking at the flowing waters of the Mersey passing by, and she felt as if she could shake him. A strange passivity seemed to have overwhelmed him, now. He was looking at the table and his shoulders seemed to have slumped. Had he really been reluctant to continue the relationship for another two and a half years? Portia felt inclined to leave Ted's and to rush around the corner to Miss Laurier's apartment in order to ask, "What should I do?" But of course she knew that Miss Laurier's function was to elucidate and not to "fix everything," as less knowing clients were inclined to expect.

Ultimately, she, Portia, would have to decide by herself if she should walk away from Louis or persist in maintaining a relationship that had once filled her life with joy, but now was making her feel jaded. Did her mother know what was best for her, after all?

CHAPTER 49

The Watcher at the Door

Teddy Laurence's weekend had been a troubled one. Not even the distraction of the youth club he ran on Friday evenings and Saturdays had been able to lighten his mood. Having suffered from a sleepless night on Friday, Teddy had, in fact, hoped that he would have been able to leave the supervision of most of the Saturday activities to Louis Lindsey, the senior boy at the club, while he, himself, caught up with paper work in the office at the back of the hall, where the youth club meetings were held. However, Louis had seemed unhappy - not quite himself - and so, Teddy had let him be.

"Is everything all right, Lou?" he had asked in a casual way.

"Nothing I can't handle, sir," Louis had answered. "Thanks."

No more information had been forthcoming and Teddy had not pressed for it. The boy had a right to have his own secret garden, after all.

On Sunday, Teddy had sat in the sitting room of his apartment, by the large windows overlooking the Mersey, the weekend newspapers and supplements piled up on the floor beside his chair, unread. For once, the river could not quieten his mind, no matter how long he gazed out at the flowing waters. Constantly, he was thinking of Susie and Isolde. Sweet naivety up against knowing malevolence, in his view. Oh! Susie had her faults and she was not above scheming, herself - and, of course, she had broken his heart. But she had a soft, vulnerable side to her as well: a vulnerable side he did not want to see crushed by the wilful embittered Isolde.

By the time he was in bed on Sunday night, a collection of short stories by Harvey Swados at hand, waiting to be read, Teddy was mentally examining his problems in a more detached way, his emotional reaction to them, at that point, having been controlled. His never-dying concern for Susie, his need to keep Isolde in her place and the ever-increasing demands on his time at work had all joined to make his life difficult, but looking at them, without emotional engagement, as a scientist might, he felt better able to cope. All the same, he wished he had gone to play with his friends' jazz band that night, in order to give expression to his feelings, instead of burying his anxieties deep inside where they could harm his body, ultimately. It had been stupid of him, really, not to have applied what he knew, in theory, to the way he conducted his own life.

Monday morning arrived and Teddy observed, as he had in the past, that the following of his usual morning routine resulted in the settling of his mind. Having arrived in Bramblewell School, he walked along the science corridor to his classroom, feeling as if everything was normal and that the events of the preceding week had happened long in the past. He noticed, though, that, unusually, the door of Isolde's office was closed, but through the small window above her door, he could see that the light had been switched on and so he reckoned she had probably already arrived. Maybe she, too, had been shaken by the events of the previous week and was not able to bring herself to look at him, as a consequence.

At the mid-morning break, Teddy went to the nearest sub-staff-room, that being a small, box room wedged between the theatrical practice room and the ballet classroom. Only Barbara Merrivale was there.

"Hi, Teddy!" she said, as she filled a white mug with tea, drank it without further ado and then, made off to prepare for her next class. Teddy made a cup of coffee for himself and then looked out of the window that provided a view of the lower part of the wood that bordered the south side of the school. The view was calming, but in his mind, Teddy was tabulating, restlessly, all the tasks that he would have to accomplish that day. It would be better to make a start on them, rather than hang around drinking coffee. He returned briskly to his classroom, noticing that the door of Isolde's office was now wide open. He did not look at her, but smiled to himself, realising that her taste for gossip had prevented her from staying too long in a cocoon of isolation.

When he entered his room, Teddy was taken aback to see Susie waiting there for him. He felt embarrassed to see her, as he had spent a good deal of the weekend wallowing in memories of her and, in particular, in memories of the way she had looked and behaved, when he had first known her. She had had, at that time, a penchant for wearing a red cocktail dress and backless red sandals, on inappropriate occasions, but since knowing Lord Bramblewell, she had learnt the art of restraint. That morning, she was wearing a finely tailored jacket, with a velvet collar, in a conservative shade of French navy, over a stiff, white, high necked blouse. Her skirt matched her jacket and her knee-length boots in tan leather set off her "look" admirably. Her shoulder–length, blonde hair, flowing freely, gleamed. She looked beautiful, of course.

"Hi!" said Teddy, walking towards her.

Susie had been looking at documents attached to a pin board on the classroom wall. Hearing Teddy's voice, she turned round quickly, a smile animating her expression.

"Teddy!" she exclaimed, unable to hide the thrill in her voice. "I'm sorry to intrude…"

Teddy took a deep breath which sounded like a sigh, as he tried to prevent himself from showing his residual feelings for the beautiful blonde in front of him.

"What can I do for you?" he asked in a way he hoped had not revealed the weakness.

The art of dissembling was not one that Susie had ever mastered or would ever consider mastering. She was honest, in her own way, and, tended to blurt out what she was thinking, in a child-like fashion.

"Rosalind Somerland told me that you had been to see her

mother recently and I was wondering…"

"Why I had gone there"

"Yes. I mean…it's not like you to talk to Liz, is it? Is something wrong? Is it something to do with Rosalind? I know she was a bit of a nuisance with that crush she had on you…"

"No! No! My visit had nothing to do with Rosalind. No…I was talking to Liz about Isolde."

"Isolde?"

"Yes."

"Oh! Teddy! Is she bothering you, too?"

"What do you mean? Has Isolde been annoying you? I thought I had solved that problem by moving her to this corridor."

"No. She hasn't been intruding on my life in any specific way, Teddy, but, always, at the back of my mind, is the feeling that she will snatch Rupert away before I can marry him. I do sense that she will not allow the wedding to take place. I am convinced that she will do something dramatic to prevent its happening. I just know she will. She's going to make Rupert remember how much he loved her and, then, he will leave me."

There were tears, now, in Susie's eyes, but she had learnt that it was not "the done thing" to cry in public and so, she stopped the tears from flowing by digging her nails into the palms of her hands, to distract herself. Teddy saw that she was struggling and so, he placed his hands on her shoulders to steady her.

"Susie!" he said, firmly. "It was not long ago that Lord Bramblewell was in the corridor out there, scolding Isolde for being rude and unhelpful in the school. He was definitely not doing so in a kind way. In fact, he sounded downright cold. And I must tell you that he mentioned you. His very words were, 'Susie is my guiding star: something you never were, Isolde, and could never be.' I think the way he felt about you was clear enough."

"Did you really hear him saying that?"

Susie's face lit up with a joy that made Teddy's heart lurch, in pain, but he smiled, although sadly.

"Yes. He did," he said.

"Oh! Teddy! Teddy!" whispered Susie, tears now flowing down her face. "Thank you,"

She put her arms around Teddy's neck and he, in response, held her until the feelings of shock and relief flooding her body had been dispersed.

With her head being buried in Teddy's jacket, Susie did not see, over his, Teddy's, shoulder, Isolde, standing wraith-like, outside the half-open classroom door, her mobile phone in her hand. Nor did she see Isolde turning then, to walk with a light step, back along the corridor, towards her own office, a smirk on her face.

CHAPTER 50

Dreaming of America

It occurred to Teddy Laurence that it was high time he invited Lynn James to have dinner at his flat, in order not only to return the hospitality she had extended to him at the start of the new, scholastic year, but also to thank her for the many ways she had discreetly helped him and guided him, during his first days in his new post.

Knowing how impressed Lynn would be, were he to adhere to correct form, he left a hand-written invitation card, in an envelope, on her desk, inviting her to dine at his riverside apartment at the end of the week. He found a reply from Lynn on his own desk two hours later. She would be delighted to accept his invitation. "How lovely!" she had added.

Teddy's culinary skills, he, himself, would not have described as extensive, but he did know how to cook a few dishes, some of which had been introduced to him by Susie, he was happy to admit. It was extraordinary, really, how good a cook Susie had been, given the fact that her own mother's skills had alarmingly not extended far beyond making beans on toast, chips and those sandwiches of white bread filled with cheese spread, which, it seems, had often been a substitute for substantial meals. The paying of the rent had been given priority, of course.

On the evening before Lynn's visit, while pondering on what the following night's menu should be, Teddy wondered if she should make a soup for his guest, using a lamb bone, carrots, lentils, split peas and onions. Something nourishing to buck her up, after a hectic week at Bramblewell, in other words. A home-made steak and ale pie was not the most sophisticated dish to offer at a dinner party, but Teddy thought he would risk preparing it, too, along with mashed potatoes, French beans and leeks. The pudding would have to be elaborate, but light. He would have to look through the cookery books Susie had left with him before choosing one, though.

The following evening, Lynn arrived wearing a sleeveless, jade green dress and with her hair arranged in an elegant chignon.

"Am I too early?" she asked anxiously, as Teddy had answered the door with his shirt sleeves rolled up.

"No! No! Come in and make yourself comfortable."

Lynn entered the apartment with which she was a little familiar having previously visited it at the end of the summer term, with a group of other teachers from Bramblewell School, after having dinner at the Fleuve Chéri.

"Come to my flat for coffee!" Teddy had said to the group of colleagues, on that occasion, and all had gone, partly out of curiosity, to see where he had moved, after selling his terraced house in Chester. They had drunk frothy coffee and had talked and watched the night falling over the Mersey and on to the Wirral, on the other side of the waters.

"Sitting room, Teddy?" asked Lynn as she hung up the coat which she had been carrying over her arm.

"Yes. Help yourself to a drink. I shan't be long?"

Lynn noticed, at once, that one of the pieces of furniture in Teddy's sitting room had been moved from the space it had occupied previously. Now, a high-backed chair and a tall, spare-looking reading-lamp were close to the window and she could imagine Teddy sitting there in the evenings, reading or preparing work for the following day.

Teddy entered the room, then, startling Lynn out of her rêverie.

"You haven't had anything to drink? What would you like?"

"Orange and soda," I think."

"Not a fine wine from France?"

"Later. I prefer to drink wine with food."

"Of course. Ice?"

"Yes, please."

"Right. Coming up."

A dining table had been set up in the corner of the room, and spread with a white linen cloth. It looked attractive, but Teddy seemed to be irritated by it, as if he felt a dining table spoiled the aspect of the room.

"I thought of turning the guest bedroom into a dining room, since this arrangement is not the best one," he said, frowning. "But if I didn't have a guest bedroom I couldn't invite anyone to stay."

"The present arrangement is fine," Lynn assured him. "I mean, the table fits into that corner nicely."

The conversation was trivial, but neither of them had the energy, after a week at school, to enter into a more fervent discussion.

"I like that chair," said Lynn, indicating, with a sweep of her hand, the high-backed chair by the window. "It wasn't there when I came here in the summer, was it?"

"No. Rebecca moved it while I was away…and I just left it there."

"Rebecca?"

"Rebecca Hampton. She stayed here during the summer holidays, while I was in France. I thought you knew."

"Oh! Maybe you did mention she'd be staying here. It must have slipped my mind," said Lynn in an apparently distracted fashion, as if the news was of no consequence to her. But she was bemused to find herself thinking of nothing else when Teddy had left the room to see if the soup was ready. Rebecca Hampton! How regularly had Teddy been in touch with her? Was she no more that a casual friend? No more than the girl who had shared a flat with his previous girl-friend, Jacqueline de Sauzon? Or was his attachment to her deeper than that? Lynn remembered that Hilary Trimm had met Rebecca Hampton in France during the party marking Teddy's engagement to Jacqueline de Sauzon.

Hilary Trimm had told Lynn how confident and articulate

Rebecca had been, those qualities, no doubt, having been the gifts of her American education and her parents' social status. Had Teddy been drawn to her qualities…or had he kept in touch with Rebecca in order to glean from her news of Jacqueline de Sauzon? No. It was inconceivable that Teddy would use the young American girl, in that way, as a mere carrier of information.

A book lying on the floor beside the high-backed chair caught Lynn's eye. She walked to the chair and picked it up, curiosity evident in her grey-blue eyes. It was a thick paperback. Lynn flicked it open. The story was set in an American, east coast college. Maybe Rebecca had left it behind. Or maybe Teddy had bought it in order to acquaint himself with the sort of college life with which Rebecca might be familiar.

Teddy re-entered the room with a laden tray.

"Have you ever been to America, Teddy?" Lynn asked, attempting to make the question sound casual.

"Not yet," he replied, putting the tray down on the linen-covered table.

Not yet? Lynn made no comment, but Teddy's words had unsteadied her. What exactly had they meant? Was she going to lose her deputy before he had properly established himself in post? Would she understand the extent to which she had been inclined to lean on him only after his departure? How would she cope without him?

CHAPTER 51

Viareggio

Having made its way through the Mediterranean, the *Sabine Estelle* on which Madame Gabrielle de Talence was holidaying, was approaching Viareggio. Passengers, out on deck early, saw the stylish resort from an advantageous angle. It looked splendid, not least because the hills of Tuscany rose strikingly behind it, while, before it, the sparkling Tyrrhenian Sea washed its neatly swept beaches.

After breakfast, Madame Gabrielle could have gone ashore with other passengers who had booked trips to Pisa and Lucca, but she decided not to. She already knew Viareggio and other parts of Tuscany well, having, in the past, taken a train from Bordeaux to Ventimiglia, following the coastal track along the Côte d'Azur, passing stations with names evocative of style and leisure - St. Tropez, St. Raphaël, Cannes, Juan-les-Pins, Nice and Monte Carlo, predominantly - and then, another train onwards to Viareggio. She was already familiar with the beaches, the passeggiata and the pineta with its shady trees. She knew the hotels she preferred - the ones with cool white rooms and gilt framed oil paintings on the walls - and she knew the restaurants which served her favourite Italian pasta dishes. Penne with a simple tomato sauce, oregano and olive oil, for example.

When she returned to her rooms, Madame Gabrielle found that the stewardess had already cleaned them. She lay down on the fresh duvet cover on the bed and tried to sleep a little, but her body was restless. She rose and put on a new, white shirt, light beige trousers, a straw hat and sun glasses - of the large type Mrs. Jacqueline Kennedy might once have worn - before, being satisfied with her appearance, going up on deck.

Although it was still morning, the heat was rising rapidly. The ship was quiet, most of the passengers having departed on their excursions to Tuscany's mediaeval cities. Turning a corner on deck, while in search of shade, Madame Gabrielle found herself in the company of a solitary man, who was leaning on a deck rail, while gazing at the glittering sea below. Upon recognising him, Madame Gabrielle gasped, in involuntary fashion.

"Mr. Mallory!" she said, almost in a whisper.

Kit Mallory turned to look at her and gave her a smile which seemed to convey a tinge of sadness as well as nostalgia.

"Have we met before?" he asked. "I have been thinking about you since the evening we met at the cocktail party. You remind me of someone."

What could she say? Should she tell him that, decades before, when she had been a foreign student in Liverpool, she had frequently seen him singing on stage in the cellar clubs of Liverpool? Should she mention how she had never forgotten the lightly scented cologne which he had been inclined to wear: one which brought to mind lemon and orange groves, exuding their fresh perfume, in the heat of a dazzling sun? But, no! Of course not!

"Maybe out paths crossed somewhere before," she said instead, in a vague and apparently rather distracted way. "I have travelled in Italy, Spain and Belgium. I have been to England."

"You have been to England?"

"Yes. But it was a long time ago."

Kit Mallory looked puzzled, as if he were searching his memory for information about her, but without success. Was she really so unmemorable? Even though he had been inclined to gaze into her eyes from the stage on which he had been performing, had she been no more than just another fan, as far as he had been concerned? An unremarkable girl of no real consequence?

"Forgive me," said Madame Gabrielle, feeling embarrassed

and humiliated. "I am tired. I should return to my room."

She made as if to turn, but then, hesitated, as if expecting Mr. Mallory to beg her to stay. He did not. But, she should not have been surprised. Many men preferred younger women and there was nothing one could do to change their preferences. There was no doubt that Mr. Mallory needed youthful beauty for company: beauty as it appeared in the form of Miss Traversi, in his case. As if on an impulse - or perhaps from vexation or even desperation - Madame Gabrielle then said unexpectedly:

"You see, I have two grand-daughters who have decided to become actresses. Oh! In a dilettante-ish way, you understnd. But I worry so much about them that I am, frankly, exhausted. You may think I am old-fashioned but I don't think the world of the stage- of performance, in fact - is suitable for girls of their type. You have had experience of the performing arts. Don't you agree with me that the ambiance is not one in which nice girls would be comfortable?"

"You know your grand-daughters; I do not," said Mr. Mallory, cautiously, looking at Madame Gabrielle as if wondering where the conversation was heading.

"Look! Here is one of them" said Madame Gabrielle, fumbling in her hand-bag and removing a photo of Marie-Colette de Sauzon, a photo in which the girl resembled Madame Gabrielle, herself, when she had been a student.

Kit Mallory took the photo from Madame Gabrielle's hand, glanced at it and returned it.

"The girl is obviously beautiful," he said.

"Thank you," said Madame Gabrielle, attempting not to let disappointment seep into her voice. He had not been reminded of her in her Liverpool days. She really had been forgotten. She snapped the clasp of her hand-bag shut and walked away without saying another word. She felt she had let herself down, yet again, having been on the point of pleading, "Remember me! Remember me!" Of course she had fallen into the infantile trap of thinking that just because she had remembered him, he would have remembered her! What an idiot she had been! Imagine what her father, the proud Count du Crâne, would have thought of her behaviour, had he still been alive! She realised, then, suddenly, that she did care immensely about the opinion her father would have had of her, especially since she had disappointed him so badly in her youth. Would that wound ever heal?

It crossed Madame Gabrielle's mind, then, that she could leave the ship at that point. She could return by rail to Bordeaux, without difficulty. The journey would even be enjoyable and, on the way, she would make an effort to put Kit Mallory out of her mind forever. But the very thought of making arrangements for such a deviation from the original plan exhausted her and, by the time she had reached her cabin, she had decided not to leave. She would endure the rest of the cruise. But oh! How she longed for it to end!

CHAPTER 52

Caterina Intrudes

"The cruise is almost through and she has been hiding in her cabin most of the time!" exclaimed Dorothy Trimm, referring to the reclusive Madame Gabrielle de Talence. "The way she has behaved is really worrying me Hils!"

"We've been doing our best, Mother. We could hardly have been expected to do more than observe," muttered Hilary Trimm, as she surveyed the contents of the wardrobe in her cabin, as if wondering what to wear over the plain, lemon dress she had put on that morning.

Dorothy sat down on Hilary's bed and sighed, in a frustrated sort of way.

"It's so annoying," she said.

"What is annoying you, Mother?"

"The fact that we have not been more successful."

"Successful in doing what, exactly?"

"I don't know...I think we should have been doing more to help Madame Gabrielle to have a nice time during the cruise. It must have been a miserable fortnight for her, being all alone. Maybe I should have knocked on her door to invite her to go for walks on deck, or to join me at afternoon lectures."

"No! I think not! We did quite enough when we held that wretched cocktail party in your rooms. Just reflect on how that ended!"

"I suppose so...But you can't take any money from the Sauzon family for doing so little, can you? You don't intend to, do you?"

"Absolutely not. I never intended to, in fact. I simply felt like going away on a cruise in order to draw a line between my old life and the one that is about to begin at Q-COLL. And I thought keeping an eye on Madame Gabrielle would be an added distraction. Your worrying about Madame Gabrielle aside, haven't you been enjoying the cruise, Mother?"

"Well! Yes! I'm especially glad that I struck up a conversation with Miss Traversi, of course. I mean, who would have guessed that her father was so well-known in the publishing world?"

"And she really is going to work for you?"

"Well! I was talking to her a few minutes ago and she told me she definitely, definitely wants to see how a small publishing house is run. She wants to learn all about the world of publishing, so that she can impress her father. I told her I'd be happy to have her working at my side. She's young and lively. I'm sure she would be an asset."

"You could be right, Mother. But, she could also pull the mat from under your feet, if you are not careful."

"Oh! I don't think so, now! She's too nice."

"She may well be nice…but what do you know about her father? Nothing!"

"Oh! Hils! Don't spoil my day! Let's talk about something else! What was I saying? Oh! Yes! You know, it's such a pity that Madame Gabrielle's romance didn't end happily. I bet she is in her cabin, at this moment, feeling awful because…"

"Because we meddled too much, Mother! That's the beginning and end of it. We meddled too much."

"Well! You are really snappy, today, aren't you? What's wrong with you? You need to go out into the fresh air. Or is it the thought of returning home and facing life's problems again that is making you so ill-tempered? Consider yourself lucky, my girl! At least you are not returning home with a broken heart, in the way Madame Gabrielle is!"

"Oh, really, Mother? Really? You have a remarkably short memory, if I may say so!"

"Oh, gosh! I'm so sorry, Hils! I did forget all about Lord

Bramblewell and Susie Sutton, for a moment! But, I do think you'll get over your broken heart when you start working again. You will, won't you? Hm? And you will find another suitor, before long. I'm sure you will."

Hilary Trimm merely shook her head in exasperation and resumed her examination of the contents of her wardrobe.

In her own rooms, Madame Gabrielle de Talence was doing much the same, with sadness in her heart. Hanging in her wardrobe, there were so many outfits that had not been worn, simply because she had not attended as many evening events as she had anticipated. What had been the point of bringing with her the sophisticated, black evening trousers that she had bought in the Rue Sainte Catherine in Bordeaux or the silver evening jacket that had caught her eye in the Rue St. Honoré in Paris, the last time she had been passing through the capital? Had the cruise been a waste of time? Not entirely, she had to admit. At least it had given her the opportunity and time to lose herself in the books she had been meaning to read for a while. The novels of Françoise Sagan always provided her with a means to escape into a stylish world, lived lightly, in which she wished she could linger, indefinitely.

With a sigh, Madame Gabrielle walked into her bathroom and there, stared at her reflection in the mirror above the sink. She could pay for injections of "fillers" at a beautician's shop, to make her skin look plump and youthful. She could attend yoga classes to make her body and limbs supple. And she could ask Agnès, her hairdresser in Bordeaux, to continue to tint her hair in ways that would make her look even younger. But what would be the point of all that? She had had an opportunity to make an impression on Kit Mallory and she had failed to do so. Instead of being swept away by him to start a new life, romantically, she would return to Bordeaux and resume her day to day routine as she had lived it before.

Three days passed and then, with regret, Madame Gabrielle steadied herself to accept the fact that only one more day and a night remained before the ship would dock in Liverpool. She dressed herself in beige, on the last full day, before wandering along the corridor where the shops were located. She tried to convince herself that she was simply having a last look at the ship before leaving it, but, of course, she was nursing the hope that she would catch a glimpse of Kit Mallory again. There was enough of the romantic left in her to wish that, upon seeing her, his eyes would light up with happiness. But she did not see him. And she spent the last night on board, lying in bed hugging her pillow, her heart feeling like a cold stone, uncomfortable and heavy.

Dawn broke. Madame Gabrielle went out on to her balcony. Sea breezes blew through her hair. She could sense that Liverpool was near. She dressed in a chic way, in black and white, and, having made her way to the breakfast room, she ate simply, choosing only sliced water melons and pineapples, yoghurt and black coffee. A news sheet pushed under her door earlier had informed her that her suitcase had to be packed and ready to be taken away by eight o'clock and that, she, herself, like other passengers, would have to go to one of the sitting rooms, before nine o' clock, in order to await the call to disembark. After eating, she went to her cabin to leave a good tip for the stewardess and then she made her way to the sitting room to wait. When her cabin number was called, she prepared to disembark without looking back.

She had to descend steep stairs to a lower deck and so she kept her eyes on each step as she went down. She did not notice Kit Mallory, therefore, until she had reached the last one and was about to step on to the level deck. He was standing in front of her, as if he had been waiting for her. Had he? Madame Gabrielle took a deep breath, her eyes brightening simultaneously. She started to smile. But then, Caterina Traversi appeared, as if by magical intervention. Caterina was full of excitement over the prospect of starting work at Dorothy Trimm's publishing house. How impressed her father would be! As for her sister Beatrice! Well! She would be flummoxed! She would not know what to say!

"Ciao! Ciao!" Caterina exclaimed, in familiar fashion, to Kit. She raised her arms and placed them around his neck.

Taken aback, Madame Gabrielle averted her eyes. She headed for the gangway, unaware of the fact that Kit was following her with his eyes, the expression in them intense and somewhat despairing.

CHAPTER 53

Jacqui

In Paris, it was the time of day, between four and seven, when the late afternoon sun delivered one last blast of heat, before allowing itself to be supplanted by the more moderate temperatures of evening. Jacqueline de Sauzon had been meandering through the streets of the Latin Quarter, in a seemingly weary manner, as if she had been exhausted by a day's studying in a library, rather than having been exhilarated by it. In recent days, in truth, she had not been able to focus on the works of France's great philosophers with as much passion as she would have wished, so depleted in energy had she become. Her lucid sister, Héloïse, having been consulted about the set-back during a telephone conversation, had immediately concluded that Jacqueline's lack of joie de vivre had its roots in her husband's neglect of her. How often had Jacqui telephoned her in the weeks that had just passed? Had he even sent text messages? How often had she, Jacqueline, tried to contact him? What? Her calls had been blocked because Jacqui had been engaged in important work or had been studying? Always? And her e-mail messages to him had been ignored?

Jacqueline had admitted that she had awoken every morning feeling confused, angry and helpless. She had had to concede, all the same, that there was still a vestige of love for Jacqui left in her: the old Jacqui whom she had known when they had been together at school. She hoped, still, that the marriage would survive the fallow period. "The tide sometimes goes out," she had said to Héloïse, as if she had been trying to convince herself, as well as her sister, that her husband's behaviour had been subject to the rhythms of nature. But Héloïse had exclaimed:

"Be realistic! Do you seriously believe that Jacqui will ever be capable of behaving correctly? Have you forgotten the way he sulked on the day you were going away to study in England? What about the neglectful way he treated you while you were over there?"

Sensing the derision in Héloïse's voice, Jacqueline had felt as if she had been slapped awake and she had realised, then, that she had probably been foolish. She had wasted too much time worrying about a deteriorating relationship between two people who no longer had a great deal in common.

Leaving the Boulevard Saint-Michel, as if seeking shade, Jacqueline took a short cut down a side street to the road in which her small apartment was situated.

"Votre mari est arrivé, madame," said the concierge as she entered the building.

"Mon mari?" asked Jacqueline, as if not understanding. Jacqui had come home? Just when he had been uppermost in her thoughts! Was that possible? Jacqueline headed for the stairs, not being fond of the ornate lift with its heavy, wrought iron gates. Her heart was throbbing loudly. At least she imagined it was.

Outside the door of her apartment, Jacqueline searched in her bag for the key which would open it. Her hands seemed to have become clumsy. She turned the key in the lock in a fumbling way and then, she pushed open the door, while taking a deep breath to control her excitement.

No sound could be heard inside the apartment. It seemed to be as empty as it habitually was. Could the concierge have made a mistake? Jacqueline went in and threw her coat on to the replica Louis XV chair in the hall, before walking into the bedroom. It was as it had looked when she had left it that morning. The bottle of scent she had used, before leaving, was still lying on the bed. Her "Made in England" hairbrush, likewise.

Jacqueline left the scene and walked into the living room. And there he was. Jacqui. Standing still, but looking out of the window, downwards to the narrow street below. He did not turn around, although he must have been aware of the fact that she, Jacqueline, had entered the room "Jacqui?" she said, as nervously as if she had scarcely known him previously. In fact, she did not know this new version of Jacqui, this young man who was now disinclined to make any effort to please her. Perhaps she should have examined his behaviour more closely and intelligently, in former times, in order to home in on signs of what was to come. Instead, she had made excuses for his lapses in conduct and had believed what she had wanted to believe.

While in England, she had known that her love for Teddy Laurence had been different from her love for Jacqui. Teddy had impressed her with his kindness, good manners and reasonableness. Her love for Jacqui had been more elemental. He had, once, made her feel vibrant and alive. But she was realising, now, that Jacqui's kind of love delivered only transitory moments of happiness. A love that was not based on consideration was not worth much, really. She should have married Teddy. What an idiot she had been to have rejected him!

Jacqui turned round slowly, as if not in a hurry to do so. His apparently casual way of responding to her, now, made her love him even less. To think of what she had given up to be with him!

"Did you bring your car?" she asked calmly.

The drive along the RN12 would have taken six hours, surely. If Jacqui had driven, he would now be exhausted. Jacqueline realised she had already started to make excuses for his behaviour. She tried to stop herself from becoming sentimental.

Jacqui shrugged.

"Yes," he answered, conveying both strength and, surprisingly, gentleness in that one word.

Jacqueline almost ran into his arms at that moment, but she restrained herself. Impulsive behaviour, in the past, had led to the creation of difficulties for herself and, indeed, had led to the marriage in which she was now trapped.

"Shall we go out for dinner?" Jacqui asked, then, unexpectedly. "There's nothing in the fridge, in any case."

"We could go out," replied Jacqueline, calmly.

What would be the point of mentioning the fact that there would have been plenty in the fridge if he had warned her that he would be arriving.

Jacqueline went into the bedroom to replace her jumper with a smart, beige blouse. She took tailored, black trousers out of the wardrobe and looked for her beige, high-heeled shoes: the ones with black toe caps that looked so Right Bank. She picked up a deep pink lipstick from her make-up tray, on top of her dressing table, and then, she decided to wear a bright red, glossy one, instead. She felt more adult when wearing red lipstick. She realised, then, that she had chosen to dress to please herself, rather than to please Jacqui.

Her preparations complete, Jacqueline returned to the living room, where he, Jacqui, was still standing. He seemed troubled. Was he trying to summon the courage to tell her their marriage was over, as far as he was concerned?

They left the apartment and walked in the direction of a nearby bistrot. The evening was still warm and the streets, busy. Jacqueline realised that had Jacqui still been capable of making her heart soar, she would not have noticed how crowded the streets were: she would have been too eagerly engaged in conversing with him, her eyes bright and her expression animated.

"This is hopeless," she thought to herself, suffering his silence.

When they reached the bistrot, Jacqui said he wanted to sit outside on the pavement terrace. Jacqueline understood he had chosen to sit there, because he believed there was less of a chance of her reacting emotionally to anything he would have to say, if they were not hidden in a dark corner inside. What was he planning to tell her?

They sat down opposite each other. Jacqui picked up the menu and handed it to her. She shook her head. Jacqui looked at her, as if wondering how often she had visited the bistrot, in recent times, and with whom she had dined there. Jacqueline, realising what was going through his mind, stared at him with contempt. The little bistrot was in a quarter inhabited by students, She had often dined in it with a bunch of friends, but not with any sole person in particular. Did Jacqui not trust her?

A waiter appeared, a long, white apron tied around his waist.

"Bonsoir monsieur, madame. Vous avez choisi?"

Jacqueline said she wanted pâté and then, steak - frites. Nothing more complicated than that. Jacqui, without enthusiasm, added that he would have the same.

Unable to bear the tension rising within her, Jacqueline leaned forward, her hands clasped in front of her on the table.

"So?" she asked. "Are you here for a specific purpose? You have not been able to bring yourself to look at me directly, have you? Why are you behaving in this way? I have given up so much for you, Jacqui. I deserve better treatment."

"I know," said Jacqui, looking straight into her eyes.

Jacqueline saw sadness in his expression. She sat back in her chair and studied his softly tanned face and his short brown hair, remembering how she had once adored the way he had looked.

"I've let you down," said Jacqui, then, his voice steady. "I hoped when I married you that I'd be able to release you from the grip of your family. I hoped that I'd set you free, in a manner of speaking. It was a romantic notion of course. Neither of us is free. You are tied to your studies and I, to mine. We are apart and our interests are so diverse that we have nothing to discuss."

"That's what grown-up life is like, Jacqui," said Jacqueline calmly.

"No. If we hadn't married, life wouldn't feel like this. Heavy and restricting,"

"You think we shouldn't have married?"

"We were too young."

"No. You were too young," thought Jacqueline to herself. "Too immature."

She leaned back in her chair, again, and watched the people who were strolling by, as if languidly, now. The waiter, meanwhile, was making his way to the table. He placed before Jacqueline a large white plate on which lay slices of pâté, toast and salad. Jacqueline looked at it without appetite.

"You are so spoilt," Jacqui then said, keeping his voice low. "There are tramps under the bridges over the Seine who would be grateful for a feast like that."

Jacqueline stared at Jacqui, wondering how he dared to talk to her in such a patronising way. She felt the back of her neck turning pink with anger. But, she said nothing. Instead, she started to eat.

"So, what shall we do?" she asked in a brittle way, after some minutes had passed.

"We could continue as we are until you have finished your studies," replied Jacqui without hesitation, as if his answer had been prepared beforehand. "We might think of a solution during that time. Something that would suit us both. A compromise."

"A compromise? What do you mean?"

"I don't know, exactly. I don't know what I mean."

"Jacqui, on the day I became engaged, formally, to Teddy Laurence, why did you appear all dressed up in your naval uniform? Why did you come to the party at all? You hadn't been invited. What was your aim? Were you hoping to make Teddy jealous? Were you imagining you could win me back? Why were you there?"

"You were the one who ran into my arms," snapped Jacqui, as if annoyed by the implied criticism of his behaviour. "I didn't ask you to do that. But, after you had so spectacularly humiliated your fiancé by doing so, I had no choicebut to marry you, to help you save face. That's why we are now locked in this marriage which I, for one, didn't want."

"How dare you! How dare you blame me! I cannot believe you have said what you have just said!" exclaimed Jacqueline as quietly as she could. She was shocked, but being aware of her surroundings, she was disinclined to raise her voice above a soft whisper. "You married me perfectly willingly," she continued. "And I certainly didn't need you to help me to save face. My family would have helped me to save face. None of us needed you. How could you possibly think otherwise, you..."

"You...what? You vulgar boy from a lower stratum of society?"

"If you still think in that way, Jacqui...If you think our relationship is always going to have the shadow of society's divisions floating over it, we..."

"We are never going to walk in the sunshine?"

"Oh! Stop being so dramatic! I'm tired and my head is sore."

"I'll take you home. We'll talk again some other time," said Jacqui, realising that too much had been said, that evening. "I'll drive back to Brittany, after that. Let's forget the steak."

"You are going back to Brest now? You can't! It's too late."

"Too late? I hope not, Jacqueline," said Jacqui.

There was a look in his dark eyes that suggested, just for a moment, that he was thinking of something other than the drive along the RN12, through the night.

Leaving Jacqueline at the door of her apartment, minutes later, Jacqui made his way downstairs, having said "Good-bye," in a casual way.

"Vous partez, monsieur?" asked the concierge, surprised.

"Oui, madame," Jacqui replied. "Il faut que je parte tout de suite."

"Ah! Quel dommage! Madame sera toute seule, ce soir, comme toujours."

Jacqui made no comment, but set off, quickly, into the dark.

He drove as if in anger, but stopped at a relais routier, on the outskirts of Paris. There, he ordered a cup of strong, black coffee and a ham sandwich. At a table by a window, he stared out at the forecourt, lit by lofty street lamps, throwing out a bright glow. Jacqui drank the hot coffee, sip by sip, in disconsolate fashion. He was furious over the fact that Jacqueline had spoken to him in the way she had. But he was angry with himself, also, for having made no attempt to create an atmosphere of harmony. Why had he felt compelled to rile Jacqueline with his ill-conceived and puerile statements? Of course he had not married her to help her to save face! He had loved her. He had loved her throughout his entire life! From an early age, he had felt a strong desire to protect her from life's vicissitudes. And during their teen years, how he had adored to go down to the beach with her, near the port of Sauzon, in order to walk along the water's edge, with her, discussing this and that. He had felt comfortable with her. Jacqueline, equally at ease, would throw off her espadrilles and would run along the sands and, then, would dance, while little waves would lap against her ankles. And he, Jacqui, would laugh. And then, invariably, they would go to their favourite café, and he would study her face, framed by her long, pale golden, sun-bleached hair, as she drank tea, English style. He remembered wanting to memorise every feature of her face, as if he were gazing at it for the last time. But he had thought their love and their companionship would last forever.

Then, he, Jacqui, had begun to lose ground in school. He had started to fail exams, while Jacqueline had made rapid progress towards a dazzling, academically-oriented future. Jacqui had, then, begun to view his relationship with her differently. He had realised, of course, that he had become jealous of her success. That success of hers had also made him feel diminished. He had begun to suspect that he would never be worthy of her, in the eyes of her aristocratic family. That knowledge was like an invisible wound: ever painful.

When Jacqueline had gone to England to study, for a gap year between school and university, he had allowed himself to slip into a state of apathy. But then, he had heard that Jacqueline had acquired a new boyfriend, a teacher, named Teddy Laurence, and the anger that this piece of information had aroused in him had compelled him to start studying again, with a view to entering the élite naval college at Lanvéoc-Poulmic, near Brest. His father had been relieved that his youngest son had finally found a goal in life. "But you must be realistic," he had warned. "Only the very best students are admitted to that college."

After working day and night in an effort to improve his academic scores, Jacqui has managed to gain entrance to the prestigious institution, but now, he was finding it difficult to keep up with the standards required. What if he were to fail a crucial examination? What if he had to accept a rôle in life lesser than the one to which he had aspired? What if he were to disappoint Jacqueline, ultimately?

Jacqui stared down at his cup of coffee. It was half empty. Half empty or half full? Like one's view of life, really. It was a trite thought. Banal. But there was peace to be found in that simple philosophy. One could travel through life grateful for what one already possessed, however little, or greedy for what one did not possess. Instead of longing for perfection - the perfect career, the perfect relationship - should he, Jacqui, not be thankful for what he had already been given in life? He was, after all, married to the beautiful Jacqueline de Sauzon. Married! And he was on the verge of destroying what he had longed to have all through his youth! What a fool he was! Should he not push his pride to one side and return to his Jacqueline? Should he not explain to her, with simplicity and frankness, the difficulties he was encountering? She had always been nurturing. She would understand.

Jacqui left the café and made his way to his car. As he approached the exit of the forecourt, he paused briefly in order to reflect on what he was going to do. Then, he decisively turned the car to the left and headed back to Paris. He owed it to Jacqueline to restore their friendship, if nothing else.

CHAPTER 54

A Teenagers' Guide

Rosalind Somerland had phoned her mother prior to catching the bus which would take her from Chester to Ellesmere Port, after school. Could she drop in for a short visit before going home to her Dad's house? Liz Laurier was, naturally, anticipating the visit with great pleasure. But she had become sensitive to the changes in tone in her daughter's voice and she had thought she had detected a trace of worry or distress in the way Rosalind had been speaking. It was Friday and two weeks had passed since the beginning of term. Was all not as Rosalind would have hoped, at Bramblewell?

Liz tidied her sitting room, collecting the books which had been lying on the sofas. She went into the kitchen, wondering if she should prepare a meal. Surely Rosalind would be very hungry after a day in school. On the other hand, Gylen's housekeeper would have prepared food too. Perhaps she had better wait until Rosalind had told her what she wanted to do, to avoid awkwardness.

Rosalind arrived. After greeting her mother, she sat on one of the white sofas and leaned back into the soft cushions, with a sigh.

"Is everything all right?" asked Liz. "Are the new girls in first year settling in? Has The Eliza Club attracted any new members?"

Liz sat down opposite her daughter and looked at her as if eager to hear her news.

"The rehearsals for the Christmas play have started."

"Already?"

"Yes. But They are not going as well as Portia would have hoped. Irene Miller has spoilt everything, really. She seems to upset everyone in the club just by being present. Portia used to be in charge, but this new girl is…"

"Undermining Portia's authority?"

"Yes. How did you know?"

"I guessed."

"Irene doesn't actually say much, but she seems to…I don't know…"

"She has an inhibiting effect on people?"

"I suppose that's what she does. Yes. In the past, Portia used to be able to persuade the girls in the club - and even the 6th Year boys - to take their acting rôles really seriously, but it's impossible for Portia to do that now, because this girl stands around, creating an atmosphere in the room. She makes it impossible for people to act properly, somehow. I don't know how else to describe what she does."

"You must give her a job to do: one which sounds important but which will not amount to much except for the fact that it will ensure that she will not be present at rehearsals. I assume she does not actually have a part in the play."

"Well! Unfortunately, she does! "

"Tell Portia to take it from her and to dream up some other task for her."

"Irene would not be pleased if Portia were to do that."

"No. She wouldn't be pleased but for the sake of the play's success and harmony in the club, Portia will have to harden her heart and tell this girl it is a bit too soon for her to appear on stage. It seems to me you are all dealing with Pluto. Irene's Pluto, I should say. I'd guess Irene is a bit older than the rest of you."

"About a year older, I think."

"A year older… Maybe her Pluto is in conjunction with Portia's Venus then and… Oh! You are not following me!"

"I'm a bit lost, Mum."

"Wait a minute," said Liz, smiling.She stood up and headed for her study, returning some minutes later with a carrier bag stuffed with handwritten A4 pages.

"I haven't typed much of this yet, or rather, word-processed much of it."

"Is it the book?"

"Yes. We'll have to sit down together to talk about its structure, one day soon."

"Have you been writing stuff about me? Or Portia and Louis? Portia needs help, Mum"

Rosalind was looking at the bag with curiosity in her eyes. She was longing to read what was there.

"I was wondering if we should try to get it published, so that other teenagers could benefit from what has been written," said Liz. "Since Venus is the planet that is strongly associated with relationships and the book will cover relationships with friends, teachers and family members I was thinking of calling it 'The Aspects of Venus.' What do you think?"

Rosalind had given a start upon hearing the word, "teachers". Her crush on Mr. Teddy Laurence had not been erased from her mind to such an extent that the thought of it no longer troubled her.

"I feel guilty about having started teaching classes in Bramblewell School and then, having abandoned those classes. I should have liked to have continued," Liz went on.

"It wasn't your fault. It was Dad's."

"No. It was my own fault. I should have guessed he might have turned up at the school's garden fête and that he would see me… Anyway, it was time for me to reveal my identity. It would not have been fair of me to have continued to teach at Bramblewell, without letting you know who I was."

Rosalind nodded but said nothing.

"Anyway," said Liz, "this book is a small attempt on my part to make up for the fact that I wasn't present while you were growing up."

"It's all right, Mum," interrupted Rosalind. "You don't have to go on and on about it."

Liz had never previously detected irritation in Rosalind's voice when she, Rosalind, had been speaking to her. But, she decided to ignore what she would normally have described as a lapse in good manners.

"I'd like to dedicate the book to you," she said, lightly, instead of delivering a rebuke.

"Oh!" said Rosalind startled. She smiled before adding, "I think it would be a good idea, Mum, to let other girls read the book. I definitely do think you should publish it. Definitely. I mean, dealing with relationships is really tough for teenagers. Sometimes I feel as if even my best friends have put me in a box in which I'm expected to behave in a certain way and that if I step outside the box - if I do something that makes me look different - my friends will go into a sort of huff."

"Which friends specifically?"

"No one in particular," replied Rosalind with a shrug. "It's just a feeling I have."

"I see...I think I have covered that sort of experience in the book actually. And incidentally, I am writing the book in a problem page style as you suggested. A problem is described by a teenager and then, the solution to the problem is given by an astrologer. I think the issues raised will be familiar to many teenagers."

"It sounds perfect. Perhaps you could call the book, 'A Teenagers' Guide to the Aspects of Venus'."

"That sounds good. How about 'The Aspects of Venus: a teenagers' guide'?"

"That's good, too, Mum."

Rosalind smiled, but seemed far away in her thoughts, now. Liz had frankly expected a show of more enthusiasm from her. Rosalind had made appropriate remarks, but without much liveliness or pleasure, really. Was she feeling unwell or simply tired? Were the problems she was having with Irene Miller really bothering her more than she had intimated? And what had she truly been trying to communicate when she had been talking about being placed in a box by her friends? The teen years were complicated. She, Liz, would have to make an effort to finish the book and to endow it with more depth. Rosalind, sensitive and easily hurt, clearly needed it and, therefore, the more quickly it was delivered, the better.

CHAPTER 55

Reading and Ignorance

Liz Laurier had dreamt of being a writer for some years, but the dream had been pushed to one side, as she had waited for a good enough reason to deliver a full-length book. Previously, her vague, unfocused desire to write had not been pressing enough to force her to make her wish to be a success in the literary world, a reality, anyway. But now, surrounded by paper in her sitting room, she felt consumed by a longing to finish her book for Rosalind, partly because it would have a double purpose. It would assist Rosalind when she had to deal with her relationships, of course, but it would, also, assuage, to some degree, her own feelings of guilt, stemming from her failure to guide her children through their early years. When she should have been reading "The Secret Garden" or "David Copperfield" to them, at bed time, she had been gallivanting in Paris and Bordeaux, pleasing only herself.

Perhaps it was the thought of Bordeaux that made the name of Madame Gabrielle de Talence slip into Liz's mind. She had become intrigued by the way Madame Gabrielle had tended to be portrayed as a complicated person, whenever she had been the subject of a conversation. Teddy Laurence, for example, had brought up her name when talking about his engagement to Jacqueline de Sauzon. Teddy had hinted that he had thought that Madame Gabrielle had been the one who had been to blame for the relationship's collapse. When Jacqueline had decided to marry Jacqui Galant, later, Teddy had been shocked, but he had, finally, concluded that Jacqueline's action, in part and perhaps unconsciously, had had its source in a desire to punish Madame Gabrielle. Maybe Jacqueline had, effectively, been saying to her grand-mother: "You didn't want me to marry Teddy Laurence? Very well. I shall marry someone you will like even less!"

Liz arose from the sofa on which she had been reclining and walked over to the bay window, in her sitting room, for no reason other than to satisfy a restlessness that had, at that moment, prompted her to move. "The Country Child" by Alison Uttley, on a bookshelf near the window, caught Liz's eye and she remembered having been moved, when reading the book, by the excitement of the little girl in the story, when Christmas had been celebrated at the farmhouse that was her home. Liz turned her head, quickly, to look again down into the street and at a pool of light shining on the pavement from a street lamp. She tried to blot out the guilt that had now come to the forefront of her mind: guilt at not having been present during Rosalind's and John's early years. To think that she had never seen the joy on their young faces on Christmas morning, as they had opened the parcels beneath the Christmas tree!

Liz walked quickly back to the sofa, sat down and set to work again. She had to make amends for her rejection of parental duty and her negation of her maternal feelings. She wondered, then, if she should mention, in the book, the undermining effect that a mother - or, as in Madame Gabrielle's case - a grand-mother could have on a young person's life. She did not want to plunge too deeply into this area, but, she felt that restricting the book to more manageable relationships would be equal to leaving out an entire section of an adolescent's life and a common source of confusion. Still, the book was to be called "The Aspects of Venus." Perhaps it would be more appropriate to devote the book to the territory of Venus, rather than increase its reach by including the dark side of the Moon: the symbol of maternity. She wanted to keep the tone of the book light and positive, anyway. She would, therefore, not mention, darkly, that life, itself, in one way or another, would deal with those who had rejected their parental responsibility or whose cynicism had blighted the lives of the young. And, she wondered, then, how life was treating Madame Gabrielle de Talence. Did she ever feel regret over the way she had crushed the hopes of Jacqueline de Sauzon or the potential happiness of Teddy Laurence? Had she ever been inclined to say to herself, at moments when she, herself, had been suffering a setback: "I think I deserve this. I am to learn something from my emotional pain and the intrusion of extreme anxiety into my life." Maybe Madame Gabrielle was too sophisticated to allow herself to think in that way, though.

In Bordeaux, that night, sitting up in her wide bed, her 'grand lit,' Madame Gabrielle de Talence, in fact, was unable to sleep. Straight-backed, in order to endow her appearance with an air of elegance, even though she was wearing a simple nightdress of broderie anglaise lined with muslin, she opened, on the quilt half covering her, the book she had chosen to help her to while away the time until slumber would finally sweep over her. In choosing "Premier Roman" by Mazarine Pingeot, her intention had been, in part, to remind herself of her youth, since it had been written by a young woman and, consequently, there was a certain candour about it: a freshness of thought and style. But Madame Gabrielle had chosen it, too, to take her mind off her own mundane problems, although, on reflection, she was not sure if it would fulfil that purpose. She had read the book before and had remembered that the way the story had been brought to a close, had been, initially, unexpected, but now, was making sense to her. The focus in the final part of that book had been on two women, who had been attracted to the same man. Madame Gabrielle knew she would be unable to read about the two women, or rather, the situation in which they had found themselves, without thinking of Caterina Traversi and the way she, herself, Madame Gabrielle, had been fascinated by that young woman's style of dressing, her way of speaking and her air of confidence, combined with a certain enthusiasm for the experience of living. Now, Madame Gabrielle could not prevent herself from wondering what had become of her, the beautiful Caterina, whose attachment to Mr.Mallory must have been obvious to other women, if not to him. Was she in touch with him, still?

As if overcome by a state of panic then, an irrational desire to go to another part of the house, as if to escape from her own thoughts, or rather, from the fear that those thoughts might make her sink into a state of despondency, Madame Gabrielle placed the book on the bedside table, pushed back the quilt and rose, reaching for the silken, eau-de-nil dressing gown, lying on a softly upholstered chair nearby. As she was standing close to the shuttered window of the bedroom, she paused to listen, but barely a sound could be heard coming from the Cours de la Victoire outside. It was late.

With a shrug, Madame Gabrielle set off across the room to descend the few steps that led to the ante-chamber where the tall, old wardrobes, with brass key holes, stood and where Agnès dressed her hair every Friday, still, in front of the Imperial-style dressing-table, with the large mirror. Madame Gabrielle left the ante-chamber quickly, the scent of pressed lavender, emanating from the wardrobes, trailing behind her. She made her way across the hall, with its marble pillars gleaming with subtlety, in the pale light of the lamp which she had switched on. She, then, made her way down the corridor that led to the kitchens, at the back of the house.

The silence of the house seemed more obvious in the kitchens, because, even when they were lit up, there was within them a certain atmosphere - created by the large ticking clock, the height of the ceiling or perhaps, the old-fashioned appearance of the furniture - that could be un-nerving if one were not used to it, or so Madame Gabrielle believed. She was accustomed to going there on nights when she could not sleep, all the same, to warm milk in a little pan or to make tea, in English style. She had always overcome her fears of the dark and had prided herself on her possession of that dignity that had prevented her from shivering, as if afraid of shadows.

That night, Madame Gabrielle felt like drinking coffee, despite the late hour. She stretched up her arm to reach for a tin of ground beans from a high shelf. She liked to drink good coffee from a grande tasse and she intended to satisfy her desire to do so, even if, as a consequence of drinking it, she would lie awake until dawn. What did it matter if she broke her own self-imposed dietary rules, for once? Could she not allow herself a little licence, now and again, to compensate for the unpredictability of life and its disappointments?

Having brought down the tin, Madame Gabrielle placed it on top of the sideboard with more force than she had intended to employ. There was a clatter of kitchen implements on a tray close by, as they were displaced. Madame Gabrielle suddenly felt an urge to cry out: to cry out to express the pain that had its source in thwarted desire and unrequited love. What had she done to deserve such unhappiness?

Madame Gabrielle stood very still, then, in order to re-gain control of herself. She could not blame Kit Mallory for the way she was feeling. He had not promised her anything. Yet, she had allowed herself to delude herself into believing he would want to stay in touch with her, once the cruise ship had docked in Liverpool, after its voyage. He had not, of course. He had fallen far short of the behaviour she had associated with him in her day-dreams. She had too readily and unwisely projected on to him qualities she had imagined he had possessed, but in fact, had not. Madame Gabrielle shuddered and her back felt cold. It occurred to her that she had succeeded in duping herself. She could blame no one for her disappointment except herself.

"I should have been more knowing and wise," she said to herself as she briskly took the lid off the tin of coffee. "If one can read, there's no excuse for one's ignorance, and that's the end of it. Voilà!"

CHAPTER 56

Liverpool Calling

"Hello-ee! Hilary? Hilary, are you there?"

"Yes, Mother," answered Hilary Trimm, in an exaggeratedly weary way, as she emerged from the spacious kitchen of her house in Chester. "You're early!"

"No. I'm not! Well! Not really. I wanted to give Kathleen time to get ready, if she's coming with us."

"Kathleen is coming with us?"

"Well! That's why I came here early, Hilary. I wanted to ask you if you'd mind if she did. You have plenty of room in your car, haven't you? Or are you taking a load of books over?"

"No. Kathleen may come with us if she wants to. But doesn't she have a routine that she follows on a Saturday?"

"No. Not really. Anyway, I'm sure she'd drop everything if I told her we were going to your college. She's very curious about your new position, Hilary. Excuse me while I 'phone her, dear. You go ahead and get ready, if you want to."

Dorothy Trimm went into her daughter's sitting-room and stood for a moment in front of the large window which provided her with a view of the terraced garden that descended attractively to the River Dee. She took her mobile phone out of her handbag and called her friend's number.

"Hello!" she shrilled. "Hello! Kath? Dorothy here! Listen, dear! Hilary is about to take me over to Liverpool to see her office at Q-COLL and it crossed my mind that you might like to come with us! Hm? You would? Well, we'll be leaving here as soon as Hilary is ready. I don't know how long she will be, but let's say we could pick you up in an hour Would that suit you? It would? Jolly good!

See you, then!"

Having returned her phone to her hand-bag, Dorothy went to the foot of the sweeping staircase in the entrance hall and called:

"We're picking her up in an hour, Hilary. You'd better hurry!"

"I'D better hurry?" said Hilary leaning over the banister. "I'D better hurry?"

"Oh, Hilary! Don't fuss. You look perfectly ready to me, anyway. Shall I make sandwiches? I mean, the café in the college won't be open on a Saturday, will it?"

"Yes, Mother. It will."

"Really? So, I could pop in there if I'm shopping in Liverpool on a Saturday? Not that I often go to Liverpool on a Saturday, but if you're ever going to Q-COLL then, you could give me a lift, couldn't you?"

Hilary sighed, gazed up at the ceiling for a moment, declined to answer and then, simply said, "I shan't be long. Incidentally, you do realise that the two of you will have to find your own way back to Ellesmere Port, don't you? I'll be staying in the college all day."

"Ellesmere Port? What are you talking about? You were brought up in Whitby Village, Hilary! Whitby Village! Ellesmere Port may be swallowing it up, but we must hang on to the old name, Hils! Anyway, yes, of course. We'll go around the shops in Liverpool One and then, we'll take a train home. Or we'll take a taxi. Kathleen will probably want to take a taxi. You know what she's like."

"I know what both of you are like, Mother. And for Goodness' sake, when we reach the college, be careful about the way you speak to me in front of students. I'm the principal of the college. Remember?"

"I shan't let you down, Hilary."

Half an hour later, Hilary drove her car out of her garage and Dorothy climbed in. Hilary started the engine again and headed out of her drive.

"By the way," said Dorothy, as Hilary looked to the left and right. "By the way…"

"Please don't talk just now while I'm manoeuvring the car."

"Very well! I shall read," said Dorothy crossly as she pulled a news magazine out of her bag and opened it at the first page.

"It's just disgraceful" she said then. "ABSOLUTELY disgraceful!"

Hilary sighed.

"WHAT is disgraceful?" she asked.

"Have you noticed how many people write 'ago' where they should have used 'before'?"

"What do you mean?"

"With the Pluperfect Tense, Hilary! An AWFUL lot of people are writing, sentences like, "'He had been there three years ago,' when they should have written, 'He had been there three years BEFORE.' It happens all the time! And DON'T let me start complaining about the way 'schism' is pronounced."

"I shan't."

"I mean, the whole world - with the laudable exception of some American academics - seems to be mis-pronouncing that word as 'skism'! 'SKISM'! Imagine!"

"Where do I go when I reach the Strawberry Roundabout?"

"Hm? Oh! Carry on for a bit. I'll tell you when to veer to the right."

"You have a bee in your bonnet about grammar, Mother."

"Well! I remember it as it was when I was a child, you see."

"Are we near?"

"Yes. Very near, now. Go right…at the next turning."

Kathleen, wearing a beige-coloured tweed skirt suit and a claret, felt hat with a peak, like one worn in "Brief Encounter," could be seen waiting in her porch, when Hilary's car rolled up her drive.

"Would you like to sit in the front or the back, dear?" asked Dorothy, popping her head out of the window beside her.

"The back seat is fine," answered Kathleen, as she climbed in, adding, "This is really nice of you, Hilary. I'm looking forward to seeing Q-COLL! It must be so exciting for you to be starting another phase of your life."

"Yes," said Hilary. "I imagine it will be challenging, but I'm looking forward to the challenge."

"What I don't understand is why you chose Liverpool. I mean, there are some lovely colleges in Cheshire and it would have been easier to drive to them in the morning, I'd have thought. Going through the Mersey Tunnel must be a bit daunting, at that hour."

"No. Not really. Anyway, I felt like a complete change and I sort of heard Liverpool calling, in a way."

Dorothy turned her head to give her friend a warning look, signalling, "Say no more on that subject."

Kathleen understood and quickly started talking about the falcons at Chester Cathedral and her own experience of watching raptors, when she had been a child in the Cheshire countryside.

While Kathleen was chatting, Dorothy, lulled by the motion of the car, allowed herself to drift into a soporific state. However, she sat up straight to rouse herself, as the car reached the north of the peninsula and the entrance to the Mersey Tunnel. Only minutes after that, Q-COLl, centrally located in Liverpool, came into view. All three women descended from the car and made for the flight of steps that led to the entrance.

"Is it a bit art deco?" asked Kathleen, once she was inside. "Or is it in a mixture of styles? I'm not well up on architecture. Oh, look! I didn't expect students to be milling around already!"

"They're enrolling for courses," explained Hilary. "A lot of them have come from abroad."

"Wasn't that Jacqueline de Sauzon girl here once?" asked Dorothy.

"Yes. And her American friend. Come on! I'll show you my office!"

Hilary's room was huge. On a large desk in the centre of the room there was a varnished wooden rectangle that bore the legend:

"Hilary Trimm. Principal. The Christina Quayle College of Languages."

"Ooh! Very grand!" exclaimed Kathleen! "I can see why Liverpool was calling! Well! Good luck to you, darling! You deserve this!"

Dorothy looked pleased in the manner a proud mother would.

"Could we go for a walk around the college, Hils?" she asked.

"Yes. Of course. Off you go! The restaurant is on the ground floor. I have work to do!"

When the two women had left, Hilary sat down at her desk and looked around her. The room was tastefully and freshly decorated in shades of cream and beige. From the window on her right, she could see the top of the Royal Liver Building: the remarkable edifice that stood majestically on the edge of the Mersey. Yes. She had done well to reach the prestigious position she was now occupying. She should be happy and satisfied. Why, then, was she feeling defeated? Why, in private, were tears never far away?

CHAPTER 57

The American Friend

As had been her custom since her return for her final year at the liberal arts college on the north-east coast of America, where she had been enrolled as a student, Rebecca Hampton woke up early in her room, in the J.Jean Lerred residential hall. After checking to see how many digitally transmitted messages had been sent to her during the night - one, she noted, had arrived from Jacqueline de Sauzon - she showered quickly. Then, after tying back her shoulder-length, dark hair in a pony tail style and putting on a white, woollen jumper and navy shorts, she set off for her usual morning run around the grounds.

It was autumn - the Fall - and tall trees bordering the small lake and the landscaped, grassy areas surrounding the residential blocks and the dining halls were shedding their leaves. As she left the controlled warmth of the res. hall, Rebecca felt herself being woken fully by the sharp air of that New England morning. She paused for a moment in order to decide which direction she should take. A couple of students, running together, were heading for the lake. Rebecca went off in another direction. At that hour, she preferred to avoid being distracted by humans.

Normally, Rebecca was acutely aware of the bucolic beauty that surrounded her at J.Jean Lerred and was appreciative of it - as a partial scholarship student, she knew she was privileged - but that morning, she ran without taking in the splendour of the claret-red, brown and ochre colours of leaves scattered over the grass. Her mind was elsewhere or rather, to be precise, on the message from Jacqueline de Sauzon that she had read quickly before leaving her room. In her message, Jacqueline had been expressing her thanks to Rebecca for the part she had played in assuring the safety of Madame Gabrielle during her cruise holiday. Madame was now safely back home, having been completely unaware of the fact that she had been watched from a distance, during her voyage. Of course, Teddy Laurence had to be thanked also. Would Rebecca pass on Jacqueline's thanks to him? Was Rebecca in regular touch with Teddy, in fact? That final question seemed innocent enough and yet, Rebecca sensed that it had been written with a hidden purpose. Jacqueline was anxious to know how close she had become to Teddy. And it saddened her that the two of them, Jacqueline and she, were now no longer as open in their communications as once they had been. Jacqueline had obviously decided that she could no longer ask a question about the nature of Rebecca's relationship with Teddy directly. She had, in fact, felt it necessary to sink to the level of extracting that information coyly. Of course, Rebecca realised that she, herself, was almost wholly to blame for this unwelcome alteration in the way they were in touch with each other. She had been tardy in answering some of Jacqueline's previous messages and had divulged little information about Teddy. Naturally, her silence would have aroused Jacqueline's curiosity.

A light rain had started to fall. Rebecca stopped running, having decided, in any case, that it was time to have breakfast. She made her way towards the nearest dining hall: Steeravant. There, from the selection of food that was on show, she chose a fruit-filled omelette, blueberry muffins and coffee whizzed up with hot milk. She carried them, on a small, wooden tray to a table beside a huge window and looked out pensively, as she took a bite out of a muffin. She had to admit that one of the reasons she had not mentioned Teddy Laurence to Jacqueline had been the fact that there had not been much to say. After her departure from Teddy's apartment in the summer, he had been in touch only sporadically and her own messages had, equally, been few. Had they both realised that there had been little point in continuing a long-distance romance, when neither had been prepared to make the sacrifices required to be with the other? She, herself, had had difficulty picturing herself embarking on a career in the Wirral – rather than in NYC - and Teddy had had doubts about moving to America, after having been offered rapid promotion at Bramblewell.

In recent weeks, Josh D. Demeter III, a student from a neighbouring college, had shown an increasing interest in her. He had invited her to play squash, to go to a small viewing theatre with him to see a season of French Nouvelle Vague films and even to attend a family get-together at a restaurant in Manhattan, one weekend. She had been tempted and yet, had finally refused those offers, although she still continued to meet him for coffee, casually. What had been preventing her from deepening her friendship with Josh D.? Her memories of Teddy? Were her feelings for him deeper than she had suspected? And if she was still captivated by Teddy, what was she going to do about that? Was she going to waste her life and opportunities pointlessly dreaming of him? Or was she going to take action either to dissolve the dream or to pursue it? Lucid thinking was required.

CHAPTER 58

The Christmas Term

Rehearsals for the adaptation of "Anna Karenina" - chosen by The Eliza Club, at Bramblewell School, to be its Christmas play, that year - had been taking place throughout November and early December. But, Mrs. Barbara Merrivale, who had observed a number of lunch-time and after-school rehearsals, had been dismayed to discover that Portia Price, uncharacteristically overcome by listlessness, had allowed her usual high standards to slip. She had even unwisely allowed the new girl, Irene Miller, to have more control of the production than had been appropriate, given Irene's lack of experience in staging plays. Were Irene to continue promoting her own ideas, Barbara felt, the Christmas production would be a dismal and lacklustre affair, performed by pupils who, by then, would be mightily tired of Irene's peremptory manner and dictatorial style of direction.

Before intervening, Barbara had taken Stella Lomas, the head girl, to one side, in order to ask her to find out why Portia had lapsed into a state of near-passivity.

"I already know what is wrong with her, Mrs. Merrivale," Stella had said. "And I was on the point of approaching you to bring up this very matter, as I was worried, myself."

"Go on."

"It seems Portia has given up any idea of pursuing a career in the dramatic arts. Rosalind Somerland is terribly worried about her, but Portia won't listen to anything Rosalind says. As you possibly know, Portia wanted to read for a degree in English Literature and Drama, her hope being that she would ultimately be able to direct plays for the theatre and to write screen plays for film and TV, as well. But circumstances have forced her to change her mind and now, she is thinking of aiming for a career in law, instead."

"Law?"

"I KNOW, Mrs. Merrivale! I can't imagine her sitting at a desk, conveyancing for years on end, either. It would suit some, but not Portia. And you can see what the very thought of it is doing to her."

"Thank you, Stella. You have been very helpful. Did you say Rosalind had already tried dissuading her from following this path?"

"Yes, Mrs. Merrivale and, what is more, Rosalind has told her that The Eliza Club's play will be a complete flop this year, thanks to the inexperience of the new girl, but Portia has paid no attention to Rosalind's warning."

Not wanting to offer advice too hastily, Barbara Merrivale gave the information Stella had provided much studied thought, but, in the second week of December, she felt she could hesitate no longer. She asked Portia to meet her in The Woodlanders, the school's little theatre, situated in the Bramblewell grounds, one morning, during recess. Portia found her teacher occupying one of the front row seats, staring at the stage.

"Sit beside me, Portia," she said, not unkindly.

Portia sat down and looked at the half painted back-cloth, up on the stage. She felt uncomfortable, having guessed what Mrs. Merrivale was on the point of saying to her.

"I don't want to interfere in your life or press you on the decisions you seem to be making about your future, Portia," said Barbara briskly. "What you do with your life, will obviously be up to you, after you have discussed the options open to you with your parents and relevant teachers and have listened to their advice. However, I shall make a couple of points of my own. First of all, you are not yet quite sixteen. Presumably, you will not leave school until you are eighteen. A great deal can happen in two years. Circumstances can change in people's lives. You, yourself, can change the opinion you have of certain people. Secondly, I should like to make the point that, in my experience, people do not excel in life, unless they are passionate about what they are doing or unless they are working towards a goal which fills them with passion."

"I understand what you are saying, Mrs. Merrivale," said Portia, without hesitation.

"You are an astute girl, Portia. I'm sure you do understand. In a nutshell, I hope you will put thoughts of what you currently propose to be your future to one side for a few months, at least. Right now, I want you to wake up and do something to inject life into the so-called rehearsals that are taking place. You owe it to me not to make a mess of this Christmas production. I have always had faith in you. Don't let me down."

"I shan't, Mrs. Merrivale," promised Portia, startled by the implied criticism. She had never before received a reprimand of such severity from a teacher.

Portia wondered how much Mrs. Merrivale knew about her private life. How did information about pupils reach the ears of teachers, anyway? Did Mrs. Merrivale know that she had decided to change the direction of her future life because she had reckoned that she would have to embark on a career that would guarantee high earnings, quite simply? If Louis Lindsey was not going to go to university, and, in fact, might even devote his entire life to caring for his ailing father, she would have to provide for both of them, would she not? The burden that had suddenly fallen on her shoulders was crushing her, though. She would have to stop thinking about it. Mrs. Merrivale was right. Anything could happen in the two years ahead of her. Louis Lindsey, after all, might abandon her, having been attracted to some other girl who was less self-possessed and therefore, less challenging than she, Portia, had been. He had implied, the first time they had met, that she was too sure of herself. She had retaliated by pointing out, with a touch of arrogance, that maybe he was simply unused to girls such as she. As she remembered the coldness in his grey blue eyes then, she felt a chill across her shoulder blades. He was proud, of course. And suddenly, it occurred to her that he would never take money from her.

As a consequence of her meeting with Mrs. Merrivale, Portia seized the reins of the slack production. She took charge of rehearsals in such a determined way that Irene Miller was aghast. However, Irene was bright enough to realise that without the support of other members of The Eliza Club, there would be no point in her making a fuss and so, she obligingly stepped to one side. Portia quickly reorganised teams. She asked Ida Traversi to be in charge of costumes and Talitha Appleby to gather and take care of props. Rosalind was given the responsibility of re-writing parts of the play that lacked pace. She was also given the rôle of co-directress, while Ida and Talitha were asked to deal with publicity and interviews, when required to do so.

Talitha was given permission by Mrs. Merrivale to spend lunch-times investigating what could be bought in the way of curios and ornaments, in the quainter shops in Chester. She was to keep a look-out for objects that would convey an impression of 19th century Russia, when seen on stage. Meanwhile, Ida set about adjusting the previous year's costumes, in order to give them a pre-revolutionary, Russian air. Three boys from the 6th Form contingent had volunteered to be actors, but there were twenty-five actresses - most of these participating in the ballroom scenes - who would be required to play extra male rôles, also.

Ida was hoping that her sister, Caterina Traversi, would come to watch the production on the night of its performance. Caterina, of course, was busy working at Trimm Publications. Her Papa, hearing about her progress, had been so impressed by her work and enthusiasm that he had promised her that she would have an important position in the Traversi organisation, upon her eventual return to Italy. In the meantime, he was considering suggesting to

Caterina's boss, Dorothy, that Trimm Publications become part of the Traversi organisation. Would she, Dorothy, have any objection to her publishing house being renamed Traversi - Trimm? Dorothy was a bit wary of the proposal, but she was not unaware of the advantages, that would flow from such a development, either. Nothing would please her more than to see her little company flourishing, after all. And she had long considered the day she had run into Caterina to have been a particularly fortuitous one. She ended up giving her consent to the proposal therefore. Caterina seemed to be ecstatic with joy over this decision, not least because she had scooped a prize that had trumped anything her sister Beatrice had done for the House of Traversi. Ida was sure that, being thrilled with her own success, Caterina would look radiant on the night of the play at Bramblewell School and that Bramblewell girls would be whispering, "Who IS she? Is she a fashion influencer? Does she have a web site? Does she write a blog?"

Rosalind was hoping her mother would come to watch the play and she hoped her father would be there, also. She had to decide, though, if she should place the two of them in seats, at some distance from each other, or if she should arrange for them to sit side by side. They talked to each other on the telephone, but communicating face to face seemed to put them both on edge, still. She knew that Susie Sutton would attend the performance along with Lord Bramblewell, of course. But what was to be done if Miss Hilary Trimm decided to come to the show as well? It would be incorrect to place her anywhere other than in the front row, but naturally, Lord Bramblewell and Susie would be in the front row too. Rosalind longed for guidance on how to deal with these problems of seating people diplomatically, but Portia, Ida and Talitha seemed to be as puzzled as she. Finally, she asked Susie what she should do and Susie told her that Lord Bramblewell had invited his sister, Lady Artemis Aethelfreda Bramblewell-Eurlinn, along with Horatio, Gwenny, Julian and Julian's friends,

Pomeroy and Tansy for Christmas and they would all be coming to see "Anna Karenina." There would be plenty of people in Lord Bramblewell's party to provide a buffer, as it were, between Lord Bramblewell and Miss Trimm. Susie had suggested placing Julian next to Miss Trimm as he was considerate and fine and would surely be nice to her, without making her suspect he felt sorry for her. Susie mentioned, then, the fact that Lady Artemis had told Julian that she had embarked on the final stages of legally disengaging herself from the Château du Crâne and that the château would, effectively, be her Christmas present to him. Julian was obviously pleased that the château would be his, de facto, but somewhat apprehensive about the responsibility that would be accompanying the present. Both he and Miss Trimm would have something in common, therefore: the start of a new, but perhaps daunting, phase in their lives.

Susie Sutton was delighted about the fact that the guests at the manor, that Christmas, would be people she already knew and liked. She spent time with Mrs. Oliver, the housekeeper, discussing the menus proposed for the festive period. Mrs. Oliver, as was the custom, would be given a holiday on Christmas day and Boxing Day and Susie had already arranged to have food transported to the Manor from a restaurant in Chester, on those days. She would have undertaken the cooking herself had fewer people been invited, but given the number expected, she had decided to seek professional help. Besides, Lord Bramblewell had pointed out that, since she was now officially his fiancée, it would be more appropriate for her to greet and entertain their guests and make them feel comfortable, rather than spend time concocting dishes in the kitchen, no matter how charmingly she would present them.

It was the custom for carol singers from Bramblewell School to visit Bramblewell Manor, briefly, in December, before setting off to raise money for charities, elsewhere in Chester. On the day before the first performance of the school play, Susie saw a group of girls, and one or two of the Sixth Form boys, advancing along the gravel drive that led to the Manor. One of the boys was carrying an ancient-looking lantern attached to a stick. As the group came closer, Susie was pleased to see that Rosalind, Ida, Talitha and Portia, well-wrapped up in their navy, woollen coats and Bramblewell School scarves, were among the singers. The great door of the manor was opened to allow them into the entrance hall where Susie was waiting, standing beside a Christmas tree, already decorated with golden baubles.

In a warm, pink dress and, festively sparkling, silver wedge shoes, Susie greeted the carollers cheerfully and gave them cheques, in envelopes, for their charities, while Tamsin, who helped Mrs. Oliver in the manor, handed out hot drinks, sandwiches and custard slices of the Cheshire kind.

"You've already told me that you will be spending Christmas with your Dad and John," Susie said to Rosalind, after drawing her to one side. "But you know - don't you? - that you will all be very welcome to come here at any time. And by the way, will your Mum be joining you, or should I ask her to come to the manor, also?"

"Dad invited her to spend Christmas with us, but she turned down the invitation. She said she didn't want to upset John. He still becomes very nervous when he sees her, you see. I think Mr. Laurence has invited Mum to his flat for Christmas."

"Teddy Laurence?"

"Yes. She told me he'd invited her and Miss James, as well."

"Miss James and your mother?"

"Yes. Mum said he had probably invited both of them because all three would be on their own otherwise."

Susie was taken aback. It had not crossed her mind that Lynn James would be on Teddy's list of very personal friends. But there was no time to dwell on such thoughts at that moment. There was too much to be done to prepare for the guests who were due to arrive at the manor that evening.

"Would you like me to come along to help you?" Rosalind

asked, as Susie quickly diverted the conversation on to the subject of all the tasks that had to be done before nightfall. Susie was grateful for the offer of help - she liked having Rosalind around, as the girl was always genuinely willing to lend a hand - but she refused the offer, all the same, kindly saying:

"I expect Portia will want you to stay behind after school, won't she? Tomorrow night will be the first night of your play, after all! We're so looking forward to seeing it, Rosie, Rupert and I!"

"It had better be good, then!"

"It will be! And don't forget that we'll need eight seats kept for us in the front row!"

"Yes. I'll see to that! At what time will your guests arrive tonight? Before dinner?"

"Yes. I'll have to spend this afternoon, checking that all the rooms are warm and cosy and that there are books and tins of biscuits and fruit and extra blankets in the bedrooms. Mrs. Oliver doesn't like me to look over what she has already done, herself, but I feel I should."

"Is she not any nicer in the way she treats you?"

"Not really. It's her manner rather than anything she says or does that annoys me. She knows she is getting under my skin and she seems to like that."

"Can you not get rid of her?"

"I don't have a good enough reason to. She doesn't put a foot wrong."

"Still..."

"Don't worry about me, Rosie. I'll be all right! Have a nice time at your last rehearsal, after school! I'll be thinking of you and wishing you luck!"

"Oh! Thank you, Susie! I'll be thinking about you, too!"

That evening, snowflakes had started to fall in the dark, over Bramblewell Manor, when the party from Ywen Manor arrived.

"The snow won't lie for long," said Gwenny. "Look! It's disappearing already!"

She stopped for a moment to admire the glittering flakes falling on to the drive, before following her travelling companions into the warm and welcoming manor. She took off her calf-length, burgundy-coloured coat, embellished with a thick, fake fur collar and cuffs and handed it to Tamsin, before exclaiming, "Oh! Gosh!" upon seeing Susie.

The future Mistress of Bramblewell looked like a goddess of femininity, having changed into a floor length, baby- pink dress which had long, slim sleeves and a V-neckline. Its delicate fabric had been cut, flatteringly, on the bias. Susie's hair, freshly washed, shone like silk and her complexion looked as pale as milk.

"You look so lovely, Susie!" said Gwenny, generously: an opinion that was echoed by the other guests.

Then, amidst the sounds of laughter and hustle and bustle, as outdoor coats were removed and hot drinks were offered to the guests, as they were ushered into one of the ground floor reception rooms, Lord Bramblewell appeared and greeted the assembled party, with affability and kindness, as was his custom. "Make yourselves at home! You must!" he insisted.

Tansy had not been to Bramblewell Manor before and Susie was looking forward to making her feel particularly welcome, as the first time Susie had visited Ywen Manor, it had been Tansy, memorable in her tangerine sandals, who had transformed her visit from being an awkward one into being a successful one.

Lady Artemis arrived shortly after the party from Ywen Manor had started to become warmly comfortable. Susie, as she greeted Lady Artemis in the entrance hall, remarked that she looked particularly well.

"Oh!" said Lady Artemis. "That will be because I feel as if a weight has been lifted off my shoulders, now that I have handed over the Château du Crâne to Julian. Honestly, what he does with it will be up to him. I don't really care, now."

"Does he know that?"

"Oh, yes! Of course! I have given him carte blanche to do

whatever pleases him."

Later, Julian told Susie that he knew his mother well enough to be aware of the fact that what she said did not always coincide with what she privately felt. He sensed that she wanted him to keep the château, but that she did, also, accept that some changes would have to be made, as a steady supply of money would have to be found for maintenance and repairs. Where was he to find it?

"Maybe the answer will come to you out of the blue," said Susie, hoping she did not sound naïve.

Julian just smiled.

The following evening, Susie and Lord Bramblewell, accompanied by Lady Artemis, her two sons and Gwenny, Tansy and Pomeroy, by the light of torches and a lantern, made their way through the small wood that separated Bramblewell Manor from Bramblewell School. Tansy found the tall, wooden gate, with a quaint handle, set in the grey stone wall that marked the boundary of the school grounds, enchanting.

"It's like something one would read about in a fairy tale," she said, her voice full of wonder.

Susie heard Pomeroy breathing in sharply, as if exasperated, but he said nothing.

Beyond the wall, there were more trees on a small, plateau-like rise and then, there was a slope that took the party down to lower ground and tennis courts and the newer school buildings. The Woodlanders, the school's theatre was among these buildings.

All was a-buzz inside the foyer of the little theatre. Mrs. Merrivale was there and obviously busy, supervising the desk where guests were handing over their tickets, while she was simultaneously shoo-ing away any schoolgirl actresses who ventured into the vicinity of the foyer, while half in costume.

"You shouldn't let the audience see you dressed up until the performance begins!" she insisted, time and time again, as excited girls tried to peek into the foyer, to see who had turned up to watch them on stage. Caterina Traversi, looking glamorous in a floor-length, dark green coat, green suede boots and green suede gloves caused a stir, as she swept into the foyer, trailing scent behind her. Mrs. Merrivale was rather lost for words, as Caterina approached, looking rather like a continental film star, but then, the party from Barmblewell Manor arrived too, and the nonplussed Mrs. Merrivale was able to say, "Oh! There's Lord Bramblewell! Please excuse me, madam," before rushing towards the front door, her turquoise bangles jangling, leaving the bemused Mrs. Devere, the headmistress of the prep school, who was helping to take in the tickets, to deal with the Italian beauty.

"Lord Bramblewell!" exclaimed Mrs. Merrivale. "Miss Sutton! How lovely to see you and your guests! Please follow me! I'll take you to your places! I hope you will enjoy the show!"

The front row seats had "Reserved" written on them and each seat bore the name of the person who was to occupy it. Susie noticed that she was close to the end of the row on the left side and that Miss Trimm, already seated and busy reading her programme, was close to the end of the right side of the row. Susie hesitated, hoping that Miss Trimm would lift her head, so that she, Susie, could acknowledge her, but Miss Trimm seemed too preoccupied to notice the new arrivals. Susie sat down, somewhat disconsolately, and then, noticed Teddy Laurence, talking to the pupils who would be playing musical instruments close to one side of the stage. She remembered having seen him standing in the same place the previous year, at Christmas, during the school play. Such a lot had changed in both their lives since then. Susie sighed as she felt her heart being stirred, but then, Miss James approached. She grasped Teddy by the arm in a way Susie judged to be familiar. What did that gesture mean? Did it indicate anything other than the fact that Teddy and Miss James were colleagues who were used to each other's company?

The lights went down and the play began. Thanks to Portia's intervention, it was spectacular. Susie was particularly gripped by the story of the idealistic Kostya, whose vision of the new met with resistance from those who were attached to old ways. In the Interval, she approached Julian in the foyer.

"You know, Kostya reminds me of you," she said.

"Really? In what respect?"

"I think you are both so nice and poetic and – wel! - decent, in a really attractive way. And I imagine that, in your head, you are mulling over new and very different ways of developing the Château du Crâne and the land around it. You are, aren't you? But you don't know how to break the news to your mother."

Julian looked at Susie pensively in a way that suggested to her that he thought she was foolish at best and presumptuous, at worst, but did not want to hurt her feelings by saying so. In reality, Julian was merely astonished at Susie's ability to read his mind.

CHAPTER 59

Konstantine

The applause that filled The Woodlanders - the little theatre belonging to Bramblewell School - on the night that The Eliza Club's performance of "Anna Karenina" had reached its end, could have raised the roof, had Lord Bramblewell not stood up, in timely fashion, gesturing his intention to make a speech.

"I should like to thank the marvellous members of The Eliza Club," he began, "for the hours and hours that they spent in rehearsals for the play staged here tonight, for our delight. I should mention, in particular, Talitha Appleby, Portia Price, Rosalind Somerland and Ida Traversi, the mainstays of the club, and, of course, their elocution and drama teacher, Mrs. Barbara Merrivale, who was a source of support and education for them while they were writing and rehearsing the play, which, you will have realised, was based on the famous book by Tolstoy. I should like to thank, also, Miss Lynn James, headmistress of the school, and her deputy, Mr. Teddy Laurence, for their leniency in allowing pupils to leave their classes to attend rehearsals, in the week before the performance and, of course, I must thank all other teachers and pupils who played a part in staging the marvellous play we have been watching this evening."

Lord Bramblewell stopped speaking for a moment, to glance at Miss Trimm, sitting in the front row beside Julian Bramblewell - Eurlinn. She was looking at the ground in front of her in a manner that suggested pensiveness or even sadness.

"I should not forget Miss Hilary Trimm," Lord Bramblewell said then, unexpectedly, and in a tone of voice that seemed to suggest he was feeling nostalgic or even sentimental. "Miss

Trimm," he continued, " the former headmistress of Bramblewell School, allowed The Eliza Club's founder members, Portia Price, Ida Traversi and Talitha Appleby, to establish it in the first place, and for that, Miss Trimm, we are all grateful."

He paused while the audience applauded.

"All that remains for me to do now," he continued " is to invite you all, on behalf of Miss James and Mr. Laurence, to make your way to the school's dining - room, where mince pies and hot drinks await you. And may you all have a very merry Christmas!"

There was a joyful murmuring in the theatre as people stood up, gathered their belongings and made their way towards the doors. Miss Trimm rose from her seat, but hesitated, as if wondering if she should approach Lord Bramblewell and Miss Susie Sutton, in order to extend to them the hand of friendship. She looked in their direction - they were still sitting down in the front row - but then, she turned her head away quickly, as if she could not bear the sight of them, chatting to each other, cosily side by side. Julian, as if understanding Miss Trimm's pain, came to her rescue.

"I apologise for this imposition, Miss Trimm," he said, "but I wonder if I could ask you to show me the way to the dining- room? Would you? I am not familiar with the school's lay-out."

He could have followed other people who were making their way in the direction of the dining- room, of course, but his intervention provided Miss Trimm with a reason to leave gracefully.

"Oh! Of course!" she responded, her face brightening.

However, just as the two of them were about to step into the aisle, Susie Sutton left her place and hurried after them. On the way back to her seat, at the end of the interval, she had asked Tansy if she thought Julian had struck her as being like Kostya.

"Oh! Very like him!" Tansy had replied.

Now emboldened by the fact that her opinion had been shared by a young woman she respected, Susie reached out to touch Julian's arm.

"Wasn't the play wonderful?" she asked excitedly, addressing both Miss Trimm and Julian. "And don't you think, Miss Trimm, that Julian is awfully like Kostya? Konstantine, I mean. He is, isn't he? Julian, you are SO like him! I'm definitely going to look for 'Anna Karenina' in Rupert's library and I'm going to re-read it, tonight! I KNOW Kostya will remind me of you, all the way through!"

Miss Trimm looked startled as if taken aback by the sight of Susie confidently addressing Julian, as if she had been a close friend of his for years. No doubt she was reflecting on the Susie she had met two years previously, when Gylen Somerland had brought her with him on his visit to Bramblewell School and had introduced her as his soon-to-be fiancée. What a gauche young woman she had been then! Miss Trimm had believed she would never learn how to behave appropriately enough to be accepted as a suitable wife for Gylen Somerland - never mind Lord Bramblewell! But now, one had to concede, however reluctantly, that Susie Sutton had worked hard to improve herself and would probably continue to do so, in order to be worthy of bearing the title of Lady Bramblewell. She, Miss Trimm, had underestimated her young rival! She watched Susie returning to Lord Bramblewll's side with a sad heart.

"Shall we go?" asked Julian, gently taking her arm

In the dining-room, the head girl, Stella Lomas, and her prefects, were ready to hand out mince pies, tiny canapés-like quiches, small, herby sausage rolls and hot drinks, to those people who were entering the room in large numbers, eager for sustenance before journeying home. In the corner of the room, Irene Miller, miffed at having been left out of Lord Bramblewell's speech, had started to play Schubert's Impromptu No. 3, in a way that seemed to express her private feelings.

Julian, in gallant fashion, would have stayed by Miss Trimm's side, but she seemed to have recovered her composure enough to release him from that duty.

"Please don't feel obliged to stand here talking to me," she urged. "I've just noticed Margaret Devere over there, by the door.

I'll go to talk to her. Do go to join your own friends in Lord Bramblewell's party. I'll be all right!"

"If you're sure..."

"Yes. Truly! Thank you for being so gallant! But I'd feel guilty if I held on to you for longer! Please do join your friends!"

Julian, though, taking a mince pie wrapped in a napkin and a mug of hot chocolate with him, went outside, by a door that was being used as a principal exit, that evening, since it led directly on to the school's drive.

The air was crisply cold and Julian supposed that the ground would be white with frost, later in the night. He thought, then, of Tolstoy's Russia and the bitter winter there. During the play he had just seen, there had been moments which had struck him as being so true to life that he could have imagined he had been watching a pre-revolutionary Russian scene, in the company of Anna Karenina, still to commit an act of folly, Princess Kitty, attractively frivolous and Konstantine, nursing his romantic notions about progress and innovation.

Julian looked up. Bramblewell territory was not far from the walled city but far enough for the skies not to be obscured by the glow of artificial lights. The stars were out. Julian thought of the Christmas present his mother had formally handed him: the Château du Crâne, deeds and all. The task ahead of him, that of retaining the château and caring for it, would be onerous, but if he could keep his ultimate goal in mind, that of retaining the château, he would simply accept, like Konstantine in Tolstoy's novel, that ideals and reality would not always coalesce in the way he might desire and he would, then, make an effort to find practical solutions to the problems that he would encounter. He would take intelligently - considered action when necessary and, with grace, would learn to live with the consequences.

Inside the school, Stella Lomas had replaced Irene Miller at the piano. She was appropriately playing a selection of Christmas carols.

Julian decided to return inside, out of the cold and into the warmth.

CHAPTER 60

Agnès

It was the first Christmas, since the marriage of her daughter to the Count de Sauzon, that Madame Gabrielle de Talence had not spent at the Château de Sauzon. She was going to miss being with Marie-Christine and Count Henri and their children in Belle-Isle, but having made up her mind, she had decided to hold fast. She now thought it was a pity that she had made this decision, though. After all, she tended to think of the Château de Sauzon, with its thick walls and imposing aspect, as a second home. But she had to admit that the thought of not going there at a busy time of year balanced the feeling of regret with one of relief: relief, above all, at not having to travel, as was her custom, on her own. When one travelled in that way, one was invariably on the alert, on the qui-vive, throughout the journey, and consequently, one's brain became over-worked and it was difficult to sleep later.

Despite the fact that she would be spending Christmas alone, Madame Gabrielle, traditional in her outlook when it came to the observance of rituals, planned to celebrate the festival with a certain amount of style. She had ordered meat from a local boucherie, good wine from the Médoc and winter foliage from a gardener in the bordelais countryside. And she had arranged for Agnès, her hair-dresser, to visit her at home, to attend to her hair style, on the 19th December.

Agnès Seurelle had noticed that, since her return from her September holiday on a cruise ship, Madame Gabrielle had been behaving in a distracted manner, as if her mind had been elsewhere. Agnès' curiosity having been aroused, she had dared, during one of her visits to Madame Gabrielle's house, to say, "Madame must have met many interesting people during her voyage, I imagine."

For a moment, it seemed to Agnès as if Madame Gabrielle was about to describe to her what had happened, during her holiday. She had given a little sigh, but then, as if deciding she could not divulge any information of a personal nature to a young girl who was, after all, no more than an acquaintance, she had held back.

On the 19th December, Agnès arrived, at the requested hour, at Madame Gabrielle's house, in the Cours de la Victoire, carrying a small case containing shampoos, mousses and styling devices. Madame Gabrielle greeted Agnès with her usual, dignified courtesy and made light conversation, from time to time, as Agnès worked on her hair. Agnès, however, intuitively became aware of a sadness lurking behind the levity. She was tempted to ask, "Will Madame be spending Christmas with her family as usual?" but she could not summon the nerve to do so. Instead she said, "Madame's hair looks particularly beautiful, this evening. I am so glad Madame has continued to have her hair coloured dark at the roots. It adds such a dash of verve to Madame's entire appearance. I am sure Madame received many compliments during her early autumn holiday."

Madame Gabrielle merely smiled and then, standing up, said, "I'll pay you now," before walking out of the ante-room, where her hair had been dressed in front of the replica dressing-table. She led Agnès across the marble-floored hall and entered a drawing-room, where there was, in one corner, a polished, wooden writing desk, in the style of the Napoleonic era. Agnès knew that in one of the desk's drawers, Madame would already have placed an envelope containing money in cash - "en liquide," as she would specify - and which she would hand to Agnès with dignity, but also with respect. The envelope was always sealed, as if ritually, with sealing-wax and, in the heat-softened wax, there would be the impression of a G, which Madame had stamped with her signet ring. Or was the impressed letter, perhaps, a C? Agnès was never sure.

That evening, just as Madame Gabrielle was about to unlock the drawer where the envelope was kept, her land-line telephone, in another room, rang. Madame Gabrielle hesitated and then, turned to Agnès, who was standing to one side, her hands clasped behind her back, and said, "Excuse me for one moment, mademoiselle." Then, she left the room with a quick step.

Agnès looked around her. She had never before had the chance to study, in a leisurely way, the manner in which the room had been decorated. There were oil paintings, in gilt frames, on the walls. They looked like original works, but Agnès did not recognise any of them. One was a portrait of a lady of some wealth, dressed, Agnès guessed, in pre-Revolutionary, 18th century costume. Others, mostly paintings of the Girondin landscape, with figures in the foreground, being less intriguing, Agnès' attention was then drawn to the dark, polished table, with carved legs, in the centre of the room. On it lay a large book, covered in leather. Was it an album of photographs? Agnès, by nature, was not abnormally inquisitive. Not to the extent of breaking the rules of propriety, at any rate. In fact, she despised one or two of her colleagues at the hairdressing salon who had a tendency to snoop. Agnès found such behaviour beneath her, usually. Yet, there was something about Madame Gabrielle that aroused in her, Agnès, the compulsion to find out more about her. Was it the aura of secrecy with which Madame surrounded herself that made one want to probe into her background? Or was it that air of sadness, that hung around her like a cloud, which made one want to help her to smile again?

Agnès threw a glance at the door through which Madame had departed. In the distance, the sound of Madame's voice could be heard. Her actual words were not clear, but she seemed to be deep in conversation with the person who had telephoned her. Agnès walked to the table and stared at the leather-bound book. She was not, in any way, psychic, or even extraordinarily intuitive, but, at that moment, it seemed to her as if the book were whispering to her, "Look! Look!"

Agnès stretched out her hand and gently lifted the cover to reveal the first page. And what she saw, she had not expected. She had supposed the book would contain photographs of Madame's family. Instead, attached to the thick, cream-coloured page, was a large photograph of a man, of a certain age, which had been cut out of a newspaper. The man's bemused expression, combined with a look of confidence in his eyes, endowed him with a certain air of old-school grandeur, Agnès thought. She, then, saw that, underneath the photo, there had been attached a piece of paper, on which had been scribbled the words, "Sincerely, Kit Mallory," in a strong hand, in black ink. The name was unfamiliar to Agnès. She gently turned the page and then, another and another. The book appeared to be chock-a-block with photos of the same man, some having been taken when he had been younger and playing in a band, of the yé-yé type, yé-yé being the word that was still used in France to describe music from the 1960s. Later, he seemed to have become an architect. Agnès assumed that "architect" meant the same as "architecte" in French.

Wedged behind one article, which had been printed from a computer, Agnès noticed a business card which had Kit Mallory's name on it. She was tempted to remove it to have a good look at it, but resisted the temptation to do so. Instead, she tried to memorise what she could see. Thankfully, an entire e-mail address was visible. Then, hearing Madame Gabrielle's footsteps approaching, Agnès hastily closed the book and moved back to where she had been previously standing, close to the writing desk.

When Madame Gabrielle entered the room, she found Agnès' face looking a bit pink, but she made no comment. She simply took the sealed envelope out of the desk drawer, handed it to the young woman and accompanied her to the main door, herself, as the house keeper had gone home, an hour earlier.

"Thank you, madame. I hope you will have a joyous Christmas," said Agnès, before walking off into the darkening evening.

Madame Gabrielle returned to the drawing room and stared

at the table in the centre. Upon entering the room, a few minutes previously, while Agnès had been present, she had noticed, out of the corner of her eye, that the leather book had been moved slightly. It had been touched. She had given no sign of having been nonplussed. She had merely chided herself, silently, for having recklessly failed to conceal it before Agnès' visit, knowing that payment would be given in that very room. Still, it would never have occurred to her that Agnès would have stooped to looking within. She had always appeared to have been a girl of the superior type. But perhaps it had been unreasonable to have expected even Agnès to have stood still in a room full of interest, for even a few minutes. Whata pity she, Madame Gabrielle, would have to modify her opinion of the girl, now, though.

Madame Gabrielle walked to the table and opened the album, turning the thick cream pages, slowly. She noticed that Kit Mallory's business card had been slightly moved from its position behind an article. At once, Madame Gabrielle felt vulnerable, but then, she shrugged. What could Agnès do with the information, after all? Weave fantasies to distract herself, during the Christmas holiday? She would not dare to mention what she had seen, knowing that if Madame Gabrielle were to hear a soupçon of gossip spread about her, she, Agnès, would no longer be visiting Madame's house in the Cours de la Victoire and would, therefore, lose a valuable source of revenue.

Agnès, meanwhile, was heading in the direction of the Cours de Verdun, where, upon reaching it, she turned left into the Cours du Maréchal Foch, before making her way past the Esplanade des Quinconces and veering left again, to make her way home, to the flat overlooking the river, where she lived with her mother. When she turned the key in the lock in the front door, Agnès heard her mother calling her name.

"Oui, Maman! Je suis là!" she replied, reassuringly.

Agnès made her way to the kitchen, where Madame Seurelle had started to prepare dinner.

"I'll take over, now," said Agnès. "Have a rest!"

It looked as if the evening meal was going to be composed of a tomato salad, lamb cutlets with lentils and, finally, cheese with fresh fruit. As she whisked oil and vinegar together, Agnès' mind was racing. While she had been walking home, it had occurred to her that Kit Mallory, whoever he was, and whatever the rôle he had played in Madame Gabrielle's life, was clearly someone of immense importance to her. But the fact that she collected photographs of him from newspapers, and did not seem to possess the sorts of photos that a friend would send, suggested that she was not in contact with him, surely. Obviously, he was English. The business card had been written in English. How had Madame Gabrielle come to possess it? She must have met him somewhere. During the cruise holiday? Had there been a holiday romance and now Madame was sad because it had ended? Had Kit Mallory not subsequently been in touch with her? The cad!

As the cutlets were cooking, Agnès set the table in the part of the kitchen that served as a dining alcove. Madame Seurelle liked to eat in an atmosphere of some formality and so, the napkins were always fresh and starched and the cutlery, although not silver, still well-chosen.

The meal prepared, Agnès sat down to eat with her mother, but she must have seemed far away in thought because Madame Seurelle eventually asked, "Is there something on your mind?"

After a moment's reflection, Agnès decided to ask her mother's advice, but she did so in the guise of a hypothetical problem.

"Maman," she said, "to what extent, in your opinion, should one interfere in the life of a person - in the life of a woman, shall we say? - if one suspects that, by interfering, one might improve the life of that woman?"

"I don't know to whom or to what you are referring," replied Madame Seurelle, "but I shall simply remind you that Advent and Christmas are traditionally times for beneficence. I dare to add that they are times, even, when miracles are believed to occur.

I concede that what I have just said will sound sentimental and illogical to a secular ear like yours, but, as a result of the sort of upbringing I had, I tend still to believe in Christmas miracles, and I shall add that I have known them to happen in small ways."

Agnès smiled gently, accepting the quiet rebuke her mother had delivered, without arguing.

"Thank you, Maman," was all she said.

Madame Seurelle looked at her for a moment or two but asked no questions. She generally left Agnès to find solutions of her own when she was dealing with life's problems. Agnès was, after all, a sensible girl who worked hard and was aware of what money could and could not buy. Maybe, after all, it was better for her to have a pragmatic head on her shoulders rather than one full of the sort of sentimental notions that might lead her into folly. Although she sometimes chided Agnès for having money-focused attitudes, Madame Seurelle was glad that her daughter was unlikely to end up as she, herself, had, spending her days wishing that she had been wiser when young. More knowing.

Later that evening, Agnès sat in the little bedroom that was her own, on a padded bench, in front of a work table-cum-dressing table where her lap top was set up. She typed "Kit Mallory" into her search bar. She, then, clicked on "Search". Several web sites, including Kit Mallory's own, appeared in a list. Agnès clicked on the Kit Mallory site. Stylish and fascinating, it was full of photos of buildings that he, Kit Mallory, had designed. And there was a form which one could fill in, if one wanted to communicate with him.

With her heart feeling as if it were on the alert, Agnès filled in her own name and address. Then, in the message box, she typed:

L'adresse de Madame Gabrielle de Talence:
122 Cours de la Victoire
Bordeaux
France.

Then, she clicked on “Send.”

“Les jeux sont faits,” she said calmly. “There is no way back.”

CHAPTER 61

The Countess

It was Christmas Eve and in the Château de Sauzon, Héloïse de Sauzon was dressing for the Réveillon meal: the traditional one, eaten late. The Count and Countess de Sauzon had returned from Midnight Mass, with Marie-Colette and Jérôme, a short time before, and having had their appetites sharpened by the cold night air outside, were anxious to sit down to the meal in the larger of the château's two dining rooms. Formally decorated with candles, Christmas flowers and white linen, the table looked as if it had been prepared for a mystical banquet, as Jacqueline de Sauzon, poetic as always, had fancifully described it one Christmas, years before.

Héloïse, earlier in the evening, had seen to the lighting of the old lanterns that had been placed in most of the windows, as had been the practice in the family for generations, on the night before Christmas. She had carried out the task as if it had been a sacred ritual, walking with a quiet step along the château's chilly corridors. It had, in fact, crossed Héloïse's mind that her insistence on taking charge of the lighting of the lanterns had stemmed from the fact that she had, guiltily, felt a need to compensate for her absence from church and the Christmas Mass, that evening. Her attitude to religion, she had tried to explain to her mother, the Countess, was one of enquiry mixed with ambivalence. The Countess had looked annoyed, but the Count had intervened. "Let her sort it out," he had said to the Countess, giving a shrug. Jérôme, who still aspired to being one of the Knights of Malta, forcefully expressed his disapproval, though, pointing out that the existence of his two recalcitrant sisters, Jacqueline as well as

Héloïse, would do little to enhance his chances of being invited to wear the robes and insignia of the prestigious Order, one day. He had not spared either of his sisters when, in pompous mood, he had lectured them in the library of the château, the previous evening.

"Are you so selfish," he had demanded, "that you do not realise that every time you step out of line, the whole family is affected? Do you ever consider the fact that what you do touches the rest of us?"

Jacqueline, astonished at having been lectured in that way by a mere fourteen-year-old boy, had been able only to gape at him. Héloïse, though, had boldly retorted;

"And did you ever reflect on the extent to which your poor marks in school, in the past, and your excessively relaxed attitude - a polite way of describing your lassitude, I should add - embarrassed your sisters, worried your father and upset your mother? Hm? And what about the treacherous way you would gossip to people outside your family about your sisters? Did it ever cross your mind that what you were doing was dishonourable? Examine your own behaviour before you start criticising Jacqueline's conduct and mine, you little hypocrite! Don't dare to presume you know how we should lead our lives!"

Jérôme, unable to parry this verbal thrust, had marched off to his room with noisy footsteps.

"What's wrong with him?" Jacqueline had asked, clearly taken aback.

"He's a fourteen-year-old-boy," Héloîse had replied with a shrug.

It was the custom, at the Château de Sauzon, for everyone to dress up for dinner in the evening, even on normal nights, when the meal was served in the smaller dining room. For the Réveillon meal, however, it was expected that an even greater effort be made to present oneself in an elegant way, because Christmas Eve was regarded as being one of the particularly special nights of the year.

Héloîse had chosen to put on a long, white evening dress, with silver threads woven into it. Her pale, blonde hair, she had decided to leave loose, to flow down her back, glossily. Her shoes, high-heeled and unadorned, were of silver satin. Looking in the cheval mirror, in a corner of her bedroom, she was admiring the way her bias-cut dress flared out at the ankles, when she heard a knock on the bedroom door. Marie-Colette, then, hesitantly walked in. The younger girl's face looked strained.

"What if they say 'No'?" she asked, referring to a promise Héloîse had made to her, months earlier, that she would ask the Count and Countess, by Christmas Eve, at the latest, if she, Marie-Colette, would be allowed to accept an acting rôle in Pierre's Laurier's film, in the spring.

"If they say 'No', the answer is 'No' and that will be the end of the matter," Héloîse replied, trying not to show that Marie-Colette's nervousness and continuing inability to deal effectively with the blows delivered by life irritated her. Jacqueline was always more understanding, but then, Jacqueline was sensitive, herself. Never had Héloîse been so conscious of how fragile Jacqueline was, in fact, as when she had arrived at the château, two nights previously, without her husband. She had visibly shivered, when Jérôme, in peremptory fashion, had demanded:

"Where's Jacqui?"

"Jérôme! How often have I told you not to ask questions in such a direct way?" the Countess had admonished him. "When will you learn to be considerate and diplomatic?"

"What do you mean, Maman?" Jérôme had asked, as if truly baffled. "All I did was to ask Jacqueline where Jacqui was."

"Let's go to the study," the Count had then said, lifting his eyebrows as he had looked at his young son.

"Me? Why? What's going on?" Jérôme had demanded, attempting to point out, by being indignant, that he was an adult and should be treated as such.

"Jérôme!" his father had said, more severely.

"It's all right, Papa," Jacqueline had interrupted, speaking softly.

Jérôme, only then becoming aware of his sister's sadness, had stared at her, nonplussed.

"Jacqui and I will not be spending Christmas together, this year," Jacqueline had explained, her voice unsteady. "That's all I can tell you."

Jérôme had looked as if he had been on the point of asking, "Why not?" but then had thought the better of it. He had ended up nodding as if sagely, and as if finally acknowledging that Jacqueline had problems to which he could not be party.

Later, Jacqueline had cried in Héloîse's room. Her relationship with Jacqui had been improving to some extent, she had said. Certainly, he had been communicating with her more often. But then, out of the blue, he had told her, in an e-mail message, that he could not spend Christmas with her.

"The reason could be connected with his work," Héloîse had protested. "You are being irrational. Pull yourself together!"

Jacqueline, though, had been inconsolable. Jacqui had spoilt Christmas for her. She would only be pretending to enjoy it, in order to keep up appearances.

"I'm sure Christmas will end up being lovely for you," Héloïse had said reassuringly, although, interiorly, unconvinced.

The Réveillon dining table, illuminated with tall candles, looked a picture of splendour, that Christmas Eve, Héloîse thought, as she entered the large dining- room with Marie-Colette. Jérôme and Jacqueline were already there, Jacqueline looking attractive with her hair arranged in a loose chignon, held in place with a jade clasp, which, Héloïse knew, Teddy Laurence had once bought for her in Liverpool.

When, after a few minutes, the Count and Countess had entered the room, the meal began, starting with the traditional first course of oysters. Marie-Colette, sitting beside Jérôme and opposite both her sisters, looked at Héloïse with pleading eyes, now and again, as if to say, "Do it now! I can't cope with this waiting any longer." However, Héloïse did not respond to the plea, but ate calmly, as if she had nothing of importance occupying her thoughts.

Jacqueline, had been made aware of what was about to happen, but she was too pre-occupied with her own problems to dwell on Marie-Colette's. She was remembering how Christmas Eve had been celebrated, two years previously, when, newly engaged, she had brought her fiancé, Teddy Laurence, to the château, to meet her family. She remembered how sincere he had looked that night and how handsome in his dark suit and white shirt, sparkling in the candlelight, like snow. Had she married him instead of Jacqui, he, Teddy, would be with her now and she would be happy. If only she had known then what she now knew, she would not have betrayed him and embarrassed him in the despicable way she had. Remembering her folly, her eyes filled with tears. "Stupid!" she thought. "Stupid! Stupid!" Was there anything more miserable than spending Christmas without one's beloved?

The oysters having been consumed, the next two courses were brought to the table, in turn. The third consisted of a turkey cooked in wine. Héloïse took a deep breath. Was this an appropriate moment to mention Pierre Laurier's request? The Count was discussing with the Countess the quality of the bird, its texture and the tastiness of the sauce. He started to talk, then, about the claret used in the sauce. Claret! The noble wine of Bordeaux! Surely this was the moment for which Héloïse had been waiting. She raised her head as if a pertinent thought had just crossed her mind.

"While I was in Bordeaux in the summer, Maman," she began, apparently disingenuously, "Pierre Laurier asked if Marie-Colette could make a brief appearance in the film."

Jacqueline, although already aware of what Héloïse had been planning to ask, gave a start as if the question had taken her by surprise. On the other side of the table, Marie-Colette stopped eating and stared down at her plate. Jérôme looked around as if not sure on whom to fix his eyes. The Countess slowly put down on her plate the cutlery she had been using and leaned back in her chair. Only the Count seemed unconcerned, continuing to eat as if nothing remarkable had been said.

Marie-Colette glanced in the direction of her mother. She shifted in her seat, ill at ease, as she became aware of the fact that the Countess' face had become pale. The Countess, indeed, seemed unable to respond to what Héloïse had said, or even to move.

"Pierre said that Marie-Colette would be on screen for only a very short time," Héloïse continued, somewhat recklessly, but perhaps hoping to make her previous statement sound less shocking by adding that detail. "No more than a minute or two."

"Pierre?" the Countess uttered, finally turning her head to look directly at Héloïse, her eyes as cold as a frozen lake. "Pierre?"

Héloïse had realised, as soon as the name had slipped out of her mouth, that she should naturally have referred to the director of the film as Monsieur Laurier.

"I'm sorry, Maman," she said, lowering her eyes.

"Have you any conception of the sort of embarrassment I have already endured in my social circle because of your own behaviour during the summer months?" the Countess then asked, forcefully, as if anger were beginning to build up inside her. "How do you think I felt when I was obliged to say to mere acquaintances, 'Oh, yes! My silly daughter has accepted a holiday job pretending to be an actress.' Can you imagine what my shame has been like? Can you imagine my humiliation as I have told people I scarcely know that my daughter had been working as an actress? Are you so ill-educated that you are unable to imagine what I have been enduring? Oh! You can protest that you are a modern girl and that my values are out-dated and ridiculous. That may be so...but they still matter to ME! Can't you see that? They matter to ME! And now, you are daring to suggest that your equally empty-headed sister be dragged into the same line of employment! You want to hurt and disgrace me even more? What do you think your grand-mother will say about this latest prank? Has it not crossed your mind that she will think I have failed in my duty, as a mother, to raise you properly? Don't you realise it will prove to her that I have not lived up to her expectations? Is that the impression of me you want her to have?"

"Marie-Christine," interrupted the Count, having calmly taken a sip of wine from one of the glasses in front of him. "Let the girl appear in the film. It will do her good. Look upon it as therapy."

The Countess stood up and stared at her husband as if he were a stranger who had said something inappropriately over-familiar. Then, she turned to glare at Héloïse, contemptuously.

"Fine!" she cried out at last. "Do as you like! All of you!"

She threw her linen napkin into the centre of the table and, with a rustle of silver-grey silk, she walked quickly from the room, leaving in her wake a silence that was unbroken during the remainder of the meal.

CHAPTER 62

Sacrifices

Marie-Christine de Sauzon went into the bathroom adjacent to her bedroom, to soak a towel in cold water. She wrung it out, noting, as she did so, that her mental agitation had led to her losing strength in her hands. It was always so. When upset, she lost the ability and motivation to do anything with energy and deliberation. She, lethargically, took the towel into the bedroom and, after lying down on the grand lit, placed it across her forehead, paying no heed to the fact that the ends if it were touching the pillow and that water was seeping into the silk pillow case. The exhibition she, Marie-Christine, had made of herself at the Réveillon meal was the only matter now concerning her. How inappropriate of her to have behaved in the way she had! And on Christmas Eve of all evenings! Had she been a newly spoilt nouvelle-riche, as yet unaware of the well-established belief that to be respected in society one had to conduct oneself responsibly, her behaviour might have been overlooked by those of charitable inclination. But, she was the carefully trained and schooled Countess de Sauzon and no excuses could be advanced for her, really.

Marie-Christine turned on her side, wishing she could stay in bed, indefinitely, or at least until those who had witnessed her faux-pas had forgotten about it. But, how likely was it that her daughters would forget her latest dramatic outburst in a hurry? She would have to apologise to them of course. As she pondered on what exactly she would say, Marie- Christine felt anger arising within her, all the same. Why should she apologise to her daughters when they had been the ones who had, initially, transgressed? Héloïse had been unpleasantly defiant, after all, hiding her recalcitrance behind a veil of fake innocence, calculated, no doubt, to rile her mother. Marie-Colette, passive and over-anxious to please, would have submitted herself to her sister's strong will without a murmur. And now, was she, Marie-Christine, required to apologise to those two, the form of response being dictated by the well-established rules of savoir-vivre? Surely not! Surely the girls were the ones who should be obliged to apologise to her, their mother, and to make amends appropriately. If only their father were not so laissez-faire! He should have jumped up to defend his wife the instant that Héloïse had made her insolent request. Instead, he had calmly, and in a self-satisfied manner, continued to eat. Was he more interested in his turkey and claret than his wife's happiness?

There was a knock on the bedroom door. Marie-Christine hesitated before responding. Were the two daughters who had offended out there? Marie-Christine could picture them, standing behind the door. Héloïse would be calm, showing no emotion. Marie-Colette would be hiding behind her.

"Entrez!" Marie-Christine called out, now on the alert.

Unexpectedly, it was Jacqueline who walked in when the door opened. The expression on her face suggested she had been provoked by compassion to visit or else had decided that a show of empathy would serve her own interests, Marie-Christine somewhat cynically guessed. Oh! The games her daughters played in their efforts to be the favoured one! And, in the end, how stupid they were, when, upon failing, they tried to punish their mother by sulking or, as had been the case in recent years, by being outrageous!

"Maman?" said Jacqueline softly, as if enquiring if her mother was asleep. Could the girl not see that her mother's eyes were wide open? Marie-Christine was not in the mood to be accommodating.

"Maman?"

"Yes," Marie-Christine replied, finally, raising herself up on one elbow, having removed the cloth from her forehead.

"May I sit down?" asked Jacqueline.

Marie-Christine, by giving a small shrug, indicated that her daughter could sit at the end of her bed.

Jacqueline sat there, placing her hands in her lap. Her shoulders were slightly hunched and it occurred to Marie-Christine that, at that moment,Jacqueline looked like a forlorn child, rather than a young, married woman. Marie-Christine wished she could respond to her daughter's apparent unhappiness, but she could not.

"Maman," Jacqueline began, "I know we have all disappointed you. I, above all. But, I, myself, am going to try to make amends. Really. Jacqui and I are attempting to find solutions to our problems."

"Why is Jacqui not here, in that case?"

"I believe he was too ashamed to accept your hospitality because he felt he had not done enough to justify my father's and your generosity in handing me over to his care."

"Ouf!" exclaimed Marie-Colette, raising her hand in a gesture of apparent nonchalance. "You are both independent enough to make your own choices, without referring to the expectations of your parents. You have pointed that out often enough."

"I know," said Jacqueline softly. "I am simply explaining…"

"Enough!" interrupted Marie-Christine. "I have no interest in hearing such explanations. Now, leave me alone."

She turned on her side, her back to her daughter. And so, with reluctance, Jacqueline left the room. How was she going to make her mother happy again? Perhaps because she had been her mother's first-born child, she had been trained to behave responsibly towards others. Her siblings, initially. But now, she felt an inner compulsion - a duty, even - to make the Countess smile again.

Jacqueline pondered on the sacrifices her mother had made in order to bring up her daughters and her son correctly, and furthermore, to live up to her own, or rather Madame Gabrielle's idea, of what a Countess should be like. The Count had revealed to Jacqueline that her mother had once aspired to being a business woman, her desire having been to create beauty products from sea weed and plants that could be found near the clear waters that washed the shores of Brittany. But, Madame Gabrielle had been shocked upon being informed of these aspirations and had responded with expressions of sarcasm and derision. A Countess in the world of business? Was she out of her mind? The old aristocracy of France could dabble only in the noble business of producing wine. Nothing else.

Cowed, Marie-Christine had given up all thought of enterprise. Had she lived a life of concealed bitterness as a result? How often had she wondered what her life would have been like had her ideas been allowed to flower? She had sacrificed her ambitions in order to devote herself to bringing up four children. And now, as she surveyed their paltry achievements, did she feel as if her sacrifice had been justified?

Jacqueline's heart was heavy as she made her way along the corridor to her own room in the château. Once there, she closed the door behind her and stood for a while with her back to it. The room had been hers since her childhood, but that night, she felt like an intruder there.

CHAPTER 63

A Caller in the Dark

Since the housekeeper, at Cours de la Victoire, in Bordeaux, had been given a holiday for the duration of the Christmas period, Madame Gabrielle de Talence had prepared her own Réveillon meal, after Midnight Mass at the Cathédrale Saint-André, to which she had been driven - and from where she had returned - in a car she had hired with a driver, for the occasion. She, generally, did not consider herself to be skilled in the culinary arts, rarely having been obliged to take to the kitchen, but she had made a good fist of a consommé, instead of oysters, steak, instead of turkey and had assembled a good spread of salads and cheeses, into the bargain. She had dressed the table nicely in the dining room and had, nostalgically, lit candles. Now, in a long, slim gown of gold-coloured cloth, and with diamonds at her throat, she was ready to sit down to eat. She felt glad that she had made an effort to decorate the dining-room, and, indeed, the house in its entirety, with dash and style, as if she had been expecting guests to join her. The act of preparation had made the night seem special and she realised that her spirits had lifted, while she had been engaged in the ritualistic activity, even though her Christmas celebration would be a solitary one.

Madame Gabrielle ate her meal with poise and attention to the rules of savoir-vivre, as if she had been sitting on her own in a restaurant, being observed by waiters. They always judged and so, she made sure they realised she was a woman who had been brought up in a certain way. Her behaviour at home was no different. She never allowed standards to slip.

When the time came for coffee, Madame decided to drink it

in her bedroom at her ease. She placed a filled cafetière, a cup, a saucer and a spoon, on a little tray, adding hot milk in a jug, before carrying the laden tray across the hall, with its imposing pillars, and into the ante-chamber, where the dressing table, at which she sat to have her hair coiffed, was situated. Then, she went up the steps to her bedroom.

Having placed the tray on a small table, she moved to one side the free-standing screen, with its panels covered in fine, opaque muslin, in order to open slightly the long and wide window, in front of which it, the screen, had stood. She wanted to be aware of people passing by, below in the street, so as not to feel so alone. Normally, solitude did not concern Madame Gabrielle, but at Christmas, she missed the feeling of cosiness that one experienced, when surrounded by a family that followed the rules of convention and the rituals that were integral to the night of celebration.

Madame Gabrielle walked over to her bed, a grand lit, covered in fine, white sheets and a snowy quilt, all of which stood out against the tall, chestnut-brown bed head. Madame Gabrielle sat on the bed, stacking copious pillows and a bolster behind her in such a way as to support her back. Then, she picked up her cell phone from the bed-side table. The Réveillon meal at the Château de Sauzon would surely be over. She would call the Countess and the Count de Sauzon, and their children, to wish them a joyous Christmas.

It was Jérôme who answered the call to the land-line telephone at the Château. Maman, he explained, had gone to her room, having been upset by Héloïse. Marie-Colette was shivering like a jelly-fish, because she hated to see people quarrelling and Jacqueline was fed-up because Jacqui had not come to the Château to spend Christmas with her. Would Grand'maman like to speak to Papa?

Madame Gabrielle reflected on that question for a second, but then, said:

"No, Jérôme. I shall call again tomorrow. I wish you all a joyeux

Noël. Tomorrow will be better."

Madame Gabrielle moved the pillows into their normal position and lay down on the bed. She regretted, now, not having made the effort to travel to Belle Isle to spend Christmas at the Château de Sauzon. Had she been there, Héloïse would not have dared to contradict her mother: that was certain. What could have been the reason for the quarrel, though? Héloïse's ill-advised attempt to turn herself into an actress? Her icy determination?

Madame Gabrielle closed her eyes and began to reflect on the Sauzon family's problems. Why had Marie-Christine's children not launched themselves into society as one would have hoped? Marie-Christine, herself, had been a model daughter. She had behaved correctly at all times. But, of course, she had not been strict enough when it had come to raising her own children. That had been the crux of the problem. Her approach to motherhood had been flawed. She should not have allowed Jacqueline, as a teenager, to consort with the moody Jacqui Galant, for a start. That boy had been completely devoid of ambition, when he had been at school. And Jacqueline's academic brilliance had filled him with resentment rather than pride. Why had Marie-Christine not spotted the problems that would ensue, were the relationship allowed to develop further? And why had Count Henri not intervened at an appropriate moment? What was wrong with that family?

Preoccupied with these thoughts, Madame Gabrielle barely noticed the sound of a car slowing to a halt and stopping, finally, in the street, below her window, but she became aware of the slamming of the car's door. She opened her eyes, then, suddenly alert. Why would a car stop so near to her front door at such a late hour? She looked at her watch. It was three o' clock. Three o'clock on Christmas morning. The door bell rang, then.

Madame Gabrielle sat up and now on edge, quietly made her way to the window. Concealing herself to the extent that she could, behind the screen, she tried to look out. There was a man standing at the foot of the stone steps that led to the main door. A tall man.

Madame Gabrielle would not normally have dreamt of unbolting the door after dark. Had the late- night visitor known her well and had he been aware of French savoir-vivre, he would have known that she expected visitors to telephone her before a visit, to arrange a time that would suit her. Tempted, therefore, not to respond to the summons to the door, Madame Gabrielle hesitated. Then, she realised there was something familiar about the way the man was standing, conveying through his posture, alone, that he was calm, but that he also expected not to be kept waiting. Madame Gabrielle could feel the throb of her heart intensifying. She turned away from the window, as if in panic, and hurried down the steps to the ante-chamber and out into the hall with pillars. She ran down the glassily polished steps to the front door, holding up parts of her golden gown, so as not to trip. She waited for a second or two as if listening, or perhaps, as if waiting for her heart to beat less forcefully. Then, she pushed the bolts on the door to one side, hurting her hands, in her hasty effort to do so. Finally, she pulled the door open.

"Merry Christmas, Gabrielle," said Kit Mallory.

CHAPTER 64

Regrets

Thankful that she had made an effort to dress up to celebrate Christmas, even though she had intended to spend the evening on her own, Madame Gabrielle de Talence took a deep breath to calm the thumping of her heart. She made an effort to smile, knowing that a smile, even when forced, endowed her with a measure of confidence and light-heartedness. She tried to look in a steady way at the tall figure of the man, standing, in the dark of night, at the foot of the stone steps which led from the pavement up to the front door of her house. Finally, she said:

"Merry Christmas, Mr. Mallory. Joyeux Noël! Please…do come in, won't you?"

Kit Mallory bowed his head slightly, in a restrained way. He went up the steps and entered the house, although hesitantly, as if he were on the verge of apologising for visiting at such a late hour. He looked around, as if he were expecting a member of the household staff to come forward to take his navy, woollen coat from him - he must have thought it was that sort of house - but no one appeared, the housekeeper having been given a holiday. In fact, the building was silent and Kit Mallory must have realised that Madame Gabrielle was alone in it, for a look of uncertainty flitted across his face, then.

Realising that the visitor had not imagined her to be spending Christmas in solitude, Madame Gabrielle felt more at ease. Of course, she knew Mr. Mallory was unlikely to be an opportunist or, indeed, the sort of cad who would not care a fig for the reputation of a lady, whatever her age, but still, she was relieved.

The electric lights in the entrance hall of the house were protected by shades which resembled glass-sided lanterns hanging from the ceiling. The glow from them, though, was not bright enough to illuminate every corner of the hall and shadows lurked behind pillars. Aware of the inadequacy of this chiaroscuro arrangement, Madame Gabrielle led Mr. Mallory quickly away from that scene, up marble steps and along a corridor to a reception room, which, when lit up, looked cheerier. Madame Gabrielle had, earlier in the week, ordered a Christmas tree to be delivered. It stood, now, in a corner of the room, looking extravagantly opulent, being covered in gold baubles and frosted pine cones. In fact, Madame Gabrielle had decorated it herself, taking as her source of inspiration, a photograph of a tree in the Christmas catalogue of a glamorous London store. There were real flowers in gilded vases here and there, also. Surveying the room, one might have thought that Madame Gabrielle had known, in advance, that some friend or acquaintance - one whom she had wanted to impress - had been planning to surprise her with a visit. In fact, she had rather hoped that at least one of her grand-children might have done so, to compensate for the fact that she had decided not to travel to the Château de Sauzon. Given the sour way she had been inclined to ladle out unsolicited advice to her grand-children in previous years, though, she could not blame them for not appearing.

While Mr. Mallory admired the Christmas tree, Madame Gabrielle walked swiftly in the direction of the large fireplace in which a "retro"electric fire, that complemented the formal and very French décor of the room, had been placed. She switched it on and then, turned to Mr. Mallory to say:

"Please sit down."

Kit Mallory placed his navy coat on a chair, close to him: a chair which looked as if it were a replica of one dating from the reign of King Louis XIV.

"Oh!" said Madame Gabrielle, now flustered. "Oh! Please forgive me."

She took the coat and left the room in order to hang it up in a wardrobe in an ante-chamber nearly. And when she had returned to join Mr. Mallory, she found he had sat down on a sofa, close to the fire, but he stood as she advanced into the room. He watched her with what appeared to be a puzzled look in his eyes.

"Is something the matter?" asked Madame Gabrielle.

She sat down on a sofa opposite the one he had occupied, gesturing that he should sit down again, but he walked towards the mantelpiece and leaned his right elbow on it. Magnificently dressed in a dark suit, starched, white shirt and grey silk tie, he appeared to be both an authoritative figure and a dashingly dangerous one. Dangerous because of the effect he could still have on romantically-inclined ladies, Madame Gabrielle suspected. Could she, herself, resist the allure of his presence? She thought of Caterina Traversi and knew she had to.

Mr. Mallory seemed to be deep in thought. In fact, it was occurring to him that Madame Gabrielle, when not looking strict and cold, was capable of appearing to be younger than she actually was. Of course, many people of his own generation were, in fact, looking younger than their chronological age. He, himself, certainly felt as if life were just beginning rather than drawing to an end. Every day felt fresh. There was still so much to do and crucially, so much yet to learn. Hungry for knowledge, he felt as if he were now quite a different person from the one he had been when younger. Then, studying had seemed a chore. He wondered what Madame Gabrielle had been like while at school.

"Gabrielle," he said, unsettling her, since he had not called her "Madame" and because he added unexpectedly, "Tell me what you were like when you were a teenager."

"When I was a student, I spent a year in Liverpool," she said, apparently shyly, while, in reality, she was thrilled to have an opportunity to speak about the time she had spent in that city.

"Liverpool? When, exactly?"

"I used to see you," she went on, as if she had not heard his question. "You would be on stage, in those cellar clubs you used to frequent. I used to stand near the stage. I had long, dark hair, in those days and, I suppose, I stood out because I was obviously French. But I never spoke to you and you never spoke to me."

Kit Mallory frowned and looked as if her were trying to recover a memory from some repository in his brain.

"It must have been stupid of me not to have spoken to you," he said, finally. "I regret not doing so. I regret so much."

Was he simply being gallant? Madame Gabrielle was not sure.

"Liverpool was such a mysterious place, then," she said, not referring to his comment, partly because she did not know if he had been sincere and partly because she did not want to think about the regrets she harboured in her own heart: ones which were a source of pain.

"Mysterious?"

"Living there was like living in a film noir. There were jazz cellars and rock music cellars and thin, cobbled roads, behind buildings. And there was a Chinatown, with restaurants and lanterns hanging outside...One dark night, I got lost in Chinatown and rain was falling down, splashing on to the dark streets. But, maybe I saw the scene in a dream. I'm not sure, any more. I'm talking too much. Would you like...English tea? I ordered some from London. Or would you prefer a glass of good claret from a left bank terroir to celebrate Christmas? By the way, how did you find out that I lived here? How exactly did you find me? Are you celebrating Christmas in Bordeaux with friends?"

Kit Mallory did not answer, but instead, sat down on the sofa. He leaned forward, resting his forearms on his thighs, while he gazed pensively at the floor.

"Gabrielle," he said then, pausing, as if suddenly not sure if he should continue.

"Yes?"

"I was hoping we could pretend to ...I mean, I'd like us to get to know each other, as if we were young...and had just met in Liverpool. But, I'd also love to know how you have lived your life since your student days. Have you enjoyed your life?"

"I settled for security when I married," said Madame Gabrielle after a pause.

"You wanted security and status," said Kit. "That's normal. Most people..."

"Status?" interrupted Madame Gabrielle sharply.

She smiled as if sourly. She, a daughter of the château, had married into the bourgeoisie and, in doing so, had not gained status. She felt tears gathering in her eyes, then. She tried to control them: it was not dignified to cry. Why was she feeling so helpless, suddenly? What was wrong with her? She knew, of course, that she bitterly regretted not having seen her parents before their deaths. She had wanted to say to them, 'Maman, don't leave me!' and, 'Papa, I'm so sorry!' At Christmas, one thought of those things. It was inevitable, if one was alone. Regrets flooded one's mind and one almost drowned in them. She squeezed her hands into fists, in an attempt to gain control of her emotions.

"I quarrelled with my parents," she then said, having composed herself. "I let them down and we were never reconciled. I had to leave home...in 1968."

The mentioning of the year did not seem to jog Mr. Mallory's memory. Of course, he would not have been in Paris at that time.

As if overwhelmed with grief and regretful thoughts, then, Madame Gabrielle stopped talking. She closed her eyes. Her lips appeared to be compressed as if she wanted to prevent other words from being uttered.

Kit Mallory stood up and walked to the mantelpiece again. He turned around and said:

"Gabrielle."

But, she looked so miserable he felt unable to continue.

Her head was now buried in her hands and she seemed to be weeping, but silently. He was finding it physically painful to see her in such a state of distress. The muscles of his heart felt constricted. What had she meant when she had said she had had to leave her home? Had she gone away voluntarily? Surely she had not been banished by her parents! What could she have done to have deserved such a fate? Kit was filled with pity. He could not bear to think of her or, indeed, anyone else - rendered homeless. But leaving her former homelessness to one side, there was something else about the woman that troubled him. From the first moment he had seen her on board the cruise ship, he had sensed, in an obscure, undefined way, that there was an element of fate involved in their meeting. Was he meant to help her in some manner? He did feel, at that moment, that he wanted very much to make her happy and, more rapidly, to make her tears disappear. She seemed to have led a constricted life. Maybe he could break the spell that was preventing her from being free.

"If you could wish for a Christmas miracle right now, Gabrielle, what would it be?" he asked.

"I'd want to go home," she said, her tears now flowing hotly down her cheeks, as she had found release in finally expressing the truth. "I want to go home."

CHAPTER 65

Overheard on Christmas Morning

Susie Sutton awoke on Christmas morning, in Bramblewell Manor, not able to focus, initially, on what was making her feel anxious. Then, she remembered that Gylen Somerland, as well as his children, Rosalind and John, had been invited to join Lord Bramblewell and his other guests for the traditional dinner at one o' clock. Rosalind was going to be one of the bridesmaids at Susie's wedding, of course, and she, Susie, was going to seize the opportunity to introduce her to June Jones, who had also been invited to the manor, that day. But, Susie was also, in extension, going to use the Christmas day celebration to try to make peace with John Somerland, as the young boy still regarded her as being antipathetic to him. She had, admittedly, been the woman who had once suggested to his father that he be sent away to boarding school, when he had been desperate to stay at home. Susie understood, now, that John would have hated to have been torn away from his sister, during an unsettled period in his life. He had, after all, shortly before, been forced to leave his childhood home in Bristol, in order to live in his father's house in Ellesmere Port and he had found the period of adjustment difficult. Susie had, later, reflected on what she had proposed and it had occurred to her that a place at boarding school was not what would have suited John at all. What he would have needed, in fact, would have been the stability of a cosy home, as well as the feeling of serenity and safety that the presence of his big sister would have given him. Would John ever forgive her for her impetuous and thoughtless suggestion? She was hoping she would be able to make amends, as she did not want to continue being disliked by him. What is more, he seemed to be adrift, still, on an ocean of confusion and, being essentially kind, she wanted to help.

Her recently acquired diplomatic skills - learnt from a book and from observation - would also have to be summoned, she believed, in order to make Gylen feel at ease. After all, he had to be feeling somewhat guilty for having given her short shrift on the evening that their relationship had ended sourly.

Little recognition, let alone thanks, had been extended by Gylen to her for the effort she had made, initially, to try to help the children to settle in his house. Rosalind had been the only one, in fact, who had seemed to appreciate all that she, Susie, had been attempting to do in order to make the transition to a new life easier. The meals Susie had cooked had been praised by Rosalind, as had the pretty clothes she had worn to make the children's environment cheerful and beautiful. Gylen, on the other hand, had rarely appeared to have noticed Susie's contribution to the assimilation of his children into his busy life. Still, on reflection, Susie had to admit that it was thanks to Gylen that she had had the opportunity to meet Lord Bramblewell and so, obviously, she felt that she had been compensated for any failings on his, Gylen's, part.

Liz Laurier had, also, been invited to the Christmas Day dinner, but Susie had not been surprised when she had received from Liz a polite, hand-written letter declining the invitation. Liz was still having difficulty communicating with John and she had thought he would be more likely to enjoy the outing to the manor were she not present. Susie, anyway, had been informed by Rosalind that Liz, along with Lynn James, had been invited to Teddy Lawrence's apartment that day. "Lynn James, though!" Susie had silently exclaimed upon hearing that item of news. Why had the headmistress of Bramblewell School had that invitation extended to her? Did she live alone? Had Teddy felt sorry for her? Or was he friendlier with Lynn than she, Susie, might have supposed? Did he consider her to be one of his closest friends, in fact? Close enough for him to be anxious to spend Christmas Day with her? Obviously, since he was now deputy head and obliged to collaborate with Lynn at work, it was natural that a friendship should develop and that the two of them would consequently meet each other outside of the school grounds, now and again. But surely, with Lynn being ten years older than Teddy, it was unlikely that the friendship would develop into a romantic relationship. What did they have in common apart from their chosen profession? Teddy's out-of-school interests seemed to centre, still, on jazz and the running of his youth club, as far as Susie knew. Lynn's life, beyond school, was a mystery. But surely she was not the type of young woman who would be drawn to dimly-lit jazz clubs, was she? Susie could not imagine her, either, supervising teenagers in youth clubs, after school hours, as if she were an enthusiastic, blazer-wearing cheer-leader. No. She was more likely to be found in concert halls, listening attentively to cerebrally satisfying music, while looking remote and sophisticated. Or else, she would be purposefully studying ancient artefacts in museums or wandering pleasurably around art galleries, homing in on paintings that challenged the brain in addition to arousing the emotions.

The time shown on the watch on Susie's bedside table was ten minutes past seven. Susie threw back the covers on the bed and forced herself to rise to face the day ahead. She reached for a long, flame-coloured silk robe, lying on a chair nearby and she put it on over her beige, satin nightdress. She slipped her feet into beige, embroidered mules with little heels and made her way out of her bedroom into the cool, but not chilly, corridor. She then walked towards a large landing, where portraits of Bramblewell ancestors hung on the walls. Susie stopped in front of one: that of Lady Maureen Athena Bramblewell. It was known that she was the ancestor whom Lord Bramblewell most respected. He had even given to Susie her cabochon ring, to serve as an engagement ring. Susie looked down at her left hand. The ring, on her third finger, felt heavy. In Susie's head, it represented duty, responsibility and the expectation of achievement. Although she was longing to be, finally, addressed as Lady Bramblewell and to call the manor "home", would she, Susie, find the price of accepting these privileges too high? To what extent would her freedom to act spontaneously be curtailed? And how little time would pass before Lord Bramblewell would realise that she was not up to the rôle she was expected to play? Would he become less tolerant of her shortcomings when her mistakes would pile up, one after another?

Susie tried to breathe deeply and slowly, to control the panic rising within her. She knew she had to stop herself from succumbing to the thoughts of self-doubt that had started to assail her. It was normal for young women to be nervous before their weddings. What she was experiencing was a natural prelude to taking her bridal vows. But, oh! Had she married Teddy her life would have been so much easier!

Susie reached out to touch the edge of the portrait and leaned her head upon her outstretched arm."Teddy! Teddy!" she said gently, but aloud, unaware of the fact that Lord Bramblewell, up early as well, was standing by a window in a room adjacent to the landing, gazing out at the grounds of his manor, as the morning light fell upon the leaf-less trees and frosted grasses. The door of the room was open and the house, being otherwise silent, at least in that quarter, Lord Bramblewell heard Susie uttering Teddy's name. He turned, without making a sound, to look through the open doorway and he saw Susie, then, framed by it, in a pose that struck him as being as elegant as that of a lady in an Alma Tadema painting. He had not flinched when he had heard her mentioning Teddy's name. She was young, after all, and it had to be expected that she would think of Teddy from time to time. Teddy would remind her of a time when the responsibilities she was about to shoulder would not have existed. However, before she could become Lady Bramblewell, he would have to make sure she was mature enough to undertake the duties that would accompany the title and, more crucially, he would have to find out whom she really loved.

CHAPTER 66

Table Manners

Only two or three minutes after Liz Laurier had arrived at her apartment in Ellesmere Port, having spent Christmas Day at Teddy Laurence's, her land-line telephone rang. She lifted the receiver and felt the gold bangle that had adorned her right wrist all day, slipping up her arm, under the sleeve of her coat.

"Hello?"

"Mum! You're back at last!"

"Yes, Rosalind. What's wrong?"

"Nothing, Mum. I'm just curious to know what your visit was like, really. I didn't call your mobile number in case you were still...you know...at Mr. Laurence's flat."

Liz suspected that Rosalind was trying to appear as if she were merely asking about a Christmas Day meal enjoyed by her mother in Liverpool and, perhaps, the journey there and back, whereas, in reality, she was essentially making an enquiry about Teddy Laurence's life style. Liz suspected that a little flame was still burning in the ashes of a teenage crush, in other words: one that was in danger of flaring up again, given enough attention.

Liz decided not to feed her daughter's imagination by giving her the sorts of details she was possibly desperate to know. It worried Liz that, despite the effort she had made, in the previous year, to help Rosalind to direct her feelings into useful, creative channels, she, Rosalind, might have fallen prey again to hopeless thoughts which would waste her time and would distract her from her studies, during a year which, academically, was a crucial one.

"It was nice," Liz therefore stated, in anodyne fashion. "The food was good. Miss James cooked a lot of it."

"Miss James?"

"Yes."

"She must feel quite at home in Mr. Laurence's flat."

Rosalind had made the remark in such a falsely casual way that, with dismay, Liz concluded that her daughter truly had been attempting to conceal her sentimental attachment to Teddy Laurence: an attachment which had possibly become even stronger than it had been previously, since now, it was secretly being bottled up, as if in a pressure cooker. Maybe Rosalind was afraid that if she were to reveal the way she was feeling to Liz, she, Liz, would betray her again, by warning Teddy that her daughter was in danger of making a fool of herself, by, perhaps, hanging around the science corridor at Bramblewell School or by presenting him with romantic poetry, dedicated to him. This, after all, was what Liz had hinted Rosalind might do, when confiding in Teddy the previous year, much to the girl's embarrassment.

"Listen, Rosalind," said Liz, affecting a coaxing tone. "I've just arrived and I simply must have a cup of tea, to warm me up. Give me a few minutes to settle down, will you? Then, we'll talk. Are you in your room?"

"Yes. In my room? You'll call me back, Mum?"

"Yes. Soon."

"I'm looking forward to hearing about...your journey and everything."

"Oh! Rosie!" thought Liz, sadly, as she put down the receiver. "You have as much interest in my journey as you would have in a plate of cold, uncooked oatmeal."

She unbuttoned her slim, midi-length, white woollen coat, happy that its soft, fake fur collar had kept her neck and ears warm, when she had stepped out of her car, now parked by the pavement outside. There had been a touch of iciness in the West Cheshire air: the sort of iciness that some would describe as the precursor of snow. A line from a poem by Robert Frost had come fleetingly into Liz's head, perhaps because thoughts of America had been prompted earlier in the day by a photograph of Rebecca Hampton that had been displayed, although not prominently, in Teddy's flat. There was a possibility that Rebecca, herself, had put it there, when she had been preparing to leave after her stay, in the summer – or, perhaps Teddy had asked her to leave a photo behind and she had obliged, after encasing it in a heavy and stylish frame. Many Americans - and Rebecca was clearly one of those - tended to be generous in their giving.

Having draped her coat over a chair, temporarily, Liz made her way to the kitchen, switched on the lights and heated water in the electric kettle. She looked at the small, Swiss watch on her left wrist. It was ten o' clock. It struck her, then, that she had left home eleven hours previously. Normally, she would have considered staying for hours in an apartment, to which she had been invited for the mid-day meal only, a serious faux-pas, but the extension of her visit, that day, had not appeared to her to have been a breach of etiquette, since Teddy Laurence had seemed reluctant to let his guests leave and Lynn had, therefore, uncharacteristically prolonged her own visit, also.

During the Christmas meal, Lynn had mentioned, en passant, the burden of having to be au fait with the language of finance, in order to carry out her duties at school. Finance, in fact, had been an area of knowledge in which she had considered herself to be wanting, when she had been wondering whether to apply for the permanent post she now occupied.

"Don't underestimate your own ability to overcome challenges, Lynn," Teddy had said, interrupting her before she had been able to list other perceived blanks in her knowledge.

Liz had noticed, then, the lingering look that Teddy had given Lynn. Had it simply signified admiration…or budding affection?

Liz opened the door of her table-top refrigerator and removed a carton of milk. She, then, reached up, into a cupboard, for a white pot, a small strainer and Darjeeling tea. After a minute of two, the tea being ready, she poured it into a porcelain cup and carried it to her living room, where she sat on a white sofa: the one beside the small, Chinese, lacquered table on which the land-line telephone had been placed. She dialled Rosalind's number.

"Mum?"

"Yes. First of all, tell me about your own day."

"Oh! It was nice. Susie was looking lovely. Dad and John were there, of course."

"I imagine Susie put John beside you, at the table."

"No. Actually, she put him between Julian and Tansy. I was on the other side of Julian and so, I could hear him chatting away to John."

"Did John respond?"

"Yes. He did. Tansy spoke to him, too. They both made John laugh."

"Really?" Julian and Tansy?"

"Yes. They were awfully nice to John."

"And you were on the other side of Julian. Is that what you said?"

"Yes."

"So…you must have talked to him, through one course, at least."

"Yes. I was able to talk to him about Owen Banks."

"Owen Banks?"

"Yes. Julian is still sharing a flat in Bristol with Pomeroy and Owen Banks."

"You sat beside Julian and you talked about Owen Banks: a boy you hardly know?"

"Well…yes. What's wrong, Mum? You sound…What should I have talked about?"

"It would have been polite of you to have asked Julian a bit about himself. You had an opportunity to get to know him and you didn't try to… Oh! Rosie! Rosie!"

"But, Mum! Julian is Héloïse's boyfriend. Well! Maybe not her boyfriend, exactly. But she does like him and he really likes her and…Well! I didn't want to interfere."

"Oh! For Goodness' sake, Rosie!" interrupted Liz, irritably. "Forget Héloïse! In my view, she sounds as if she's…"

"What's wrong, Mum. I've never heard you sounding this angry."

"No. Of course you haven't. I'm sorry. It has been a long day."

"Did you not enjoy…?"

"Christmas dinner with Mr. Laurence? It was fine. It dragged on a bit. That's all. Listen! I'm tired, Rosie. I'd prefer to talk about it at some other time."

"All right, Mum. I'll leave you. But, call me later when you feel better. Promise?"

Rosalind had sounded baffled and sad and Liz was now furious with herself for having soured her daughter's happy day. She who, as an astrologer, was supposed to be able to stand back, in detached fashion, in order to analyse relationships and the emotional responses they engendered, without judgement, had failed to control her own reaction to what her daughter had told her. She had not, in fact, realised that the maternal bond binding her to Rosalind - a bond which had previously been weak - had now become unquestionably strong. She felt as if she really had turned into a modern version of Mrs. Bennett: the fussily match-making mother in "Pride and Prejudice". In other words, she had become a woman desperate to ensure her daughter would have access to appropriate resources in adulthood, along with a kind and decent husband. If only Rosalind had seized the opportunity to engage in conversation the flawlessly polite, the attractively kind and - one might as well admit it - the immensely charming possessor of land and property, Julian Bramblewell-Eurlinn, who knew what sort of friendship might have developed? Mr. Teddy Laurence and Owen Banks - or Peregrine-Hugo, as Rosalind had once called him - would have been very quickly forgotten. Of that, Liz was certain. After all, they had lived principally in Rosalind's imagination and, in their imagined form, had no more substance than princes in a fairy-tale. Had Rosalind been given wise advice prior to the Christmas Day dinner, at Bramblewell Manor, she might have ended up writing poetry for Julian - not for Teddy Laurence - that very evening:

Liz sighed. She should not have shown her irritation over the way Rosalind had behaved, all the same. Had it not been for Rosalind's own even temper and sense of fair play, the conversation might have ended differently, with her, Rosalind, bringing the telephone call to a close, abruptly and in a huff. She, Liz, was very lucky to have a daughter like Rosalind and she knew she should make more of an effort to demonstrate her appreciation.

It struck Liz, then, that one way of diverting Rosalind's attention away from Teddy Laurence would be to give her tasks to do, at home, in connection with "The Aspects of Venus." The purpose of this strategy would be to render Rosalind so busy that she would have no room, in her crowded mind, for thoughts of Teddy. She, Liz, could also arrange for her to have weekend riding lessons at stables in Cheshire. Liz could not help reflecting on the fact, also, that, as a result of having these "finishing" lessons, Rosalind - were she to run into Julian Bramblewell-Eurlinn again - would undoubtedly be ready to impress him. But, wait! Wasn't such scheming ridiculous?

Liz went to bed, that night, wondering what sort of person she, herself, had become. It was normal to do one's best for one's child, but surely behaviour had to be measured! Liz felt, in a vague sort of way, as if she were teetering on the edge of some Dante-ish morass. It was not the desire to divert Rosalind's attention away from Teddy Laurence that was bothering her: in steering Rosalind away from Teddy, her behaviour was justifiable, obviously. No. It was the fact that she was attempting to push Rosalind towards Julian Bramblewell-Eurlinn that was giving rise to feelings of anxiety. She suspected – or rather knew – she was taking a step too far. Rosalind was young, of course, and still required guidance. To what extent, though, could a parent steer a daughter - or son - in a certain direction and do so, with an easy conscience? Liz could argue that, being an astrologer, she was helping Rosalind to live, according to her lights. And although she had not studied Julian's astrological chart in any depth, she had noticed that his Sun was in conjunction with Rosalind's Midheaven. In other words, Julian, simply by being in Rosalind's life, would improve her position in society. Were Liz an ambitious mother, the presence of this aspect - this connection - across the two charts would be enough to convince her that a friendship - and later, a firmer relationship - between the two, should be pursued. The rest - the additional aspects, challenging or otherwise - could be sorted out in due course. But were Liz to interfere any further than she already had, would she be breaking her own code of ethics?

As Liz was struggling with these thoughts, Teddy Laurence, in his apartment in Liverpool, was sitting in the comfortable chair near a large window in his living room, his body stretched out in a pose that suggested extreme fatigue. He could not understand why he was feeling so tired, though. He had cooked much of a meal and had contributed to a lively conversation, but that was all he had done that day, really. Of course, his two guests had remained in his apartment for quite a while after the end of the meal and talking could have tired all of them. The hours had slipped by, though, with no one present paying attention to the sky darkening outside. However, Lynn had finally gasped when she had, in absent-minded fashion, looked at her watch around eight o' clock.

"Oh, no!" she had exclaimed, startled. "That can't be the right time, can it?"

Lynn and Liz had both stood up at once and there had been a scramble to look for coats and to assemble other belongings: the heavy boots that had been taken off in order to be exchanged for the more comfortable footwear that had been thoughtfully brought by the two women; the presents that been given and received; the coats that had been hung up to dry. Teddy had insisted on his two guests having one last cup of coffee before leaving, but finally, they had been off.

Teddy had cleared up a little, but had decided, shortly afterwards, to sit down with a cup of tea, in the chair by the window. Sensing that he was now drifting into sleep, though, he straightened his back in order to stay alert. He knew that were he to fall asleep, he would wake up cold and with stiff limbs. He forced himself, therefore, to go to the kitchen, to make another attempt at finishing the washing up. On the way there, he switched on his CD player and the corridor leading to the kitchen was filled with a sound of music that Teddy would once have described as being numbingly monotonous, but which recently he had begun to use deliberately to bring order to his brain when his thoughts were straying into negativity. Teddy turned the volume to "low". His apartment had been sound-proofed, but it was late and he wanted to make completely sure that no noise would filter down to the flat below, where an old-ish couple, who went to bed early, lived.

In the kitchen, Teddy put plates and cups away in a cupboard. And as he did so, he suddenly thought of a puzzling incident that had taken place three days before Christmas. He had gone to Louis Lindsay's house with books which he felt sure Louis would benefit from reading during the Christmas holiday. Just because Louis had decided not to apply for a place at Cambridge University did not mean, after all, that he could give up studying. In fact, the opposite was the case. Louis had to continue to study in order to be ready to seize those opportunities that would present themselves to him in the years that were ahead.

Teddy had parked his car in a convenient spot and then, had walked around a corner, in order to approach, on foot, the house where Louis lived. As he had turned that corner, though, he had seen the door of the house opening and two women in semi-uniform emerging, followed by a man who had remained on the threshold, as the women had made their way to their car, parked a short distance along the road. Teddy had assumed the man to have been Louis Lindsay's father. He had looked thin and undernourished, as if he had been ill, but he had also looked as if he had been beginning to make a recovery. The women, whom Teddy had taken to be carers or nurses, had cheerily waved, before they had climbed into their vehicle.

"Ta-ta, love!" one of them had called. "See you next time! Take care, love!"

The man at the door had watched until the women had driven away and then, had gone back into the house. He had seemed to have been capable of walking, albeit with the help of a stick. He had unquestionably not been as incapacitated as Louis had once suggested and, crucially, he had not seemed to have been unhappy at having been looked after by strangers, as Louis had also intimated he would be. Teddy had left the books on the step and had walked away, to avoid an embarrassing encounter, while wondering why Louis had lied, or rather, had appeared to have been lying. Why had he exaggerated the severity of his father's poor health in order to provide himself with an excuse for not rising to an academic challenge? And was it actually the thought of the academic challenge that was sapping his confidence or was it the suspicion that he would not be able to cope socially with life at Cambridge? In that respect, had his relationship with the more sophisticated Portia Price not actually helped him, but rather, had made him aware of the gaps in his own knowledge, when it came to social etiquette?

Teddy returned to his living room, his mind troubled. What time was it? Half past ten? Was it too late to call Louis Lindsay's mobile number? Perhaps. He sent a text message, instead, that being, "Where are you?"

Louis Lindsay, at that moment, was leaning against the gates of the Church of St. Nicholas, the sailors' church, near Pierhead, where the Mersey softly lapped against the landing stages that accommodated the ferries that crossed the river. Louis often went to that spot at night, simply to calm his mind and to think. He liked to be close to the statue of the mother and her little boy, in the grounds of the church. He knew he was being fanciful, but nevertheless, when near the statue, he imagined that his own mother- the mother he had lost - was not far away. The statue, for him, had become a strong symbol of the maternal love he had known only fleetingly.

When he received Teddy's message, Louis responded by phoning and agreeing to drop into Teddy's flat for a few minutes. He walked along the side of the river quickly, having suspected, from the tone of Teddy's voice, that something was amiss: something needed attention. The night was chilly and Louis, his shoulders hunched under his dark woollen jacket, put his hands in his pockets to keep them warm. He wondered what could be wrong. Had the Somerland boy run away from home again? Or had there been some mishap connected with the youth club? "On such a night as this," he thought, "things happen." Christmas was not over and he felt, still, a kind of breath-held tension in the air.

After talking to Louis on the telephone, Teddy had gone directly to his computer which had been set up on a narrow table, in the corridor that led from his living room to his bedroom. He had switched on a new acquisition, this being a white-light lamp beside the screen, and then, had thought for a moment, as if wondering where to begin. But now, he was preoccupied with searching through lists of video films on YouTube. As he had suspected, there were many short films that provided good advice for young people on how to improve their performance when speaking in public or when present at an interview. There were also etiquette classes. In fact Louis could learn everything he needed to know about social behaviour, from the way to conduct himself when dining out to the correct clothes to wear on formal occasions. All that he had to do was to consult the World Wide Web. Of course, he had to know first, though, what he should be looking for. Perhaps he actually needed personal tuition, Would he be prepared to dive in at the deep end and travel to London in order to be tutored there? It occurred to Teddy, then, that he, himself, could pay for a London course, or perhaps even two, presenting them to Louis in the guise of a present to thank him for the voluntary work he had done at the youth club in Liverpool. After all, the hours Louis had spent there had barely been acknowledged, ever. It was time that they were, in fact. It was Christmas after all.

The door bell rang. Teddy stood up and went to greet his visitor, with a determined step. The boy had to be taken in hand.

CHAPTER 67

Tansy

After spending Christmas at Bramblewell Manor, Julian Bramblewell-Eurlinn accompanied his mother to London, where she had an apartment near Mount Street. Then, he continued onwards with her to Ywen Manor, where she was planning to convert empty buildings in the grounds into a home for herself.

Julian went up to Bristol early, five days before the new term began, to the flat he shared with Pomeroy and Owen. In fact, Pomeroy had already arrived. He had previously told Julian that he had had a "brilliant" holiday at Bramblewell Manor and so Julian was surprised to find him sitting in the kitchen, his elbows on the table and his head in his hands as, brow furrowed, he read Antonio Damasio's book about Descartes with an earnestness that suggested he was looking for an answer to a problem, or else was desperate to distract himself. When Julian asked, "What's wrong?" Pomeroy answered in a resigned way that suggested he thought there was no point in concealing what had happened to him. His relationship with Tansy had ended. It had been foundering for a while but had come to a complete halt, abruptly, when he and Tansy had been taking it in turns to drive back to Bristol from Bramblewell Manor.

"But, what did you do? What did you say?" asked Julian, shocked. "Presumably, you quarrelled over something. Did you?"

"Somewhere in Wales, when I had taken over the wheel and she had settled in the front seat, beside me, I told her...Well! I didn't say that I was bored exactly, but I told her that our lives had become a bit predictable, really. We followed a routine. You know...lectures...lunch in the Union...tutorials..."

"What were you expecting?" interrupted Julian, looking baffled. "Afternoons at the Zoo?"

"I just thought that we needed a break from each other so that we could try something new, separately."

"A new relationship, you mean."

"I didn't say that exactly."

"Do you have anyone else in mind?"

"Anyone else? No. There isn't anyone else. Not yet, anyway."

"So, how did Tansy…?"

"React? She was upset, obviously. Well! Not obviously. I didn't know how she was going to react. But, yeah…She was upset. She sort of became …silent. And then, I started shouting…just to get a reaction from her."

"Were you out of your mind?"

"I know. I know. I know. I shouldn't have. It was awful. She reacted as if I'd hit her. You know…"

"No. Actually, I don't know. What exactly did she do?"

"She sort of crumpled up in the seat and stayed like that until we had reached Bristol. I drove up Goldney Avenue and was about turn into Regent Street when she said she wanted to come here, to this flat, first, to collect some belongings she had left here. And so, I drove her here and she gathered up everything that was hers, without saying a word, and then she left. Her face was very white. I was going to follow her but I decided to watch from the window instead. She sat on the wall outside for a long while. She must have been shocked. I mean…I'd never shouted at her before."

"Why would you? Tansy, of all people!"

"I know. I hate myself. Actually…would you go to see her? She isn't answering her 'phone. I'm worried about her. Will you check that she is all right?"

"Yes. I'll go to see her," said Julian, his expression grim. "I'll go now."

Julian had known Pomeroy since their time together at boarding school. They had been class - mates there from the age of twelve until the age of eighteen, and ties of loyalty, based on long-standing friendship and shared experiences, bound them still. However, there were times when Julian found it hard to recognise the Pomeroy he had known growing up and this was one such occasion. Pomeroy's concern, Julian had noted, had been for Tansy's well-being: it had not been generated by a desire to resume his relationship with her. Therefore, there would be little to offer by way of consolation.

Julian strode along St. Paul's Road, before crossing Pembroke Road and continuing in the direction of the Students' Union. Momentarily, he wondered if he should drop into the building to see if the shop was open. Then, he thought the better of it. How would a present possibly help to mend a broken heart? It would create no more than a momentary distraction and since the giver would not be Pomeroy, it would mean little. Julian headed instead for Victoria Square and crossed it, taking the diagonal path amongst the trees. There were leaves still on the ground. "Like fallen tears," thought Julian, unexpectedly lyrically.

Boyce's Avenue seemed busy. Despite the fact that the late afternoon sun was losing strength, suggesting it was time for people to return home to a cosy hearth, the cafés were still doing business. Julian paused briefly to look at antiques in a shop window, his mother's new home in mind, before striding across the main road to Princess Victoria Street and, then, heading down The Mall.

Tansy was slow to answer the call of the door-bell in her upper floor flat when Julian rang. She looked relieved to see that it was Julian who had arrived, when she finally did open the door. But, he, Julian, was disturbed to see how changed she was in appearance. Her expression showed signs of strain and she seemed to be having difficulty moving. It was as if she had been ill for a long time and, as a consequence, had been drained of energy. She was dressed in a grey jumper and blue jeans and was wearing, also, thick, white woollen socks. But, over these clothes, she had put on a pale blue, fluffy, polyester dressing gown, of the type that one could buy in supermarkets. Julian realised that the garment was acting as a kind of comfort blanket for Tansy. She was clearly suffering, the initial emotional pain having transferred itself, in part, into her body. Julian helped her to return to her sitting room, where an electric fire was thankfully heating the space adequately. A soft lavender sofa had been pulled to the centre of the room and turned so that it faced the fire and Tansy must have been lying on it, for a woollen blanket had been cast aside there, presumably when she had been summoned to the door. Julian helped her to lie down again and covered her with the blanket. It was white and heavy.

"Where do you keep the spare pillows?" he asked. "Are there any?"

Tansy looked at Julian for a moment, as if not comprehending, but then, told him there were some on the top shelf of the wardrobe in her bedroom. Julian fetched two and placed them under her head. He became aware of the fact that she was shivering. He wondered when she had last eaten or had even drunk anything hot.

"Tea?" he asked.

She shook her head.

"I can't" she said, but then, changed her mind. "I mean, yes! Tea please, Julian. But wait! I'll make it."

She tried to raise herself on one elbow, but Julian told her to lie down again and to keep warm. He went into the small kitchen and found wrapped bread, as well as butter and an unopened carton of milk, in the fridge. In a cupboard, he came across a mundane tin of beans beside a small tin of Royal Oscietra caviar, which had presumably been given to Tansy as a Christmas present. The bread would be palatable enough if toasted, he hoped. He switched on the toaster and tipped the beans and a thick slice of butter into a small saucepan, remembering that he had once been told that anything cooked in butter would be good. There was not much else in the kitchen cupboards, anyway. Obviously, Tansy had not been inclined to go shopping upon arriving back in Bristol, Given the state she must have been in, it was surprising that she had even made her way to her flat, on her own.

The beans having been heated, Julian buttered the toast, cut it up into small squares on a large plate and took the food, as well as the tea, into the sitting room.

"Try!" he urged Tansy, as she looked at the simple feast with some reluctance. He scooped up a piece of toast and some beans on a spoon and held the spoon in front of her mouth.

"Oh, Julian!" she said and tried to smile, although in an exhausted kind of way.

"Have you not slept?" Julian asked.

"I have a bit," she answered, adding, "but, I wake up and I wish I hadn't woken up. I don't know why…I don't know why Pomeroy has had this effect on me. Well! Maybe I do. I can't cope with male anger, you see, and I never thought Pomeroy of all people, would lose his temper with me. I expected too much, obviously. I think it's hard for men to live up to the expectations I project on to them. And then, I can't cope with the emotional consequences of what I do. I can't cope when male anger is directed at me."

"And why should you?" said Julian, feeling anger rising within himself at the thought of the gentle Tansy being treated badly. He realised he had better go out for a while to cool off.

"I'll do some shopping for you," he said abruptly. "What would you like? Lucozade? Does that appeal?"

Tansy nodded.

"Try to finish your tea," he urged her. "I'll be back soon."

"Take the key," she murmured. "It's in a dish in the kitchen."

She closed her eyes, then, as if sleepy, but her expression looked more relaxed than it had, when Julian had first arrived.

Outside in the street, Julian took his mobile 'phone out of the pocket of his jacket and sent a text message to Pomeroy, the message being:

"Tansy coping. Staying at her flat tonight to make sure."

Then, he made his way to the shops in Princess Victoria Street, where, in addition to Lucozade, he bought enough supplies to last Tansy a week, so that if she were unable to leave her flat during that time, she would not be hungry. On a whim, he added pudding rice and custard in a tin to the food he had bought, having remembered that Gwenny had once told him that, when recovering from winter illnesses, her body weight having dropped as a consequence, all she wanted to consume was nursery food, simple and unchallenging to the stomach.

It became dark quickly. That evening, as Tansy slept sporadically on the sofa, opposite the fire, Julian, who had sat down on a rug, on the floor beside her, decided that, the next day, he would try to persuade her to go with him to the university's medical services on St. Michael's Hill, to ask if she could be allowed to be absent for a few days, at the beginning of term, to give her the opportunity to regain her mental and physical strength, along with her composure. After that, he would drive her to Ywen Manor, to stay with Gwenny and Horatio. It was better that she not be left alone. Solitude was fine for some and effected healing, but Tansy would respond better to cosy cosseting. Her mind, if not stimulated or kept busy, could drift quickly into excessive negativity, Julian suspected. Her emotions, if not properly directed, could render life sour.

After some hesitation, Tansy agreed to Julian's plan, the next morning and, as a result, he was soon driving her out of Bristol, in a north-easterly direction to Ywen Manor. He had telephoned Gwenny in advance and she, shocked by what he had told her, was ready to welcome the undermined Tansy with warmth and sympathy and a hot drink in a cosy kitchen.

Julian had planned simply to leave Tansy at the manor and to return to Bristol straight away, but Horatio stopped him.

"Mother wants to see you," he said. "I think she thinks the news is good."

"What news?"

"You'd better talk to her."

Julian found his mother in one of the buildings at the rear of the manor, talking to a young architect.

"Ah! Julian!" she exclaimed, warmly. "What do you think of the American loft look? White walls, white floor..."

"Horatio said you had good news."

"Ah! Yes! I've been contacted by a chap who wants to buy a piece of the Château du Crâne from you."

"Buy? What are you talking about? I'd have thought you wouldn't have wanted the château to be sold."

"Well! The chap wants to buy only a part of it. I'm wondering if you could lease it to him instead of selling it to him, actually. Is that permissible under French law? I'm not sure. But whatever you managed to do, you would surely end up with money that would help you considerably to pay for the repair of the rest of the château. I think there is nothing for it really but to sacrifice a bit for the sake of the rest. Anyway, you could contact the chap who wants to buy a bit to see what he is like. I told him that the château is no longer mine and that he should talk to you."

"Is he British?"

"Oh, yes. He lives not far from Bramblewell territory, I suspect. In the Wirral, in any case."

"Well...that sounds...good. At least it will be fairly easy to make enquires about him, I imagine."

"Come into the manor and I'll give you details of how to get in touch with him. He's expecting your call. Oh! He's been in contact with the fellow you know in France, as well. The son of one of the Counts du Crâne who sold the château to our family, in the first place."

"He has been doing his homework, hasn't he? What's his name?"

"Mr. Mallory, I think. Yes. Mr. Christopher Mallory...Known as Kit. You should talk to him, Julian. Maybe something could be arranged."

"A good deed brings its rewards," said Tansy with a gentle smile, when Julian explained to her, before leaving, what his mother had told him. "Thank you for what you did for me, Julian. I felt as if I'd never be able to get up from that sofa in my flat…but I feel so much better now."

Julian abhorred physical violence, but as he drove back to Bristol, he reflected on the fact that words could deliver blows that were almost as harmful as those that were physical in origin. Tansy's reaction to Pomeroy's words had convinced him of that. The mind and the body were intertwined in ways that were not yet widely acknowledged, but deserved to be.

CHAPTER 68

The Letter

After celebrating Christmas in Belle-Isle, Héloïse de Sauzon decided to spend a week or two in Paris, living in the apartment of her sister, Jacqueline, while considering, seriously, how she was going to fill in the remaining months of her gap year, before beginning her life as a university student. She had left Belle-Isle, knowing that her mother was still angry about the fact that she, Héloïse, had arranged for her younger sister, Marie-Colette, to appear in a film. In the Countess de Sauzon's eyes, such behaviour was considered to be infra-dig. Now, Héloïse, was waking up, nightly, knowing she had had strange dreams. She had associated them with her mother's displeasure, although she knew there had not seemed to have been an evident connection. Each time, upon wakening, she had been aware, also, of the fact that she had been dreaming in vivid, luminous colours and had assumed that natural chemicals in her brain had been responsible for that phenomenon. Had those chemicals been stimulated by the extreme feelings of remorse she had felt as a result of hurting her mother, in the way that she had? She had wanted to make amends, but at the same time, she had truly felt that the new experience of being in the lime-light would help her excruciatingly shy sister to emerge from under her shell and she had not wanted to dissuade Marie-Colette from appearing in the film for that reason. Besides, the Count de Sauzon had seemed to think that Marie-Colette would benefit from the experience.

On the fourth morning of her stay in Paris, Héloïse went into the kitchen at breakfast time, knowing that she looked tired, given the dark shadows under her eyes. Jacqueline, dressed in a white shirt and blue jeans, folded to a level slightly above her ankles, was already there, engaged in preparing good coffee. She carried the percolator to the table with care since she was wearing pale blue court shoes with very high heels, which were not conducive to good balance.

"Tu as bien dormi?" asked Jacqueline, a trace of anxiety evident in her voice, although she was smiling.

"Better than on Tuesday night," answered Héloïse in order to reassure her. Jacqueline always felt unsettled, when those on whom she depended in some way did not behave as expected. The thought of Héloïse's restless nights had been making her nervous, although what she had feared had not been clear.

"I like being here, incognita," Héloïse went on, comfortingly as if to persuade Jacqueline she was happy. "One is not known and not noticed in a big city."

"A letter arrived," said Jacqueline, then, without taking up the conversation. "By post."

"What?"

"This letter."

"For me?"

"For you."

Jacqueline handed her sister the thick, cream-coloured envelope she had been keeping in the pocket of her jeans.

"It's addressed to both of us," said Héloïse blankly.

"But, your name is first."

"The post mark is Parisian. Who sent it?"

"Find out!" Jacqueline retorted before shrugging as if in exasperation.

Héloïse tore the envelope open, pausing only a moment to note the fragile, blue tissue lining. Inside, on thick, creamy paper, there was a hand-written letter from an Antoine du Crâne. He wanted to know if he might be permitted to arrange to meet either Héloïse or Jacqueline with a view to establishing some sort of regular contact with one or both of them, since, after all, they were his blood relatives."

"Blood relatives?" said Jacqueline, as if baffled.

"He's the chap Julian met," said Héloïse. "Didn't Julian mention him to you?"

"Yes, but…he didn't mention anything about our being blood relatives."

"When I was talking to Julian, last summer, in Bordeaux, we worked out that Grand'maman might be the missing sister of the Counts du Crâne."

"Missing sister? What are you talking about?"

"Julian told me that when the Château du Crâne had been sold to his grand-mother by the three sons of the old Count du Crâne, the brothers' sister had not made an appearance. Julian did know, though, that the sister had been called Gabrielle."

"But…"

"Do you remember the diary I found on the night of the big storm in Belle-Isle?" interrupted Héloïse, in a rush, before Jacqueline could continue.

"Of course I do! It was Grand'maman's diary."

"There was a line in that diary that escaped our scrutiny because so much else was holding our attention."

"Which line?"

"Madame Gabrielle said that her brother had gone with her to the Gare St. Jean in Bordeaux to pick up a friend from Liverpool and then, that her brother had driven the two of them back to the château."

"Yes. And?"

"Which château, Jacqueline?"

"I don't know…It didn't cross my mind."

"Well, Julian and I think she had been referring to the Château du Crâne…and that means that we are descended from the Counts du Crâne."

"On our mother's side of the family?"

"Yes."

"And... that means...doesn't it?... that we are descended from the Angélique who wrote the journal that the Bramblewell schoolgirls found in the Château du Crâne."

"Exactly. The Angélique of the legend and the curse."

"No! Mon Dieu! It's not possible! I mean, Maman would have known! And Grand'maman would surely have told all of us that we were descended from old nobility on both sides of our family. She wouldn't have concealed information like that from us! Did she feel that the mistake she had made in 1968 had been so great that she could not even mention the family that had banished her, subsequently? Surely not! I'd find that hard to believe!"

Jacqueline sat down on a kitchen stool, crossing her legs at the knees and clasping her hands in front of them. She looked at her sister as if trying to take in the implication of what had been revealed to her.

"I think I should arrange to meet this Antoine du Crâne," Héloïse said thoughtfully, looking as if she had not been listening to her sister's words.

"Yes," Jacqueline agreed. "Yes. You must."

After paying due attention to what she would write, Héloïse sent a letter to Antoine that same day, by regular post, but appending her e-mail address to speed up communication. A meeting was arranged, therefore, almost as soon as the letter had been received.

On the day of the rendezvous, Héloïse chose to wear pale grey trousers along with a very short, grey jacket and a grey blouse, adorned with opulent frills. After rejecting two pairs of shoes that she had tried on, she opted finally for white, court shoes with heels so high that they equalled those on Jacqueline's pale blue shoes.

"The blouse is excessively fussy," said Jacqueline.

Héloïse exchanged it for a pale grey waistcoat.

"Better?" she asked.

"Honestly! You look like a business woman, now!" said Jacqueline, disapprovingly. "Antoine du Crâne will think that you are in pursuit of hidden family money!"

"Oh! Jacqueline! Please!"

"I am serious! Our clothes communicate messages about us and our concealed intentions!"

Héloïse changed again, into a pink, flouncy dress, a long beige jumper and knee-high, pale beige boots.

"Surely my hairstyle is feminine - looking enough," she thought, shaking her head so that her glossy, flaxen locks rippled down her back like a stream. She shrugged then, in a "that will have to do" fashion, but before leaving for the meeting, she put on soft pink lipstick to complete her "look".

Antoine du Crâne's apartment was situated beyond a wrought iron gate and a courtyard. The stately walls of the apartment building, as a whole, were pale blond and the mansard roof, greyish blue and slated. Héloïse acknowledged the building would have been, at one time, an "hôtel particulier" owned by an aristocratic family, before the Reign of Terror. She went up to Antoine's apartment in a lift which had an air of elegance, from times gone by, about it. She rang the bell beside his door and waited until a housekeeper opened it and invited her to enter.

Antoine du Crâne came out of one of the reception rooms smiling and greeting his newly-found cousin with great charm. He was nicely dressed, Héloïse thought, in the English-gentleman style that Frenchmen who were anglophiles favoured. Leading Héloïse into the book-lined room from which he had emerged, he explained, without preamble, that he had known of her existence and that of her sisters and brother for some time. In fact, his father had been keeping a watchful eye on her family, from a distance, for decades. However, his father and he, himself, had felt that what might have been perceived as an intrusion might not have been welcomed by either Gabrielle, who was very proud, or her family and so, neither he nor his father had attempted to make contact. However, once he, Antoine, had met Julian Bramblewell-Eurlinn, he had felt confident that an approach by him might be appreciated. He had gleaned from what Julian had told him that she, Héloïse, had realised that Madame Gabrielle de Talence, had, in fact, been named Gabrielle du Crâne, at birth.

Héloïse had felt as if a small bird had fluttered its tiny wings within her heart when Antoine had mentioned Julian's name, but she attempted, now, not to allow any sign of emotion to register on her face.

"A very fine fellow is that young Englishman" Antoine added, with sincerity.

"Yes," agreed Héloïse, but did not dare to say anything else, for fear of revealing her wistfully growing attraction to Julian: an attraction nurtured by his absence. She had begun to understand that a new love had to be protected by concealment, in order to give it time to put down roots in darkness, as it were, and to grow in strength, so that no careless remark, no passing comment, thereafter, from a competitive friend or even a sister, could destroy it.

Antoine paused, bemused, as if he had guessed what Héloïse had been thinking, but then, he looked serious as he expressed his wish to become acquainted with her family, little by little, and, in particular, with Madame Gabrielle de Talence, herself. It had been his father's wish to make contact with her and, once, had tried to do so, but she had apparently been resolute in her determination to cut her brothers out of her life. They had not communicated with her when she had been banished from the Château du Crâne and had had to rely on the kindness of friends, initially, until she had recovered from the shock of her father's rejection, her mother's passive acceptance of his decision and her brothers' failure to assist her, even in secret. Why should she help her brothers to assuage their troubled consciences, now that the years were passing? For all she cared, they could suffer. They could not be suffering more, in any case, than she, herself, had suffered in her predicament, before she had found her feet and had learnt how to survive, by dint of effort and the application of cool intelligence to her problems.

"It was arguably his fault," said Antoine, with a hint of an ironic smile, while looking up at a portrait-sized photograph of General De Gaulle, hanging on the wall. "My grand-father - your great grand-father - was extremely Gaullist. Why would he not be? De Gaulle was a truly great man. I admire him, myself. I read the books he wrote assiduously and I am in awe of him, as a consequence. Of the man he was."

"But Madame Gabrielle took part in those demonstrations in 1968, in the streets of Paris, to criticise only De Gaulle's government, surely. The demonstrations were a visual criticism of the government. Not of the man, himself."

"Ouf! More than criticism!" interrupted Antoine. "But, whatever the reason for it, that action, on Gabrielle's part, led to her banishment from the Château du Crâne: her family home. She was never to return. My grandfather could not cope with the perceived dishonour she had brought upon the family. And so he disowned her. Totally."

"But she was so young! And she had been misled by other students. Or rather, by one in particular."

"Is that an excuse? Are we not responsible for our own actions, even when young?"

Héloïse nodded thoughtfully. Of course, Antoine was right. Youthfulness was not an excuse for allowing emotions to drown one's ability to think, prior to taking action, especially if one had enjoyed the privilege of having been educated well. How could she think otherwise? But then, she remembered that it had been Teddy Laurence who had expressed his horror at the way Gabrielle had been treated by her father. He had found it hard to believe that a father could have cast a daughter of his own out of her home.

Héloïse mentioned Teddy Laurence's objections to Antoine, bringing to his attention, in particular, Teddy's dismay at the lack of compassion shown, the unwillingness to overlook the folly of youth and the inability to effect a reconciliation.

"But, presumably this English friend of yours did not live

through World War II in France, did he?" asked Antoine rather sharply. "So much went on during that war! Even today, there are families in which the subject is never raised. It's complicated. Can one fitfully judge the actions of people who went through that war, if one has not endured their war-time experiences or lived in their war-time environment? But, enough! Let us drop this subject! What is important is that we have found each other and that, with luck, there will be a long-awaited reconciliation with Madame Gabrielle...thanks, of course, largely to young Julian. By the way, he'll be coming to see me again, in due course."

"What? Here in Paris?"

"Oh, yes. Here in Paris. Maybe soon."

CHAPTER 69

Traversi-Trimm

For some months, Caterina Traversi had been in almost complete charge of Traversi-Trimm Publishing. Dorothy Trimm, who had offered the position to her and who now trusted her to deal with the bulk of the work on her own, dotted in and out of the offices - or the uffizzi, as Caterina was inclined to call them - for short periods daily but, largely, left Caterina to make decisions as to what to publish and whom to employ.

Caterina had never before been respected in the way that she was now. The realisation that employees at Traversi-Trimm took her seriously and did not regard her as being a mere dilettante, playing at being a business woman, took her by surprise and forced her to look at herself and the world around her differently. "What are you? A publisher!" she would nevertheless say, when looking at her own reflection in a big mirror in her bedroom, in the apartment that she had rented in Little Sutton, to the south of the Wirral, as if she could not quite believe that she was the bearer of so many responsibilities. At home in Italy, constantly undermined and criticised by her mother, she had grown up feeling, essentially worthless. She recognised that fact now. She could detach herself from her feelings and could analyse the reasons for their power over her, in an objective way, even though she knew that she could not subvert their control completely. She still felt guilty at having failed her mother in some unspecified way. She suspected, though, that she had simply not been the type of daughter that had been desired. And in lucid moments she acknowledged the fact that she would not have wanted to have resembled Beatrice, her mother's favourite, in character or behaviour, anyway.

Caterina's father, aware of his wife's inability to dispense motherly love, when dealing with Caterina, had tried to compensate by showering his daughter with money and presents. Caterina had taken advantage of his largesse, making impulsive demands, constantly. She had asked for a sumptuous apartment in Rome, for example, and had requested new clothes with the coming of each season, along with money for fine art, to hang on her walls. She had loved the paintings she had bought, but generally, after shopping sprees or visits to auction houses, she had been left feeling dissatisfied and unfulfilled. Now she recognised that her dissatisfaction had stemmed from the fact that the money she had spent had not been her own: she had not earned it. The job Dorothy Trimm had offered her in the Wirral and the training Kit Mallory had given her, while she had been working for him, had been spell-breakers. They had given her the keys that had enabled her to leave the invisible cage in which she had been held. Now, she was able to give expression to the talents which had previously been squashed and hidden.

Dorothy Trimm, motherly by nature, despite the brittleness that had always been a feature of her relationship with her own daughter, Hilary, had noticed the change in Caterina. A wish to consider the solutions to problems that arose, with an attitude that was mature and modest, had replaced her former petulant belief that her Papa's money would extract her from every jam. Dorothy noticed, also, that Caterina was now looking even more beautiful than before. It was as if she had awakened from a sleep and was now fully alert. Yet, underneath the pleasing façade, Dorothy was aware of a sadness that sometimes made Caterina look wistful and distant.

"Is there anything troubling you, pet?" she asked Caterina one day, when bringing to her desk a cup of coffee, which had been made by the new, gleaming, chrome machine which Dorothy had acquired for her own office and which she had been anxious to use.

The question had come out of the blue and Caterina did not know immediately how to respond. Was anything troubling her? VAT? Authors' contracts? Quibbling proof-readers?

"Boyfriend trouble, I mean," persisted Dorothy, ever the inquisitive one.

"I have no permanent boyfriend, now," answered Caterina, cautiously.

"I think you had a bit of a thing about your boss on the ship, didn't you? Kit Mallory, I mean."

"Oh! He was…nice. Yes. But…"

"But, too old for you?"

"No. Not that. I don't mind dating someone older…but, there was…"

"What?"

"Someone else in the picture."

"The French woman, Madame Gabrielle?"

"Yes. There was the French woman. I thought…Anyway, it doesn't matter now."

"Hilary and I noticed that there was a frisson in the air when Mr. Mallory met Madame Gabrielle. She seemed to be thrown by your presence, when you turned up, of course."

"Was she?"

"My dear! She couldn't bear to be in the same room as you! Don't you remember? You must have noticed."

Caterina looked down at her desk and then said:

"She had tea with me, once."

"Oh?" said Dorothy, raising her eyebrows, as if saying to herself, "I bet that was an interesting experience!"

Caterina lowered her eyes again and looked away, imagining the pain Madame Gabrielle must have endured simply because she, Caterina, had been present on the ship. But, what was an attractive woman expected to do in such circumstances? Life was unfair, in the sense that natural beauty was visited only on some. In any case, her youthful beauty had not always served her well, as it had attracted, principally, the sort of men who had not wanted to help her to develop her own character. Madame Gabrielle might have been cheered to have heard that soupcon of information, along with the news that, although Caterina had been working in the Wirral for months, Kit Mallory, who lived there, also, had made no attempt to contact her, for any reason, even though she had been interviewed by reporters from two local papers, to which she knew he subscribed.

As if reading her thoughts, Dorothy asked:

"Have you been in touch with Mr. Mallory recently?"

"No. Not at all."

"That's a pity, seeing as he lives so near here."

"If you are insinuating that I accepted this post in order to be near him, I can assure you that I didn't, Dorothy," said Caterina, firmly. "I really, really wanted to do this job and I can honestly say I have been thrilled to have gained so much experience. Believe me when I say that Mr. Mallory has scarcely figured in my thoughts. I've had a marvellous time working for you."

"Yes. And your being here has been marvellous for me, too. Trimm Publishing would have sunk into oblivion without an injection of Traversi money. Your father has been astonishingly generous. But, what I was going to say was that Kit Mallory will be telephoning you soon, if he hasn't already done so."

"Really?"

"Yes. He got in touch with me this morning to find out if I minded if he offered a job to you that would take up two days of your time and would mean your travelling to Paris."

"With him?"

"No. I don't think so."

Dorothy smiled gently upon seeing the look of disappointment that had flitted across Caterina's face.

"I told him that you were largely in charge of Traversi-Trimm and that you would make your own decisions," she added, kindly.

Caterina nodded, looking thoughtfully into the distance.

"Maybe you'll meet someone nice in Paris," suggested Dorothy, then. "I shouldn't be surprised. You are a beautiful young woman."

She leaned forward, her two hands on Caterina's desk.

"Whatever you do, don't waste your life dreaming of the what-might-have-been, pet," she urged. "Think of what happened to my Hilary. She wasted years waiting for Lord Bramblewell to fall in love with her. I actually think she thought he would do so, eventually, just because she was besotted with him. Of course, if A is attracted to B, it does not always follow that B will be attracted to A, in the game of love! How many women fail to grasp that basic fact? And, just reflect on what happened to my daughter in the end! Did Lord Bramblewell fall for my capable, loyal, educated Hilary? He did not! He fell for Miss Susie Sutton: she who was sans education, sans breeding, sans anything at all except her red sandals and her short, red dress. What I am impressing on you, Caterina, is this: if you don't see a light in a man's eyes, the first time he meets you, forget him. Find someone else."

"Find someone else," said Caterina, echoing Dorothy's words, as if in a semi-trance. "You are probably right, Dorothy. One can waste too much time dreaming and, through doing that, blocking other options."

"You're a sensible girl, pet," said Dorothy. "You deserve better than a man who hasn't bothered to call you until now."

The next day, Caterina's young personal assistant, Polly, asked if she, Caterina, would accept a telephone call from a Mr. Kit Mallory.

"Yes," answered Caterina, revealing neither delight nor surprise, despite the fact that her heart had started to beat quickly with the thrill of anticipation. She lifted up the receiver of the land-line telephone on her desk.

"Mr. Mallory?"

"Miss Traversi! May I call you Caterina, as before?"

Caterina laughed softly, indicating her assent, while becoming aware of the fact that Kit Mallory's voice, firm and commanding, was having the effect of making her feel protected. She wanted to say, "Ah! Good! You are here, at last! Now, you can take over!" But, of course, she could not say that. She listened, instead, with pleasure, as he congratulated her on the way she had transformed Dorothy Trimm's publishing house, in just a few months.

"It's part of the Traversi brand, now" explained Caterina. "I follow the directions given by my father. Some of them, anyway. I'm kept busy."

"Of course. And for that reason, I'm beginning to wonder if you will actually have time to carry out a small task for me…as a favour."

"A small task?"

" You would be required to travel to Paris to carry out the task and I have to tell you, straight away, that you would probably have to spend two or three days there. Could we discuss this over lunch or dinner, if you are interested?"

"Would this proposed task be, in any way, connected with Traversi-Trimm?"

"No. Not at all. It would be in connection with property I intend to buy in France. My own knowledge of French is not at a high enough standard for the level of conversation required and that is why I thought of you, since I know you speak French fluently, in addition to English and your native Italian, obviously."

Caterina hesitated, but for only a second.

"I'd like to meet you for lunch," she said, even though she knew that s soon as she met Mr. Mallory she would not be able to resist agreeing to his proposal, thus seizing an opportunity to please him. But, she was curious, also. What sort of property did he want to buy in France?

"You would?" she heard him saying. "Good! Where would you like to eat? And when? What about tomorrow at the Fleuve Chéri in Liverpool?"

"I'd prefer to stay in the Wirral, since I'll have to return to work quickly, but tomorrow would be fine. How about eating at

Cataphora, in Birkenhead?"

"Agreed. Mid day?"

"Fine."

The following morning, Caterina, who always dressed well, went to even greater lengths than usual to look both chic and pretty. The cream, crochet dress, over a silk lining in a matching shade, which she had decided to wear, had been fashioned to emphasize her slim waist. Her cream shoes of Italian leather, Tuscan-made, had unusually shaped high heels which drew attention to her fine ankles. Her glossy hair, her artful make-up and her hands softly scented, all contributed to the aura of specialness that she exuded. She questioned herself as to what her motives were in making such an effort to look attractive, but she convinced herself, finally, that she would do as much if she were preparing to go out to lunch with anyone, really. A client or a friend, for instance. Lunch in a nice restaurant presented one with the opportunity to dress up and so, why would one not seize the chance to do so? Mamma had always taught that one should wear clothes that were likely to enhance the beauty of one's surroundings, with the secondary consequence of making the experience of going out to a restaurant, a theatre or a concert hall as lovely as possible for one's partner, as well as for others present. Life became more amusing - or more tolerable - when one adorned it with prettiness and frivolity.

Caterina met Kit Mallory at Cataphora at the appointed hour. He was looking elegant in a dark, charcoal suit, a freshly starched, white shirt and a sober, grey tie. Caterina had wondered how she would react when she would see him. Would she be overwhelmed by emotions she would be unable to hide? In fact, what happened was that she managed to appear calm, outwardly, while being aware of the heavy beating of her heart. She was somewhat alarmed by its force. Still, she smiled while hoping her smile had not lit up her face so that it resembled that of an ingénue on a first date. She wanted to look indifferent: it was a mistake to look too enthusiastic. Enthusiasm robbed men of the thrill of the challenge.

All Italian women knew that.

The two of them, Mr. Mallory and she, were shown to a table beside a window which presented them with a view of a quiet road where greenery was in abundance.

"I'll get to the point quickly," said Kit, although he had started, in a distracted manner, to peruse the menu that had been handed to him by a waiter.

"Yes?"

"I'd like you to meet a man in Paris who knows a lot about the property I want to buy. He has old ground plans and he will be able to tell you a great deal about the history of the place, some of that history having been passed down only orally in his family. He said that if I were to fly over to Paris, he'd provide an interpreter - and, actually, his own knowledge of English is good - but I said I'd prefer an intermediary to represent me. I was thinking of you, at that point. I trust you and I know you'd be discreet."

"I can take a day or two off in order to fly over to Paris," said Caterina. "I like any time of year there."

"I'm delighted."

"I take it that this is an architectural project that you are taking on."

"Partly. It's an old piece of property near Bordeaux."

"Bordeaux?"

"Near Bordeaux. I should tell you that I want to buy one side - one flank, if you like - of a château. The Château du Crâne. About a quarter of the building, in other words."

"The name of that château is very familiar. My sister, Ida, was there last summer, during the shooting of a film."

"Yes. I heard about that. The woman who owns the château - or rather, used to own it - mentioned the film. She has handed the property over to her son, now."

"Oh."

Caterina knew it would be unseemly to ask probing questions of a personal sort, but her curiosity had been aroused by the fact that Kit's voice had softened slightly when he had said "Bordeaux" and "Château du Crâne." To calm her thoughts, Caterina looked down at the menu that had been left in front of her. It had been hand-written that day, on thick, cream-coloured paper, its pages bound together with a length of blue cord.

"I'd like to begin with something simple," she said, making it clear that she thought it was time to order. "I usually have soup before dinner in the evening, but I think I'll have some now, instead of an hors d'oeuvre. Plain celery soup, I think. What about you, Mr. Mallory?"

"Kit."

"All right. Kit, then," said Caterina, apparently lightly, but without looking up. She seemed to be absorbed in reading the rest of the menu, whereas, in reality, questions were forming rapidly in her mind. Why did Mr. Mallory want to buy a quarter of a château, so far from home? What were his plans? What was his purpose? As soon as the word "Bordeaux" had been uttered, Caterina's senses had been on the alert. She had, of course, remembered that Madame Gabrielle lived in that city. To think that she had once felt sorry for that older woman! But, now? Caterina suspected she had been out-manoeuvred by her! Mr. Mallory was clearly about to buy a quarter of a château, no less, in order to be near her! But, was that really what was happening? Had age and experience triumphed over youth and beauty? Had Madame Gabrielle, during the period that had elapsed since the end of the cruise, managed to capture Mr. Mallory's heart? Was that possible? But wait! She had to accept that Madame Gabrielle was much closer to Kit Mallory, when it came to age, than she was, herself, obviously. They would have memories of times that had passed to share. And, realistically, what had she, herself, expected? A proposal of marriage from this much older man, who had never steered a conversation with her towards the subject of romance? She had imagined, in the past, that he had loved her a little. But he, more than she, would have been aware of the inappropriateness of a liaison, given the difference in their ages and, frankly, the difference in their wealth. Kit Mallory was rich but the Traversi family was richer and knowledge of that fact would have bothered a man like Kit Mallory.

Caterina hoped her face showed no sign of her inner distress, although she knew that the joy that had enlivened her expression when they had met, a short time before, had disappeared like bubbles in soda in a crystal glass.

"By the way..." she said, sitting up straight hoping that by disciplining her body she would also discipline her wandering thoughts. "What is the name of the person I shall be meeting in Paris?"

"Antoine du Crâne," answered Kit, leaning back in his chair and looking business-like, again. "His father spent much of his life in the Château du Crâne, before it was sold to the Bramblewell-Eurlinn family. I'll send you, by e-mail, some of the topics I'd like you to cover during your conversation with him."

"Thank you," said Caterina, adding, "Shall we order, now? After soup, I'd like chicken cacciatore. Adelina makes it for me from time to time. I'll judge whose recipe is the better one!"

"Adelina is still with you?"

"Oh, yes! She stays in my apartment in Little Sutton and looks after me, still, although I do wonder sometimes who is taking care of whom! She is happy here, though."

Kit smiled but in a restrained way. He was wondering if he should mention Madame Gabrielle's name. After all,, Antoine du Crâne might bring it up in Paris and it would look as if he, Kit, had been trying to conceal a relationship with Madame Gabrielle were that to occur. For the sake of clarity, he would have to explain the background to his decision to buy one quarter of the Château du Crâne. But as he was about to do so, he heard Caterina saying:

"I assume your acquisition of a portion of the château near Bordeaux is, in some way, connected with Madame Gabrielle de Talence. Are you acting as her agent? Or has she been giving you advice as to what sort of property to buy for yourself?"

Kit responded by telling Caterina, calmly, that he was going to buy part of the château so that Madame Gabrielle could live there when she wanted to. Caterina thought he could have softened the information in some way. Could he not have said the château was going to be used by friends as a holiday home? Shocked, her thoughts began to fall into a state of disarray, quickly. She tried to focus on what her father had been saying to her in previous days. Impressed by her work at Traversi-Trimm, he had confirmed that she could return to Italy to take control of part of the Traversi organisation, at any time she wished. She had said "Not quite yet, Papa." However, now, the thought of leaving the Wirral was beginning to seem desirable. She would have to think seriously about what she should do.

Caterina's silence induced in Kit Mallory feelings of guilt. Maybe in being honest, he had been brutal. Could he not have been more gentle while simultaneously uncovering the truth? He would try to compensate by ensuring Caterina would be booked into one of the best hotels in Paris and would have a room with an interesting view. No! She would have a suite! And there would be flowers and chocolates awaiting her. But then, he wondered if such an action would be wise. Would the girl be confused by it? How would she interpret such behaviour? Why, in any case, had he asked her to go to Paris for him when the task was straightforward and could have been carried out by a professional interpreter? Why had he asked her to lunch, in fact? Had he wanted to know if he was still attractive to her, now that she had started to make a success of her own life? One could ask oneself too many questions, of course. Maybe the unconscious mind was best left undisturbed.

Kit flicked through the pages of his menu.

"Celery soup and chicken cacciatore, did you say?" he asked. "I'll have the same."

Caterina nodded but did not comment. It struck Kit that her expression, at that moment, resembled that of a pale lady in a

Renaissance painting: the type of secret-hugging lady who once would have made men dream and would have left them to wonder which philosophy was guiding her.

Caterina was far from being philosophical. She was angry, now, but was trying hard not to reveal the fact that she had descended into such a state of raw emotion. A man had invited her to lunch to tell her that he was intending to buy a piece of a castle for another woman: her aging rival! And, he wanted her, Caterina, to help him to carry out the transaction, in effect! What subtle cruelty was this? Was Mr. Mallory, in fact, aware of what he was doing? Was he simply cruel or so stupid that he was oblivious to the pain he was capable of inflicting thoughtlessly? Could she, now, go to Paris, having become aware of his apparent, dodgy taste for Schadenfreude? Well! Yes! Why not, if Mallory was paying the bill? Paris wasn't Florence, but it still could be lovely! Besides, it was always interesting to meet new people and Antoine du Crâne had a particle in his name, to show he had come from the nobility. He might even be nice.

CHAPTER 70

Correspondence

Rosalind Somerled opened the window of her bedroom and leaned out, allowing the soft rain of early Spring to refresh her face for a moment or two. Down in the garden, behind her father's house, the colours of wet grass and foliage on the high hawthorn hedge that ran along the back boundary, looked darker than they normally would when the weather was dry. The scent they exuded, when they were soaked with rain - a nettle-ish one - seemed stronger. "More dense really," Rosalind thought.

It was a Saturday afternoon and a time usually reserved for pleasant pursuits: a visit to Liz Laurier's apartment down-town, for instance, or, as had recently been the case, a short journey to a riding school beyond Chester, for preliminary lessons that Liz had insisted on booking for her daughter. However, instead of passing the time in that invigorating way, Rosalind had announced earlier that, all afternoon, she would be revising for the national examinations that would take place towards the end of the summer term. The girls in her class at Bramblewell School had been strongly advised to do so, and most, it seemed, had been intending to comply with the instruction, although all had thought it premature.

"It's ridiculous!" Portia Price had protested, in fact. "Talitha probably needs to begin to revise early, because she has to go over notes several times before she remembers them. She says so, herself, doesn't she? But I reckon that I shan't need to. Neither will you, Rosie. Or Ida. Do you think anyone will actually check what we've revised each week?"

Rosalind had not known how to answer that question. And,

she had decided, in the end, that her teachers probably knew the best way to go about revising given their experience. Perhaps it would be a good idea to follow their direction. Or to try to, anyway.

After having a mid-day meal of slowly cooked stew and berries with yoghurt, which the housekeeper had prepared early, prior to taking the rest of the weekend off, Rosalind had gone up to her room, to start studying, but she was now finding it difficult to settle. Her mother had lent her a favourite CD of minimalist music, in the hope it would help her to stop her mind from wandering, but Rosalind was yet to listen to it. She was finding it hard to do anything, really, a lethargy having crept over her. All she wanted to do was to look out of the window at the rain, the grass, the hedgerow and the field beyond, as if giving the natural world her attention had become important.

She was aware of the fact that, downstairs, her father had turned down the volume on his radio, even though he liked to listen to jazz programmes on Radio 3 on Saturday afternoons. Her brother, John, was being very quiet as well. They were both, of course, making these sacrifices to help her to study. Rosalind felt profoundly guilty, therefore, for wasting time. And yet, she could not pull herself out of what seemed to be an energy sapping state of passivity. What was wrong with her?

The advice given at school had been unequivocal.

"Begin early!" Lydia Dacre-Hill, teacher of English, had commanded forcefully. "Begin now, during the Spring term! Count the number of weeks that there are between today - today! - and the date of the first exam. Work out how much you can revise during each of those weeks and, then, write out for yourselves personal revision plans. Be realistic, but set targets, also. And if you begin to despair when reflecting on the amount of work that you will have to cover, remember this: your grand-parents had to sit much more difficult exams when they were young. Oh, yes! They did! If you bear that in mind - the fact that your grand-parents had to memorise more - your own exams will not seem to be as daunting as all that!"

Having folded the sleeves of her soft, grey, cashmere jumper up to her elbows, Miss Dacre-Hill had then written, on the classroom's white board, a set of rules that had been based on her own experiences as a school-girl. "Don't procrastinate!" had been the first rule. She had written it in big letters.

"Don't procrastinate!" Rosalind ruefully said to herself, as she returned to the table that had been put in her room so that she could use it while studying. Already, she had become an expert in the art of procrastinating, it seemed to her. The need to arrange the books on the table in neat piles, so that each book would be easily accessible had provided her with her first excuse for delaying the moment when she would have to start working. Then, she had noticed that the books on a nearby shelf also required her attention. They, too, had needed to be tidied. After that, she had decided to go down to the kitchen to fetch a cup of coffee. Finally, it had occurred to her that she, basically, lacked will power. She was not made of the right stuff! She had no right to call herself a Bramblewell girl! Or...maybe she simply worked best when she was under pressure and time was short. Weeks and weeks were to pass before the exams would begin. Maybe that was the source of her problem: the fact that her exams seemed to be as far away as the stars.

Rosalind's mobile phone began to ping, then. She picked it up. A text message had arrived from Héloïse de Sauzon! "Any news of Julian?" she had written. That was all!

It occurred to Rosalind that Héloïse rarely asked for news of anyone else, now. Her mother had warned her that she, Rosalind, was being used as a conduit through which news of Julian flowed to France, but perhaps, in Héloïse's position, far away and desperate to know what was happening in Julian's world, any teenage girl would behave in the same way! Rosalind sent a text message to Debbie, her old school friend from Bristol days, whose father, coincidentally, owned the flat in Clifton that Julian, Owen Banks and Pomeroy were renting that year. A minute or two later, Debbie sent a message in return: one that stated: "Sending e-mail." That surely meant that Debbie had news to pass on! Rosalind switched on her lap top and, while waiting for it to warm up and, of course, for Debbie's message to arrive, she jotted down notes about all that she, herself, wanted to ask or to mention.

1. Was Debbie being encouraged by her teachers to begin revision early?
2. A little piece of information! Mr. Teddy Laurence had telephoned her Dad, Gylen Somerland, one evening, to arrange for Louis Lindsay, Portia's boyfriend, to tutor John, once a week for a few months. Her Dad had been delighted, as he knew John thought highly of Louis.
3. Susie Sutton's wedding was imminent! She, Rosalind, would have to have fittings for the dress she would wear as a bridesmaid. She had not seen Susie's dress, but she had been told that little crystals would be sewn on to it.
4. She, Rosalind, had been collaborating with her mother on the writing of "The Aspects of Venus: an astrological guide for teenagers." It would have a question and answer format, and would be as simple as it possibly could be.

Debbie's message arrived as Rosalind was wondering what else to jot down.

"Guess what! Guess what!" she had written in a breathless way that Rosalind knew her mother would describe as "a Madame de Sévigné style." Intrigued, Rosalind read on quickly, but was soon biting her lip in dismay. Pomeroy and Tansy seemed to have quarrelled. Debbie had seen Tansy with Julian in Clifton, from time to time, but recently, she had been with Owen Banks, a lot. Debbie had seen them together in a supermarket in Princess Victoria Street, crossing Victoria Square, going for a meal in a restaurant in Regent Street and walking in the direction of the Downs, when a circus had come to town! Owen Banks had taken Tansy to a circus?

Rosalind felt as if her head had started to spin, while imagining that, simultaneously, her blood had turned to ice. Tansy and Owen Banks! Owen Banks! When she had been a school girl in Bristol, she had had such a crush on him! It had consumed her to the extent that she would take the long way back to her grandmother's house in Cotham, after school, in the hope of catching a glimpse of him running down the seven steps from the Wills Memorial Building! She had dreamed that, one day, he would give her an engagement ring of Bristol diamonds, in the unusual gardens of Goldney Hall!

Oh! She liked Tansy. She had met her the previous Christmas, but - honestly! - she, Rosalind, had been attracted to Owen Banks before Tansy had paid attention to him! She had to win him back! She simply had to! Of course, thinking practically, she would have to be accepted as a student at Bristol University before she could make further plans - and that would not be easy! Never had the need to excel in school been more crucial. Rosalind sat upright and reached for a pile of books, dragging them, then, close to her. Filled with a new energy, powered by determination, she opened the first.

CHAPTER 71

The Chemistry of Love

Having been told by Antoine du Crâne that Julian Bramblewell-Eurlinn would be visiting Paris before, presumably, much time had passed, Héloïse de Sauzon was wondering if she would be able to persuade her sister, Jacqueline, to invite him to stay at her flat, as, indeed, she had on a previous occasion, when Julian had been in Paris. The problem was this: how could she, Héloïse, raise the subject of Julian's visit without unintentionally letting the intuitive Jacqueline know that her interest in Julian had now become more than casual? So much could be given away by the sparkle in the eyes, the warmth in the voice or the faltering over a word or two. She would, actually, have shared her secret with Jacqueline had it not been for the fact that she had become embarrassed by it. In the past, she had been the cool, emotionally detached sibling. Jacqueline and Marie-Colette, while growing up, had expected her to sort out their emotional messes for them and to help them to view their situations from a logical perspective. Even as a small child, Héloïse had been able to think lucidly enough to perceive the apparent lack of reasonableness under-pinning behaviour. Her parents' disagreements and arguments, for example, surfacing usually at dinner, in the evening. But Héloïse's gift for logical deliberation had been undermined, during the previous year or two, by emotional attachments. First, she had been drawn to Teddy Laurence and, now, even more forcefully, she was attracted to Julian Bramblewell-Eurlinn.

Through study, Héloïse had learnt that the transition from adolescence to adulthood had brought about changes in the balance of chemicals swilling around in her head, and, she now assumed that whenever she thought of Julian, parts of her brain became flooded with oxytocin and endorphins. Although she felt as if she were swimming in an emotional swamp, she was not sure if what was happening to her was enjoyable or unpleasant. Her heart had started to ache - or so it seemed - with a longing to see Julian again but she felt ashamed of the fact that she was giving in to the sorts of romantic feelings that less cerebrally directed girls regularly experienced. What was love anyway? What did the words "I love you" actually mean? "I want to devote myself to making you happy"? "I want you to devote yourself to making me happy"? Had the poet, Pierre Reverdy, been right in claiming there was no such thing as love: only proof of love? Whatever love was, it had to be handled with intelligence. Rather than suffer the pain of unrequited love, was it not more sensible to devote oneself to someone who returned one's offering of affection? What was the point of drooling over a photo, a scribbled note, or romantic poetry, waiting for some tardy, would-be beloved to make up his mind? If he was too stupid to see what he was rejecting, why would one want him, anyway? Héloïse realised that her thoughts, when they turned in this direction, had Teddy Laurence: as their focus: he who had ignored her throughout the previous summer. The humiliation stemming from his rejection still had the ability to sting. But when she had finally accepted that he had no wish to have any kind of relationship with her, her emotional attachment to him had largely changed to pique. She was well-educated, accomplished and pretty. She was not given to whimsy or unpredictable flights of fancy. She had been brought up in a château, for Goodness' sake! What more could Teddy want? The American girl, with her showy love of intellectual pursuits and her sporty confidence?

Héloïse suspected, or rather hoped, that Julian could perceive what she, herself, essentially was and could understand that she had value. During the first occasion on which they had had a proper conversation, he, Julian, in a light-hearted manner, had suggested that the Angélique curse would perhaps be broken if the two of them were to marry, Héloïse had gathered that he would not have been averse to such an occurrence. Had her head not stupidly been filled with thoughts of Teddy Laurence, at the time, she would have paid more attention to that conversation. Julian had been fascinating. And gentlemanly, in that engaging British way that would-be gentlemen, all over the world, wanted to emulate. And he was as handsome as a golden prince of legend. Her parents would have adored him, had they met. Would they ever meet him? Would she, Héloïse, be given a chance to make amends for the off-hand way she had treated him previously? Or had he already dismissed her as being - well! - not quite what he had initially imagined? Héloïse would often come to in the morning knowing that, in the half-sleeping, half-awakening phase, she had been dreaming of Julian. She knew she had visualised him standing before a large fire in the hall of a manor house on a winter's day or striding through a sun - filled meadow in summer. And although she was aware of the fact that these scenes were no more than the tropes of romantic novels, she found herself becoming seduced by them to the extent that she would deliberately recall them, from time to time, during the day. Simultaneously, she was trying to arouse the critical faculties of her brain, but it appeared to her, on occasions, as if her pre-frontal cortex had gone into "le melt-down": an expression Talitha Appleby, one of the Bramblewell girls staying at the Château du Crâne, the previous summer, had often used when giving reasons for her own behaviour. Héloïse did not want her mind to become so overwhelmed with - what? - passion? - that she was rendered incapable of retaining cool mastery of her conduct. A line spoken by a character in one of Racine's 17th century plays, "Phèdre," came to mind, the elevated words being:

"Ma folle ardeur, malgré moi, se déclare."

She feared that her crazed love might reveal itself, in spite of her effort to conceal it. She had to retain mastery of herself. She could not allow herself to let down her guard, especially if she were to meet Julian again. Even the most ill-educated coquette knew that, in such a situation, it was important to appear to be unobtainable or, at least, difficult to impress.

One evening, in Jacqueline's flat, while Jacqueline, assiduously observing classic rules, was preparing coquilles St. Jacques, épaule d'agneau and tarte tatin, Héloïse seized the opportunity to say, with apparent casual indifference:

"You know, you should invite Julian to dinner when he comes to Paris. I'm sure he'd prefer to eat here, in your apartment, than to eat alone in restaurants or at his hotel."

"When will he come to Paris?" asked Jacqueline, who had been looking at the lamb in the oven, but who, now, straightened up abruptly.

"I don't know. Maybe you could ask him. Maybe he could stay."

"Here?"

"Well…yes."

"How could he? You are in the room he occupied before. Do you expect him to sleep on a sofa? And anyway, why don't you invite him, yourself? You know him better than I."

"This is your apartment. You should be the one who should invite him," retorted Héloïse. "To dinner, at least."

Then, she shrugged and did not continue.

Jacqueline sighed, as if exasperated. She did not, after all, want to reveal to Héloïse how much she, herself, was drawn to Julian. She made a show, therefore, of having been pushed into saying:

"I'll send an e-mail message to him. He gave me his e-mail address and mobile phone number while he was here."

Julian was duly approached in this way and he responded quickly. Yes. He would love to accept Jacqueline's invitation to dinner and was looking forward to seeing Héloïse, as well. He would be staying in an hotel in the Rure Saint- Honoré and would arrive, in fact, in about a week's time.

A week passed. Jacqueline had given no indication of having

arranged with Julian a date for his visit to the apartment. Annoyed at having been kept in the dark and finding Jacqueline calmly making coffee in the kitchen, one morning, Héloïse bluntly asked:

"So, when will Julian be coming to dinner?"

"I haven't made any definite arrangement with him," replied Jacqueline, in a way that seemed to Héloïse to imply that she might not bother to do so.

"He should be in Paris soon. He will be expecting you to call him," said Héloïse, trying to disguise the urgency in her voice by pausing, before adding,

"You cannot simply ignore him. That would be discourteous. What will he think of you - of us - if you fail to contact him?"

Jacqueline shrugged her shoulders and pouted, in the French way, as if she did not care what Julian thought.

"Marriage hasn't helped you to grow up, has it?" said Héloïse, a touch of iciness now evident in her tone. "I mean, you are still as vague as ever."

Jacqueline put down, on the kitchen table, the cafetière she had been holding. She tightened the belt of the floor-length, silk dressing gown she was wearing and lowered her eyes, as if reflecting on what had been said.

"I don't know what you are talking about and I don't want to quarrel," she stated quietly, then.

Héloïse, when aroused to anger, would not normally express what she was feeling in speech. What would be the point of doing that? She would indubitably open a wound that might never heal and she would be obliged to apologise, thus extending the embarrassment for all parties concerned. However, on this occasion, she found she could not stop herself from giving expression to the opinion she had formed of Jacqueline's behaviour.

"I think you are addicted to the sensation of being in love," she said, sitting down in a chair opposite her surprised sister. "When you fall in love, all sorts of chemicals are released in your brain. Dopamine, oxytocin, endorphins, serotonin...Who knows?

All of them, for all I know! But, when you are brought down to earth, finally, by the fact that the maintenance of a relationship means shouldering responsibility, you want to run away to hide in candy - floss clouds again, where you will not have to grapple consciously with the difficulties of everyday living. In other words, when the feeling of euphoria, induced by being in love fades, you flit, like a butterfly, to someone else, so that you can lose yourself in dreams, again. When you fell in love with Teddy Laurence, you were besotted with him for months, while living in a foreign land, far from your family. Then, you took Teddy home to the Château de Sauzon for Christmas, and real life intruded. You had to come to terms with Madame Gabrielle's opposition to the match. It was all too much for you and…"

"No! Stop!" interrupted Jacqueline. "No! That's not true! It simply isn't! What makes you think that you have any notion of the thoughts going through my head? And do you think all this talk about chemicals is likely to be of use to me? Oxytocin? Serotonin? Are you qualified to use these words correctly? I think not! As far as I know, you have not extensively studied the natural sciences!"

"I believe that the events I witnessed at your party, when you became engaged to Teddy Laurence, summed up your character," stated Héloïse, coldly. But, she was clutching her left wrist tightly with her right hand, behind her back. She was not enjoying the confrontation any more than Jacqueline was. However, she continued:

"When you ran into Jacqui's arms, that day, you were, in my view, running away from your responsibilities. You wanted to hide in your candy-floss clouds again. Of course, you subsequently had to marry Jacqui, in order to cover up your infantile behaviour, to the extent that was possible and to salvage the honour of your family. But now, married to Jacqui, you are bored. Real life is becoming difficult. And you want, predictably, to flit like a butterfly, in the direction of someone else. Well! I am warning you, Jacqueline, that I shall not allow you to disgrace yourself again by harming Julian."

"Julian?"

"Oh! Don't pretend to be so innocent! So unknowing!"

"Don't lecture me!" exclaimed Jacqueline, white-livid with contained rage. "Are you so faultless in your own behaviour that you think you can justifiably criticise me?"

Héloïse, realised that she had stepped over a prohibited line, as it were, in expressing an opinion she should have kept private, for the sake of peace and the maintenance of decorum.

"I'm sorry," she said. "I shouldn't have spoken in that way. Please accept my apology."

She walked around the kitchen table to give Jacqueline a hug.

"Sisters quarrel," said Jacqueline generously, if a little coldly, adding, "especially when they are squabbling over a young man."

Héloïse drew away and looked at Jacqueline quizzically.

"What do you mean?" she asked.

"I know what this sort of obsession is like," said Jacqueline, in a way that suggested she was being kind. "And I wish you well. He is nice."

"Who?"

"Julian, of course. He did tell me, when he replied to my e-mail message, the date of his arrival. He would have arrived last night. If you go to the Rue Saint- Honoré or thereabouts, you might catch a glimpse of him. I should imagine he'd go for a stroll after breakfast, don't you? Please invite him to come to dinner tomorrow night. I'll cook boeuf en croûte. Do you think that would be appropriate?"

Dumbfounded, Héloïse only nodded. She saw one of her jackets draped over a kitchen chair and, as if distracted, she picked it up, before leaving the room.

"Bring me a baguette on your way back," Jacqueline called after her, indicating that life would continue as before, despite the verbal spat.

Frowning, Héloïse went to her bedroom. The Rue Saint-Honoré was chic. What should she wear to impress? She pulled out of the wardrobe, red corduroy trousers. She could wear them with red, ballerina shoes, a beige jumper and a matching beige grab bag. Would she pass muster? She hoped so.

"Ciao, Jacqueline," she called, before going down into the street. There, she decided to go on foot across the Seine, past Notre Dame and then, onwards to the Rue Saint-Honoré, in the 1st arrondissement. A growing excitement consumed her and so, the walk did not seem to take long. Soon she was passing the Church of St. Roch and then, she became aware of the fact that she was on truly historically notable, if blood infused, territory. Had prominent revolutionaries not met in this very street in the 18th century? Had Queen Marie-Antoinette not been taken along this very road on her way to the guillotine? Marie-Colette, excessively sensitive, had once said that her spine had tingled when she had visited the street and that she would be reluctant to go back to it. Héloïse paused but, a second later, she interiorly shrugged and walked onwards. There would be time to ponder on France's history on some other occasion. And then, she saw Julian in the distance! She was sure it was he! She recognised his stride, his height and his blond hair. She felt a thrill going through her entire body. It was as if a bucket of ice cubes had been poured down her back and some weighty object had simultaneously been aimed at her heart. Julian was making his way in the direction of the Champs Elysées or, perhaps, in that of the Place de la Concorde. She would have to dash to catch up with him.

Taking no notice of the astonished looks she was given by passers-by, Héloïse sped along, her long hair becoming tangled and messy.

"Julian!" she called, recklessly. "Julian!"

At last, he turned round and astonished, he opened his arms to catch her as she tumbled into them.

"Julian," Héloïse gasped, reeling with exhaustion and out

of breath. And it was only then that she became aware of the young woman at his side. With her hair styled in an urchin cut and coloured blonde, the new-look Tansy took a step back as if surprised by the exuberance of - and familiarity implied by - Hèloïse's greeting. Embarrassed, Héloïse extricated herself from Julian's arms. Without a word, she turned and retraced her steps quickly, although too confused to be really sure of what she was doing or where she was going.

CHAPTER 72

A Suit Pressed Too Quickly

For her visit to Antoine du Crâne in Paris, Caterina Traversi of Traversi-Trimm, wanted to project an image of herself as being stylishly business-like, in order to look as if she were a serious representative of Kit Mallory's company: not a mere messenger girl with a side-line in translating. Being Italian, she was well aware of how important the concept of bella figura was. It had been a well established component of the culture in which she had been immersed from childhood onwards. Therefore, in order to make a good impression on the man who would be observing her appearance as well as her conduct, she chose to wear, on the morning of her visit, a dark grey skirt suit with a white waistcoat and pale beige high heeled shoes with black toe caps. Momentarily, she considered wearing white shoes with lower heels, instead, but thought that such a choice would look too predictable: one that would be chosen by those who lacked confidence in their own conception of style. Over her shoulder she slung a small, grey, quilted bag that matched the suit in colour. It was stuffed with tissue paper and served no purpose other than to look decorative. Her make-up kit, digital devices and purses were placed in a more copiously sized grab bag. Caterina also squeezed in there a book about writers, poets and artists who had drawn inspiration from sojourns spent in Paris: a book she would skim-read, if, by chance, she was required to wait in one of the reception rooms before the interview would begin.

Breakfast, in the form of hot coffee, croissants, apricot jams, butter and fruit had been brought to Caterina's suite in the smart Right Bank hotel earlier and had been left on a small, round table, covered in a white cloth. Caterina, upon seeing the food laid out, had initially wished she had requested something more substantial, as, in the Wirral, she had become used to eating breakfast à l'anglaise, having acquired a taste for bacon and eggs with sausages and tomatoes, toast and tea. "Never mind," she thought. Perhaps Antoine du Crâne would take her to a splendid restaurant for lunch.As she checked the contents of her bag to make sure she had all she needed, Caterina wondered what he, Antoine du Crâne, would be like, in appearance as well as personality. Kit Mallory had told her that he was probably around forty and had seemed to have been "perfectly amenable" when conversing on the telephone. Well! She would know soon enough if this assessment had been accurate.

A car had been ordered for her by one of the hotel's staff, in accordance with instructions communicated by Kit Mallory. Having settled herself on the back seat, Caterina asked the driver to take her directly to the apartment building where Antoine du Crâne lived. The journey lasted only ten minutes. It would, in fact, have been shorter had there not been delays caused by the slow progress of condensed traffic. Having arrived, Caterina stepped on to the pavement and took in the aspect of the pale blond building and the grey-ish blue mansard roof with the appreciative eye of the student of fine art and history of art that she had once been, albeit briefly. She wondered if, in Napoleonic times, the building had been occupied by one of the Emperor's military officers and if, in the era before that, the Ancien Régime, it had belonged to a splendid marquise - all powdered hair, voluminous skirts and fine jewels – living lavishly, before the streets outside her domain had run with aristo blood during La Terreur.

Caterina shivered at the thought of what the inhabitants of the building might have endured, or at least witnessed, during those ill-starred, blooded times, as she went up to Antoine du Crâne's apartment in a lift with wrought iron gates. She rang the bell of the apartment and a uniformed housekeeper opened the door and stood back to allow Caterina to walk into a wide entrance hall, where wood-panelled walls were covered in framed, modern art work, and, more traditionally, where sofas with gilded frames, upholstered in pink, were ranged in a spaced out way, against those walls. Caterina followed the housekeeper, with interest, into a reception room, which, from floor to ceiling, was lined with books. And a second later, before she had time to look around, Antoine entered the room.

He was tall without being excessively so. His hair, straight and still brown, was not brutally short, but not long either. A lock of it fell over his forehead, so that he had the appearance, rather, of a concert pianist who had just played a lively piece by Liszt.

"Allow me to introduce myself, mademoiselle," said he in English. "Antoine du Crâne, at your service."

It occurred to Caterina that the man's accent had sounded a touch American. It seemed to her that this was unusual, given his stock, since the aristocracy of France and Italy generally showed a preference for the English accent traditionally used by professors at the universities of Oxford and Cambridge: the sort of people who pronounced "controversy" correctly. Perhaps Antoine du Crâne had spent some time at Harvard, though. Or some other Ivy League university. Caterina studied the expression on his fine-featured face. He was smiling as if in a bemused way, but the serious look in his eyes suggested he was not a frivolous man. Caterina thought she would find him agreeable.

"Mademoiselle Caterina Traversi," she said, holding out her hand. Antoine took it in his and bowed in order to deliver the baise-main which, in line with correct protocol was no more than a mock kissing of the air above her skin. Caterina had expected no less than this show of continental gallantry, but nevertheless, she was enchanted by it, partly because in England, where she had been living long enough to have become accustomed to its ways, the baise-main was rarely delivered. Perhaps it was regarded, there, as being too continental and showy, quite simply.

Antoine, as he had bowed his head, must have spotted the book in Caterina's bag, for - rather precipitously, Caterina thought - he said:

"I see we shall have more to discuss than the ground plans of the Château du Crâne. On the subject of books, tell me, mademoiselle, do you think one's reading of, say, a novel is enhanced or diminished by one's acquaintance with the personal history of the writer?"

Taken by surprise, Caterina hesitated. Antoine's opening question was one with which she had never had to deal, when meeting a man, in a formal situation, for the first time.

"I think," said Caterina, after pausing to ponder on what she would say. I think that a novel should be judged without reference to the character or life-style of the writer, but I have to admit that, often, once I have discovered how the writer has lived his or her life, my views about the book are coloured by this background knowledge. I do read literary biographies, but I suspect myself of doing so because I am entertained by tittle-tattle. Fundamentally, my interest in people and their lives is no more serious than the interest that a common gossip would have in them. I read hefty books, but tragically, I am not at all high-minded."

Apparently astonished by the candidness of this answer, Antoine, at first, smiled in a quizzical way and then, laughed, but not unkindly.

"Mademoiselle," he ventured, "if you will permit me, I shall take you for lunch to a restaurant much used by stylish writers and, indeed, le tout Paris, There, you will be able to observe, to your heart's content, the day-to-day behaviour and, frankly, the indiscretions, of a fascinating crowd. But, I beg you not to gossip about these people until you have returned to England!"

"You have a sense of humour, sir!" said Caterina, smiling slowly in the coquettish way that had served her well in times past. "I accept your invitation with pleasure."

Antoine gave a slight bow, before pointing out:

"But first, we must work!"

He walked towards the book cases lining one wall and removed four leather-bound volumes which he, then, placed on the polished table in the centre of the room. One of them, Caterina observed, contained folded ground plans of the Château du Crâne. Antoine spread them out and then took larger maps and plans from a drawer under the surface of the table. One of these looked complicated and detailed.

The next three hours seemed to Caterina to pass quickly, as Antoine explained to her the architectural features of the château and the topography of the land around it. Caterina became aware of the fact that, at times, Antoine spoke to her as if she were his equal: at other times, as if she were his student. She had been required to concentrate so hard on the information being presented to her that she had not noticed when Antoine had begun to talk in French instead of English and she, herself, had, in absent-minded fashion, responded in the same language.

Finally, perhaps because a clock had struck one, somewhere in the apartment, Antoine judged that he had said enough. He took Caterina to lunch in a handsome restaurant which had rather an air of the Belle Epoque about it. There, they enjoyed crêpes aux fruits de mer, steak-frites and crème au caramel. As they ate, Caterina glanced at Antoine's hands. They were as fine and sensitive as those of a musician. Yet, they also had an outdoor look about them, as if they were capable of manual labour. Caterina was pleased about that. She assumed that that was because a man whose hands indicated that he could protect her in a storm, or could build a shelter for her in the throes of some other catastrophe, made her feel secure, on a primitive level. She was not drawn to passivity. Now and again, Antoine would lean forward to reveal to her discreetly who such and such a person was at a table nearby. Caterina realised that she was enjoying his company, for he was witty without being cruel and attentive without being paternalistic. She was unsure of how he felt about her, though. But, unexpectedly, he, then, with a changed and indecipherable look in his eyes, asked briskly:

"Will you be meeting the young heir to the Château du Crâne as well, while in Paris?"Has Mr. Mallory arranged for you to talk to him?"

"The heir to the Château du Crâne? I know nothing about him, except for the little my sister told me about him, last summer," said Caterina. "Is he in Paris at this moment?"

"Currently, yes."

"I'm sure Mr. Mallory, himself, will have already arranged to meet him somewhere else. I was given only one task to do. You see, I am not actually employed by Mr. Mallory."

"I know. I know. But, with your permission, I'll ask him to arrange for you to be his intermediary when he needs to communicate with me again, in the future. In other words, I should very much like to see you again You, specifically."

Caterina visibly drew back and looked at Antoine in a questioning sort of way. She was attracted to him, but would not, herself, have dreamed of showing her hand, as it were, so quickly. She wondered why such a sophisticated man had suddenly thrown aside his air of dignified nonchalance, in order to allow her to see an eagerness that, frankly, persuaded her to be guarded. She had been warned by her father to be wary of men who would lavish praise on her only because she was rich. It was not romantic to think in that way, he had conceded, but it was better to be realistic, in the beginning, rather than be hurt, ultimately. She liked Antoine. She liked him very much, but she would have to investigate his background before any relationship with him could develop. Especially now. She wished he had not been so precipitous in revealing his eagerness. She was also conscious enough of her own previous patterns of behaviour to know that there was also the danger of her losing interest in Antoine if she felt that she had completely conquered his heart. At that point, she would begin to question his judgement. Her successes while working for Kit Mallory and Dorothy Trimm had done much to boost her self-esteem, but still, old doubts remained lurking at the back of her mind. Her mother had never obviously liked her. How could anyone else value her? If her own mother could not love her, how could anyone else do so? Antoine du Crâne might have been attracted to what was visible, but would he be repelled, ultimately, by the inner Caterina: the one who had nothing to offer, really, but self-doubts, hours spent on self-adornment, to conceal what was real, and childish crying in the night, that sometimes went on and on?

Lunch drew to an end with Caterina in pensive mood. Antoine who had realised that he had pressed his suit too quickly, was largely silent as he drove her back to his apartment where she had left papers she wanted to take away with her. He wondered why he had revealed his hand in such an uncharacteristically brazen way, he who was normally so careful not to drop his pose of indifference. What strange impulse had possessed him to speak in the frank way he had? He gave a sigh of exasperation and, at that moment, had to brake suddenly, as a girl with long blonde hair, attempted to step from the pavement in front of the car, but then, drew back and turned to walk rapidly in another direction.

"I think I've seen her in a photo," said Caterina, but in such a distracted way, that Antoine feared he had lost her attention and, more crucially, her interest, indefinitely.

Héloïse de Sauzon, shocked at having failed to pay attention to what she had been dong to the extent that she had made a car brake precipitously, as she had stepped off a pavement's edge, made her way rapidly up the Rue Royale, hoping to conceal her embarrassment by mingling with crowds of tourists and photographers who were lingering there. In the Place de la Madeleine, she stopped, finally, to come to her senses and to look for a café. Minutes later, she found one, down a side street, and she sank, with relief, into a chair on the terrasse. She realised she had lost control of her rational mind. In silly, school-girlish fashion, she had persuaded herself that her encounter with Julian Bramblewell-Eurlinn, that morning, would have been of the highly romantic, eau-de-rose sort: the type described in novels. Instead, she had found Julian with another girl: a pretty, English-blonde girl, looking like a fresh rose-bud in a pleasant garden, after summer rain. How stupid of her, Héloïse, not to have realised that Julian would have decided that her character was not to his taste. He had probably found her conceited and so, had chosen someone kinder and more reasonable to be with him in the city of love and light. She had lost him, in other words. And she would probably never arouse his interest again.

When a waiter approached her table, Hèloïse ordered an Italian cappuccino. She hoped its smooth and frothy creaminess would warm her up, as she could feel her blood turning cold, as if from shock. She had been reluctant to telephone to Jacqueline, since she had not wanted to lose face, as it were, by relating what had happened. And she had not wanted to hear words of sympathy either. She really was too proud to listen to conventional murmurings of compassion even when offered by the sister to whom she had once been close. However, Jacqueline had to be told the story at some time. Héloïse took her phone out of her bag and called Jacqueline's number.

"I'm glad you called," said Jacqueline at once. "I've just been talking to Julian."

"Julian?"

"Yes. He has agreed to come to dinner tonight, instead of tomorrow night, but he'll be bringing a friend with him."

CHAPTER 73

Nuit Blanche

Julian Bramblewell-Eurlinn had been keeping an eye on Tansy since the day after the abrupt ending of her relationship with Pomeroy. Julian had noticed that although she, Tansy, had appeared to have been behaving normally - attending lectures, performing household chores, shopping in Princess Victoria Street - she had seemed to have been doing so listlessly, as if her energy had been spent. Her eyes no longer sparkled, Julian had noticed, their gaze now being that of a person devoid of hope. Her smile, once warm, now seemed to be merely polite.

Tansy's dip in energy had worried Julian to such an extent that, when he had been making plans to go to Paris for a long weekend, he had decided to take the dispirited girl with him. He had thought it unwise to leave her alone in her flat, even for forty-eight hours, without the distraction of his conversation, in case she would have occasion to tumble into a deep or deeper depression. He had already fallen into the habit of meeting her every day, either in the Students' Union building or at her flat, after lectures in the late afternoon, prior to taking her out for something to eat in a little bistro, where he had discovered that, despite her depleted appetite, she could be persuaded to eat a dish of couscous. And, during these excursions to the bistro, he had tried, periodically, to point out to her that Pomeroy's disappearance from her life had simply created a space which someone like Owen Banks might eventually occupy. However, this argument had generated neither hope nor consolation, and, indeed, had not drawn Tansy out of her gloom, to any noticeable degree. When had a broken heart been mended solely by logic, after all? "There is more to life than being criticised and undermined by Pomeroy," Julian had persisted in arguing all the same, but Tansy had not been in the mood for accommodating such a view.

A line from Petrarch's work, which Owen Banks had quoted, one morning, when talking about Tansy, had been hanging like a rain cloud over Julian's head, the line being:

"E veggio 'l meglio e al peggio m'appiglio."

How often, like Petrarch, had people known the better road to take but had stayed on a worse path? Tansy had undoubtedly realised that, logically, she should have paid attention to Julian's advice to forget the past and to look forward, instead, to meeting people who would be more supportive and encouraging than Pomeroy had ever been. But her emotional response to having been abandoned by Pomeroy had been so overwhelming that it had undermined all rational thought. When Julian had told her that he had booked two air tickets to Paris and two rooms in an hotel in the Rue Saint-Honoré, though, Tansy had felt her poor heart becoming less sore and her brain less frozen, and she had - almost in the detached and bemused way of the Tansy of former days - acknowledged the truth underpinning the belief that women, no matter what their intellectual status, could be mollified and cheered by the thought of going on holiday or visiting a glossily stylish shop. A woman, no matter how attached she was to abstract thought and serious discussion, was still a child of Venus, as Julian's mother had once pointed out, when she had been talking, in a light-hearted way, about astrology.

Julian had been delighted to see Tansy's mood altering when he had given her details of their itinerary for their weekend break, but he had been taken aback when, in preparation for the trip, she had changed her appearance startlingly. A hairdresser in Clifton had cut her hair in an urchin style and had bleached it blonde. The new look had endowed Tansy with an air of vulnerability, but also, originality, and it had occurred to Julian that perhaps this was the first indication, on her part, that she had decided no longer to be the person she had, consciously or unconsciously, become while she had been in Pomeroy's company, playing a secondary and supportive rôle, only, while he had been the star, as it were: the leading player in his own drama.

The journey to Paris had been devoid of upsets. The flight from Bristol had been smooth. In the taxi from the airport to the centre of Paris, Julian had pointed out to Tansy various districts that he had recognised and he had derived some pleasure from seeing the enchantment in her eyes as she hadobserved the clothes and behaviour of people in the streets. She had never visited Paris previously and so, simply by being in the city of light and art and intellect, she had felt the thrill of anticipation, as if she had been a child on Christmas Eve, waiting for Santa to arrive. Could they go for a walk in the Champs Elysées later? Could they visit one of the famous cafés where the Existentialists had hung out, on the Left Bank? Could they spend time in Montmartre where so many artists had once lived? Julian had said "Yes" to everything, while hoping that Tansy would have a more realistic picture in her head of what was possible, the next day.

After a comfortable night in the Rue Saint-Honoré, they had set off the following morning to see the city. But, no sooner had they stepped into the street than, at a spot near the old Hôtel de France et de Choiseul, Héloïse de Sauzon had unexpectedly appeared, running towards Julian as if she had anticipated an enthusiastic welcome. Nonplussed, Julian had looked at her, startled, and at that moment, Héloïse had stepped back, having noticed Tansy, standing by his side. Then, appearing to be both embarrassed and disappointed, she had turned and had walked away quickly.

"Don't you want to go after her?" Tansy had asked, having realised, at once, what had been going through Héloïse's head. "Who is she?"

"Jacqueline de Sauzon's sister, Héloïse. She was at the Château du Crâne last summer. I did talk to her a few times."

"And?"

"And…nothing! Nothing! I mean, I did like her at first, but… there's an inconsistency in the way she lives her life."

"I don't know what you're talking about."

"She can't…Excuse me."

Julian's phone had alerted him to the arrival of a text message.

"It's from Jacqueline," he had said.

"Héloise must have phoned her. Just now. I shouldn't ask, but…"

"But what is she saying? She has invited me to dinner. I stayed with her the last time I was in Paris and I told her I'd be back, this weekend, but that I'd be booking into an hotel."

"It's possible Héloïse has just contacted her to ask her to invite you to dinner. Does she stay with Jacqueline?"

"Yes. I think so…when she's in Paris."

"So, what will your reply be? To the invitation, I mean."

"I regret I can't. I have a friend with me."

"No! Don't refuse! Héloïse will want to see you. You should go!"

"Too late. I've pressed 'Send.' Do you really think I'd leave you on your own?"

The reply to Julian's message had arrived five minutes later. Jacqueline had written:

"Bring her or him. Both of you will be welcome."

"Are you up to meeting people?" Julian had asked. "I don't mind what we do."

"I think we should go," Tansy had answered, remembering the pained look in Héloïse's eyes. She had wanted to make it plain to the French girl that she and Julian were simply friends. Good friends, but still just friends.

In the early evening of that day, Héloïse de Sauzon dressed for dinner as if she had been planning to dine at La Tour d'Argent, rather than in a small dining room in her sister's apartment. Her dress, which she had bought on her way back to the apartment, after she had recovered from the shock of seeing Julian with another girl, was a short, pale golden cocktail one, which was similar in colour to the blonde of her hair, but which shimmered more. She went into the kitchen to show Jacqueline what she had chosen, but Jacqueline, in the throes of preparing soup and beef, merely commented:

"It suits you, but put on an apron. I want you to wash some fruit and put out the cheeses. Use that big plate, but put a napkin under the cheese."

"How much time do we have?"

"They'll be here in half an hour, if not earlier, I expect."

"You're surely not going to use all of these cheeses, are you? Brie de Meaux, Camembert de Normandie, Roquefort…Three will be enough. No?"

"No. Put out seven."

"Seven? No! Far too many! We are providing dinner in a small apartment on the Left Bank: not a banquet in a château in Bordeaux. Whom are you trying to impress, anyway?"

A suspicious thought briefly insinuated itself into Héloïse's mind, then. Was Jacqueline attracted to Julian, as she had previously suspected? Was Jacqueline, in fact, trying to impress him by showing off her newly-acquired skills in the kitchen? Héloïse dismissed that thought quickly, though. Jacqueline was too spontaneous to be coldly subversive. No. The rival who should be occupying her attention that night should, naturally, be the girl whom she had seen by Julian's side in the street, earlier in the day.

"Will you keep an eye on what's in the oven?" Jacqueline asked then, adding, "I have to go to change my dress!"

Héloïse nodded, bending down to peer through the glass door at the decorated pastry covering the beef. She sat on a kitchen chair, close by, and tried to calm herself. But, five minutes later, the door bell rang. There was nothing for it but to let the guests in, without Jacqueline.

Tansy, her expression kind, smiled in a sympathetic way, upon seeing Héloïse, pale but composed, framed by the door and lit by the light behind her. Julian behaved as if nothing was amiss. He made no allusion to having seen Héloïse earlier.

"Hello! Lovely to see you," he said, as he took off his coat. "This is Tansy, a friend of a friend."

"A friend of a friend," echoed Héloïse, looking suspiciously at Julian.

"Yes," said Tansy. "I'm just one in a group of Julian's friends."

"But, you are here in Paris, with him…with Julian…and alone?"

"Yes. I was unwell and Julian thought he'd take me with him this weekend, to cheer me up."

"Ah! How kind!" said Héloïse, still wary and unsure of the nature of the relationship. Responding to the feminine need to size up the other, she studied what Tansy was wearing: a short, black evening dress; black high-heeled shoes; a single row of pearls; just a little lip-stick. A conventional way of dressing, then. Predictably English. But that hair-style, though. How would one describe it? Artistically avant-garde? The girl was an enigma.

Jacqueline appeared and offered an apéritif and then, everyone sat down to dinner. The conversation flowed, but it was superficial. Topics ranged from the English weather and English gardens to French weather and French vineyards. All the while, Héloïse watched Tansy out of the corner of her eye, seizing opportunities to glance properly at her, now and again. By Héloïse's reckoning, the way Tansy looked at Julian - gratefully, respectfully - did not suggest that her friendship with him was casual, even if he, Julian, was not aware of his companion's adoration. Not at that moment, anyway. But he surely would become aware of it, at some point. The friendship would progress to another level. Of that, Héloïse was certain. And, more chilling still was the fact that Julian had felt so sorry for Tansy that he had taken her with him to Paris! Paris! Would a young man who was entirely indifferent to a girl's charms take her to Paris? No! Héloïse felt as if her heart had been thumped, when she realised this and consequently, by the time the evening was drawing to a painful close, she was feeling worse than she had felt earlier in the day. Her discontent was made more irritating, furthermore, by the fact that Tansy seemed to be a good sort, of the English type. Had she been crafty and mean – spirited, Héloïse would not have minded disliking her. But, she had, instead, to admit that Tansy was the kind of girl that Julian deserved.

That night, after the dinner guests had gone away into the dark, Parisian night, Héloïse went to bed and tried to sleep. She wrapped herself in her quilt as if it were a cocoon and tried, unsuccessfully, to direct her thoughts away from Julian and Tansy. It was impossible to do so, of course. She sat up, knowing that she was going to have a sleepless night: a nuit blanche. Thoughts were racing around her head: thoughts of the type that left her feeling anguished. Her heart-beats, she could feel through her skin. She could blame no one but herself for her pain, of course. She had been stupid, stupid. Why had she flirted with Teddy Lawrence during the previous summer? If she had thought that, by doing so, she would make Julian jealous, the strategy had misfired. She should have realised that Julian, being English, would have reacted differently from the way she would have expected a Frenchman to have behaved. Frivolous flirting, on the part of a girl, simply bored young and intelligent English boys. They either did not understand what was going on or else, felt insulted and sought someone else, more deserving of their attention. She remembered that Jacqueline had told her as much once and she should have paid heed to what her sister had said. Oh! Why could she not think and behave and look like milky-skinned Tansy - the Tansy who, no doubt, would be at home racing around a hockey field, behaving like a good sport, happy to hand out cucumber sandwiches and pour tea in the tea tent and all of that other stuff that she, Héloïse, had read about in novels of a very traditional, English type?

She got up and went into the kitchen. She let water flow slowly from a bottle into a glass and then, she sat down at the kitchen table and sipped it. Next, she stood up, restless again and turned on the small-screen TV on top of a cupboard. Jacqueline liked only tiny TVs; she thought they were the only ones that were chic. Héloïse shrugged. A late night film was being shown. She turned the sound down so that her sister would not be disturbed. She watched, not really understanding what she was seeing and not caring either.

When light began appear in the sky, she was still there, in the kitchen, tired, but feeling strangely stronger. Such was the power of the dawn. It brought hope. Maybe she could still capture Julian's heart. She simply had to find a way of doing so. Every problem had a solution, according to her calm and patient father. Well! She was her father's daughter and she would find one!

Jacqueline entered the kitchen to find Héloïse there with dark shadows under her eyes.

"Couldn't you sleep either?" she asked. "Have you made any coffee?

"Not yet. Why couldn't you sleep?"

"I was worried about you?"

"Worried about me? Why?"

"You seemed so…I don't know! Listen! I keep meaning to remind you that Marie-Colette will presumably be summoned to Scotland by Pierre Laurier before long, so that she can be filmed. Why don't you come with us?"

"You know quite well that Maman wouldn't hear of such a thing. She doesn't trust me to look after Marie-Colette. But what is the connection between your excursion with Marie-Colette and the fact that you are worried about me and why are you worried about me, anyway? You haven't answered that question?"

"It doesn't matter."

"Oh! It doesn't matter! It doesn't matter! What kind of answer is that? You really annoy me! You pretend to be helping me, but you never do. I have always been the one who has helped you! And now, when I do actually really, really need helpful advice, you can't persuade yourself to help me! You are hopeless! You always have been! You pretend to be mysterious, but your mysteriousness is a sham: a cover for your stupidity!"

Tears hot in her eyes, Héloïse left the kitchen and made her way quickly to her bedroom. There, she lay down on her bed, rolling herself round and round in her quilt. Why had she spoken in the way she had? She had exchanged angry words with Jacqueline on previous occasions, but she had never before accused her of being stupid. How could she face her again? She should have walked out of the room, before words of anger had been uttered. Now damage had been done: the insults could not be retracted. She would have to apologise at some point, of course and Jacqueline would forgive her but would regard her as being less noble, indefinitely.

In another part of Paris, Julian had also had a sleepless night. He went downstairs to the room in his hotel where breakfast was being served, shortly after six o' clock and was shown to a table near a glass wall that overlooked an inner courtyard, where green plants grew. The young waiter in attendance, careful and conciliatory and obviously a beginner in his profession, assiduously paid attention to the way the croissants were presented and the coffee poured. Julian drank black coffee slowly and soon felt more awake, his brain and senses having been sharpened. He had not been able to interpret the way Héloïse had behaved the previous evening. Her glacial expression had been at odds with her politeness, correctness and even charm, on occasions. What sort of message had she been trying to communicate? Had she been annoyed? Tansy had gone to great lengths to explain that she had been simply a friend. What more could have been done?

On the way back to the hotel in the taxi, Tansy had said:

"I imagine that, in Héloïse's position, I'd have been wondering what exactly had been behind your decision to bring a strange girl to the dinner party. Had I been Héloïse, in fact, I suspect I'd have thought you might have done that either to insult me or else to avoid having a quiet conversation with me. Did that cross your mind when she was being frosty? Do you know what I'm talking about?"

"I wish I did," Julian had said, staring out of the window of the taxi, while watching the lights of Parisian street lamps, slipping by,

He had not been able to erase the pained and hostile look in Héloïse's eyes from his memory all night and even now, he could imagine her sitting on the other side of the table, looking arch and cool. Had she been deliberately trying to elicit an emotional response from him, the previous evening?

"Ice Princess," he thought.

The waiter brought a coffee pot with a white napkin wrapped around it.

"More, sir?"

"Yes, please," said Julian, in a distracted manner, angry with himself now, for having wasted the possibility of having had a good night's sleep through worrying about a girl who had probably still not stopped playing games with his emotions. When would she grow up?

CHAPTER 74

The Distant Hebrides

A great deal of persuading, on the part of Héloïse and Jacqueline de Sauzon, and, indeed, the Count de Sauzon, had taken place before the Countess de Sauzon had allowed her youngest daughter, Marie-Colette, to agree to take part, briefly, in the filming of "The Quest of Angélique". The fact that the filming was to take place in the distant Hebrides, off the west coast of Scotland, had been the least of the Countess' objections. So entrenched had been her opinions regarding the unsuitability of the venture that, at one point, it had seemed she would never give in. But then, Pierre Laurier, himself, had intervened promising that he would make sure that Marie-Colette would be comfortably accommodated with her sister, Jacqueline, and that, of course, Jacqueline would be allowed to take part in negotiations on Marie-Colette's behalf. The Countess had given her consent frostily, emphasising, as she had done so, that Marie-Colette had always been a "much loved and precious daughter." Over-hearing her mother uttering those words, "much loved and precious," Marie-Colette had been shocked, having previously been the target of her mother's ire, so often.

Easter arrived, then, and the Sauzon sisters found themselves flying from Paris, via Glasgow, to a white-shored island, washed by turquoise waters. It seemed very far away. Marie-Colette thought, though, that, visually, the island resembled Belle-Isle to some degree, but that the air that was breathed there was different and that the brooding atmosphere that emanated from the silent hills was unsettling. But she kept those views to herself.

A house had been rented for the sisters. It looked traditional but had a large extension at the back. In the original part of the house, there was a bedroom and a large bathroom upstairs, while downstairs, there was a nicely furnished sitting room and a kitchen. In the extension, there was an upper bathroom and bedroom, with a wide landing, at the top of the stairs: a landing that overlooked the sitting room below. It was like a balcony, in fact. On the ground floor, also, there was a kitchen.

Marie-Colette had assumed she would be sleeping in a room next to Jacqueline's and she looked at the way the house had been constructed with dismay. She was wondering if she should ask if she would be able to sleep on a sofa in the sitting room, close to Jacqueline's room, rather than in the second bedroom on her own, in the other part of the house, when Jacqueline said:

"I expect you will want to have a bathroom all to yourself. Do you want the larger one?"

"No. You have that one," answered Marie-Colette, bleakly, assuming Jacqueline meant that she, herself, did not want to share.

"I think it's sensible that we have a bathroom each," Jacqueline went on. "Filming begins early and if we have to get ready in a rush, after wakening up, we shall need to have a bathroom each. It makes sense for us to sleep in different rooms as well, for the same reason."

"Yes. That would be best," said Marie-Colette, but without conviction. She was not looking forward to sleeping so far away from her sister, in a strange house and in unknown territory.

"We can have dinner together, of course," said Jacqueline, sounding business-like. "Chez moi! Let's have a look at what has been left in the kitchens."

The girls found the fridges and freezers laden with food and Jacqueline had no difficulty in assembling a good salad and then, a main dish from lamb cutlets, potatoes and green beans. Marie-Colette realised that Jacqueline would be anxious to talk to her parents, or maybe even Jacqui, on her mobile phone and so, after dinner, she retreated to what was to be the part of the house she would occupy. She noticed, as she was going through the connecting door, that the door knob seemed to be loose.

Marie-Colette heated ground coffee in a saucepan in her own little kitchen. She poured the infused coffee into a blue and white striped mug that she had found hanging on a hook and then, she went up the wooden stairs to her bedroom. There was a sloping sky-light in there, one which gave her a view of a hill top and the sky. She stood on tip-toe and tried to see more. There were no houses in sight. Just acres of heather-covered moors and marshes. The quietness of the landscape was making her nervous. Only the ticking of a clock in the sitting room below could be heard. She went downstairs again to fetch her white, silk pyjamas from her trolley case and then, went to the bathroom to prepare herself for bed. Having completed her night-time ritual, she fetched an alarm clock from her hand luggage and having set it for five, as Jacqueline had told her to do, she took it upstairs. Slipping between the cold, white sheets on the bed, she shivered, even though an electric radiator had been turned on in the corner of the room. She felt tense as she watched the sky changing colour, through the sky-light, but eventually, tiredness overwhelmed her and she fell asleep.

The pink streaks of dawn had started to appear on the horizon, when Jacqueline, in her own room, awoke, horrified to discover she had slept through the ringing of her alarm clock. She went down to her kitchen and heated water and milk, before taking to Marie-Colette a cup of café au lait and three biscuits, which looked like "Petit Beurre" ones but did not taste quite the same.

"The car will come for us in an hour. Drink this and hurry!" said Jacqueline, in the anxious tone of one who had meant to wake up earlier.

Marie-Colette felt heavy-hearted. But, she pushed back the white sheet and blanket and the substantially padded quilt covering them and stood up. The sky was starting to lighten. As bidden, she made haste.

When the car arrived, she was driven with Jacqueline to a beach backed by white sand dunes and spiky marram grass. Pierre Laurier, his film crew, his equipment and his vehicles were already there. Marie-Colette was taken to a trailer in which costumes were stored. There, she was given a long skirt and a blouse to wear. Her hair was left to tumble down her back loosely. Then, she was made-up in another trailer, in a subtle way.

"What sort of shoes shall I be wearing?" she asked.

"No shoes," was the reply.

A piece of bronze cloth was, then, tied around Marie-Colette's waist to add a splash of muted colour to the grey of her blouse and the dark blue and white of her long, rough skirt.

"You're ready," she was then told. "Go to see Pierre!"

The first scene was set up so quickly that Marie-Colette was in the thick of it before she had time to become nervous. She was asked to stand on the beach, close to the water's edge, her head held high. Her face had to communicate a range of emotions, she was told: fear, followed by resentment and then, disdain. No feeling had to be exaggerated, though. She had to look as if she were in control of her reactions as she would watch a young actor, in 17th century garb, leading his horse, along the beach towards her. Marie-Colette saw him in the distance, preparing himself for the command: "Action!"

"I cannot stay," said the young actor, when close to her, his tone both fearful and apologetic. "The Red-Coats are already searching Barra. They will soon be on their way here. I have no choice but to leave for France and exile."

Marie-Colette put up her hand to stop him speaking. And as she looked at him, the young man who, in the film, was leaving her and her unborn child to face social opprobrium and a life of poverty, she felt rising within her the anger that Angélique's grandmother would have felt, standing in the same place, but in another time. In a strong and scathing voice that even she did not recognise as her own, Marie-Colette, uttered the words she had learnt from the script:

"I curse you!" she cried, her voice rising above the noise of the waves hissing and rolling forcefully on to the beach, leaving foam behind. "I curse you and your children and their children and their children's children. Only when one of your descendants marries one of mine will the spell be broken!"

The face of the young actor standing before Marie-Colette became pale, as if he had been shaken by the force of her words. He mounted his horse and departed at the gallop.

Pierre Laurier, who had been sitting in a canvas-backed chair, stood up, looking as if he could not believe what he had just witnessed. He had been considering hiring an actress to dub Marie-Colette's words on to the sound-track, had the girl spoken her lines too softly. The voice he had just heard, though, loud and potent, must have sprung from some emotional depth previously unstirred.

Marie-Colette was looking anxiously in Pierre's direction, seemingly having reverted to being shy. She was trembling as if cold. She took a few steps towards Pierre and then, started to sway as if she had been overcome with dizziness.

"Give her a chair," shouted Pierre. "It's the shock of having been in front of the cameras for the first time. Nothing more."

"I should take her back to the house," insisted Jacqueline, having run up from her position on the side lines and having pushed her way through the members of the film crew who had started to crowd around Marie-Colette.

Pierre hesitated and then, shrugged.

"Call for the car," he shouted to an assistant.

"I'm just tired. That's all," murmured Marie-Colette, while allowing Jacqueline to lead her through the group of onlookers, and onwards, across the sand towards the car which had been driven off the single track road and on to the grass at the edge of the beach.

"You'll go back to bed as soon as we reach the house," said

Jacqueline, helping Marie-Colette into the back seat, while trying not to show that she, herself, was feeling ill at ease. She had never before heard the voice that had come out of her young sister's mouth and she had felt her body becoming rigid with alarm upon hearing it.

In the house, Marie-Colette slept for most of that day, waking now and again for only a few minutes at a time. She would look up at the sky, through the sky-light, on those occasions, and then drift once more into a state of dream-less oblivion. In the late afternoon, Jacqueline brought soup and bread.

"Do you feel like getting up?" she asked.

"Not yet."

"Do you feel weak?"

"Not really. I just want to hide under the covers and to forget."

Marie-Colette fell into another deep sleep, and awoke, when the sky was dark. As she recovered consciousness, she thought she heard a board creaking on the stairs. She sat up quickly and turned on a lamp that was on a small table beside her bed. "Jacqueline?" she called. "Is that you? There was no response. Only silence. Marie-Colette strained her ears to hear the ticking of the clock, in the sitting room, but she could not detect it. Then, her body became rigid with shock as the loud sound of a heavy object crashing to the ground could be heard somewhere downstairs. Fear gripped Marie-Colette's heart, then. It began to beat with exaggerated force and the skin on the back of her neck felt chilly. What was she to do? Hide under the covers? No! She should remain sitting up, surely. Her mouth felt dry. What could have happened? Was someone down there? Or had something fallen? Maybe that was the answer. Something heavy must have toppled over. What if it had been the fridge in the kitchen? It had, after all, been laden with food. Was it even possible that such a thing could occur? She tried to think rationally. And then, it crossed her mind that if the fridge had fallen, the electric cord might have been dragged from the socket in the wall. She would have to investigate.

There was nothing for it but to go downstairs. It was then that she thought of using her mobile phone to rouse Jacqueline by ringing her number. She took her phone from her handbag which was by her bed. She switched it on. A message appeared, that being, "No network coverage". Marie-Colette read it with incredulity. How was that possible? Jacqueline had been using own her phone earlier.

Frustration lent Marie-Colette strength. She threw back the bed covers and looked for her slippers on the floor. She could not see them and so, put on canvas espadrilles instead. She felt alert now. She left her bed and flicked a switch on the balcony, at the top of the stairs. The lights came on in the room below. The wooden stairs creaked as she descended.

In the sitting room, everything seemed to be in order. The clock was ticking now. She walked into the kitchen, expecting to find the contents of the fridge or even a cupboard scattered over the floor, but everything was in place. The larder, too, was in an orderly state.

The chill of fear now gripped Marie-Colette. She knew she had not imagined the creaking on the stairs or the noise of a heavy object crashing to the floor. But there was no evidence of anything having been disturbed. She stepped back into the sitting room and studied it carefully. And then, she noticed a framed picture standing erect, supported by a cushion, on an arm-chair. It was a print of what seemed to be a Victorian painting of a broodingly desolate moor. A piece of tartan cloth was lying, ragged and stained with mud, on the grass, in the foreground. Marie-Colette recognised the style of the painting but not its executor. However, she felt sure she had previously seen it, the painting, hanging on the wall, above the arm chair. The nail on which it had been hanging was still in the wall, in fact. Marie-Colette now, boldly took a step forward and raised her hand to touch the nail. It was not loose. She tried to pull it from the wall: it would not budge. Gently, she touched the picture and tipped it forward. The string behind it was not broken. It was not even frayed. It was attached to two hooks firmly screwed into the back of the frame.

Marie-Colette placed the picture back in position in front of the cushion. She knew that it had not been on the chair before she had gone to bed; she would have noticed it. It must have jumped off the nail and on to the chair: that had to be the only feasible explanation. She shivered and realised that her body was as cold as ice. She went up the stairs and slipped into bed. It was only then that it occurred to her that she should have gone through the connecting door to Jacqueline's part of the house to waken her. But she was fearful of going downstairs again. She had been brave for a few minutes but now, she was terrified. She pulled the quilt up to her chin and waited for dawn.

CHAPTER 75

Aftermath

Maie-Colette de Sauzon lay on her back, trying to sleep in the small bedroom, where she was spending a second night. She was conscious of the fact that her heart was forcefully beating. It was that beat that was annoyingly preventing her from drifting into slumber, she reckoned. She tried not to move and eventually her forced stillness led to drowsiness and that drowsiness to sporadic napping.

She must have slept more soundly, then, because an hour or two later, she was aware of having been woken by a shimmering glow, shining through the skylight on to her face. For a second, she imagined she was back in Belle Isle, in the Châreau de Sauzon, on a moonlit night. But then, she recollected where she was and she remembered, too, with misgiving, that her sister, Jacqueline, was in another part of the house and, therefore, was not companionably near.

Marie-Colette, despondent in solitude, knew she did not possess the strength of spirit to be able to spend an entire night awake and alone and helplessly unsupported. Not that particular night, anyway. She decided, therefore, that even though the thought of her earlier experience now filled her with so much fear that her breathing was becoming faster, she would force herself to go downstairs again, in order to pass through the connecting door to the part of the house where Jacqueline was. There, she would have to spend the rest of the night lying on a sofa, but that was of little consequence, if sleeping there meant she would be near her sister.

Marie-Colette sat up and, as if mechanically, pushed aside

the sheet, blanket and quilt before reaching for her light-weight dressing-gown which she had left at the foot of the bed. Then, she looked for her espadrilles. She found them below the bed and having tied the laces around her ankles, ballerina-style, she walked towards the skylight and gazed upwards. The Moon, a white luminous globe, was full and looked large in the sky.

The thought of going downstairs was daunting. Marie-Colette remembered the fallen picture and the creaking stairs and she hesitated as memories of Breton legends about ghosts and premonitions, read at home in Belle-Isle, came uninvited into her mind. One of Anatole le Braz's books of collected tales had been in her father's library at the Château de Sauzon for years. Marie-Colette had often looked at it, but now, as a chill at the back of her neck made her shiver, she rather wished she had not. She told herself that if she were not to go downstairs, though, she would have to remain up in her small bedroom until dawn, her body alert and taut, while her ears strained to hear any sound coming from below. Besides, she was feeling thirsty. She wanted to prepare a hot drink with Jacqueline, to chat and to pretend that life was normal.

Marie-Colette advanced towards the top of the stairs, she switched on the light that illuminated the room below and then, she started to go down, pausing on each step to listen. She could hear only the ticking clock. When she had reached the last step, she made haste to walk swiftly across the floor, towards the connecting door, passing on the way, the fallen picture on the armchair. She glanced at it, noting it was still in the position in which she had last seen it. She reached forward and put her hand on the door-knob, then, and turned it slowly. But, it disengaged itself from the door, and she found herself holding it. Had it been deliberately broken? It looked as if it had been severed in half. Marie-Colette began to breathe audibly. But then, before panic could turn to frantic breathlessness, the door opened slightly by itself, as if offering her an invitation to enter. Had it not been properly closed, initially?

Marie-Colette gave it a slight push and it opened more widely. She went through into Jacqueline's side of the house and her breathing became more regular.

She was about to advance towards the stairs that led to her sister's bedroom, her intention being to ask where the spare blankets were kept, as she intended to sleep on the sofa. But then, she noted that the main door of the house was open and light was streaming in.

Marie-Colette thought it odd that Jacqueline would not have locked the door securely. Imaginative and poetically inclined she might have always been, but Jacqueline was still scrupulous when it came to carrying out duties. Why had she left the door open, then? Had she gone out into the garden to look at the Moon?

Marie-Colette went towards the open door and then, stood on the threshold and looked out. There was no sign of her sister. She took a step or two outside and then, dragging her hand along the smooth, whitewashed stone on the side of the house, she walked a little further. There was a garden beyond the gable end of the house, or rather, the remnants of a garden that had been neglected and was full of tall grasses and nettles. It had once been enclosed by large, grey stones, piled up to form a wall. Here and there, they had fallen and so, there were gaps. Marie-Colette advanced towards one of those gaps and looked into the partially enclosed space.

She stood there, surveying the scene for a moment or two, before noticing a young man leaning against the wall on the opposite side. It was difficult to distinguish his features despite the fact that light was beaming down from the Moon but she could tell that he was pale-haired. Oddly, she did not feel afraid.

"Qui êtes-vous?" she asked. "Who are you? Have you seen my sister?"

The young man stood up straight and Marie-Colette imagined he was about to take a step towards her, but still, she felt no fear. She noticed, now, that his face was gaunt and his expression, troubled. She sensed that he was desperate to say something, but was unable to. His face was so full of sorrow that Marie-Colette felt compassion for him. But then, he was gone. It was as if he had disappeared when she had blinked. Stunned, but surprisingly calm, Marie-Colette approached where he had been standing, aware of the fact that nettles were stinging her ankles. She looked down at the grass, illogically, as if wondering if he had been swallowed by the earth below.

As if mesmerised by the grass where the young man had been standing, Marie-Colette continued to stare down at it, seemingly unable to move. Perhaps she would have stayed there until daybreak had Jacqueline, unable to sleep because of the moonlight shining through her own window, not decided to place a coat over the un-curtained pane of glass, in order to darken her bedroom. She dragged a chair across the floor and positioned it under the skylight. Standing on it, she undid the window-latch and pushed the glass, having decided to allow a burst of fresh air into the room, first. She looked out at the same time and it was then that she saw Marie-Colette, motionless in the old, enclosed garden.

"Mais, qu'est-ce que tu fais là?" asked Jacqueline aloud, being both surprised and irritated.

She climbed down from the chair and put on her coat over her pyjamas. Then, she went downstairs, her annoyance intensifying when she saw that the front door had been left open.

"Marie-Colette!" she called. But the young girl did not stir. Reaching her, Jacqueline found her in what appeared to be a semi-trance. Had she been sleep-walking? Jacqueline led her gently inside the house and helped her to lie down on the sofa. Then, she went upstairs to find blankets with which to keep her warm. The girl would return to full consciousness when she was ready to. Jacqueline felt sure she had simply become over-excited since the day had been an eventful one. It was not surprising, in fact, that Marie-Colette had not been behaving normally, given her high level of sensitivity and her nervous disposition.

Having found blankets in a cupboard, Jacqueline returned to the ground floor and tucked them around her sister.

"Ça commence," said Marie-Colette, suddenly, opening her eyes wide. "Ça commence."

"What is beginning?" asked Jacqueline, her curiosity aroused. "What are you talking about?"

But Marie-Colette was already sinking into a deep sleep and did not reply.

Meanwhile, in the Chàteau de Sauzon in Belle-Isle, that night, Héloïse de Sauzon, who was spending a few days at home, had awoken from a fractured, restless sleep, her mind in turmoil, Prior to having gone to bed, she had allowed her thoughts to have become swamped with remorse and as a result, her dreams had been filled with dark omens in the form of swooping raptors: large grey birds with cruel eyes. What had she done to deserve such unpleasantness? Was her conscience punishing her for…what? For having behaved with unpredictability and a lack of good manners when she had been in the presence of Julian Bramblewell-Eurlinn in Paris? She would not blame him if he did not now want to be associated with such a fool as she! Her behaviour had been so out of character that whenever she thought of it, now, she felt like curling up in a ball of embarrassment and hiding. What had happened to her rational brain? If only she could talk to Julian, now, in a sincere way, without pretentiousness or fake flirtatiousness, she would try to explain that she had not been herself. She would admit that, in the manner of an ingénue - a provincial among sophisticates – she had failed to behave in a dignified manner. But, would she ever again be given the opportunity to talk to Julian? Was it not more likely that he would avoid her in the future? Maybe she would never see him again! The thought of his absence from her life was unbearable. What could she do to bring about a rapprochement? She possessed his phone number, of course. Did she dare to use it? At that very moment? At such a late hour? It was the middle of the night in Bristol. Perhaps she should not disturb him…and yet, if she were to wait, her courage might fail.

Héloïse reached for her phone - she had left it on a bedside table - and she scrolled through the numbers in her list of contacts. Before she had allowed herself time to consider seriously what she was going to say, she touched Julian's number on the screen, but she almost switched off her phone in panic as his began to ring. However, she then heard Julian's voice and she could not. He was sleepily saying, "Hello? Is that you, Héloïse?"

"Julian!" she found herself replying.

"Is something wrong?"

"No. Nothing. I simply wanted …to hear your voice."

She realised she was sounding gauche and unattractively shy. Had Julian answered "Why?" then, she would have known she had made a mistake in calling him. Instead, in tangential fashion, he started to talk about his flat-mates, Pomeroy and Owen and how they had been keeping him awake earlier, with their raised voices as they had been amusingly arguing about burnt quiches. Who had left the oven at too high a heat? They had been very funny but annoying, all the same. Such was life in a students' flat in Clifton!

Héloïse began to laugh. Julian, having no doubt sensed her anxiety, was making conversation easy for her. Maybe he had realised she had something of some import to say, but needed to be coaxed into saying it. His consideration deserved frankness on her part. She would find the strength to tell him what was on her mind. After all, what did she have to lose, now? Besides, it was possible Julian had realised already what had been behind the pose of confected insouciance that she had paraded in front of him, pointlessly. She would begin by apologising for her behaviour.

In Paris, Antoine du Crâne was also enduring a sleepless night. It was not unusual for him to stay up late while working on this project or that, but it was not his custom to torture himself either, by mulling over mistakes he had made. It was not his practice, after all, to make many. He could not rid his mind, though, of the way he had mishandled his congress, on a personal level, with Miss

Traversi. He had sent her a letter apologising for his inexcusably over-zealous attempt at establishing a lasting relationship with her, but she had replied only with a short but polite message, with the consequence that he had no idea, now, as to what her private opinions about him were. Was it possible that she was the type of woman who would interpret his enthusiasm as vulgarity or as a masked suggestion that he, the rich suitor, thought she was easily bought? How could one know, in advance, that that was the view to which a woman might adhere? After all, other women interpreted tardiness and indecision as insults, did they not? There was the possibility, too, that Miss Traversi simply did not like him, of course! What a blow to his ego! In any case, he wished he knew what exactly was going on in the mind of the enigmatic Caterina in order to settle the matter.

Restlessly, Antoine paraded around his apartment. He was wearing a full-length dressing-gown in silk. It was patterned in shades of burgundy, ochre, olive and grey and he had acquired it in London. Whenever he wore it, he felt as if he were a proper English gentleman of the type required to behave in a certain, considered manner: a manner that he, himself, tried to imitate when he was in company and behaving formally.

Windows in Antoine's sitting-room provided him with views of the Eiffel Tower, with its long beams illuminating the dark sky. He momentarily, thought of a painting by Chagall. The Moon was supposed to be full that night, but as if it were contributing to a philosophical puzzle, it could not be seen. Just like the answer to his own problems, Antoine thought, the Moon was hidden: obscure. And yet, he knew that despite the agitated state of his mind, deep within him, at that moment, there was a conviction that the tides of fate were about to turn. Would his next meeting with Miss Traversi, then, be a fortunate one?

Antoine was feeling unwell, now. The fragility of his health was a secret shared only by his housekeeper. Should he wake her to ask her to make her way in haste to the all- night pharmacy to fetch medicine for him? No. Such behaviour was inconsiderate. He would lie down on the sofa in his study, instead, and would try to control his emotions by feeding his prefrontal cortex with problems of a more concrete nature.

The clauses in the contract that Julian Bramblewell-Eurlinn had asked him to draw up should keep him mentally occupied until dawn.

CHAPTER 76

Drama in the Cathedral

Dorothy Trimm was concerned about the fact that her daughter, Hilary, had left Bramblewell School without having had an opportunity to say "Good-bye," formally, to the teachers she had known there. Obviously, she had not been adequately thanked in public either, by Lord Bramblewell, for all that she had done to promote the school that, after all, bore his name. It irked Dorothy that Lord Bramblewell, himself, had not already followed the steps she had recommended to correct this oversight and the plan she had drawn up for him to approve and so, when she approached his manor, with the intention of reminding him that it was high time he did so, she was in no mood, when the door was opened, to listen to the protestations of the housekeeper, Mrs. Oliver, who, as always, was trying to discourage her from entering.

"He is not to be disturbed, madam," Mrs. Oliver said, her mouth drawn into a grim line.

"Nonsense!" declared Dorothy. "He will see ME! And well you know it!"

She proceeded to make her way into the large entrance hall and up the great staircase, shouting, "Rupert! Rupert! Are you there?"

Lord Bramblewell appeared, all in a tizz. Naturally, upon being told why Dorothy had visited, he apologised in an effusive way for his lapse in good manners, much to his visitor's satisfaction. Of course, the matter had been on his agenda for months - Lynn James had even mentioned it - but, in recent weeks, it had slipped out of his mind, preparations for his own wedding having preoccupied him. Would Dorothy, herself, help him by proceeding with the arrangements for a dinner or a buffet for Hilary? Would she find out from Lynn what the most suitable dates for such an event would be? Dorothy did not have to ask for his approval. She could simply arrange the entire evening without his consent. Dorothy assured him that she would be delighted - DELIGHTED!- to be of assistance to him in that way and resolved, on the spot, to make sure her daughter's days at Bramblewell School would be celebrated in a manner that properly reflected her status.

Dorothy's first port of call, after talking to Lord Bramblewell, was Lynn James' office. The new P.A., ensconced in the ante-room, a pleasant young girl called Karen, showed her into Lynn's room, without making a fuss.

"Your new secretary is so much nicer than her predecessor was," said Dorothy, once she had closed the door. "I'm so glad that the dreadful la Delamar was moved away from the main office. Can you imagine what would have happened if she had managed to re-conquer Rupert's heart again and she was now wearing his ring? She would be making our lives unbearable! His, as well!"

Lynn smiled, but diplomatically made no comment. After all, Isolde was still working in the school, at the end of the science corridor.

"How can I help you, Dorothy?" she asked. "Please sit down."

"Well!" exclaimed Dorothy, slightly histrionically, as she drew a chair up to Lynn's desk. "I've finally been asked by Lord Bramblewell to proceed with the organising of an event for Hilary. I've mentioned this before, Lynn, but I've been waiting and waiting for Rupert to tell me that my plans have met with his approval. He has been busy, of course."

"Actually, I, myself, mentioned to him that something should be arranged. But, you are right. He has been very busy and..."

"Yes, I know," interrupted Dorothy. "And so have you, dear. That's why I'd be the best person to organise the whole thing."

"That would be very nice of you, Dorothy. How is Hilary, incidentally?"

"She is well. I think she finds the Christina Quayle College quite different from Bramblewell, in many respects, but I don't think she actually regrets her decision to move. She still has her house in Chester, of course, and drives through the Wirral in the morning and when she returns home in the evening. Sometimes she calls in to see me in Whitby. It's nice for both of us."

Lynn nodded, but said nothing. It had occurred to her that Hilary had made her decision to leave Bramblewell School without reflecting long enough on what the consequences of her decision might be: the longer drive to work; the more daunting administrative tasks; the lack of contact with old friends, like Lord Bramblewell…

If these drawbacks had crossed Dorothy's mind, it was clear that she was not going to mention them. After conversing with Lynn for a few minutes longer, she said she would be on her way, asking, as she made for the door, if Lynn thought it would be a good idea for her to call on Liz Laurier. Or would Liz be a persona non grata at the dinner for Hilary, given the opposition of so many teachers to her presence in the school the previous year?

"Oh, gosh!" exclaimed Lynn. "You mustn't leave Liz out! Imagine how her daughter, Rosalind, would feel if her mother were to be excluded! Lord Bramblewell, too, would expect her to be invited."

"Of course. You're right, Lynn. I'll drop in to see her before long."

In fact, Dorothy delayed her visit to Liz until the evening before Lord Bramblewell's wedding, possibly because she was hoping to extract from Liz her views on the match. Liz, though, made it clear, when Dorothy arrived, that she was expecting a client and would not have a great deal of time to chat. And although Dorothy strayed, undiplomatically, into territory that Liz preferred not to discuss, the visit ended amicably enough, with Dorothy reminding Liz that they would possibly see each other, the following day, at the grand wedding in Chester Cathedral.

Dorothy had parked her car opposite the house in which Liz's apartment in down-town Ellesmere Port was located and so, she was well placed, when she had climbed into it, to observe the arrival of the mysterious client to whom Liz had referred: a client who was still to drive up. Since other cars had been parked on the same side of the road as Dorothy's, she reckoned hers would not stand out and that, therefore, her presence, within her car, would not be noticed by Liz's client. Should she wait? She could not resist the temptation to do so. Liz had seemed very anxious for her not to know the identity of the client. Why? Dorothy made herself comfortable in the car seat and took her phone out of her hand bag. She would call Hilary. She had not spoken to her since the evening before.

The conversation had barely begun, though, when Dorothy was startled to see Susie Sutton parking a Bramblewell car in front of Liz's door. The following day's bride! Dorothy watched her getting out of the car and buzzing Liz Laurier's bell, before turning her head to look up anxiously at Liz's windows. Why was she there? Was she having second thoughts about marrying Lord Bramblewell? Or was she worried that Isolde Delamar might spoil her wedding day in some unanticipated way?

Dorothy dropped her voice as she conveyed a report of what she was seeing to Hilary. She did not hesitate, while she was doing so, to mention the fact that Hilary had played a considerable rôle in making Susie's life difficult, by helping Isolde Delamar to secure an administrative post in Bramblewell School, thus creating a situation that Susie had found difficult to endure. Was it Hilary's cold refusal to accept any responsibility for Susie's pain or the sight of Susie, herself, looking fragile and vulnerable that softened Dorothy's heart at that moment? Whatever the reason, she found herself wanting to help the young woman. Despite her inclination to deliver a sharp riposte, now and again, Dorothy was fundamentally kind. She, also, had a sense of fair play and she did not like what Hilary had done one bit. But, how could she be of assistance to Susie, without barging into Liz's flat and offering to over-see the preparations for the wedding at Chester Cathedral? On the other hand, she did not actually need Susie's permission to carry out such a task. She could drive to the cathedral directly, at that moment, to check that all was being done to ensure the wedding would be a success. After all, she was a trusted friend of Lord Bramblewell and she was good at organising events. The people hired to decorate the cathedral would be grateful to her for rushing to their aid, given her knowledge and connection with the Bramblewell world, would they not? She had actually been intending to call at Kathleen's house, before going home, but initially, she could drive onwards, to Chester, to see what was happening at the cathedral and to make sure that all was well.

Dorothy usually drove to Chester at a leisurely pace, in order to take in the views, which were always a delight, but that evening, she drove a little faster. Within twenty minutes, Chester came into sight, flaunting its white and black-timbered loveliness. Dorothy left her car in a car park and made her way to the cathedral on foot, heading, first, in the direction of the Town Hall and then, St. Werburgh Street.

Entering the cathedral, Dorothy felt, as always, as if she were stepping into a world belonging to the past: one illuminated by elegant stained glass windows and warmed by marvellous tapestries on the stone walls. "What a truly beautiful setting for a wedding!" she mused, as if she were appreciating that fact for the first time. She made her way into the dramatic interior and then, saw several young men and women - their demeanour exuding confidence and purpose - walking around, talking in clusters or looking up at the lights. An older woman, with a clip-board and tablet, seemed to be in charge of them. Dorothy guessed they were all employees of the events-planning company hired by Lord Bramblewell to make sure the wedding proceeded without a hitch. Dorothy heard the woman in charge saying, "I'll check now," and then, she walked off in the direction of the Refectory.

Dorothy sat down to wait for the woman's return, her hands

resting on her hand bag, which she had placed on her lap. From time to time, she looked up at a stained glass window, thinking of nothing in particular except its extraordinary luminosity. And it was while she was in this largely passive state that she suddenly became alert, having heard one person, or maybe two, approaching a table that had been placed some distance behind her and, then, putting down something heavy upon it. There had been no reason, really, as to why Dorothy should have homed in on that sound, in particular. The young people walking around in front of her were carrying out their tasks in just as distracting a way, after all. Later, Dorothy would suppose that her intuition, at that moment, had been heightened.

Dorothy turned round and saw Isolde Delamar standing at the table, engrossed in the task of removing papers from a cardboard box and handing them to Eva Derbyshire, the previous year's head girl at Bramblewell School.

"What in the name of creation are they up to?" Dorothy wondered. "And why is Eva, of all people, with that woman?"

Dorothy's mind was racing. Was it likely that Lord Bramblewell would have asked Isolde to help with the preparations for the wedding, given the fact that he was well aware of how Susie felt about her? Definitely not! Dorothy stood up. Almost on tip-toe, she made her way towards the two who were busy piling papers on to the table. Dorothy was not noticed, in fact, until she was standing beside Isolde. Becoming aware of Dorothy's presence, suddenly, Isolde gave a start. She stared at Dorothy, a look of horror and then, defiance on her face. Eva Derbyshire became pale and stepped back, as if she were about to slide away.

"Oh! No you don't!" exclaimed Dorothy, seizing Eva's wrist firmly. "Don't try to run away or I shall telephone your mother and, furthermore, I'll make sure she is removed from the social committee, on which we both sit, and that she will never be elected on to it again!"

It was a threat that sounded alarming enough to make Eva's

body become rigid with shock. Isolde Delamar was staring at Dorothy as if she did not know what to do next. Then, she seemed to have realised that she had to spring into action and she began, furiously, to put back into the cardboard box the papers that she had been removing from it.

"What's in here?" asked Dorothy, letting go of Eva's wrist and seizing the box.

In the struggle that ensued, Isolde tried to pull the box out of Dorothy's hands but Dorothy resisted the attack and held on tightly. The young people working in the cathedral, noticing that something was amiss, hurried towards the two struggling women. Isolde, realising that she was not going to overcome Dorothy, released her grip on the box, with the result that the contents tipped on to the floor. Defeated, she ran from the cathedral.

"I'm fine," said Dorothy to the young employees who had gathered around her by this time. "I'm fine. Really. But, thank you."

Turning to Eva, then, she said coldly:

"You have a lot to explain, haven't you?"

Eva picked up one of the papers that had tumbled from the box. It was actually a booklet, its cover identical with the cover of the official booklets that contained the Order of Service for the wedding that was to take place the following day. She reluctantly handed it to Dorothy who started to flick through it. Everything about it seemed normal at first. But then, when Dorothy reached the two pages in the centre, her heart seemed to jump, so great was her shock. Printed across those two central pages was a large photo of Susie Sutton in the arms of Teddy Laurence, her head resting on his shoulder, an expression of peace and familiarity on her face, as if she had returned to a safe haven. Furthermore - and crucially - Susie was dressed in a chic suit that had been bought after her engagement to Lord Bramblewell had been announced. Everyone who was acquainted with Susie would be aware of that. Dorothy understood what the photographed implied and what the consequence would have been for Susie had the fake booklets been circulated among the guests in the cathedral the following day.

Eva was now weeping.

"Come to sit beside me," Dorothy ordered her, leading the way to the nearest chairs.

Still distraught, Eva did as she was told. Dorothy felt somewhat sorry for the girl but still wanted to extract answers to many questions.

"I shall not reveal what you have done," said Dorothy firmly, "if you tell me everything. Come on! Stop crying and start talking! Hurry up!"

Eva's story unfolded between sobs. Isolde Delamar was her cousin, Aware of the fact that Eva, upon finishing school, had been terrified of going to university and had been searching for something to do locally that was less challenging, but high-status, for months, Isolde had made a pact with her. If she, Eva, were to help her to become Lady Bramblewell, she would give Eva a job at the manor, as a personal assistant and lady's maid.

"A lady's maid?" gasped Dorothy. "You? You want to spend your life ironing hoity-toity Isolde's petticoats? Polishing her jewellery? What is wrong with you? You were head girl of Bramblewell School! A leader! Honestly! I despair! The founder of Bramblewell School expected her girls to be educated to a level that made them extraordinary! Have you lived up to her expectations?"

Eva began to whimper again and Dorothy realised that her association with Isolde had left her psychologically fragile.

"There! There!" she said. "I shall not tell your mother about this aberration - shall we say? - but you must allow me to help you. I think, in fact, that you should enrol yourself in the Christina Quayle College of Languages, this year. You can still live at home, but you will have taken a step towards becoming a university student and you will acquire a knowledge of another language or maybe two. Furthermore, you will meet other young people who are preparing for further studies, also. You can think about applying to university when your confidence has returned and you are a year older. The head of Q-COLL, as it is familiarly called, will of course be known to you - and so, you won't feel as if you are completely on your own. Now! Dry your eyes and help me to separate the fake booklets from the original ones. Oh! And if Isolde Delamar tries to contact you later tonight, tell her that I shall be watching out for her. If she ever comes anywhere near Bramblewell territory again, she will regret it. Do you understand what you must say?"

"Yes, Mrs. Trimm," said Eva, quietly.

"Good! That's settled, then. Now, let's set to work! I shall take the correct booklets away with me to keep them safely in my own house for the night and I shall shred the others. Help me to load the boxes into my car, will you? Then, you can go. And make sure you never misbehave again, Ever! I shall be watching you, also!"

The boxes safely installed in the boot of her car, some minutes later, Dorothy slid into the driver's seat. However, before starting the engine, she took her mobile phone out of her handbag and rang Kath.

"Put the kettle on," she said. "I'm on my way! You won't BELIEVE what has just happened!"

CHAPTER 77

Kath as Confidante

Dorothy Trimm parked her car outside Kath Yarrington's house and then, hurried through the prettily scented garden, the solid heels of her shoes clicking on the path. Kath, who had been hovering by a window, awaiting her arrival, opened the front door before her friend reached it, ushering her then, quickly, through the hall, obviously all agog to hear her news.

"We'll go into the conservatory," she said. "Jeremy's in the sitting room, working. You know what he's like: his papers are spread out everywhere. Apparently, his study isn't big enough!"

"Should I say 'Hello!'?" asked Dorothy. "No! I'd better not. He'll start talking to me about some medical matter or other and I'll be there all evening. Come on! Let's go through to the back, then!"

Kath made tea, while Dorothy made herself comfortable in the garden room. The sun had not yet set and its golden rays shone through the glass panels covering a quarter of the roof.

"Now!" exclaimed Kath, bringing a tray and placing it on the coffee table. She handed Dorothy a linen napkin before sitting down in a cosy chair opposite her friend's.

"Now!" she repeated. "Tell me all about it!"

She leaned forward and picked up a plate on which scones swathed in cream and crushed strawberries were arranged.

"I made these earlier," she said, "and I've put fresh strawberries on them because you found my jam too sweet the last time you were here."

"Yummy!" exclaimed Dorothy. "How unusual!"

"Now!" said Kath again, more forcefully this time. "Spill the beans! And begin at the beginning!"

Dorothy related the events that had taken place in the cathedral in Chester moment by moment, from the arrival of Isolde Delamar and the surprising appearance of Eva Derbyshire to the discovery of the printed photograph inserted into the Order of Service booklet.

"And here it is!" exclaimed Dorothy with a flourish, handing Kath a copy of the booklet, open at the appropriate page.

Kath leaned forward to take the booklet from Dorothy's hand and, having cast her eyes on the photograph, she gasped as if she had had a shock. Without thinking, she put her hand up to the pearl necklace around her throat and pulled at it so fiercely that the string broke and the pearls scattered over the floor.

"Never mind!" she said in an absent-minded way. "I'll pick them up later. They needed to be re-strung anyway. What's important is this photograph. You say you confiscated all copies of the booklet?"

"Yes! They are all in the boot of my car. Eva Derbyshire helped me to carry them outside. Oh! The silly girl won't cause any more trouble. She's too afraid that I'll tell her mother about her behaviour!"

"But, Isolde Delamar has scarpered?"

"Yes. She took to her heels."

"You see, that's what bothers me. She could try to do something else tomorrow. What has she got to lose now?"

"We'll talk about that in a minute. What I want to discuss with you, first, is this photo."

"What about it?"

"Well! Isn't it obvious from what Susie is wearing that the photo was taken not long ago? It was certainly snapped after the engagement to Lord Bramblewell had been announced because it was after that time that Susie started wearing up-market clothes. So...what is she doing in Teddy's arms in the photo? Did Isolde Delamar actually know something about Susie and Teddy that no one else knew?"

"You mean, you think…? No! I don't believe it! No! No! What you are implying is simply not feasible. Susie was Teddy's girlfriend at one time after all, wasn't she?"

"But, she isn't Teddy's girlfriend now! At least, she shouldn't be!"

"So…do you think we should ask her why she was in Teddy Laurence's arms?"

"I jolly well think we should ask her exactly that question for poor Rupert's sake, but I know that she is visiting Liz Laurier at the moment and besides, if she is unaware of the existence of this photo, it might not be kind to upset her. There could be an innocent explanation as to why she was in Teddy's arms, you see."

"Yes. Of course there might be a perfectly innocent explanation, but I can't help wondering why she was visiting Liz Laurier on the night before her wedding."

"What shall we do, Kath?"

"Why don't you call Teddy Laurence? Do you have his number?"

"Actually, I do…Do you really think I should call him?"

"I think you jolly well should and for two reasons. Firstly, he should be made aware of the depths to which Isolde Delamar is capable of sinking, I mean, she is presumably still employed in the school."

"Oh! Not for much longer! Surely!" interrupted Dorothy.

"And secondly," Kath continued, "he will be able to tell you exactly why Susie was in his arms! The reason could be quite innocuous, as you have pointed out, but if he starts to flounder in the way a fair number of men do when they have been caught out doing something not very nice, you'll know that something shabby has been going on. I don't believe, any more than you do, that Teddy Laurence is the type to deceive, but it's best to check so that a cloud of suspicion won't be hanging over him. Just do it!"

Dorothy took her mobile phone out of her box-shaped handbag and located Teddy's number. He answered almost at once and having been given details of what had been shown in the photograph, he was able to explain that it, the photograph, would have been taken, obviously surreptitiously, shortly after he had told Susie that Lord Bramblewell had upbraided Isolde Delamar in the science corridor of Bramblewell School for the disrespectful way she had been talking to various people in the school. Lord Bramblewell had also made it plain to Isolde that Susie was the one he loved.

"When I told Susie what Lord Bramblewell had said, she collapsed with relief into my arms," added Teddy.

"Oh! I understand, now!" exclaimed Dorothy. "That is such good news, Teddy!"

"What?" whispered Kath, leaning forward. "What is he saying?"

"It's all right!" Dorothy assured her. "Nothing to worry about! What, Teddy? Oh! I was just talking to my friend, Kath! We'll see you tomorrow!"

Having completed the call, Dorothy recounted to Kath what Teddy had told her.

"Cool!" exclaimed Kath.

"Cool? What are you? A teenager?" retorted Dorothy. "Honestly! Sometimes I think you are becoming as bad as those misguided and irritating people who say, "I was sat there" and "I was stood there"!

"Will you forget about grammar for a moment and concentrate on tomorrow's wedding? Listen! I think it could still be wrecked by this wretched Isolde."

"How likely is it that she will have a back-up plan, though? This booklet was obviously meant to be her coup de théâtre. There is a chance – don't you think? – that she doesn't have anything else up her sleeve. Unless she is going to be awake all night cooking up another dastardly scheme, the marriage will go ahead without a hitch. That would be my guess. She'll watch from a distance seething with rage, but she will know that she has lost the battle."

"Yes. But, that will make her very dangerous, Dorothy. She'll be back when Susie, Teddy and Lord Bramblewell least expect to see her and she'll attack. You can bet on that. I also think that we should keep a look-out in the cathedral tomorrow."

"Yes...You are right. She probably will be back and I bet Teddy has realised that also. He won't say anything to Susie but I'm pretty sure he'll stay at Bramblewell just to be ready to protect her. He'll never get over Susie, you know. Never. I really believe that."

"What about the headmistress?"

"Lynn? Hm...Not sure. He seems to be very attached to her, but he is a bit younger than she is. Would SHE find HIM interesting? That is the question, as Shakespeare would say."

"And wasn't there an American girl?"

"Oh! You can forget her! I'm sure we shan't see her again. A long distance romance? Never works, dear. Never works. Now, are you going to make more tea? We need to decide where we shall situate ourselves tomorrow so that we shall have all corners covered, just in case...It's going to be a long day, Kath. A very long day. Make sure you have a hearty breakfast."

CHAPTER 78

Wedding Day

Susie Sutton awoke in her bedroom in Bramblewell Manor, knowing that the most important day of her life - her wedding day - had finally dawned. By the end of the morning, she would be Lady Bramblewell, having risen, like the heroine of a romantic novel, to a position she had previously only attained in dreams. Or would she? The thought of Isolde Delamar's lurking presence was one which Susie could not force out of her mind. Would Isolde be hiding in the cathedral? Would she try to prevent the marriage from taking place in some dramatically unexpected way?

There was a quiet knock on the door.

"Come in!" called Susie, sitting up. She had told Mrs. Oliver that she was not to be disturbed that morning and so, the person outside the door was probably one of the bridesmaids. It was Rosalind, in fact, still in her nightdress and dressing gown, but clearly wide awake and in high spirits.

"What would you like for breakfast?" she asked. "I could fetch something on a tray."

"Don't worry about me, Rosie," answered Susie." Look after yourself! You have a long day ahead of you, too!"

"Oh! Surely tea and toast, at least!"

"All right! But bring enough for yourself as well!"

Susie realised, then, that her head was beginning to hurt. She poured water from a decanter on her bedside table into a glass and swallowed all of it. She wondered if June, her chief bridesmaid, had woken up. It had been a while since she had had a long conversation with June and it was because of that lack of contact that Susie had become aware of the extent to which she had depended upon her friend's unqualified support, when life had been difficult, in the past.

When both she and June had worked together at the Tectum accommodation agency, in Chester, Susie had, also, rather enjoyed the way June had placed her on a pedestal. June had clearly been impressed by her admired friend's apparently glamorous way of living, the outer trappings having consisted of a wardrobe full of up-to-date clothes and a house that was all her own. What, in June's opinion, could have been more desirable than the Susie lifestyle? Naturally, when the engagement to Lord Bramblewell had been announced, June had been genuinely pleased, but without any expectation that she, herself, would benefit from her friend's good fortune. Such loyalty and modesty, Susie felt, had to be rewarded. June had been asked to be the chief bridesmaid at the grand wedding, but she deserved to be thanked in other tangible ways, also.

Susie pushed back the white quilt, sheet and blankets covering her and swung her legs out of the bed as if she had been alighting from a car, in the way her tutor in gracious living and etiquette had recently taught her. She walked over to the nearest window and pushed the heavy curtains fully open. Down below, the trees and lawns of the park surrounding the manor were absorbing the early sunlight. Susie felt an urge to run out on to the grass, bare-footed, in order to feel sensually at liberty one last time, but then, she reined in her thoughts. Lord Bramblewell would surely expect his bride to be more circumspect on her wedding day, of all days.

Susie sat down in front of her dressing-table, then, and looked at her face in the large mirror. There were shadows under her eyes but they could be concealed with make-up. First, she would have to have a warm bath. Then, she would have to prepare herself for the arrival of the hairdresser who was going to wash and style her blonde locks. The make-up artist would arrive at the manor a short time after that. There was so much to do!

There was another knock on the bedroom door and, this time,

it was June who entered. Already, dressed in a long, slim, ivory gown, covered in pearls, she looked like a princess. Even her skin had acquired a glow that became her.

"Oh, Susie!" she said. "This is too lovely for me."

"No. It's just right," said Susie, sitting down on the edge of the bed. "But listen, there's something I want to arrange with you."

"Yes? Something you want me to do? What is it?"

"I want to talk about my house in Whitby Village," said Susie. "You know that I still go there from time to time, but from today onwards, possibly not as often as before,"

"Yes," said June.

"I don't want to sell it, but…"

"Do you want me to keep an eye on it?"

"Sort of. It takes only fifteen minutes to walk to it from where you live with your parents. Isn't that right?"

"Yes."

"Well, I'm aware of the fact that you want to be close to your parents, as they are not in good health, but I also know that you'd really prefer to have a place of your own and I was wondering if you'd like to move into my house. Would you? I'll call in from time to time but not often. Only when I need a break from life in the manor. You'd be doing me a favour. And don't even think of paying rent. I wouldn't accept it."

"Oh, Susie!" gasped June. She put her hand up to her throat, as her face turned pale. "This is the best present anyone has EVER given me. I'd never have saved up the deposit for a house of my own! I don't know what to say! Honestly! You don't know what this means to me!"

"Oh! I think I do, June!" said Susie, remembering her own struggles. "Come on, now! Don't cry! You'll spoil your make-up! And besides, there's something else I want to ask you."

"What?"

"Well, Lord Bramblewell has pointed out that I'll have so many duties to fulfil as Lady Bramblewell that I'll need a secretary to look after my social diary. I was wondering if you'd consider leaving the accommodation agency in order to take the job. Would you? I know that I can trust you, absolutely. And we'd have a lot of fun gossiping, wouldn't we? Just like the old days!"

"Oh! Susie!" Of course I'd love to have the job! That would be brilliant!"

"That's settled then! I'm glad! Thank you! I sort of knew you'd say 'yes'!"

"You really, really have no idea what all of this means to me. My life is going to change so much!"

"And for the better, I hope. Just like mine."

"I don't know what…"

"Listen! Go to your room and calm yourself down. Don't forget that I'll be relying on you later to make sure I don't make a mistake!"

When June had gone away, Susie looked for her hair-dryer in one of the drawers of the dressing table and having located it, switched it on. It was she who needed to calm down, as she was beginning to feel nervous. She directed the jet of warmth gushing out of the dryer at her hair and then, ran it up and down the skin of her arm, imagining that she was lying in warm sunshine on a beach. She felt better. But she could not waste any more time. The future Lady Bramblewell had an important engagement to fulfil!

A few miles away in the Wirral, Dorothy Trimm was also on the point of sprucing up her appearance, in preparation for the wedding. First things first, though. In her kitchen, she made a cup of tea and an omelette. The ceremony in the cathedral would be long and she knew she would have to eat adequately beforehand in order to have the strength to see it through. Besides, she would have to have sustenance to help her to stay alert, in case Isolde Delamar would decide to make one last attempt to destroy the bride's happiness. Of course, were Isolde to do so, she would ruin herself socially in Cheshire. On the other hand, she had probably gone beyond the point of caring about her diminishing social agenda.

"She's like a scorpion," Dorothy muttered to what she assumed to be a neighbour's cat that, to her surprise, had jumped on to the window sill outside her kitchen. "A scorpion! I honestly think she would readily sacrifice herself, if that sacrifice would result in her destroying Susie as well. There are women who are like that, you know! Stupid but deadly! I sometimes think my own daughter comes dangerously close to being one of them, mind you!"

Dorothy had bought a new outfit for the wedding: a pale blue dress with a fitted jacket in the same material. There was already in her possession a pale blue cloche hat which matched the dress and she had decided to wear it, but had asked a dressmaker to add a pale turquoise band to add contrast. When her dressing was complete, Dorothy studied her reflection, front and back, in the long mirror on the landing. She decided that she looked very smart and was therefore satisfied. The hat was rather out of date in style, but that would make it a head-turner, so to speak, although obviously not to the extent that it would be impolitely distracting.

Dorothy and her friend Kath had decided to go to the Cathedral together, in one car. Kath arrived to collect Dorothy an hour and a half before the ceremony was to begin, in fact. Then, after Kath had driven to the car park in Chester, the two of them went on foot to St. Werburgh Street. The cathedral doors were open and the atmosphere was festive.

"Any sign of her?" asked Kath. "Isolde, I mean."

"No," said Dorothy. "But then, she could be anywhere, couldn't she?"

"I'll go to the cloisters right now," said Kath. "I'll have a look around. Are you going to stay here? I'll see you at the end of the ceremony, anyway. Somewhere or other."

"Yes. Cheerio, then. But wait! What are you going to do if you come across her? We haven't actually talked about that."

"I don't know, but I'll think of something if I have to."

"That's all very well, but I reckon we should have some plan in mind!"

"Actually, I don't REALLY think that she'll turn up! Do you?"

"I don't know..."

"Honestly? After what happened last night? I don't think so."

"I hope you're right, dear. But I'll hover around here at the back, all the same. Oh! There's Stella Lomas! She's a discreet girl, I'll ask her to keep her eyes open, too. So, I'll see you in an hour and a half's time or thereabouts."

"Agreed. If we miss each other, we can meet in the car park."

In Bramblewell Manor, meanwhile, Susie, helped by her bridesmaids, was stepping into her bridal gown. Floor-length, slim, white and cut on the bias, it sparkled when she moved, since it had been studded with tiny crystals, all sewn into the satin by hand. Being simple in conception, the dress had an uncomplicated allure, rather than an overly sophisticated and stiff appearance. For that reason, Susie had asked that her hair not be rolled into a smooth chignon. Instead, she had requested that it fall in soft, shiny waves to her shoulders. Around her head, she had chosen to wear a circle of leaves and flowers that had been plucked from the greenhouses behind the manor. She had been offered a Bramblewell tiara to wear by her future husband, but she had decided that she would reserve that bejewelled treasure for the grand celebration that would be held in the evening, She would wear it with an old-fashioned perfume created in the 1950s: a scent that rather evoked the atmosphere of a stylish ball, in a grand manor house, like the one soon to be her home. When walking down the aisle, she wanted to look, in contrast, rather like an unknowing ingénue: sweet-natured and as fresh as the flowers she was wearing. Susie, as always, was conscious of the messages conveyed by clothes and the effect they had on the beholder.

After Susie's dressing had been completed, the bridesmaids left, June being the last to go. Susie breathed in deeply. The minutes were passing quickly. She felt the chill of nervousness on her skin, again, but nevertheless, she made her way to the door, fighting the temptation to allow her thoughts to drift towards negativity. She had attended to all that could be controlled. She had to trust that all else would be well.

Through her mother, with whom she had infrequently been in touch, Susie had let her father know that she had wanted him to give her away on her wedding day. However, he had sent a message in return, declining the invitation. He had regretted the fact that he would be unable to attend the wedding, but had wanted his daughter to know that he had felt honoured and flattered to have been even considered for such a rôle, given his negligence in the years that had passed. Naturally, he had wished Susie well and had promised he would be thinking of her on her wedding day. Susie had not pressed him to change his mind, but there had arisen, then, the puzzling matter of whom she should choose to accompany her down the aisle of the cathedral. Lord Bramblewell had suggested that she consider one of his nephews, Horatio or Julian. Susie had not hesitated: she had chosen Julian. Now, he would be waiting for her, downstairs.

Having glanced in the cheval mirror near the dressing table, one last time, Susie left her bedroom and walked along the corridor to the head of the grand staircase. Down in the entrance hall, Julian was standing alone, looking magnificent in morning dress. At that moment, Susie could think of no other she would have wanted as her companion during the drive to the cathedral. She realised how much she trusted him and the extent to which she felt at ease in his company. But what she valued most of all was the fact that, like Lord Bramblewell, he had never become angry with her, no matter what he had privately thought of her. She intensely disliked men who expressed their anger loudly. Gylen Somerland's bad temper had terrified her, even though she had had to conceal her fear, for the sake of his children.

"You look beautiful," said Julian gallantly, when Susie had reached the foot of the stairs. "Uncle Rupert will be stunned."

Susie smiled but said nothing other than "Thank you!" a cold wave of nervousness now having seemed to have anaesthetised her throat. Her intuitive faculties, though, had become sharper. She sensed that there had been a degree of restraint in the way Julian had spoken to her.

"Is there something wrong?" she managed to ask.

"No! No!" Julian assured her, but without elaboration. "Let's go, shall we? Are you ready, Susie?"

The dark grey, Bramblewell car was highly polished, but stylishly devoid of ribbons. Susie made herself comfortable in the back seat and Julian helped her to fold her dress, in such a way as to avoid over-creasing, before he joined her. Lord Bramblewell's driver started the engine and Susie looked silently out of the window as the car moved slowly through the grounds of Bramblewell Manor, heading for the gates and the main road beyond them. There, the driver would turn the car to the right and then, would drive Susie and Julian to the City of Chester, proper and, specifically, to St. Werburgh Street and the doors of the cathedral.

As the car neared the Bramblewell gates, however, Julian unexpectedly leaned forward. He asked the driver to stop the car and to take a short walk to check that the gates were actually open. The driver alighted from the car without question. It was as if he had already been told that Julian would make the request.

"Susie," Julian said quietly, then. "I think there is something I should mention to you at this point. I was asked to say nothing until we had reached the cathedral but my conscience has been telling me that it wouldn't be fair to spring a surprise on you, there."

Susie felt a wave of fear now sweeping over her. She looked at Julian as if aghast. She could not imagine what he was about to say to her, but obviously, it was something that was making him feel uneasy.

"What is it? What's wrong?" she asked, her voice sounding like a little girl's.

Julian took hold of her hand. His skin felt warm. Hers was cold.

"What's wrong?" Susie repeated. "Tell me!"

Julian hesitated. He glanced out of the window beside him but then, turned to look directly at her.

"When we reach the cathedral," he said, "Teddy Laurence will be waiting for you."

"What do you mean? Why? I'm not going to marry Teddy!"

"No. Of course not! But, Uncle Rupert felt that Teddy should give you away, during the marriage ceremony."

"But, that's…Why? I mean, why can't you do it? Why did Rupert think Teddy…? It was his idea that you should give me away. What's going on?"

Susie's voice had become even more child-like. She sounded as if she were about to cry. Julian looked at her in a way that suggested he was not sure how to explain to her why Lord Bramblewell had decided, the previous evening, to ask Teddy to accompany her on her walk to the altar. Julian, too, had been surprised to hear about the change in the plan and had wondered why Teddy had agreed to it. Perhaps Teddy had immediately understood the symbolism of the gesture and the effect it would have on Susie's attitude to him after her marriage. That outward sign of an inward change would be significant, surely.

Julian held Susie's hand tightly, as if he were hoping the touch of his own hand would steady her.

"Uncle Rupert wanted you to be sure that he was the one you really wanted to marry. He mentioned something about the way you had said Teddy's name on Christmas morning. You were standing in a corridor in front of a portrait of Lady…"

"Oh!" interrupted Susie as if suddenly remembering the moment. "He must have been…"

"He overheard you," Julian continued. "He wasn't spying on you, of course, but he did happen to overhear what you said, or rather, the way that you said it."

"But, why didn't he talk to me about it?"

"He needed time to think."

"So, doesn't he want to marry me now?"

Susie was on the verge of tumbling into a state of panic, as she envisaged her most cherished dream slipping into a dark hole in space. Why had she been worried about Isolde Delamar's strategies when she had stupidly been the creator of her own misery? But then, through the shady cloud that had descended on her, she heard Julian saying:

"Don't be absurd! Of course he wants to marry you. He just wants to be sure that you want to marry HIM! He wants to be sure that you are ready to be his wife and that you are prepared to forsake all others, as the saying goes."

"Oh! Julian! I'd never betray him. I just wouldn't. I mean...No! I couldn't! I'm not Anna Karenina!"

"What has made you think of Anna Karenina?"

"Well, the school play, last Christmas, was about her, wasn't it? Remember? I'm not like her, Julian. I swear I'm not! Why is this happening to me? Why is Rupert putting me through this on my wedding day? How could he?"

"He was let down badly by Isolde Delamar, you see...He has to be sure."

Susie's mind was in turmoil. Surely Lord Bramblewell knew that she was not like Isolde and never would be! Should she marry him: a man who was capable of upsetting her in the dramatic way he just had? Did she know him as well as she thought she had known him? Had he been more concerned about her friendship with Teddy Laurence than she had ever suspected? What else was there to learn about him? What should she do?

"Shall we drive on, Susie?" Julian was asking gently. "It's up to you. Are you ready?"

Susie was now thinking of the night she had been offered her engagement ring: a beautiful ring that had once belonged to a cherished Bramblewell ancestor. She thought of her visit to Ywen Manor and the way she had been welcomed by the Bramblewell nephews, Horatio as well as Julian, and by Gwenny. She thought of Bramblewell Manor and how she had grown to love it and care for it. And then, she thought of Lord Bramblewell, himself, and how he had kindly opened the door to a life she had never before experienced. He had had every right to question her fidelity, given the way she had whispered Teddy's name at an inappropriate time. How would she have felt if she had heard him whispering Isolde's name on Christmas morning? Tansy had been right when she had pointed out that she, Susie, had been expecting Lord Bramblewell to have been exceptionally tolerant. Was she not fortunate, in fact, that he was giving her another chance to be his bride?

"I'm ready," she said, squeezing Julian's hand. "But… what are you going to do when we get there?"

"I'll have a place reserved for me, somewhere. Don't worry about me!"

During the remainder of the drive to the cathedral, Susie was silent, but she held on to Julian's hand tightly, as if she were trying to draw strength from him. Soon the car swept into St. Werburgh Street. Susie saw the open doors of the cathedral and, on the other side of the road, a crowd of well-wishers starting to applaud. Her face became animated. The future Lady Bramblewell was ready to slip into her rôle.

As she descended from the car, Susie became aware of Teddy, all dressed up, walking towards her. He looked mystifyingly untroubled. Behind him could be seen June, steady, still and smiling. Had she known about the Teddy plan, earlier that morning? Surely not! Beside her were the younger bridesmaids, Rosalind, Ida, Portia and Talitha, elegant in a youthful way, like Spring swans, floating on Chester's River Dee. Susie looked up at the sky. A falcon was circling the cathedral before swooping down to return to its place of rest. Susie took hold of Teddy's arm. She, now, felt comfortable and calm, as if she had stepped on to a stage to take part in a performance for which she had prepared well.

Inside the cathedral, she moved forward at a stately pace, Teddy by her side. There was music playing. She did not recognise it but she thought it sounded glorious. She glanced to the left and right and noticed Miss Trimm and how pale her face was. She searched the crowd for a sighting of Isolde but she was nowhere to be seen. Then, she became aware of Lord Bramblewell waiting for her with Horatio, his best man, by his side. She smiled at him, her beloved Rupert, and he smiled back at her, relieved that she had arrived.

The ceremony proceeded without an interruption. Susie drifted through it as if in a dream. When she emerged from the cathedral, she waved to the people outside who were generously cheering, before she stepped into the Bramblewell car. As Lord Bramblewell joined her, she caught sight of Julian and they exchanged knowing looks. Julian was smiling as if he were silently saying, "Well done!"

At the back of the cathedral, Dorothy was waiting for her friend, Kath. But before Kath's arrival, Stella Lomas, in a girlishly elegant, calf-length dress and an appropriately pretty picture hat, with a chiffon band around the brim, approached her.

"I should have pointed out earlier that you look lovely, dear," said Dorothy, "Very jeune fille!"

"Thank you, Mrs. Trimm," said Stella, appreciatively. "It was nice of Lord Bramblewell to have invited me. It was a wonderful wedding, but I think I should point out that Miss Delamar was outside, in the crowd in St. Werburgh Street. I saw her."

"Did you? When?"

"A couple of minutes ago. She noticed that I was looking at her and she stepped back then. I couldn't see her after that."

"That's very interesting, Stella. Thank you for being so observant, dear."

Dorothy turned to Kath who had just arrived, anxious to discover what had happened.

"Did you hear that?" Dorothy asked. "Isolde is still on the prowl!"

"Oh, no! Does that mean I'll have to keep watch all through the evening celebration as well? Come on, Dorothy! Enough is enough!"

"I agree, dear. Susie Sutton is married. I think we can have a bit of a rest, now! But, we should still be observant."

At the manor, food had been provided, in the form of a buffet meal, for those who were hungry after attending the marriage ceremony at the cathedral, but the main celebration was to take place in the evening. Dorothy and Kath had decided to attend both the early afternoon and evening events.

"Just in case," said Dorothy. "You never know! Ooh! Look! A whole, big, Stilton cheese! It must be ages since I tasted Stilton! Can you see the spoon? What are you going to eat, dear? It's all a bit salad-y, isn't it? Is there any soup?"

Upstairs in the Manor, Susie was resting before preparing for the evening event. The new Lady Bramblewell would have to look her best, then. The dress she was going to wear - a slim, heavily bejewelled and embroidered gown, which had a high, pearl studded neckline and long, thin sleeves which were puffed at the top - was hanging up in her walk-in dressing room. Her satin, high-heeled shoes, which were also heavily embroidered with white and silver threads, were by her dressing table, waiting for her to put them on. Susie walked from dressing room to bedroom, touching the dress and the shoes, over and over again, as if to ascertain that they really existed, just as she had once walked around her house in Whitby Village, touching the walls and the staircase to make sure that they were not part of an imagined chimera. She looked at her left hand, from time to time, to ensure that the heavy, wide, golden band was still adorning it. All was in place, of course. The dream had come true. It was difficult for Susie to stop herself from crying with relief and gratitude, but she succeeded. The new Lady Bramblewell had to set an example, after all, even in private.

That evening, all those who had had the good fortune to have been invited, enjoyed the most splendid of celebrations: a celebration which evoked the atmosphere and style of a former era. Chandelier-lit and scented with essences of roses from the gardens of Cheshire, the ballroom looked like an illustrated page from a child's book of fairy tales. The pale, floor-length curtains had been drawn back to provide a view of the flood-lit terrace and the starless sky above it.

Susie was at the centre of attention all evening, Lord Bramblewell being happy to allow her to be in the limelight. He was proud of her. She had played her part splendidly that day. He turned to her to tell her so and she smiled with pleasure, happy that she had not let him down. While she had been listening to him, though, she had noticed, out of the corner of her eye, Teddy Laurence talking animatedly to Lynn James. She, Lynn, chic in a long, sleeveless, cream dress, with a high, round neck-line, her long hair, loose but elegant, had been looking completely at ease in his company. Was Lynn the reason why Teddy had looked so composed that morning? Susie, when later reflecting on his tranquil demeanour, had been mildly puzzled by his lack of overt sadness. After all, he had loved her so much, once. Had Lynn been his distraction? Well! It did not matter any longer. She, Susie, had let him go.

It was black- dark outside the manor, that evening, but by the light of a small torch, a cloaked woman was making her way, swiftly, through the trees that had stood, knowing and wise, in the Bramblewell grounds for centuries. After crossing an expanse of grass, the woman headed for the kitchens. Then, after looking through one of the windows, she approached the heavy door that led to a white-walled passage where coats were hung up. She knocked on it.

"What are you doing here, Miss Delamer?" asked Mrs. Oliver, having responded, in a tetchy manner, to the hammering on the door. "Can't you guess we're busy?"

"I have to talk to you."

"I don't think so."

"Oh, yes! You do!" insisted Isolde, her tone slightly threatening.

Mrs. Oliver, obviously fuming, returned to the main kitchen.

"Tamsin, take over, for a minute," she ordered in a peremptory manner. She took her coat from a peg by the door, then, and stepped outside with Isolde.

"Listen!" she said, after checking that no one had followed her. "I don't know why you are here. I did as you asked, last night. I handed the photo you gave me in a plain envelope to Lord Bramblewell and said it had been delivered by hand but that I hadn't seen who had left it. However, as is obvious, your plan to stop the wedding from taking place did not succeed. You played a losing hand, Miss Delamar. There is no more to be said."

"But, I want you to carry on helping me! We can get rid of her, if we stick together."

"Carry on helping you? I am sorry, Miss Delamar. Why should I risk being dismissed from a job I like and, frankly, need by trying to destabilize my employer?"

"Your employer? I'm talking about Susie Sutton!"

"And I am talking about the new Lady Bramblewell, Miss Delamar. Good-night!"

Shocked, defeated and alone, Isolde Delamar stood still as the kitchen door was shut and locked. She then slipped, like a cat, into the night.

CHAPTER 79

Resolution

Photographs of Lord Bramblewell and his bride appeared on the web sites of society magazines only hours after the wedding had taken place. In Paris, the following morning, an astonished Jacqueline de Sauzon scrolled through them on her computer, stopping now and again to note the bride's poise and her smile: a smile which enhanced her appearance to an extent that persuaded Jacqueline it had been practised many times prior to the event's occurrence.

Jacqueline checked her mail-box, then, to see if anyone had written to her to make comments that echoed her own opinions. In fact, a message had arrived, during the night, from Rebecca Hampton. Rebecca, on the east coast of America, had been studying the photos, too, via the world wide web, and had expressed surprise that Susie Sutton had not backed away, at the last moment, from the daunting prospect of becoming a Bramblewell bride. Rebecca, in fact, had thought that Susie would have scuttled back to Teddy Laurence, having been intimidated by the challenges that being a Bramblewell would entail. But perhaps Teddy had acquired another girlfriend? It occurred to Jacqueline that the entire purpose of Rebecca's message had been encapsulated in that final question. Rebecca had not really been interested in the fate of Susie Sutton. She had simply wanted to know if Teddy had a girlfriend. Jacqueline was disappointed that Rebecca had not been more candid. When the two of them, Rebecca and she, had shared a flat in Liverpool, as students, they had exchanged information about their thoughts and intentions in an honest way. Why was Rebecca being coy now?

Jacqueline had to admit, though, that, like Rebecca, she, herself, had had initial doubts about Susie's ability to cope with the duties that were now hers. However, the photos of the wedding were suggesting that her fears had been groundless. Cheerful, optimistic Susie had risen to the challenge with aplomb. How different she was now from the way she had been when Jacqueline had first met her, though! Susie had made it clear, then, that she had social aspirations, but her red cocktail dress and backless, scarlet sandals, coupled with her rather louche and easy nonchalance, had suggested she had a long way to go. By Sauzon family standards, at any rate. But now, one could learn lessons from Susie's dogged perseverance in her pursuit of a goal, although, obviously, one could not overlook the fact that she had coldly and selfishly stepped over Teddy Laurence in her eagerness to climb the social ladder.

Jacqueline's interest in the new Lady Bramblewell's transformation had been triggered, in part, by the fact that she had been considering changing the direction of her own life. She had started to think about doing so during her visit to the Hebrides with Marie-Colette. Far from her usual environment - the cafés of Paris where intellos gathered, the bookshops of the Boulevard Saint-Michel and her Left Bank apartment - she had had time to reflect on her life, her troubling marriage and her relationship with her family. She had thought often about her mother, the Countess de Sauzon, and, specifically, her mother's thwarted ambition which had left her feeling unfulfilled. It had once been the Countess' cherished desire to found a company, small or otherwise, which would have as its focus the manufacturing of beautifying products, made from the flora found by the sea, but this desire had been suppressed, since the mere mention of it had resulted in her being contemptuously derided by Madame Gabrielle.

It seemed natural, now, to Jacqueline that her mother would be interested in the world of business. Her father, the late Hubert de

Talence, after all, had been a business man. It was not inconceivable that his only child would have inherited from him the drive to succeed in that field, even though Madame Gabrielle had insisted on preparing Marie-Christine for another rôle. Jacqueline had begun to wonder if she, herself, had been carrying within herself, genetically, her mother's latent flair for business or if her growing desire to make her mother's dream a reality had arisen from a feeling of guilt over having let her mother down, combined with the related wish to make amends and to please her.

Jacqueline had begun to wonder, too, admittedly more fancifully, if her visit to the Hebrides had been neither accidental nor coincidental. If she, herself, were to set up a beauty business, of the type her mother had envisaged, but in the Hebrides, rather than in Brittany, it would be so far away from France that surely its existence would not embarrass Madame Gabrielle. Perhaps she, Jacqueline, could begin on a small scale by opening a beauty clinic and thalassotherapy centre, which would provide a few treatments. Perhaps she could find a large enough house for sale that she could convert. She would have to contact someone in Paris who had an acquaintance with Europe-wide law and who would be able to advise her. It crossed her mind, then, that her newly-discovered cousin, Antoine du Crâne, might be the best person to approach, initially. She would talk to her mother about the project also, in the hope that she would be persuaded to take an interest in it. At first, the Countess would be fearful, since she was capable, still, of being intimidated by Madame Gabrielle, but gradually, her fear would turn to pleasure, surely. As for the Count de Sauzon, he would simply shrug. And Jacqui? Perhaps he would not mind that his wife had found a consuming interest that would divert her, while he was at sea. In any case, she would have to finish her studies in Paris first, but having a goal in mind would make a difference to the way she perceived her life there.

When she thought about the change that she was considering, Jacqueline realised that she had started to feel the pull towards it on the night that she had found Marie-Colette standing in the moon-lit, Hebridean garden, staring at a stone wall. Jacqueline had assumed the girl had been sleep-walking, but now she was not sure. Marie-Colette's insistence that something was beginning had been puzzling, then. "Ça commence," she had said, firmly. But, when questioned the next day, she had looked blankly at Jacqueline as if she could not remember anything that had occurred the night before. She had insisted that she did not like "her" side of the rented house, all the same, and had refused to set foot in it again. Jacqueline had tried to chivvy the girl into cheerfulness until it had been time to leave. Back in France, Marie-Colette had been sent by her mother to rest for a fortnight in a clinic near Vannes, when the episode in the Hebridean house had been reluctantly described to her, but she, the Countess de Sauzon, had managed to stop herself from saying, "I told you so," much to Héloïse's relief as well as Jacqueline's.

On that moon-lit night, the one that had enticed Marie-Colette into a Hebridean garden, Antoine du Crâne, far away in Paris, had also been unable to sleep. Wearing navy-blue monogrammed pyjamas, acquired in London, and a silk dressing gown, he had lain down on a sofa in his study, in order to settle a bout of queasiness. Then, at dawn, he had gone into his library to search for a philosophical work that would calm him. To which writers should he turn? To Pascal? To Montaigne? To the Greeks? He had felt as if he had been tumbling into a state of desperation, when his search had come to nothing. What a self- indulgent feeling that had been, though, given the ease of his circumstances! Desperation, indeed! How had he dared to imagine himself falling into despair when he had known that people had been sleeping under the bridges of Paris, homeless and destitute, for years? They were the ones who were familiar with the real face of despair. But, on the other hand, ease of circumstances had never cured him of his self-doubt. Although he had hidden his condition well, he had been of a nervous disposition, even at the best of times, all his life and therefore, the thought of the day ahead of him, a day that would possibly be emotionally draining, had played havoc with his mind and body. He had already been compelled to take two fizzy tablets dissolved in water to lessen the effect that his thoughts had been having on his stomach. What had been making him feel worse had been his assumption that Miss Caterina Traversi, whom he had arranged to meet in the morning, had once mentioned, en passant, that she had always had a taste for the sang-froid of the idealised British gentleman that she had encountered in fiction. He had been able to imagine her being drawn to that kind of man. What would she think of him, Antoine, were she to discover that his cool self-possession had never been more than a sham?

He had known that Miss Traversi had already landed in Paris and that she would be arriving at his apartment around eleven o' clock in the morning "Bon sang!" he had muttered. What sort of power had the young woman been able to exert over him to have induced in him such a feeling of helplessness? The meeting, after all, was to be no more than a business engagement. Miss Traversi would simply be discussing with him, in French, some of the details that Mr. Kit Mallory had requested be clarified with regard to the leasing of a section of the Château du Crâne. Mr. Mallory had wanted to buy, but Julian Bramblewell- Eurlinn had been disinclined to grant permission for such a sale, foreseeing difficulties when the question of inheritance would arise. Mr. Mallory had clearly been sympathetic to Julian's desire to repair the château with care and with due respect for its past, but Mr. Mallory's heirs were unknown. It would be folly to assume that they would possess the same level of interest in the château's history as had been shown by Mr. Mallory. The conversation with Miss Traversi, in the morning, would deal with such issues and would be straightforward, but the emotional tension created by her mere presence would be overwhelming. Antoine simply hoped that he would manage to conduct himself without making a fool of himself as, apparently, he had done, the last time they had had a meeting in Paris.

Not far away, in a hotel room in the 1st arrondissement of the city, that night, Caterina Traversi was sitting up in bed, making notes for the meeting that would take place in the morning. At the same time, she was trying to recall in detail, the way she had parted company with Antoine du Crâne on the previous occasion they had met. He, Antoine, had seemed exceptionally anxious to see her again and she had drawn back, as if by reflex action. Numerous times since then, she had mentally gone over her reasons for having behaved in the way she had and, finally, she had concluded that her inner panic had not been a reaction to Antoine's character: it had been connected solely with her own. In fact, on reflection, she had found plenty to admire in Antoine's behaviour. She had found him to be not only knowledgeable but interesting, after all. She had been able to listen to him without feeling tired. Additionally, she had been charmed by the fact that he had verged on being a trifle eccentric, eccentricity being a trait that rather amused her. And, in the end, after much thought, she had realised that her own behaviour had been driven by fear: fear that Antoine would discover her inherent worthlessness were he to be given the opportunity to know her better. She had been afraid that, for him, such an experience would be similar to his buying diamonds and, later, discovering that he had been duped, as they had really been only poppet beads made of plastic.

Caterina leaned back into the pile of white pillows that she had assembled behind her and then, reached for the remote control object lying on the bedside table. She turned down the sound of the flat-screen TV on the wall opposite her bed and then, closed her eyes. She had to stop thinking about herself negatively.

She had, after all, worked hard for Mr. Mallory, she had been given a position of responsibility by Dorothy Trimm and Papa had been pleased with her success. She had achieved a great deal on her own, in fact, in a short time. Why then was a voice inside her head still telling her that she was not good enough? Was what one did not part of what one was? Or was that too existentialist a concept for her unconscious mind to accept? She did not really understand existentialism. Had it been discredited as a philosophy? Maybe she should ask Antoine du Crâne to explain it to her. Or perhaps she had better not waste Mr. Mallory's time or Antoine du Crâne's, for that matter, the next day, by bringing up private preoccupations for discussion. She fell asleep while still sitting, exhausted by those troubling thoughts she had been entertaining.

In the morning, resignedly, Caterina dressed herself in a fine woollen, sleeveless dress, in cream flecked with beige. She had a matching coat to wear with it, the coat having, additionally, a beige velvet collar and cuffs, which endowed it with an air of pale luxuriousness. Her make-up completed, with her red lipstick having been applied, she looked out of the window of the hotel room: a room situated three floors above ground level. The sun was shining on to the street below. Was the temperature going to rise and if it were to do so, would the velvet trimmings on her coat look excessively out of season? Well! It was too late to change into another outfit now. It was time to set off.

She arrived at Antoine du Crâne's apartment exactly on time. Antoine opened the door, himself, when she rang. He looked pale and she unexpectedly felt a wave of tenderness sweeping over her. Was he ill? He was being very polite, Very correct. What could she say to make him realise that she had not been offended the last time they had met? She had simply been building defences to protect herself from having to deal with rejection, ultimately. She followed him as he made his way to his library. He stood aside to allow her to enter first. She was aware of the fact that he was feeling awkward and was treating her as if he were afraid that she might run away, were he to utter some opinion of which she did not approve.

"Antoine," she began to say, but then, stopped suddenly as she saw him leaning forward to clutch the edge of the table in the centre of the room. Now, his face was flushed. He placed his hand on his stomach as if he were feeling acute pain there.

"Antoine!" Caterina now cried, as if afraid. "Antoine, what is wrong?"

But he could not answer and so, Caterina rushed from the room.

"Madame! Madame!"she called, hoping the housekeeper was, in fact, in the apartment. "Madame! Are you there?"

"Ne vous en faites pas, mademoiselle," said the housekeeper without a trace of panic in her voice, as she came out of the kitchen.

"Hurry!" Caterina cried, her nerves taut. "We need a doctor! Which hospital is near? Hôtel Dieu? Call its number! Please! Don't you understand? Monsieur le Comte is ill! Oh! Listen! What's the emergency number? I'll talk to the operator, myself! It's 15, isn't it? Isn't it? Are you understanding me?"

"Mademoiselle," said the housekeeper bafflingly calmly. "I have been working for the young Monsieur le Comte and his father for years. This happens. I shall call the clinic. He goes to a clinic in Passy. Perhaps you could go back to him to tell him what I am doing?"

"What?"

"Go back to talk to him. Tell him Nadine is telephoning to the clinic."

"Are you…?"

Caterina did not finish the question. At a loss for words, she rushed back into the library. Antoine was sitting on the floor, resting his head on a chair. She knelt beside him and placed her cool hand on his forehead. His skin was very hot.

"You must have a fever," she said, "but Nadine is telephoning to the clinic. Someone will be here soon."

Antoine made an attempt to nod, to show that he had understood.

"I'll stay with you until then," Caterina added. "And I'll come with you to the clinic, if you like." She put her arm around him, moved to do so out of compassion, but also, out of a strengthening attachment to the man who was in need of her care. Was he really normally dependent on only the seemingly complacent Nadine?

An ambulance arrived from the clinic and two medics, dressed in white, took Antoine away to the chic 16th arrondissement, Caterina following in a taxi. A doctor, at the private establishment, said she would be allowed to wait, assuring her that she would be able to see Antoine within half an hour. She sat in a very white waiting room, in which contemporary art work provided spots of colour on the walls. She was the only occupant of the room and her thoughts began to drift. She remembered a conversation she had had a long time before with her sister, Ida. At first the conversation did not seem relevant to the shock she had just had and she wondered why it had come to mind, but then, she realised that it was connected with the way she had reacted to Antoine's near-collapse. Ida, at that time, had just begun to study astrology at Bramblewell School and was at home in Italy, for a holiday.

"I am convinced that you have the sign of Cancer on your Ascendant, Caterina," she had said, indulging in guess-work rather than practising her astrological calculations. "I've been watching you and I'm sure you do."

"What does that mean? What are you talking about?"

"You need to care for people. To nurture them."

"I need to nurture people?"

"Yes. Absolutely."

Caterina remembered smiling indulgently and paying no further attention to what her young sister had said, but now, those words of hers had started to make sense. The feeling of being needed by the sick Antoine had made her suspect that she had found her destiny, somehow. She realised that she actively wanted to care for him kindly and to support him and to make sure that he was happy. She wanted to advance from being preoccupied with her own problems to sharing his. She felt as if she were ready to grow up psychologically, in other words, in the field of human relationships: not just in the world of work. The shock of seeing

Antoine suffering physically and, in fact, the fear of losing him, had forced her to view her life from a different angle.

A doctor entered the room. Caterina stood up.

"Has he recovered, doctor?"

"Oh, yes, mademoiselle. But, I recommend that he stay here, in order to rest, for perhaps a week, as he has done in the past."

"Does he come here often? Is it permissible for you to tell me what is wrong with him? Does he have a stomach ulcer, for example? He was clutching his stomach. That was the first thing he did."

"He has told me that you are a close friend and he has authorised me to talk to you. He may have an ulcer, caused by a bacterium. We'll have to do some tests. But I think that his attack is more likely to have had a psychosomatic source. Have you heard of Generalised Anxiety Disorder?"

"I have not heard the name of the condition before, but I can guess what it is. Are you suggesting Antoine has it?"

"Yes. I believe he does."

"This is my fault!"

"No! No, mademoiselle! Not at all! This has been a long-standing problem! But I imagine that you might well be part of the cure!"

"May I see him?"

"Yes. You may, but do not stay at his side for long, today."

When Caterina entered Antoine's room, moments later, she saw that his eyes were closed, but he opened them as she approached his bed.

"You looked so pale," she said. "I thought…I don't know what I was thinking. This is my fault, isn't it? I know it is. I am so sorry."

"It's not your fault," Antoine assured her, looking straight into her eyes.

"I have to return to the Wirral…but I'll stay in touch…at least until I am sure you are all right."

"That would please me very much."

Through communicating with Antoine in e-mailed messages, subsequently, Caterina became better acquainted with him than she might have done had she had awkward, stilted conversations with him during little dinners in Parisian restaurants or trips to the theatre. She found it was easier to reveal what was in her heart through the medium of the written word, as did he. The relationship developed quickly, in fact. After a month, Antoine flew to London and then, travelled by land to Chester. Caterina showed him the old Roman city and her favourite spots in the Wirral. She introduced him to Dorothy Trmm. And one day, she took him over the river to Liverpool and there, while they were walking along by the Mersey at Pierhead, admiring the stately buildings overlooking the water, Antoine stopped and asked her to marry him. He advised her not to rush into making a reply. He would wait for her to make up her mind.

That evening, Caterina went to see Dorothy Trimm at her home in Whitby Village.

"What do you think of him, Dorothy?" she asked. "You have met him. Are we suited to each other?"

"Very much so," said Dorothy. "The only thing I have against him, pet, is the fact that he'll possibly take you away from the Wirral too soon! I've started to depend on you. Where shall I find someone who will be able to replace you?"

"We'll look for someone together. Someone really well qualified and nice. And I promise I shan't leave until we have found someone suitable."

"Shouldn't you talk to your parents about all of this? Not just the proposed wedding but the fact that you could be moving away sooner than expected. I mean, your father has recently invested a lot of money in Traversi-Trimm and might prefer you to stay with me a bit longer."

"That's another reason as to why my replacement should be really talented. I might have to ask Papa to help us. You wouldn't mind if he took part in the search, would you?"

"Not at all. I'd be delighted."

The next day, Caterina told Antoine that the answer to his question was "Yes!" He was thrilled, naturally. At once, the two of them decided that there should be ceremonies in both France and Italy. First, there would be a formal civil wedding at the mairie in Paris, Then, some days later, there would be a religious marriage in Italy, and this would be followed by a grand celebration for both families. To her father's great pleasure, Caterina decided that she wanted the Italian ceremony to take place in the cathedral of Santi Pietro e Paolo in Castelnuovo di Garfagnana, where he, her father, had grown up and where his parents - her paternal grandparents - still had a large house.

"The cathedral is very attractive," Caterina explained to Antoine. "There are important works of art inside."

"And Castelnuovo di Garfagnana, itself, is ..."

"In Tuscany. It is enchanting. You will love it, as much as I do."

There was much to consider and much to arrange, but Caterina left the bulk of the preparations required for the celebrations in Italy in the hands of her great-aunt, Signora Elisabetta, whose taste she admired. And since she, Caterina, was travelling from Cheshire to Paris and back once a week and had much to do at Traversi-Trimm, into the bargain, Antoine, himself, took charge of the arrangements for the civil wedding that would take place at the mairie in the 4th arrondissement of the French capital. For the most part, as he pointed out himself, he simply had to gather together the documents that were required, including birth certificates. Caterina sent for what she needed in the way of documentation from Italy and, on one of her visits to Paris, presented Antoine with a large envelope containing all that would have to be handed over at the mairie

A night or two later, after Caterina had returned to the Wirral, Antoine checked what was in the envelope. And when he saw Caterina's name written on the documents that had been enclosed, he thought that the world had ceased to spin. Certainly, at that moment, his heart had seemed to have stopped beating. He leafed through all the papers before him in a frantic way, as if not believing what he had seen, but the name continued to appear again and again: Caterina Aubaine Traversi. Caterina Aubaine Traversi! On the birth certificate, Caterina's father's name was given as Giovanni Franco Aubaine Traversi. The name "Aubaine" had been bestowed on Caterina through her father's family. The Italian line. How had that happened? Antoine put his hand up to his forehead in a gesture that suggested he did not know what to do next. He had to think, but his brain seemed to have become frozen. Then, he pulled himself together. He looked at his watch. It was almost midnight. It would be eleven o' clock in the Wirral. Was it too late to call Caterina? He knew it was inconsiderate even to think of telephoning her at that hour, in fact, but he could not resist.

"I have to ask you something in connection with the documents you have given me," he said quickly, having made the call through her land line.

"Yes? Is something missing?"

"No. I simply wanted to ask you about the origin of your middle name: Aubaine. It's important that I know."

"Why? Because it's French? I know only what Papa once told me."

"What did he say??"

"Oh! He once explained to me that one of his ancestors had been a French soldier who had been, in fact, in one of Napoleon's armies at the Battle of the River Trebbia in 1799. The French were fighting the Austro-Russians and were defeated. The soldier - I believe his name was Jean Aubaine- was badly wounded. He was taken to an Italian village. I don't know who took him there - presumably his comrades - but because he was considered to be dying, he was left in the village. It seems he recovered. He must have stayed in Italy and, of course, must have married. That's all I know, really. I wasn't paying much attention. There must be some reason as to why the name Aubaine has been retained in the family, but I don't know what it is."

"But, didn't I tell you…?"

"Didn't you tell me what?"

"That Jean Aubaine was…No! It was Julian…Of course it was Julian!"

"Julian?"

"I was telling Julian all that I knew about Jean Aubaine not long ago."

"What's going on, Antoine?"

"Tell me: does your sister, Ida, know the story about him? About Jean Aubaine?"

"Possibly not. Papa only mentioned it to me in passing. I don't think Aubaine is registered as part of her name, actually. Or Beatrice's. But, anyway, why do you ask? You are being very mysterious, I must say."

"It's nothing. You know how much I like history! I was curious. That's all."

"May I go to sleep now? I am very tired."

"Of course. I'll call you again, tomorrow."

But, the next day, just before lunch, it was Caterina who called Antoine.

"What was all that about last night?" she demanded.

Briefly, Antoine explained that there was a possibility she might be descended from the man who had been cursed by his, Antoine's, own ancestor: Angelique's grand-mother, on a remote Hebridean island.

"Oh!" Caterina exclaimed, a laugh in her voice. "The story from the film? Do you mean…you think that when we marry, the spell will be broken? How odd! I must tell Ida!"

"Why are you laughing? Don't you believe in curses?"

"Of course not! Listen! My family is no more unfortunate than anyone else's! In fact, we have been well off, in the material sense. People who believe in curses, in fact, curse themselves by making themselves miserable and fearful. That is all that happens. One could also argue that people who curse others do much the same to themselves, because they have to live forever afterwards with the guilt that swamps their thoughts. I am surprised that someone like you would even bring up this subject! What do you think is going to happen when we marry? Do you imagine there will be a sign in the sky? Antoine! Come on! How lucky you are that someone as sensible as I am will be marrying you!"

In fact, the sun was shining, on the day of the civil ceremony at the Parisian mairie in the 4th arrondissment. Caterina wore a short, white dress of Breton lace over silk. Later, with Antoine, she repaired with their guests - guests who included Ida in their number, since she had been allowed to have three days off school so that she could attend - to a very good restaurant near Notre Dame, where they all dined on oysters and champagne and toasted each other with great ceremony. As Caterina pointed out to Antoine - after he had started to tuck into beef cooked à la bordelaise - spell or not, they felt no different from the way they had felt before their marriage and nothing dramatic had happened either.

However, unknown to the new bride and her husband, on that distant, Hebridean island on which Marie-Colette had been filmed, a double rainbow had appeared in the sky at mid-day. Such a sight was not unusual – but, in the evening, people were to report seeing "a strange light" which would seem to "dance" over a hill top before descending into the sea. Then, it would rise again towards the sky. "It's a spirit being released," said a woman of a certain age to three holiday-makers - bird-watchers - on a beach, before she walked away towards white dunes topped with marram grass. The three noticed she had left no footprints in the sand, but did not comment on that fact to each other until later in the evening, when they had returned to the hotel where they were staying.

"Well! That was odd!" one of them said and then, was silent.

Five days later, a grand wedding ceremony took place in

Castelnuovo di Garfagnana. Signora Elisabetta had surpassed expectations in the artistically gifted way she had arranged - or, rather, had stage-managed - the proceedings. Caterina looked splendid in a long, white, taffeta dress, which had a voluminous train, attached to it. On the way into the church, it, the train, was carried by Ida and two cousins as well as Beatrice. Caterina, initially, had not wanted Beatrice to play a part of any significance during the ceremony, but, at the last minute, had asked her to and Beatrice had accepted her rôle, for the sake of appearances. "I hope I shall not regret this," Caterina had murmured, upon extending the invitation, but Beatrice rose to the occasion and behaved in an acceptable way, for once.

The setting, in the cathedral of Santi Pietro e Paolo, was gorgeously baroque with lit candles, glorious music and guests in their finery creating a special atmosphere. Later, everyone went to the Traversi family's ancestral home: an extremely large villa, surrounded by gardens, on the edge of the town. Long tables had been set with fine cloths, Tuscan plates, glass goblets and silver. The conversation flowed, amidst much jollity. Only Signora Elisabetta became a little sour when a French guest, sitting beside her, mentioned Caterina's good fortune, in having been able to marry a French aristocrat with a particle, since she, Caterina, was bourgeoise.

"Good fortune?" snapped Signora Elisabetta. "I think Antoine du Crâne is the fortunate one, madame. Look at him! Is he not a little fragile? The family he will have, in due course, will be lucky to have had a shot of good, strong, down-to-earth, Italian blood injected into it!"

As the afternoon wore on, Héloïse de Sauzon asked Julian Bramblewell-Eurlinn, who, like herself, was a guest at the wedding, if he wanted to go for a walk in the town.

"Let's find a café in a piazza!" she suggested.

"All right," said Julian following her, as she made her way through the olive trees in the garden. "But, I thought you'd want to stay here. I thought all girls liked weddings! You like weddings, don't you, Héloïse?"

"I know you are teasing me! But you know as well as I do that the love that leads to weddings is no more than a collection of latent qualities within oneself which are projected on to the object of one's fascination. "

"Really?"

"Yes! Really! Shall we go down to a café or not?"

"Carry on!"

They started to walk down a hill, in the direction of the centre of town. Héloïse gave Julian a sideways glance. In the sunlight, he looked so …golden and English and, in a story book way, enchanting. Her heart gave a lurch.

"Marriage is quite different from romantic love," she said firmly, in an attempt to calm the beating of her heart. "It requires practical skills and the ability to deal with challenges in a pragmatic way."

"Hm! Sounds tough! But at least we shan't need to get married now. I was talking to Antoine and it seems the spell was broken when he married Caterina! That's good news, isn't it?"

"Oh, but…"

"But?"

"Well…"

"Well?

"I could help you, at least, to restore the Château du Crâne to its former beauty. I have lot s of ideas…"

"You mean…you want to marry me. You do, don't you?"

"Stop teasing me."

"Will you marry me, Héloïse?"

CHAPTER 80

The Party

The end of the year examinations, which would take place during the summer term at Bramblewell School, seemed to hang like rain clouds over the otherwise sun-filled days, whenever Bramblewell girls gave them some thought. There were distractions during that term, of course: tennis matches in the ball courts below the wooded rise; rounders in the lusciously grassy playing field; and the change from winter clothes to the sky-blue dresses, baby-blue cardigans and panama hats which Miss Trimm had wanted for her girls and which Miss James had retained as part of the school uniform. All served to lighten the atmosphere within the school and to lift the spirits.

For Rosalind, Portia, Ida and Talitha, though, there was no escape from the fact that their year group would be required to sit national examinations which would be supervised in the long assembly hall, where Lord Bramblewell's ancestors would be staring down from portraits hung high on the walls. And the thought of sitting exams in those formidably formal conditions was daunting. Rosalind suffered from headaches nightly, as she contemplated the consequences of possible failure: disappointment on the part of her father; uneasiness on the part of her brother. But, the examination period, in fact, passed without anguish. In the end, anticipation proved to have been more painful than the actual occurrence.

During the three weeks over which the exam period had extended, Teddy Laurence had been busy, overseeing the administrative tasks that had preceded the delivery of each exam. Karen, the young secretary working in the ante-room next to

Lynn James' office, had been obliged to work late almost daily, since Isolde Delamar was no longer in the school to assist with the more usual day-to-day duties. There had been a few applicants for Isolde's post, but none of these had been in a position to step into the job immediately. Then, out of the blue, Lynn had received an e-mailed message from Lee Chan. Was the post still vacant? Lee had loved Hong Kong and specifically, the glamorous office in which she had worked, the high end shops which she had weekly frequented and the fast pace of life she had found exciting. But, she had missed her family and relatives in Liverpool and she had wanted to return to the Wirral so that she could be near them. Were she to be offered her old job at Bramblewell School, she would seriously consider returning speedily. "How soon can you be here?" Lynn had replied, adding, "Lord Bramblewell has suggested that your salary be increased substantially, if you decide to return. He wants to acknowledge your former hard work and loyalty as well as the fact that you have acquired new technological skills in Hong Kong. We can all benefit from what you have learnt." Days later, Lee was on a flight to London, her present-laden trolley case in the hold, her wrist encircled in jade and gold, her heart singing.

While Teddy and Lynn had been busy with duties connected with the daily running of the school, Lord and Lady Bramblewell had been thinking about the social side of life there. It was imperative that, before the end of the school year, an event of some sort be arranged, to celebrate the time that Hilary Trimm had spent in post as head-mistress. Lord Bramblewell had invited Dorothy Trimm to be in charge of this project but had not been told how much progress had been made. He, therefore, invited Dorothy to tea at the manor to discuss the matter, in Lady Bramblewell's presence. Dorothy had had difficulty persuading all the teachers at Bramblewell School to agree on a restaurant that would be suitable for the event and was still in the throes of negotiation. She had been angered by the attitude of a few teachers who had disliked Hilary and who now were being obstreperous.

Upon arriving at the manor, she decided not to complain about the unhelpful ones, though, since a complaint would only make her look weak. She merely mentioned the fact that some of the teachers at Bramblewell School had favoured a dinner at the Fleuve Chéri in Liverpool, given its proximity to Teddy Laurence's flat and the chance that he might invite them there for coffee, after the restaurant had closed for the evening. Others had expressed a preference for Foxglove and Fern in Ellesmere Port, since it was closer to their homes. Lady Bramblewell, who had listened carefully to what Dorothy had been saying, interrupted at that point.

"But, this is silly!" she said. "We could have a party for Hilary here, couldn't we, Rupert? There would be plenty of space, obviously, no one would be obliged to leave early and the atmosphere would be more relaxed, wouldn't it?"

Dorothy hesitated. She reckoned that warm-hearted Susie had spoken spontaneously without having given any thought, at that moment, to the way Hilary would feel about returning to the manor in which she had once romantically dreamed she would be living one day. Lord Bramblewell, on the other hand, realised why Dorothy had paused and he generously spared her the embarrassment of floundering over a response by enthusiastically saying to his wife:

"That's a splendid idea, Susie! But, before we start phoning the caterers and party planners and all the rest of it, I think I'll telephone to Hilary, myself, to find out if she would actually like to have a large party organised in her honour. Given the discreet way she left the school, she might prefer to celebrate her time at Bramblewell more quietly, with just a few friends to whom she was close. Who knows?"

Lord Bramblewell was as good as his word. The next evening, he telephoned Hilary, when she had arrived home after a day at Q-COLL. She had begun to prepare a meal in her spacious kitchen, when she heard her land-line telephone ringing in the living-room. Removing her apron, she hurried to answer the call, sitting down, first, on the arm of a sofa before she lifted the receiver. When she heard Lord Bramblewell's voice on the line, she reached out to touch the back of the sofa to steady herself and then, she turned to look wistfully out of the large window that provided a view of the terraced garden that dipped down to the waters of Chester's River Dee. It had been a while since she had heard Rupert's voice and she realised, at once, the extent to which she had missed hearing it. She felt herself mentally and physically weakening, as the old desire to please him, no matter what the cost to herself, surfaced. And then, she heard herself saying:

"Yes. All right, Rupert. A party at the manor would be lovely. Thank you."

Hours later, she sat up in bed, her restless brain preventing her from sleeping, as she chided herself repeatedly for having agreed to Rupert's request. How was she going to endure an entire evening watching Susie Sutton playing the part of the benevolent hostess and, furthermore, playing it well?

Susie, that evening, was feeling equally anxious while thinking about the same event. Having been eager to prove that she could make a success of her rôle as Lady Bramblewell, she had seized the opportunity to have a big party at the manor when that opportunity had presented itself to her. But later, she had realised what an ordeal the evening might be for Hilary. Susie would readily admit that she, herself, had ruthlessly climbed the social ladder, but she had never been a deliberately revengeful person. And although Hilary had been mean to her, she had no desire to be spiteful in return. She would try to make the party at the manor as pleasant as possible for the former head-mistress, out of decency. After all, by behaving in that way, she might even persuade Hilary to become a friend. Not a close one, of course, but at least one with whom she could be on reasonably good terms, for Lord Bramblewell's sake.

In the days that followed, Susie worked fast, because time was short. She had once read that a hand-written message always impressed and so, she slipped a hand-written note into each envelope before she inserted the invitation card. Her hand-writing had not always been good, but she had trained herself to write in a flowing, joined-up style that made her look educated. She wondered how many teachers would respond, in timely fashion, to her R.S.V.P. plea and was delighted when the replies started to roll in quickly. Most of those invited wanted to attend. The party would be big! It would be a great success. Rupert would be pleased.

Liz Laurier had been one of those who had replied to her invitation at once. Although the academic year she had spent at Bramblewell School had not always been a comfortable one, given the fact that the creation of her post had been controversial, Liz had been happy to receive Susie's note and formally printed invitation card, since a party at the manor, to celebrate Miss Trimm's years as head-mistress of Bramblewell School would provide her with the opportunity to meet again some of the kind friends she had made while she had been teaching there, incognita, and whom she had not seen since the day she had decided to leave, quietly.

"What are you going to wear, Mum," Rosalind asked, the next time she visited Liz's apartment and saw the invitation card propped up on a shelf. "You'll have to wear a long dress, won't you? Don't you think so? Will you let me choose one for you?"

"You can offer your opinion, certainly," said Liz, carrying an armful of gowns from her bedroom into the sitting room and laying them on a sofa.

Rosalind, at once, suggested that Liz choose a summery, white dress, with tiny pink flowers printed all over it, the waist-line hoisted as high as that of a Regency heroine in a romantic novel. Lynn smiled in an indulgent, "That's very nice and I'll think about it," way. But, on the evening of the party, she put on a slim, chic silvery white dress, with matching shoes that shimmered like moon-light. She did not want to be completely eclipsed by Susie Sutton, who would be dressed up to the nines, the party being the first social event she would be hosting at the Manor, as Lady Bramblewell.

In fact, on the evening of the party, Susie was dressed simply in white, in a dress that was draped to resemble the gown of a Greek goddess, her hair in a pony-tail style. Hilary Trimm, who arrived at the manor at exactly the time the party was due to begin, had chosen an equally simple look: a long, fitted, beige dress worn with pearls. Susie and Lord Bramblewell greeted her warmly and soon, she was encircled by former colleagues - Thetis, Anna Layne, Savannah - who looked delighted to see her.

The ball room at the manor started to fill up and a jazz band began to play. Guests were talking in animated fashion and Liz, with a glass of apple fizz in her hand, moved from one group to another, giving a nod of recognition here, a cheery "Hi!" there. Julian Bramblewell-Eurlinn was standing by a window that opened out on to the terrace, a beautiful, young woman, whom Liz took to be Héloïse de Sauzon, by his side. Rosalind had told Liz about their engagement and, seeing Héloïse for the first time, Liz had to concede that, visually at least, the girl was arresting. Liz could understand why Rosalind had been fascinated by her French poise and her air of what New Yorkers might have called "entitlement." Her long, blonde hair flowed down her back, part of it being bound by a ribbon, in the style of Botticellli's Venus. She must have known that the apple-green, chiffon gown she had put on would be likely to render her unforgettable, so self-aware did she appear to be. Liz was pleased that Julian was not looking at her as if mesmerised, though. He seemed rather to be bemused. He conveyed to Liz the impression that he had the measure of the posturing girl, but for one reason or another, had decided he wanted to remain with her. Liz had heard that he had given her a ring with a single stone. A large, but not vulgar, emerald from South America. It had once been given to a Bramblewell forebear, who had been an explorer of the Amazon, as a token of gratitude for some action unknown. The ring, like Susie's, was a Bramblewell heirloom, then, but it was a more exotic one than Susie's. What a pity Julian had not waited for Rosalind, Liz unrealistically thought. Given her romantic imagination, Rosalind would have woven stories around a ring like that.

Liz hesitated before approaching Julian and his fiancée, wondering if the fact that she was miffed about Julian's choice would be obvious. But, in the end, good manners dictated that she offer her congratulations, with as much warmth as she could muster. As she made her way through the chatting guests, Liz saw Julian turn his head to look in the direction of an alcove where Teddy Laurence was in conversation with Lynn James. Liz noticed that Lynn seemed to be at ease and happy, her hair loose, her long, white, sleeveless dress a picture of European stylishness. Teddy, as if becoming aware of the fact that he was being watched, looked over Lynn's shoulder and Liz saw him glancing at Héloïse and then, exchanging a look with Julian which seemed to imply complicity. What did it mean?? Had there been a gentleman's agreement of some sort? Liz did not know what to think, really, but guessed that they had at least spoken to each other about Héloïse at some point.

It seemed to Liz that time had slowed as she had evaluated Héloïse's character and had observed the glance that Teddy and Julian had exchanged, but, in reality, only a second or two had passed. Reaching Julian, she touched his arm gently.

"Julian!"

"Oh, Liz! Hello! You haven't met Héloïse before, have you?"

"No. I haven't. But my daughter, Rosalind, has talked about you a great deal, Héloïse."

"Rosalind? Oh, madame! She is charming! We were friends last summer."

"Liz!" interrupted Julian, as if having no desire to be reminded of the summer at the Château du Crâne. "I'd better tell you that Dorothy Trimm is desperate to talk to you about your book. I think she wants to publish it."

"My book?"

"Haven't you written a book about astrology?"

"Well, yes. With Rosalind. But, I didn't think Dorothy had any intention of publishing it."

"She seems to want to. That's what she is saying to all and sundry, anyway. I'm happy that she is going to do this for you. But Liz, despite my own family's interest in the subject, notably that of my mother, I cannot, myself, accept that there is any moral justification or logical basis for..."

"I know exactly how you feel and why," said Liz, stopping him from continuing. "But, 'there are more things in heaven and earth, Horatio, than are dreamt of in your philosophy.' Julian, I should say! Not, Horatio!"

"Ah, yes. Very amusing! Actually, I do admit that Shakespeare alluded to the stars now and again. I bow to his wisdom, even though we are talking about the 17th century now, aren't we, Liz?"

"Dorothy Trimm is over there!" Héloïse exclaimed then, having taken note of the easy exchange of words between Julian and Liz with mild irritation. "She is talking very loudly!"

Above the heads of a number of guests, Dorothy Trimm's voice could indeed be heard, saying:

"I just don't understand it! All these people wandering around the country with Queequeg-inspired tattoos all over their bodies! What is going on? In which sphere, pray, are tattoos judged to be attractive? Honestly! It's as if we are returning to the days of blue woad!"

"Dorothy!" said Liz quietly, having reached the woman she could not help liking, despite the forthright nature of her opinions. "Dorothy!"

"What? Oh, Liz! Yes! I want to speak to you! Come over here to the window seat so we can talk! I understand that you have changed the format of the book you have been writing and that, now, your daughter, Rosalind, is collaborating on the project with you. If you are wondering how the news reached my ears, it did so through Caterina Traversi, who was told about it by her sister,

Ida, Ida being…"

"One of Rosalind's best friends."

"Exactly, Come on! Let's sit down, dear."

Making herself comfortable on the window seat in one of the alcoves of the ballroom, Liz explained:

"Rosalind and I thought a question and answer format would appeal to teenagers."

"Yes. Caterina Traversi was keen to have a look at it. And my new assistant thinks it could be a big seller in America."

"Your new assistant?"

"Yes. Caterina will be leaving soon to live in Paris and Rome, although she'll be visiting Traversi-Trimm in the Wirral regularly, too. We advertised far and wide for someone good enough to replace her and, at last, we struck gold! We hope so anyway! She'll be coming here, tonight! You'll meet her! Oh! There she is!"

"Caterina?"

"No! The new girl! Rebecca Hampton! My new assistant!"

Liz looked in the direction of the steps that led down to the ballroom. She saw, standing at the top of them a young, lithe, sun-tanned woman, with sleek, shoulder length, dark hair, dressed in a one-shoulder, navy gown that oozed Park Avenue sophistication. So! That was Rebecca Hampton! The girl who had spent the previous summer in Teddy Laurence's apartment, if the rumours had been correct. With a confidence based on a familiarity with such events, she, Rebecca, descended the steps as if used to having the eyes of a crowd upon her. And as if knowing where to look, she turned her gaze in the direction of the alcove where Teddy Laurence was standing. He was staring at Rebecca as if she were an apparition. He put his hand on Lynn's shoulder, as if to steady himself, and Lynn, then, lifted her own hand to place it on his. It was a moment of such tender familiarity that Liz turned her head away, feeling as if she were intruding. She had already realised, though, that Teddy, given his pallor, had not known that Rebecca would be coming to town.

Throughout the evening, Hilary Trimm had moved quietly from group to group, thanking this person and that person for good wishes and, in the case of teachers, for years of support, in the form of good work and forbearance. Having completed those duties, she went into the adjoining room where a multitude of dishes, hot and cold, were laid out in the form of a splendid buffet, but she could not eat. She could not help remembering the scene Susie had staged in that very room on the night she had first attended a party at the manor. She had boldly arrived without Gylen Somerland, her companion at the time and had histrionically fainted, making believe she had been fragile and in need of protection. Lord Bramblewell had allowed himself to be taken in. On that night, he had decided to look after her, in the way he would want to look after a stray kitten, probably. "Susie played to win and she won," Hilary thought, wryly, adding with bitterness, "Well! Good for Susie!"

The memory of that night was now making Hilary feel ill. She knew she needed a breath of fresh air. Moving quickly, she made her way across the ballroom to where long windows opened on to the terrace, lit by floodlights. The windows were ajar. Hilary pushed one and it opened easily. She slipped outside, trusting that she had not been observed.

Standing on the terrace, Hilary looked out at the dark lawns and the black shapes of the trees beyond. The ballroom had seemed to be so hot that Hilary was now able to tolerate the chill in the air with equanimity, even though her arms were bare.

Unknown to her, at that moment, she was being watched. Isolde Delamar, dressed in a long, hooded cloak, had been skulking around the grounds of the manor all evening. Seeing Hilary standing alone on the terrace, she realised that an opportunity was being presented to her: an opportunity that simply had to be seized. She clutched the trunk of a beech tree and watched Hilary with interest, her eyes glistening like those of a wild animal about to home in on its prey.

Guided by the beam of the flood-lights illuminating the manor, Isolde, wraith-like, crossed the lawn quickly. Within seconds, she was standing close to the stone balustrade which marked the edge of the terrace. She gazed up at Hilary and Hilary returned her look, in a way that implied she knew what Isolde was going to say, or rather, going to offer. It was obvious to her that Isolde would suggest that they undermine Susie.

"Let's join forces!" Isolde said eagerly, adopting a persuasive tone. "We can come up with a plan, if we work together!"

Hilary's gaze changed from being one of disdain to one that was inscrutable. Isolde perceived a certain hesitation beneath the air of confidence. The uppity Miss Trimm was being tempted! Isolde took a step forward.

"In every beautiful garden, there is a snake, Hilary," Isolde then unexpectedly heard someone saying, in a voice that was cool and controlled, the accent an acquired, arch one.

Hilary Trimm turned around. Susie Sutton, having stepped out of the ballroom, had come into view. A calm, dignified Susie Sutton: the new Lady Bramblewell.

"Come inside, Hilary," Susie said kindly, holding out her hand. "It's cold out here."

EPILOGUE

On an August morning before dawn, in a room on the ground floor of the Château du Crâne, previously used by Julian Bramblewell-Eurlinn's mother as an office of sorts, but which Julian had now suggested be used as a study, Héloïse de Sauzon was sitting at Aethelfreda's former desk, making notes on loose sheets of A4 copy paper. Close to the desk, several large books - mainly about the history of art - were stacked within reach. Héloïse had been assiduously studying reproductions of portraits of ennobled ladies in an endeavour to find inspiration for the creation of her own wedding dress. Her marriage would take place in the Cathédrale Saint-André in the Place Pey Berland, in Bordeaux, and, given the splendour of the Gothic cathedral coupled with the inherent honourableness of the young man she was going to marry, the dress, in order to be equal to the status of the occasion, had to be magnificent. To be precise, it had to be heavily bejewelled or ethereal or else, so simple in its conception, that the perfection of its lines alone would draw gasps of admiration. It had yet to be decided whether she, Héloïse, would take full charge of the creation of the dress, using discreet seamstresses in the locality to carry out her wishes, or if she would approach a designer in Paris, as Madame Gabrielle had suggested, and not without insistence. Madame Gabrielle was always Madame Gabrielle, even though there had been a certain softening of her character as circumstances in her life had changed and she had felt less alone.

Héloïse was sitting close to an open window. The shutters were already pushed back and the fresh, gentle air of the Gironde was drifting in. Héloïse whimsically remembered that Montesquieu, the seventeenth century writer, who had lived not far away in fact, had stated, once, that France had the best of climates. That morning, in the Gironde, Héloïse was inclined to agree with him. She turned on a small CD player that Aethelfreda had left behind and located the fourth movement of Mahler's fifth. The music reminded her of the day Julian had asked her to marry him. He had done so in a light and friendly way, but she had had no doubts about the seriousness of his request, or the fact that marriage to Julian would provide her with the emotional security that she had decided she had previously unknowingly craved. Now, she would admit that before Julian had entered her life, her preferred way of behaving had consisted of her attempting to dominate her emotional longings by nurturing her cerebral development – frequently by reading the works of Voltaire. Since her engagement to Julian, though, she had felt those defences, built of erudition and near-cynicism, coming down. She had imagined herself, in fact, as an ice sculpture, melting, bit by bit, in the warmth of Julian's love. She was annoyed with herself for having had recourse to the language of romantic novels - of the type Jacqueline still liked - in order to express something that was indefinable and, sometimes, overwhelming. But, how else could she describe the way she was feeling? In such circumstances, one found oneself helplessly reading poetry or gazing at photos of the beloved. One could not help it.

They had wandered through Caslelnuovo di Garfagnana, that afternoon on which Julian had suggested they marry. The reception, following the marriage of Caterina Traversi and Antoine du Crâne, had been in full swing but probably she, Héloïse – and Julian, also – had felt a need to leave the party in order to breathe in a less heady atmosphere for a while. A light breeze had made olive trees, in a nearby grove, rustle their leaves, but, in the streets, that exuded the charm of centuries past, the air had wrapped itself around Héloïse like a blanket. In a square, at a little table outside a café, they had ordered strawberry ices and cool drinks and, then, had continued to wend their way through the town, barely noticing where they were going, their focus being on each other. They had talked and talked. Julian had spoken about his plans for the Château du Crâne and the land around it. Héloïse, unsure of herself for once, had listed her aspirations with an air of uncertainty. She wanted to obtain a degree, she had said, but she would apply to Bordeaux-Montaigne University, instead of the Sorbonne. Was the campus situated in Talence? Later, she might study for a further degree at Bordeaux University's Institute of Vine and Wine Science. in order to be of help to Julian when he would attempt to resurrect his vineyard. Such was his determination that she was sure he would have his own Bramblewell wines one day! Julian had told her, then, that one of the potential drawbacks of marrying him would be the near-obligation to attend familial gatherings at Bramblewell Manor, at least once or twice a year. Héloïse had said she did not mind. Susie would be a rival, of course, but that rivalry, rippling under the surface of their lives, would stop her, Héloïse, from becoming complacent.

Bramblewell! Héloïse would not have wanted to lose touch with the world of the manor or the school, in any case: she was too interested in the way the lives of those who were connected with Julian, in some way, would unfold. Rosalind Somerland had told her that Liz Laurier's book, "The Aspects of Venus" - to which she, Rosalind, had contributed - would be published soon. Héloïse, could not wait to read the book, given the fact that it seemed to cover the full range of romantic attachments within the Bramblewell world, from Lord Bramblewell's and Susie's to that of Teddy Laurence and...Well! That was still to be decided. Everyone's identity had been heavily disguised, Rosalind had said. Would she, Héloïse, be able to guess which confected couple would represent Julian and herself?

Day was breaking. Héloïse turned her head towards the window and briefly closed her eyes, while light settled upon her face. Another day with Julian. Did she deserve such happiness? She felt she could not waste a minute of her life in order to merit being with him. She stood up, feeling the need – Voltaire-like –

to drink morning coffee to give her brain a boost. However, she knew she would have to start to limit how much of it she drank. After all, she wanted her skin to be well hydrated, so as to be in perfect condition on her wedding day.

In another part of the Château du Crâne, on that August morning, Madame Gabrielle de Talence, who had spent the night, restlessly, rose to push open the shutters of a window in the large, first floor bedroom where she had tried to sleep. The sun was rising. Soon, it would be high in the sky, pouring its warmth down on to the vineyards of her beloved Bordeaux: the terroirs of the left and right banks of the Gironde; the gravelly soil and the clay.

Tightening the belt of the light dressing gown she had put on, she went out of the bedroom, then, and into the corridor beyond, walking along its length with the assured step of a woman who was familiar with her surroundings. Only the fact that she stopped now and again to gaze - in a way that suggested she was feeling nostalgic - at some tapestry hanging on a wall, or a painting in an old, gilded frame, indicated that she had not visited the château for a while. In fact, fifty years had elapsed since she had lived there. At that time, she had been the beloved daughter of the noble Count and Countess du Crâne, then alive. But, that had been before her father had cast her out of the family. Over the years she had sometimes expressed anger about her expulsion, but most of the time she had been tortured only by guilt. Now, at this stage in her life, she felt pain: the pain that accompanied the knowledge that she had never been able to speak to her parents again. Her father had refused to see her, even when he had been dying.

Mr. Kit Mallory had decided to acquire a wing of the Château du Crâne principally for her use, out of compassion. When he had seen her crying, at her home in the Cours de la Victoire in Bordeaux, he had been deeply moved. Madame Gabrielle had felt embarrassed, later, at having succumbed to such a display of weakness. How deplorable that a woman of her social standing had allowed herself to have been broken by a mere memory of the unhappy consequence of her misguided, youthful behaviour. Those tears of hers had humiliated her, but Mr. Mallory had been much affected by them. He had subsequently expressed his desire to buy a wing of the château when he had made contact with Julian Bramblewell- Eurlinn, the new owner. Julian had resisted the temptation to sell, though, not permitting himself to be drawn into such a transaction by the promise of a large amount of money which he would have been able to use at once. He had decided that a lease and a steady rent would be preferable in the long run. Had he sold, he would have lost control of the way that the Mallory section of the château would have been used by successive generations. Therefore, a leasing contract - a contrat de location – had been drawn up and Mr. Mallory had been told that he would be able to occupy his part on the château immediately.

He, Mr. Mallory, had made a show of asking Madame Gabrielle if, as a favour, she would stay in his part of the château as often as she could - at weekends, perhaps - since the demands of his own business prevented him from making use of the property in any way other than as a part-time residence.

Would she keep an eye on it during his absences? The property needed to be lived in, cared for and appreciated. Madame Gabrielle had known that Mr. Mallory had not wanted her to think that he had offered her the use of the Mallory section as a charitable gesture, provoked by pity and so, she had entered into the game, pretending that she had not realised what his real motivation had been. Of course, being an intuitive woman, she had also been aware of the fact that there had been another reason for the excuse Mr. Mallory had concocted: he had not wanted her to think that he had offered the leased property to her as a present and a prelude to his asking her to marry him. He was as proud as she was, herself, and he would not ask such a question were he not sure of a favourable reply. In fact, she did not know how she would answer, were the question to be posed. Her attraction to Mr. Mallory, after all, had been based on qualities she had attributed to him a long time before, when she had projected her romantic notions on to him, and although the attraction to him was still active, her cool, rational brain had started to over-ride it. One should never draw too close to one's idols. It was an old adage, but still a valid one. Once the mist of her illusions had started to clear, she had gradually become aware of Mr. Mallory's human moods, orientations in thinking and habitual behaviour. Could she make the adjustments that would be necessary to accommodate them? Could he become used to her ways? She had begun to wonder if she should have agreed so readily to living in the château at his request, even. But, how could she have resisted the temptation to return to her old home which she had missed so much?

Madame Gabrielle now started to feel unsteady as she walked along the corridor that she had once known so well, her reaction to her surroundings having developed from being emotional to being physical. She stopped and leaned against a wall as she began to feel a tightening of the muscles around her heart. She needed something to revive her, to give her strength. Would a cup of coffee be enough? She would go downstairs presently. She would have to retrace her footsteps, though. The staircase ahead did not belong to the Mallory section. She could use it, of course. Julian would not mind. But, she did not like to. Julian had obviously wanted to retain the staircase because its upper part led to the room in which Angélique's diary had been found. The famous diary!

Perhaps Julian was planning to turn the room into one of the château's attractions, for the benefit of visitors.

The story of Angélique and the curse had begun to perplex Madame Gabrielle. Her rational brain, trained to be Cartesian in its approach to life's problems, was inclined to reject the idea of curses having potency. Surely only those who were ill-educated or suffering from a psychological disorder were inclined to believe in their efficacy. But, there had been a few occasions, all the same, when, in moments of undermining doubt, she, herself, had pondered on the sequence of events, the decisions taken, the encounters and the relationships that had led, eventually, to the marriage of her nephew, Antoine du Crâne and the dazzling Caterina Traversi, one descended from Angélique's curse-casting grand-mother and the other, seemingly, from the man who had spurned that grand-mother, thus provoking her into threatening to destroy the happiness of generations that were to follow in her own family as well as his.

But, had the curse done so? In lucid moments, she, Madame Gabrielle, could not accept that there was enough evidence to support that view. And yet, as Antoine du Crâne, himself, had explained when he had met her, something odd had seemed to have been afoot. If Caterina Traversi had not quarrelled with her sister, Beatrice, and if she had not decided to seek employment near to where her sister, Ida, had been at school, and if she had not subsequently, wandered into a café where, by apparent chance, a certain newspaper had been left on the table that had happened to be vacant and, then, if she, herself, Madame Gabrielle had not decided to have a holiday on a cruise liner and if Hilary Trimm and her mother had not been free to voyage on the same ship… If! If! If! But, was not the whole of life like that for everyone? A succession of ifs and a collection of possibilities? Was one really expected to believe that there was some master plan, directed by a force unknown, behind it all? Was life really so mysterious? Surely there was a rational explanation for all that seemed to be numinous. In a less advanced era, after all, people believed the Sun travelled around the Earth! Ideas, like knowledge, evolved and would continue to do so. Anyway! She would reflect on it all at another time. Right now, her head was hurting her.

She pushed open a window in order to allow fresh, morning air to enter the corridor. Down in the courtyard of the château, Julian Bramblewell-Eurlinn, dressed fetchingly in blue jeans and a white shirt, a dark blue jacket of semi-19th century design slung over his shoulders, was walking towards the draw-bridge, with Héloïse by his side, her favourite blue jeans, rolled up above her ankles.

Madame Gabrielle had dined with the two of them the night before and they had been charming. They had explained to her their plans for the château: their intention to turn it into holiday accommodation, without altering the interior to a noticeable degree. Like any young couple, they had light-heartedly disagreed about this and that. Héloïse had wanted the furnishings to be white: entirely white. Julian had expressed his preference for a more traditional look, in keeping with the era in which the château had been built. But, he had also wanted one of the large spaces on the ground floor to be used to exhibit contemporary works of art whereas Héloïse, having acquired a taste for acting, had thought the focus should be on something more lively: Shakespearean drama performed in the castle grounds, perhaps. "As long as 'Henry V' is not staged," she had laughingly added.

"But, who will come to watch it?" Julian had asked.

"People in Bordeaux," Héloïse had retorted, "They are cultured, after all! And besides, lots of English people have holiday homes in this area. Lots! You know that! One sees them everywhere! In Libourne, in Arcachon…"

Madame Gabrielle had smiled with indulgence at their youthful enthusiasm and their dreams. They had been at ease in each other's company. They would be happy throughout their lives. She had been sure of it. When she had been young, she had been happy too, she had wistfully remembered, then. And her thoughts had turned for a while to Liverpool, at one time her own city of youthful imaginings, with its splendid waterfront and the lapping waters of its river. She had woken up each morning, while she had been there, thinking that the day ahead would be full of fresh adventure. Her life had been infused with the energy that had had its source in love, in the knowledge that she had found someone who had conformed with her inner image of perfection. That had been how she had experienced love, at any rate, even though the young man who had attracted her attention had been no more than a handsome youth on a stage: one who had slipped away, whenever she had thought he had been within reach. Could that feeling of youthful passion for life, for living, be recreated now? Could she cast her cynicism to one side and embark on another stage in her life with the hope in her heart that her story would have a happy ending? La petite Agnès, her hairdresser - an enthusiastic reader of eau-de-rose romantic novels, after all - would be disappointed were she not to marry Mr. Mallory! Well! Maybe for Agnès' sake, she would be more welcoming the next time Mr. Mallory visited Bordeaux. The ice in her soul would have to be melted before then, but maybe that golden couple, Julian and Héloïse, would bring about that dissolution with the warmth of their affectionate response to her.

Down in the courtyard, they, Julian and Héloïse, were now standing, looking upwards. Héloïse was pointing at the blue, slated roof, or rather, was sweeping her arm and hand in a curve that replicated the gesture of a ballerina. The sun's slanted rays were shining down on the two of them. It occurred to Madame Gabrrielle that a child might imagine them to be a prince and princess standing before their fairy-tale castle.

Catching sight of Madame Gabrielle, now leaning forward so as to be seen, Julian called:

"Come to lunch, later, Madame!"

She waved in such a way as to say, "Volontiers!"

Ah! Julian! His love and tender concern for the château was so deep, so instinctive that Madame Gabrielle could imagine that he had been descended from Bordelais nobility. Perhaps his ancestors had been in the region at the time of the Angevin dynasty? She did not think she was being fanciful. Yes. The château, once her beloved home, would be safe in his hands. She felt hopeful suddenly and, simultaneously, she felt the pain around her heart lessening, the tightness being released. Who had written that one could breathe only in a world full of hope? Malraux?

Two hours later, in a different time zone- and, specifically, in Liverpool, Madame Gabrielle's city of dreams, Teddy Laurence was in the kitchen of his apartment pouring tea into a cup. While he did so, he listed mentally - as was his custom - the items that would be on his agenda for the day ahead. He liked to follow a timetable, even though he was still on holiday - the start of the new term at Bramblewell being some weeks away - because he felt so satisfied when he managed to complete the tasks on his list before evening. More importantly, he knew that fixing his mind on a series of goals helped him to rein in his thoughts when they strayed on to de-stabilising or perplexing matters. He could cite, as an example of these, the fact that Rebecca Hampton had re-entered his life, bringing, in her wake, not so much joy as questions. The subsequent change in his once-developing relationship with Lynn James was another disturbing preoccupation. Lynn was now being wooed - in a charmingly old-fashioned way - by another young man. What had he, Teddy, expected to happen, though? Had he believed that Lynn would patiently wait for him to make up his mind as to whether he wanted to be with her or with Rebecca? When he had given that question some thought, he had realised the extent to which Lynn would have judged such presumption on his part to have been arrogant- or even naïve. Naturally, a young, sophisticated woman like her would not wait for a fellow who wavered in an insulting way: one whom she would now consider to be too young to be of interest. And as a consequence, he had lost her! It served him right, of course. He accepted that fact – at least, in abstraction. Every day that passed, though, he found he was regretting the path he had chosen. Oh! He revelled in Rebecca's company. Who would not, given her wit, her cool, interestingly detached way of viewing the world and her New York-ish air of knowingness? However, that enjoyment was soured by his creeping suspicion that Rebecca was merely using him as a stepping stone to something - or rather, someone - whom she judged to be better. By "better," she would mean someone of higher status, socially, he had realised. His relationship with Rebecca, in fact, was beginning to resemble his previous relationship with Susie

Sutton. Rebecca had even candidly expressed her admiration of Susie's achievements! She, Rebecca, was mentally tougher than Susie, of course. Susie still revealed her fragile side, riddled with uncertainty, from time to time.

He reflected often on the negligent way he had treated Lynn on the night of the party at Bramblewell Manor, when Rebecca had made her stagey entrance, out of the blue. Lynn had been gracious, afterwards, all the same. His good relationship with her, at work, would survive although it would never, now, be anything other than a professional one. A wave of near-despondency sometimes swept over him when he thought of Lynn's heart being captured by a more dashing beau. Should he, himself, move away from Bramblewell territory now? He was still being offered posts in schools in the north of the Wirral, after all. Could he un-nerve Susie by straying even a little distance away, though? Intuitively, he felt that knowledge of his very presence close to the manor endowed her with the courage she needed to play her new rôle. Isolde Delamar, after all, could be watching everything that was happening in the Bramblewell world, while waiting for an opportunity to strike again. Surely he should stay close to the manor if only to protect Susie from Isolde's attempts at revenge?

In Whitby Village, Dorothy Trimm was planning the day ahead. She would drive into the town centre of Ellesmere Port to do a little shopping and then would make her way to Kath's for morning coffee and a chat. She would discuss with Kath the news that apparently had been buzzing around Bramblewell School for days. It was believed that there was a possibility that Lynn James would become engaged to the young man she had met on the night of the party at Bramblewell Manor. Would she subsequently move away were she to marry, leaving the post of headmistress vacant? Was there a possibility that Hilary could then re-apply for her old job?

Out of the corner of her eye, Dorothy had partly observed how the meeting between Lynn and her new beau had taken place that night. When Lynn had noticed that Teddy had fixed his eyes on Rebecca Hampton, she had slipped away into the mass of guests, leaving the way clear for Teddy to go to speak to Rebecca, without having to make excuses to her, Lynn, for doing so. Stella Lomas, who had been invited to the party as a representative of the pupils at Bramblewell School, had quickly walked towards Lynn and had engaged her in conversation to distract her and to spare her the embarrassment of looking abandoned, as it were, if only for seconds. Such diplomacy on Stella's part would suggest that she would go far in life. One could be sure of it.

However, at that moment, also, Susie had stepped through the French windows from the terrace, with Hilary Trimm at her side. Intuitively, she had seemed to have taken in what had been happening and had acted swiftly. As if gliding like a swan in water, she had led Hilary towards Julian and Héloïse, leaving her with them while disengaging from their company a distant Bramblewell cousin who had arrived from his travels, earlier that afternoon. Dorothy had guessed that the cousin, Crispin, an explorer and writer, had been just a little older than Lynn. Dorothy had seen Susie leading him towards the young headmistress, while obviously saying, "There's someone I want you to meet!" Dashing but sincere and "frightfully handsome" - as Dorothy would describe him to Kath - Crispin spoke several languages and lived in a large apartment in a palazzo in Florence. Lynn had seemed impressed. Crispin, in turn, had boyishly seemed to have been enchanted by the young headmistress with the long, dark hair. Had a spark been lit?

"Well, Kath?" Dorothy asked, upon arriving later at her friend's house. "What do you think will happen? I discussed the matter with Hilary on the telephone last night and I have to say, that she did not seem AWFULLY keen to return to Bramblewell School. I thought she would be desperate to, now that she has reconciled herself to the idea that Susie is Lady Bramblewell and always will be. I thought Hilary would simply want to be near

Lord Bramblewell again. She does miss him. A lot."

"Hm! I don't know," said Kath as if thoughtfully. "You know Hilary better than I do, obviously, but, honestly, would you go back if you were in her position?"

Hilary Trimm, at that moment, was placing her bags on the back seat of her car, before slipping into the driver's seat. Although students had still not arrived at Q-COLL, she liked to do administrative work in the college each day, in order to prepare herself for the term that would start in a few weeks' time. She had so many ideas floating around in her head and so many innovations that she wanted to introduce in the college! Oh, yes. The college! Her college! Her mother had spoken to her on the telephone about the possibility of her, Hilary, returning to Bramblewell School. She had half-heartedly toyed with the idea, but only for an hour or two. During the party at the Manor, after all, having seen how competently Susie had been playing the rôle of Lady Bramblewell, she had decided she would have to say "Good-bye" to Bramlewell School and Bramblewell Manor, definitively, to avoid the pain of observing a younger woman excelling in the rôle she, herself, had once coveted. . Bramblewell School was her past; Q-COLL was to be the foundation of her future. She had to embrace life at the college with as much enthusiasm as she could muster and make a success of her life there.

"Chin up, Hilary!" she had said, echoing a command often directed at her by her mother.

Once she had made that decision, Hilary had become energetic. She had begun to plan with determination. Many students at Q-COLL were away from home for the first time. Never having endured the severing experience of boarding-school life, they were homesick. Hilary had decided to look for creative ways of dealing with that problem. At Bramblewell School, a matron in a woollen cardigan would sympathetically distribute tea and biscuits, but Q-COLL's students would need to be approached in a more grown-up way. Or would they?

In addition to pacifying the emotionally distressed, Hilary wanted to introduce her students to drama, since there was no established dramatic society in the college. A drama club would be a distraction for those who were pining for home - as well as a means of encouraging the awkward to speak in public with aplomb. She had considered asking Barbara Merrivale to come to work for her, but she had then realised that The Eliza Club at Bramblewell School, without Barbara, was unimaginable, How about Teddy Laurence, though? He knew the ropes and he still ran a youth club in Liverpool. Would he be willing to help in his spare time?

Those thoughts filling her head, Hilary hardly noticed her drive through the Wirral and the Mersey Tunnel. Then, after she had arrived in Liverpool, the hours at Q-COLL seemed, to her, to pass quickly. In the mid-afternoon, the weather being fine, she decided to walk down to Albert Dock, to view an exhibition of French 20th century art which was being displayed at Tate Liverpool. She was now in a happy mood. Suddenly, the future seemed to be full of choices. Her experiences and knowledge would be of use to the young students in her care to an extent she had not initially anticipated.Having left the college, Hilary made her way down sloping streets, heading in the direction of the art gallery. A cool breeze blew up from the river and, feeling chilled momentarily, Hilary pulled the edges of her beige, tailored coat together. She wondered which paintings would be on display. Could she hope that a Matisse would be there? A Chagall?

When she reached Pierhead, Hilary saw a young man, whom she recognised, sitting on a stone step gazing at the Mersey. She had seen him before, on one occasion, when she had driven through the gates of Bramblewell School, at the end of a day, there. He had been standing in the lane outside, deep in conversation with Portia Price.

"Oh! That must have been Louis Lindsey," Barbara Mertrivale had said, when Hilary had made enquiries. "I'll have to intervene.

He's going to de-stabilise that girl, if I don't." Hilary had, then mentioned the boy to Teddy Laurence, in the hope Teddy would chase him away, but Teddy had spoken highly of Louis. He had, also, talked about the boy's extreme lack of self-belief. Teddy had later told Hilary that he had offered to arrange for Louis to have instruction in social etiquette and the way to behave during interviews, pointing out that having knowledge of that type would help him to feel at ease during his first days at Cambridge, but Louis had firmly - and even angrily - declined the offers and it was not clear still if he would ultimately apply for entry to Cambridge, anyway.

Looking at Louis – or rather, the disheartened slump of his shoulders - Hilary instinctively sensed that what he essentially feared was home-sickness though. Yes. Just that. Pondering on this realisation, Hilary, as if inspired, remembered that she had heard Julian Bramblewell-Eurlinn talking about a young woman whom he knew- one called Tansy- who would be going to Cambridge to further her studies. Yes. On the night of the party at Bramblewell Manor, when Susie had left her in the company of Julian and Héloïse, she had heard Julian saying, "Tansy will move to Cambridge. She has found out that Pomeroy will be staying in Bristol and so, on my mother's advice, she has decided to go elsewhere rather than risk running into him in the Students' Union Building." Julian had then commented on how much Tansy would be missed by her friends at Bristol. Was anyone kinder or more gentle? Hilary reflected on those words. She could not help wondering if Tansy could be persuaded to keep an eye on Louis were he to go to Cambridge. Maybe Tansy would meet him when he arrived, even? She would ask Teddy to talk to Julian about the possibility of making an arrangement of that nature.

Hilary approached the stone step where Louis was sitting. He looked up, the sun dazzling him, at that moment. He tilted his head to one side.

"I'm Hilary Trimm," she said.

He began to stand up and she indicated that he should sit down again. She sat beside him.

"You know, Louis, we all make mistakes in life, but the most potentially dangerous ones are made when we are young," she then said, without preamble and in a conversational way.

Louis made no response but looked straight ahead, as if construction work in Birkenhead on the other is of the river, was a riveting sight"Centuries ago," Hilary continued, "boys of your age and younger went off to sea, from this port, not knowing what lay ahead of them and discovering, eventually, that they would have to learn bits of new languages, new rules for behaving, new ways of approaching people…"

"Where are you going with this?" asked Louis, although not abruptly.

"Even in your own country," Hilary said calmly, "you could find yourself in a place where you might have to learn a different way of expressing yourself and new ways of conducting yourself. It wouldn't mean that, after your voyage, so to speak, you couldn't return to your Liverpool home and resume your old ways while you were there. It would be like living in two countries, Louis, travelling when necessary, from one to the other."

Louis nodded as if understanding what Miss Trimm was saying. He looked thoughtful for a moment and turned his head, then, to watch the River Mersey flowing towards the open sea. Suddenly, the world beyond the great port seemed to be beckoning.

ASTROLOGIAL DATA

LORD BRAMBLEWELL

Ascendant 28 Cancer
MC 1 Aries
Sun 29 Capricorn
Moon 1 Leo
Mercury 23 Capricorn
Venus 9 Capricorn
Mars 13 Sagittarius
Jupiter 22 Capricorn
Saturn 14 Gemini
Uranus 23 Libra
Neptune 6 Sagittarius
Pluto 4 Libra

DOROTHY TRIMM

Ascendant 11 Aries
MC 4 Capricorn
Sun 12 Libra
Moon 26 Capricorn
Mercury 2 Scorpio
Venus 24 Scorpio
Mars 7 Taurus
Jupiter 8 Aquarius
Saturn 4 Cancer
Uranus 22 Libra
Neptune 5 Sagittarius
Pluto 4 Libra

JULIAN

Ascendant 2 Aries
MC 1 Capricorn
Sun 24 Sagittarius
Moon 16 Pisces
Mercury 15 Capricorn
Venus 29 Scorpio
Mars 23 Virgo
Jupiter 28 Capricorn
Saturn 0 Aries
Uranus 2 Aquarius
Neptune 26 Capricorn
Pluto 3 Sagittarius

HÉLOÏSE

Ascendant 26 Libra
MC 1 Leo
Sun 28 Libra
Moon 19 Scorpio
Mercury 15 Scorpio
Venus 26 Libra
Mars 9 Virgo
Jupiter 18 Pisces
Saturn 0 Taurus
Uranus 8 Aquarius
Neptune 29 Capricorn
Pluto 6 Sagittarius

ISOLDE

Ascendant Unknown
MC Unknown
Sun 21 Scorpio
Moon Aries
Mercury 15 Scorpio
Venus 6 Scorpio
Mars 24 Aquarius
Jupiter 3 Pisces
Saturn 9 Sagittarius
Uranus 20 Sagittarius
Neptune 4 Capricorn
Pluto 7 Scorpio

SUSIE SUTTON

Ascendant 27 Cancer
MC 1 Aries
Sun 6 Gemini
Moon 12 Leo
Mercury 19 Gemini
Venus 21 Aries
Mars 17 Leo
Jupiter 4 Libra
Saturn 0 Pisces
Uranus 21 Capricorn
Neptune 20 Capricorn
Pluto 23 Scorpio

TEDDY

Ascendant 28 Capricorn
MC 3 Sagittarius
Sun 15 Libra
Moon 11 Pisces
Mercury 1 Scorpio
Venus 16 Scorpio
Mars 13 Cancer
Jupiter 29 Virgo
Saturn 11 Aquarius
Uranus 14 Capricorn
Neptune 16 Capricorn
Pluto 21 Scorpio

LIZ LAURIER

Ascendant 15 Libra
MC 20 Cancer
Sun 18 Scorpio
Moon 0 Taurus
Mercury 1 Scorpio
Venus 4 Capricorn
Mars 11 Virgo
Jupiter 26 Libra
Saturn 17 Libra
Uranus 29 Scorepio
Neptune 23 Sagittarius
Pluto 25 Libra

PORTIA PRICE

Ascendant 2 Aries
MC 1 Capricorn
Sun 9 Pisces
Moon 8 Taurus
Mercury 15 Aquarius
Venus 16 Aries
Mars 6 Sagittarius
Jupiter 3 Gemini
Saturn 15 Gemini
Uranus 21 Aquarius
Neptune 7 Aquarius
Pluto 15 Sagittarius

LOUIS LINDSEY

Ascendant 26 Virgo
MC 2 Leo
Sun 20 Taurus
Moon 19 Scorpio
Mercury 25 Aries
Venus 8 Aries
Mars 26 Aries
Jupiter 21 Pisces
Saturn 26 Aries
Uranus 12 Aquarius
Neptune 12 Aquarius
Pluto 7 Sagittarius

KIT MALLORY

Ascendant Unknown
MC Unknown
Sun 29 Leo
Moon Aquarius
Mercury 24 Leo
Venus 21 Cancer
Mars 20 Gemini
Jupiter 29 Virgo
Saturn 20 Cancer
Uranus 17 Gemini
Neptune 4 Libra
Pluto 10 Leo

MADAME GABRIELLE

Ascendant Unknown
MC Unknown
Sun 4 Capricorn
Moon Virgo
Mercury 12 Capricorn
Venus 7 Sagittarius
Mars 22 Capricorn
Jupiter 9 Capricorn
Saturn 6 Virgo
Uranus 28 Gemini
Neptune 15 Libra
Pluto 16 Leo

CATERINA TRAVERSI

Ascendant Unknown
MC Unknown
Sun 17 Scorpio
Moon Capricorn
Mercury 8 Sagittarius
Venus 1 Libra
Mars 16 Scorpio
Jupiter 10 Virgo
Saturn 1 Aquarius
Uranus 10 Capricorn
Neptune 14 Capricorn
Pluto 20 Scorpio

SIGNORA TRAVERSI

Ascendant Unknown
MC Unknown
Sun 18 Sagittarius
Moon Virgo
Mercury 22 Sagittarius
Venus 15 Capricorn
Mars 20 Pisces
Jupiter 17 Sagittarius
Saturn 10 Gemini]
Uranus 17 Libra
Neptune 3 Sagittarius
Pluto 1 Libra

ROSALIND

Ascendant 7 Pisces
MC 21 Sagittarius
Sun 21 Leo
Moon 14 Gemini
Mercury 29 Leo
Venus 14 Cancer
Mars 19 Sagittarius
Jupiter 6 Cancer
Saturn 13 Gemini
Uranus 22 Aquarius
Neptune 7 Aquarius
Pluto 12 Sagittarius

TANSY

Ascendant Unknown
MC Unknown
Sun 5 Pisces
Moon Libra
Mercury 23 Aquarius
Venus 26 Aquarius
Mars 3 Libra
Jupiter 7 Cancer
Saturn 6 Aries
Uranus 6 Aquarius
Neptune 28 Capricorn
Pluto 5 Sagittarius

Printed in Dunstable, United Kingdom

66167949R00353